THREE BROTHERS FROM VIRGINIA

THREE BROTHERS FROM VIRGINIA

An Epic Tale of Love and Liberation in the Civil War

Andy Lazris

DEDICATION

In writing this book I was inspired by Boris Pasternak's characters Yuri and Lara who, in the depths of helpless despair and war, discovered a passion and an oasis of their own by turning their backs on the mores of a self-serving world that sought to stifle them.

This book is dedicated to all those who fight for happiness, freedom, and love even when they feel powerless against the unrelenting force of society's shackles. Great people and movements are born when a few brave souls discard the rules of homogenous accommodation, and when emotion and goodness prevail over staid conformity. These are our heroes, even if their existence is often derided and ephemeral.

The Civil War was many things to many people, and without a doubt, it shaped our nation's future. Congressman Thaddeus Stevens hoped that the war had been a transformative moment when he spoke to Grant's vice-presidential nominee soon before his death: "If you and your compeers can fling away ambition and realize that every human being, however lowly born or degraded by fortune, is your equal, that every inalienable right which belongs to you belongs also to him, truth and righteousness will spread over the land." The Civil War never achieved the hopes of its most passionate and forward-thinking dreamers. It is a war that we are still waging today. To the three brothers from Virginia, and all of those who buck the status quo to fight for something better, I dedicate this book to you.

Art
The cover design and all drawings in the book were crafted by my mother, Marilyn Lazris, the best and most underappreciated artist I know. Thank you, mom!

Rejoinder
This book is historical fiction, and as such, it takes liberties with its depiction of characters, locations, and events. Many of the people in the book are real, and typically their dialogue is verbatim or paraphrased from what they said in life. But since real and fictional characters co-mingle, engage in events that are based on fragments of historical truth, and often animate purely fabricated situations that create a mood or backdrop to the story, caution is advised. I have tried to depict the battles, riots, military units, landscapes, and other substantial moments of our Civil War as accurately as possible, with poetic license taken when the historical record was sparse. Events are depicted through the eyes of the three brothers and are thus subject to their interpretations as well.

The backdrop of much of this book is Washington, Virginia. While some events described in the book did occur in Washington—from the encampment of a federal army to the creation of a unit that fought in the Civil War and was led by Colonel Kemper—the majority of what transpires in this tranquil Virginia town is entirely manufactured, including many townspeople, such as the doctor and the main characters, who did not exist in reality. I have visited Washington many times, have climbed Old Rag—the mountain that itself is a character in the book—and have admired the landscape and orchards in the Shenandoah Valley with joy and awe. I always imagined how such a bucolic place like this participated in, and was changed by, the events of our Civil War. I encourage anyone to visit Washington and Old Rag; these wonderful spots are infused with history and beauty that inspired me to place this story in their shadows. A climb up Old Rag will allow you to read this book with a broader perspective and will transport you into the world of Paul, Luke, and Matt. Make sure to bring water!

INTRODUCTION: RESURRECTION

Loosely affixed to the blue-tinged monotony of the Shenandoah ridge sat a pinnacle of rocks, distinct from the rest, seemingly pushing to get away. The locals called this peak Old Rag. As Matt stared at it wide-eyed on this darkest of nights, he could feel its anger, and he swore that its rocks glowed a haunting orange, trying to tell him something of great urgency.

"Matt!" shouted his father, yanking his sixteen-year-old son's attention away from a trance. "Have you heard anything I been saying?"

"Yea, I heard," Matt snidely uttered. "I just don't want to listen." His eyes again snuck up to the peak, but his father quickly pulled him back.

"Look at me, Matt. All I want is what's best for us. We been living here as long as you been alive, even longer. Your mother died having you, and that left us alone, just me and you and this here land. We found a life here. It's been good to us. I was nothing before I found this place."

Matt interrupted him. "You didn't find this place," he snarled, with eyes brewing with indignation. "Someone give it to you, out of pure charity. You couldn't hold a job up North. You even tried the army and failed that too. Then a friend in your New York army group who hearkened from Virginia, he knowed of this place, and he helped you get it and get it going. I know the story, Dad, and I ain't in any mood to hear it again. It don't make what you are doing right. That's all I know."

Matt glanced up one more time, but the night's intense blackness engulfed the rocks of his mountain. They were gone, and Matt stood alone. That reality only accentuated his fury, as he clenched his fists and fought off angry thoughts.

"I want my brothers," he shouted sharply, his piercing voice slicing through the night's silence. "It's my job to protect them. And I want my mamma back!"

"She's dead, Matt, dead from delivering you."

"No!" Matt shoved his father, breathing deeply. "The one who gave birth to me, I never know her. She ain't nothing to me. You know who I mean. Don't be like the rest of them who live here and pretend that Momma was nothing more than some slave to you. My real mother raised me and my brothers. She was your wife. She was everything to us, smart as a whip, kind as can be. She was my momma. What you did today was disgusting. Don't pretend she don't exist. You don't get a right to do that!"

"Matt," the man sighed after a brief silence, "you got to understand. She is black. It ain't so simple down here. There are rules, and we broke proper every one of them. But now, we got no choice. Either we leave this place, or we give in to what they say. Your momma, she knows that. This was all her idea. To save her boys. To keep our life. That's the price she wants to pay for her family."

"And what's your price, Dad?" he asked cuttingly. "Seems like you get off scot-free."

Matt felt his indignation dig into his father. The man took a deep breath, and his dreary eyes wilted just that much more. In the moonlight, Matt saw lines and wrinkles on the man's face that aged him well beyond his years. He looked like a broken man.

"My price," his dad whispered, "it's more than you can ever know."

With that Matt's hands relaxed a bit. He peered at his dad through more sympathetic eyes.

The doctor had come by earlier today with a contingent of townspeople. He always seemed pleasant, the doctor did. Always smiling. The people around him looked up to him with an air of respect. He had been meeting with Matt's dad a lot these past few months. Matt listened in sometimes, when he could hide just right. He heard what the doctor had to say. The doctor claimed that there were rumors about what was going on in Dad's house. That Dad's orchard—which is what this land was, mostly apple and pear trees—was doing just fine, not so good or bad as farms go, just fine enough to allow Dad to make a living. But, said the doctor, if those rumors were true, then this orchard would probably be burned to the ground—not by the doctor of course, but by less-scrupulous people in town. Those were some of the doctor's words. And lots of talk of politics, of how the North was trying to make life down here harder, about how all Virginians had to hold onto their values more now than ever.

Then this morning the doctor comes back with those townspeople, and before the sun crossed the horizon, Matt saw his momma being led off the farm by a few of them he did not even know, her arms in chains, her face serene and silent, and these people just laughing and chatting like it was just any day to them. His dad was nowhere to be seen.

Matt knew this day was destined to come. His momma told him herself, not but a few days ago. She said it was OK; she was going to another farm down South, just for a while, until things settle down here. "Take care of your father," she said with a smile that glowed of pure goodness. "He will be a lonely man. And watch out for your brothers. Especially Paul! He has fire in him. He needs a steady hand."

"You told my brothers you is leaving? What's they saying about this, Paul and Luke?" Matt asked his mother, lying on her shoulder as she stroked his thick brown hair.

"They understand," she whispered. "And so too should you. We will all meet again in better times. Your father will make sure of that."

And then they took her away in chains. Matt cried for hours, so helpless, not even able to say a proper goodbye. His momma smiled all along, breathing a peace that he could not understand. But Old Rag wasn't smiling. Even then, with just a flicker of sun touching the peak, anger spewed from its burning rocks.

"Then what's going to happen to my brothers?" Matt asked his father after a long silence. Aside from bright stars above and sparkling candles in the house windows, darkness draped the landscape. Matt could barely make out his father's silhouette.

"They will have to live in the slave quarters now, of course, and be treated like everyone else," he said. "At least, we have to make it seem that way, to the folk in the town, to our other slaves here. But Matt," he said, as though through a smile, "me and you, we are two clever men is what we are. And we are sneaky as catfish. We know the rules, but that don't mean we got to always follow them all the time. We just got to be careful."

"Then we can have them in the house with us, talk about stuff like always, play games, be like we always were? Is that what you are saying, Dad?" His eyes opened wide.

"They are my boys, Matt, no less than you are. And I love them as deep as any man loves anyone. I lost the love of my life today, and I ache more than you can ever know." He paused and seemed to choke on his words. Matt knew his dad was crying, because he pushed out the last words splattered with tears. "I won't let nothing happen to them or you ever, I promise! I lost too much today! I ain't losing no more, ever, I promise that, Matt. I promise you with all my heart and soul!"

And at that moment, Matt lost every bit of anger and fear that had suffocated him all day, and he engulfed his father in a deep hug. Tears flowed from both of their eyes as they stood as one beneath the obscured shadow of mountains staring down from above.

Two years from that date, Matt's father would be dead, the victim of a sickness that all the doctor's leeches and bloodletting could not cure. Matt knew that a heart so broken as his father's could never heal. Still, Dad kept true to his word, and the three brothers were stealth enough to fool them all, growing into men together upon the hallowed ground of their orchard, separated from the destructive sameness that defined the world outside of its boundaries.

After Matt took control of the land—with the help of one of his father's friends from New York, who barreled into town and paid a drunk overseer a good wage to never come back again—the orchard thrived. In fact, it grew so prosperous that it was the envy of Rappahannock County, putting out bounteous quantities of some of the best pears and apples that any man from this hilly land had ever tasted before. There was a secret to that success, one so well guarded that it never trickled beyond the sanctuary that was their farm, one that sat in the heads of three young men whose love of land and of each other propelled this place beyond anything otherwise conceivable.

Matt peered up, under the bright sun, his face and hands splattered with mud. There, beyond the pond that they had engineered and built, stood his brothers, talking about something big and important as they always seemed to be doing, something to make the orchard even better and the space within it livelier and more interesting. And high above that was the rocky peak of Old Rag, serene and gray, relaxed as it pushed itself just a bit farther away from the staid Shenandoah line, its cold water flowing down into their pond and feeding everything around them.

PART I

Genesis

And the serpent said unto the woman, Ye shall not surely die: for God knows that when you eat of [the apple] your eyes will be opened, and you will be like God, knowing good and evil.

1

Keep their eyes closed, son, and keep the gates up high. What lays outside should never enter their thoughts and minds. Promise me that. Promise me.

A splash of sunshine snuck through a fading night sky, instantly warming the air just enough. They were here! For years all that Matt had ever wanted was to show his brothers this small slice of heaven that sat apart from the venomous world about which his mother had always warned him. Surely, coming here did not breach the tocsin that she so vehemently pounded into his mind. *Keep them safe, within the gates, away from all that blows beyond.* This was a special place, the mountain that fed their farm, that hovered over it like a smiling angel, that gave them the power to stay strong against the tide of society's ensnarling sting. This could be their last chance to see it all together. To Matt, it was a necessary journey, despite the risks, despite the poor timing.

How could Old Rag possibly turn against them?

And yet, on this day, their lives would change forever, and even Old Rag could not protect him and his brothers from the tsunami that Matt inadvertently unleashed.

Paul seemed to know. He never wanted to come here; he fought it to the end. But that was Paul's way, and so Matt dismissed his brother's defeatism. Paul slumped under a thick bed of white pines, his arms crossed against his chest, staring at the ground, silent. Yes, silent; that was Paul. Strong and tall, with a long dark face that conveyed both passion and skepticism; he refused to engage in this quixotic venture. He had come only to protect his other brother, Luke; that's what he told Matt. It was a bad idea.

"But it's what Dad always wanted for us," Matt had pleaded to Paul.

Paul could only shake his head. "I know I have no say," he told his older brother. "But Dad wouldn't have done it now. He would have known that with Lincoln's possible election, it's not safe to be out here among these vultures. Dad would never have let us go. Mom would have taken you to task if you even mentioned it. You must know that, Matt."

"But it may be our last chance!" Matt pleaded.

He needed to bring his brothers here! This place, it flowed through their blood; it fed their farm. How could they not experience it, at least just this once? To be here with them, that is what Matt needed more than anything else in the world! And with so much changing, so much uncertainty gusting across the horizon, the opportunity seemed to be evaporating quickly away.

They were here, so why did Paul fret? All was going as planned.

"We made it," Matt said to his brother. "You will see! Wait until you see!"

Paul just shook his head with unconcealed disdain.

A raging river soared through the gorge below, and from it darted their younger brother Luke, short and a bit plump, glowing with excitement. He shook off his wet shirt like a dog. His visage glimmered with a naive wisdom that defined who he was. He had built their farm into something amazing, something beyond what seemed to be possible. And for his success he credited no other than Old Rag itself, lauding the perfect mineralized water that this precious mountain fed to their land. Now, for the first time, he immersed himself in the cold, flowing stream, oblivious to any discomfort, basking in a moment that he had so long craved. There was no question that Luke was going to join Matt on this venture despite his brother's skepticism. Luke needed to be here just as much as Matt needed him to.

And so, Matt smiled, looking away from Paul and focusing on his other brother.

"I took samples," Luke exclaimed in a deep voice that had recently thickened after his seventeenth birthday. "I will bring them home. How wonderful to be so close to its source! I think that if we can get the acidity just right, growing grapes next year will be as easy as pie!"

Paul growled. "Enough with your damned grapes! We have to get up and down this piece of dirt before it gets dark. We're already two hours behind. If you plan to study every rock and drop of animal piss while we're climbing, we may not make it back until after Mr. Lincoln wins the election next month. Can we get this over with, or do you want to take another swim, brother, maybe even go to sleep in your precious water?"

It was an arduous journey to get here, and Paul was easily shaken by adversity. Every dog that barked, every distant light that flickered from someone's home, filled him with consternation. Why were they taking this chance, he repeatedly asked his brother? How could the reward possibly justify the risk? Especially in these times, weeks before the election, when every white citizen of the county wanted nothing more than take out their wrath on a renegade slave or two, why now?

Matt just smiled. "You always say you want to leave the farm, that you're a prisoner there," he said to Paul, who stood a good six inches above Matt's scrawny frame, forcing Matt to peer up. "Well, Brother, here we finally is! I got you here and I will get you home, and no one will be the wiser. Dad took me here so many times. I been up it, and it's like I seen heaven. And sometimes, sometimes I think that the mountain, it speaks to me. When you get to the top, you will be thanking me, Brother."

Paul laughed—a dubious and irreverent laugh at best—as they trudged through mud, looking for the trailhead, Luke shivering through his plastered smile. "If the mountain starts talking to you, Brother," Paul said, "I won't be thanking you. I'll just finally realize that you lost your fucking mind. It gets dark earlier now than when we were supposed to come here last month. Have you taken that into account?"

"I ain't an idiot," Matt said.

"Really?" Paul smiled. "Are you sure?"

Matt laughed. "Well, I am an idiot, we always agree on that. You two are the smart ones. But I been planning this trip for more than a year. If Izzy hadn't showed up last month, we could have done it then. That's what I was planning, and we would have had two hours more of light. But it still ain't too dark to do this, Paul. Trust me. I ain't ever let you two down in my life. Daddy told me to protect you, that was his dying words. And I won't never do nothing other than that."

"Don't listen to Paul," Luke said, placing his arms over both his brothers' shoulders. "I can't wait to climb to the top of this hallowed spot and view the landscape from its peak, Matt. I already swam in its veins and tasted its blood, and now I want to feel the immensity of its splendor!"

"God help us," Paul said, pushing Luke's arm away and shaking his head. "Enough of your banter. No more crap about the mountain's Christ-like stature, OK? Let's just get up and down this rock and get back home before the lynch mobs execute their own version of God's sanctity and passion."

"You got nothing to worry about, Brother," Matt smiled.

Paul stared into his brother's eyes. "Matt, I love you, but you are white," he said curtly. "Me and Luke, we're not. I'm glad you are so confident. I'll kiss you when we get home safely. Until then, let's have less preaching and a bit more action. Let's go."

Keep their eyes closed, Matt. Keep them behind the gates. Don't let the world swallow them. Promise me that, promise me that forever.

Dark clouds swirled above them, as brisk winds started whipping through the barren trees, blowing off stray leaves and dead branches. The ground was muddy, and there were fallen trees everywhere. To get to Old Rag's rocky head meant to climb straight up through the forest until it gave way to nothing but boulders and open air. Matt was not sure exactly which way to go, although he concealed his ignorance. Just go up, that's all he knew. Time ticked away faster than he had hoped. *Where was the top?* he wondered. *How far away could it be?*

Beads of sweat plummeted from his scalp, his shirt now completely drenched. *Where the heck were the boulders? We should be there by now! What if we don't make it?*

Paul was right. The trip was precarious. One mistake, one delay, could have devastating consequences. And what he had not told his brothers was that he had made a mistake—a big whopper of a mistake—that put them in great peril if they didn't get home in time. This should have been a seamless trip. Matt's plan was perfect. And yet, here they were, hours behind, as thick clouds hovered above them portending a possible late-autumn storm. If that occurred, my God, then what? Matt knew that he should probably turn around and get back to the farm. A horrid wave of trepidation overcame him.

Where the heck is the peak? Why is this taking so long?

They had planned to make this journey in mid-September, after the harvest was done, when the fruit had been picked and the days were still warm and long.

"We'll go on a Wednesday. I got the day picked and everything, and it's all going to happen this time," Matt had told his brothers. "It'll be perfect, we'll finally do it, and you two, you'll be so happy, but not half as happy as me. I just can't wait. I have goose bumps thinking about it!"

Every Wednesday the three boys took a break from their labors, at least for part of the day; that was a pact they had made with each other after Dad's death. They spent time in the big house, reading books, Paul cooking them a feast, the three of them discussing politics and farming and everything under the sun. When Mom and Dad lived, Wednesday was their day of rest, of solitude with the family; weekends were always too busy. And so, the brothers promised to make Wednesday an untouchable sanctuary after losing their parents. What better day to make the trip to Old Rag?

Each boy had a role on the farm. Paul managed the finances, Luke managed the logistics of feeding and growing and harvesting and irrigating, and Matt maintained a good relationship with the townsfolk and found buyers for their fruit. After Dad's death, their farm flourished and grew, and rather than hire more slaves—they all feared bringing more people onto their secretive and protective oasis—they made up the slack themselves. They worked that much harder, almost every day, from dawn to dusk, and then they read and planned bigger things through much of the night.

Except for Wednesdays. That was their special day, the day they reserved for themselves, for intellectual and emotional journeys that transcended the monotony of an endless barrage of pears and apples. This was the day on which they again became the sons of Jake and Mary, who raised them to be much more than mere farmers, and who insisted that they nourish and care for each other and for themselves.

So, it was on a Wednesday that Matt insisted they were to climb Old Rag, the day he would show this holy place to his brothers, who until now could only marvel at its majesty from behind their farm's closed gates. It had to be a day with good weather, enough time, and not much work. There was only one Wednesday that fit the bill, in mid-September, but year after year it did not work out. Matt was insistent that this year he would make it happen, and it seemed like it just might.

But then, it didn't.

Out of the blue and without any warning, Dad's old friend Izzy decided to come to town on that very day. He came from

New York, a salesman of used clothes, and a good friend to the boys. In fact, Izzy chose this time because he knew they would not be very busy. He loved to sit with them in the big house, to talk about all the many changes that were brewing in the nation, and the upcoming election that he was sure Lincoln would win. He brought them books, and they ate copious amounts of food, laughing and arguing deep into the night. No, Matt's brothers would never agree to climb any mountain when Izzy came to town.

And so, Matt had to wait, wait until after they sold their fruit, wait until mid-October, when storms could strike suddenly, and when the sun dropped early from the sky. This was not the best time to go, but Matt was insistent! They would wake up at 3:00 a.m., go up and down quickly, and wander home under the cover of darkness. He planned it so perfectly that it had to work. It just had to!

But then, the day before his trip, he met with the doctor. And that's when he learned something that should have given him the sense to cancel the trip, because after that meeting he knew that coming here could have disastrous consequences should anything go wrong.

So, he convinced himself—knowing well that he did not have the heart to cancel this trip yet again—that nothing would go wrong. It would work out. Old Rag would protect them.

Keep their eyes closed, Matt, and keep them forever behind the tall gates of our farm.

The sky had now completely darkened; the winds blew hard into their faces.

Where were the damned boulders?

"Paul, you ever read the chemist Lavoisier?" Luke called out to his brother, who now was far ahead, pushing away dead branches as he marched rapidly up the forested ascent.

"You going to name-drop with me, Brother?" Paul screamed back, not even turning his head. "You think you can stump me about French philosophers? Not on your life! Now, though, I'm focusing on something a bit more mundane. Trying to fix the foolish plan of this idiot," he said, pointing to Matt.

"Don't look at me!" Matt shot back. "I didn't say nothing."

"Lavoisier is not a philosopher, Brother," said Luke. "He's a chemist. And he showed how important acid and base are in everything we do, how they can alter the nature of substance. I'm reading about French grape horticulture, and Lavoisier contemplates using ammonia or citric acid to improve soil acidity, and I realize that's the magic formula: grapes need a proper acid environment, and through Lavoisier's work, I know how to attain that. We can make a canal from the pond, regulate the mineral-rich water that flows to us from this peak (which I will be able to do once I analyze these samples), create the ideal acid environment, and then we are growing grapes and making wine, just like Thomas Jefferson did. What do you boys think of that?"

Paul shouted from his perch far ahead. "Jefferson was an idiot. I hope you know that! He pretended to be a great innovator, but he merely chewed up his land with tobacco and used his slaves to do all the work. Classic white Southerner. And you know what white Southerners like to do, Brother? They like to beat and whip slaves that wander too far from their farm. Is your French chemist going to save us from that, Brother? Because if not, we should stop talking about nonsense and start moving our asses up this mountain before we live to regret it."

Matt was drenched with sweat. Should they turn around? He had lost all sense of time. What if they didn't get down before dark? What then?

Suddenly a burst of sun spilled upon them, and the trees seemed to disappear. There they stood, in front of a large boulder, and everything looking up was rocks. They were here! Matt smiled. He had no way of knowing what time it was, but a certain intoxication expunged rational thought or worry from his brain at that moment. A wave of calm flooded him, and he felt energized.

"Let's go up, boys," he said, patting each brother on the back. "Finally, you can share this place with me, just like I done with Dad so many times. Paul is right. Let's go!"

The sky opened up beneath hovering dark clouds. Across every vista lay a wide horizon with no limitation or constraint. Matt felt the power of this place flow through his body, and despite all his qualms and worries, nothing else mattered. Up here he was free, he was alive, he was with the two people who he coveted the most in this world, all alone but for God and peace! This is why he had brought them here. Now, now they would feel what he did, and they would understand.

There was little banter on the way up. Matt leaped up onto rocks, through small caves, and around jutting edges that could toss any careless person two thousand feet down should they lose their grip at the wrong time. Every corner brought a new vista, an interminable strip of farms in the valley on one side, and on the other, the majesty of the Shenandoah range carpeted by bright red and yellow leaves that stretched endlessly in each direction. Matt watched Paul's demeanor change rapidly. His brother stared off into the horizon and seemed to gain strength with every passing turn and climb. He looked almost invigorated, like a fire had been lit behind his muted visage.

"That's our farm down there, Matt," Luke pointed out when they reached a ledge that Matt estimated was halfway up. "Do you see it? I can make out the pond. You can almost grab it with one hand."

"Up here," Matt said, "everything is small. We is bigger than everything. Even our farm. All those people, them farmers who scare Paul so much, their rules that tell us what we can and can't do. We're bigger than all of that. It's like, we is transformed into God himself."

Paul, hands on hips, staring forward, just nodded. "Let's go," he whispered. "I want to get to the top. I don't want to hear your crap about God. This isn't God. There is no God. This is a mountain. And I will admit, it's transcendent. But it's a mountain. Let's go! You two mules are slowing me down."

"See, Brother," Matt whispered to Luke, who marched astride him, transfixed by the magical scene all around them, dark clouds and swirling winds punctuating its wonder, "even Paul knows what I am talking about. You see why I had to bring you here? And it only gets better. It only gets more amazing. You will see."

Luke draped Matt with his arm, a huge smile commandeering his serene face. "I feel Mom and Dad here, Brother. Thank you. I'm sure Paul feels it too, even if he will never say so."

Matt nodded, as tears trickled from his eyes.

They hit a few dead ends where the rocks stopped and revealed no path forward, sometimes bringing them to precarious drop-offs that opened up vistas and views of even more rocks. Matt studied the landscape a bit, usually silently, and then changed direction. One mistake, Matt knew, could be fatal. Somehow, he did not remember the way up, although he hid this fact from his brothers.

Darkness grew denser; a thick sheath of swirling black clouds now fully obscured the sun. The winds picked up; even the views grew narrower and more shaded. From over the Blue Ridge range, flashes of lightning burst through the din, as thunder rumbled around them. Matt's trance, this moment in which he and his brothers stood apart from the world, suddenly evaporated. He became overwhelmed by a wave of terrifying fear.

We ain't going to make it! We'll never get down in time. We got to turn around!

"I think we seen enough," Matt cried, his voice barely carrying through the wind's howls.

"No," Paul yelled, far ahead of them and climbing over some steep rocks. "I see the top. I'm going there. You can wait, but I am not turning back. Not now."

"We got to turn around," Matt yelled, even as his brother disappeared from view. "Paul, we got to get off this mountain. We don't got time. We got to leave now!"

Matt hyperventilated; he was almost hysterical. What had he done? He had planned this trip perfectly; there was no room for error. He knew that if he didn't get down tonight, get back to the orchard by tomorrow, then he and his brothers and everything they had ever worked for could be in grave danger. "Paul," he yelled again. "Goddamn you, Paul, get down here now!"

Luke moved to his brother's side and put his arm around Matt's shoulder. They both sat on a rock, and Matt just kept shaking his head. "What's wrong, Matt? Tell me." The wind was so loud now that Luke had to scream.

"We got to get back."

"Or what?"

Matt's face did not change. "Or we is in a big heap of trouble. All of us. Even our farm. We is in even more trouble than you can ever know. I totally messed up, Luke. We got to get down. We got to get down right now."

"Matt," Luke calmly said to his brother, leaning against him. "It will be OK."

"I promised Mamma I'd take care of you," Matt cried out, tears dropping from his eyes. "Now look what I done! Now look at the mess I caused! Why did Izzy have to come on that day, on our day? Why then? If he had just not come, then everything would be right. Now look at the mess!"

"Matt, I promise you, you always have taken care of us, and you always will. It will be OK."

Just then the sky opened, and a deluge of rain spilled upon them. Thunder rocked the landscape and bursts of lightning shot out from everywhere all at once. They were trapped here, and Matt knew it. A rush of thoughts flooded him: should they try to get down the mountain tonight and risk falling off, or could they make it home in the morning and risk being detected by some of the locals as they trekked back to the orchard in daylight? All these thoughts jumbled into a morass of regret and fear, as his entire body shivered from the wind and rain. And all he could think of was, where the heck was Paul, and why did Izzy have to come on that day?

"No," he spit out through accumulating water. "It won't be OK. It ain't never going to be OK again."

2

September 1860, six weeks before the trip to Old Rag.

His name was Isadore Snout, Izzy for short, and he was the reason Matt and his brothers had delayed their trip to Old Rag and were now in their current predicament. Somewhere in his forties, Izzy appeared no younger or older than he had when Matt was a kid. His incessant laughter and bouncing head obscured any memorable physical traits other than a large mop of wavy black hair, thin neck, and short stature. He walked with a bounce in his step and rarely stopped talking, sometimes with a hint of an accent, but usually with an inflection of bland Americanism. He had been a frequent visitor to the farm when Matt's dad was alive; he stayed over sometimes for weeks at a time as he and Jake talked and laughed deep into many nights. Now his visits were less frequent and more abbreviated, and so Matt dared not miss his chance to see Uncle Izzy.

He had lived in New York all his adult life, emigrating from Germany as a young boy. "Well, let's face it, the Germans wouldn't call it Germany, because it was kind of sticking off the edge of Poland," Izzy had told the brothers. "And my name was not Snout, it was Stapinsky, but what can I tell you? It's better to be a German Jew than a Polish Jew in America, not that being any Jew is exactly a gold star in this world of ours, so I made myself German, and I made myself Snout, and damn it, I'm sticking by that!"

His parents died young, he said, and his other relatives took him in and hoped to make him into a rabbi. "First off, no thank you. That's not exactly a position of upward mobility in the world, and it's as boring as shit, so no, that was not going to happen, believe you me. And I had bigger dreams. I heard about people going to America, so I took off one day, doubt they even missed me, and here I am, not as easy as all that, but I'll spare you the details. Great men have great tales, boys, and lesser men have lesser tales. My tale is about the size of a pebble!"

Izzy Snout worked with a clothing distributor in New York, delivering every type of trousers, shirts, dresses, and wardrobes across Maryland and Virginia. His clothes were secondhand, but, as he told his young friends, "No one here needs to know that. And unless someone tells them, these people will never figure it out." He had a large buggy with two geriatric horses, and he traveled around the eastern border states selling his wares to a large contingent of steady customers. Often, he could unload an entire wagon in three weeks and then gallop back up to New York to gather some more, although more frequently he hung around the farm with the three brothers.

During his unannounced visit in mid-September, he parked himself in Jake's old room, unloaded his stuff, and asked Paul to cook him some corned beef, his favorite meal. A giddy Paul quickly complied, grabbing a pile of books Izzy had brought him and delving into them before he could even say hello.

"I made us chicken tonight, Izzy," Paul said, beaming even as he turned pages in the books. "Tomorrow we can do the corned beef. I even have a big jar of mustard, brown and hot, like you like! I have so much to talk to you about!"

"Well, Paul, that's good, because I have so much I want to hear."

It became quickly clear to Matt that Izzy was there to stay for a while; in an instant his dreams of a September trip up the mountain evaporated.

The next morning Izzy hovered over Matt's bed and startled him. "What time is it?" he asked the man, who was chewing on something and making some terrible sounds.

"Time to start my deliveries," Izzy casually said. "I'm hoping you'll come with me, just me and you for a change. I never get a chance to talk to you, well, with your brothers all over me the whole time. What do you say, Matt?"

"Sure!" Matt proclaimed. How could he say no?

Izzy loaded his cart with some selected clothes, and they stammered off the farm, bouncing and shaking all along, a row of blue mountains glowing on their left as the sun slowly rose high in the sky. They were going to a few farmers' homes, and then they would make the trip into the town of Washington. The first stop was a nearby farm belonging to one of Matt's dad's few friends, a man named Marshall Jones.

"These farmers are all straight shooters down here," Izzy said to Matt. The buggy bounced over a long, rocky driveway onto Marshall's farm as a squadron of dogs chased them. "In New York, we expect some haggling when we sell shit. Here though, you give them a price and that's what they pay. Haggling comes more naturally to me. You start high and go low. Everyone thinks they get a bargain. Here I've got to start lower, and I'm never sure where that should be. It changes from farm to farm. I like Marshall. So, I give him a decent price. When we go to Ned Gravley's farm, I will get some pleasure gouging him. It's the only power I have over these people, many of whom I detest! My little way to dispense a bit of Northern justice."

"You don't like Ned?" Matt asked. "I do a lot of business with him. He seems like a swell guy."

Izzy slapped him on the back. "He's not. But that's OK. It's not your job to dispense justice. That's my role in life. You've just got to manage your dad's farm. And you are doing a hell of a job of that. I'll take care of screwing the people who are bastards. That's what God put me on this world to do!"

After selling the farmer two hats and a pair of slacks, Izzy said it was time to see the doctor.

"You sure we got to go there?" Matt said, swallowing hard. "You don't even like the doctor, and you always fight with him. Besides, Jessie is home, and it can be uncomfortable."

"I like being uncomfortable, Matt, you should know that," Izzy said to him. "The only thing I like more than being uncomfortable is making other people even more uncomfortable and sparring with the doctor, which is one of my favorite hobbies!"

They rode up the main pike toward the town of Washington, the endless row of blue mountains brighter and more prominent as the sun raced into a cloudless blue sky.

"The doctor is good to me, Izzy," Matt said at one point when Izzy started talking about how he planned to swindle the man. "And he was good to Dad. He ain't that bad as you make him."

"I miss your dad, Matt," Izzy said, seeming to ignore Matt's comment about the doctor. "But, you know Matt, I saw him change in his last year of life. He missed your mom terribly, and he was lost when she left. He started relying on the doctor more; he and I used to ridicule that dumb doctor all the time, but all the sudden, your dad started defending him and his ways. Your dad said some bad things about abolitionists—about the Republicans—and how they would destroy the sanctity of the South. Shit like that. I called him on it, and he usually laughed and backpedaled. But this place, it has a way of indoctrinating even the best among them. And the doctor, he has a power over weakened people like your dad was then, a subtle form of control, one that is almost infectious. I see through him. But, your dad, I think he got lost in the doctor's allure. He became a different man."

"He seemed the same to me, Izzy," Matt said. "He always was good to us. He spent so much time teaching us everything, kept us safe. He helped turn the farm into what it is. He was a great man."

Izzy rubbed the boy's head. "I know that, Matt. I'm not disparaging him. It's just that this place, it's like an infection that distorts the brain, and the doctor is the guy who grows the bugs. I tell you this only to protect you. You have to respect the doctor and to never defy him, because he has power beyond anything or anyone else, but don't ever fall for his tricks; don't ever believe him. That's all I'm saying. You have to protect your farm and your brothers from his meddling, but you also can't let him get into your mind. I will mess with him. That's my favorite sport. You can just watch and enjoy!"

"He's OK, Izzy. That's all I'm saying."

Izzy smiled. The carriage bumped and shook along the lonely dirt road, as Izzy changed the subject and gabbed about the upcoming election.

Last night Izzy spoke a lot about the election, and both of Matt's brothers were rapt in the momentous events that were sweeping across the nation. Being isolated within their farm's bubble, Paul and Luke craved information from the North. And Izzy told them everything! He brought them several weeks of newspapers, mostly the *New York Times* and *Herald*.

"These are banned down here," Izzy said, "because they have a law down South that you're not allowed to tell the truth. Fake news is what they call what Northern papers publish. I call it the facts."

He handed an ecstatic Luke several books about grape horticulture and some new farmer manuals from Europe. He gave Paul a new version of Gibbon's *Decline and Fall of the Roman Empire*. "Read it close, Paul," he told him. "You'll see a lot of disturbing parallels between Rome's fall and where we are now in the country, believe you me!"

And then, on Wednesday, when the boys had free time, the four of them sat in the big house's main living room, a crackling fire-spewing warmth and comfort, the succulent odor of Paul's feast laid out in front of them, and they laughed and talked and forgot about everything else.

"When Jake died," Izzy said, "I was ready to bring you boys up North. You were sixteen years old, Matt. Paul was an angry young fourteen-year-old, and Luke, you were thirteen and quiet as shit. I remember the three of you got together, and you came out as a unit and told me, 'Izzy, thank you, but no thank you, we're staying.' Just like that. None of you wanted to leave. None of you would allow it."

"Maybe a big mistake," Paul muttered as he chewed on potatoes, corned beef (with mustard and chopped cabbage on rye bread, just like Izzy liked it), and assorted roasted vegetables. "I was too young to understand how precarious it was to stay here. That was the time we should have gone."

"We couldn't leave, Izzy," Matt said to him, peering away from Paul. "We promised Mom and Dad we would stay and make something of it here. And that's just what we done!"

"It took a lot for me to convince the idiots in this town to let you boys stay here and run the farm yourselves," Izzy said, talking as he ate, making loud chewing sounds as the food sputtered from his mouth. "I had to swindle the doctor into believing that I'd be watching over you and that you would have adult supervision. I tossed him a few free 'high quality' shirts to sweeten my argument a bit. I hired an overseer who took a big salary to stay away and keep his mouth shut. I had to make sure, Luke and Paul, that you talked in your dumb slavery inflection when you were with anyone other than Matt and did not go into the big house ever when someone was around. You all agreed to it, and you made it work. It's kind of amazing you did. I assumed the doctor would figure it all out."

Paul laughed. "The doctor is an idiot!"

Why did they all hate the doctor so much? Matt wondered. *Dad always said that the doctor would help him, would be there for the boys. And he always was!*

"Well, Matt, paying off the overseer to stay off the farm was a big part of it," Luke smiled. "He paid Pete more to stay off the farm and pretend to be here than if he actually had to work. And Pete was so lazy that he bit at that immediately. Once Pete was gone, we had a little freedom. As we do today. That was all Matt's idea! My big brother kept us safe, Izzy. He deserves all the credit."

Matt laughed. "Pete's a dumb guy, dumber even than most of them, even dumber than me! But it's 'cause of you and Paul, that's how I had the money to do that. You made this farm work and gave us a lot of cash. I used that to buy off anyone who I worry about, including dumb Pete, and to make all the farmers around here happy. It's been a good swindling! I'm glad we didn't leave. This is our home."

"Our sanctuary." Luke nodded. "Everything outside its walls is corrupt. This is where we will be forever."

"Our prison," Paul snarled. "In here, we're sitting ducks to the passions of the doctor and his flock, people who are always poised to take out their wrath on a pair of Negroes who are not apt to follow God's grand script of passive enslavement. We are nothing here, no more than ants ready to be squished. I hope Lincoln wins. I hope he fights a war against these people and beats the crap out of them. But I don't intend to hang around here and wait for that verdict. If things start to get ugly, I will be out of here in an instant. This may be a prison, but it's difficult to lock up a Cocklin."

"And you would just give this all up?" Luke asked incredulously. "The world outside is not a friendly one, Brother, not North or South. You tell him, Izzy. Tell him the facts. This is not a prison. This is a sanctuary. This is our home."

Izzy grabbed a pile of corned beef, doused it with mustard, and shoved it in his mouth, drips of yellow goop sliding down the edges of his lips. He had only one thing to say.

"Paul, what did you whip up for dessert? I'm starving!"

Now Matt and Izzy strode down Main Street in Izzy's buggy, a small contingent of people dashing back and forth in front of them, finely painted houses astride small shops, horses tied to wooden poles. It was a picturesque town seeming to shine beneath the backdrop of the blue mountains; from here, the mountains were like an orderly line that sliced through the sky, Old Rag's defiant ugliness not visible from anywhere in town. Through it all, Izzy did not stop talking. Matt was never sure exactly what he was ranting about much of the time, because the chatter could bounce from one topic to another in a matter of seconds. But, nonetheless, Matt enjoyed it!

"We're here," said Izzy, as he parked his cart along the town's one paved street.

As they meandered up a manicured path replete with blue-and-pink bushes that led to the doctor's white-painted house, the silhouette of the Blue Ridge Mountains hovering brightly in the background, Izzy leaned down to Matt and whispered in his ear, "This guy scares the living crap out of me, even though he is the world's greatest idiot!"

"He ain't that bad," Matt whispered back.

"Just watch me play with him!" Izzy chuckled.

Just then, the door opened, and the doctor, smelling of perfume, greeted them.

He was not a tall man, nor particularly thin, but he seemed to be both as he stood at the door with an erect stature wearing a very fine, pressed brown blazer. His face was wide, with a gray mustache and goatee upon his otherwise clean-shaven white skin. His hair lay back neatly; it was short and thick, perfectly groomed. He had neither a prominent nose nor chin; both were hardly noticeable. And as he looked upon the visitors, he displayed a subdued elation, one that seemed more forced than genuine.

Last night Izzy had told this to the boys: *I hope he wears that brown jacket I sold to him last year. I told him it's made of imported silk, and I got him to pay a pretty fortune for it. In fact, it's sewed from New York wool and belonged to a Negro minister who died in it before the church sold it to me, and then I swindled it on him. It gives me a perverse pleasure to watch him wearing it. A tiny victory for our cause. What can I say?*

"Ah, Doctor, what a pleasure to see you!" Izzy said with a chuckle. "I love your jacket."

"As do I," the man uttered in a stilted, slow infection. His large mouth remained permanently stuck in a half-smile. "I do believe that it is one of your finest products you have sold me. Please, both of you, come in, come into my humble abode. Matthew, I am so glad to see you too. A very nice surprise indeed!"

The doctor slid through his simple and elegant parlor and led them to his study, surrounded by books and elaborately framed impressionistic paintings and a row of skulls lining the back wall. He stood stiffly and formally, gesturing for Izzy and Matt to sit on the couch. But instead, Izzy plopped into the doctor's favorite chair, something he surely must have known would irk the doctor since he had been here many times before. But, as was typical, the doctor did not flinch. It was rare anything could fluster this very disciplined man.

It was clear to Matt, though, that Izzy was trying to irritate him. It was so uncomfortable being here, not only because he was afraid Izzy would get the doctor mad, but also because Matt really didn't want to see Jessie, the doctor's daughter, who likely would be hovering if she knew he was here. Matt kept looking around, squirming in his chair, wondering what Izzy would say next.

"Hey Doc, you got any of those sandwiches and iced tea like last time?" Izzy asked him in a gruff New York drawl that was very distinct from his usual inflection. "I remember those were good."

The doctor smiled, a bit uncomfortably. "Why of course! No hospitable Virginia host would fail to offer his guest refreshment. But I do remember, Mr. Snout, that your people have very peculiar laws, and that you cannot eat both meat and cheese at the same time, for whatever barbaric reason there is for such a thing.

So, out of respect for your antiquated customs, please tell me, would you like chicken or cheese in your sandwiches, because I do believe that on your last trip I offered you both."

Izzy nodded and stared hard into the doctor's beady eyes. "That is true. We do have laws. And some of them don't make sense. Something you people down South can certainly relate to. I'll take the cheese."

A small bowl of peanuts sat near Izzy's chair, and he shoved a handful in his mouth, chewing loudly.

"So, what is the word in New York about Lincoln's chances of winning?" the doctor asked him, seemingly oblivious to Izzy's antics. "My understanding is that your city is ambivalent. You are about to elect a mayor who states that he would go with the South if the country split up. That is hardly an endorsement of the Republicans! We in Virginia are a civil people, and we don't want war, but we also will not tolerate Lincoln."

"Well," said Izzy, his mouth full of food, "it takes a civil people to start a civil war, or so I heard."

The doctor forced a smile. "My understanding too is that the Jews are less in favor of splitting from the South. I know that you people worship the god of money and that you have a pecuniary addiction to our cotton. Besides, your Bible is a virtual endorsement of slavery!"

"Well, Doctor," he said with a smirk, gulping down the last of his nuts, "I can't speak for all the Jews or for all the New Yorkers, just the smart and handsome ones like me. By saying the Jews are for the war, I assume you are talking about Rabbi Morris Raphael from B'nai Jeshurm, that's who endorses slavery, and to be blunt, Doctor, he's a horse's ass who gets more support from the gentiles than from us, believe you me. The rest of us, we're a bit more ambivalent. Something about human chattel that rubs us the wrong way, especially given our history of being in your chains for most of our existence."

Just then Jessie, the doctor's daughter, strolled in wearing a long, pink flowing dress that her father had bought for her out of Izzy's stash. She showed it off for the boys, smiling with large crooked teeth, and winking at Matt, who instantly turned away. She was less than five-foot-tall and quite plump, with short brown hair and large breasts that she always found a way of highlighting. She poured tea into Izzy's and her dad's empty cups and then approached Matt. "Would you like extra ice in yours, Matthew?" she asked him softly, her tiny eyes staring into the whites of his. "I know how much you like ice, especially since you make this place so hot."

He nodded no.

"Do you like my dress, Matthew? Daddy bought it for me for my birthday. I don't turn eighteen for several more weeks, but he thought that it was perfect for me. I bought it thinking that you would, at least that's what Izzy told me."

Izzy said that? Matt twisted his glace to Izzy, who winked at him.

Jessie had never been Matt's favorite, for reasons that stretched back to their time together in school. She had not even paid attention to him until recently. But now, every time he meandered into the doctor's den, there she was, shoving her breasts into his face, smiling at him with a hypnotic glance. He tried to be nice, as he did on this day, but deep down he was repulsed. "It's a nice dress, Jessie."

"Thank you, Matthew," she smiled, kissing him on the head with her slobbering, wet lips. "You are just the sweetest boy ever. And you look so handsome today!"

Izzy smirked, almost coughing out his sandwich. He stood with tea in hand, and with his other hand, he slapped Matt on the back. "Let me tell you, Jessie," he spoke to the doctor's daughter, even as his hand sat on Matt's shoulder. "Matt himself picked out that dress for you. He said, Izzy, I know who would look perfect in that dress, the doctor's daughter Jessie, and he made sure that I didn't sell it to anyone else in this country until you were able to see it first."

Matt grimaced at his friend. What the hell was Izzy doing? Izzy gave him a covert wink, and then Matt forced a smile.

Soon enough, Jessie wandered back into the kitchen, and these two men continued to spar. Why did Izzy insist on fighting with the doctor, constantly disparaging him and making him seem reprehensible? In fact, the doctor had been nothing but good to Matt, he was respected by all who lived here, and he never bothered Matt or his brothers. He had also been his father's friend and helped Jake find his way down here. Of all the people in town, why did Izzy detest the doctor above everyone else?

And for that matter, if he so despised the doctor, why was he trying to push the doctor's daughter right into Matt's lap? Was that just one of his games, or did he have another purpose?

"We make clothes in factories all over New York," Izzy continued, "all of high quality, like the ones I sell you. In my city alone we have more manufacturing capacity than your entire South, and that's just the tip of the iceberg of what Northerners can produce. If there's war, those factories will be making uniforms and guns. How do you people think you have any chance against us if there is war?"

The doctor laughed. "It seems to me, Mr. Snout, that in the panic of 1858 we down here did just fine, while you and your factories collapsed and your people crumbled. Don't doubt our resolve. You would best to be respectful of us, even a bit fearful."

"And you have slavery too, doctor, and thousands of Negroes who will slit your throats once they know they can run up North and be free. Not only can we outgun you, but we have an army of people right in your backyard willing to kill for us. What can I tell you?"

The doctor laughed, in an almost mechanical way. "Our Negros are docile and appreciate the life that we give them; they won't turn on us. What do they have up in your New York?

I understand the Negro can't find work, is starving, is treated poorly by his white brethren. That he is kicked and killed and ridiculed. If you call what we have slavery then what do you have?"

"We call our thing freedom," Izzy casually said, as he slurped down the rest of the iced tea.

Matt was getting antsy. His skin started to itch, and he felt twitchy. He needed to end this mindless banter, to get out of here before Jessie returned or before these two men tore each other apart. He could barely tolerate it anymore!

"Aren't you supposed to be buying some clothes, Doctor?" Matt blurted out, standing up and cutting off one of Izzy's rants. "Not to be rude, and I know you two men got a lot to discuss, but I reckon you should buy your clothes soon so I can go back to the farm. It's harvest season, and even though I got me a good and loyal overseer, I like to look over the slaves myself, and I don't want to spend all my day here when I need to be over there."

The doctor laughed proudly and placed his arms around Matt's shoulders. "So true, son, so true. We are just having a little fun, but work is work, and you do need to return home. Mr. Snout, let's you and I walk outside and take a look at your wares. If war does come, and I pray that sensible minds will make sure that it doesn't, but if it does, the most upsetting part of it will be that I can no longer buy your fine clothes! Come, let's look. I will need to stock up."

"It'll likely be a short war." Izzy laughed. "So you have little to worry about."

"Touché, Mr. Snout," said the doctor. "I hope there is no war, no Lincoln, no secession, and no fighting between us. Let us hope calm and noble minds prevail and that Northerners and Southerners reach into our Christian souls to find common ground and mutual understanding."

"Doctor, I don't have a Christian soul, but if I get one, I'll let you know. Until then, this old Jew will at least be able to keep you well dressed."

They rode back rapidly along the wide dirt road that connected Washington to the many Southern farms and orchards dotting the valley along the Shenandoah chain. The sun had started to descend.

"Why you say all that stuff to Jessie about me?" Matt asked him. "You know what I feel about her."

Izzy pulled the cart off the road and brought his horses to a halt. He stared hard into Matt's eyes, and his visage of levity instantly evaporated. "Matt," he said, his very slight Yiddish accent that he had so carefully suppressed slipping out just a bit, "your dad, before he went completely off the deep end, said something to me after your mother left. He said, 'Izzy, you make sure if anything happens to me that my kids are OK.' That's what I've done. I play with the doctor because he likes it, and—what can I say—it makes you look good the worse I look. I also make sure that he and his daughter continue to like you. Don't ever let her know how you feel. The more she likes you, the more you will be in the doctor's good stead. Look, I would prefer you boys don't stay down here. I wish you would get your asses up North. Until then, what can I tell you, we all just have to play the game."

Izzy paused, seemingly considering his next words before uttering them. "One of the things that Paul requested, and that I have for him, are maps and information regarding the underground railroad. That cannot be seen by anyone. Do you understand me? Paul knows that, but I only tell you because there may be a time you have to let those two boys off the leash. Things could get that bad, Matt, and when that happens, you have to be prepared to help them get away."

Matt nodded. "I don't think we need that, Izzy," he said. "I can just free them anytime, and I would too. The doctor, I'm sure he'd let me too. He's not so bad after all."

Izzy's visage twisted, and his voice became firmer. "Matt, trust no one. On one! Not the doctor, not his daughter, not the birds who fly around. There will likely be war, and once that occurs,

God help us all. They will discover your brothers, and then they will destroy everything you know. Promise me, Matt, that if the shit hits the fan, you will let them go. Promise me!"

Matt sat quietly, somewhat taken aback, nodding his head up and down.

And then, Izzy laughed. "I only tell you this not to berate you, but because I understand what it's like to be at the mercy of other people. My people have been—"

"I know," Matt smiled. "Your people been beaten and slaved and tortured for two thousand years, and they only survived by making no trouble, staying smart, and keeping away from harm's way."

"No, Matt, five thousand years. We have been tortured for five thousand years. Don't forget the Babylonians. Never forget the Babylonians. And we still are in danger every day. One bad move and we are in the doghouse again. So, we are careful. As you should be. Because these people here will not be happy if they know what is really going on with your farm. They can never know."

"OK," Matt said.

"Well then, let's get home for dinner! I'm starved. What did you think of those sandwiches?"

"Terrible!" Matt laughed.

"Yes, terrible! God help you if you marry that girl. She makes a terrible sandwich, that much I can tell you. Let's go! Being here with you boys, that's the best food any man could ask for!"

Poor Izzy! Always fearful and paranoid. And at the same time, always so funny and lighthearted. Matt quickly dismissed Izzy's fears. He was more concerned about Izzy's quip about marrying Jessie! That, Matt knew, would be worse than the five thousand years of misery Izzy's people had to endure!

3

During Izzy's brief stay, Paul found a bit of a spark again. His mind had wandered to the darkest of places during the past few months. He knew that it was harvest time, that he needed to focus on sales and production, that the crop this year seemed better than ever. It was difficult managing so many trees and so much fruit with just a few slaves. But, all three brothers worked incessantly, and Ruth's two boys, they could do twelve men's work in a day; they were quiet and efficient, and Ruth drove them hard! Sometimes Paul would laugh with them, but they had very little to say. For some reason, they gained solace in their work and wanted nothing more than that.

"We've got excess fruit this year," Paul had said to Matt a few weeks earlier. "I found a few markets up North, distributors who are willing to come down here and see what we have. Izzy contacted them for me. The prices they are willing to pay are far better than what we're getting here. Our profit margin will soar if we sell to them. Maybe then we can hire some laborers for harvest; they have people up North willing to help out for a small wage. Then we can plant more trees. I've been even eyeing the land that abuts ours from the Sanders's farm. Sanders is an idiot; he never uses that land. I say we offer to buy it, have Luke push out our irrigation ditches that way, and plant a whole new crop.

Luke and I have been talking. He has ideas of what may grow best."

Matt nodded vehemently from side to side. "We can't do that, Paul," he shouted at his brother. "You keep saying all these things. You always do good with our finances, you figured out how to sell our stuff better than anyone, you know how to package it and make it last longer—you do all these things. But I know these people who live down here. We can't be stealing other people's farms. We can't be selling to people up North or bringing them down to work on our farm. Down here, you bring in more slaves, that's what you do if you need more people to do work. I know what you is saying, Paul, but you don't know these people. They won't let us do all that stuff you is always saying."

"Fuck them, Matt," Paul snapped back. "We don't have to drop down to their level. We need to show them how things are done. Believe me, they may yell and scream, but soon enough they'll be emulating us, just like they've done with our irrigation and our planting techniques. You don't think they want to be more successful? You can't subvert our progress just to satisfy their ignorant minds!"

"The answer is no," Matt insisted. "They is all on edge down here these days. They talk on and on about the North and how terrible everyone is there. We can't take a chance and start selling to Northerners, hiring Northerners. You ain't all that smart all the time, Paul. I know you think you is, but you don't know these people. I will tell you when we can do stuff like that. I know better than you about that stuff. And I'm in charge of this farm. Now ain't the time to be doing this stuff!"

Paul's heart sunk as he smiled knowingly at his brother. "Just say it, Matt. You are the master. I am your slave. That's what it comes down to. Eventually, I knew you were going to say it."

"That's not what I'm saying, Paul. You always put words in my mouth. I am just saying, now ain't the time to do that. And all your financial ideas, they don't always work out. Sometimes you got these ideas and you just want to do them right away and you ain't thought everything through, like you did with them stocks you tried to buy with our money, before Izzy stopped you. That's all I is saying."

"And you are also saying," Paul said to Matt, staring him hard in the eye, "that you are in charge. That your word is final. That Luke and I, we're just your slaves. You wouldn't even have this farm if it weren't for us, Matt. I don't discredit your contribution to our success, but you have to know, it wasn't substantial. If we had followed your lead, we'd still have three trees and a flooded farm."

"I ain't disagreeing with you, Paul, and I ain't saying you is a slave. I never ever treated you that way. But I know these people. And I got to do what I think is right."

"Because you're the master," Paul said to him.

"No," Matt said. "Because you is pigheaded most of the time, and Dad and Mom told me to make sure you don't do nothing too dumb! You always got these ideas, and you always got to have your way and do everything the minute you think about it. We is successful because we do things slow, because we make sure that everyone in the farms around us benefits, and we don't rouse no suspicion. That's my job on this farm, to make sure we don't get in no trouble. My whole role in life is to make sure we is safe, that our farm stays out of harm's way. You and Luke, I know you two did all the stuff to make it successful. But when I get an idea that I think could harm us, that's when I put my foot down."

"And that's when you put us in chains," Paul said. "Because we're your slaves."

Matt grunted and shoved his arms in the air. "Forget it!" he cried out and then turned and marched away.

But in the end, Paul knew he was right. He was just a slave. Despite all that he had accomplished, he would never receive credit. Despite all that he envisioned, his ideas and plans would be contingent upon satisfying the moronic inhabitants of this county, people who viewed him and his brother as sub-human. He had never been off the farm, never seen the world but for a distant glare. He lived on an island surrounded by sharks. Paul's path to the world beyond was through what he read, what his dad and mom had taught him, and what Izzy fed him. He always felt elated when Izzy came to town! He gobbled up news of politics and culture, read through books of history and philosophy, discussed religion and slavery and so many ideas considered taboo by any of those who lived around his island. He craved those moments.

But they were all too fleeting.

Paul's "stock mistake" that Matt continued to remind him about occurred two years earlier. Yes, Paul had become cocky; he was the first to admit it. They sold so much fruit and kept their overheads so low that they accumulated excess money. Paul had an idea to put some of it into stocks.

"People are making a fortune investing," Paul had said. "We are just sitting on this cash. We can't expand our farm, we are at maximum capacity, we don't dare hire more slaves, so why not invest?"

Izzy had been over the house for a few weeks that winter, and he was receptive to most of Paul's ideas. But not this one.

"I work with a man named Abe," Izzy said. "He runs our business. He buys the clothes and finds salesmen like me to sell them. When the money is good, he takes some of it and saves it for a rainy day, much like the story of Joseph in the Bible tells us. (I know you don't like the Bible, and you don't believe in God, Paul, but there are some stories worth reading, and that's one of them, believe you me!) Abe says to me, Izzy, the gentiles, they like to put their money in stocks, and good for them if they succeed. But for me, he says, I want control of my own finances. I will put my money into more shirts, more carts, more salesmen. This I can control. Stocks I can't control. One bad turn in our country, and those stocks drop like a man falling off a cliff. Why trust the whim of others when we can be in control of our own destiny? That's what Abe taught me."

It took a lot of convincing for Paul to eschew his investment ideas, and Matt in the end prevented him from doing it. "We don't need to make more money," he told his irate brother. "We got to be sensible. If these people think we're rich, if they knowed that we got our money in speculation with the Northern industry types, they will get suspicious. Besides, if we lose that money, it will put our whole farm at risk. We will be indebted to others. And Daddy said to never let that happen."

Three weeks later, in 1858, the entire stock market collapsed. Matt never said anything to his brother about the near disaster that Paul's rash idea could have instigated, not until his recent allusion to it, but Paul felt just a bit muted after that, and he knew that Matt had gained the upper hand.

But one thing would always be true. Paul knew that, in the end, he was just a slave. He watched Ruth and her two boys. They had been here for as long as his dad had; he bought them decades ago when he purchased the farm. The boys were old now, older even than Izzy, and they too had not been off this land, had not interacted with any other people, did not know how to read or write (and had no desire to learn), and just went through their daily tasks, day after day, month after month, year after year, until they grew old and gray and empty. He had tried to talk with them, but they never sought to engage him. They wanted to remain separate from the brothers. Paul respected their wishes.

But he so feared becoming just like them.

He had so many ideas! So much ambition! He had already accomplished more in his brief life that most of the farmers here ever achieved. He and Luke had created an agricultural masterpiece! They had introduced the most advanced science and engineering, the most efficient business practices, and their efforts were rewarded by their consistently superior results. And yet, although he lacked much of an ego, Paul could not help but feel slighted that he had to conceal what he had done behind an illusion of what the world wanted to see: he was just a dumb slave. Matt received the credit. Paul and Luke had to forever be shoved into obscurity. There was nothing else that could be said.

"Isn't it enough that we know the truth?" Luke tried to tell his brooding brother. "Why do you care what people in the outside world think? The three of us know. Izzy knows. Ruth and her boys know. To live for acclamation by people you neither respect nor care about seems like an unsatisfying goal, Brother. It's your inner sense of achievement that should drive you. Stop focusing on what you can't control."

"It doesn't bother you, Luke, that we are stuck here, that we have to play our roles whenever any idiot walks on our land, that we have little control over what we do? It doesn't irk you that at any minute the doctor or any of his cronies can walk on this land and whip us or kill us or sell us off, like the inhuman creatures they think we are? Think about what we could achieve if we weren't the slaves that we are! Our mother was stripped from us so we could continue to playact for the people who live around us. We don't know if she is alive or dead, if she is being raped and tortured. We don't have anyone to give us the warmth and compassion that she did. How is that OK, Luke? How can you be happy being on this farm knowing that what happened to Mom could happen to us?"

"Matt won't let that happen," Luke said, a pensive smile sewn upon his face. "And none of your fears will transpire as long as we have Matt. They haven't yet. We are safe here, Brother. We can revel in our accomplishments. We can float upon our pond and survey all that we have achieved. Out there, beyond the fences, that's where danger lies. In here, we are the masters. We control our own fate."

Increasingly, Paul did not see things that way. He looked up at the mountains—the blue chain that stretched far to the north—and he dreamed of running off. He closed his eyes and envisioned a better fate for himself, one in which he could excel and be amply rewarded. He dreamed a lot. The monotony of his current existence ate at him. He was a feckless creature going through the motions, a slave at the mercy of an illusion that was as precarious as the flimsy fence that surrounded this land.

Sometimes he thought of his mother, her tranquil face smiling at him as a child, and he shuddered. How could that have been allowed to happen? Why was everyone so forgiving of so heinous a crime? He had been robbed of an affection and intelligence that he craved so much. And yet, no one seemed to bat an eye.

Paul sat with Izzy on a warm September day as they looked through the rows of apple trees ready to shed their fruits.

"You know what I think sometimes, Izzy," he said. "I think, Ruth's two boys, they've never been with a girl. They can't ever be fathers. They can't ever know love. Sometimes I think of how nice it would be to be in someone's arms. To have someone love me. And then it hits me, that will never happen. I am in the same predicament as they are. I will never feel that kind of love."

Izzy laughed. "That's for the best! The one good part of your current state of bondage is that you don't have to be a slave to the female species. Believe you me, it's not worth it. They charm you and then entice you, and before you know it, they entrap you and suck out all your vital juices. I have spent my life avoiding them! You think you are a slave? You need to hang around married men. Then you will see what slavery is really all about!"

Paul chuckled. "At least you have the option to think that way. I don't. My fate is sewed by others."

"Paul, my good friend, you think too much! That's a good thing, but it can be a dagger." He then paused and peered around through the trees. "If you do come North, I will get you started with work. I know people who will put you up. It's not so pretty a life as you have down here, but you will be free. Free to be hungry and dirty and to walk through shit and to look at broken buildings and to be taunted and abused by the Irish. But free nonetheless"

"That sounds like heaven." Paul gleamed.

"Despite all this beauty down here," Izzy mused. "I usually can't wait to get home. I have never seen a place so graced with God's wonderment and so shit upon by man's ignorance and hate as the towns of Virginia."

"Don't forget, Izzy, the God of these people, the same one that everyone seems to believe in these days, He's perfectly fine whipping Negroes and treating us like cattle. So, He makes some nice mountains and gives us fresh air, only so his taskmasters can accomplish their vile tasks more easily."

Izzy smiled. "For an atheist, you certainly know a lot about God!"

"Believe me," Paul said, "God is everywhere. That's what they tell me. And that's why my mother was taken from me and why I can't leave these gates. But—and I don't share this with my brothers, so please don't either—I am thinking of getting out of here soon, of leaving these gates behind me. I appreciate all the maps and the advice you've given me. I would want nothing better than to live in filth and to work for you."

"Why not just tell them?" Izzy wondered. "Matt says he will free you. You can come back with me."

Paul nodded. "It's not that simple. They won't easily let me go. They'll try to convince me to stay. Lay guilt all over me. Talk about how I am abandoning them. How the world out there is worse than I really think. And the people who live here, the doctor and all his brood, they aren't going to let Matt just free a slave and send him on his way. They have their customs and values! And that includes chasing us down and whipping the shit out of us. Matt has no power when it comes to defying the customs of Virginia. He tells me that every day. He may offer to free me, but in the end, he never will."

Izzy nodded. He understood. "Study the maps," he said. "I will be waiting."

On his most lonely days, on days where he did have some time and space, Paul would wander out to the copious trees and sit down. He often brought a book, even when the temperature dropped and the land was covered by frost and snow. He peered through the forest that he and his brothers had created, up to the mountains and clouds, and he imagined his own freedom. These trees sat stuck in the ground, producing fruit for others, never able to achieve anything on their own. Paul could relate to their predicament! And the mountains stared down at him, permanently crippled by their weight, having peered at generation after generation of animals and humans who used and abused this land, whose own avarice and vile intentions had tainted the wondrous valley beneath their shadows. He stared at the one mountain that stood out from the others, Old Rag, its craggy rock head seeming to laugh at him.

"I got away from the others," Old Rag said to Paul. "And now look. I am still stuck. My top has been stripped away. Was it worth it?"

Paul nodded. "Yes," he said to the mountain. "Because you are free from the chain. You are your own self." And, in Paul's eyes at least, Old Rag smiled back.

These days of farming were becoming more emotionally arduous. Even picking apples dug at Paul. Why was he doing this? For whose benefit? Had all his education and ambition led him down this path forever? Was this all there would ever be?

Since being a young boy, after his mother was stripped from him, Paul had buried himself in the kitchen. There he gained a peace and solace he knew nowhere else. There he could accomplish something palpable and something instantly rewarded. At first, Ruth was reluctant to relinquish her kitchen to the angry young boy. But Jake insisted, and then upon Jake's death, Paul gained his own autonomy. Ruth knew that when Paul was in a cooking mood, she better just give him some space.

"Just don'ts goes and mess my kitchen up," she would yell at him. "And puts everything back where you gots it from! You understand that!"

"Of course, Ruth, I'll be good."

She would shake her head. "Good? You is a good boy, Paul. Deep in your heart you is. But good is not how I would describe you in any other way. You is an explosion waiting to happen. Just don't let it go off in my kitchen!"

"Yes, Ruth, I promise. You want me to bring you and the boys something when I'm done?"

"Damned right I does! You better! We always love your cooking. Just don't mess my kitchen!"

"You will not be disappointed!"

"I's better not be. I never has yet." And she would laugh and walk away.

Paul created his own recipes; he told Matt what to buy, and he made do with what he could get. He never consulted books or asked for advice; everything he cooked and created percolated in his mind. He could spend hours in the kitchen, and when there he lost himself in the task at hand. His mind smiled. He peered up at Old Rag and offered the old mountain a bite.

"If only I could, Paul," the mountain said to him. Yes, even Paul heard the mountain talk!

"One day," Paul said, "you will lead me to freedom."

And Old Rag nodded. Indeed, he would!

4

Luke gazed at the majestic pond as its surface rippled in a soft, warm September wind. A crystal-clear image of the world around them reflected upon it like a mirror: a line of blue mountains, an intense sky with puffy white clouds dancing across the landscape, trees whose leaves were fluttering in their colorful glory, and the one peak that stood out from the rest—bold and distinct. He smiled with a certain pride sitting here on the water's banks, because he knew that this slice of defiance and beauty, this testament to knowledge and innovation, was his child, built by his vision and his careful planning, the very nidus of the farm's special place in the world. To some, it was just a small pond. To Luke, it was God's gift to him and his brothers. It was his parents' souls. It was life itself.

September was harvest time, when Luke and his brothers and Ruth's boys picked and packaged their crop of apples and pears nearly every day. Everyone worked hard, and Matt even contemplated hiring some extra hands from town to do some picking, something he did with great apprehension given the secrets that no one here wanted to be revealed and exposed. But Matt was a genius in this way. He knew how to conceal certain realities, how to instruct his brothers how to play their roles when others were watching, and how to feed people in the town with gifts and jobs such that they often looked the other way even if they did harbor some suspicions. This September, after Izzy left word that he would be coming to town, Matt pleaded again to hire some people, just a few, just for a few days, but Luke and Paul pushed back.

"We will do it ourselves," Luke said. "We want to spend time in the big house with you, especially Wednesdays, and especially after Izzy arrives. We want to be free to talk and to plan. We don't want anyone soiling the purity of our island or causing us any apprehension."

"It ain't like Izzy's gonna help," Matt said. "He's just gonna slow us down. We can get three Negroes from the Baker farm. They pretty much done with all their picking anyway. They won't say nothing to no one."

"We will take care of the crop ourselves," Paul stated more emphatically. "We don't need anyone else. We always do it ourselves."

An exasperated Matt just tossed his arms in the air. "Fine," he cried. "You both know best, I guess. I ain't worth shit here anyway. We'll just let the crop rot on the trees until we get to it. That's just fine with me. It ain't like I care. It's just money."

Luke, smiling pensively, kissed his anxious brother on the head. "We love you, Brother," he said. "You are amazing. And you may be right. Let's see. Any way we can keep people off our sanctuary, though, is preferable to the alternative. We just want to try. If you agree."

Matt, breathing hard, nodded up and down.

Now Luke sat on his perch at the Southern end of the farm, peering over the pond, rapt in its ripples, studying the water's motion, assessing which dams needed some adjustment. A bright September sun shined upon his neck. His mind floated upon the pristine waters.

Ten years earlier he sat in this very spot as rain pummeled the farm, producing floods and deep mud that hampered the growth of their trees. His eyes moved from drop to drop, puddle to puddle, stream to stream. His mind absorbed everything and twisted it into another reality. He envisioned the pond, which at that time did not exist. He could see it, could taste its waters, could feel its nourishing flow.

"What are you doing out here, Luke?" his mother asked him on a cool, wet day so long ago. She sat beside him and encased him in her warm hug, kissing him all over the face. "You'll freeze to death."

"You know why I am here, Momma," he said softly, smiling, peering forward at the land.

"The pond?"

Luke nodded up and down.

"Tell me all about it, Luke!" she said to him, rubbing his thick, wet hair. "Show me where it will be, how it will flow. Let me see what you see! I want to see it in my mind like you do."

Luke glowed. He spoke quickly and with great energy, telling Mamma everything, showing her, pointing, explaining. They stood up and trudged through the mud; both were oblivious to the rain, both were talking and laughing and looking. It was as if she finally understood!

"God gives us all this magical water, Mamma, and it's filled with His bounty, with nature's fertilizer, coming right down from that big beautiful mountain," Luke said. "He gives it to us, and it's our job to control it and use it to our benefit. Think about it, Mamma. All this water is flooding us. It's our enemy. But with just a little bit of effort, once we learn to control it, we can transform our farm and our land into God's great masterpiece, into a thing of beauty and energy. If we control the water, if we make it our friend and not our enemy, then we will have more fruit than you and Daddy can ever imagine."

"God?" his mother laughed. "I don't think it's God, Luke, that makes our choices. I don't even think there is a God. Even if there was, Lukie, we are in control of our fate, not Him."

Luke peered into his mother's inviting eyes. "This water, it comes from the mountains, from up there." He pointed through the dark sky. "It is God. Not the God you and Daddy tell me doesn't exist, not the one you say the slaveholders use to hurt people. But our God, Momma. The one who watches over us. The one who lives up on that mountain. He gave us this gift. It's up to us to use it and turn it into magic!"

She rubbed his head. "Are you sure you're only eight years old?" She laughed. "Well, maybe you are right, Luke, it makes sense. This piece of land here, where the water all seems to sit and flood everything, that could be the very pond you always talk about. We can dredge the land and make it deeper. Then we can divert the stream here and fill it up. Put up those dams you talk about. And then control where and when the water flows to every part of our farm. I can see it. No more floods. Perfect irrigation. Custom fertilization. I can see it, Luke. I really can!"

He grabbed his mother tightly, rain draping his face, so comfortable was he against her warm body.

He spent so many days here, watching, and then measuring, and finally writing everything down. He drew out his idea in great detail. Sometimes his mother would sit with him, and they would review the plans together, modifying them with every storm.

"Do you think Daddy will do it?" Luke asked.

"I talk to him about it every day," she said to her son. "He wants to. But you know your daddy. He has to do it right. Find out how to pay for it. Make sure anyone we hire is safe. But I showed him your plans. I walked him through it. He's as excited as we are."

"Yay!" Luke cried out.

But then, just like that, his mother disappeared, dragged away from their farm, gone forever from his life and his heart.

The loss stung Luke hard, and he stopped thinking about the pond or anything else.

It was on a September day a year later that he sat alone again in the rain, watching, looking, studying. On that dreary day, his father walked out and sat quietly beside him.

"We're going to do it," Jake said, with little inflection in his voice. "I hired us twenty Negroes from town once the harvest ends. I rented the machines we'll need to dig them ditches and the holding pond from your sketches. I have material we can use to build dams. I am doing it for your mother. This was always her dream. I want to see what you and her are always gabbing about. We're going to do it, Luke. By spring, it will be real, and you won't have to sit out here in the rain no more."

Luke leaped upon his father and hugged him. Jake, as was his want, rubbed Luke's back and started shedding tears. He cried often these days. *But this time*, Luke thought, *they were tears of joy*.

A year later, he had his pond, and his farm prospered like no one could ever imagine. Now he sat beside it, thinking about his mother and father, knowing that their souls drifted through the clear water and over every ripple.

As the sun beamed on him during a break from a long day of labor during a prolific September harvest, Luke slipped back into reality and peered at his red raft. Despite a brisk autumn breeze that blew against his hide, he decided to launch it into the pond's cool water.

With a few logs and a piece of old burlap doused with red paint, he had constructed this raft out of a need to be closer to the water, and on many warm days and star-filled nights he sat upon it, in God's waters, and lost himself in contemplation. This was the heart of an alternative world in which he and his brothers lived, one eschewed by the mores of a corrupt society that failed to encase them within it, and by the dangers and rules that pounded upon their gates every day. Even as Matt worked tirelessly to keep their oasis safe, and as Paul reminded him incessantly just how precarious it was, Luke knew that here, in this place, with Old Rag's blood flowing and nourishing the land, they were free. Here they could always be happy. Luke slurped up the farm's beneficence, never wondering what could happen if its walls were pierced, so sure he was of the sanctity and security of this place. Nothing good existed outside of the orchard's fences. Nothing for him or his brothers. And so, he sat on his red raft with the pond's cool waters soaking his pants and feet and thought only of trees, of the waters, of the fertile land, and of what more he could achieve upon this hallowed spot of earth. He stared into the sky and across the ripples of his pond, and he smiled.

"Yo, Brother," Paul called out from the far bank. "You working or dillydallying in there? We don't have much sun left; we have a hell of a lot more to do. Izzy will be here damned soon, and Matt's getting antsy from all the unpicked pears that are ripening fast."

Luke smiled. "I won't be long. I need a little mind massage, Brother. I think I found the perfect spot to grow our grapes and where to build a new dam. I really think we can pull it off."

Paul shook his head. "Good luck with that, Brother. But for just a minute, can your mind focus on the here and now and get out of its dream state? Your idiot brother Matt, who has no idea how the money-flow works when we try to get top dollar for our fruit, thinks we should bring the entire pear crop into town to sell, but I know up North there are better markets. I've researched and written to some, and we can increase our profits considerably if we move in that direction. I'm going to talk to Izzy about it. Will you back me up on it, Brother?"

This was too much mindless chatter for Luke. He closed his eyes and drifted, his mind floating through his many ideas, all exciting and grand. Paul, as usual, marched away in a cloud of grumbles.

Even on the warmest days, the pond remained cool and clean. There were no mosquitoes hovering upon its surface, no slime or crud that gathered in its cracks. Luke had designed it to be alive. He had read a great deal about the agriculture practices in Germany, as well as what little was written about the successful Amish farmers in Pennsylvania. Irrigation and fertilization proved to be of utmost importance; one could not rely on the whims of nature to help fruit reach its optimal potential. The land in Virginia was caked with clay, so Luke devised ways of softening it and making it more fertile. He implored Matt to purchase livestock, whose excrement provided an excellent fertilizer source when properly distributed and manicured. And then there was the water, saturated with minerals and chemicals that were beyond even Luke's most sanguine expectations.

The pond itself was not stagnant. Its water always moved, and even when its banks flooded, the tenth canal diverted it off the farm's land and back into the stream beyond, preventing any further soil saturation or erosion. And so, the pond actually was part of the river; it was, as Luke always said, alive; it was God's reflection on earth. He measured its chemical content and adjusted it with regularity. He made sure all livestock grazed beyond its flow so their activities did not alter the purity of its water. It was the heart of everything here, of the farm's success, of its special nature, and of what a bunch of slaves and a single decent white man were able to accomplish on this sacred piece of dirt that, before their presence here, was nothing but a useless stretch of mud and puddles and malnourishment.

A woman standing on the pond's edge called over to Luke and woke him from his trance. The sun was beating hard on his face, and he was thinking about his mother, who he had lost at too young an age, but whose wisdom and goodness reverberated within him always. He opened his eyes and looked up at a heavyset woman in her late sixties; she had short gray hair, a simple and muddied dress upon her, and muted black skin. His raft had drifted toward the bank and was lodged there. He smiled at her. "All good, Ruth?" he asked.

Not one to smile or reveal too much of herself to anyone, Ruth respected and seemed to love Luke and his brothers. She acknowledged their place on the farm and was content with her own role on it. Together with her husband Isaac, who died a few years ago, and their two grown sons who were now close to forty, Michael and David, she and her family were the only other slaves on the orchard. They oversaw the trees and land, took care of the livestock, monitored the pond and its canals, and did whatever else had to be done, from woodworking to some simple blacksmith duties. Ruth kept the main house clean and, when Paul was not in one of his cooking moods, kept the brothers well fed. She typically ate with her own family in their cabins, although she had an open invitation to eat with the brothers in the main house anytime she chose. Sometimes one of her sons would join the brothers, but it was rare; Luke knew that both Michael and David felt somewhat alienated from him and his brothers and never were fully comfortable being with them.

When Isaac died, Matt felt compelled to replace him with another slave. "He was a hard worker," Matt said of Isaac. "We ain't gonna be able to do enough without him."

Before Paul could even stamp his feet, it was Ruth who muffled Matt's ill-advised suggestion. "Excuse me for saying so, but that ain't a good idea is all I's saying," she said to Matt in a curt, if courteous, tone. "We don't need no more slaves here. We don't need none of that. We don't need no one else snooping around here. What we got here, your daddy would be so proud of it. What you done here, it's the most beautiful thing I ever seen. Me and my boys, we is thankful every day, and we will work harder to make sure nothing ever changes. All's I got to say, and I won't say no more, is if you get Luke to stop floating on the pond all day and get him to do a man's work, and you get Paul to spend more time picking and less time cooking during harvest and leave that to me, well then, I don't think we need another set of arms around here who will likely have too many eyes and see too much, is all I's is saying. We's all can do it ourselves."

"I can work harder too, Ruth," Matt said to her.

She nodded. "I ain't saying nothing about that. You can say it. You is the master here, so I got nothing to say about you. But the other two, I think they need a little push and someone to say to them in no uncertain terms that if they wants to continue living this way, they gots to do a real man's work once in a while. That's all I gots to say."

Luke loved Ruth; he wished she were more open, more affectionate, and less distant. But that was her nature, and it was not his role to push her in any other direction. As he stared up from the raft at her, blocking the sun from his eyes, he smiled.

"My boys is taking a small break for lunch, and we's gonna sit in the cabins a spell to rest from the sun. I will start cooking dinner if you's wants me to. I can get on that soon as you say."

"Paul said he wants to cook tonight," Luke responded. "Matt got some real plump chickens from town, and Paul has some ideas about how he wants to cook them. You know that Izzy is coming, and Paul loves to cook for Izzy! We can bring dinner out to you, or you can come in with us. Izzy loves seeing you. Always your choice, Ruth. But I will warn you, we will be eating late."

Ruth, with a face devoid of emotion, just shook her head. "I figured as much," she said. "You tell old Izzy to come by the cabin. Me and the boys always likes to sees him. Gods only knows how long he will be able to come down here with all the trouble in the world these days. But that Izzy, he always seems to finds himself a way. He is a crafty man at that, a lovely and crafty man."

Luke laughed. "I will!" he said, and then his eyes brightened. "Ruth, let me show you where we're going to plant our grape vines! Izzy plans to get me all the material we need to start. I'm going to build a new dam after the harvest. Do you want me to show you? If we can grow grapes and make wine, well—that will put us in another level. Your boys can enjoy it too!"

Ruth looked down and shook her head. "Luke, you is a good boy, and I loves you like a son, and your mamma and papa will always hold a big place in my heart, but sometimes, you say things that is so far out in another world that I got to just turn away. I's is going to the cabin. You tell your brother Paul that if his chicken is half good to bring us some tonight. We are good eating late. And you make sure that Izzy he comes by and kisses us all hello!"

Luke pushed the red raft farther toward the center of the pond, away from the eddies and flow. He closed his eyes and lay there, content in his place, unimpeded by the harsh vibrations that drifted out of the minds of less-sanguine folk. Here he was on this raft in a place that no one ever believed could exist. Here he was with his brothers and with Ruth's family living a life that no one could believe was possible. Why should he think that there were any limits to what he could accomplish?

He recounted the stories his father and mother told about how Dad came to purchase Mom and Ruth's family. They used to regale the boys with the tales at dinner, laughing and arguing about what was real and what was fantasy, and Mamma, she told him about it too sometimes late at night when she sat with him and eased him to sleep. They talked about a lot, him and Mamma, about the farm and how to make it better, about the world out there beyond its borders. She was never scared, not here; even when she left the farm those many years ago, she did so by her own accord, totally out of love, so she could protect their oasis and her husband and boys from the world's maleficence.

"They are scared of me," she told her young son with a smile. "They always have been, all except your daddy. And so long as I stay here, none of you, and nothing that we are trying to do here, will ever be safe. That's why I am leaving, Luke. Remember, my dearest young man-boy, I plan to come back, one day, when the time is ripe and when the world changes just enough, as I know it will. But until it does, you have to stay here, do what your daddy says, never try to change them that live outside our land, because those people they can ever be changed. They are what they are. You can't convince them even with the best of logic to be otherwise. Always be content and protective of what you got inside, and never wander outside its gates, even if you are curious, because what you find is never going to be as good as you think and certainly not as good as what you got, and it is more dangerous than you realize. Because, Luke, you know I am not one to believe in God and all the other myths the white people push on us, but I do believe in salvation, and this place here, this is what salvation is. Cherish it!"

And then, like always, she would say, "Did I ever tell you how me and your daddy first met?" as though she never had. She liked to talk about it! They both did. It seemed to make her smile and forget everything else.

Daddy bought this land from a friend of his who he met at a fort in New York during his army days, a man named Bob, who stayed in the military even after Daddy left, and who had connections down in Virginia. He implored Daddy to try his hand at farming, since Daddy had proven to be less than competent at almost anything else. *There's a farm down near a place called Washington,* Bob told him. *And they grow fruit. It's never lived up to its potential. Its owner is a drunk and sold off his slaves and was driven out. I can get it for you cheap. I can get you started and tell you how to make it sustainable. I think it is something that can turn around your life, Jake, especially with a child coming to you and your wife. If you're willing to make a go of it and to change your ways enough to not scare off the natives.*

Dad agreed after much discussion with his wife. He had no fear of going South and trying over again and was willing to sell all his meager resources to make it happen. He knew nothing about farming, but Bob was able to give him a crash course, and Bob (who was from a family of money) even sent friends and family over from time to time to help Jake out. Before Dad finalized the purchase, Bob told him the most important thing of all, one thing he implored Dad to never forget: he had to abide by the rules of Virginia if he lived down there, and one rule was that he had to buy slaves. Maybe five or so was all he needed for an orchard like this, and he could hire more part-time during harvest, but there was no negotiating about that. Without slaves, the townspeople would not be welcoming of a Northerner moving into their midst. Dad was not happy about the prospect, but he agreed. He had some money to do it, and Bob told him about the slave auction and how to buy what he needed.

It was the most uncomfortable place I have ever been, Dad told them. *I stood there just dumbfounded, my mouth open, my gut nauseated, just watching people being marched by in chains, whip marks on many, faces drawn. And then I heard a voice.*

"You look like you are a man who doesn't belong here," a woman on the slave line said to him. "In fact, it looks like you don't know what you are even doing. What's your deal?"

Dad turned and locked eyes with a thin woman, dark black, with piercing yellow eyes. She stared hard into his. She wore chattels on her arms and legs; her ragged skin was covered by linear scars and open sores, but all he saw were her eyes. He was drawn in.

"You talking to me?" he asked her, shocked by her audacious behavior and hypnotic beauty.

She smiled, her bright white teeth large and prominent. "What do you think? I'm looking right at you; somehow you think I'm talking to the walls?"

He laughed. "I see why they got you in so many chains. Let me guess. You've got a big mouth, and your master has had just about enough."

"How many you looking for? You got a big planation, small farm, or what? How many slaves you need?"

Luke's dad could not pull his eyes away from this incredible woman. "You trying to sell yourself? Why should I buy someone who's got a big mouth and is evidently a troublemaker? Although I'm guessing you come cheap. What skills do you have?"

She nodded, as though she saw through him. "No, I don't give a damn if you buy me or who buys me. I could care less who owns me because, in reality, no one ever will. I will say that if I do have a big mouth it's because I have a lot to say. And if you want someone who actually knows how to grow things and make farms prosper—because I can look at your face and see that you don't—then you may want someone like me, something my dumbass master didn't quite understand. But I am not selling myself. If you need four slaves, I'm here to tell you that I know the people you should buy, and I promise you that you will thank me till your dying days."

According to Luke's recollection of the story, the two of them spoke back and forth for almost an hour, before the auctioneers insisted that he let her move on to other potential buyers. But between insulting each other with open smiles and talking about the state of farming in Virginia, she did have something to tell him.

"There's a family of four: a lovely man and woman and their two boys. They are on my farm, great workers, willing to listen and do what they are told. They are models of decency and hard work. But my master, who is the face of evil and idiocy, thinks that they are in alliance with me, just because they treated me with kindness, and so he's selling them, and in this auction, they will be separated, each sold to different masters, and their lives, what little lives they have, will be destroyed. If you need four slaves, take them all. Don't let them get split up. You'll get more than their price, and you may actually be doing a good thing."

He nodded when she uttered those words, and she pointed them out. He watched the four of them huddled together, bonded by love, draped with dread and fear. That was enough for Jake. He walked up to the auctioneer and bought them for their stated price, which was less than he hoped to pay. Their names were Ruth, Isaac, Michael, and David. Then he asked about the woman.

"Her?" the auctioneer asked, laughing. "Well, she does come cheap; that's for sure. But her master prefers she be sold somewhere far South. He prefers her to suffer. In fact, he made me promise she'd be sold to someone strong with the whip. You want her though, I'm happy to get rid of her, and I can tell her master that she was bought by someone who seems far firmer than you."

Four months later, Jake's wife gave birth to Matt, and two weeks after that she died. His wife's untimely death was a bittersweet moment for Luke's father, who had already fallen in love with this big-mouthed slave, with whom he spent hours every day talking about farming and life and politics while gazing into her deep eyes and sometimes embracing her with the most passionate kisses he had ever known. Her name was Mary, and she had stolen his heart. When Matt's biological mother died, his father mourned the wife who he did love in a certain way, but then he quickly turned to the other woman whom he loved with a depth of heart he could not have ever imagined possible. Together they built a thriving farm. Together they had two children, Paul and then Luke, whom they raised to be smart and proud men who would never bow down to a slave society that sought to emasculate them and infuse them with false notions of honor and chivalry and God.

Luke smiled whenever he thought of his mom and dad. How delighted they would be with how much this place, and their sons, had grown! He knew that somewhere his mamma was watching over him, and that one day she would return.

The brothers sat with Izzy that night, glowing in the fire's warmth, as he relayed tales of impending doom and war and chaos. Luke had shown Izzy where he intended to plant the grapes, and Izzy brought Luke several books on the matter, all of which Luke imbibed voraciously.

"What do you think Momma would think about the grapes?" Luke asked him. "I can imagine her big smile and the wonderment in her eyes and her pride and joy."

"I think she'd call you a damned fool," Paul countered. "Grapes. Jesus Christ, Brother. There are so many better things we can do with the land."

"I think it's perfect, Luke," Izzy said to him, chewing Paul's chicken as he spoke. "You can make wine, the best wine in Virginia. We can even make it kosher, and I'll sell it up in New York. There's not much to doing that, believe you me. Just tell them it's kosher, and they'll believe it! They just have to know that God blessed it."

Luke smiled. "It will be blessed by God, Izzy," he said. "God is here, on this farm, in its waters, flowing everywhere, bringing us the bounty and freedom that we all have, every day, together."

"Jesus Christ!" Paul laughed. "God again? The same God that the slaveholders use to keep us in bondage? That God? Did you ever listen to anything Mom and Dad told us?"

"It is ironic," Izzy said. "These people like using the Old Testament God to prove that their slavery is sanctioned by the Bible. They hate Jews and everything we stand for but love using our holy book when it justifies their disgusting ways. And let me tell you this about that: our God was no fan of slavery, believe you me. He is misunderstood. You have to give Him a break!"

"Still," Paul said, "Mom and Dad taught us to reject all religion, that it is used as a way to keep people down, to enslave them. All this talk about God makes me sick."

"Not me," said Luke. "Me and Mamma talked about God all the time. He watches over us and gives us His life's blood so we can be safe here and thrive. There is no Bible, Brother. There are no holy words you have to utter. You just have to peer into the sky and see the craggy old mountain that looks over us and gives us the water that nourishes our land and our souls. That is

God. And Momma, she knew, she understood, and she is watching over us as well."

Paul bit into his chicken quietly. So too did Matt. Izzy chewed more voraciously. "Your mother would have loved this chicken," he said. "It's damned good. Damned good."

"It is," said Luke. "It's perfect."

5

"Mathew, sit down, sit down, welcome! My daughter will be by soon, so I want to ask you if you have thought about what I said to you last week?"

From the orchard it was about two miles north to Sperryville, a small hamlet with a few shops providing food and farm necessities, then from there another six miles to Washington, which was where the doctor and anyone who was anything in Rappahannock County lived. Those eight miles could be a treacherous ride when the road was saturated with mud, but on a dry day a good horse, like Matt's brown stallion that he called Horse (he had a hard time coming up with a proper name, so he ended up with that one), could make the trek in a half hour or so. The doctor called this town "Respectable Washington," to distinguish it from the nation's capital, which he considered a moral and physical cesspool.

It was early October, a week before Matt's revised date to climb Old Rag with his brothers, when Matt rode off to see the doctor, who had beckoned him there for a conversation. Main Street sported many small and brightly colored houses where county leaders, affluent farmers, and professionals like the doctor clustered. A few inns and watering holes sat between the grand homes—everything you might need if you came to visit these parts. The town, with its small roads and businesses and schoolhouse, sat in the shadow of the Shenandoah foothills, now teeming with bright orange and yellow trees. It was always meticulously clean. Matt had gone to school here a bit, but when his dad died, he had to stop and tend the farm. Since then, he came in for supplies and when invited by the doctor, who liked to periodically converse with the "young man" to make sure all was well at the farm.

"Your dad was a good man, but he was a Yankee," said that doctor to him soon after Jake died. "He did not know our ways, and he engaged in, shall we say, some actions of questionable morality and civility. You are born of the South, young man, and I want to be your guide, your adapted father, to help you with the gargantuan tasks that lay ahead, and to teach you how to be a dignified Virginian."

Last week the doctor, who always sat in his study with a pitcher of sweet iced tea on a small white marble table, asked Matt to stop by, to pose just that question: Had he thought about what he said to him the week before about his daughter?

"I'm sorry, sir," Matt answered, sitting on a small rocking chair straight across from the doctor's desk. "I don't remember exactly what you're talking about."

"You know my daughter, of course, Jessie," he smiled, his white, straight teeth jibing well with his overall demeanor of civility and erudition. They all knew him here in Washington; he had money and influence, and he cared for the people's health as best he could. When there was a civic meeting, a fundraiser, or a town hall, there would always be the doctor, front and center, having something important to say, which he uttered without bravado or coercion, always offering to lend a hand. Since the death of his wife nearly a decade ago, his young daughter Jessie, now eighteen, always stood at his side. He owned no slaves and had no servants; just he and Jessie managed his modest home and practice, and it was rare they were ever apart.

"'Course I know Jessie," Matt answered back, somewhat quizzically. He looked at the doctor both with warmth and fear. Matt kept quiet most of the time with the doctor, always afraid he may say something dumb, like talking about how Luke or Paul did this or that amazing thing. Instead, when he mentioned his slaves, he ridiculed them and emphasized their lazy ways, crediting himself for working the farm and making it into a success. That's what the doctor wanted to hear, so that's what Matt fed him, and in that way, he could keep his brothers safe beyond the watchful glances of Washington's citizens who had come very close to driving Matt's dad away and burning the orchard to the ground. He and the doctor got along very well, just so long as Matt never said too much.

"Well then, Matthew, a strapping young boy like you needs a woman, you know that. You can't go on forever alone. And Jessie, she has an eye for you. She likes your visits here, likes pouring you a cup of tea. She has many suitors in town, many farmers who come to me and ask about her for their sons, but I know that it's you she really wants."

This was not the first time Matt heard those words, and each time he denied hearing them before. It wasn't something he wanted to discuss with the doctor. "She's a good girl, I know that, Doctor, and pretty as a whip. It just I ain't in a place in my life where I can be interested in those matters," he said, knowing, in fact, that she was neither of those things, at least in his eyes. "Besides, she takes care of you, and the Lord knows that you need her a lot more than I do right now."

Izzy's words bounced in his brain. *Never let the doctor know your feelings for her. Always pretend that you like her; you have to keep them on your good side, what can I tell you?*

Matt started to sweat a bit as he squirmed in his chair.

The doctor laughed softly and nodded his head. "I can't hold her here forever, Matthew. I can hire a servant should I require an assistant. She's a young girl, she needs a man, and I'm afraid, despite your protestations, that the man she wants is you. As her father, I approve of her choice, and I told her that I would do what I could to make sure the two of you establish a friendship that may lead to better things." He sipped his tea and looked up at the boy. "I want to bring her to your house next week, maybe on Wednesday, when my schedule here is light. Your house slaves can make us lunch, and I will leave the two of you some time while I tour the ground with your overseer just to learn the secret of your success. What is his name again, your overseer?"

"Umm, it's Peter, sir. Peter Jones. He's a good man, although he's off next week for a family function, and I'll be running the slaves myself that time. And Wednesday, that ain't a good day for me, sir, not next week at least. I have meetings set up with vendors. Would the following week be just as good, so long as it ain't on a Wednesday?"

Matt's hand was trembling, and he could see the doctor's tiny eyes wandering in that direction.

The doctor's demeanor changed a bit, and his eyes tilted back up and pierced Matt's glance, broadcasting a small whiff of suspicion. "I think you should be careful letting your overseer be absent for so long. No, I insist on next week. I will change my schedule. Let's make it Thursday if that is better for you. I will not take no for an answer. I will walk the grounds myself, assuming your slaves can show me around (you've told me how slow and stupid they are, so I do not have high expectations), and then you and I can talk afterward about your farm, my daughter, and perhaps our future together. Why, per chance, is Wednesday not as good for you? What will you be doing, especially with your overseer being absent? I would assume you are not planning to leave the farm."

Beads of sweat spilled from Matt's brow, and he desperately wiped them off.

"Of course, sir, I ain't planning on leaving the farm, not with Peter gone and all. I ain't that stupid. But Wednesdays is my financial day. I got someone coming over to look over all my finances for the year is all, and it won't be easy to change that, that's all."

October in the valley meant cool temperatures, but Matt was bursting with heat. Soft breezes rolled through the doctor's home, and again the doctor glared at him with dubious scrutiny. "You are OK with us coming by, aren't you, son?" the doctor asked sternly, staring at Matt's saturated and telling brow.

"Of course, sir, of course," he said with a bit of a tremor in his voice. "I invite you both over on Thursday. I look forward to it, sir."

"You do like my daughter, don't you?" the doctor asked him. "I can't imagine why any man would not, but I want to be sure that I am not pursuing a path for her that is ill-advised. I care about Jessie more than the world itself. It is a great honor that she has affection for you. I would be very displeased if that affection were not fully returned."

"Of course!" Matt said with a stutter. "Jessie, she's great!"

Do everything you must to keep the doctor on your side, even if it means coddling up to his daughter.

But, in fact, there was no one he more despised than the doctor's daughter.

An image from his school days flashed beyond his eyes. His father had recently banished his mother from the farm; Matt knew that people in the town were riled up by his mother, but he did not know why or even the extent of the town's collective indignation. His father was frightened. After Momma left in chains that dreadful night, Jake sent his son to school. There he met Jessie and her contingent of boyfriends, the most prominent among them being a boy named Jude, tall and burly, always having to say something nasty.

Jessie always kept a posse of boys by her side. She slithered between them, and they seemed to always jump to her every command and whim. Even then her dresses were cut low, and her legs found their way of rubbing against those of her companions. Sometimes her hands would slide up Jude's back, even during class. He nodded and smiled.

"Looks, it's the Negro-loving son of the witch," Jessie would say to Matt whenever he came to school. "How are you, Negro boy? I hear a rumor that you are black on the inside and that your blood is black too. Jude, should we see if that's true? Should we cut him up a bit and see what his insides are like?"

Jude laughed. He marched in front of a tremulous and scrawny Matt and shoved him hard to the ground. "Nah," he said. "Ain't worth it. We already know that his blood flows black. That he's Negro through and through. My dad says that his dad made love to the Negro witch and that the two of them was hatching plans to burn our whole town down and make a slave rebellion here. His son ain't too far from the tree; that is for damned sure, especially with the two witch kids still with him on the farm."

Matt lay on the ground peering up at Jessie, who stood above him and spit in his face. "You are right, Jude," she said. "My daddy says the same thing. He says it would be best if Matthew's dad just up and died. That would be God's will. Maybe Daddy will help God in that way." She spit again, and then she and her four boyfriends marched away laughing, Jude's arm draped over her shoulder.

Day after day, Jessie did not relent. Day after day, Jude shoved him down and Jessie spit on his face. Even after his father pulled him from school, needing him on the farm, Matt's few trips into town were met by Jessie and her posse. Sometimes, behind Jake's back, they threw rocks at him. Sometimes they walked by him innocuously, and she whispered. "Negro lover," in the vilest of tones.

When Jake died, her attitude did change. She spent more time with the doctor and less with Jude and the other boys. When with the doctor, her demeanor toward Matt was one of deference and friendship. But even then, until very recently, when he was walking alone on the streets, she would often whisper "Negro boy" as she passed by.

Suddenly, though, everything had changed. Jude rarely came to town. Jessie spent all of her time with the doctor. And now, for a reason he could not fathom, she peered at him through loving, glassy eyes.

The doctor methodically sipped his tea. He said nothing for several minutes, peering ahead into empty space. His tilted eyebrows had not yet returned to their more serene state, and Matt knew that he was contemplating something, perhaps concerned about what Matt may be up to. Why else did he insist on visiting the farm, something he had not done for years? And why on the very day that Matt had so carefully planned to bring his brothers to Old Rag? Did the doctor know?

"You been reading about the politics of the other Washington, the vile Washington over across the Potomac?" he finally asked, as again a smile graced his face. "You know what is going on in the world, Matthew?"

"Some, sir, although we farmers, we don't got much time for politicking and all. I know there's an election coming up soon and lots of fighting about slaves and such, not that any of that is new or different, at least as I see it."

"Well, Matthew, this county, it's mostly made up of farmers, and I would venture to say that you may be the only one who's not up on the politicking, as you so casually call it. This, Matthew, is a moment in history where our values and our culture will either live or die. There is not just an election coming up. This is a test for who we are as a people. Are we Jeffersonians, the sons and daughters of our noble founders who—like Mr. Jefferson, General Washington, and Madison and Monroe—harken from the great state of Virginia? Or are we greedy industrialists and abolitionists who seek to enslave the white race and turn our backs on the values and mores upon which this nation was built?"

Of course, Matt spent most of his time hearing the other side of things from his brothers and Izzy, but with the doctor he played ignorant, not wanting to say something that may be misperceived. "I know that a man named Lincoln is running for president and that he wants to get rid of the slaves, but I heard that even if he wins that there ain't much he can do anyway being with Congress and the courts already filled with Southern men who wouldn't let him do nothing bad. That's why I don't make much of it."

The doctor laughed again. "Well, son, you may be right. There is not much he could really do. But that's not even important. This man is a symbol, a symbol of Northern oppression over our values and our culture, a symbol that the corrupted people north of our border feel they can tell us what we can and can't do. If he wins, Matt, there are few states in the South that will stay in the Union. They feel they've been bullied too much already, and this election is the last straw. If that happens, then Virginia will have a big decision to make. Frankly, son, I don't know which way she would go. It could mean war."

"Do you think he may win, sir?" Matt asked, truly curious as to the doctor's take on that matter. "Lincoln, I mean? You think he will win the election?"

The doctor put his chin on his hand. He waited a few seconds before answering and then did so in a calculated manner. "I see it this way, Matthew. The firebrands in the Deep South, they are itching for a fight. Unlike us in Virginia, they cannot even look at a Northerner without feeling a need to upchuck. So, although we do have a candidate in the Democratic party, a man named Douglas who is hated by all but, as flawed as he may be, would win an election if he alone ran against Lincoln, the Deep Southerners were not satisfied with Douglas, and so they nominated a second Democrat, a good man named Breckenridge, who they hope will attract more broad appeal since he is a Northerner who is sympathetic to the South, but who will likely split the ticket. That will make it easier, although not certain, that Lincoln will win. I support another option, a man named Bell, who seeks to quell the hostility and put Union over sectional squabble; he is the only candidate who truly wants peace and who understands the Constitution, and he is the man I endorse, and who I hope Virginia and the other border states will vault into the White House, assuming the election is divided and is decided in the House of Representatives, our only hope for peace. That's where we stand, Matthew. It's a battle brewing for which side of the Mason Dixon line is going to control this nation and whether the time has come to have two countries and not one."

"Well, I guess in its heart it's about whether we gonna have slaves or not, right, sir? Up North, there are people who think we'd be better off just freeing the slaves and having people work for wages, while down here, we want to preserve what we got."

"And do you agree with that, Matthew?" asked the doctor, his eyebrows again pointed down as he pierced into Matt's visage.

Matt had already said too much. Too many echoes of Paul's interminable discourse on this matter rang in his head. If he opened his mouth again likely something would spill out that may offend the doctor's good senses. So, he chose his words carefully, straddling a narrow line. "Me, I don't know. They say the Negro is inferior and is best served on the farms under our whips and guidance; although some of mine, they are good workers, sir, and smart too, not that I think that means freeing them, just that I kind of know why they may want to be free."

The doctor laughed. "You do know how to dance around an issue, don't you, son!" He then nodded and stood. "Do you know much about Thomas Jefferson the scientist? We all know him for his Declaration, and for his presidency, but he was also an outstanding farmer and a scientist of great renown. And he did weigh in on the issues of Negro intelligence. Let me show you something that may alter your thinking a bit."

They meandered through a small kitchen into an office that was spacious and dark. Books rose high upon well-crafted bookshelves along the walls, a few open books and newspapers scattered on the floor. There were an exam table and a desk; this was where the doctor saw patients as well. In the room's corner, somewhat conspicuously, sat five skulls, human skulls, although Matt could not determine if these were models or were real. The doctor led him there.

"What do you think of these skulls, Matthew? Does anything stand out when you look at them?"

Matt peered at the heads, strolling from one to another. Were they different colors? Different shapes? "They are different sizes," he finally said. "I guess some are kids, some adults?"

"No, Matthew, they are all the same age. All young men. And yes, they are of different sizes. Do you know why?"

Matt shrugged. The doctor then reached behind the skulls and retrieved a set of metallic sliver calipers that he snapped like a pair of scissors. "You can measure the difference in size between them quite easily. Then you can quantify those differences and calculate an average if you measure enough skulls. Mr. Jefferson did just that, and he wrote about it. In fact, his scientific conclusions are quite revealing."

The doctor moved from skull to skull, put the calipers from ear to ear on each, and then read the measurement of the skull's size. "You see, Matthew, on the left we have the smallest skull, the size of an average Negro. On the right is an average Caucasian, like you and me, which is the largest skull. Near the Caucasian is an Indian, a species of human that Mr. Jefferson believed was capable of civilization, just on average a little smaller than the white skull. And do you know what these two skulls are in the middle, each being smaller than the Indian's but larger than the Negro's?"

Matt nodded no.

"They, son, are mongrels. They are the skulls of people who have one parent who is Negro and one who is white, a very unfortunate practice carried out by many otherwise honorable slave-owners in the South, including, quite tragically, Mr. Jefferson himself, as well as your own father. In other words, Matthew, the children of this aberrant breeding produce a head size and therefore an intelligence level that is less than even that of an Indian."

"Intelligence level, sir? You saying that the bigger heads mean smarter people?"

"Yes, son, that is what I am saying. That is a scientific fact. Skull size correlates with brain volume, which correlates to intelligence. On the left is the Negro, a far less-intelligent breed of human, likely closer to ape than a person. To the right is the white man, the pinnacle of intelligence. But with the mixing of races, we are bringing our intelligence down even beneath that of an Indian and more toward that of an ape. Soon we will be little better than the Negro himself."

Matt stared at the skulls. He said nothing for a moment.

"That is what we are fighting for, Matthew. I am not in line with the firebrands from the South in my defense of slavery. I wish we never brought a Negro into this country, and my inclination is to expunge them from our glorious land before they contaminate the sanctity of the white race. But until we do that, it is essential that we keep them enslaved and away from the lot of decent, intelligent white people, because if we do not, and breeding occurs between races, then soon enough we will be the inferior species of human in these United States, and it will be only a matter of time before the Indian again rules this land and uses us as his slaves. That, Matthew, is why Lincoln must not win this election, and why, if he does win, we have to fight him with all the power we can muster. It is not about slavery. It is not about state's rights. It is about the very survival of the white race in America."

Matt mused about the skulls, moving from one to another, hardly listening to the crux of the doctor's lecture. "You know what's funny, sir?" he said. "One of my broth—" He quickly stopped himself and peered up at the doctor, whose eyebrows had again furled downward. "One of my field slaves, who has a brother, he got the biggest head I ever seen, 'cause when I wear a hat and then sometimes lend it to him on a real hot day, it don't ever come close to fitting on his head." Matt laughed. "I call him boulder brain sometimes 'cause of that big head of his!"

The doctor did not smile, and he stared deeply into Matt. "What are you insinuating, son? That this slave harbors intelligence that is beyond even your own?"

"No, sir, I ain't saying that. I'm just saying he's got a freakishly big head." Matt laughed again, thinking about a time when he and his brothers were having a snowball fight last winter and Paul told him to aim for Luke's head because there was no missing that target! "I guess that with all this science and stuff not everyone fits exactly what Mr. Jefferson was saying. Maybe some of the Negroes, well, I guess they can be a little different, not that they is smarter, just that they can have a really, really big head." With that, Matt just burst out laughing.

But not the doctor.

He waited a few moments until Matt settled down, all along staring at the boy. Then he lifted his calipers. "I know the slave of whom you speak," he softly uttered. "He and his brother. I knew their mother, and I know much else about them, more than perhaps you realize, including your father's pact with Satan in creating them. I hope they are both good workers who understand their place on your farm and that they have not put any ideas in your head, son. I look forward to meeting both of them too next Thursday. Maybe we will do our own little experiment on your farm. I will bring my equipment, and we will see if Mr. Jefferson's theory applies. I do know that once in a while a Negro may fall out of his predestined condition, and when that occurs, he can be very dangerous and needs to be dealt with harshly. Do you know what a slave rebellion is, Matthew?"

Just then the door opened, and the doctor's daughter walked in. Jessie wore her same long pink dress with her breasts bulging out from the top. She smiled, her crooked front teeth obscuring any other features that Matt may have noted on her face. Matt was already sweating, and Jessie's appearance right then and there gave him a bit of relief. He smiled at her, and she smiled back.

"Want some tea, Matt?" she asked in a sweet, high-pitched voice.

"I would, Jessie, thank you."

Matt peeked at the doctor, who continued to snap his calipers back and forth, a more sinister grin plastered on his face, as he looked at Matt's knowingly.

"Jessie, dear," he said to his daughter, "we will be visiting Matthew for lunch next Thursday. How do you like that?"

Jessie smiled. "I like it just fine!"

Negro Lover.

What could it all mean?

And Matt sweated even more. Thursday. He would have the farm ready. Just as long as he would be able to get off of Old Rag on time, and have everything ready for the doctor's visit, then what could go wrong? Ruth would cook a proper lunch and have it ready. He and his brothers would have returned the night before, and they would be in their slave clothes in the cabins.

He nodded up and down, smiling at Jessie. Why did the doctor want to bring her to the farm? What could this be all about? He could sense something behind Jessie's eyes that frightened him a bit. That girl he had known all those years, she could not have simply disappeared and become the smitten princess who thrust her heart and breasts upon Matt's lap.

But enough of that! Next week he would take his brothers to Old Rag. That was all he really cared about! And he had pushed the doctor's visit off just far enough to make the trip possible. It was another successful interaction with the doctor! Sometimes, Matt even surprised himself with his ingenuity.

6

Swirling wind swallowed the background din as rain poured upon him, rendering him almost blind. Bursts of thunder cracked across the sky, vibrating off rocks illuminated by flashes of lightning. Paul stood firm upon a podium up in the sky; from here he could peer down at the world from every vantage, a tiny world over which he now stood supreme. All around him was blackness. His arms outstretched, he yelled into the air, not even able to hear the words soaring out of his mouth, as cool water pummeled his tongue and clogged his throat.

"Bring it on, bastards!" he shouted. "That's all you got? After all this time, you have nothing else? You feckless sons of bitches, this is your one and only chance. You hear me? I'm talking to you! Either you stop me here and now, or I swear to you, you will pay the price, because Paul Cocklin has woken up! You understand, you bastards? You kept me tied up for eighteen years, but that ends today, and I'm coming for you, all of you!"

A crash of thunder shook him for just a moment as it reverberated through the narrow, precarious rocky perch upon which he stood at the edge of Old Rag's peak. But it was not enough to muffle a decade of indignation and humiliation that brewed within him, here in this singular spot that hovered over everything around it, here within a symphony of discordant power that nature itself thrust at him from everywhere all at once, drawing out incipient angst that Paul had suppressed for far too long. It all became clear to him at that moment in an unremitting harangue that nothing—not time, not weather, not even danger—dared try to dampen. Paul did not know how long he stood upon the peak of a rock-faced mountain, but when the storm finally dissipated, when he stood alone in the hazy darkness saturated from head to toe with frigid water, and when the winds quieted just a bit, he could hear distant shouts from his brothers below, and only then did he step out of an intense trance.

Paul hyperventilated, exhausted. "I'm here," he cried back.

He lifted his black hands and looked at them. They looked different from before, their very presence on his body possessed a significance that he never really comprehended. Here, at this moment, in this singular spot above the world, he was a free man, and the power of that thought sent tremors down his spine. These hands, their color, confined him to a lifetime of slavery in the land below. But up here, he was free; to nature, he was just another rock, another thing upon another of its mountains, nothing more or less. And nature did not judge its rocks by their color. His body, beaten and exhausted, Paul knew that he could never again be happy in the world below.

"I'm here," he said again. *What time was it?* he wondered. How long had he been up here? His body felt very strange. His head was spinning, as though he were in another space and time.

His brothers made their way up as Paul stood there paralyzed. He looked at them suspiciously. Did they want him to go back down? He did not say a word.

Matt, drenched with water and visibly shivering, glared at his tall, powerful brother. "What the heck you dillydallying up here for? We got to go! We are in a big heap of trouble if we don't move fast."

Luke stood beside Matt, engulfed in a tranquil smile dropping of water. "Matt, we're not going to make it down tonight.

Let's go back to the cave we passed, we can sleep there while the storms pass. I don't think God's lightshow is over yet."

"No," Matt said frantically. "You don't get it. We got to get down to the bottom now, tonight, back to the farm. We can't wait another day. We got to go now."

"Matt," Luke said pensively. "If we try to negotiate those rocks in this darkness, we will fall to our deaths. One mistake and we drop off an edge. And the rocks are wet. We need to spend the night up here. Come on, let's get to the cave." A burst of thunder shook them. "We don't have much time."

"You don't get it," Matt screamed. "We are in big trouble if we don't get down. It's Wednesday. Tomorrow's Thursday. I got to be back by Thursday. All of us got to. I can get us down. Let's go, Paul! Damn it, let's get going!"

"Matt," Luke reiterated, putting his arm around his brother's shoulders, "whatever it is can wait. We will spend another night here and walk home after darkness on Thursday. It will give us more time together, up here, on your favorite mountain. I'm glad you brought us here, Matt. It is magical."

Matt, though, shoved his brother's arm away and seemed almost hysterical. "I hate this mountain! Why did it do this to us? Why is it trapping us here? We got to get off this mountain! We got to get down. Paul, let's go. Luke, just shut your trap and stop all your high-handed thinking. We are getting down tonight. We got to be home by Thursday. You guys don't get it. You don't get it at all!"

Paul listened to the distracting banter between his brothers, and it only pushed his mind farther into the morass from which he seemed to have just escaped. Every meaningless word they uttered stabbed him. He could hardly bear it. "I'm not going anywhere," he finally said. "I'm staying here."

Matt screamed again in an almost incomprehensible rant about this being Wednesday and that being Thursday and they were in a heap of trouble and they had to go down tonight, which even Paul knew was not possible. But Luke, deflecting Matt's tirade, seemed to comprehend the gravity of Paul's words.

"Brother," he said pensively to Paul, "you can't stay here. There's nothing up here for you. You won't survive."

"I'm not going back down," Paul said to his younger brother. "I tasted it, Luke. Don't you taste it too? Up here we are human beings, not objects that are owned and bartered. Up here we are free. I can't give that up."

Luke just shook his head. "It's an illusion, Brother," he said, smiling brightly. "You're still on their land here. They have chased down escapees up here on the mountains, sent their dogs after them. No, Paul, this is just an extension of everything you despise. It only seems different tonight. We have but one sanctuary that keeps us safe, and that is our farm. That's where we must get to. Come down with us."

Paul paused and hyperventilated. He knew that Luke spoke out of love, and yet, his brother's logic did not persuade him as it had so many times before. "That's the illusion," Paul finally uttered. "That our farm is really going to protect us. Did it save Mamma? Does it really make us free? At any point the people from town can burst through the front gates and impose their will, the South's will, on us, because really, we are no more than their slaves whether inside their gate or out. They own us, Brother. We are not alive down there, not even on our farm; we are but chattel in the grasp of monsters."

The winds howled, and rain again started dropping upon them. Matt's ranting did not wane, but Luke was able to convince both his brothers to meander down the rock about a hundred yards where he remembered passing through a small cave. "We'll just wait out the storms until they pass," he said to both brothers, each of whom sought to move in the opposite direction. "Then we can decide."

As he slipped over the rocks, holding tightly to wet, mossy boulders and wondering where the mountain's edge lay, Paul pondered his options. There was a way to traverse these mountains, tiny trails in the woods, homesteads and farms that could be negotiated carefully, which may enable him to find his way North, past Harper's Ferry perhaps, to a spot on the underground railroad, and eventually to New York. He had spoken about this to Luke in the past, but his more pragmatic brother dismissed it as folly; even Izzy's maps did not persuade him of the possibility of escape. But the thought never left Paul's mind, and now, up here, he tasted it like a succulent steak.

The cave was merely a bend of rocks, but it kept them dry as the storm surged voraciously outside of its hundred-thousand-year-old walls. The temperature dropped sharply, and all of them shivered in there, wet and cold, exhausted and hungry. Matt never stopped talking and yelling, but when he finally sat down, he took some deep breaths and then said, "We are in a heap of trouble, and I don't know what to do." And then he broke into a hysterical fit of tears.

That's when Matt told them about the doctor. "He wanted to visit me Wednesday, with his daughter. I don't know why all the sudden he wants me and Jessie to be dating or something, and he's more suspicious. I can smell it, so when he gets like that, I say, come over, see the farm, just not on Wednesday, that's our day, but I ain't about to tell him that. I come up with this or that excuse why he can't come that day, especially this Wednesday, since we ain't got no other chance to come up the mountain. But he insisted. He wants to fix me up with his horrible daughter, Jessie. He wants to see the farm, so I thought I was clever, and I told him, come Thursday, that's tomorrow. 'Come then, and I'll show you around.' So," Matt said, pausing, "that's what he plans to do."

The gravity of Matt's rambling soliloquy hit both brothers equally hard. Luke said nothing, his smile obscured by the cave's blinding darkness, and his thoughts unrevealed. But Paul was not so muted.

"You did what?" Paul shouted harshly. He could not see either brother, other than when lightning flashed and their images briefly appeared, but he yelled in Matt's direction. "Are you a fucking moron, Brother? You told him to come to our farm tomorrow? Do you know what you did, Matt? Do you know what's going to happen when he shows up there and finds no master, no overseer, and his two most suspicious slaves—the sons of Dad and his banished mistress slave—gone with the master? How the hell do you have the gall to expose us to that type of danger? Do you have even a tiny bit of brain in that warped skull of yours? Jesus Christ, Matt, you just signed our death warrant!"

"That's why we got to get down," Matt said tremulously. "I ain't thought we'd get stuck up here. I had it all planned out. We'd be back in plenty of time. This mountain, it sabotaged us. It's evil."

"No, Matt," said Paul. "You sabotaged us. You and your idiocy. I'm sorry. But that's the harsh truth. And now my mind is made up and clear. I am not going down there. Not now, not ever. Whatever deceptive protection our farm conferred on us has just been shattered by Matt's imbecilic move. We go down there, and the doctor will be leading us out in chains, just like he did to Mamma."

"We got to get down the mountain now," Matt pleaded. "Once the rains stop, we can do it, right through the night, just being careful, then we can hustle back and get there by dawn. We got to!"

Paul sucked in a deep breath of air. "No, I'm heading North. Just as soon as dawn comes, I'm taking my chances up here. We're only a few days from Maryland, and there we can find people who will be willing to help. My mind is made up."

For a while, only the wind and thunder provided any answer to Paul's declaration. And then finally, and calmly, Luke chimed in. "We have to consider all our options and their ramifications," he stated. "Let's not be rash here or jump to conclusions.

The world is changing, and you both know that. In three weeks, there's going to be an election. There's a chance Lincoln will win, and everyone down here will be so focused on that, they won't have time to be worrying about a master and his two slaves who wandered off and left the farm unsupervised. Let's think about our options. Perhaps walking back to the farm in the early morning and getting there before the doctor arrives."

He paused for a moment, hushed by a blast of thunder. "What if we borrow a few horses as soon as we hit the first farm?" Luke asked. "There were many there. Again, if we are clever, we can hop on a couple, race back home, and then let the steads go, no one the wiser as to how they wandered so far from their homes."

Paul shook his head. "Even at best we wait until dawn, we climb down the mountain as fast as we can, that doesn't leave us enough time to get back to the farm in time. Most likely, we'll be stopped by someone. There's no one who lives down in the valley who is not going to be suspicious of two Negroes and a white man hiking in from the mountain. No one."

"Paul," Luke said to his brother, "we are smarter than them. We will find a way home."

Paul laughed. "You are living in a land of illusion, Luke. You view our little piece of land as an island that is somehow protected from the world. But is it really? It's more like a teetering rock sitting in the middle of a volcano. We sit on it and think we're safe, but in a second a spray of lava can come our way and kill us all. That's your precious farm. It is no less a trap for us than it was for Mamma. A delusion. Why don't we all just leave? Let's head North. Matt, you can free us, and we can leave this place. We can leave right now. This may be our ticket out. If Lincoln does win and there is war, we can fight for everything we believe in. We can restart our life up North. Izzy has promised to help."

"They will chase us down," Matt shouted. "They'll kill us. We'll lose everything, our farm, everything we built, all our future, everything we spent our lives making so great, even Dad's bones that is buried down there. We just got to get down there tonight. All this talk, it's just delaying us. I know I screwed up. Now let me fix it and get us down."

"It can't be done," Paul snapped. "Not in the dark. Not without a path. We only have one choice. It's time we face reality and head North, where we all really belong."

For a moment there was silence. Matt stuck his head out as fierce winds and water suffocated him. Then he cursed, cursed the weather, cursed the mountain, and cursed the doctor and his horrible daughter.

"Matt," Paul told his frantic brother, "don't berate yourself. Yea, you screwed up, and we are in deep shit because of what you did. But it was going to happen anyway, at some point. We were just pretending on the orchard. We were playacting. The truth is that we are just slaves in a land of slaveholders. We can think we're not because you treat us well and we live a decent life. Eventually, those people outside of our gates will do us in. That moment may have just come, Matt, and it's time that we brothers make a decision."

More silence, more wind. Everything was black. And then thunder and lightning crashed upon them and caused the cave to shake. Paul peeked out. It was raining even harder now.

"Let's not get ahead of ourselves," Luke quietly said. "There are options."

"Back to us stealing horses and getting away with it?" Paul laughed. "I'm sure the white folk will be OK with that!"

"What about this," Luke continued. "Matt pays Pete to stay off the farm, so obviously he won't be there when the doctor arrives. Rumor is that he does a lot of drinking and spends freely. Matt can just tell the doctor that Peter was supposed to be on the farm, and he abandoned it, probably drunk. We all were collecting soil samples for the farm when the storm came and pinned us in. Matt was just as shocked as anyone that Peter left the slaves to run free. It's Matt's word against Peter's. It's the word of the kid he wants his daughter to marry against the word of a drunk. That's how we handle this."

Paul laughed again. "Wow, Brother, you have a dark side! You want to ruin a man's life by lying about him, just to save our hides? I'm impressed, Luke, surprised and impressed."

"Ain't gonna work," Matt said. "I told the doctor that Peter's taking the week off. Said he was gone."

"Wow, my other brother, just how much can you screw up in one night?" Paul said.

"Listen, we have to make the story tight," Luke said. "You, Matt, have to be firm and convincing when you talk to the doctor. We were collecting samples of soil on Wednesday because we are planning to produce a crop of grapes, and you intended to surprise the doctor with this news when you saw him Thursday. You had me and Paul come with you to help out. Peter was gone, but he promised to have someone cover the farm while we were on our journey, and when we did not get back in time due to the storm we weren't worried because Peter assured you that the farm would be watched, if not by him, then by a designate of his. That's our story. Peter will have to pay the price so we can survive."

"That ain't fair, and it ain't true," Matt cried out, hysterically. "Peter, he done everything we always asked of him all this time. We can't just fry him like that. Besides, if we do that, he will tell the doctor what we did, how we paid him off to stay off the farm, and we are all in more trouble than we been in before."

"Again, Matt, it's your word against his. You can't waver. You have to be firm and convincing. I understand that you feel badly about harming an innocent man. But is he really innocent? He is an overseer of slaves. He is a terrible man. To save our farm, save our sanctuary, you don't think it's justified to sacrifice a man like that?"

"I don't know," Matt said. "I just don't think it'll work. The doctor, he won't believe it. He ain't that dumb, and I think he's on to me anyway. That's why he is coming over. This will just be the last straw."

"Matt," Luke continued calmly, "this is not a game. This is our lives, it is our entire world, it is the legacy of Mom and Dad and everything we've ever done. As Paul said, you inadvertently committed an error that not only put your brothers at risk but put everything we have spent all our sweat and passion creating at risk. Your shortsightedness threatens our very existence. So, Brother, you have to do whatever it takes to correct your error. And sacrificing a drunk Negro-beating ignorant man to achieve that seems more than worth the price. Do you understand, Matt?"

"It ain't going to work," Matt cried out. "The doctor will see right through it. He ain't so dumb."

Paul's mind was pointed North, but he heard his little brother's desperate pleas and knew that, at least not yet, he could not simply run away and abandon Luke to a horrid fate below. He took a deep breath and accepted the fact that he had to help his brothers get through this morass.

"Matt," Paul said to his older brother, "your precious doctor actually is that dumb. They all are. Don't be fooled by their haughty language and fancy clothes. These are idiots pretending to be what they are not. I think that for once, Luke is making some sense. You play your role, my gullible white brother, and we'll play ours. We'll hang out in the slave cabins. We'll do our sad faces and 'yes, sir, massa' and all that crap. We'll pin this on Peter, for whom I have not a whiff of sympathy. And then, in about three weeks, the doctor and all those so-called smart people who live down there in their insulated world of horrors will have to deal with a presidential election that is going to throw their world upside down. At that point, they won't give a shit about us. I guarantee it. We just have to weave a story that is credible to the doctor, you suck up to his precious little daughter, and soon enough he will have bigger problems on his hands than the likes of us."

"And then, Brothers," said Luke, "we can resume our lives as though Matt's error never transpired, and I am confident we will grow the best damned grapes the state of Virginia has ever seen. The samples I collected up here is our ticket to a new agricultural triumph for the Cocklin brothers. We can start the irrigation ditch soon, and I will plant the vines when they arrive. Within a year we will be producing the best wine in the valley."

Paul swallowed his annoyance with Luke's flight of fancy. He was impressed with how quickly his little brother was able to maneuver into a warrior! *Let him dream*, Paul thought. *As long as he fights!*

"Matt, you are in charge," Paul said in a more subdued voice, his transient dream of running up North delayed just a bit—he didn't have Izzy's maps and had not prepared, and besides, he could not just abandon his brothers, because if he did not return with them, then the doctor would punish Luke for sure. "Our fate is in your sweaty white hands, Brother. Don't blow it this time."

Matt started crying, and Paul slid over and gave him a hug. He whispered in Matt's ear, "I love you, Brother. Never forget that. Never." And Matt bawled harder, hugging his young brother tightly.

Paul smiled. He placed his head on a rock, shivering just a bit, and peered out of the cave, as pulsating winds pushed beads of rain off the cave walls. He was proud of Luke's passion, and he would stand by him, at least for now. And he had faith in his older brother, whose smarts and guile had saved their hides many times over the years. But he knew too that the taste of freedom this mountain gave him would not easily evaporate. From that moment on, he thought of only one thing: how was he going to run away and get North. The farm was not an oasis to Paul; it was not safe from the vicissitudes of malevolence that swirled all around it. Rather, it was a holding cell, a place to hide for a bit until he could concoct a better plan. Somewhere up here on this mountain was a way out, and he was determined to find it. But for now, he was comforted by the fact he was here with his brothers, and nothing could ever be better than that!

7

Morning dew draped the horizon, wet grass, and bright orange sky hovering upon the range of hazy blue mountains. Old Rag stood firm, seeming to nod and smile, watching over them as they limped back to the farm, the sun barely rising in the east. They had made it!

Bloodied and exhausted, the three brothers separated at the gate. A nocturnal jaunt down the mountain became possible after the storms drifted away and a big, full moon illuminated the mountain and their path off of it.

"God is with us," Luke smiled. "He lives on the mountain. He was not going to abandon us. He led the way."

"Shut up," both his brothers snarled, almost simultaneously.

"We did it," Luke said, nodding. "We outwitted them. We are back here. Nothing lost, nothing to fear. Paul and I will be in the cabins and then start work on the fields. Matt, you wash up."

Just then, as if waiting behind a rock or tree, the doctor's carriage trotted through the farm's gates, sliding past the three brothers as though oblivious to their presence. The doctor's proud white horses seemed to dance upon the muddy ground, while Jessie, her face glowing and her dress red and revealing, pushed her head out of the window and nodded to Matt.

"You work too hard," she cried to him. "Come in and clean up so you can show me your farm!"

Stunned, Matt nodded. He peered at his brothers. Luke pointed forward, and Matt ran toward the house, flanking the carriage on his way. Luke and Paul wandered to their cabin.

"We made it, Paul," Luke said. "Just in time."

"That's not good that the doctor saw us come in," Paul whispered to Luke as they darted to the cabins. "Something is wrong. Did you see the man's face? He knows."

"We just have to get through this day, Brother," Luke said to Paul, who had been quiet and contemplative all during their journey down. "Tomorrow will be brighter."

"We'll see," Paul said.

Luke knew that his brother was swimming in a vat of contemplation that transcended the here and now.

"We will make it work down here, Paul," Luke smiled, placing his arms high over Paul's shoulders. "We always do. Just like Momma said we must."

"We will see" was all that Paul said in response. He was limp as he walked. He seemed totally drained.

In the cabin, Luke used a rag to wipe the blood off their arms and legs. He handed Paul a shirt and had him change into it. They had scraped over rocks, tumbled down a few, tripped over roots, and fell face-first upon muddy dirt. They had not eaten or drank for almost a day and had not slept for longer than that. But Luke felt alive and vibrant. He would pull his brother through this. He knew that he had to.

"It's early," Luke said. "Maybe we can get a bit of rest. There's not much work to do, just some cleaning, and of course the new irrigation ditch. That can wait. Do you want to sleep?"

"No," Paul said. He did not look at Luke; his glace seemed to be in a different space and time. Luke could do nothing to engage him.

"Why do you think the doctor came so early?" Luke wondered aloud. "We barely made it back in time. So very close. I am glad we ran those last two miles! It was a good idea."

"It doesn't matter," Paul said. "Somehow, Brother, I know that it doesn't matter. We shouldn't have come down here. We had our chance. And now, we let it slip away. Something is terribly wrong."

Luke peered at him. "What?"

"I don't know," he said. "But we don't belong here. I feel like I'm in a foreign land. Nothing feels right. There's something that is wrong."

Just then, Ruth pushed her way through the front door. She was breathing hard, which was uncharacteristic of her. She was frazzled, almost frantic. Luke stood up and grasped her.

"Ruth?" he asked.

She shook her head vehemently. "It's bad," she said, her eyes filled with tears. "It's be really bad. You's boys are in a heap of trouble. We's all is!"

Something dropped in Luke's gut. He turned to Paul, whose flat expression had not changed. Then he twisted back to Ruth. "What?" he asked.

She sat down on a log and caught her breath. Then she peered sharply into Luke's eyes. "The doctor," she said, "he and two men, they's come trampling on the farm yesterday when you's was all gone on your trip. They starts to look around. They comes and gets me and the boys. 'Where is they?' the men shout at us. They push at my boys, who just keeps says, 'We's don't know, we's don't know nothing.' So, they says to me, 'Where's is your master, Matt, and his two slaves? Where is the overseer, Peter, where is he?' And I say to them that I's don't know nothing about nothing. I says the master, he may be out just a spell, and last I know that Peter, he's been drinking in the main house all night and that's where he usually sleeps off his bender when he does that. I thinks as fast as I could, that's what I done for you dumb boys! But, those men, they didn't buy nothing."

Paul barely budged from his perch, peering up at Ruth with a melancholy acquiescence. But Luke pushed her harder.

"You did a good job, Ruth," Luke said. His characteristic smile had faded. His mind churned with possibilities. He needed to know more. "That's exactly what you were supposed to say. Did they leave you alone after that? What came next?"

She cried a bit, and Luke rubbed her back, draping her with a hug. "What happened next?" he goaded her.

"Wells," she said, looking from one brother to another, "he stayed here most of the days is what he done. He told my boys, 'You's gonna pay for this is what you's is going to do.' The two men with him, they's up and pushed the boys around and then told them to gets to work, which is what they done. The doctor man forced me to make them food, and then one of them, he rides his horse away, says he's going to get the overseer and find out the truth. 'And you better be right with your stories,' he says to me. 'Or I will whip your boys till their skin falls off their back!'" She then broke down in a fit of tears.

"We're screwed," Paul muttered from the back.

"No," Luke said. "We're not. It's our word against Pete's. He's a drunken fool. We have to let Matt know."

"Matt's being played, Brother," Paul said, in a flat and quiet inflection from the bed on which he sat. "I give the doctor credit. He didn't buy Matt's story for a minute. He knew that the excuse Matt concocted about being busy on Wednesday was a farce. He waited, and he pounced. I'm sure he knows the truth by now. He's playing Matt right even as we speak, I'm sure of that. The doctor is clearly not as dumb as we all thought. We're fucking screwed."

Luke twisted back to Ruth. His mind spun out of control. The game was hardly over. He needed to think! "Did they bring Peter back here?" Luke asked her. "What did they do next?"

"I's don't know," Ruth cried. "The carriage left late in the night, but those two mens, they stayed here. I see's them in the woods talking and smoking. Me and my boys, we stayed in our cabins. I been's up all night, scared to death is what I was, watching for anything, afraid for my boys! Why? Why did you boys do it? You puts us all in harm's way! Why?" And she dropped into a fit of tears again.

"Talk to Matt, Ruth. This was his brilliance," Paul said with an uncomfortable laugh. He stood up and meandered to the cabin's door, peering up at the mountains. "I think our best chance, to be honest, is to make a run for it. To get back up there. We're sitting ducks down here."

"They'll shoot us down if we run," Luke snapped at him. "Be smart, Brother! Be calm! If we play our roles, the doctor will be stymied. He has no evidence that anything transpired other than what Matt tells him. Ruth did her part. We just have to do ours."

"Think about what is going on right now, Luke." Paul laughed again, still staring into the sky. "The doctor is with Matt. He is asking our dear brother what he did yesterday. And do you know what Matt is going to tell him? That he was here all day. Here with us. The doctor will probe a bit, and Matt will fall right into the doctor's trap. He will lie, and the doctor will call him on it. He has us in his grasp, Brother."

"No," Luke said. "We need another story. That you and I were in the fields. We fell asleep there. They saw us when they came in this morning. They saw we were dirty and exhausted. Why not tell them that we were working so hard that we fell asleep in the fields? Matt can say that he thought Pete was here all along, that he didn't mean to fall asleep, maybe that he fell asleep too, or was out a bit on an errand and he assumed that Pete was there, something like that."

Luke's mind flew from one thought to another. He started to tremble. He did not know what to do.

Paul swung his face toward his little brother. "Don't you get it?" he snarled. "Matt is telling the doctor something completely different. He is saying that we were here all day. That Pete was on vacation. Just the opposite of what Ruth said. Just the opposite of what you want us to say. It's over, Luke. The gig is up. Matt's folly is reaping its rewards. I think, Brother, that we have to run, before it's too late."

"No!" Luke yelled. "That is not an option. We have to stay calm. We will have an opportunity to turn this in our favor. We just have to wait for it. We have to be smart. We will be able to twist the story when we have to. We just must remain calm."

"Ruth," Luke said to her, "go back to your cabin. You and your boys, spend the day as you usually would; have breakfast and start cleaning the southern fields. Box the dropped pears that are still intact, just like always. Do nothing different. Say nothing other than what you already said. We will take care of the rest. I promise. Just don't act frightened or change your story. That's what they're looking for."

Paul laughed as Ruth darted out into the cool October air. "How long are we going to play the fools?" he asked Luke.

"As long as it takes, Brother. As long as it takes."

The sun now draped the clearing sky. Luke wandered out, stealthily moving around the pond. He perched himself behind a tree and watched. The doctor's carriage remained parked at the big house. He looked that way for a few long minutes. Soon enough, Matt and Jessie drifted out, the latter laughing as she draped her hands around Matt's back. They tiptoed through the mud and then disappeared into the western apple orchard, their voices trailing off.

Luke watched the house some more. *Where was the doctor?* He wondered too about the other two men and about Pete. He needed to gather more information before he could make his next move.

Old Rag's reflection danced off the pond as it flowed quickly, releasing the rain waters into the main outlet dam. It must have rained several inches last night, he knew. He peered for a moment at the spot he wanted to dig the new irrigation ditch for the grapes. In his mind, he thought about the best way to proceed; it would be about twenty-five yards long and did not have to be very deep or wide.

Suddenly he heard a commotion from the cabin. He could perceive the echoing din of Paul's voice, and then a shot of a gun! His thoughts instantly collapsed. He looked around and then stood up.

Before he could even take a step, a hand grabbed him from behind. He twisted backward, looking into the grinning face of a mustached white man. And then, in an instant, the man's fist slammed into Luke's face, and everything became black.

8

The doctor snapped his calipers around as though ready to chop through someone's neck. Paul watched the man march back and forth, clearly brewing with certain awful thoughts that had not yet found the proper words through which he could express them. Behind him in the living room of their house—where Paul and his brothers had spent countless invigorating hours debating politics, planning upcoming planting seasons, or quietly reading—stood two other men, farmers both, rifles in their hands, staring voraciously at the slaves as the doctor paced, waiting for some rendering of justice. Beside Paul was his brother Luke. The two stood against the back wall, arms in chains, staring silently forward.

Matt was conspicuously absent.

"When you think about it, gentlemen," the doctor finally uttered, his face curled up and his finger waving forward, "there was no crime committed here. We can accept young Matthew's word that he had left with these slaves for good reason, to collect samples and bring them back, and that he had assumed to be back before being stranded by the storms. We can also assume that, by Matthew's account, Pete, his overseer had been contracted to be here, and if Matthew and his party came back late by no fault of their own, then Pete was bound by our laws and customs to remain here until the owner returned." He paused, staring hard at both Paul and Luke. "And yet, gentlemen, something smells fishy. This is not as it seems."

"These two boys is trouble," said one of the farmers, whose name was Ned, the very one who had punched Luke an hour earlier. "They ain't what they seem to be is darned right, Doc. They is the sons of that witch slave that was speaking sacrilege and traitorous words those years back, who lucky for all of us we got wind about and her sexual escapades and her living in the main house with Jake, God rest his demonic Northern soul, and the two of them likely plotting to start an insurrection. Yes, Doctor, we did indeed rid ourselves of that witch, and then God Himself smote her heathen husband, but I said it then and I will say it now—so long as her sons remain alive in our town and in this county, there is no end to her influence over them and their influence over Matt, and that means this place is a bed of plots for slave insurrection and murder and other such villainy all right in our backyards. I don't believe young Matt for a minute! I know what these boys likely was doing for two days off the farm. They was going on one of their secret trips to gather arms and meet with co-conspirators and the like. Who is to say otherwise? I am sure they already poisoned his mind, just like their mom done to old Jake."

The other farmer, a short and stocky man named Henry, who seemed to wear a pleasant face, laughed. "You are crazy, Ned," he said. "These boys are imbeciles, especially the plump one. You ever hear them talk? They are docile as cows. Matthew, he's been a good farmer and a good citizen. Let's not start stretching stories from the past and then dreaming up crazy ideas of what's going on now. Matthew is young and he doesn't know all our ways and he made a mistake to be out with his slaves and leave his farm unattended, and we are all on edge because of the election in three weeks, but we shouldn't be jumping to conclusions and selling this boy down the stream prematurely."

"I don't buy that for a second," said the first man. "These boys are the devil's reflection. They have Matthew under their spell. And they probably, like their mother, aim to kill us all."

"Gentlemen, please, we are civilized here, let's have a more reasoned assessment of the situation," said the doctor, as he opened and closed his calipers menacingly. He then marched over to Luke and placed the calipers from ear to ear. He calculated Luke's head circumference. "And yet we have an interesting scientific conundrum. The Negro is an inferior creature, but this one, this plump one as you call him, his head is far larger than not only the average Negro, but also larger than that of most White people too. A Negro's brain is not capable of high-level thinking, not like we are, so when you find one with a larger brain, you do have to wonder if within that skull his more animalistic tendencies are more advanced. Slaves with brains such as these are the very ones we worry most about, the very ones capable of insurrection and murder. They are more intelligent predators. This other one," he said, pointing to Paul, "he has a big head too, but not of the same size. I have frankly never seen a Negro with so large a head as the plump one."

Paul surveyed the room. Many possible scenarios jumped in and out of his mind. If he and Luke quickly rushed these feeble men and subdued them, they would never have time to react before having their guns stripped away. Paul presumed he could still hold and fire a rifle even with his arms in chains. He could shoot all three of these men and bury them deep beneath the pond, while he and his brothers escaped to the mountains and into the veil of darkness and safety.

I should have stayed on that damned mountain, he thought, as his fists clenched. *And where the hell is Matt?*

He peered at Luke, who just smiled as always, despite the gravity of their predicament, despite his swollen black eye and bruised cheek. *How blank was his brother's mind?* Paul wondered. What would it take for him to finally realize that this oasis, this farm that he touted as being beyond the grasp of the vile world's tentacles, was and never would be safe, and that because of Matt's error their lives and existence were in peril forever more? Did he realize just how precarious their situation was right now, how powerless they were in the presence of these men?

"I is wondering if I can goes and tend the farm some more, Mister Doctor sir," Luke then blurted out in his well-rehearsed slavery dialect. "The sun, it's setting soon, and massa Matt says if we don't get the apples down, they is going to rot and there will be a lot of hell to pay for that. He can be cruel if we don't do right by him, Mister Doctor sir."

The second farmer laughed. "This boy may have a big head, Doc, but he is dumb as they come!"

What game was Luke playing? Or did he believe that by acting the fool he could persuade these villains to simply go on their way? Life here did not work that way!

"Matthew is with my daughter, showing her the farm," said the doctor. "His overseer, Peter, who indeed is a known drunk and malcontent, will be here shortly. I am sure their stories won't jibe, and it's up to us to render judgment and a verdict. I understand mistakes were made, perhaps innocent mistakes, but we can take no chances like this, not in Virginia, not during these perilous times."

"We can shoot the smaller-headed one," Ned said, raising his gun toward Paul. "I don't like what I see in his eyes. It's like he's already plotting to get us."

Ned's words shook Paul a bit, and he looked sheepishly at the ground. *If I can kill one of these cocksuckers before they kill me, that would at least allow me to die with a modicum of self-respect. Let this moron come a bit closer,* Paul thought, *and I'll pounce on him so fast he won't know what's coming. Luke can take down the slovenly guy, and then I will kill the doctor, shoot him with the very gun now pointed at my face.* He smiled a bit beneath is indignation, imagining executing the deed.

"We are civilized people," the doctor said to the farmer. "We don't shoot people, even slaves, without a fair hearing. And even then, we will hang them if we find that they are complicit of a crime. Even in doling out punishment, we must adhere to our values, Ned, and guns are so Northern. Perhaps a dozen slashes on each of their backs may be sufficient. Perhaps, like with their mother, we will have to banish one or both out of our county, sell them down South, and then help our poor naive Matthew, who has never purchased a slave in his life, find a suitable replacement."

"You can tell they work in cahoots with each other and with Matt and probably a whole army of others, white and Negro, who they meet off their farm when we ain't suspecting it," Ned said again, his gun still pointed at Paul's head. "You split them up, sell one of them off. That may square it. I mean, after the lashes, of course. They need those lashes. Their skin is far too pristine for a proper and obedient slave. There ain't a single scar I see on either of them, and I aim to fix that error before the day is done."

"Excuse me, sirs, and Doctor sir," Luke said again, bowing his head. "I is just saying the sun, it's going down, and we have picking to do, or massa Matt, he is going to be angry at us, so mad and so angry that I's is scared, mister sirs."

"Your master hardly seems that way," Ned said to Luke, whose head was pointed down and whose chained hands were shaking. "And you have not a single mark or brand on your skin. Why are you so scared of him?"

Luke's head popped up, and he stared hard into Ned's eyes. "Oh, Mister sir, you don't knows! You don't knows his cruelty! He locks us in a small box without any light, no windows, and he leaves us in there for days and days, no foods or waters or nothing, mister sirs, and at night he walks around and throws rocks at it, makes noises like the devil he does, and when he lets us out he says, 'You never do that again, or next time you will meet the real devil for sure!'" Luke put his head down again. "Please, Mister sirs, Doctor, Mister sir, please let me go and pick the fruit, or I is so scared for what he will do!"

Henry laughed. "See what I'm saying, Ned? See what I'm saying, Doc? This boy is dumb as shit! You can't fake that much dumb! I say let him go and pick some apples. I need them apples anyway. Have a crop I am selling tomorrow to a vendor from Richmond. I would hate to lose out on that sale. Let the boys go to do some picking, and we can keep an eye on them when we talk to Matt. No point in making us all suffer because of something that ain't our fault anyway."

Ned, whose gun remained raised and pointed at Paul's skull, shook his head. "Christ, the harvest is damned near over. How much picking are we talking about? It's probably just a few stragglers on the ground. This boy is just playing you. I say we shoot them both in the feet, then let them go gather whatever fruit they is talking about, and then, unless there really are some worthwhile barrels they bring in, we hit them with twenty lashes tonight. That's just for starters. What do you say, Doc?"

The doctor seemed pensive, snapping his calipers as he paced across the room. "No, gentlemen, no. Let's be smarter. Twelve lashes, that is something I can live with. But that is not enough. One of these boys has to be sent away. Maybe both. I think they are having undue influence over our young Matthew. I do agree, some of their mother's blood is flowing in each of them, and my confidence in anything they say is suspect. They are vicious animals with no credibility. They speak in the devil's tongue."

Then the doctor paused. "We know that if Lincoln wins the election, there will be slave insurrections all over the South. We must be assured that there are none in the great town of Washington. These boys could well have been plotting something on their journey out of here, like you say, Ned. I don't discount the possibility. We will give them lashes tonight. I leave that up to you, Ned. They must know the limits of what they can and can't do in our county and in the Commonwealth of Virginia.

But then we must devise a more final solution, so we never have to face apprehension about what misdeeds are being perpetuated behind these gates. I will wait for Matt and hear him out. This is his farm, and by our values and customs, he deserves to have a say, assuming I ascertain that he is not poisoned already by the venom these boys have spewed upon his innocent soul. Bring these boys to a quiet spot, don't remove their chains, and administer the lashes as you see fit. Just don't kill them. Justice needs to be more calculated, more commensurate with our mores and after a proper and fair proceeding, as is our way in this great Commonwealth."

Paul shook. He was virtually paralyzed. He peeked up at his brother, who still smiled sheepishly. Why was Matt leaving them here alone? Had he lost all authority on his own farm? It was incredible how thin the veil was that separated this place from the world around it. Just how feeble was Matt's power here—it crumbed the very minute that the doctor marched upon their "hallowed" ground. The level of paranoia that flowed across this land had reached epic proportions in the wake of the upcoming elections. Now Paul and Luke would be its victims.

He had never been whipped before. Never been struck by anything other than a friendly hand slapping his head. What would be worse: the pain of the lash pulling the skin off his back, or the harrowing realization, despite so many years of delusion, that down here he was not a man; he was a mere animal at the whim of a tribe of white savages who held all the power and had a noose always and forever around his neck, a noose they could hang to a tree whenever they in their vile minds felt belittled or needed to pretend that they were more than the feckless imbeciles they actually were. He should have stayed up on the mountain. Every part of his gut told him to do that. And where the hell was Matt?

The two farmers, who laughed and spoke in a gibberish tongue, led the brothers outside, pulling them by their chains.

An Indian summer (as it was so recently called) had swept across the valley. It was warm. Paul started to sweat. Paul looked to his left as they slid past the pond, and he could see Ruth and her family standing quietly by, watching, likely worrying. Luke's red raft fluttered in the pond, stuck against one of the dams, bouncing up and down without a purpose and with no one to rescue it from the tides of nature that pinned it down. The doctor remained in the house, probably waiting for the overseer to come, whose own truthful story would completely contradict anything Matt had to say.

Was Matt really with the doctor's daughter? Why had he not insisted he be in the house when his brothers were chained and interrogated, his house, Matt's house, where he was supposed to call the shots? It just deflated Paul all the more. If Matt could not stand up to the doctor today, how could he ever be counted on to prevent his brothers from being tortured and expelled, even murdered? Dad had not been able to stop these same people from banishing his mother in chains. In fact, Jake was complicit in carrying out the deed! Why would Jake's son be any different?

A river of sweat dropped from Paul's brow. For the first time, he was scared to death.

"Please, Mister sirs," Luke then called out, "cans I go pick some of the green apples for massa Matt? I is so afraid, Mister sirs!"

The second farmer laughed.

"Your master is with the doctor's daughter," said Ned. "He ain't gonna be seeing you tonight. She's got strict instructions to keep him away from the house for now, so he won't be saving your vile asses this time!" And then he laughed, loudly and joyfully, slapping the second farmer on the back. "You got nothing but God sitting in judgment of you, and you will be punished in a way your misguided master would never allow. That job the Doc left to me, and when I get done with the two of you, there ain't gonna be much left for your master to do to you, or much skin left on your murderous backs."

They slid past the pond and toward the dense shadows of the eastern pear orchard as the sun rapidly plummeted. Ned, who seemed to be calling the shots, told a sycophantic and unquestioning Henry what to do. "Tie the one with the plotting eyes up to the tree over there," he said, pointing to Paul. "I want his shirt off, and I want him tied damned good. Let the big-head go. Take off his chains and let him do some picking. But if he doesn't fill at least one barrel with them green apples he's talking about, I plan to shoot him down just for lying. I don't care what the damned doctor says about that. I plan to do justice my own way today."

Henry nodded obsequiously. He pulled off Luke's chains even as Ned strapped Paul to the tree. Paul looked at his brother from the corner of his eye, barely able to see him, hoping that perhaps his fate would be better than Paul's.

"Thanks you, Mister sir, thanks you. I will fill up two barrels, and you cans be proud of old Lukie, you will be for sure." He smiled brightly.

"Wait," Ned said. He walked methodically to Paul's brother, pulled out his rifle, and without a moment of hesitation, fired it at Luke's left foot. The explosion rocked Paul's brain, and he watched his brother cry out in agony and collapse to the ground. Tears flew from Paul's eyes, as he gritted his teeth and said nothing. Intense rage built within him. He pulled on his ropes, but there was nothing he could do to release himself. He was helpless.

"Get the hell up," Ned screamed at Luke.

"Now why in God's name did you have to do that to the boy, Ned?" Henry asked. "He's as dumb as a doorknob. He ain't done no harm to no one. And he needs to get my apples."

"You get the hell up, big-head," he said again to Luke, yanking Paul's brother off the ground. Paul peered at Luke's face. Luke sewed a smile back on his visage that seemed as genuine as any Paul had ever seen on his brother.

"Thanks you, sir," he said to both farmers, bowing his head, clearly in pain but trying to conceal it. "I's OK, don't you worry. I understand why yous all had to do that. I's been bad, and I deserved every bits of that; you can rest assured! Now if you don'ts mind, I intend to pick you those apples." He limped off, blood trickling from his sandals, but hardly dented by the bullet that shattered his foot.

Paul turned toward the tree. He heard the farmers crunch through some dried leaves in his direction. Ned laughed, but said nothing Paul could hear. Paul was proud of Luke; his brother was so damned brave, so willing to do whatever it took to get through this. And he also thought of Matt; these people had deceived him, which is why he wasn't here. When he found out what happened he would certainly become unhinged. It was up to Paul to be equally brave. This was his moment of truth.

From behind him, as though an electrical bolt bursting through his brain, he heard Ned snap the whip at a nearby tree. "This is going to hurt like crap on that virgin black skin of yours," the farmer said to the back of Paul's head. "I suggest you don't ever forget what happens here today. Don't never! Because I ain't afraid to shoot you in your black heart if you do. You ready, boy?"

Paul nodded up and down.

He felt a small whiff of wind cross his bare skin, and then the whip struck, stinging every fiber in his body, causing him to wince. That's one, he said to himself. Just eleven more. It struck again, and Paul was ready for it. He winced, and he gritted his teeth, his hands clenched closed. Then another hit. Then another.

He looked up, past the fading sun, and saw the mountains, Old Rag standing proudly in front of the monotonous blue chain, looking down upon Paul, watching. He stared hard at it each time the snap of the whip tore more skin off his hide. Four. Five. Six.

I'm going up there, he said to himself. *There's only so much these people can do to me. They can tie me to a tree and whip my skin. Or they can try to kill me. But no matter what they do, I will be free. And that's how it's going to have to be.* Eleven. Twelve.

"That's enough, Ned. That's the twelve lashings doc told you to do."

"No," said the farmer, who laughed good and loud. "Not for this boy."

The whip struck him again. Thirteen. Fourteen. Paul just stared at Old Rag, imagining he was up there still, safe in the mountain's grasp, a free man. At this horrid moment, it really didn't matter how many times the whip tore at his skin. Today would soon be over. He needed to be ready to plan for tomorrow. As he peered up through bursts of agonizing pain, the old craggy mountain gave him solace. It stood apart from the others. It was brave and strong. Its rocky face pushed away from the monotonous blue ridge that hovered behind, freeing itself from the bland sameness of its brethren. It seemed to be talking to Paul, beckoning him back. Paul closed his eyes, sensing the power of an attainable freedom in the midst of a shower of impuissant pain.

Twenty-one, twenty-two.

It didn't matter. Paul had tasted freedom, and he knew at that moment, in that horrid place and time, as he looked into the sky smiling, that he would find it again.

9

T he chill of a dark autumn night descended upon the three brothers. The day's warmth and comfort dissipated amid a cacophony of snapping branches and howling wind. From across the horizon, a storm was coming, a storm that this place and these people had never before imagined possible.

Matt hurried across the foreboding shadows of his farm, slipping on a few branches and rocks that were obscured by leaves. He breathed heavily, frantically. He knew that time was short. Hyperventilating, he dashed into one of the slave cabins, guided toward his brothers' home by its flickering candle. His rapid breaths were visible as a frozen mist that drifted from his mouth like a plume of smoke. When he arrived, Luke stood, staring hard at his brother.

"How much time do we have?" Luke asked him in a calm voice.

"It ain't gonna be too long," Matt said frantically. "Ruth, she give five or six glasses of wine and fed him like a pig. He ate like he ain't never eaten before. And now he's just snoring on the dining room chair, for how long I don't know. The doctor, he's down in Richmond for a few days. He took his daughter with him, so I don't expect any visitors tonight either."

"Well then," Luke said, "Let's sit down and figure this mess out."

Matt could not help but notice his other brother Paul sitting silently in the room's dark corner on a pile of hay. His face, when the candle's light struck it, was blank. His emotions seemed drained. He peered elsewhere, severed from this place and the conversation that percolated around him.

Luke pointed to a cot and motioned for Matt to sit down. The wind howled outside. It was frigid.

"We have few options, Matt," Luke said. "We are stuck with an overseer in our midst permanently, a town of suspicious eyes glaring at us and not likely to pull their gaze away anytime soon, and a likely inquiry to determine if Paul or I, or both of us, will be banished from the farm. It could go one of several directions. But we do know that if the election launches Lincoln into the White House, as Izzy and others think is inevitable, there could well be war. And with war, there will be change. What that change means to us we don't know. It could improve our lot. It could make things worse. But I feel strongly that we can't sacrifice what we built here until we know. Paul wants to get out now. I understand why my brother thinks that way. But I feel patience is our best course. To give up everything we have created here in the presence of an unknown future seems both negligent and foolhardy."

Matt shook his head violently. "No, Luke, you ain't being sensible. This place, this farm, that's all it is. It's a piece of dirt stuck in a pile of mud with enemies all around us and now some of them living right inside too. We got nothing to fight for no more. Paul is right, and he got the scars to prove it, and I ain't gonna let that ever happen again. We can build the same thing somewhere else. We got the know-how, we got the brains, and we got each other. But in Virginia and all that's going on around us, we will never have peace in this place. Peter, he used to be happy to let me pay him off. He used to leave us alone, but now that the doctor got to him and told him what he got to do, he is a monster. He answers to the doctor, not to me. I got my balls taken away from me, and I don't know if they ever coming back."

Matt halted his words for a moment when he heard Paul wince and clench his fist.

"Paul, I beg you, tell me what you thinking now," Matt pleaded, so despondent over his once-strong brother's descent into silence and paralysis. "Just tell me, and I'll do it!"

Paul remained like a rock, barely twitching. Finally, a short string of words slipped through his lips, no inflection or emotion tied to them. His body remained stiff, as though glued to the hay.

"We need to leave" was all he said.

"No," Luke countered. "We have to stay. We are smarter than they are. We can figure this out!"

To that, Matt lost his cool, glaring at Luke with an uncharacteristic indignation.

"Your brother, he's already been whipped once. You got shot right in your foot! There seems to be no limit to what these people think they can do on my farm. I got no power here; they do, and they dispense their justice as they see fit. And they done all this to you because we took one trip away from the farm. We didn't even do nothing wrong. All of this happened because of that dang darn mountain, the one that I thought was standing over us and protecting us, but Old Rag, it let us down. It sold us out. And I ain't intending to stay here anymore to find out what that mountain or these people plans to do to us next. They led our mamma in chains off our farm just because she loved my dad. I ain't making the same mistake. It's time that we leave. Paul is right. We got to go, and we got to go now."

Luke smiled. He stood up and put his arms on his brother's shoulders. He stared gently into Matt's eyes. "It's because of Mamma, it's because of Dad, that we have to stay. They sacrificed their lives to make this place ours. What we have done here is a testament to them. All that they are and all that they were is sprinkled on this land. Every successful crop we cultivate resurrects their souls. Every innovation we introduce makes them smile. If we leave here, we will be leaving them behind. I can't do that. We need to give it a chance. Even with everything that's gone on, we need to give this a chance."

"For what?" Paul's voice slid out like a grunt from the room's corner. Matt could see his eyes shriveled and yellow, staring hard at his younger brother. "You know what I saw today, Brother? That man who holds the whip, Peter, the one we were so proud that we outwitted, you know the man, Brother, the dumb white guy who pushes us down and kicks dirt in our face, you know what he did today? The sun was hot today, and that man took your red raft and sat on it in the middle of our pond. Then he calls out and tells me to bring him a glass of Ruth's iced tea. He made me march into the frozen pond fully clothed to do that. And when I handed him the drink, he told me that I was a good boy, and as long as I know my place, I will not get whipped anymore. And then he sent me on my way. Through my eyes, I saw then and there that this place now belongs to him and his puppet master, the doctor. You say Dad and Mom live here still? Well, if that's so, they are about to be murdered again by the same bastards who killed them the first time. The fact is, Brother, their lives are not on this land. Their lives are in us. Everything that is important and meaningful, it lives within us, not on this corrupted slab of dirt that is at the mercy of the doctor and his gang. The gates are a rouse; they've been penetrated. This sanctuary is a prison. And for the first time in my life, I find myself agreeing with Matt. Either we leave here, or we die, and Mom and Dad die with us."

"Can we wait at least until after the election?" Luke asked. "If we just run away, we will be left with nothing. We will start from nothing. If there is a war, and we move up North, we will start with nothing in a land that has nothing to offer us but bloodshed and destruction. Despite everything, this is still our safest place to be. They need our fruit. We feed half this town with the profits from what we are doing here. They need us. If there is a war, they will need us and our produce even more. And with war they will leave us alone. Momma always told us that."

"It ain't so simple, Luke," Matt snapped, staring harshly at his intransigent brother. "I've been with the doctor today before he left for Richmond. He told me in no uncertain words that every slave will have to be watched like a hawk because more than anything he fears that they will rebel if Lincoln wins. There ain't gonna be no respite. With war or without it, we ain't gonna be safe here. So, I got a plan. I want to free the two of you. I want to free Ruth and her family. I want to put the farm on the market. We got the most productive farm in this whole county. It's folly to think it ain't gonna sell. I got a guy in town who's willing to sell it for me so long as he gets some money out of it. He knows I'm good for my word. Then me and you and Ruth and Mike and Dave, we all get the hell out of here. We go north, or we go west, it don't matter where. We just get the hell out of here. If we got to work washing dishes or cleaning shit off the floor, it's better than this. One day we can get enough money and buy a farm of our own somewhere far away from here and make it into something amazing. But I ain't staying here. Not after they whip Paul and shoot you. Not after they took over this place and pushed me aside like a little child. Staying here ain't worth grapes, it's not worth the pond, it's not worth nothing."

Paul stood and meandered over from his corner perch. "Brother," he said, staring into Matt's eyes, "you are exactly right, and I am with you and appreciate your clarity. But I have to tell you, you are putting faith in people and institutions that will turn on us. These people, these demons, they will never let us just march away. They will never let you free us. They will never let you sell the farm. They would rather us be dead than free, because if we're free, then they lose. They would assume slaughter us first and burn this place down. It doesn't matter if we are growing food that they need. They don't care. Protecting their

way of life is more important to them than pragmatic consider-
ations such as survival and profit."

"Then what would you do?" Luke asked his brother.

Paul stood up. His shirt was off. The scars of his whipping
were still raw. "We run," he said. "We run into the mountains.
We run fast. If Ruth and her family want to come with us, that
is their decision. But the three of us, we take our chances on
that mountain. I have maps and information to get us up North
through the underground railroad. Izzy has promised to help
us once we get to New York. If you two don't want to do it, then
I will do it alone. But I'm not playing these games anymore. I'm
not staying on this tainted land and pretending it is safe. I'm
not making deals with these people and thinking that they will
adhere to them. This place is the embodiment of hell. And the
only way out of hell is to run as fast as you can. You run and you
don't look back. And that's what I intend to do."

"Brother," said Luke, as calm as always, seemingly not shaken
by Paul's words or impacted by his brothers' pleas, "those mountains aren't safe. And even if you get North, you'll arrive with
nothing. It seems like a fool's errand."

"The only fool in this equation is you, Brother. Do you think
the doctor's good word and the overseer's whip is a better choice?"

"It's a transient price to pay to preserve what we have."

"It's a ticket to an early grave, and not a game I'm willing to
play any longer!"

Matt stood quietly as his brothers jabbed with each other.
How did all this happen? One innocent trip to Old Rag had triggered a cascade of circumstances that in an instant incinerated
everything that they so carefully constructed. Matt did not want
to leave the farm. This was where he had lived his whole life. This
was the place of his birth. This was where his father and mother
sacrificed everything for him and his brothers. This was where
they built the pond and cultivated the most valued produce in
the state. This was where he and his brothers had grown into the

men that they were, where the echoes and laughter of Mom and Dad and Izzy reverberated off the walls and brought life to this place, transforming it into a temple of knowledge and passion and love. He listened to Luke and felt swayed by his brother's argument. He listened to Paul and felt deflated.

Earlier today Matt sat with the doctor. It was in the doctor's sunroom, along with the books and the skulls, where he, the doctor, and Jessie spent a good part of two hours. Jessie brought them lemonade, and for a time she stood behind Matt breathing softly on the back of his neck and shoving her breasts into his back. Sometimes her hands, small and plump, rubbed his head and caressed his skin. He was not sure how he felt when she did that. There was certainly something enticing about it. Her touch triggered emotions within him that he had not really experienced before. But, within the depth of his soul, she was still a horrid creature in so many ways.

As they sat together, Matt had a lot to say to the doctor, and he did not hold back. Matt berated the doctor for ordering his brother to be whipped. He said it just wasn't right. It wasn't right that Luke be shot in his foot and treated the way he was treated. It wasn't right that Matt would be lied to so he didn't know anything of what those farmers were doing to his property and on his property. The doctor in his serene and methodical way disagreed.

"In the civilized world of Virginia we have rules and customs that transcend the authority of land ownership, son." The doctor rubbed his brow and twisted his eyes, spacing contemplative silence between his sentences. "Each individual in the Commonwealth has rights, and we hold those rights as dear as did Mr. Jefferson. But as a society, we also have laws and mores which makes those rights possible. If one individual threatens the glue that ties us together, then in fact his freedoms challenges the freedoms of everyone else, and thus we must step in and curtail him. You, Matt, inadvertently invited danger and disarray upon our land when you left your farm and slaves without any supervision, especially during these dark times when such foolishness can kindle insurrection. You've treated your slaves softly. That is your way. For you, it works. But for us as a people, for us as a Commonwealth and a nation, for us whose values were forged by no less men than George Washington and Thomas Jefferson, it is dangerous and incendiary. We had to put your slaves in their place so that they know that they are not merely at the mercy of your rules and supervision but are beholden to this community as well. We needed to provide an overseer who we can watch and regulate so we know your farm will never be a threat to our way of life again. Matt, you're a good boy. My daughter likes you, and I like you. I hope that one day you become part of my family. But you are naive. You are the son of a man who did not truly understand our ways, and so you have little room for error. I apologize for what had to happen that day. I assure you that as long as your course is righted it will never happen again."

Jessie stood behind Matt rubbing his neck. She smiled. He could not see her, but he knew that she smiled with her crooked teeth in a way that was hardly appealing. And then inexplicably, at that moment, despite all of her dark past, she stood up for him. She said to her father, "I met those two slave boys, Daddy. The one you say has a big head, he is as dumb as a blackboard. He knows one thing and one thing only. He knows about farming. He can talk your head off about farming. He's like an idiot savant when it comes to that topic. He doesn't know much else but that. Maybe that's why his head is so big. I don't think there is an evil thought inside that boy's head. That may be a reason why Matt's farm is doing so well. I'm not taking anything away from Matt because he's a genius that way too. But this boy is something strange and special. And I think it will be terrible to take him away from the farm."

"What about the other brother, Jessie?" the doctor asked. "The one who was whipped. What you think about him?"

Jessie rubbed Matt's neck that much harder. She rubbed it so hard it even started to hurt. Then she said, "I don't know about him. His eyes, they are a little scary to me. He seems quiet enough. He doesn't say much. He's strong and is a good worker. He does what Matthew tells him to do. But somehow, I think there is something behind those eyes. I can't tell what."

Matt looked at the doctor and said, "These two slaves, they help me run the farm. They are docile and obedient, and I can't run the place without them. They been with me from the start. There ain't never been noise from my farm or from them or me or no one. We've only done good by this town. I ran my farm just fine without all this interference, without my slaves being shot and whipped. I don't like that you tell Pete what to do to run my farm, 'cause it's my farm, and he's in my employ, and it's up to me to tell him what to do. I don't like this man answers to you. I don't like any of this."

The doctor laughed boisterously. He waved his daughter over toward him, and she obediently marched by his side. Her hair was tied back in pigtails, and she wore one of Izzy's flowery dresses that flowed to the floor. She stood almost statuesque, staring sensually at Matt as her father spoke. "Right now, son, this town is frightened of your farm. It has done well by all of us, but that doesn't mean that we can simply give it a free pass. Your father's ghost and what he did still lives there. And you are his son, and those two slaves are the sons of his mistress. No one in this town will feel comfortable unless they are sure that there is no mischief among the three of you. Your overseer, Peter, he claims you paid him off to stay away from the farm. Now, I know he is a drunk and a scoundrel, but he does have a reputation as a firm and decent overseer, and until we all believe that that you are using him properly, we cannot possibly trust you to oversee him." He paused and sipped his tea.

"I'm going down to Richmond tomorrow with my daughter to speak with people in the assembly who represent our county.

Everyone is uneasy because we don't know what's going to happen when this week is over. There is great fear that Lincoln will win. But even if he doesn't, even if Douglas or Bell win, it doesn't mean that things will be any better. Down South several of the states are intent on leaving this Union, no matter what. They've been waiting for an excuse and that excuse has now come. They hate Douglas as much as Lincoln. They are not likely to be content with Bell. They detest everything about the North. My belief is that they have already crossed beyond the line of disunion and will accept no other course. I have no doubt there will be secession, and Virginia will have to make a choice. But regardless, during these times, no one can take a chance that your slaves or any others are going to cause trouble."

Jessie smiled and said, "He is looking out for you, Matt. I want to be there for you too. I want to be by your side. I want to be part of your life. I hope you understand how much Daddy cares and wants things right. Isn't that right, Daddy?"

"It is right, darling," the doctor said, kissing his daughter on the cheek. "Matthew, if after all this nastiness quiets down, if you want a different overseer and you want to manage the farm differently, that is your prerogative. But for now, please follow my sage advice and do as I say. Any move otherwise could easily instigate suspicion and overreaction. We are civilized people, but we're also living on the tip of a matchstick. Many among us are not so patient as I am. Like with Ned, the man who shot and whipped your slaves, who is a good and decent man but one who knows that his life and livelihood are put at peril by the forces of disruption, I can only contain them if you cooperate. And, Matthew, I hope you also heard my daughter's words. It would mean a great deal to me if your courtship with her moved forward. My daughter is my precious gem, and I respect and like you enough to know that she would be lucky to have you as a husband."

Those words sent a chill down Matt's spine. Now as he sat with his brothers in this cold cabin on a dark and stormy night, he didn't know what to do. He understood Paul's anger; he also understood Luke's hope that this moment would pass, and things could be as they once were. He wanted to believe that more than anything. The prospect of leaving this place and all that they had built here sickened him. But the fear of staying sickened him even more. He always relied on his brothers for direction, and now the two of them sat upon conflicting poles of opinion.

He looked at Luke, whose smile seemed as vibrant as ever. "So, Luke, you think we could ride this out? I want to believe that. But how? How can we do that when our heinous overseer is watching our every move? How can we do that when the doctor and the townspeople will have their eyes on us every second of every day? Christ, Luke, we know what these people are capable of. They shot you in the foot, and they whipped my brother. I can't tolerate that ever happening again!" Tears rolled down his eyes when he uttered those words. The very thought of his predicament and his failure to prevent it—and the fear that he had instigated it by going to Old Rag—drained him of all strength.

Luke, whose serenity almost seemed hypnotic, glared at his brother sharply this time. It was as if he had a sudden revelation. "Matt, Mamma made the ultimate sacrifice to assure our lives here in this place would continue. The question I have for you is whether you're willing to do the same thing for us?"

Matt looked at him quizzically. What could he mean? What sacrifice could he make to right all that was wrong? Matt nodded his head up and down. "'Course I will. Anything."

Luke continued, "I've been thinking of all the possible scenarios here, Brothers. To me, there is one person in this entire calculation who has the most power over our fate. He comes across as a man of civility and succor, but in fact he is the architect of all our troubles. And that man is the doctor."

"The doctor is the only friend we have," insisted Matt. "He is the one that saves us every time there is trouble!"

Paul's voice bounded from the room's corner. "Although I can't believe I'm even saying it, the fact is that Luke is right. It was the doctor who insisted that our father sell our mother down South. He arranged my whipping, and he alone placed our farm under his lens. I think he murdered Dad as well, as you well know. And I don't think he would have any qualms about killing us and taking our farm, all in the name of values and civility, of course. Matt, I love you, but your eyes are blind. That man is not our friend."

Matt turned to Luke. "And what's the sacrifice you asking me to make, Luke?" he asked his brother. "And what's it got to do with the doctor? Because I'm willing to do whatever it takes to make our life the way it was. And I am also willing to go with the two of you up into the mountains and run as far away as from his place as I can. I'm willing to do either. But if I can keep this place and keep our life, that's always going to be my first choice."

"That can never happen, Matt, "Paul said. "This place is poison. We have to run away."

"This is what I have to say, Matt," Luke stated calmly. "And hear me out both of you before you throw daggers down my throat. Because on the surface what I am proposing is going to sound both cruel and suicidal. But if our goal is to reassure the doctor, then the way to do that is through his heart. He wants you to marry his daughter. What I am asking of you, Brother, is that you do just that. You bring her on the farm. She lives with you in the big house. With her here, the doctor will never worry about what goes on. He will leave us alone."

From his corner, Paul laughed loud and hard. "Well, Luke, I think you actually did me a huge favor. You proved my point by trying to do just the opposite. What you are in fact saying is that the only way to preserve this fabricated world you worship is to utterly destroy it. You bring the doctor's daughter here, and our world is gone. There is no lying on the red raft and reading books. There is no discussing philosophy and religion and politics in the house. There is no time for me to cook dinners. We become slaves and nothing more. If Matt marries that girl and she lives here, then even our illusion of freedom will dissipate. The doctor's eyes will be on us every second of every day through her. We will be slaves, no less than that, slaves to our master, slaves to this horrid community and the man who assaulted us. Congratulations, Luke. You just proved that the only way to remain here is to become slaves."

To Matt, the very thought of Luke's idea curdled his stomach. Everything about it seemed wrong. Not only would he be stuck living with her for the rest of his life, sharing a bed with her, forced to have intimate moments together; But with her on the farm, the three of them could never be brothers. They would have to be master and slave. It made no sense.

"Hear me out," Luke said. "This is a vast sacrifice I am asking of you, and one that we all will have to endure. But with time the girl herself may change. She may become softer. I talked to her when she was here the last few days. I talked to her about farming. She seemed interested, and she seemed to like me. I told her that I like to read books about farming as I sit on that red raft. And she was intrigued. You see, as long as I'm not a threat, as long as I'm here to help you, Matt, the doctor's daughter will accept me. I may not be able to be in the big house, not all the time at least, and I may not be able to be myself around her, but I will still do the things most important to me. And you, Paul, you can do the same. You can cook when you feel compelled, because when Matt asks you to do that, then you'll do it. And I'm sure she will be very pleased to know that you can make amazing meals for her husband. You can still do all the planning and financing of our farm, just so long as you give Matt credit. The three of us can sit together, especially on the days and weeks that she visits her father, long stretches that will occur very frequently given their tight relationship and his loneliness. We can sit together either here in this cabin or in the big house, and it will be like old times. Izzy can even join us; she is unlikely to stay when he is here! We will be free to be ourselves beyond the shadow of her presence and the doctor's piercing eyes. You see, our alternative universe does not have to die. It just has to adjust to a new reality. If we do this thing that I'm talking about, if Matt is willing to make the ultimate sacrifice, then we will be able to be the people we have always been."

Paul suddenly bounded up and grabbed his brother by the chest. "You listen to me, Luke," he shouted with unmuted fury in his voice. "I don't want to hear any more crap about your alternative universe. Even if it did exist in your mind, it's dead now. It's like your goddamned red raft that now is occupied by Peter as he sits on your precious pond and pees into it while he tells us what to do. That's your fucking alternative universe. It's gone. You bring the doctor's daughter here, you're only going to make things worse. She is the doctor's reflection. She is the devil. She will see right through your game. And even if you fool her, it doesn't matter; we have the doctor's overseer watching us day and night, and he won't be easily fooled by your nonsense. If this is all you got to offer, then my mind's made up. I'm leaving this farm the first chance I get." He relaxed his grip on Luke's shirt, and then he pushed his brother away.

"Brother," Luke said softly, hardly flustered, "you're just not patient enough, and you lack vision. With time this will work. We'll grow grapes and make wine. We will talk about politics and philosophy. We will sit on that red raft and enjoy the splendor of the mountains on a warm summer day, reading about grand and lofty topics. All that will happen because we will make sure it does. The doctor's daughter will be our path to that possibility. No, Paul, the alternative universe is not dead. It just has to adjust to the times. This is our land, and we design it always to meet our needs."

Paul stared hard at Luke and then marched away. He walked out of the cabin into the howling winds and darkness. Matt watched his brother disappear. So many thoughts jumbled his mind that he didn't know what to say. The very notion of him being with that girl barred him from thinking rationally. But then again, her breath and touch on his neck did feel nice. The sweetness she showed toward him was at least a bit tempting. Maybe she had changed. Maybe what his brother said was true. *If you take care of the doctor's daughter, then you've taken care of everything.*

"You think that we can get Jessie to let us do those things like you say?" Matt asked Luke. "I mean, I see what you is saying. In some ways it makes sense. But it scares me, Luke. Because Paul is right. We make one mistake, and they can come on his place and just destroy us. And it can happen before we know how to react. You asking me to commit my life to the doctor's daughter, and yet we don't know what that will mean to me to us or anything. I may be stuck forever in something that's worse than even now."

"I thought this through. I think it is our best chance. If it doesn't work out, if things start going the wrong way, then we will leave. I promise you that. We'll disappear one night into the mountains when she goes off with her father, and we'll never look back. I have faith, Matt. I have faith in you and Paul and me and in this land where our parents sacrificed so we could flourish. It has never let us down. And it is surely better than anything outside of its fences. This is our world, our alternative universe, our heaven. It is perfection. How could we abandon it without a fight?"

Matt stared pensively at the ground. So much uncertainty clanged within his brain. He alone had placed his brothers and his farm in this predicament through his own foolishness. Now he had a chance to redeem himself and make the ultimate sacrifice. In fact, he wanted to do it. He wanted to do it to make up for what he had done wrong. He walked over to Luke and hugged him strong. He sobbed as he did so. He sobbed for the love of his brothers, and also out of fear for the path he was prepared to take.

"And what about Paul?" he whispered to his brother's shoulder. "How you convincing him to go along with this plan? I don't think he was in a mood to listen to your reassurances right now. I ain't sure he will even stay. And more than anything else, I can't bear to have him leave us. We have to stay together!"

"Leave Paul to me, big Brother. There's only one week until the election. This is not a good time for him to be running away or for any of us to be running away. This is a dangerous time. We need to stay put at least for a while, and let's let this thing play out. I have that much time to work on him. And what about you, Matt? How are you going to do your part?"

Matt, stared into the darkness. "I guess I'll ask her to marry me," he said. "And I'm guessing she'll say yes. And then we'll get married, and she'll move in. That's what I intend to do. Soon as she and the doctor get back from Richmond, that's what I intend to do."

They remained buried within each other's hugs for what seemed like hours. Paul never returned. Not that night at least. Not while Matt was there. Eventually, Matt meandered back to the main house. The following morning, he found Paul working in the fields. Paul had nothing but a blank stare on his face, and he did not utter a word. Matt understood. He wasn't in a talking mood either.

10

Despite a few violent evening storms, the unusual warmth of early November persisted. Leaves fluttered across an otherwise barren ground where rotting apple and pear cores sat as fodder for deer and rabbits. Unlike the farm's human bondage, these creatures came and went as they pleased, jumping over or burrowing beneath the wooden fence that the doctor's men recently reinforced. Luke laughed as he thought of it—animals freer than humans. Paul would appreciate the irony.

His mind raced as he put his plan in motion. He knew time was a precious commodity. The election would strike this land in a mere five days. Paul had distanced himself from Luke, working hard from dawn to dusk in the fields, eyes peering far away, a mind that seemed to be contemplating other things. Paul said nothing to his brother, ignoring him whenever Luke tried to engage him. Instead, Paul interacted obsequiously with Peter, who came to like Paul. "Best worker on this farm," Luke heard Pete say to the doctor's daughter about Paul when she inquired how the slaves were doing. "He does what I tell him to, and then he comes and asks for more. Brings me liquid refreshment when I ask, even walks through the water when I am on the raft. I like the boy. Like him a lot!"

When Pete uttered those words in Luke's earshot, Luke knew that the overseer was being duped and that Paul was concocting some kind of plan of his own. It made Luke smile, even if he trembled a bit, wondering what was brewing within his brother's mind.

Luke marched around the farm with Matt and Jessie that day; the happy couple grasped each other's hands and occasionally snuck in a kiss. Jessie liked to have Luke around when she visited Matt; she asked him frequent questions about farming, which he happily answered with a bounce in his voice. This of course was all Luke's idea. Since he instructed Matt on how to pursue a proper courtship with Jessie, he made sure that he was nearby to help out when needed. That's why Luke endeared himself to the girl and acted like her cute little pet. He just wanted to hang around and slip in an idea here and there.

In this instance, after hearing Pete's comment, he grasped an opportunity to extoll Paul. It was all part of his grand scheme of utter manipulation, a plan that had been progressing even more smoothly than he envisioned. If he could endear this naive and lovestruck girl to Matt's two brothers, then perhaps she could dissuade her father from selling one or both of them off the farm.

"My brother, he is a goods worker that's sure. But you know, Ms. Jessie, he can cook like nobody could cook before! Oh my God, you tell her massa Matt, tell her how my brother cooks! He can turn chicken like you see on the ground into a meal fit for a king! Ms. Jessie, you have to have my brother cook for you, and you will see what I says is true. Wait till you see! Right, massa Matt, right?"

Jessie smiled and patted Luke on his head. She did that often. "Well, thank you, Lukie," she said. "Matthew and I would always appreciate a magnificent meal cooked by your brother. Once we get married that is. Matt, why didn't you tell me that your slave Paul is also a cook? No wonder you love these slaves so much! I want to help you make this farm as successful as it can be. And,

Luke, you are just so smart about everything farming! I want to hear more about those grapes you told me about. That sounds intriguing! We can make our own wine here. And I'm sure you're the one to do it. Have you heard your slave talk about the grapes, Matt? How wonderful!"

Luke played the game well. She was putty in his hands. All was progressing beyond expectation!

Matt proposed to Jessie on the last day of October, All Saints Day. Luke told him exactly what to do. He was to first ask the doctor's permission. As per the script, Matt promised the doctor that Jessie would have the life of a queen. And that the slaves on his farm would be Jessie's slaves as soon as they were married. Jessie decided that both Luke and Paul were crucial for the farm's continued success. Apparently, the doctor argued with her, but Jessie never lost a fight. Paul and Luke would be staying. And while Luke would remain as the brains behind the operation, Paul, the best worker Pete ever saw, could spend some time in the kitchen, whipping up a big meal from time to time.

On a cloudy day in early November, Luke found his brother in the field spreading compost around the trees. Paul of course ignored him, but Luke inserted himself between his brother and a large pear tree.

"It's only been a few days, Brother," he said to Paul, who continued to shovel piles of dark, aging dirt as though Luke were not there. "Do you know how far we've gotten? Matt is engaged and will marry Jessie within the month. The doctor has agreed to let us both stay here. I can continue as the farm's horticulture expert with endless access to the red raft. You can cook and read your books and of course covertly manage our finances. It's as if our world is slowly returning to its natural state."

Paul, without flinching, lifted a pile of the brown dirt high and dumped it on his shorter brother's head. His stern facial expression did not waver; his mouth uttered not a single word. He then dug up another pile of dirt and resumed his composting.

Luke smiled at him, even as pieces of rotting leaves and vegetables caked his face. It didn't matter. It was all working out. Paul would appreciate it, eventually.

Later that day, as the trio meandered through the farm, Luke spotted Pete sitting on his red raft, humming a tune as he kicked up water. Luke pointed his finger at Pete and looked at Jessie. "I don't know, masa Matt," he said. "But that man likes to lies on that raft all days and all night. Remember, Ms. Jessie, how you said how you wants me on that raft to think and think and think of so many things? Remember? But that Pete, he just sits on it all day, evens when he is says he is working, and he makes Paul serve him, and all of that all the time he coulds be working and I coulds be thinking and I says, to myself I says, 'Poor Lukie!' Whys, oh whys does he does that to me? What you think, Ms. Jessie?"

Jessie of course patted him on the head, and she giggled a little. "Well, Lukie, that raft should belong to you, and your overseer should be out on the fields, making sure that the work is done, not dillydallying on the pond. Matt, I think you're treating Pete much too kindly. He shouldn't be lounging on that raft. If he's not working the slaves, there is work he could be doing himself. Matt, you are too soft on everyone. You have to be a little bit tougher with your people."

"Yes, Jessie," Matt said with a bit of a smirk. "I'll let Pete know."

Luke nodded his head and smiled. Without any question, his plan was working out to perfection.

Early morning one Saturday, just three days before the election, Jessie and Matt brought Luke into town. Other than on their trip to Old Rag, Luke had spent every bit of his life within these fences. But Jessie insisted on escorting him to spend time with her father. She wanted to show him the farming store in town, so he could see firsthand all the many tools and gadgets that may help him in his work. She was excited to hear what he had to say and to show him off for the doctor.

"Wait until Daddy hears about your grapes, Lukie! He will be so impressed!"

This was Luke's first trip to Washington. He rode on the saddle behind Matt and held onto his brother as tightly as he could. The ride was in fact a little bit frightening. Matt was not the best horseman in the world, and the road was wet and bumpy.

When they arrived on the well-manicured main street, several boys spotted the trio and drifted over, blocking the way. Later, Matt told Luke that these were the boys who bullied him in his youth, the very ones who had an interest in Jessie and were part of her posse. They were not happy with how matters had resolved since Matt's plot was uncovered after Old Rag; Jessie's courtship with Matt, the fact that the witch-slave's children were not banished from the farm, and even Matt's continued ownership of that cursed piece of land ate at them. One of them, a boy named Jude, had a broad body and a neck that resembled a tree trunk. He had a particular antipathy toward Matt for many years. If any boy had bullied Matt, Jude was certainly on the top of the list. Luke could smell Jude's disdain for his brother before he even looked into the boy's sinister eyes. And now, as Matt entered the town with his slave and his fiancée, Jude and some others were there to greet them.

"So, this is the freak with a big head," Jude said, pointing to Luke. "The son of the slave bitch your father fucked."

Jessie scolded him. "Jude, you be good. Or I will tell my daddy what you're saying."

Jude and the others looked at each other, laughing. "All of a sudden, Jess, you is going to be a sweet little princess and Matt is the one you decide to be with? After all those years and all those things you said about him, how he be the son of the devil, how the slaves on his farm is going to kill us all, how we should go and burn the whole place down? Now you're going to up and marry him? You go tell your dad whatever you want. But me and the boys, your former friends, the ones you fucked in more ways than one, we ain't having nothing of this."

And with that, Jude marched to Luke and shoved him hard. Luke easily could have remained upright by pushing his center of gravity forward, but instead, he limply fell to the ground. He cried out that he was hurt, and he begged his master for help.

"Now you see what you just did?" Jessie yelled at the boys, who seemed genuinely stung by Luke's frantic hollering "He's just an innocent numskull, never hurt anyone, he never could. You go away now, or I swear, Jude, you and all of you will feel my daddy's wrath before nightfall!"

A few of them scattered, and Jude stood alone, breathing hard, grimacing, hands on his hips. He pointed to them with a stiff finger. "Matthew Cocklin, you better watch your ass. When you ain't looking, when you don't got this princess to protect you, we'll be coming for you. And we will find you! You is as good as a piece of shit being trampled by a horse's foot." He shot one more piercing glance at them and then hustled away.

Luke, hardly flustered, enjoyed walking through the town, sewing a dumb smile on his face that never faded. Jessie even bought him a piece of penny candy, after which Luke seemed so happy that he nearly fainted. He did enjoy the vitality of the main street, the rush of people who hurried by, and even the few menacing stares that surveyed the hand-holding couple and their peculiar slave.

From every corner, and in every store, Luke palpated a great deal of tension in the town. People were clustered together speaking, whispering, and arguing.

Jessie brought her two companions to the periphery of one such group, a few farmers, the town's lawyer, and of course her daddy. The men pontificated what might happen should Lincoln win. Was he going to win? How were the electoral prognostications faring? The doctor knew that the Deep South states— "those uncivilized bastions of anger and overreaction that had no sense of how to play this game, and God forbid they pull us deep into something that is not in our own interest"—might flee the Union, but would Virginia follow? And if there was war, and the next president chose to fight to keep the Union together, what would that mean for the Commonwealth? What would it mean for all their farms and their livelihood? Could Virginia remain neutral? Could there be peace after Tuesday? They tossed out their sundry thoughts and fears all at once in a cacophony of opinion, until the doctor bowed and walked away, moving toward another group of seers. Then he spotted the trio and gravitated in that direction, his daughter smiling and giddy as he approached.

"Ah Jessie, and my soon-to-be son-in-law Matthew, how pleasant to see you," the doctor said, shaking Matt's hand and kissing his daughter on the cheek. "As you see, we are solving the world's problems today! In a few days we vote, as does the country, and never in my life has one election meant so much." He paused for a moment and then glared at Luke. "I see you brought the slave genius savant. What do you say, is it, Luke? What do you think may happen after the election on Tuesday?"

Luke reacted quickly. He stuttered a bit and bowed to the distinguished man. "All's I knows doctor sir, and all's I ever wants to know, is that when planting season comes in the spring that we's all is ready, no matter who sits in that White House over there across the river, because it don't matter not who is in that house or not, because every one of them appreciates a good pear!"

The doctor laughed loudly, and Jessie patted Luke on the head.

"See, Daddy, see! See what I told you! He is so smart and so wise! And so very sweet!"

They wandered to another group of men, where Luke recognized Ned, the farmer who had shot him in the foot and whipped Paul that harrowing night. About eight men were yelling at each other, none of whom could possibly be hearing what the other was saying. One of them, a stocky man with a worn-out face and a large hat on his head, was holding a gun, waving it back and forth.

"Boys, boys," the doctor said, inserting himself in the center and quieting the melee. "Let us be civilized Virginians here. Speaking without listening is a trait they employ up North and has no place in the great city of Washington and the great Commonwealth of Virginia."

"Well, hello to you, Doctor," Ned said. He peered over at Luke and laughed, then turned back to the doctor. "Maybe you can help clear up these misguided people's error of ways. They is saying that we should vote for Breckinridge come Tuesday, and that either he is picked or there ain't no reason to stay in the Union anyway. Now, I heard you talking about Bell as being our best chance of keeping the Negro-loving Lincoln out of the White House, and you ain't as hard on Bell as some of these boys seem to be. So you tell us, Doctor, why do you think we should cast our lot with Bell?"

The doctor grasped his chin between two fingers and squinted, his brain carefully contemplating what to say, which was his wont. Luke was fascinated by the doctor's theatrical posturing and how quickly it engrossed and quieted all these angry men! Finally, the doctor lifted his finger and spoke.

"Our representative to Congress, Thomas Babcock, he is a firebrand; he wants us out of the Union. Hell, boys, the only reason he is not Speaker of the House is that his candidacy was sabotaged by Northern unionists. Now, he comes from Appomattox, so is not exactly representing our interests here in Washington, but even he would tell you that Bell would be a fine representative of our interests and certainly the only man other than Lincoln who has a chance of winning this thing."

"I do respect Tom Babcock; I voted for him two times already and would vote for a third," said a small man in the crowd, who precariously grasped three bags of seed as he spoke. "But he's dead wrong on this, and so are you. I hate to contradict you, Doctor, but I must. Bell, just like Douglas, wants each state to decide about slavery inside its own border, which is well and good, but I can tell you here and now, all that is going to do is leave the new states in a constant state of war, and mark my words, gentlemen, if I can even call some of you that after hearing your idiotic talking today, the Northern bankers and industrialists and Jews, who all back the Negro cause, they are going to make sure the new states end up free, and in ten years with Bell in office we will still be fighting this thing, but this time with less clout and less resolve. That's what Bell got in store for us. It's just delaying the inevitable. I'd rather have it out now. I'm voting for Breckinridge. He's the only one who speaks for me."

"A vote for Breckinridge is a wasted vote," said Ned vehemently. "You ain't much into math, Crow, but me and the doctor, we ran the numbers. You get the South behind Bell, and just a few states up on the border and in the West pick him, which I am sure they will, then Lincoln can't win, and the race will be tossed into the House of Representatives, where Bell has a great chance of winning the thing, because we have a lot of power there. And not only do he win it, but he ain't about to bite the hand that fed him. He knows from the get-go that he won because of us here in the South, which is where is he from anyway. He's beholden to us. That's why we vote for him. He can win, and he will be our best chance. Why would you vote Breckinridge, who has no chance to win?"

"I'm not selling my soul out to some Northern pretender just because of your fancy math," the short farmer said.

Ned waved his arm at the man called Crow. "You want war? You think that's a good thing for your orchard, for this town, for us or our boys? We had years and years of Northern presidents who leave us alone. Bell will be one of those, and he will leave us to handle our Negroes without all the meddling that these other people keep talking about. But if you vote for Breckinridge, then all we got is Lincoln, and then we are standing in a pile of shit, beholden to South Carolina or having to cower to the North, and either way that ain't good for any of us."

"Ned," another man in the crowd said, "you smell like you already been standing in a pile of shit!"

The doctor shook his head quietly and calmly, as he always did. He looked at the short farmer. "Crow, what you say does not make sense. I've known you since you were a boy, and I know your father. And I understand why you would be angry and be fed up with any man like Bell who is willing to compromise with the North. But Bell is not our enemy. He is one of us. He is acceptable to the Northern moderates and an enemy to the abolitionists. He is no threat to our way of life. He'll be working with a Southern Congress and a Southern Supreme Court. And he will fight for us, I assure you. Would you rather our course be dictated by the brain-dead leaders of South Carolina and Georgia, whose only goal is to spread the institution of slavery so they can profit from selling their slaves, whose own goals subvert our ability to prosper in the Commonwealth? The firebrands from the Deep South have poisoned our minds. They want to sow chaos into our country. We in the Commonwealth are prospering because we remain on good terms with the North, while adamantly preserving our ways. Breckinridge brings us Lincoln, which brings us secession, which puts South Carolina in charge of our fate. Bell allows us to continue our current path. What do you think makes more sense?"

There was a silence. Then the man with the gun spoke softly.

"Maybe, Doctor, some of us don't want to keep wondering what's next that the Northerners will come up with to screw us even more. Maybe we think they is all at the mercy of their own Negroes and abolitionists and ain't never going to change. Maybe we ain't happy with this Union. Maybe it's time we do break away. You say South Carolina will be in charge. I don't think so. In just a short matter of time, we Virginians be running the show. We always do! I got faith that we'd be better away from the North and to take our chances with people who got the same ideas as us than keep playing a losing game."

"It is a conundrum," the doctor smiled. "There of course is no right answer. Mr. Jefferson called it a fireball in the night. The divide between North and South is inevitable. It's just a matter of when. But frankly, boys, I do not think this is the time. And I don't want South Carolina to force my hand. I want any decision the Commonwealth makes to be done with thoughtfulness and integrity."

"If Lincoln wins and we go to war, you going to support Virginia joining up with the South?" Crow asked the doctor.

"I will support the will of the people." Then he then pointed to Luke. "You see this slave? I asked him what he thought. And you know what he said? As long as he can keep growing pears, then he really doesn't care who wins. Maybe that should be our mantra, boys. We should hope for the scenario that enables us to continue growing pears." He then laughed. "Make sure to be at my house on Tuesday after supper. Horatio Moffett will be joining us, and we will talk and have cigars and some bourbon as we get word of the election results. The telegraph is just one house removed, and I have been promised updates every fifteen minutes. For now, I bade you farewell. I will be lunching with my daughter and her fiancé."

He bowed and waved his hand. Luke followed behind, briefly peering back at the group of men. Within seconds they were shouting at each other just as they had done before the doctor intervened.

That night Luke sat at the edge of Paul's cot, where his brother lay silently, staring up at the roof, breathing slowly and methodically. Luke moved close to him, trying not to invade his brother's space, but very much needing to talk to him.

"I feel your pain, Brother, but you have to understand. These people are easily manipulated. You give them a script, and they will do exactly what you ask of them, without knowing they are doing it. Jessie is already our greatest ally! And you had to be in the town today. The man who shot me, I stood near him, and he didn't care. None of them care. They are so preoccupied with the election and what it portends, and their honor and the great Commonwealth, that their eyes are far away from what we are doing. I think we will be fine."

"I am glad that you think we will be fine, Brother." Paul breathed softly without inflection.

Luke looked at his brother, who was clearly submerged in angst and discontent. How could Luke persuade him? "Brother," he said, "I know you don't believe me. I see what you are doing. You're just playing the role of the good slave, I assume, so they leave you alone. And then what? You just wear a mask the rest of your life and lose your soul? No, my brother would never do that. I know what my brother would do. He would wait until the moment is right and, knowing that Pete will not suspect it, would bolt out of here and run. Run to where, Paul? No matter what the result of the election, these people and many others in your path will not tolerate a runaway slave."

"You are right, Brother," he said in a voice devoid of deflection. "Jessie is a wonderful girl, and Ned, he's not such a bad guy as long as we stroke him enough. So, let's keep growing our apples and pears for them. Let's plant grape vines and make our own wine here. And what else? What else do you want to grow so we can feed our oppressors as we wilt on their land and never can be men? Should we live a life as slaves forever and stroke all their brows and thank them for not whipping us and putting us in chains, just so we can stay on this God-given farm of ours and hope that maybe we can sneak in dinner together, or secretly read a book, or make Matt look smart? Is this what you want me to wait for?"

"Brother, you are thinking too much about this," said Luke, smiling. "We grow our produce because we are the best farmers in this land, and we can be proud of our accomplishments. We don't need external validation to know what we have done here and what we can continue doing. And if there is war, and it ends with the victory of the North, then what we have created here will feed not our oppressors but our saviors. Look beyond tomorrow, Paul. We have proven our ability to flourish in this place and to excel. I am showing you that our success can continue unabated. I need you with me."

Paul sat up. He seemed neither angry nor particularly despondent. He put his arms on his brother's shoulders and looked smilingly in his eyes. "I love you, Luke. I always will. You and I view the world through unique lenses. I don't share your optimism. I can never be the man that Mom and Dad hoped me to be while hiding behind a fence and begging to be pet like a dog. If there is a war by the North against these demons, I don't want to be on the sidelines. I don't want to help these people in their war effort by feeding them as they fight for my slavery. I do appreciate all that we accomplished. You are amazing, Brother. And I hope you are right. I just can't hang around to find out."

Luke nodded. He understood. He hugged his brother and lay his head on Paul's shoulder. "You just be careful," Luke whispered. "I love you too."

Time was ticking quickly. Luke continued to play the game. It was now two nights before the election. Previously engulfed by frantic babble and arguing among its citizens, Washington faded into a hush. A few people traversed the street, all quietly, none interacting. It was eerily silent. Jessie and Matt picked up a few supplies from the doctor, taking Luke along because, well, Jessie wanted him there. They rode back in the late afternoon on an empty road and arrived at the farm.

From the South a strong wind blew across the valley; the doctor said it was going to be a nor'easter, windy and wet. Luke smelled the intensity of this storm; years of experience enabled him to predict the weather fairly capably. This one would be one for the books. When he had a brief moment, he whispered into Matt's ears. "We have to tie down some of the newer trees, and we have to clear the fields of all debris. And we have to keep the outlet dam wide open."

Matt nodded.

By late evening the wind picked up dramatically. The few leaves remaining on their trees flew off and fluttered through the night air. Now the branches were bare and exposed. A few started to snap. It was dark and cold. Rain had not started, but Luke could feel the air's thick moisture accumulating. When Jessie stepped away to use the privy, he implored Matt to push Pete a bit harder to prepare the farm for this storm. They needed to tie down the trees!

"You want to go to the main house, Jess?" Matt asked his fiancée when she returned. "It ain't really safe with all these branches and the like flying about. I got to get Pete moving to tie some stuff down. I'll come in after a bit."

"Can Lukie take me there?" Jessie asked. "I would feel safer."

Matt nodded. "You hurry back, Luke. We need all hands to get this place ready for the storm."

"Yes massa, Matt, sir." Luke bowed. "I will takes Ms. Jessie to the main house and come right back to helps out. Ruth can watch her in the house and keeps her safe. I's be right back. You's always right about this stuff. You's so smart, massa Matt."

Through the swirling wind and drops of cool water, Jessie and Luke crunched over branches and crispy leaves. The light of the main house led them forward. Jessie held Luke's shoulder. And then suddenly, she stopped. She twisted Luke and stared sharply into his eyes.

The house's light struck her face, and Luke stuttered. What he saw sent a chill down his back. She peered at him with a sinister smile. Her eyes were wide open, with her eyebrows pointed inward. She almost looked like the devil. She took her right hand, which she had used repeatedly to pat his head, and instead reached down his pants, grabbing his groin. She stroked his balls a few times and then, leaning forward, licked his face. Then she squeezed him, and he let out a squeal. She relaxed her grasp.

"We'll have some fun, Lukie," she said in a firm, deep voice. "You boys have been playing right into my hands. You're like putty to me. You've made my job so easy. I knew Matt was not the brightest boy in the land, but I didn't think it would be this easy to take his farm and slaves and make them my own. My daddy was right; getting control over all of this, this wonderful farm, this place that will help us earn the money we need, it is worth the price of marrying your feeble master. I have to say, Luke, I know you are an imbecile and probably don't understand a word I am saying, but I want to thank you. It's almost like you knew what I wanted and helped me to get it. You may be smarter than you realize." And then she laughed, sliding her hand out of his pants.

Luke stood there, stunned. What was she saying?

"You go back to the fields, Luke, and go help your master make sure my farm stays safe." Her sweet voice returned. "I'll be fine getting to the house, my house, myself. I will have Ruth prepare me a bath. I'll be there very naked. Do you ever wonder what I look like naked, Luke?"

His heart started to flutter. He said nothing.

"Well, soon enough, you'll see. You'll see it all. Soon enough I will be calling the shots, and you will belong to me, to do as I command. And I do have some very erotic and sensual dreams about you, Lukie, that I do have! But for now, go help your master. We don't want this storm to threaten our precious trees. I have a lot of plans for this place and for you, Lukie, my cute little smart man. Soon enough, thanks to you, they will be real." She kissed him on the cheek and wandered into the light, as her voice faded into a flutter of laughter.

She was gone. And as the wind and rain accentuated, saturating his skin with chilling moisture, Luke stood in shock. What could she be saying? He turned and walked slowly toward Matt. He was doing the manipulating, not her. What could she even mean?

The wind blew a small branch into his chest, and he yelled out. It hurt, and it dropped him to the ground. From there he watched helplessly as the storm brewed above him, threatening everything he knew, everything he assumed as truth, everything he had worked so hard to create. His groin started to throb; his breath was short. He lay there for a few minutes, and then he propped himself up.

We have to tie down the trees.

Sometimes, the simplest thoughts can be the greatest solace in the darkest of times!

11

Two weeks earlier, before Luke was hit by Jessie's shocking revelation, and when Paul and he still chatted with some levity, Izzy made one final trip to the farm.

"Pretty big contrast from just a month ago, wouldn't you agree, Izzy?" a newly animated Paul said to his friend as they huddled with Luke in their slave quarters. It was cold. Damned cold. "When you came in September, we were in the big house by a fire talking about Julius Caesar and the fate of the American republic. Now we live in here under the rein of a gas-bloated doctor, everything stripped from us, speaking and acting like fools, and the best we can hope for is that we're not whipped. Good life, huh?"

"I don't come down to freeze my ass off in this cabin and listen to tales of suffering, believe you me," Izzy said to them, buried in a blanket. "I can do that in New York. With bigger shitheads than you two. But I have to say, I am devastated, and this damned election means more now than ever. I need to get you boys out. Somehow, I have to get you out."

Izzy slipped over from Warrenton, where he had made one last delivery of clothes before dashing up to New York where he would cast a historic vote for Lincoln in a few days. He stopped by the farm just for one night; he had heard about some trouble in little Washington and hoped it did not involve his boys. Sadly, it did.

"Ruth gave us a feast at least," Luke smiled, sitting on a bale of hay, seeming comfortable. "Good food, good friends, good conversation, and some new books about grape harvesting. What could be better?"

"Better?" Paul said. "What could be better? How about I don't have whip marks on my back that sting like they're fresh? How about Matt isn't hobnobbing with the doctor and fucking his daughter, who is haunting this place like a witch from hell, as his voracious overseer with the brain of an ant treats us like dogs? That might be better."

Izzy nodded his head. "Yea, the feast isn't quite as tasty as usual, not under these circumstances." And he threw a piece of chicken into his mouth, chewing loudly. "It's still tender, don't get me wrong, thanks be to God, to Ruth. But you know, I had to sneak in here. Ruth helped me slip by Matt, said that he and his wife were 'busy' in the main house, lots of noises coming from there, so she said."

"Oh, yea, believe me," Paul laughed. "They don't conceal their bedroom fun. You can hear their squeals deep in the pear orchard, and most of the birds fly away in shock! Good advice for Ruth to slip you past his witch wife. I just don't know how you'll get us out. This place has eyes everywhere."

Izzy drank wine, something quite uncharacteristic for him. He was visibly disturbed. "New York City, it's not going to vote Lincoln, but the state will. The entire North will. He is going to win. And within sixty days, if you want to believe the seer Henry Clay, this nation is going to be at war."

Luke smiled. "The doctor believes that Bell has a chance," he said. "With Bell there can be peace."

Izzy spat out his wine, choking on it. "Are you fucking crazy," he shouted back at Luke. "I believe that your misguided Matt has been quoting the good doctor lately, but et tu, Lukas? Et tu?

Here's a fact, Luke. Lincoln will sweep the North, Breckinridge the South. So where does that leave Bell? He's a nothing, a nobody. He doesn't even have a party. I'm glad the bastard doctor is voting for him. At least he'll get that one vote. I'd hate to see him embarrassed."

When Izzy drank, he spoke quickly and incoherently in a Yiddish accent. He went on and on about how the brothers had to get out and get out fast. "Don't trust anyone," he slurred. "Not even Matt."

"Matt is still with us, Izzy," Luke pleaded, after Paul had argued just the opposite. "He is playing his role, but he will protect us. It doesn't matter who wins the election. It doesn't even matter if there's war. Matt will be here for us, always. Of that I assure you."

"Now I need to drink some wine," Paul snarled.

"Beware the son," Izzy said to the two brothers, after drinking his second cup of wine. He seized a chunk of chicken and shoved it in his mouth. "So with the father, beware the son. My people have been fearing the son for hundreds of years. You boys best take the same advice!"

"Amen to that," said Paul, pouring more wine in Izzy's cup. "Tell my brother. He thinks the world is as pure and pristine as ever. And that our brother is the same man he always was."

Luke just nodded. His face reeked of its usual tranquility, it was unmoved. "Matt is playing his role," Luke reiterated. "He is doing what needs to be done to obfuscate what we have created here. He's sacrificing so we can preserve this farm, our paradise. Short-term hassles, yes. But long-term security. Worry not, Brother and Izzy. Matt is and always will be our ally."

"Obfuscate?" Izzy laughed. "That's a new one for me! You boys are certainly enlarging my vocabulary!"

"I don't think he used it in the right context," Paul snarled. "And by the way," he said, lifting off his shirt and showing his back to his brother, "this is not just a hassle. It hurts like hell.

I don't even sleep at night sometimes. And despite your delusions, Brother, there is more of this coming our way! There are a few days until the election. We hang around here, and the bastards who did this to me will be running the show, not Matt."

Izzy nodded up and down. "Beware the son," he said again. "Five thousand years of persecution has taught us a thing or two. Running is not a bad option. It never is. That's why people like me are still around. And why we are always ready to run. I just have to figure out how to get you boys out!"

"I thought it was three thousand years," Luke said

"Nope." He chewed some more chicken and shivered a bit in his blanket. "Five thousand. We've been running for five thousand years. That's why I'm so goddamned fit!"

Luke still did not flinch. "You are prone to hyperbole, Izzy, and this non-kosher wine may be tainting your Hebrew soul." He smiled. "Dad was not a man who listened to these people. He hated slavery. He never sold out. He died a broken man, but a man who protected us to his last days. Matt is the same way. He loves us, Izzy. He loves what we created here. That will never change. We can take our chances out there in the world, with its sullied morality and hateful people, with a bigotry just as voracious as what is just more overt in the South, or we can stay here, in this paradise we created, made safe by our brother, by our orchard's success, and by the fact that if we all play our roles, then, as Mamma said, the fences will protect us."

"Like the fences protected her?" Paul snarled.

"Luke," Izzy said, standing up and flicking him on the head, "get off your ass and smell the grapes. This is just a farm, like a million others all over the country, except this one is infested by vermin and tainted by poison. It's just a piece of freaking dirt plopped down in some garden of shit, and even though you may feel it's the promised land, it ain't; I assure you. We Jews died a thousand deaths by hanging on to Israel and getting decimated time and time again, thinking it was paradise, our promised land, thinking God would protect us. Those of us who survived ran away from paradise and ended up in New York. Food's better too. Not as warm. But a hell of a lot safer, believe you me!"

"It's the same damned line, Izzy," said Paul, picking at the chicken. He never drank. Never dared to dull his senses. Ate smartly so he could remain strong. Everything he did was for a purpose. "You won't convince my brother. He will be drowning in his precious pond and tell you how wonderful the water is from down below. We mock Ruth and her boys for being religious. That they have turned to a fabricated God to achieve salvation, instead of tackling their bondage directly, a God given to them by their captors. It's nuts, right? But how much better is my brother's illusion? How much better is it to believe that this farm is some form of salvation, even as his brother gets whipped, even as his other brother falls prey to our tormentors, even as we have lost every bit of security and autonomy we ever knew? Why is that not any more delusional than the self-abrogating faith that Ruth and all the docile slaves down here have chosen to follow? Ruth and Luke both are doing just what the masters want. They are finding peace with the status quo, finding solace with some false savior who will one day deliver them from slavery even as they remain in chains. What slaveholder wouldn't endorse that!"

"It's going to be a hell of a grape harvest this year, Brother," Luke retorted. "I'd be ashamed if you miss it, Izzy. You seem to like this tref wine. I plan on making crates of it."

The night was winding down. Matt could be back soon. Peter might make his nightly rounds. Izzy would have to leave. Paul peeked outside. His heart was racing. Time was precious. There was one more task to accomplish, one more favor he needed from his friend before he darted off for New York. But Izzy, his mind activated by fermented grapes, would not shut up. He gabbed about Lincoln, the Irish in New York, the fate of his clothing business amid the shadow of war, and how the Jews had escaped

Roman bondage. His thoughts leaped from one idea to another. Paul's patience was running thin.

Time was running out.

Paul peeked out the cabin's open window. Old Rag glowed in the distance. It was staring at Paul, speaking to him, firm and unwavering amid the world's chaos and Izzy's endless chatter.

"Izzy," Paul finally shouted, his voice sharp and stern. "I need to talk to you. Alone."

The room dropped into a sudden silence.

A rooster cockled outside. Luke smiled. "You want me to leave, Brother?'

"I do, Luke. I need to talk to Izzy before he has to travel North. We don't have much time. There is something I have to tell him. Alone."

Luke nodded. He smiled at Paul and, saying nothing, wandered out into the cold night.

A few insects chirped, as Luke's footsteps drifted away. Paul peered outside. There was silence.

Izzy sat and stared at him, suddenly silent. For a moment, neither of them uttered a word, their eyes saying more than anything else could. Then Paul spoke.

"I read the book," he said. "It's kind of vague. Lots of things left up to chance. But you think I can do it?"

Izzy nodded in the affirmative. "If anyone can, it's you. Let's face it, Paul. Two rules apply. Dodge the bastards. And head up North."

"That I can do," Paul said. "Then someone will meet me in Frederick?"

Izzy nodded. "Some of the best people I know."

"OK," he uttered, as a large smile overtook his face. "OK."

Izzy paused for a moment. "What about your father's letter?"

Paul nodded. "That's what I need you to do for me before you leave. It's in the big house, in the room where you usually sleep, under the bed, in an envelope. Peter the overseer is going to make rounds soon. Matt and his princess are likely tucked away in his room. Do you think you can sneak in and get it before you leave? I don't want to head North without it."

Izzy nodded, suddenly quite sober and earnest. "Of course," he said. "My carriage is off the farm. I'll have to leave here when that bastard Pete comes by. I can dash in and get the letter. Do you want me to bring it to New York?"

Paul nodded yes. "I'll get it from you there. In a few days."

"I take it Luke doesn't know?"

"No," Paul said. "He can't. He won't go. And he'll try to talk me out of it. I just don't need that. I will miss him terribly. I fear for his life. But I know his limitations. He is not a man who relishes the unknown."

"Unless the unknown involves grapes," laughed Izzy.

"Right," Paul said, putting both his hands on Izzy's shoulders. "Unless it involves grapes."

12

Wind and rain shook the farm to its core; it was November 6, the nation's election day, and no torrent of adverse weather was going to deter the people from this county from swarming the polls. It was a simple choice, Matt had told Paul. Bell or Breckinridge. Union or secession. Matt intended to follow the doctor's lead and vote the former. Paul hugged him, tighter than usual, and told his brother to make a good choice.

"You could vote for Lincoln," he had said to Matt. "Or, at worse, Douglas. That would make a statement."

Matt shook his head. "No, it ain't like that, Paul. They know who you vote for here, even if they ain't supposed to. The doctor, he says neither of them is going to get a single vote in the county, and I don't even think they is on the ballet. It's either Bell or Breckinridge. Anything different is a wasted or even dangerous vote. I ain't taking a chance like that!"

Paul hugged him again and then wiped a tear away. *Don't fall apart,* he chided himself. *Pretend it's just another day.*

He pulled away from Matt. "See you soon, Brother. You know I love you, right?"

Matt nodded, smiled nonchalantly, and then dashed into the rain, where a long and wet ride to town awaited him. Paul watched him go, grinning amid a surge of deep affection.

His brother would be OK. Often dimwitted, not always able to figure people out, but OK. In these times that may just be enough.

Now, five hours later, Paul stood in the main house's kitchen cooking a big turkey dinner, by permission of the farm's owner, who happened to be Matt. Pete popped in and out, drenched with water. He had been spending the day, along with Luke and Ruth's two sons, managing the overflowing dams. He grabbed food here and there, but asked Paul, "When's that damned grub going to be ready? I am hungry as a starving cow, and besides, boy, we need you out there doing a man's work, not this sissy cooking that your idiot master put you up to. We got a lady here for that!"

"You won't be disappointed," Paul told him.

Pete nodded, took a whiff from under the lid of a pot, and then hit Paul on the shoulder. "I can't wait, boy. I am fucking starving!"

Earlier, knowing he could not get to the polls, Pete gave Matt his proxy ballot. "I'm a Breckinridge boy," he told Paul later. "Doc and others, they like this guy Bell, but Bell he's just a limp prick, can't pick a side. I say we vote for someone who's got our interest in mind. And if it means war, then that by God's will, I'm ready to take up arms for my Lord and my Commonwealth and blast those motherfuckers from the North right through their cocks."

Paul could not envision how a Breckinridge victory, or even a prolonged war, would benefit a guy like Pete. But Pete, like every poor slob who lived here, leaped on the jingoistic train, riding God and country as a reason to turn his back on self-interest and common sense. Pete was a tool of men like the doctor, although he would never know it; his passion emanated from being part of the club, knowing that as bad as things were for him, at least he was better than the Negro, who he could push around and torture at will. Pete was higher up on the social chain because there was human chattel forever lower than him. If slavery disappeared, where would that leave Pete? He would just be another poor bastard tilling for a low wage and at the mercy of the South's laconic planter class. So, Paul got it, although he had no intention of hanging around to see how it all turned out.

He yanked a large bottle of red wine from the cabinet and popped the cork. Then he dumped some of it in the sink. From his left pocket he took out a small, clear glass bottle, and he poured an odorless liquid into the wine bottle. He then recorked the wine.

"Now, whats in God's name is you up to, Paul," said Ruth, who stealthily hovered at the kitchen door and surprised the boy, almost causing him to drop the two bottles. "Whats you put in that wine bottle? Is thats poison you put in there? You trying to poison someone with that, someone like Pete? That whats you aiming to do?" Her voice accentuated with each word as she stared into his eyes knowingly.

Paul gasped a bit and shushed her. "It's not like that, Ruth. It's a medicine they use for horses, calms them down. I'm just trying to relax Pete tonight, with the election and all. I worry about how he may react if the result is not exactly what he is hoping for. God knows what he'll do if Lincoln wins. He could get so mad he'll beat the lot of us, or worse. I figure if I knock him out for the night, it's good for him and us. I'm sure he'll thank me for it in the morning." He placed the bottle back up on a shelf.

"That ain'ts right!" Ruth chided him. "You can'ts go and play God, Paul. The Lord, He works in—"

"Pipe down, Ruth," Paul snapped uncharacteristically. "I've heard enough about your God and all the good He does us. I don't wait for your God to help me, Ruth, and I don't worry about how He is going to judge me because the way I look at it, all these men, from Pete to the doctor to the farmer who whipped the skin off my back, it seems that your precious God is caring for them just fine. So, enough crap about God!"

She stared at him unfazed. She walked toward him, as he hyperventilated and peered back at her through bulging yellow eyes. She placed her worn hands on his face and rubbed it. "Paul, God is good. He don'ts always seem it here on earth. But He is testing the righteous always. And you's is a good boy, Paul, so don't do nothing dumb to change that in God's eyes. In the final judgment, He will punish the wicked and reward the righteous. You's want to spend eternity with men like the one who up and whipped you, then you go's ahead and poison Pete. But Paul," she said, staring lovingly into his eyes. "I wants you to be with us in eternal heaven with Jesus Christ looking over us and rewarding us for our patience and goodness. Do what's you's gots to does. But, Paul, I beg you, for the sake of your momma and daddy and two brothers, respect the law of the Lord." And then she calmly slid away.

Paul breathed hard. He then turned his attention to the turkey. He loved Ruth, whom he had known since he first had a conscience. But her parochial views glued her to this reality by delivering her hope for a mythical afterlife where all the injustice that dominated this existence would be magically reversed. Paul harbored no such illusion. He hated those to be the last words he spoke to Ruth, but time was short, and he needed to take matters into his own hands before his narrow window drifted away.

The storm raged unceasingly outside. Darkness descended on the land. This day, November 6, would usher in a change of epic proportions. Where it would lead, no one could know, but the world would never be the same once the storm ended. Paul understood its implications. So too did Matt.

Matt sat with a group of men in the doctor's lounge. They all chatted about more mundane issues as they dried off from the sloppy storm. They staggered in, a few at a time, shedding layers of clothes and laying them near a crackling fire. Matt recalled that just a few days ago he wore bare skin outside as he worked under a penetrating sun. Now he gravitated close to the fire.

Slowly and with a shy posture, Jessie entered the lounge. She smiled at her fiancé and then slid near her father, who as usual sat front and center, this time sharing the podium with another man who was just as well dressed and carried a similar dominating presence in the room.

"Ah, Jessie," the doctor said, motioning to the other man. "You know Horatio Moffett, who runs the law office in town."

"I do, Father," she said sweetly, bowing to the man. "How are you today, Mr. Moffett?"

"Ma'am," he said with a smirk, "I am just as uneasy and anxious as every other man in this room. I just choose not to show it."

A gust of wind blew hard into the house, as a part of a tree snapped off and crashed to the ground. Everyone peered outside, one man rushing to the window to take a closer look. "It's OK, Doc, just on the front yard, can clean it up tomorrow."

"What can I do for you, Jessie?" the doctor asked his daughter.

She told her father that she wanted to leave the house and sleep elsewhere. She had no intention of staying here all night with these cigar-smoking men who talked too loudly, cursed too much, and likely would make a ruckus until the sun rose in the morning. Matt told her she could stay at his house. Pete would be there and could look after her, and Paul the slave was cooking a big meal.

Father and daughter argued back and forth, in a most civilized and polite manner, as Matt looked on curiously. The doctor did not want his daughter out in this storm, although Jessie believed she would be safer on Matt's farm than here with these angry men. Anyway, she said, it was a very quick ride as long as one of the farmers here agreed to take her. Finally, exasperated, the doctor consented. He sent Henry, the same farmer who had been on Matt's farm the day Paul was whipped—the one who did not do the whipping—to bring Jessie over.

"And Henry," the doctor told him. "Hurry back. You know I'll be worried."

Jessie rushed over to Matt and whispered into his ear, "I love you, my future husband!" and then ran out the door, wearing a heavy raincoat and hat.

Just as she left, another man walked in, young and gawky, who meandered over to the doctor with some papers that were kept dry in his pocket, harboring a despondent snarl. "Some of the New England states already are reporting results," he said. "They are all going to Lincoln."

The doctor seized the papers and stared at them, before handing them over to Mr. Moffett. He put on a set of narrow reading glasses and studied the papers for quite a while. All the others in the room were in a hush, waiting for some word from these two sagacious men.

The doctor, in his usual manner, took some time to answer. He scratched his chin and peered inquisitively into the blank air. Then he said: "No surprise. New England has voted for Lincoln, five states so far. Well, men, we have one chance to pull this off. That's if enough men of reason in the border states vote for Bell. We know the Deep South scoundrels picked Breckenridge already. I heard in some South Carolina counties he was the only name on the ballot. But we in the border states, who have more at stake in keeping this Union whole than in watching it tear itself apart, we would do best we vote for Bell." The doctor stood and walked between his guests, looking from one to another.

He continued: "Some of you in this room don't agree, and I respect you for it. You voted your conscience. Your hope is that if the South goes with Breckenridge, maybe the North will split between Lincoln, Douglas, and Bell. If that happens, maybe the math will work out. We've talked about this over and over again. The math can never work out. We just don't have enough votes down here to win this thing outright. Our only chance to win is if no one gets a majority and the election is thrown into the House of Representatives. But men, it has to be Lincoln and Bell if we stand a chance in the House. If it's Lincoln and Breckinridge, no Northern or Western state will go with a man who seeks to extend slavery everywhere. Lincoln will win that contest for certain. But they may go with Bell, at least Pennsylvania and New York, and some of the Western states, and if we in the South choose Bell, then he will be our next president. That's our only hope."

Mr. Moffett sat near the doctor, nodding. He seemed to agree. But then he said in a similarly erudite manner: "The flaw in your reasoning, Doctor, is that nobody up North will vote for Bell. I think you falsely presume that Bell and Lincoln might split the Whig faction, and then maybe Douglas as the only acceptable Northern Democrat will win enough delegates to prevent Lincoln from sweeping the North. But Bell never will take a single state up there. He reeks too much of Southern hegemony despite his alleged neutral stance. Those are scoundrels up there, Doctor. They've proven that over the years. And Doctor, I want the Union as much as the next man in this Commonwealth. But look at these returns. Five New England states, all solidly for Lincoln. That shouldn't surprise us. But what is surprising is that the Democrats are getting no votes at all. Nor is your man Bell."

"It's early yet, my friend," said the doctor. "New England offers no surprises. We will see how this fall on the more reasonable Northern states, as well as those of us on the border of the South."

Matt listened to the discourse with a keen ear. The doctor had talked to him ad nauseam about the math. The math would have to be perfect, the doctor said. Anything less than perfect would certainly lead to secession. If Lincoln won, the Deep South would pull out of the nation immediately. So, to the doctor, it all came down to Bell. Bell would have to get enough of the border states, including Virginia, and to grab a few of the Northern states, especially the big ones, to get the second-most votes on a split ticket. If no one candidate won a majority of electors, then the top two finishers would fight it out in the House, and in that venue, the doctor argued, Bell could win. Like the rest of these men who sat in his study that night, as the soggy man from the telegraph office burst in and out bringing election returns, Matt smelled that the doctor's calculations were not working out as he hoped.

"Do you know, Doctor," Mr. Moffett said, "that Governor Letcher, our governor, supports Douglas!" He laughed. "Can you imagine? And our president, the lame Mr. Buchanan, who is from the North, supports Breckinridge. Our world is indeed quite perplexing these days."

"Well, our ex-governors, Wise especially, and Ruffin too, they are big Breckinridge men. There are no prominent names North or South pushing for Bell. It seems as though this country is as divided as it has ever been, with each side looking for the most extreme candidate. I will be disheartened if the Commonwealth picks Breckinridge, but I know, Horatio, that it is a possible outcome I will have to accept," the doctor chimed in.

Just then the gawky telegraph boy burst in again, shaking water all over the doctor's study. He placed a piece of paper into the doctor's hand, which the doctor studied intensely. The doctor shook his head, and Matt could see his entire face sink. "Looks like Pennsylvania is solidly Lincoln," the doctor said. "That perplexes me. Breckenridge is from that state. He is the vice president of the United States. President Buchanan endorsed him. Why would Pennsylvania not even consider him, or at least Bell, but instead cast their votes for Lincoln, well knowing the consequences that such a short-sighted action will have on our Union? Not even a single nod for Bell. I'm just confused."

Moffett patted the doctor on the back. "Even in Pennsylvania, Doctor," he said, "even there, the animosity toward us is too great to overcome. Your man Bell, he's not willing to address the slavery issue at all. In Pennsylvania, they insist that the slavery issue be addressed. They don't want it to spread. And so, we are giving them no choice but to vote for Lincoln. Breckenridge, he became a tool of the Deep South. Pennsylvanians will never vote for him. They view him as a turncoat."

One of the farmers spoke up. "I don't view him as no turn-coat," the farmer said. "I think Breckenridge is our man. I think we're fooling ourselves to think that a vote for Bell is gonna do no more than delay what's coming our way. Hell, no one wants war. But we don't want those people from up there, those people who think they know better than us and who should tell us what to do, we don't want them to win this thing. It's time to end it here and now. To hell with Bell! Let Lincoln win. Let's get out of this Union while we can and show the North what we is all about, and we will whip their asses!"

A chorus of hurrahs bounced through the room. Ned, the farmer who had whipped Matt's brother, spoke up next.

"The way I see it, boys, those sissies up North don't know what's coming their way. Let them give it a try. They may got their factories and bloated egos. But we got guns, and we know how to use them! Bring on the war! I voted for Breckenridge. And I hope we pull out of this Union just as fast as South Carolina, and we stand firm and dare those bastards to try to stop us!"

"Doctor," said another one of the farmers in a quiet voice, "let's say that Lincoln wins, and let's say them people down south, they pull out. I ain't so sure us putting in our lot with them makes good sense. Most of my crops I sell up North. What about Virginia being neutral? What about all the border states being neutral? There are ways to do it you know."

"That's a bunch of bullshit, and you know it," Ned said. "Neutral? No. No one is neutral today. Everyone got one side or the other. If you compromise, especially with those people up North, they will pretend to be all nice and then kick you in the balls the next minute. There is no neutral, Ron. You're either with us or you're against us. There are two sides here: the ones who is sensible, and the assholes."

Mr. Moffett spoke up. "Think about what a neutral Virginia would mean, Ron. If the North doesn't let the Southern states go, then the war would have to come through Virginia. So, one way or the other we would get involved. And if we did stick with the North as a neutral state, then we as a slave state will be so outnumbered that everything we believe in would be threatened. The only way to preserve our way of life here in the Commonwealth under those circumstances is to either go with the South, and God help us all if we do that, or only go North if they pass a constitutional amendment guaranteeing our right to hold slaves forever."

The doctor nodded. "I agree, Horatio. If this country splits, we have to go one way or the other. My hope is that if we do go with the South, we will be in a position to lead the new government that is formed rather than follow the spitfires from the Carolinas whose brains are somewhere in their asses, if you will excuse my vulgarity. We have leverage in this or any nation that is formed. I would hope that if Lincoln wins and the firebrands down there pull out of the Union one after another, which is what I fully expect those people to do, that we don't follow suit. We must hold out a bit and use our leverage. We extract concessions from them. We make sure that we're running the show. Virginia is the greatest state in the Union, the embodiment of our founders and our most prestigious presidents. Whichever side has us is likely going to win this thing. Let's make sure that we do not commit until that is made quite clear."

Violent winds bashed into the doctor's house as he uttered those prophetic words. The foundations seemed to shake. It was now close to 11:00 p.m. From the rain-soaked tundra outside, the tired and weary telegraph boy flew back in. He handed a piece of paper to the doctor. The doctor studied it carefully, as Mr. Moffett looked over his shoulder. The two of them nodded simultaneously. The room fell into a hush.

Matt sat still, his stomach gurgling uncomfortably. What would this portend? For his brothers? For his farm? If there was war, would he have to fight? Matt knew and liked many of the men in this room, even those who wanted war. He had assisted some along the way. But now to him, they were more of a mob than anything else. He could feel the tension rising. The fury. Almost everyone in this room was looking for a fight. Nothing else seemed to matter.

The doctor crumpled the paper and spoke up. "It's looking bad," he said. "New York, New Jersey, Delaware. All for Lincoln. Most of the West is not back yet, but I don't think they'll change the math. No one up North voted for Bell. Virginia is too close to call my friends. Even our county looks like we split between Bell and Breckenridge. Tennessee and Kentucky are too close to call. The rest of the South states, of course, chose Breckenridge. Now it doesn't matter. Just one more Western state goes for Lincoln, and he's won this outright. He may not even need that."

Mr. Moffett put his face into his hands. "There will be many long days ahead for us," he said. "Many long days. We will have to try to figure this out. We will probably watch this country dissolve in front of our eyes, but we in Virginia are better than that. We'll need to make some sense of it. As the doctor says, let's not rush to judgment. We must stay calm and be the civilized men in the room."

"I'll make some sense of it," Ned said. "I'll get my guns ready and start putting a regiment together from this here county. Not too early to start that now. There is a war coming, and I'm damned glad of it!"

The hurrahs erupted throughout the room.

Matt sat isolated among the boisterous clatter. The doctor looked despondent, chatting with Mr. Moffett. He periodically cracked a smile as he spoke to his good friend. The rest of them, all these farmers and townspeople who could lose their lives and livelihood from what might soon transpire, they all seemed giddy and drunk. The whole thing hit Matt hard. He felt like he couldn't breathe. The winds and rain swirled outside with great intensity as Matt stared into a world that he had never before perceived to be possible, one now spiraling out of his control. What would he do?

Five miles to the south, the smell of turkey and sweet potatoes flooded the main dining room in Matt's big house. A single plate sat on the table filled with scraps of food and a half-finished cup of wine. In fact, it was the fourth cup of wine that Paul poured for a thankful Pete. His face on the table and his arms sprawled forward, Pete snored loudly. He could not be aroused. Otherwise, the house was empty. Paul hustled around. He ran upstairs in and out of rooms in which he gathered carefully concealed items. A backpack. Clothing. Empty bottles. He rushed down and went to the kitchen. He opened the cabinets. Bags of dried fruit. Nuts. Freeze-dried meats. He shoved them all in the backpack. He then filled the bottles with water and opened up a fresh bottle of wine, filling one of the bottles with that. He then draped himself in one of Matt's warm raincoats and peered around one last time.

And then, with not a whiff of hesitation, Paul darted into the darkness of the storm. He peered across the row of cabins just to see if Luke's candle was still flickering. It was. His brother was probably awake, waiting for him to return. But Paul could not afford a delay. This was his moment. The entire town would be occupied watching their manicured society implode in the volcanic eruption that this election delivered to their front stoops. There would be a little concern about one runaway slave.

Paul sloshed over wet grounds and dashed past the front gate. For only the second time in his life, he was outside of the orchard's walls. He stopped for a second just to see where he was going. He needed to take the main road south for a few miles and then head west to the mountains. He would follow the path upon which he and his brothers had tread on that day that opened his eyes to another reality, on that day before his skin was scarred by the white man's whip, on that day where he grasped a wisp of freedom. That's where his body ushered him, to the mountain that stood apart and beckoned him to come. He intended to climb Old Rag in the dark and then follow trails north. He'd been reading all about them. Small Indian trails. His destination was clear.

As he hustled down the long gravel driveway, he suddenly stopped, gasping. He heard the sound of a galloping horse rushing toward him, although he could see nothing. Paul was stunned. Who could this be? There were no trees to hide behind, nowhere to run. His heart raced. With no other options, he fell to the ground and lay flat on the wet grass, staring up as he saw the outlines of a horse quickly approaching, puffs of billowing smoke soaring out of its nostrils. A burst of lightning struck the sky, and he could perceive the silhouettes of two people on the horse, the one in the back much shorter than the other. The horse pounded its way closer. Its loud hooves vibrated across the ground, and he lay there, hoping to remain concealed, afraid to lift his head, fearing he could be trampled or sighted. Just then another burst of lightning struck simultaneous with a loud clamor of thunder. He peeked up as the horse dashed by him, only a foot or two from where he lay. He could see the eyes of a girl sitting in the back, and she was staring right at him. Ever so briefly he perceived a sinister smile on her face as their eyes met. And then the horse was gone, up the driveway, and into the orchard gates. The rain fell harder. Silence otherwise cloaked the land.

Paul stood up, his heart beating through his chest. He looked around to see if any other danger was heading his way. He recognized the girl; it was Jessie. What was she doing back on the farm? Many fearful thoughts threw daggers at his scalp. What if she saw him? What if she found Pete passed out at the kitchen table? What if she tasted his wine and saw that it had been spiked by a powerful sedative? Paul thought it through. He would be far away by the time she could garner any help. But he had to run and get into the trees quickly. And that's exactly what he did.

Slicing through a dense darkness, deflecting sheets of wind and rain, Paul's legs pushed him forward. As another burst of lightning illuminated the horizon, Paul saw where he had to go. It was as if someone was lighting a beacon to show him the way. Paul ran fast, for at least an hour, maybe more. He did not tire. He knew the way without even thinking. And he smiled a big smile, because he could smell his freedom. He pushed himself toward it with nothing in his path that could possibly deter his strength and resolve. Freedom. That's what this election was all about. But Paul did not have the patience to wait. He was going to grab it on his own.

13

Through the last remnants of a dying wind, Luke heard the patter of footsteps outside his cabin. They approached slowly and deliberately, as if they harbored some apprehension and doubt; there were starts and stops in their movement, contemplative hesitation. The steps were soft, surely not those of the overseer or even Matt. Luke smiled. His brother had returned.

Paul's absence portended many possibilities, but Luke refused to even acknowledge the one he most feared, that of flight. Paul hinted at it. Izzy gathered for him booklets that Luke knew were designed to facilitate an escape to the North. Matt made nothing of it, but Luke understood. Paul was assessing the feasibility of an escape.

Luke knew that his brother's mind swam with passion and indignation. He could not transcend the simple fact that on this farm he lived as a slave, as an inferior to those who he believed were not his equal. It mattered not to Paul that here his life was in many ways charmed, that here he lived with his brothers and best friends, that here he could reach a potential that would evade him everywhere else. Here was his home, his sanctuary. Here he had thrived and helped to build the region's most successful farm, spearheaded its financial prowess, and had time and resources to explore politics, arts, and sciences more than could any free landowner or laborer. Here he became himself, beneath the shadow of majestic trees and mountains, in one of God's most hallowed and bucolic settings—preparing fine meals in their small mansion and lounging upon their own private lake. This was paradise, although Paul never could accept that fact. One tiny gnat chewed at his brain and made him perpetually uncomfortable: he knew that he was a slave.

Times were difficult, as Luke freely admitted, but they had been this way before. As a potential war loomed all around them, they would have to adjust, as they did when Matt courted Jessie and they moved back to the cabins for at least a while. After Momma's exodus so many years ago, and after Dad's death, a similar shadow of fear and peril hung over them, but they overcame those obstacles and thrived even more. Luke knew that they could achieve the same result again. This is what Luke preached to his brother incessantly over the past many weeks, as he watched Paul's energy and optimism fade. Paul never recovered from the Old Rag trip and his subsequent whipping. He lost his soul that day. He started peering beyond the farm toward a nebulous salvation, one that Luke knew simply did not exist. Here was their home and their salvation. Here was where they needed to be.

Don't ever cross the safety of these fences. Do you promise me, Luke? That is why I have to leave you—to assure that you can remain here beyond their claws, beyond the specter of their power and hate. Here, under the watchful eyes of your father, you will determine your own fate. We will meet again, my son. I can't wait to see how you have grown! Just promise me that you will never ever leave this farm!

His mother's words reverberated off his skull on this dark night. Paul had heard them too. Certainly, he would heed Momma's last wish and comply.

"Don't let some phantom of hope dim the light you already have here with us," he had said to Paul only yesterday. "Out there is uncertainty. In here, we have our ingenuity and our special place. It's not perfect, but it's better than anything else out there. It is Mom and Dad's legacy. It is love!"

The footsteps approached again after a brief pause. They moved more quickly, crunching leaves and sticks that had blown across the land. Luke smiled. What would he say to Paul? He could not act cocky. Not tell him that he told him so. He would bury his brother in a hug and let that be his only response. In the end, Paul was passionate, but he was also sensible. The world out there was no place for him. He would not thrive there; his skills would not be appreciated. Besides, he had a responsibility to this place and to his brothers. He would never simply abandon them. Paul was not that type of man.

The footsteps stopped, and the cabin's door creaked open. Luke stood and stared, a candle in his hand, a smile of pure ecstasy sewed to his face. And then, against the swirling darkness, he saw a figure walk in. He peered at it and stood stunned. His smile and everything else that reeked of any joy and happiness within him instantly evaporated and was no more.

Paul stood upon the very rock where he had tasted the sweetness of freedom on that fateful day long ago. It had been an amazing journey to arrive here. He evaded Jessie and the riders who swept onto his farm and almost trampled him, dogs that chased him behind the Johnson farm and threatened to expose him or tear him apart, a treacherous hike up dark, slippery rocks whose edges dropped like cliffs that could end his life in an instant. But here he was now, on Old Rag's pinnacle, while the world down there, a world of flickering lights that seemed so insignificant and far away, drowned in a vague confusion wondering what the most recent election would portend.

Paul did not have time to find out.

He peered into a dark sky, swallowing sweet and moist wind, and he shouted out, "I am free!" He said it again and again. It was intoxicating. He could not say it enough.

For a while he started to laugh, and then cried. He pointed his fingers at the lights below and cursed them all; he cursed the doctor, cursed the farmers who whipped him, even as he laughed at their feckless ignorance, their inability to stop his trek to freedom. Walking out of the farm was the most difficult thing he had ever done. It was where he was born and where he lived his entire life, where he grew and prospered. It was where everyone he loved lived, or had once lived, and where his comfortable life was scripted. He had become a creature of habit there; it was a place in which he knew his role and where each day was the same as before. It was a part of him.

But even before being ridiculed by the doctor, whipped by the farmer, forced to act a fool and live in a slave cabin, made to share the farm with a girl whose vile nature stunk like a rotten pear—even before all that, Paul knew he had to flee. He had found something better up here on a mountain he had stared at from afar day after day and year after year, something he felt and knew to be right, something that may not be as comfortable and conditioned as his life on the farm, but something that he craved. He read about those slaves who had achieved freedom, who had run from their horrors; some of them now lived in dire poverty up North, and others like Frederick Douglas rose to great heights. But despite their status and their achievements, all of them had something he could never have: freedom. He saw them in his eye and knew that he could stay here no longer.

Luke told him otherwise. Those slaves were abused, he said; they lived in horrid conditions, and they ran because they had no choice. Paul's situation was far brighter; he would be running from a safe oasis toward uncertainly. Why would he do that? But Luke did not understand the pain that reverberated in Paul's shackled soul. He never could. And so, Paul did not engage him or argue the point. He simply sprinted away from his purgatory to a fate he knew must be far better. He did not look back.

He stood up on that rock at the top of Old Rag, providing an open view of the Shenandoah valley, and he knew that up here no one could tell him what to do or how to act. Yes, there was love on his farm, there was comfort, and there was a predictable and tranquil life. But even if Lincoln won, even if by some miracle the masters treated their slaves with some degree of decency, that was not good enough for Paul. He had tasted freedom for a brief instant in this very spot, and it tasted good. To achieve it permanently, he would have to shed the comfort of his life down there and embrace uncertainty and peril across the top of these mountains. He loved something even more than his brothers and the creature of habit he had become. He loved himself. And he could only be himself if he were free.

Taking one more look, Paul moved forward, through the dark woods and into the unknown. He was heading North, across old paths about which he had read, through a landscape that could easily swallow him whole. But he moved quickly and without hesitation. The farther away he drifted from all that he had ever known, the less he thought about his brothers and his former life. They would always be there, in his mind and in his heart, but on this day, on the day of an election that would change the world, Paul sought something more.

"Hello, Lukie. You are looking fine today. May I come in?"

It was Jessie! She wore a puffy red dress, and her hair was windblown, bursting out of its ponytail. She smiled, her crooked teeth glistening against Luke's tremulous candle light. She took off her dark coat and moved in front of Luke, whose entire gut was splayed on the floor, lacking clear thought or emotion. He was totally stunned, devastated. What could this mean?

Luke had mentally discarded that brief encounter with her a few days ago, the one in which she grabbed him below and claimed to have manipulated Matt into taking this farm. She was probably just a bit drunk, he surmised, probably just playing around. Her behavior subsequently convinced him that he was right. This game and its rules were his; he called the shots, she and her father were his unwitting victims. But now, now with her here, with her eyes as sinister as they were back then, he harbored doubts. His body shook as he stared back at her sheepishly.

"This farm is such a special place," she said, placing her stumpy hands on Luke's shoulders. Her eyes were sinister, glaring at him hungrily. "And you made it that way. Good for you, Lukie! You are not as dumb as you look and sound! But I only joke with you, you know that. Under that serious exterior I know lives a wild beast. You get my blood rushing, Luke. I want every bit of you. And tonight, I am going to get my first taste." She kissed him on the lips, although his mouth remained tightly shut.

"You know," she said, moving toward his cot and untying her dress, "your brother, I saw him running from the farm. He was lying down outside the gates as I rode in, and we both looked into each other's eyes. I could have sounded the alarm, Luke. I could even have trampled him. But you know what I did? I let him go. When I turned around a bit later, I could see him running off into the woods. If he had been caught, he would likely be whipped or hanged. No one likes him. I could just tell my daddy that he tried to touch me. I can say anything at all, and they will believe me. But tonight, I decided to show mercy to your brother. I let him go. And I did that for you."

Luke stared at her in disbelief. Paul had actually run away? How could he? Was he OK? Would he come back? Why did she let him go? How could Paul be so foolish and selfish to leave his home? Cold air whistled through the cabin, but Luke, standing speechless and clothed only by shock and impotence in Jessie's shadow, started to sweat profusely. He did not know what to do.

Jessie then pulled off her dress. Beneath it, she wore a white corset under which her large breasts bulged. "You are in luck tonight, Lukie. I am having my menstrual bleeding. Do you know what that means? You probably don't understand. But all you have to know is this. We can have wild sex in here knowing that no one will bother us and knowing that I can't get pregnant. The overseer is dead asleep and is bound to stay that way for quite some time, likely thanks to your brother's perfidy. And Matt will be in town for most of the night, if not until tomorrow morning. And with your brother having run away, well, that leaves time for us to have some fun, the first of many times I hope."

Luke nodded his head and backed away. He could not even utter any words. What was she saying?

"Are you aroused?" she asked him. "I am sure this is the first time. I'll tell you what to do; I'll lead you each step of the way. Don't worry; I don't have a lot of expectations tonight. This is just an introduction. I am guessing that after a few times you'll get much better at it. You'll even like it and crave it like all the boys do in town. I am rather good at this, so consider yourself a very lucky boy! And as long as you satisfy me, sweet and innocent Lukie, as long as you cooperate, we can keep doing it for as long as we want. But," she said, walking toward him and pulling off her corset, her breasts hanging out and bouncing as she stepped, "I do hope your realize who is holding the cards on this farm from now on, and what the consequences may be if you cross me. If you don't satisfy me, if you don't do everything I want when I want it, then I will just tell my daddy that you tried to rape me. It's really as simple as that. I want you badly, Luke, but I need you to want me too. Anything short of that, and Jessie will not be happy. If Jessie's not happy, poor Lukie likely won't survive the day. So, are you aroused?"

Sweat poured off him in droves. His body shook. He stared at her; he had never seen a woman naked before. It did instigate a strange tingling within him, especially below. But he did not know what to do. He half hoped that Paul would pop into the door and save him from this. But then what? Would he kill her? Then they would be forced to leave this place. What good would that do?

She reached into his pants and grabbed him, just like she had done the prior night. She rubbed her breast against his chest and kissed him all over his face. And she smiled. "It's getting very large," she said. "Just like I hoped. You are aroused! And you are such a man!"

And with that, Jessie started to undress him. Luke stood still as she did it. He breathed methodically. His mind tried to reason through this catastrophe. Let her have her way. What did it matter really? Was he betraying Matt by enabling this? Was he relinquishing his own sense of worth and decency? Or was he doing whatever it took to save the farm? He knew it to be the latter. And so, he let her have her way with him. And if she came again and again, he would continue to do the same. And in an odd and almost frightening way, he lost himself in the moment, shut his eyes, and started to enjoy it. Waves of utter pleasure launched him into another plane. As she put him inside of her and cried out hysterically, he smiled and swam in the moment, all along thinking about the grapes and what a wonderful crop they could have by this time next year.

In the distance, Paul saw smoke puffing out of a chimney, and he took a sharp turn to the left far off the tiny Indian trail. A spattering of mountain people lived up here, fiercely independent and not favorable to visitors, especially those with black skin. A few of these houses had dogs, and so Paul needed to take a wide berth around the home. Sometimes one of their inhabitants could be out hunting, and there is nothing they would like more than to find and shoot a runaway Negro. He was taking a chance even traversing this path by day. But last night he learned that the evening was not necessarily any safer.

He had been crossing a small stream, its cold water running up his leg. He stopped for a moment to drink. He still had bottles of water and packages of food in the backpack, but any nourishment he could gather on the trail would save him from exhausting his supplies too quickly. The moon was bright last night, and it illuminated his journey up and down two large peaks and through some dense forest. He made good progress. But then, at that stream, he heard the howl of wolves. First, there was one seemingly ahead of him. Then a few more. Their cries inched closer. They seemed to be lurching at him from every angle; he could hear the methodical crunching of leaves as they approached. He stood in the water, helpless. Earlier in the day he almost ran directly into a black bear who was foraging for nuts in a grove of trees. He quickly turned around and marched backward. His more rational brain told him that it was too close to the hibernating season for a bear to be interested in eating a person; it would surely need to be gathering food for the long winter ahead. But wolves don't hibernate. And they like meat. He knew that very well.

He decided to meander along the stream, despite the fact that on this cold night its frigid waters were saturating his shoes. He shivered just a bit, but slowly moved onward. Perhaps, he reasoned, the wolves would be unable to track him in the water. And then he did something either brilliant or suicidal. He took out several packages of food from his backpack, all of the meat and turkey he had prepared, and laid them on the side of the stream. Then he continued forward, through the water. He heard the howls fade away. Soon they were gone. A few hours later he returned to the site where he had left the food, and it had been ravished. There was nothing left. And no sign of any wolves. He decided to move about a mile away and fall asleep against a tree, keeping his backpack and all its contents far from where he rested.

He had been traveling for over a day now. He walked for eighteen hours straight after summiting Old Rag. He slept for only a few hours that night, and now, with the sun rising, he aimed to make more progress. Maybe it was wisest to walk in the day anyway? Although he could run into an errant hunter, he could also better see and thus avoid their homes. Still, he moved quietly and with great trepidation, slowing his pace just to be sure he was as stealth as possible.

His wet feet were starting to ache, and now he had no food. At a certain point, when he finished the last of his water and his small canister of wine, he tossed the backpack down a mountain ledge far into the wooded morass below, where he knew it could never be found. He had no idea where he was, or how much longer it would take to arrive in Harper's Ferry, his first major destination. Once he got there, he would have to be very careful; the local population was not sparse, and a federal outpost there would certainly have patrols out all night. He had read about the underground railroad enough to know that he should probably avoid that town, so he devised a plan to get around it, one that involved floating in the Potomac River past the most populous part of town and toward Frederick Maryland, which was his ultimate destination. The river's current would be moving in his direction, but with all the recent rain it could be ferocious, and rumor had it that the river was cold and filled with rocks. Still, he had little choice.

Close to sunset, Paul sat on a rocky ledge that provided a panorama over the entire Shenandoah Valley. It was marvelous. He had no food and had found none on the trail. But that was OK. A man could survive weeks without eating. And the many streams he traversed provided more than adequate hydration. It was cold, and he shivered even within his parka and blankets; he kept those with him even after he tossed his backpack. As he peered across the land, he thought of the election, wondering about its outcome and what reaction it engendered in Washington and beyond. He dwelled on his brothers, how they would react when they learned he had left. Would they pursue him? Would they hate him? He had no desire to hurt anyone or instigate their ire. And he did have some remorse, especially given all the difficulty he had already encountered and knowing what lay ahead. Still, he had persevered. He did not know how he would possibly survive the river journey, or even how he would necessarily find the safe house he had read about in Frederick. But somehow, he knew he would.

He looked across the valley and put his hands around his mouth. "Day two of freedom," he yelled to the innocent stretch of nature. "No one has stopped me yet! And no one ever will!"

On the farm, one would not necessarily know that an election had occurred that tossed the young American nation into a quagmire likely to tear it apart. To those who lived here, there were more basic tasks about which to be concerned. A storm had swept through, and a lot of branches had to be removed and cut into firewood. Pete the overseer woke up Luke that morning, as well as the other slaves, telling them to get their butts in gear and start preparing to work. He brought a small bag of biscuits and some bacon that the "woman of the house" had prepared.

"Matt, he came back last night, not saying much I reckon," Pete said to Luke, seeming almost kind and wanting to chat. "That scoundrel Lincoln won he tells me, and then he asks for Jessie and marches over to his room to get some shut-eye. Hey, where is your brother, Paul? He ain't in your cabin from what I can see."

Luke shrugged. So, they didn't know yet? Maybe Jessie had said nothing at all. If so, then Matt didn't know either.

"Well, I wouldn't be surprised if he's already out there working. He knows what to do, your brother does. Smartest slave I ever seen. If I had me a couple of Pauls on a farm, I could make this place hum like no one ever seen. Well, eat your breakfast and get out on the fields in a half hour or so. I got to go wake up the others. Ms. Jessie, she just tells me to give the bacon to you. She said you deserve it."

You are a God, Lukie! A sensual black God! I will give you more than you ever imagined; you deserve so much more than you have now, and Jessie is your path to nirvana! Sleep well, you firey boy! I will make sure to nourish you in the morning, just like you did for me tonight!

A few hours passed, and Luke quietly meandered toward the northern corner of the farm. There were damaged trees here and a large number of fallen branches that needed removing. He looked up into the mountains, toward Old Rag, and he wondered about his brother. There was nothing he could do now. No one would find him there. They could not possibly know where to even look. That is assuming Paul even survived the first night. His fate rested now only in Old Rag's holy hands.

He examined the ground, pushing away some leaves and sticks. This is where he intended to plant his first batch of grapes. It seemed to have a perfect mix of sun and moisture, and the waters of Old Rag fed its soil brilliantly through his canals. The planting would have to occur in early spring, and hopefully, he would be able to convince Jessie and Matt to order cuttings from France, where the best wine grapes grew. After last night, it seemed that Jessie may be willing to give him almost anything.

Ruth and the boys remained aloof all day; Luke knew they were clearing areas to the South where the big pear trees lived. He hoped that those trees had survived without too much damage; they were the most vulnerable of all the fruit trees on the orchard. Suddenly, from the direction of the house, he heard a horse moving swiftly toward him. Luke stopped for a moment and peered up, his mind blank and his face drenched with sweat, as he watched it approach. On it rode Matt and Jessie. Matt stopped the horse, and the two of them dismounted. Luke glanced over at Jessie, who winked back at him. He smiled, mostly because he was happy to see Matt. He swallowed any apprehension that he felt from seeing her here, deflecting his eyes from her body and from distracting thoughts that entered his mind.

"Well, Luke, as I'm sure you heard, Lincoln won last night," Matt said, approaching his brother in a friendly manner. "Apparently in a landslide. The whole North went for him. South Carolina, they is already talking about seceding before even Lincoln gets a chance to take off his pajamas. It's a royal mess is what it is!"

"Excusing me, Master Matt, and ma'am, but unless it helps to somehow get these sticks off our farmland, then I's don't knows or cares too much about all that stuff, because that storm that blew through, it's what made the royal mess, is what I'm saying."

Jessie laughed, and then, in her puffy white coat and with her hair back in a neatly groomed ponytail, she walked over to Luke and patted him on the head, kissing it gently. Her lips felt different to him now, and part of him started to throb. "Why, Lukie, I didn't know you could be so funny! You look like you are in a very good mood. Did you have a nice night, because it seems like you are absolutely glowing!"

"Yes, ma'am, I's slept good in the night, thanks you for asking. It's going to take days to clear off this place. Can't worry about no election. Thems things come and goes like the wind. But it don't mean we don't got to do our work, unless that man Lincoln he aims to comes down here and helps us."

Jessie chuckled again and kissed him over and over on his head.

Luke's heart raced rapidly as he pushed his every thought elsewhere.

It's a perfect location for the grapes. They would prosper quickly here!

"You seen Paul?" Matt asked him. "We ain't seen him all morning. And Jessie tells me that when she came back last night, our fine overseer was as drunk as can be, snoring on the kitchen table. Was Paul back in the cabin with you last night?"

Luke paused for a moment, contemplating his words. "I reckon," he finally said. "I'd been so deep asleep, I reckon he come in at some point, start complaining about this and that like he does all's the time. I do remember that, and then when I wakes up this morning, and Miss Jessie she sends over a nice breakfast for us, Paul was nowhere to be seen. Must be out there somewhere."

"Well," Matt said, "Ruth and the boys, they been all over the farm, and they didn't see him either. No one has. I just fear for him. All those branches falling, the pond; I hope he is OK, is all I'm saying."

It was a few hours later, as Luke finished his dinner in the cabin, and the temperature started to fall, that once again he heard the crunch of leaves moving in his direction. His body locked, and he feared what might occur. But quickly he realized that these steps were different. They were loud and erratic. They stumbled. This was not Jessie. It could only be Matt.

Sure enough, Matt wandered in. His face was devoid of all emotion; he looked drained. He walked past Luke and then sat on Paul's bed, peering at the ground for quite some time. Luke watched him, peeking inside the soul of his brother, and knew that Matt was brewing with pain.

"He run away, didn't he?" Matt finally asked his brother.

Luke nodded yes. "I think he did. He talked about it. I didn't think he would go through with it. But I am sure that's exactly what he did."

"Did he tell you, Luke? Did you know?" Matt looked up at him. His eyes were welling with tears.

Luke nodded no. "I don't think he would tell us, Matt. He couldn't face doing that. He loves us too much. But I guess, he just felt like he had to do it."

Matt nodded. He then leaned over to his brother, put his face on Luke's shoulder, and openly sobbed. He cried for a long time; Luke's shirt was soaking wet when it was all over. Luke stroked his brother's hair. He smiled. He smiled from knowing how much Matt loved his brother. He even kissed Matt on the head. So much pain. He understood.

Finally, Matt lifted his head and wiped his eyes. He tried to smile too and peered at his brother with such intense affection that it nearly sent tears to Luke's eyes. "Then it's just me and you?"

Luke nodded.

"I know why he done it, Luke, don't get me wrong. I get it. This is going to be tough times for us here, and with Jessie on the farm—which I will remind you was your idea—well, we have to be extra careful. Everyone in town, they are mad as hell about the election, about South Carolina, about all the hotheads and the cold heads, and about just everything. This could be a mess. And that's not what Paul ever wanted. It's just—" He stopped for a moment and swallowed another burst of tears. "It's just, I would have hoped he would have said goodbye!" He cried out the last words and then collapsed again on Luke, bawling hysterically until finally they both started to cry.

The night passed quickly. It was cool but calm. The two brothers hugged and sat together for a while upon Paul's empty cot.

"What am I gonna say to them?" Matt finally asked him. "When do I tell them I think he run away? And who do I tell? Pete was drunk. They will surely take it out on him, and who knows who we may get next if that happens. I don't know what to do, Luke. I just don't know. Will they go after him? I want him to be able to get away. I don't want no one hurting my brother!"

Luke rubbed Matt's thick, matted hair again as more tears fell. "How about this," Luke ventured. "The storm was terrible.

Paul made the dinner and ate it with the overseer; that much we know. But then, when he wandered home, he fell into the pond and drowned. Maybe he drank a little wine after the overseer got drunk. And we know that Paul doesn't drink. That could be our story."

"But, don't we need to show them his body or something? They ain't just gonna believe that."

"It's too cold to scour the lake, so it will have to wait until spring. I can say I heard something plop into the pond late at night, and that Paul never came back after that. We can make it stick. It will take everyone's mind off him and give him a fighting chance."

"OK," Matt said. He stood up and again wiped his eyes. "I'll go with that. I'll go with whatever you say, Luke. You are the only smart one left on this farm now."

"Brother," Luke said, grabbing Matt by the shoulder. "Jessie may know the truth. She was riding in when Paul likely left. She could have seen him. I just need you to know that."

Matt nodded. "Do you think he's OK?"

Luke said nothing. They both stared out to the mountains, to their mountain. Old Rag would take care of him; he knew that much at least.

It was dark, and the street was quiet. Even the houses in this cluttered town seemed asleep. Paul slid by as softly as he could, his own black skin and muddied clothes perhaps camouflaging him against the backdrop of an intense November night. He rapped at the door again; he had done it a few minutes earlier and then, hearing no response, ducked into some shrubs at the front of the house. Now he tried again. He was desperate. He was starving. He had not eaten for three days. His last drink was from the Potomac, which he promptly spit out. So, he knocked at the door.

This was the right address. It met the right description. Why was no one home?

Finally, a candle flickered upstairs, and he could see it bounce down a set of steps through the window. What if this was not the right house? What if someone here called the alarm? At this point, what choice did Paul have? He had nowhere else to go.

The door opened slowly, and an elderly white woman answered it. She wore a bonnet on her head, and a long wool nightgown. Paul stuck his head in. She gasped.

"I traveled here from Virginia," Paul said. "Across the mountains. Please, I beg you, I need help."

She waved him in, peeking up and down the street. She seemed totally startled. "We weren't expecting anyone tonight. We have two already. Who sent you?"

"I came on my own," Paul said.

"Oh my, look at you. Soaking wet. You look hungry. Please, come in. Let me get you clothes and some food. No one could have followed you? Are you sure you came safely?"

Paul nodded. "Then is this the right place? Am I on the railroad? Am I safe?" Hunger and cold meant nothing at this moment; after all he had been through, his near capture at Harper's Ferry, diving into the river, bashing into rocks, barely staying afloat, and then wandering the streets of this huge town hoping to find an elusive house that he had read about on a piece of paper Izzy had given him and which had become illegible, thinking that it was all for nothing, that he would never make it, not a chance. "Am I safe?" he asked again.

"Yes," she said sweetly, putting her small arms on his shoulders. "You are safe. We will take care of you."

And with that, he fell to the floor and started to sob. Every bit of pain and fear and anger melted into a rush of pure relief. He had made it. He was free. He stood on his knees, barely able to muster a word, but cried out, "Thank you," before drowning in his tears again.

More footsteps trickled down the stairs, and three other people now stood over him. One was an elderly white man and then two Negroes, a young woman and an older man, the latter holding onto the girl as they both glared at him.

He stood up and wiped his face. "I'm sorry. It's just been a long journey." He extended his arm to the black man, who smiled at him with a warmth that sucked Paul right in. "I'm Paul. I'm from Washington Virginia. I ran off on the night of the election, and I've been wandering here over the mountains ever since. Thank God I found it. I never thought I would."

"Well, Paul," the middle-aged black man said to him, "you talks too damned good to be a slave from Virginia. Unless them people treats you a lot better than we got done to us over in North Carolina. In which case, why the hell you's running away?" He laughed deep and hard and slapped Paul on the back. "My name is James, and I am pleased to make your acquaintances. These are our two hosts, Jenny and Michael, and they been ferrying slaves up North for lots of years. They probably saved hundreds by now, is that right, Jenny?"

"Three hundred and fifty-five, including Paul. And we haven't lost one or had one returned."

He laughed again hard. "Tomorrow night we's is heading to Baltimore and then up to New York, the last stop on our journey. That good with you, Paul?"

Paul nodded.

"And this here is Smiles," he said, pointing to the young lady who stared at the ground and did not show any inflection in her face. "I pulled her off the farm one night because I hads to do it. We ran off in the woods and prayed hard and then joined up with some of God's people who is doing His work to help the slaves, and they brought us to Jenny and Michael. It's a miracle we got this far, but we did. And now her hell is over and me and her, and now you, maybe we can live in peace. Especially now with a man in the White House who may look over us and protect us forever more."

"Then Lincoln, he won?" Paul asked, still wiping tears from his eyes.

"Damned right he done win! You think God would have it any other way?"

Paul looked at the girl. She seemed unable to talk. Like a statue. Her timid beauty glowed against the room's flickering candle. He could not pierce her exterior at all. But something about her fascinated him. He stared at her for a few seconds.

"Does she smile?" he asked James. "I mean, that's her name. Does she do it?"

"Well, nots for you, Paul, she don't know a damned thing about you. She don't trust men after what this poor girl been through, and I doubts she'll be talking to you any time soon. If you's is lucky enough to see her smile, well then, Paul, you'd have to earn her trust, and then you's will see why she has that name."

"Are you her father?" Paul asked. "Or husband?"

James laughed again. It seemed to Paul that this man should be the one called smiles given his boisterous personality. "Paul, you is sure brewing with a lot of dumb questions after all that traveling and running away you been doing and all that hunger and misery you probably have. No, Paul, I is just someone who looks out for her; we been on the same farm with the same son of a bitch master since she been born. I did my best to protect her there, but I couldn't do no good after a while. I's had to get her away. We's will all be together a long time, Paul, the three of us will as we move up North. You have lots of time to ask a whole bunch of dumb questions, and you'll be happy to knows that I'll have time to give you a whole lot of dumb answers. But for now, get some food these fine people is offering you, and get some dry clothes on, because you's is quite a mess!"

Paul smiled as he continued to sneak peeks at the mysterious girl. He was safe with these people, and he could hardly believe his good fortune. This shy girl intrigued him, and he could not look away. He peered into her dark black eyes, hoping to get something back, but she merely looked at the ground. That was OK. She would learn soon enough to trust him. They all would. The world had changed, and Paul was moving into it as a free man, one who could make a difference, one who could be himself and demonstrate the wisdom and strength and goodness that brewed within him from all of his years on the farm, an inner soul that he had to conceal and curtail for far too many years. He nodded to James and then walked to the kitchen with Jenny, who was the first angel he had ever seen. Thoughts of his brothers and of the farm faded fast behind him. These were his people now, and this was his future. He could not be happier.

PART II

Exodus

And the Lord said, I have surely seen the affliction of my people which are in Egypt, and have heard their cry by reason of their taskmasters; for I know their sorrows; And I am come down to deliver them out of the hand of the Egyptians, and to bring them up out of that land unto a good land and unto a land flowing with milk and honey.

14

"You look blacker than usual," laughed John Campion when Bobby Jeffrey trounced in the door. "And you reek like you walked through a river of shit. Maybe you are really a piece of crap disguised as a Negro!" He laughed again, good and hard, in a thick Irish accent that he had acquired during his youth on the Kerry Peninsula. *Kerry's not the most high-brow of locations,* as one of them told Paul.

It didn't matter to Paul. John was one of the nicest men he had met in New York, effortlessly bantering with his African American roommates rather than spewing out racist epithets like most of the others who resided here, especially while drunk.

John and his wife moved here in 1851, at the tail end of the Irish famine. As a fisherman on the peninsula of Kerry, he had been able to survive for a spell on marine life as the potato crop perished across his island nation. But when he could no longer sell fish to his starving neighbors, and when half the population disappeared, John knew that he had to leave too. So, he and his wife sailed to America, along with half of Ireland. He found odd jobs with Collin Ryan, who owned a series of tenement apartments in the farthest corner of Five Points, including this apartment on the third floor of a collapsing wooden structure that was decades old. With Collin's help, John and Sarah subletted their one-bedroom flat to any decently behaved runaway slaves that Collin said would help pay rent.

Bobby Jeffrey just smirked. He got along with John and his wife, Sarah, even if he said very little to either of them. Bobby had been living here for over two years after running off from a South Carolina plantation. He shared the tiny apartment with them and held a steady job as a chimney sweep, which enabled him to pay the rent. Bobby swam through chimneys all over the city. He never came home with anything less than a thick coating of soot and a noxious odor seeping from his pores.

"Used to been three other Negroes was here in this flat," Bobby told Paul and James when they arrived in New York after leaving Frederick. "Cholera gots them last fall, before the winters come. It's one sickness after another here, and theys was too weak, no job, hardly enough food to makes it to the next day. Collin and Reverend Tappan both does their best to take care of the Negroes here, God bless their souls to the boths of thems, but those Negroes died an ugly death, and poor John, he needed help with the rent, so goods thing you's come along when you's did."

As the African American population in Five Points dwindled, most having been chased further north in the city, especially after the riot of 1834 in which the Irish burned the buildings of black residents and killed scores of them, Bobby was one of just a few dozen left. Most of them were here under the watchful eye of Collin Ryan, who owned two buildings in Five Points, and stuffed runaways into the apartments of his tenants, mostly young Irishmen unable to maintain their rent without the borders.

Few area residents wanted African runaways to live in Five Points, or so Collin told Paul when he showed the trio of runaways their new lodging. "But if you keep your mouth shut, your smile turned on, and don't steal no jobs from the hardworking folk who live here, then they will leave you alone. They will never like you, but they will leave you alone. They know you are helping their brethren pay for lodging, and so they'll leave you alone. Just don't make trouble. You got it?"

Collin spoke bluntly but gently. Paul trusted him from the moment that their eyes met.

Paul and James marched through lower New York, largely ignoring anyone they passed.

"I always wonder if this is mud or it's shit we's walking through," laughed LB. That's what Paul called James, who now was his constant companion. LB: Laughing Boy. There was rarely a time this fifty-year-old man did not smile or laugh, no matter what the circumstances.

"The mud smells like shit, and the shit smells like mud, so I reckon it don'ts matter to really care. People in this town shit and piss wherever they please. Hell, I seens rivers of pure refuge flowing down Baxter Street after a good storm, the rains picking up all the shit the people been dumping from every ass in every tenement in Five Points, and it don'ts smells any more or less worse than the backyard of our own apartment, with its own piles of shit all over the place."

"I'm getting used to it," smiled Paul, as he sloshed atop the soaked cul de sac of Water Street along a stretch of crumbling four-story wooden tenements, one of which he and James had lived in since coming here in November. Four months in this place. Freezing weather. Scant food. Just the occasional job that never lasted more than a few hours or days. Brown snow caked the streets, with rivers of refuge slicing out small crevasses of space through which one could walk. But it was all thawing now. It was almost fifty degrees today. The frigid drafts of wind that swept through his third-floor apartment abated just a bit. He smiled as he walked, comfortable now, having a glimmer of hope.

"Don'ts get too's happy with the warmth," Bobby had warned him earlier. "You boys aint's smelled nothing yet, until you get a whiff of the odor around here once the heat comes up. That's when the sickness hits. And sometimes the smell, it's so bad, you's just prays you's is going to catch something and die!"

This corner of southern Manhattan was called Cow Bay, because it sat along a defunct cow path that had once meandered through the wilderness of New Amsterdam decades ago. In fact, Five Points, as this area was called, because its center was marked by the confluence of five streets, had emerged in New York rather auspiciously. It once was the home of a five-acre lake called The Collect, a bucolic spot in the woods with Bunker Hill overlooking it. In the winter New Yorkers would come here to skate, as onlookers sat along the shaved ridges of Bunker Hill. But then commerce moved in, as it always does. Factories surrounded the edges of the lake, and within years it was noxious and polluted. So, the powerful real estate interests who craved more land had a brilliant idea: knock down Bunker Hill and use it to fill up The Collect. Which is what they did.

And on that day, Five Points was born. It soon became the home of saloons, dance halls, and the most dilapidated tenements in the city, most of which had no windows, no ventilation, no sanitation, and some of which burned down in the winter to be rebuilt the following summer. The buildings often sunk into the soft mud that covered The Collect. Conditions were so bad that only the poorest souls moved in, forced to pay most of their wages for a place to sleep. The Irish and Germans came first, along with some African Americans, but a riot in 1834 drove out most of the latter, and soon this spot became an enclave for the Irish. Five Points was part of the powerful Sixth Ward; it had its own firehouse and police station that kept the peace based on its own rules and hierarchies, and it was perhaps the liveliest and deadliest place in the entire city.

Paul and LB meandered along unpaved streets. Even now, early in the afternoon, peddlers and salesmen crowded every inch of every street, pushing through masses of slowly moving people, yelling out in so many languages and accents what wares they were trying to unload, as loud music shot out of the bars, and prostitutes stood against every wall. Paul received a rapid lesson about the vices of Five Points from Collin, who warned him to stay away.

"You are here, the three of you, under the sponsorship of Reverend Tappan, a great man, who has done all he can to help your people find jobs and a livelihood and pay your rent until you do," Collin told Paul, LB, and Smiles in his thick Galway accent after they landed in New York that winter. "Stay away from drink, women of the street, and fights. Any of that will get you kicked out of my abode. The reverent is a good man, but not one who tolerates sinners. Nor do I."

And since Five Points was a bed of pure sin, as Paul quickly discovered, that lesson was a good one to heed. Both men never strayed from the center of the street. They kept their eyes peering forward and their ears shut to everything but each other, even as they dodged peddlers and people that darted toward them without any regard to their presence, as well as piles of mud and crap that seemed ubiquitous.

To Paul, it was all exhilarating, even in the frozen winter. He could come and go as he pleased, could say what he wanted, could try to make something of himself. Although the latter proved elusive for both men, given the paucity of jobs available to African Americans in the city, the very idea that he could find any job excited him.

"The Irish gots themselves a stranglehold on employment, on the docks, on the construction jobs, on every store and factory in this city," LB bemoaned, even as he laughed. "You's gots to hands it to them; they sure figured it all out. I means, everyone hates them the samesss as they hates us, but while we's is finding nothing anywhere save a small job here or there, they organized and figured it out."

Paul agreed. "They took over all the jobs on the East River and Hudson, I read about it. The Longman's United Benevolent

Society kicked out every Negro from the docks and wharfs about two years ago. Only Irish were employed after that. You can't show your black face there without getting it bloodied. Collin is no friend of them, and he told me to stay away. Kind of ironic calling it the benevolent society!"

"Boy," LB laughed, "your words is so confusing that I's don't know what the hell you's is saying half the time. Tone it down. Sure, the Irish took over the jobs. Just say it like that. You don't's need all those fancy words. Smiles told me she thinks you's is talking tongue."

"That's because I've been working with her to improve her diction a bit," Paul said. "She is very hesitant. She hardly talks. I'm just trying to help her out."

"Well, you mights want to back off," LB told him. "Because that poor girl been through enough abuse, and she don't need to be exposed to a big-headed and big-worded boy like you! Gives her some space, and she will feel more comfortable with you. Right now, she's clamping up whenever you walks in."

Paul nodded and looked down. He so much wanted to connect with Smiles. Her big black eyes pulled him in; her face expressed a warmth and pathos he had never seen before. He tried to speak to her so many times, and she seemed almost scared of him, always clamping up and looking away, quite the contrary of her interaction with LB, to whom she showed a big white smile and pure radiance. Even when she held John and Sarah's baby, who she watched during the day in lieu of paying rent while they were out in their jobs, she smiled and sang and was filled with a sparkling halo of happiness.

"Maybe you can talk to her," Paul implored LB. "You are her husband after all! Tell her that I'm OK!"

LB laughed. "Yea, I's her pretend husband so Collin let her live with us, but it ain't like I can tell that girl what to do because she done does whats she wants. Wasn't ain't no chance in hell that a pious man like Collin would let a single girl stay with two men the likes of us. So, hell, we's is married in his eyes, but she is like my daughter in God's eyes, and that's how I sees her. You wants to talk to Smiles, you better learn to be less of a pompus ass." And with that, LB slapped Paul hard on the back.

They crossed Bowery and Catherine Streets. The buildings were a bit taller here; most were concrete and not crumbling, unlike the wooden slums infesting Five Points. Some had stoops and stairs where people congregated, and clothes hung from the rafters. Almost everyone had white skin, although the dress varied. Vivacious peddlers still pushed carts down the muddy streets where the stench was a bit tamer. Paul noticed the Jews who seemed to dominate the pushcarts here and who stood outside the storefronts that lined the area. Some had hats and long beards down the side of their faces. There were fewer taverns and bars, no dance halls or prostitutes, and more people selling sundry wares. A deafening din flooded the air.

A warm March breeze whipped through the streets. To Paul, it felt so fresh. Sometimes he thought about the farm and his brothers. He could smell the pear trees as they blossomed in the spring. He could taste the meals that he and Ruth had whipped up. The blue backdrop of sky and mountains sparkled in his eyes as he imagined a life gone by. And now here he was, in the filth and crowds, with few prospects for work available to him and hateful eyes peering at him everywhere. But he was free here, and he spent his days taking everything in, even what he did not necessarily relish.

"Paul!" came a shout from a small patch of grass on the far side of Bowery in the direction of Chatham Square. The crowds of peddlers and rushing horses and people blocked Paul's eyes from the source of the cry. But the voice, he knew that well.

"Izzy?" he called back. He looked everywhere, and then, across the square, he saw his undersized friend pushing his way through a crowd of families and horses. They ran rapidly toward each other and leaped into a deep hug!

It had been too long, and Paul shed a few tears as he held this man, this great man, rubbing his back. Somehow being with him here, in this place, it was so refreshing, so genuine, as though it were the first time he had really been able to know him as a man. He pushed him away and laughed.

"Man," Paul said to him. "You look like you plumped up a bit. You've been spending too much time down on the farm. How are you? How are my brothers? How is that bitch of a girl who Matt married? Tell me everything!"

Izzy turned to LB, who ran to catch up. He stretched out his arm. "James, I presume? Collin told me all about you. I am Izzy Snout and have the unfortunate bad luck to be a friend of this jackass who you are living with."

LB laughed. "Well, you's is a perceptive man, Izzy Snout! This boy has some real problems that I'm working hard to fix. He's a tough project, that much I do knows. But I do love the guy!"

"As do I!" Izzy, standing firmly on the ground of his city, glowing in a way Paul never before saw.

It was in fact Izzy who had alerted Collin about Paul's need for housing. Izzy sold his clothing supplies to many of the Tappan refugees, some of whom Collin found homes for in Five Points. In his seventies, Lewis Tappan, a Congregational minister who tended to embrace a more Unitarian approach to life, helped bring runaway slaves into the city and to establish them with lodging and jobs. Izzy and Collin, who came from different worlds, found common cause and quick friendship when working with Tappan. And as soon as he heard wind of Paul's escape to New York, Izzy let Collin know, so he could find him a place to live. Collin needed three tenants to live with the Campions, so it was fortuitous that Paul happened to be traveling with James and his "wife."

"Well, Izzy, she ain'ts exactly my wife," LB laughed. "I knowd her since she was a baby, and I got her out of that slice of hell where she and I was enslaved, and there is ain'ts no way I could ever leave her alone. So, to Collin, she is my wife. But you look like a man who don't cares about all that stuff."

"What are you saying, James?" Izzy said, slapping the man on the back. "We Jews don't have morals? Or we salesmen don't? Well, either way, you are right, I don't much care. I can do without Tappan's incessant moralizing, and for that matter Collin's too. But they are good men, doing good work, so I will not reveal your charade, and may I say, congratulations on your fake marriage. Mazol Tov!"

Izzy chatted with Paul about his brothers as LB quietly looked on. "There's war in the air down there, Paul," Izzy told him. "What can I tell you? The jackass doctor is talking all high and mighty about how the South should make him president, so he can fix the sectional problem. Virginia is like God to that man; and he is Virginia's Jesus! It will be Virginia that will be the glue that keeps the nation together, he keeps saying. That's all well and good. Him and the farmers are still buying my clothes. So, I don't cross the man. But believe you me, I always have a bit of vomit on my lips when he talks."

"Is Matt buying into it?" Paul asked fearfully.

Izzy shrugged his shoulders. "He's with the wife day and night. What can I tell you? I don't get a chance to talk to him because her claws are aimed at my face all the time. You know your brother. He's not the brightest star in the sky! I can't tell if he's sucking up to the doctor or playing along. I've spent more time with Luke. He's so focused on the grapes that he can't talk about much else. I did get him the seeds and fertilizer he wanted. But he wanted me to tell you something. He said, 'Ask the idiot if freedom feels as good as a dip in the pond?' He really misses you, Paul. I'll be going back down in a few weeks, and I'm going to stay for a while, if Luke needs me to. Even though Luke pretends nothing is wrong, he seems to want me around. But before I leave, I'm getting you a job! You are too fucking smart to be wallowing here on the streets. I have got someone who wants to talk to you—my friend Abe. I told him everything. I told him that I promised you a job in peddling. He's my supplier, and he's a good guy. With him on your side, it may even feel better than a dip in that damned frozen pond!"

Abraham Strauss, like Izzy, was a German Jewish immigrant who came over in the 1840s.

Strauss opened a used-clothing store on Chatham Street and soon after hired a young Jewish immigrant named Izzy, who became one of his top salesmen, especially when Izzy proposed peddling the used clothes to farmers in Virginia, some of whom he had come to know through Jake. "Abe is pretty progressive. He needs his Southern customers to stay afloat, so like most people in this city, and most Jews I know, he's torn about this damned fight that's brewing. But I told him, war or no war, I'll peddle his stuff down there, so he owes me one. And he needs someone with the financial smarts you have. He's never hired a Negro before, and he's suspicious. But just dazzle him with your stuff tomorrow, and I think he'll fall for you in a second."

"So, when do I meet him?" Paul asked. "And what does he want me to say?"

Izzy put his arms around both men. He smiled, and then he laughed. "Come to my flat, gentlemen. I will give you a good sandwich, brisket on rye, the biggest pickle you have ever seen, and a few pairs of used clothes that don't happen to be filled with shit. We'll talk about how you can dazzle Abe and get that scent of shit off your hide. And James, I'll get you a job too, if you don't mind pushing carts."

LB smiled. "You are one goods man, just like Paul said of you," he said with a grin. "And you knows this boy well. I'll make sure he keeps his mouth shut when he meets with your man. He does that, and he can be a pretty impressive guy! Now what the hell is a pickle?"

That night Paul tossed and turned on his hard-wooden floor. The temperature dropped, and the wind whistled through copious cracks in the walls. There were no windows, and the air was thick and noxious. He heard shouts from the streets below, cursing, a few gunshots. Sometimes there would be bursts of laughter. The baby was crying, and Paul could hear Smiles stand up to comfort him. Bobby snored from the corner of the room, and he could hear John whisper something to his wife. Above them, the older Irish couple was again banging the floor; LB said they were either punching each other or having sex. It came about the same time every night. The walls, floors, and ceilings were porous to a cacophony of life to which Paul had become accustomed over the months. Usually, they did not bother him. But tonight, he could not sleep.

Seeing Izzy was like a dose of adrenaline. It infused him with both confidence and will, while reminding him just how little he had accomplished since achieving his freedom. Tomorrow he had to prove himself. It was time for Paul to shine.

He peered at Smiles as she cuddled the baby. Her face was angelic. He could sense the goodness that seeped from her pores. Her beauty stunned him. He snuck a peek whenever he could; when she caught him looking, she tossed a vicious stare right back. Even in this frozen, noxious, vociferous box in which all of them were crammed, on top of one of many saloons and dance halls that cluttered this muddy old former lake and shook the building at its core, she sat calm and firm, as though nothing could ruffle her inner goodness. Even after everything she had been through in North Carolina, some of which LB relayed to Paul as they wandered Manhattan's dirt streets, Smiles remained unfettered. Paul stared at her, and his heart beat hard. He would prove himself for her. Somehow, that meant more than anything. And then he put his head on an old pile of clothes, shut his eyes, and started to dream.

It would be one of the last few peaceful sleeps he would have here for a very long time.

15

"He's was a nasty man, fat with globs of skin rolling down his gut and arms, and he smelleds of mildew, like an old rotten cat or something." Smiles peered down at the sullied floor when she spoke to Paul that night. She pushed close to him. Paul said nothing as he looked into her eyes, listening, rapt. He felt her warmth, imbibed her breath. It was magical; Smiles was talking to him! Despite everything that had happened today, if this was the result then, to Paul, it was well worth it!

Everyone was asleep, all but she and Paul. Bobby Jeffry snored loudly, and the baby occasionally let out a high-pitched squeak. The streets of Five Points exploded with their usual rowdy havoc, as a strong wind shook the rickety old wooden building.

Smiles had sat with the others across the room, staring at a bruised and isolated Paul, her face reflecting a sympathetic pathos. Paul looked back into her large, melancholy eyes and asked if she was OK. She smiled big and happy, and nodded yes. It was the first time he had seen that smile directed at him, the one she usually reserved for LB or the baby. And he smiled back.

And then, to Paul's utter exhilaration, she stood up, slid across the room, and sat by his side. She then started to tell him about her former master, the one who started raping her before she even turned 12, who whipped James, who treated them like animals. Her voice was calm; it was if she felt comfortable sharing her pain with this man who she watched suffer tonight, suffer to save her.

"The son, he's was worstest of all," she said to Paul, their eyes locked. "Thought he was Christ Himself, carried himself around like a king, and downs there, on that farm, he's could do whats he wants to do. He would whip a slave fifty times because he wanted to, or because he's been having a bad day; you just had to hope you's wasn't in the way of his moods. He come into my cabin too sometimes. His father, he lets me have my own cabin, because he wanted to make sure I was alone when he comes in, and the son, he could come too." She said it all without inflection, but Paul could sense her discomfort.

Soon after landing in New York she had opened up to him a bit about her life on the plantation, but he interrupted her to correct her grammar. "You don't have to talk that way anymore, Smiles," he had said, gently, or so he thought. "You don't need s's after those words, and there are just a few other minor changes you can make to your speech to sound as intelligent as you really are."

He was just being nice, but when he said that, her eyes twisted into something vile, and she turned away. She did not talk to him for weeks, and then only spoke sparingly, usually about something mundane. After relaying something to him she always ended by saying, "I's hope you can understand my simple words, with all your high and mighty smarts and all."

Nothing Paul did or said could rehabilitate his tainted image in her eyes. He tried and failed repeatedly. And so, he was left gazing into her large, dark, melancholy eyes, kept away from this woman who so entranced him. He thought about her day and night. It consumed him.

"I beg you, James, at least get her to talk to me," he entreated his friend.

LB formed a wall around Smiles. He would talk to Paul about almost everything, but not about her. "If she wants to talks to you, you's will know. Until then, my advice is to back off. She been through enough than to have to deal with the likes of you."

Paul persisted. "Why does she hate me, James? Because of the grammar? I haven't done that in months. I'm leaving her alone." They wandered the docks of the East River looking for work. "She is so sweet to almost everyone, even people she doesn't know. To me, she seems ready to slice me up every time I smile at her."

LB laughed and draped his thick arm over Paul's shoulder. "Smiles, she don'ts does much small talk, and when she does, she does it to be nice. But with you, she ain't about to do it; she expects more from you. Either she likes you or she don't. What she tells me about you, Paul, is that your ass is bigger than your brain, but you's don't know the difference between the two, so you just talk out of your ass most of the time and fart from your brain." He laughed big and loud.

"She said that?" Paul asked, laughing himself. "Really?" She was amazing, he knew that, smart as a whip, but so distant, so mysterious. He was desperate to show her who he really was.

"I think she wants to likes you, Paul, she really does," LB said. "But you gots to earn it."

In his many attempts to do just that he struck a brick wall.

But tonight, she sat by his side and spoke softly to him, her eyes staring into his as she shared every pain and horror with him. Her body lay snuggly against his. Her warmth filled his emptiness. His heart beat fast. He dared not interrupt.

She told him about her plantation, the overseer and master, the whippings and rapings. And she told him about LB, how he watched over her, how he sacrificed himself to quiet the master's rage against her and others. "He been whipped and kicked and beaten more than any man's could ever endure, and even after all thems whippings and pain and suffering he would comes to me and say, 'Smiles, are you's OK,' that's what he always said, and that's because his heart is so big that it can't be hurt by any man no matter how mean he is. That heart, it protected me and everyone else."

"It protects me every day," Paul whispered back to her. "He is a saint."

Smiles nodded up and down, laying her head on Paul's chest. His heart raced. He so much wanted to rub his hands through her thick, knotty hair. To caress her face. To tell her that everything would be OK. But all he did was to listen, and to stare.

"What you's done tonight, Paul," she whispered from his chest, "you's reminded me of him. Only, with you, I felt like it wasn't my father pulling me away from danger. It was," she smiled and peered up at him, her eyes so dark, so intoxicating, "it was you."

Only three hours earlier, though, Paul was not in such a blithe state.

It was a cool March evening, and Paul visited Abe Strauss with Izzy at his small secondhand clothing store on Chatham Street just outside Five Points. A swarthy man with tan skin and thinning black hair, Strauss had immigrated here from Germany twenty years ago. He pushed carts on the street before working himself up to a point where he could purchase a store. His years as a cartman provided him with enough contacts in the neighborhoods of Lower Manhattan to have access to a steady supply of used clothing and a cadre of eager customers. It was a brilliant idea, or so he said. Buy old clothes cheaply that people wanted to discard, employ local Jewish women to repair the clothes in their tenements, and then resell them on the market at a far higher price. He had many people to pay along the way before he could turn a profit: those who sold him the clothes, those who repaired them, and those who sold them. He did some business in his store, but most of his success came from men like Izzy, who took his used clothes to places far from New York, where buyers did not know that they were secondhand and were willing to pay a steep price for high-quality New York fabric.

"Dear Izzy and his good friend Paul, come in, come in," Abe Strauss bellowed in a deep, inviting voice. He hugged them both, his long beard tickling Paul's face. Paul felt as though he were in the grasp of a bear. "Welcome to my humble abode here in the slums of New York!"

In a thick German accent, Abe described his business model to Paul and took him on a whirlwind tour of his store, deplete of anything but racks and racks of sundry clothes that consumed every inch of space. Paul wondered how any customer could sensibly find what they wanted, what size anything was, where different items were stored, or even what things cost. This store was the very epitome of chaos. As Paul meandered through the tiny facility, Izzy boxed merchandise for tomorrow's scheduled run to Virginia. He nimbly plucked items from the racks as though he knew where everything was.

"Have you been following the uproar after Lincoln's election? This whole succession thing is bad for business, that much I know about it," Abe said to Paul. "As a Negro, you probably see things a bit differently than me, since Lincoln wants to free your people," he said, laughing. "I sympathize with your position. We were once slaves too, you know!"

"I know," Paul chuckled. "For five thousand years, or so I'm told"

Abe slapped him hard on the back. "Yes! Exactly!"

"Izzy," Abe cried into the jungle of clothes. "Come with me and Paul into my office. Let's talk business before you drop to sleep. Paul, let's go to my office."

They stepped over a few bags and into a tiny room, sweltering and musty. Food lay scattered on the floor, the chipped wooden desk obscured by papers and apple cores. Abe pushed a few chairs together and entreated Paul to sit on one, as he sat down as well. Izzy wandered in a few minutes later.

"You elect a president who says he wants to do nothing more than stop the spread of slavery. Otherwise, he has many good qualities, wants to build railroads and improve roads and canals, improve the banks. That's an agenda all of us can live with. But the slave thing, it can't let any American see clearly; they just know they are on one team or another. They are for the slave-holders or against the slaveholders. And they could agree on everything else in the universe, they could be identical twins and share every thought and idea, but if they differ on that one thing, on the slave thing, well then, they won't even look at each other, because they hate the other team. That's our mess, and let me tell you, Paul, as Izzy well knows, it's not good for business."

"It's not good for anything," Izzy said. "You can't even have a conversation with anyone without getting your head shot off. What can I tell you? You have to watch every word you say."

"Which," said Abe, with his big baritone laugh, "is not something my friend Izzy is capable of. Watching what words he says. They fly out of his mouth like the diarrhea of cholera!"

"If I offend someone, I just tell them I'm a Jew, and they don't know anything about Jews, so they think, poor guy, he probably didn't mean it, it's just the way those people are."

"Unless he offends a fellow Jew," said Abe. "In which case he says he's from Poland, not Germany, and they forgive him just the same and feel sorry for him."

Izzy sang Paul's praises for many months, and Abe was happy to meet him. Abe spoke to Paul bluntly and intelligently, as though talking to a peer, not like he was talking to a "Negro." Paul took an instant liking to the man.

"Izzy tells me you're the smartest boy he knows, and that's saying a lot coming from this bastard, who thinks most people are complete idiots, which they are, I grant you that," he said, slapping Izzy's hand. "I do have two needs that you may be able to fill. First, I need to know more about Negroes and their buying patterns. There are large Negro communities in the upper part of the city, in Brooklyn and even the Bronx, and we have never been able to market our clothes to them. But they need clothes like anyone else, and I don't know where they get them. I would want you, Paul, to be my salesman to that community. I need you to seek them out, talk to them, and see if you can develop a whole new customer base. Although people like Izzy will likely continue to wander into the South even if there is a war between the two sides of our country, our sales will certainly suffer, and we need new customers."

Paul nodded. He did not know too many other African Americans in the city, nor had he been to many of their neighborhoods. He had wandered up north on many occasions, to the hills of upper Manhattan, where on particularly dour days he would sit and look over the city and its expansive waterways and contemplate his life. He would think of his brothers and his farm, of the troubles that greeted him here, of LB and Smiles, and he would wonder where his fate lay. Big thoughts! He passed through some black neighborhoods on his way, but never stopped to speak to anyone. That was particularly true now that the city was tearing down Seneca Village to make way for a large park that would fill the city's center, scattering many black inhabitants all over the city and its outer limits. But he could do what Abe asked, and he told him as much.

"That should be no problem for me," he said. "I have a friend who can help as well. He has been peddling goods up to those areas. We should be able to get you a loyal base."

"Do all Negroes talk like you?" Abe then asked him. "You talk better than even the Irish."

Paul smiled. "Where I come from, yea, it's me and my brother, and we don't try to speak any less than our intelligence allows."

"He uses such big words," Izzy said, "that sometimes I get aroused."

Abe just laughed. "Well, don't be too smart around our customers," he said to Paul. "They don't need to think you're trying to outsmart them."

Abe then told him about the second part of his proposed job. "Izzy says you are a financial genius, that I could make a bigger buck if I had someone doing my books and watching my cash a bit closer. So, I thought, why not you? I have a mess of papers somewhere here. Maybe you can come in for the next few days and make sense of them. If I like what you do, then you got yourself two jobs."

They said their goodbyes. Paul hugged Abe and then gave Izzy a note for Luke, one he had been writing for the past few weeks. He missed his brother immensely and worried about him down there. When people spoke flippantly about the sectional crisis brought on by Lincoln's election (or as Mr. Strauss referred to the president, the much taller and uglier Abe), Paul thought only of Luke and his naivety, how Luke's myopic view of their farm might cause him great harm should the South pull away from the Union and unleash a deleterious racial fury that a civil war could instigate.

("I can't get your brother up here safely, not yet," Izzy had told him, when Paul asked. "But he's not going to want to come here anyway. He's got his grapes. Remember?")

"Well, the only good thing that may come of a civil war is that I don't have to make any more interminable trips to the doctor's house," Izzy said, putting the last box on his cart, the sun starting to drop below a smoggy horizon. "He said he wants to show me his skull collection, evidently to demonstrate how dumb you and your brother are. I'm sure he'll pull out a Jew skull too, and it will be sitting right near his skull of a rat. God help Matt; I can't believe he's stuck with that man's daughter."

"Give him my best too," Paul said. "I don't have a letter for him, but I think about him all the time. I hope he is OK. That he doesn't resent what I did."

They embraced, and then Izzy's rickety carriage bounced past Chatham Square toward the East River docks. It was getting dark, and Paul did not want to be alone in Five Points by himself at night.

"One more thing, Paul," said Abe, darting out after him as he turned to leave. "Lewis Tappan, he might be the link to the Negro market. There will be a lot of refugees and runaways once the war starts, and from what Izzy tells me, they all come through Tappan. They will all need clothes. And I've got clothes. So just a thought. Once you show me your stuff next week, we'll talk dollars and cents, but Paul, I like you, and I think we'll do a great job together." He grasped Paul's hand with his thick, hairy fingers and squeezed very tight. He then nodded his head and bounded back into his store.

The streets of Five Points flooded with people toward the end of the day—peddlers trying to unload their final wares often at a reduced price, men and women returning home from work, many others trickling into the taverns and pool halls that by 8:00 p.m. would be crowded and raucous on every night of the week. Close to Cow Bay, where Paul lived, not a single building was without a drinking establishment on the ground floor, and the mostly Irish crowds started to gather soon after the sun dropped into the Hudson.

As a lone black man in an Irish enclave, Paul often garnered hostile stares and gestures from many of the people passing by, especially toward the evening. Some of the larger dance halls hosted African American performers and patrons, and in the Five Points, as long as they were in the right place at the right time, which Paul was not right now, no one accosted African Americans.

As it happened, LB was hovering outside their building, and Paul offered to take him into one of the nearby dives for a drink to tell him the good news. Paul had enough money for two beers, and this was a German-owned bar that never minded if a few stray African Americans wandered in early in the evening. LB was a regular here, and although Paul rarely if ever drank, he too liked to sit and relax with his friend from time to time, so his face was not unknown.

Darkness descended upon them.

As Paul told LB about his good day and the prospects of a high-level job with a reputable clothing dealer, several ears pointed in their direction. The bar started to fill up, a background din escalating around them, causing Paul to speak loudly, gloating about how with his skills and intelligence he planned to turn Abe's business around.

"They say they are smart here," he called out. "They keep bragging how smart everyone is in cosmopolitan New York. But this Negro from Virginia seems to be smarter than the lot of them."

More bodies and ears inched toward them, a few indignant eyes. They were listening to Paul speak. Paul was oblivious, gulping a large pale beer and feeling more giddy than usual. He was laughing as he degraded every ethnic group he had encountered, until LB finally hit him on the side of the head and told him it was time to leave.

Up in their small, cold room the baby was crying. Smiles tried to coddle it the best she could, singing it songs in the sweetest voice that Paul had ever heard. John and Sarah had not yet returned from work; Sarah, in fact, often stayed overnight to babysit her employer's young boy, leaving her baby more and more to Smiles. When that happened, John spent the bulk of most nights in the taverns, sometimes returning very late and very loud. Bobby Jeffrey (or BJ, as they now called him) sat in the room's corner, counting his unsold matchboxes, while some coins and bills lay near his side. He peddled matches all over town, mostly in African American neighborhoods, and walked miles every day. He was chewing on a cooked potato and some pieces of white bread.

Paul was hungry. "What do we have left?" he asked, not sure exactly who he was asking.

"There's be some potatoes in the cupboard if you wants to makes those—the gas is working today so maybe worth a try—and some bacon left which we should cooks tonight before it spoils," Smiles whispered. "And please keeps you mouths closed, or this baby will be crying all day and night! And by the ways, I's hope you can understand my simple words, with all your high and mighty smarts and all."

A noxious cloud of excrement hovered near the wall where Paul stood. He looked down through a crack in the wall (which they called their window) and saw a few people defecating in the back court. Just at that moment, through the darkness, he spotted four or five men, wearing hoods on their heads, rush by the people in the courtyard and into the building.

Not thinking much of it, he said, "I'll get the water going. Maybe five potatoes for the three of us? We have about a dozen left."

Just then there was a knocking at the door, and then a pounding. It was loud and strong. The baby screamed, and BJ looked up from his chores.

"What that?" he asked.

The pounding intensified, with some bellowing voices mixed in. "Open up now, goddammit, or we will bust this door down," came one cry, echoed by others that were similar.

They looked at each other, especially Paul and LB. "What do we do?" Paul asked. "Who are they?"

LB shrugged his shoulders. "They know we's here, given that loud Irish baby who won't shut her trap," he said. "Maybe it's nothing?"

In Five Points, they knew, it was never nothing.

LB asked who it was, and the gruff voice of a man with a thick Irish accent simply said, "Open up now."

LB looked at Paul, who peered back at him. BJ hid his money and matches behind him and stared blankly at the door. The baby cried hysterically, as Smiles continued to sing, although her eyes too were peeled toward the door.

LB opened it.

Four men rushed in, all wearing hoodies, two holding guns, one a night stick. They looked fairly young. They stood for a moment and stared at Paul, all of them.

"That's him," one of them said.

Another nodded.

"Shut up that fucking baby!" the first one screamed at Smiles. "Or I will fucking shut you up."

"You boys was in the bar," LB said out loud. "I seed you's there. We don't wants no trouble. We is good people in here. We is renting from the Campions, who is a tenant of Collin Ryan. You knows who he's is. Everyone knows Collin Ryans. That's the Campion baby my wife is watching. He wouldn't want no harm in his building."

"That boy," the leader said, pointing to Paul, "is the Negro who said some shit that was offensive to us. We don't mind you boys being here, but when you open your mouth and say such things, it offends us. It offends Collin too. You think you are better than us, boy? Smarter? That's why you said in there. And we don't take kindly to those thoughts or words. Do we, boys?'

They all shouted in agreement.

The baby cried again. The leader pointed to Smiles and gestured for one of his tall, gawky associates to move toward her. The man grabbed the baby and wrested it away from Smiles, before she knew what was transpiring. The baby cried even louder. "Put the baby outside the door," the leader told him. "She ain't going nowhere. She's fucking annoying as shit."

Smiles shook her head. "Please, I's didn't do nothing, can I go out with hers and just hold her there?"

"Maybe," said one of the other men, "you would be best to shut up."

LB gave her the silent sign, by putting his finger over his mouth. He then said to the leader, "My friend drank too much. He's is sorry, he is. He's doesn't thinks that way, none of us does. I woulds be happy to give you some food and refreshment for your troubles, and I promise this won't happen again."

"It don't work that way, nigger," the leader said to LB. "We don't like that there are any Negroes here. We don't like it at all. Collin wants to put some up, well, we don't mess with Collin, but even he knows that when rules are broken, then we have a right to take the law in our hands. This boy has to be punished. That's why we are here."

Paul, less scared for himself than for what he may have brought on to the others, stepped up to the leader. "I'll take whatever you need to give me," he said. "Just leave the girl alone. That's all I ask. Let her go, and then do with me what you will."

The leader laughed, and the others followed suit. "You are one uppity Negro, ain't you? You and your fancy words and ideas. And don't you think, boys, he seems to like that girl. And she's a pretty girl, ain't she? Maybe that will be your punishment, boy. We'll let Peter here fuck the shit out of your girlfriend there. And you can watch. And then maybe next time you'll think twice before opening your mouth. What you think about that idea, Peter?"

The small man they called Peter nodded his head and smiled, every tooth bright yellow.

"She's my wife," LB said, with a tremor in his voice. "You wouldn't be hurting him. You's would be hurting me."

The leader laughed. "I'm happy to hurt both of you. You may not realize it, old man, but this young friend of yours has his eyes on your girl all the time. Peter, go on. And if anyone tries to stop us, I will shoot him." He lifted his gun.

Paul trembled. With little thought he darted over and tackled Peter, pounding his head onto the floor. A gunshot went off, and the baby's shriek reverberated across the hallway. Paul grabbed

Peter and lifted him up, holding the small trembling man in front of his body, as blood trickled from a slash in his head. "You touch the girl or go close to her," Paul said, "and I will kill this man. You shoot me, you'll hit him. We don't want trouble. We want you out of here. That's all."

The leader laughed, his gun pointed at Paul's head. The baby continued to cry; LB and BJ stayed silent. All eyes were on Paul. "I don't give a shit if I hit Peter; it's collateral damage. He's got consumption anyway, don't got too long to live. Besides, you kill him, it gives me every right to kill you."

Paul nodded. "Then kill me. Kick the living crap out of me. Punch me until I'm unconscious. I don't care. Just leave the girl alone. She did nothing wrong. I did. You can inflict your harm on me."

The men looked at each other. Paul could feel and smell Peter's excrement rolling down his leg. He continued to tremble. But his eyes remained firm, not wavering from their piercing stare directed at the leader, whose name he did not know. Minutes ticked by. No one flinched.

The leader smiled, then nodded. "OK, boy, you got yourself a deal. We beat the living shit out of you in the courtyard, and we leave the girl alone. We ain't bad people, and we got nothing against any of you, but sometimes you got to be punished. That's the law of the land around here, and if you people want to stick around, you better figure that out fast."

Paul nodded in agreement. He let Peter go, who scampered quickly behind the others.

"Give the girl her baby back, and let's lead this Negro down to the courtyard," said the leader.

Just then Collin Ryan and two other men burst in. One was carrying the baby, whose cries had not diminished at all. "What the hell is going on in here?" Collin asked.

"This man was gloating," the leader said pointing to Paul, instantly cowering a bit in front of Collin's stern visage. "He said

he was better and smarter than the rest of us. We were just showing him some justice."

Collin looked at each of the men. "Well, he's a hell of a lot
smarter than the four of you assholes, that's for sure. He's right
about that. Then again, this wall is smarter than you four. Who
gave you permission to trespass in my building and threaten my
tenants?"

The leader slid his gun in his pants and waited a moment
before answering. "We was just taking justice in our own hands.
If you had heard what this boy said, you'd of told us to do just
what we did."

Collin laughed. "You think? No, these are good people. All
of them are. Sometimes people talk too much, like him," he said,
pointing to Paul. "But he causes no trouble, he works when he
can, he pays his bills, and he's good to the others. So, I don't give
a shit. But if you think you're right, we can take the matter to Mr.
Biggelow. Is that what you want?"

Ernest T. Biggelow was the chief of Engine Company 21,
where Collin too was a fireman. No one had more clout in Five
Points and the entire Sixth District of New York than the chief of
EC 21; that's where votes were tallied and justice was dispensed.
Everyone, even these four men, knew that simple fact.

"I know for a fact that Mr. Biggelow ain't no fan of the
Negro," one of the men said. "He don't like them here. He said
so himself."

"You may be right," said Collin, calmly. "But he lets me keep
them in my buildings. As long I vouch for them, which I will do
for these people any day of the week. And if there is one thing
Mr. Biggelow hates more than anything else, it's a bunch of assholes who trespass on private property and threaten one of his
friend's tenants. So, what will it be, boys?"

They turned their heads toward each other. The leader apol-
ogized, and they slowly filed out. The man holding Sarah's baby
handed it to Smiles, and the baby quieted instantly.

"I'm sorry for the trouble," Collin said to them. "Not all of us are like that, but there are always a few in every bunch, and they give us all a bad name." He then turned to Paul. "But they are right about something. You had better learn to shut your trap sometimes."

Paul nodded, his face turning red. Collin nodded back, and, after LB offered thanks and apologies, Collin and his men slid out into the chilly night.

And now, three hours later, only he and Smiles lay awake. The baby was sleeping by her, and Smiles was starting to doze. Ever so slowly, her head slid down and rested on Paul's shoulder. He grinned from ear to ear. He wished he could stay here forever, by her side, being her protector, earning her love. Today was a great day for Paul, despite the minutes of terror that were some of the worst he had ever known. As Izzy trampled down to Virginia to see his brothers perhaps for the last time, as the world stood on the verge of a war that might rip this nation's gut apart, as Paul hovered in a feckless fog amid squalor and hatred, he could do nothing but smile, stoking the thick black hair of the girl on his shoulder, enjoying every second of a happiness he had never before tasted.

16

warm breeze and bright sunshine draped the three of them as they sat in the courtyard just a bit dazzled. Between refuse and garbage and the crumbling buildings that proliferated in Five Points, amid the bars and taverns and rowdy neighbors, on this small patch of grass that lay below their stoop, a sparkling blue flower sprouted from the ground and hovered majestically over all else.

Somehow, as winter turned to spring, this was a sign.

"It be amazing, that's much is what I figure," LB said to Paul and Smiles, the three of them encased by an unusual moment of peace. "So many peoples shit down here on this here grass, I guesses that we gots ourselves enough fertilizer to give us this tiny bits of beauty."

Smiles leaned toward Paul—her delicate hand discreetly rubbing his leg and igniting firewood in his pattering heart—and she nodded. "It's more than that, James. More than just the results of a winter's worth of shitting. It's what we needed for sure," she said. "It's just perfect. Perfect." And then turning to Paul she said, "Do we pick it and put in up in the room, in a glass of water?"

"It would look perfect in your hair," Paul said. "It was meant to be with you."

He wanted to lean down and kiss her as their eyes met and seized each other's. The magnetic spell she cast on him was overwhelming! The flower, the warm air, a blue sky bereft of clouds—in this place of great beauty he knew only his desperate longing for her, and felt only his beating heart.

Did she share the depth of his affection? Did he dare try to let her know?

But alas, despite the mirage of freedom that escape cast upon Paul, he was not at liberty to express his desires even here. A certain fabricated reality continued to chattel him, a pretense that he could not easily shake, one that betrothed Smiles to LB and thus wedged a wall between his heart and his actions. He remained a slave both to circumstance and to those whose approval he could not live without.

Don't fool yourself, Paul. The world outside the gates, it's not as free as you may think. In here, we are as free as we make it. But out there, whether North or South, they have rules, rules that don't make sense, rules that can muffle your humanity as much as can slavery itself, and rules that are also much more harsh on the Negro than on anyone else. Beware, my passionate son, beware of temptation that can lead you down a road filled with danger. Never let down your guard, and never assume that you are a free man if you ever dare step outside of these gates. Rules are no different than chains, my son. Rules are just as toxic and just as arbitrary. Rules can just as easily kill. Beware!

Paul was rational, and he understood the limitations of his freedom. But here, staring into Smiles's dark and enticing eyes, feeling the touch of her fingers caressing his warm and hungry skin, he did not much care about all that. He loved this girl! He needed her! Damn the rules! Damn it all!

And so, he reached down and touched her, and that made her smile.

"I wish I could tell my brother all about you," he whispered to her. "To bring you to our pond, show you what we did there. My God, that would mean the world to me!"

"I's wants to tastes those grapes of his," Smiles laughed, staring deeply into his eyes. Her hand slid up and down Paul's legs. "They's probably tastes so good. So succulent. So sweet. So very sweet. Like my boy. So sweet." She peered into his eyes as she uttered each word, grabbing every bit of his soul.

"Well, Paul," LB said loudly, slapping Paul on the back and shaking him just a bit. "Times we goes and gets to works. And Smiles, you's gots to get to that baby. Let's not forget who's we is and where we's is. That ain't something that we can't never forgets! Take a last look at the flower both of you's, and then I's will cut it down and bring it in. It's sure an amazing sight, that much I does knows."

Sometimes LB had to shake them out of their trance lest their passions get the best of them. He was, after all, her husband! And so long as that charade remained alive, Paul and Smiles had to be careful.

And so it was—they cut the flower and leaped out of their transient moment of fantasy. It was time for work, for following the rules, for playing the game.

Paul knew that the blue flower was indeed a sign. He had struggled in New York, Paul would be the first to admit that, but now the tide had perhaps begun to turn. He stared at Smiles through a lens of passion he had never before known. And tomorrow, he and LB would push the first of Abe's carts into the Negro areas north of the city and stake their claim as the best African American salesmen New York had ever seen. *"No," Paul corrected his friend. "The best salesmen, period!"* It was a start. But, to Paul, it was not enough. Like the blue flower that germinated within the defecation of a hundred other souls, this moment was a sparkle of color, an opportunity growing in the dirt of despair. There had to be more.

For these many long and dreary months he lived in Manhattan, work was sporadic. Sometimes he would help LB push his carts across town that were packed with various sundries (these days LB peddled buttermilk due to a surplus at the docks); on other days a position would open up on a construction site or in a warehouse, something very rare and transient and subject to the whims of Ernest T. Biggelow, who ruled over the Sixth Ward like a tyrant. To be robbed of work and forced to grovel for the most menial of jobs irked Paul, who had so much to offer, so much energy left untapped.

"They says that when the weather warms up there'll be a ton more work for us," LB had told Paul during those dark winter days. "Theys be building the park uptown, and more housing for the displaced Negroes there, and so they may have Negroes working in some of thems jobs, and there ain'ts no Engine Company 21 bullies to be telling us that we ain'ts able to do a job that they saved for the Irish. Be positive, my friend; like you tells me and Smiles every day, at least we is free men now."

Yes, Paul knew, he was free. Free to be the man who he always knew that he could be!

Paul placed his hands on LB's shoulders, gazing at the man's serene face, the face of a man who had been through the farthest reaches of hell and somehow continued to have faith in humanity. "This is our moment, James. This is when we need to step up and make a difference, to show why we deserve to be not only free, but to have the same rights and opportunities as everyone. I want to be that person who can convince the most virulent Negro-hater that he is wrong, and that he should embrace us because we are amazing."

LB laughed, big and deep. He rubbed his tall friend's thick black hair. "You's can change the world, Paul, of that I am entirely convinced. But even Fred Douglass didn't just show up in New York and start making speeches. It takes time, my friend. And a hell of a lot of patience. Which you ain't so good at. And also at shutting your trap sometimes, that is what else I would says you need some work on."

He had tried to make contact with Lois Tappan, the most prominent abolitionist in the city, the man who had financed his journey here and who subsidized his housing. On many a day, Paul strode to the Tappan mansion and asked if he could talk to the great man. At every juncture, his request was rebuffed.

"I really think I can help," he pleaded with a meticulously dressed African American butler who opened the door. "I have skills and knowledge. I can speak to crowds. I just need a minute with him!"

The elderly butler barely altered his expression. "You and every other Negro who comes knocking at the reverend's door day after day," he said in a crisp Boston dialect, "you all are the next Frederick Douglass. Isn't that what you were going to tell me next? You are the next Frederick Douglass?"

"No, not at all!" Paul pushed back.

Of course, that is exactly what he was going to say.

"You know," said BJ in their suddenly hot tenement room later that night as he was sorting matches, "you know, I knows some people. Not Reverent Tappan, but just as good as he, I knows people."

He must have overheard Paul telling Smiles about his failed attempts to penetrate the movement. He spoke with her a lot about what was transpiring across this city, how he was trying to find a voice in the endless discourse that struck him everywhere he walked and worked, among every white man and woman, in the newspapers that lay wet and muddied on the street, in the whispers of black folk who were both hopeful and afraid but largely shut out of the conversation.

Would there be war? What will Lincoln do? What will Virginia decide? Paul wished he could be down there, just a fly on the wall of the doctor's study as all these allegedly great men determined which path Virginia should take, even as every other Southern state defiantly marched out of the country, even as the impotent president sat back and did nothing. What was the doctor thinking? How was it all affecting Matt and Luke? Would Virginia join the hotheads from Carolina or stay with the Union?

So much did Paul want to be involved! This was his moment, and all he could do was be thankful for an opportunity to push a cart filled with used clothes. Is that all that freedom would deliver to him?

"You know," BJ repeated, "in my church, Shiloh Presbyterian, over theres on the corner of Prince and Marion, Reverend Garnet, he's been preaching the gospel of abolition all along, that's what he's been done. And he is in with the big dogs, the ones you wants to talks to. This Sunday, our old pastor, Reverent Pennington, he's coming to talks with Reverent Garnet. Oh my, thems two, they hates each other, that much I done do knows, but this Sunday they's plan to bury the hatchet and makes a big giant speech about the future of our peoples here with war coming and all."

"What about?" Paul asked. "What are they talking about?"

"What I hears from my sources," BJ said somewhat emotionlessly as he slid matchboxes into various piles, "and don'ts you goes and repeat it, but both of them, they's be burying the hatchet, and I thinks they plans to talk about Negro soldiers, trying to get us an army here in New York to be ready when the wars does come. That's what I hears at least. If you want, I can tells Reverent Garnet about you? You and all your fancy talk and big ideas and all, he may wants to be talking to you. I's is going to see him tonight to meet over the prayer book this Sunday. You tell me, and I's will give him the good word."

Smiles, who cradled the sleeping baby and leaned against a snoring LB ("I's gots to take care of both my babies these days," she often told Paul. "They sometimes naps at the sames time!), could only laugh. "Oh, that's so precious I's can't even believe it!" she said, rubbing Paul's head. "Yes, Billy, you tells the minister that our Paul here is ready to bow down to God and Jesus in the church and join them in their crusade for the Lord. You go ahead and tells them that!"

BJ nodded. "OK, then I certainly will."

Smiles rubbed Paul's back quickly and then peered into his eyes. "What a day this will be! Paul Cocklin will be finally finding God! Glory be! Ha ha!"

"Glory be," BJ cried out from the other side of the room. "Glory be to God."

"I'll go to church to find who I need to find," Paul whispered to her, somewhat uncomfortably. "I don't care about any of that. I am not selling out. I'm just going as a guest."

Smiles, though, staring at him with a playful and loving glance, kept having some fun at his expense.

"Ain't you going to praise the Lord, Paul?" Smiles asked, her grin wide. "Don't you believe in the Lord's glory? Say it, Paul! Says it!"

He nodded side to side, smiling. Boy did she know him! "Fine," he said softly. "Glory be."

"That's all you's got to say to the Lord? Just a whimper of praise? That's all you are goods for?"

"Glory be!" he yelled out, shaking LB out of his slumber with a shriek that caused everyone to laugh.

Shiloh Presbyterian Church was ministered by the very controversial Henry Highland Garnet. Garnet had gained notoriety for once suggesting that African American slaves murder their masters, and then later encouraging all African Americans to migrate to Africa, something that put him at odds with both pro-slavery forces and also such well-known abolitionists as Willian Lloyd Garrison and Frederick Douglass. But Garnet's abolitionist resume was otherwise impeccable, and he was on the front lines, helping black Northerners in New York. One of his major campaigns focused on organizing African American troops in the case of war, a cause that Paul had been yacking about to LB and Smiles for weeks.

It was Reverend Garnet's call for black troops that brought the church's former minister, James Pennington, back to New York; he and Garnet could not stand each other, but both strongly advocated African American involvement in any pending civil war. Pennington, who now ministered in Connecticut, was banished from Shiloh after being arrested for protesting the segregation of New York's streetcar system. Now he returned for several days to meet with Garnet. Both men continued to lecture about abolitionism. Both were close to Tappan. Maybe this was Paul's ticket into the movement. Maybe BJ, of all people, would lay the path he so needed.

During the darkest of times, when Smiles watched the Campion baby day and night, when LB and even BJ were off peddling their wares, when the odor of defecation and the sting of cold winds blew inside his concrete prison, Paul liked to meander through the city.

He left early most mornings, saying goodbye to Smiles (who quietly reciprocated with her intoxicating eyes!), and wandered up, through Manhattan's densely populated areas, past the African American shanties, toward the wilderness beings razed to create a large public park, and into the hills and rivers of upper Manhattan where no one lived and where few faces could be found. Deer shot across his path, wolves howled, the crackling of crusted leaves with some remnants of snow followed his ascent. Often the winds whistled and struck his skin like daggers, as the cold air enveloped him and caused him to shiver. But he climbed the highest mountains despite all that, near some tall oaks he had named and considered friends. From there, he could see through the leafless trees a panoramic view of the city below and the two large waterways that squeezed Manhattan Island into a vice. He could sit here for hours, wondering what he needed to do to escape from his rut, why he had failed, what his future might hold. He dreamed as always of a fanciful reality, imagining that someone would discover his skills and intelligence, that he would be asked to help, that he would give speeches alongside Frederick Douglass.

Look, Jimmy, look. That's Paul Cocklin, the man I told you about, the man even more important than Fred Douglass, the one whom President

Lincoln relies on. And just to think, he was just an escaped slave who had to push carts and bow to the Irish before finally being discovered. Such an inspiration is he!

Back on the farm he used to hide himself in the pear trees, playacting great scenes of triumph where finally the world recognized his genius, much like he did on the hills of Manhattan now.

"And now, Mr. President, I want you to meet this fine young man, his name is Paul, and he has shown us the way to shore up the economy while at the same time feeding most of our poor."

"Paul Cocklin! Yes, yes. I have heard of you, young man. I can't wait to hear what you have to say!"

Too often, during his trances within the thick bed of pears, Ruth had to awaken Paul and remind him that he "is just beings a horses ass when he shoulds be doing some real work, for God's sake!"

He had been a slave then, with nothing other than empty dreams fluttering through his mind. Now, though, opportunity finally discovered him, and perhaps it offered Paul a chance to break through. Being with Smiles opened his heart and spurred him to be something special, someone great. Knowing that Izzy and LB would be always at his side—such good friends were a precious gift—and having found a place with Abe, all of this lofted him into a certain state of satisfaction, of real achievement.

But, with the echoes of war reverberating across the land, with the fate of his people in the balance, Paul needed to do and be more. This was his time! His life was no longer a game to be played out behind fences that could not be straddled. It was no longer a flight of fancy to be interrupted by the calls of duty and the reality of his status as a perpetual slave. This, Paul knew, was real. It was his time!

Up here, on the lonely hills of Manhattan, Paul dreamed. He tried to expunge the filth and failure that were his constant companions down below. It was up here that he drafted his letter to Luke, the one that Izzy would deliver to his brother on his trip to Virginia, which was his proclamation of emancipation. And it was up here that he gathered enough strength and resolve to face yet another day in an unwelcoming land of jungle tenements that mocked his freedom and tried to strip him of his dignity as a man. Although few men believed in him all these many months, his inner strength had finally persevered, and now he had found a voice and a few influential ears.

It was time to take the next step.

"I's always did believes in you, Paul," Smiles said to him one morning. She coddled the baby back and forth, but found a way to lay her long, soothing arm upon his back and to rub it so softly. "I never doubted you. Ask James. I told him every days, 'That son of a bitch is going to do something amazing, of that I'm sure,' is what I saids to him. 'In that pigheaded skull of his is goodness and smarts and ideas that could change the whole world.' I watched you, Paul, and I was just waiting for you's to figure out who you's is and what you is capable of being. I still is always scared you's going to do something dumb, but I am here by your side if you do or don't, and I'll help you all's I can so you can be the person I know you really is."

Her smile lit up his soul. As difficult as it was, he never interrupted or corrected her slavery dialect that she refused to relinquish. It gnawed at him that she would not let him teach her, that she did not realize how much her language held her back; and even when she talked about God and Jesus, he did not tell her that those were slavery ideas as well. He looked past that now and felt only her warmth and intelligence. Because deep down, Smiles saw him for all he was; she recognized the very qualities that he most embraced in himself, and she seemed to share with him the love he felt for her

That night as they sat in their small room, all in their same positions, eating the same potatoes, smelling the same stench, the baby crying just the same way it always did, Smiles nestled just a bit closer to Paul as he read her the front page of a newspaper he had found in the garbage. BJ had been carefully putting his matchboxes into small piles, saying every now and then how he would have "a greats opportunity if there be war, cause in war everyone they needs matches, that's much I knows," until he looked up and stared at Paul.

For a minute Paul feared that BJ was onto him and Smiles, and so he pushed away a bit. BJ curled his brow, and then asked, "Hey, did I tells you that I talked to the reverent last night? I don'ts remember if I tell you or nots."

Paul nodded. "No, Billy, you never did tell me. I figured you forgot."

BJ hardly looked up from his task. "No, I ain'ts forgot. It was the first things I says to them. I says, 'Reverent, I gots this boy who lives with me. He's smart as a whip, so smart I don't knows what he says half the time, and he comes from the South, from Virginia I thinks, and he wants to help out, help out the Negroes, wants to talks with you.' And the reverent he says to me, he says, 'Billy, you tell that boy to come on Sunday, listen to what me and Reverent Pendleton says, and you tell that boy to find us after we talks, and we will be happy to hear what he has to say.' That's what I means to tell you. I ain't not forgot! I told him right way."

"Thank you, Billy. Thank you," Paul said.

Billy nodded up and down, peeking up. "Praise be God," he uttered.

"Praise be God, Billy," Paul returned.

Smiles started to giggle. She looked away from Paul but lay her hands discreetly on his back and seemed to be spelling out a word. Or was it a heart? It was a heart! My God, it was a heart!

Paul melted. He smiled and just sat there, her hands tracing the heart over and over again.

The idea of going to church rubbed Paul the wrong way. Smiles sensed Paul's angst. She always did. But there she was for him, loving him, helping him. If there was a God, Paul knew that He had given this girl to him. This was Paul's gift from heaven!

The world was in a spiral, and people were talking about war, about freedom, about the end of slavery. He thought of Luke on the farm. How amazing would it be if Paul, donning the uniform of Union, freed his brother and helped to push the South into the pitiful ditch in which it deserved to rot? If he and Luke and Matt could walk together as three brothers, free to be themselves, could stroll past the doctor encased in dignity and power—propelled by a freedom that Paul would help to achieve—and spit on him, walk past Ned and all those other farmers as free and proud men, and then, together, together as brothers, go find Mamma and be a family again. And as he stared at Smiles, he knew—just knew, from the depth of his heart—that she would be there too, as would LB and Izzy, all of them, free to be themselves in a changed world, a world that Paul had helped to make into a better place for everyone.

"I'll go there Sunday," Paul said to himself. "Fuck the church and all it represents. I'll go to meet those men. And they will finally see the man who I am. The man I was always meant to be."

It was Friday. The next day, as soft sunshine caressed them, LB and Smiles brought Paul into the tiny ally behind their tenement. Smiles held the baby, and LB had a box, which he gave to Paul.

"A gift from us, to the next Fredrick Douglass," LB said. "Or, as you's always tells me, the next thing even better than Frederick Douglass is what you really is!"

"Not better," Paul said "Just different. What is it? What's in the box?"

"Open it!" Smiles prodded him. "Go on, we's all excited to sees what you thinks!"

Paul looked from one to the other, a comforting contentment flowing through his veins. He undid the box, and there inside it was a jacket, a fancy striped blue-and-white sports jacket, and also a pair of slacks. He peered at LB and shrugged.

"It's church clothes," LB laughed. "Abe, he done found it for you and wants you to have it as a gift. He says he knows your size just from looking at you. Trys it on! You's need to dress like a good church boy if you wants to go and impress those men. Try it on."

Paul did just that. And it fit perfectly!

"Look at the pocket, Paul," Smiles said. "Look what's there."

Paul did. It was a lapel! The blue flower! They had made a lapel out of the blue flower!

Tears started to trickle down Paul's eyes. He did not know what to even do.

Smiles hugged him, gentle and deep. And she whispered in his ears, "I love you so much, my wonderful man. Just don't be arrogant and dumb."

Paul nodded. He was so happy. Just so happy! Unfortunately, Paul either did not hear, or refused to abide by, Smiles's sage advice. Happiness, as with all else, was only as good as the rules allowed. This was something that a giddy and confident Paul always seemed to be very quick to forget.

17

Every day I fight to grasp the meaning of my freedom. Since liberation, my heart has been pulled from my gut. I have been physically and emotionally assaulted at every turn and have been denied access to any means of attaining true autonomy and self-sufficiency, being excluded from both the political and economic realms of society. The white men around me are devils who, with some notable exceptions, look down at me with obvious disdain. My fellow Negroes disparage my intelligence and assail my spirit, refusing to leap out of the vice of servitude that their white masters, and their fabricated God, have tied around their necks. And thus, I stand alone, basking in freedom that only resonates with enduring pain. But still, dear Brother, I prefer this state to the horrid cruelty and wanton violence perpetrated on us in Virginia. Here at least I am a man, I can come and go as I please, I have the opportunity to turn my lot around and make something of myself. For now, at least, I still have hope, as no law or chain can stop me from becoming the man I know I am, from becoming an influential force of positive change in the world. Somewhere out there lies redemption, and in my unshackled state I will forever fight until I find it.

Luke looked up at Izzy after reading the first paragraph of his brother's letter. "Kind of dark, don't you think?" he said to his friend, as both sat by the pond on a windy March evening.

Izzy laughed. "Well, he wrote that a while ago, and he has the job with Abe now, and other things, so, you know, what can I tell you? Maybe things will turn around for him."

"It's a terrible place, New York. I don't know why anyone would want to live there."

"The food's not bad there, Luke. It's pretty damned good in fact. Pretty damned good."

Luke stared across the pond and tossed a rock in, the centrifugal rings of water spreading out and dissipating upon a brown, grassy shore. He peered at the dams that surrounded his masterpiece, and the permanence of the water that filled it. This was water that trickled down from the bright blue sky; it fell upon a majestic mountain laden with ageless boulders and minerals crafted by nature over the course of millions of years before traveling on its raucous journey to their farm and beyond, carrying with it sediment that nourished the land. This water was everywhere at once: the sky, mountain, stream, pond, and even in his trees and crops, regenerating itself over and over again through evaporation and rain. This cycle opened Luke's eyes to the perseverance of nature. People came and went, wars were fought for senseless reasons, hate spread its wings and then had them clipped, but this ongoing cycle of renewal, the one that flowed through Luke's pond and into every part of his farm, it was not fickle at all. It was the meaning of everything, a buffer to the ephemeral world beyond its shores.

And so, when Izzy clamored on about Paul and New York and a war that was brewing across the land, Luke remained tucked in his tranquility. Only one thing bothered him now, and he hesitated to tell his old friend about it. But finally, he did.

"I have my red raft," he said to Izzy, staring deeply into the good man's eyes. "And even with all that has transpired here, I sit on it and see only beauty. Mountain peaks, Old Rag standing firm and proud, blue skies with puffy white clouds, a forest of bounteous trees, the majesty of this place we created here.

When I look farther, I can see the grape vines you brought me. I planted them on the eastern shore, I restructured the acidity of the dirt there by modifying water in the irrigation ditch, and I think I have it perfected. This summer we will watch them grow. It doesn't matter that everyone is dying outside these gates, that forces of ignorance and hate will clash over their opposing arrogance, that Paul says he is free but is suffering every day. The only thing that matters is love. And once you find and grasp love, then, my good friend, the other distractions and the senseless clamor of life's charade simply melt away. For me, this place is love. I don't care about vague concepts of freedom and war and even the fact that I am technically a slave; Paul's theories are abstractions that do not lead to happiness. I just have to embrace my love, and from there, all goodness will fill me and allow me to change the world."

Izzy scratched his unshaven chin and looked at Luke quizzically. Darkness had begun to descend upon them, and his stomach started to rumble. "You telling me that you're in love?"

Luke nodded. "Yes, I am madly in love, Izzy. I am in love with what this place is, what it represents. I love my brothers, and I love you. But, if I were to walk out of these gates, as I've done before, it all changes, Izzy. It's not the same. It's as if, this love I feel, it gets sullied and it wilts. And Izzy," he said, his eyes welling just a bit, a heaviness filling his head, "sometimes, the dirt from outside, it finds its way in. Sometimes we inadvertently let it in. Sometimes. "

Luke paused, finding the words difficult to elucidate. Izzy looked at him, waiting, cautiously anticipating.

Luke turned his eyes toward the ground. He threw another rock into the pond. "I did something horrible, Izzy. Something destructive to everything I love. And I don't know how to fix it."

For the first time, a tear rolled from Luke's eyes in front of another man. He did not conceal it. The tears grew more voluminous and then dropped into the pond in a deluge, adding yet one more ingredient to the pond's brew.

"Luke," Izzy said, sliding beside him and putting both hands on his shoulders. "What's wrong? Tell me."

Luke looked up and forced a smile. "When Matt's gone—he spends a lot of time trying to make good with the community, talking with the doctor, meeting with representatives of the peace party, with the farmers who want to start a military regiment to be ready in case there is war, with people in the town as they all wonder what's going to happen next—he leaves his wife here. She sleeps in the main house. But at night, she comes here, she comes here with me. And she does things."

"My God, Luke. What the fuck do you mean? What things? What is she doing?" Izzy stood up. He could barely contain his rage.

Luke threw another rock. The sun descended quickly, painting a red streak across the pond that fanned out to create a watery rainbow. It was so majestic, so beautiful. "Please don't overreact, and please never tell Paul. He can't know, Izzy. Promise me that. In the end, the small insults that the world jabs at us don't amount to more than a bruise, as long as we can contain them. But, Izzy," he said, tossing more rocks through unsullied waters, "she has been a menace, and I want you to know, just because I need to tell someone. She comes in here at night, and she pulls off her clothes, and she makes me do the same, and she hits me and tells me to do things, and that if I don't do them, she will tell her father that I raped her. So, I do those things. I think about the grapes and the pond, and I release myself from the painful dungeon she throws me in, and then, with my mind floating elsewhere, I can do what she wants. She comes rarely; most nights she leaves me in peace. I created my own purgatory, Izzy. I forced Matt to marry her so that we could be safe. Maybe this is my sacrifice to the sanctity of this place, of this farm that I love so much. Maybe I have to do my part so that we keep our oasis intact."

"Bullshit," Izzy cried out, his eyes slicing into Luke's face, his puffy black brow flagellating. "Have you told Matt? Does he know? Screw that, Luke. No. That's not a sacrifice. That's called rape. That's called abuse."

"Yes," Luke smiled. "And I'm a slave. And that's the doctor's daughter. Who will they believe?"

"If you tell Matt, then…."

Luke nodded no. "What can he do? She is still the doctor's daughter. They would kill me for sure. They would kill him too if he defended me, and would kill you. I'm sure she would implicate him and you in the plot to rape her. And then we would lose our sanctuary. We would lose everything."

Luke tossed in another rock. Cool air descended upon them from the sky. The heavens darkened. Luke peered up at his friend. His face continued to reflect pure tranquility. Just telling Izzy about it released him from any angst. "Let's go in the cabin," he said. "Unless you have to get up to the main house."

"Fuck that," said Izzy. "I'm not going to the main house. You can't just tell me that and then think I'm going to sit down with that witch and break bread with her. Luke, you don't tell me that shit and expect me to just say, 'Yea, it's OK, let's wait it out.' Bullshit, Luke. I need to get you out of here. If you're not willing to tell Matt, if you have no faith that your brother can save you from the bitch he's married to, then you can't stay here any longer. Why else would you tell me this, Luke? Why would you tell me if you didn't want me to do something?"

"Then let's go in the cabin." Luke stood and marched to his wooden shack. Izzy followed behind him, ranting. They sat on Paul's old bed, and Luke lit a few candles. He peered at his friend, who was breathing heavy, punching his fist into his hand, seeming ready to explode.

"Look, Luke," Izzy finally said, his voice a bit calmer, "I understand what you are saying. You want to keep your farm. You want to wait it out. But it doesn't work that way, not here. What can I tell you? These people are nothing short of evil. That bitch, she has your life in her claws now. When this happens to my people, we run. You have to run, Luke! Hide out in my cart. Let me take you to New York with your brother. Even that is better than what you have here."

"Could you stay the night with me here?" he asked Izzy. "She won't come if you are here."

"Luke, we have to tell Matt. He will leave with us if he knows this."

"Then," said Luke with some indignation weaved into his voice, "the farm will die."

"Fuck the farm," Izzy shouted. "Like I said, it's a piece of dirt. Dirt is dirt, grapes are grapes. The Jews understand that once you place your faith in dirt, in land—"

Luke cut him off. "I know, Izzy. I heard it. But this is not just land. This is a sanctuary upon the earth that is beyond any equal. You people think Jerusalem is somehow holy. It's a desert, Izzy. You can't even grow a weed there. But here, look at what we've done here. And when the grapes start to flourish—"

Izzy cut him off. "Do you trust Matt?" He stared into Luke's dark eyes. "Do you?"

The question pushed Luke off his train of thought. He was not prepared for it. He turned away and started kicking dirt on the cold floor. "I don't know," he finally uttered.

"Why, Luke?"

Luke lifted a handful of dirt and threw it out the door. Luke stared outside at the bright stars as they reflected off his pond. And he smiled. "There are times, Izzy, he comes in here and he talks about the doctor and some of the people in town, and he seems to like them, maybe even respect them. He says that some of the young men in town, the kids he always hated and who abused him, were starting to recruit people into the Washington Grays, a new army unit they are putting together. They have a leader now, a guy named James Lawson Kemper, who Matt says is a great guy, a farmer, a patriot. Those are Matt's very words. And

Izzy, when Matt talks to me about what's going on in the South, about the secession and about the Virginia Peace treaty, he always tells me what the doctor thinks, as though what the doctor says is the factual account that he believes. He spends more time off the farm than on it and has not asked me even once about the upcoming crops, the grapes, anything. He is absorbed by the world out there, by his father-in-law, by the lore of Virginia. He has changed."

Izzy nodded his head despairingly. "That's just what happened to your father," he said. "The same bullshit. The same brainwashing. Luke, you shouldn't trust him. He may already be lost."

"No," Luke said with a smile. "He is still my brother. I know he loves me. He never comes with Jessie to see me, only by himself. He talks with me as he always has."

"And what about the doctor's daughter? Does he love her?"

"Maybe," Luke said, finally looking up at his friend. "He treats her that way. He holds her close, kisses her on the cheek, seems giddy around her. And she always pretends to be a doting wife when she is in public, although with me she tears him apart, calls him horrible things, thinks he is an idiot. If I tell him what she is really like, the things she says, the insults she hurls in his direction, the things she does to me, he wouldn't believe me. He wouldn't believe anything I tell him about her. You ask if I trust him. The answer is, I am his brother, but I am also a slave to him now, one who needs to know my place and to do my job. I don't know what he would do if I told him."

Izzy just shook his head. "My God, Luke, you poor thing." And he reached over and buried Luke in a hug. Then he pushed Luke away. "I am not tolerating your pigheaded obstinacy. You are coming with me. If you don't trust Matt, good, I believe you. But I am taking you away."

Luke just nodded, side to side. "No," he said. "I won't ever leave this place."

As the wind whistled across the bare trees, footsteps approached. First Luke heard them, and then, when he asked Izzy to stay quiet, Izzy did too. "Is it her?" Izzy whispered.

"No," Luke said. "Too loud. I've gotten very skilled at determining when she is coming alone. I can hear two discrete sets of footsteps now. It may be the happy couple."

Sure enough, Matt and Jessie slid into the cabin, both with smiles on their faces, both giggling.

"Izzy!" Matt said, stretching out his hand and shaking Izzy's. "I didn't know you got here already. You know Jess, the doctor's daughter, my wife now. You sold her the last two dresses she got; one was a pretty blue, and one, what's it, honey, is it red?"

"Yes," Jessie said, "Red. Both beautiful. Thank you for them." She bowed to Izzy.

Izzy just glared at her, right through her, and Luke feared that, being the person he was, Izzy would say something, here and now, something to reveal the fact Luke had spilled the beans.

"Massa Matt," Luke said, instantly transforming his dialect like a trained linguistic master, "Mr. Izzy comes by to see Ol' Luke, that what he's done doing, is all. Came here first before the main house, because he knows how hards I work, and I always says, just like Ben Franklin, early to beds and early to rise makes a man healthy and wise."

"Healthy, wealthy, and wise," Jessie corrected him, patting Luke on the head

Luke laughed, hard and gruffly. "Luke ain't not gonna be wealthy anytime soon, Ms. Jessie," he said. "That's why I leaves that part of it out!"

Jessie laughed with him. "You are too funny Lukie," she said. Then she turned to Matt. "Are you sure Luke has food for the night? And are you going to invite Izzy up to the house for dinner?"

Matt nodded. "We seen your cart here, Izzy, so we said you must be down visiting Luke. We got a dinner and everything ready for you, a guest room all made up. With all the stuff going on down here in Virginia and all of that, we know you want to sell your wares fast and get out, especially with the vote coming so soon and all, the vote to see if Virginia is staying or going with the South. We can bring Luke some leftovers later. You ready to come up now, Izzy? It's so good to see you."

Matt did not even acknowledge Luke. It was if he was a ghost; he only looked at Izzy, and Luke was sure that Izzy knew that too.

"I'd like to spend a little more time in the cabin, Matt," Izzy dryly responded, looking at Luke as he spoke. "If that's OK with you and your precious wife."

"Have you heard from Paul up there in New York? Not sure that's where he was headed, but I'd like to know at least he's doing OK. Would make me sleep better at night."

Jessie hugged Matt. "He worries so much about his slaves, even the ones who run away. He is so kind a man."

Luke peered at Izzy, whose eyes bulged, and whose fists were clenched. God only knew what he might do or say! "No, Matt, there are hundreds of thousands of people up North, and more slaves that escaped from Southern bondage than any man can count. So, no, I haven't seen him. But I'm sure he's happy to be free. Who wouldn't be?"

"He had a pretty good life here, Izzy," Matt said.

"Well," Izzy smirked, "I guess that explains why he ran away."

For a long, uncomfortable moment a thick silence enveloped them. The candles flickered in the darkness. A soft wind blew across the pond. A solitary owl sang into the night air.

"I's be OK here, Mr. Izzy," Luke finally said. "Go eats with them upstairs. Ruth, she can whip you up something fine, and you's will be happy you dones it, of that I am sure."

"No, Luke, I'm going to stay here with you tonight," he said, and then he turned to Matt. "Matt, I do appreciate the offer, and I'm sure Luke and I would appreciate you bringing us a plate of whatever Ruth is cooking; we aren't picky. I have some catching up to do with my friend here. Frankly, my people have a lot more in common with the enslaved than with the enslavers."

Matt looked stunned, as though he did not quite comprehend what Izzy had just said. "So, you coming up to sleep in the house? It gets cold here at night, Izzy."

"Oh, really," Izzy laughed. "And somehow that's OK for Luke? Things have changed a great deal here in just a few weeks, what can I tell you? Better to freeze with the holy than bake with the sinners—that's what my bubby always said. You people believe in a place called hell, right? I understand it's pretty damned warm there. That's why sometimes it's better to be cold."

"Izzy!" Jessie giggled. "I think you have us all wrong. Luke is treated very well by us. He will tell you that. On this farm, all the slaves are. We love Luke, we really do."

"'Love' is a funny word, Jessie," Izzy said to her in a harsh tone. "It can mean a lot of things. But I sure don't think it means what you think it does. Luke understands the meaning of love. Do you?"

"Oh, Izzy, they's does love me here, you knows that. And I loves thems too!"

Izzy nodded. He took a few deep breaths and kicked a little dirt on the ground.

Then he turned to Matt and forced a smile. "It's been a long day, and a stressful one, Matt. I'll be more comfortable here tonight. Tomorrow I'm going to take my wares to town before you people instigate a war in the name of keeping men in bondage, you know, in the name of your honor. The only tragedy of the war you are about to start is that I will lose my best market. Virginians are the dumbest and most gullible customers a New York salesman could ever find. It will be a shame to lose you."

Matt looked at him, seemingly bewildered. Jessie stared knowingly into Izzy's eyes and then kissed her husband on the cheek.

"We'll bring you some blankets and food," Jessie said, shifting her visage into one of naive joy. "Let's let them catch up. Come, let's go, dearest Matthew." And they slipped out.

Izzy stood up and walked to the wall. He then yelled something completely unintelligible, clearly in another language ("Gay Koffin Yom!") and then kicked a bunch of dirt into the air. A dust cloud floated up, Izzy coughed. "Bastards," he uttered. "I could wring their fucking necks."

"You asked me if I trust Matt. What about you?" Luke asked him.

"I don't know," Izzy said. "He is pretty dumb. He may not know what's going on. Then again, what can I tell you? I knew his father, and this is just a bit of déjà vu. The doctor is very adept at casting spells, especially ones that can deceive the weak minds of Cocklin men. And those breasts of his wife are likely not helping matters much either. I think he's a lost cause, if you ask me."

"I'm glad you're staying here tonight," Luke smiled. "And you even were able to get me a hot meal and some blankets. She must like you."

"Bite your tongue," Izzy snapped back. "I don't date Christians, especially ones who came out of the devil's womb." He then paced a bit along the wall. "But I do have an idea."

Luke peered up at him.

"I'm making a delivery to the doctor tomorrow," he said. "I'll try to convince your brother to join me and then to see exactly where his mind is with all of this. I promise I won't tell him anything about what you told me. I just don't want to leave you alone with her. That's my only concern."

"She never bothers me during the day," Luke smiled. "Daytime is for work."

"Good," he said. "But goddamn it, Luke, if I think that Matt has gone to the dark side, I don't give two craps about you and your pond and your farm and your damned grapes. Let me tell you this about that: you are coming with me back to New York, and there's not a damned thing you can do to stop me! Jesus Christ, what has become of this world? This is the pit of hell! You poor kid. You damned poor kid! I am not leaving you alone down here if I don't think Matt is on the up and up. What can I tell you?"

Luke sat back. He was glad Paul was safe, if not yet happy. But New York was not a place for Luke; he could never leave his sanctuary despite the blight that now infested its soil. He would wait it out. *Why did I tell Izzy?* he wondered. He had not intended to, and yet he felt compelled. He knew that Izzy would be furious and could potentially say or do something counterproductive. But it was also possible that Izzy might find a solution, one that enabled Luke to remain on the farm and somehow extinguish the precarious flame that he had unwittingly kindled. As Izzy paced back and forth in the small cabin, Luke peeked at him lovingly, hopeful. Tonight, at least, Luke would be safe. Perhaps Izzy would find a way to stay here with him. That is what Luke craved the most.

18

Matt could hardly recall how the conversation had escalated to this point, with these two men who Matt loved and respected locked in a staring contest. They talked past each other as each coldly stabbed the other with a conflicting point that the other regurgitated and spit back. The doctor always proclaimed his adherence to a "discourse of civility" whereby his words would be soft but firm, his ears always open, and a mutual respect never relinquished. "That was the way of Virginia, of Thomas Jefferson," he said. Today, it seemed, he had reverted to the ways of Neanderthal!

"Jefferson?" Izzy threw back at him, laughing. "You mean the man who planted slanderous lies about his former friend John Adams in the 1800 election? The man who split up his slave families and had a fifty-year affair with a slave girl half his age, producing many, many, many kids, who he freed as the price to keep her as his whore? The man who squandered all his money on extravagances and then begged Congress to buy his books just so he could pay his debtors? The civility of that Jefferson?"

Barely chewing at the bait, the doctor merely said, "Yes, that Mr. Jefferson, that very one."

It was as if, Matt thought silently from a seemingly invisible perch in the room's corner, *neither of them could hear the other, nor did they want to.* They were both just making their points, oblivious to what the other one was saying. It was their very own civil war right in the doctor's study!

Horatio Moffett was late, and Matt wished he would just show up to end this little sparring match between two hard-headed men. The main event was a discourse that the doctor set up between Izzy ("An abolitionist Jew from New York," as the doctor referred to him) and Mr. Moffett, the county's representative to the Virginia Secession Convention, "and a man of great intelligence and civility."

Matt and Izzy had been walking the town for most of the morning before arriving at the doctor's home. Izzy went from house to house and farm to farm, selling the last of his clothes on this final junket to Virginia before secession might be declared at the Virginia convention on April 4, just five days away. "It's a pre-war sale," Izzy proclaimed. Everyone had questions for the New Yorker, wondering how things were up North, and how Northerners would react if Virginia seceded.

"Not that I give a damn," said one farmer, who bought two pairs of slacks and a quilted hat. "Let 'em come. We'll whip the crap out of them. I'm already in the Washington Grays, and Colonel Kemper's been by the farm earlier today and told me that we are ready to fight should we need to. I'm guessing that they ain't so well prepared up North."

Izzy laughed. "Our mayor, Fernando Wood, already declared he's going with the Confederacy. But what can I tell you that you don't know already? Once there's war, the North will fight. The Irish don't like Negroes or anyone else for that matter, but they are pretty pissed off that the South is trying to tell them what to do. Believe you me, they'll be grabbing their guns and signing up for war as soon as bullets start flying. You boys may be good, but you don't have any idea what it's like to be fighting against a swarm of angry Irish!"

Between houses and farms, Izzy asked Matt a lot of questions about Luke, some of them just a bit pointed. "So, you don't invite him in the house anymore, not even when that wife of yours is gone? You don't spend time with him at his cabin? You used to talk all the time."

"That's the deal we got, Izzy," Matt finally said. "It's Luke's idea. We supposed to lay low, to pretend, until all this washes over that 'I'm the master and he's the slave.' Luke said to me to take no chances. Once Luke says it's OK to act normal around him, then it'll do it in a second. But he wants me to pretend, to act, so they leave the farm alone. It's all Luke's idea."

"Your little wife, the one you used to say is the daughter of Satan, you sure as hell seem pretty damned close to her, all lovey-dovey and crap. What can I tell you, Matt? If your kissie lovie theatrics is all an act, you're a far better thespian than I would have guessed."

"I like Jessie," Matt said. "She ain't the girl she used to be. She's changed, and I do like her. But Luke's my brother. I'll do whatever he says. I just don't want to get none of us in trouble. Jessie likes Luke too. But I ain't quite ready to tell her about who he really is. Not yet."

"Not ever!" Izzy snapped sharply, staring at Matt in an uncharacteristically firm glance. "Not ever, Matt. Don't trust the secret of your brother's intelligence to anyone. Especially not her."

Especially her? Matt did not understand why he would pick on Jessie, especially given how much affection she seemed to have for Luke. But Matt did not have time to ask Izzy. They arrived at the doctor's humble abode just that moment.

Jessie was back at the farm, and so there were no cups of iced tea poured, no snacks sitting out, just pleasant conversation in the doctor's study as they waited for Mr. Moffett to arrive. The doctor had invited Izzy over to buy a few shirts and then to speak with Washington's representative to the Virginia Secession

Convention. After all, Izzy could provide valuable information to Mr. Moffett that the county representative could bring back to other wavering delegates to the convention. Apparently, no one yet knew which way they would vote next week: to remain in the Union as a neutral state, or to join the South in a new Confederacy that had been recently declared.

"The objective, of course," said the doctor with a small tilted smile, rubbing his face gently with his left hand. "is to avoid war. To also prevent the Commonwealth from being a staging ground for war between the two childish sections of our great nation. I expect Virginia to exert enough influence to stop this madness. We no more want to join forces with the ignorant firebrands of the Deep South—to call Jefferson Davis our president—than to remain in the Union under the ape-like tyrant Abraham Lincoln. No, we want nothing to do with those scoundrels. As our nation dissolves, only one state can effectively intervene, the very state that led us in our revolutionary battle against tyranny, starting with Mr. Jefferson's declaration in 1776. But should your Abraham Lincoln decide that he must assail the states that have chosen to dissolve their bonds to Union, should he raise arms against the Deep South, we in Virginia will not stand by and allow that to transpire. We will not be the bloody battlefield in a spat between two children, and we will not let the abolitionist armies invade our lands and exert their misguided will upon us. We will reluctantly join with the South and stop you, should you chose to ignore our wisdom and guidance."

Izzy nodded, as though he agreed. "As an immigrant to this country, it's hard for me figuring out what your revolution was even about, especially since England was even more progressive than all of you. Your Mr. Jefferson didn't help create a country based on high-minded ideals. He was just protecting his slaves and his ability to push the Indians further west, so he could maintain his wealth and position. What can I tell you? He and his so-called disciples, including the great George Washington, were in a shitload of debt to England, and rather than work and pay the loans back, they figured, what the hell, a good war can help us just erase the whole thing as we sit on our butts and have our slaves work for us. And now his brethren want their way again; they want to have their slaves and be lazy and take advantage of the Northern industry; anyone who disputes the actions of the great slave states is declared an abolitionist and unpatriotic. Everyone who talks about abolition is jailed down here—quite a way to honor Mr. Madison and his First Amendment of free speech. Yes, your revolutionary heroes certainly did leave you a worthy legacy down here in Virginia, one that you are continuing to this day."

The doctor did not bend. He merely nodded in apparent agreement. "Mr. Jefferson was a realist, as are we in Virginia," he said. "You Jews, you are far too universal; you have no particular loyalty to any nation or state, to anything at all except for yourselves. But we are different in Virginia; our first objective is to protect our Commonwealth and all the values upon which we have built this great nation. We understand, as did Mr. Jefferson, that for us to persevere as the beacon of hope and progress in a world where the strong try to subjugate the weak, we had to divorce ourselves from England or we would have been forever beholden to their aristocratic laws and their control over us. They feared us, because our way was superior to theirs, and they knew it. And Mr. Jefferson knew too, as do we all in Virginia, that the Negro and the Indian cannot be allowed to spread their blood to the white man, cannot be allowed to be anything more than fully subjugated, or our culture, our society, all that we represent, will dissipate. We are a white, Christian race, the best of the best, the city on a hill, and we are in a pitched battle against lesser people and lesser races that seek to push us off that perch. As soon as we fall prey to universalism, to moral weakness, to a need to pity the lesser races and incorporate them into our body politic, as soon as we mix our blood with theirs, then on that day, we will die.

Virginia is fighting for our survival. We choose to fight on the side of Union, for the government and culture our founders created. But if the Union bows to inferior ideas and races and heeds the self-destructive words of abolitionists and warmongers, then we will have to fight that Union with all the strength we have. We will have to fight it, sir, so we can assure that it will survive."

"Well, Doctor," Izzy smiled, "at least we agree on Mr. Jefferson."

"We do indeed."

The conversation swam around Matt like an insect he could not swat. He felt like he was in the big house months ago, sitting with Paul and Luke and Izzy as the three of them slid from topic to topic, agreeing and arguing, seeming to revel in their mastery of everything, while building ideas and thoughts that bounced across the walls with an obvious electricity, but which Matt never could grasp.

There was a knock at the door. Thankfully, Mr. Moffett had arrived! A tall but unassuming man, Horatio Moffett lived nearby and frequented the doctor's abode with some regularity, including on the night of Lincoln's election. A noted lawyer, he served as the Rappahannock County Commonwealth attorney and was voted unanimously onto the secession congress as Washington's local representative. He was not a man laden with grand ideas or concrete opinions; often he liked to chew on thoughts with the doctor so as to better solidify his position.

After making congenial conversation about the weather and the upcoming planting season, and about a recent court case over which he presided regarding a stolen violin that was being used to store chicken feed, Mr. Moffett introduced himself to both Matt and Izzy, and the four of them settled into the doctor's library.

"Your skull collection never ceases to amaze me, Doctor," Mr. Moffett said, wandering over and rubbing the collection of bones. "It is a very graphic reason why we in Virginia must take up the mantle of righteousness and assure that emancipation never occurs. Like you, Doctor, I wish the Negro never landed on our shores, but now that he is here, it is up to us to slow down his procreation and to assure that nothing the North does enables his release into general society."

Izzy laughed. "My goodness, Mr. Moffett, you sound just like Abraham Lincoln!"

Moffett's face nearly dropped to the floor. He tried to say a few words, but they came out as gibberish.

"Ignore his brashness, Horatio," the doctor said. "He likes to incite us. It's his people's way."

"What I mean," Izzy continued, "is that Lincoln has never said he wants to get rid of slavery. He just doesn't want it to grow or to expand. Exactly what you seem to be saying."

"You are quite misled," the doctor said. "The Republicans and abolitionists are working hand in hand to release the black race upon us, to free the slaves, to give the Negro equal rights, to soil the white race with mongrels that push us back into primitive days, to give the Negro an upper hand in the inevitable clash of the races that will consume our nation and the world. We are reasonable people in Virginia. We want neither war nor the horrid path that abolitionist Republicans seek to lead us down; we are looking for a compromise that will benefit us all. Horatio, tell this New Yorker what the moderate voices in the convention are saying and see if it is something he thinks they can stomach up North."

Horatio Moffett nodded and cleared his throat, looking more at the doctor than at the two guests. He seemed to be a bit shaken by Izzy's rude behavior, as he told the doctor later. "We need assurances from the North," he said meekly, "that those states that wish to part with the Union will be allowed to go their own way without any interference from the government of Lincoln, that the remaining slaveholding states that elect to remain with the Union will have (through a Constitutional amendment) perpetual protection of their slaves that cannot be rescinded even by another amendment for at least a century, that there will be no war started by the North against the Southern states, and that certain safeguards be placed that enable agrarian states to continue to have a voice in the political sphere, although we may become a minority."

Izzy nodded. "What can I tell you? It's not gonna happen," he said.

"That's it?" the doctor shot back. "Mr. Moffett offers a reasonable way to preserve our nation, and without a thought or discussion you simply discount it? How horribly ironic that you in the North call us unreasonable!"

"I'm just saying," Izzy coolly responded, "people up North are sick of having to have their leashes yanked by you people. If there is a war, that's why it's going to happen. Too many demands by you people. Not enough willingness to change and adapt. We don't want to be your lapdogs."

"It seems to me that you people up North would covet a situation where the Deep South states walk away from the Union," the doctor said with a clever grin. "How many times has South Carolina or Georgia thwarted the cause of the Union and sought to pull us down to a lower level of prosperity? How many times have they held us back from greatness by demanding an agenda that curbs our ability to prosper as a nation? Don't forget, Georgia was a colony of criminals, and South Carolina a colony of lazy wretches, and ridding our country of those people would be a blessing that we should all desire! Let them go, that's what we say, and provide us with enough security so that we can maintain our way of life and our position of power within the Union so that we don't fall into the grips of the abolitionist states who seek to destroy what we in Virginia stand for, which, incidentally, is the very core of what our founders fought for. The only thing standing in the way of a grand compromise is our newly elected president and his abolitionist sycophants. We don't want war in Virginia. We want the Union. We want prosperity. We want to have a mutual understanding of what it means to be an American and seek to silence the malcontents, North and South, who want otherwise. We are a white, Christian nation. We must protect that in every way we can."

Izzy laughed. "You see, Doctor, the white Christian thing, you're not really pulling me on your side whenever you say that. It's kind of a little frightening."

"Touché," said the doctor. "We are pleased to include the Jews too. As long as you know your place."

"Like selling you pants?"

"Precisely. Is that so terrible.?"

Izzy nodded, hardly flustered. "No, you are a good customer, I have to admit." Izzy twisted to Horatio Moffett and glared at him with a smile. "So, Mr. Moffett, how do you intend to vote? Because I'm no seer, but I can tell you, no one wants the Southern states to run away. Not in New York at least. We have a lot of economic baggage sitting down there; we want their cotton, and they are a major market for our goods. So, if your vote is to stay with the Union only if the North lets the Union dissolve, I don't think that is a feasible plan. Just one New Yorker's opinion."

Horatio Moffett seemed a bit unnerved. He peeked at the doctor, then at Izzy. "I plan to vote for the Union," he finally said. "With certain stipulations. But if your president fires one gun in the direction of the South, I will change my mind in a moment. No one in the South wants war, including the states that have already left. And war will devastate the Commonwealth. If there is war, the blame for that sits squarely on the lap of the president and the Northerners who elected that buffoon to office."

Izzy nodded. "Well, I understand your position, Mr. Moffett. But the North is not going for that. What can I tell you? They take the Constitution seriously and intend to hold these *united* states together. You people down South seem content to treat our Constitution like a paper rag that you can wipe your butts with and then, whenever the wind doesn't blow your way, say, see, it's just a bunch of shit we can toss away. What we want is to keep our country together under a set of laws that the founders created. So, I think we have here what your Mr. Jefferson would call a pissing contest between two burly drunks."

The doctor and Mr. Moffett looked at each other quizzically, and Izzy just burst out laughing.

"Do you seek a race war, Mr. Snout?" asked the doctor, very sternly, staring hard at a smiling Izzy. "As much as we fear a racial dilution of our national greatness, so too do we tremble at the prospect of a race war. In Abraham Lincoln, the Negroes of the South have found a new Moses, and who is to stop them from breaking the chains of their masters and slaughtering every one of us knowing he is their savior? Once the North fires on the South, the door is open for a slave insurrection that will not only bring down the South but will destroy the entire white race in America, North and South; soon enough we will all be *their* slaves. That is what we fear, and what you should fear as well. One bullet in our direction by the North, one cannon fired at us, and Virginia will reluctantly join forces to avert that inevitable outcome, because once the Negroes know that a Northern army will be at their bidding, nothing will prevent them from slaughtering and subjugating the white race. In nature, everything is an incessant battle between races and ideas, and there is but one victor. If we lay down our guard and allow the enemy to have the upper hand, then we will have quickly lost the war."

Mr. Moffett nodded his head. And then there was silence.

"The shit's gonna hit the fan, Matt," Izzy said to him, as the sun descended and they trotted slowly across the Shenandoah ridge back to the farm. The specter of Old Rag still shimmered above, although its gloss was a bit faded by shadows cast upon it. Cool air blew at them from the south, the very direction in which they were traveling. The wind and the words bit into Matt, as he stared forward numbly.

"It's going to hit the fan damned hard, what can I tell you? And when it does, Matt, you got to do everything you can to protect the people on your farm. If you run off and join this war, there is no guarantee that Luke will be alive when you come home."

"Why would you say that?" Matt asked him. "That makes no sense at all. Jessie will be there. The doctor too. They'll get us an overseer who has our interest in mind. I ain't worried, not that I'm ready to hop over and join the Grays anytime soon. The doctor told me, he said, Matt, your place is by my daughter's side and on your farm. You'd be doing more for the cause of Virginia if you keep your crops growing fast and strong than if you give up on that and pick up a gun. Besides, as you well know, Izzy, I ain't much of a warrior."

They turned onto the long dirt road that meandered onto the orchard, blurry mountains fading behind them. Izzy stopped for a moment and peered into Matt's eyes with a visage of foreboding that Matt had never seen. "There are forces afoot, Matt, that you may not fully understand."

The wind blew briskly, and an orange glow filled the sky.

Matt did not understand.

"These people will not alter their way of life. They won't. They may be hiding behind a mask of civility and pretend they are all nice and good, but they aren't. Believe you me, Matt, we Jews have been in this spot more times than I can tell you, which is why I am in America now and not Poland. We know when to run. We trust no one. And there is no one I trust less than your father-in-law. He's just one asshole among many, but a lot of people like him, and even those who don't, well, they pretend they do. These people will murder any slave who threatens their way of life. They don't view people like Luke and Paul and your mother as humans. Killing them is like swatting an ant. The great Mr. Jefferson had no problem doing just that even as he helped to create the world's only democracy. They don't see that as a contradiction; in fact, they see the two things as supporting each other."

Matt remained dumbfounded. What did Izzy want him to do? "Then what, Izzy?" he finally asked.

"Protect your brother. Don't leave him alone, not with your wife or her father or any of them. And if you go to war, God forbid that, Matt, we only have one option. You send word to me up North; you get it to me any way you can, through any salesman coming from New York, through any soldier or straggler you find, you let me know, and I will come down here and take over your farm. I'll be the overseer while you're gone. I'll take care of Luke and the others, and I'll make sure your farm is safe. Believe you me, that's the last thing this salesman wants to do, but for Luke, I'll do it. In an instant."

Matt nodded. "That seems bat crazy, Izzy. It won't come to that. I don't even think there will be a war, and if there is, I ain't going, and if I do, Jessie will stay around to protect Luke and the farm. And even if not, there ain't no way I can get no word to you. I wouldn't know how. And even if by some miracle I did, and somehow you snuck down here between armies killing each other, you think the doctor will just let you run the farm, just like that, after how you talked to him and Mr. Moffett? He was ready to tear your eyes out."

Izzy nodded. The sun descended quickly, and little light remained but for some flickers ahead. The wind blew that much more forcefully, and Izzy's thick black hair ruffled around like a mop being shaken. But his face looked serene, and he placed his hands on Matt's shoulders.

"Trust no one here who has a white face," Izzy said. "You should trust the horses more than them. I am sure there are good people among the whites here, but the doctor owns them, like he owns you. So, watch your back too. Be clever. I can't say more than that. You've known me all your life, Matt. Just trust me on that. What can I tell you that you don't know already?"

"Why can't you say no more?"

"Trust me." He smiled, kissing Matt's head and then neighing his horses forward. "I'm sleeping with Luke tonight. I need extra blankets. You should spend more time with him, Matt. I see you getting dumber and dumber every day you hang around all these high falutin Southerners. You need to have some conversations with more people with brains. Me and Luke got small brains according to the doctor. But at least we have brains nonetheless."

They crossed onto the farm. A lit candle flickered from Luke's cabin. Izzy drove his horses quickly in that direction. He hoped to God that Luke was there alone. If not, he did not know what he might do.

19

Whispers of war spread throughout the city like a hurricane. People could not talk of anything else. To most, it seemed to be an exciting moment, a time for flexing muscles, for finally breaking through the gnawing tension that so many years of accommodation and unresolved indignation had sowed. Few, even the Lincoln haters and Democrats, believed that the Southern states were anything more than scoundrels and seditious traitors. Talk of armies and fighting and finally shutting those bastards up trickled through the din of more conventional conversation. Juxtaposed were taunts about Lincoln and "the damned Negroes" and the "dumbasses" running this country, but that did not mute the jingoistic cries for war.

A moment of decisiveness came upon New York and the rest of the country quickly. South Carolina threatened to take over all federal forts along its coast. Lincoln and his secretary of state, William Seward, drew a red line, saying that any seizure of federal property would be tantamount to treason. And so, the two sides stood face-to-face, neither flinching, even the slightest mistake likely to precipitate an all-out war. If Lincoln was aggressive, then the border states like Virginia, that just voted to stay with the Union, would bolt. If he did nothing, then the United States of America would cease to exist. Would Lincoln reinforce the forts? If so, would South Carolina attack a Union Garrison? If that happened, what would Virginia and Maryland do? Would Washington then be surrounded by hostile forces? And what would New York's reaction be, especially given that its mayor claimed allegiance with the South?

Paul digested the chatter and mused over what it might mean, but he nestled himself in a more concealed space now, a spot so soothing and tranquil that it isolated him from reality, leaving him less concerned with anything but his happiness. It was if he was transported to Luke's red raft, placidly oblivious to a world that twisted and twirled around him. He was in love!

A warm April breeze and the bright sun lit up Paul's spirit. He walked down Mott Street hand in hand with Smiles on a busy Saturday, with so many different faces and languages bouncing between street carts and horses that no one seemed to notice these two dark-skinned people in a sea of mostly white. They leaped over mud and flowing refuse, large piles of manure, and streams of human waste, stepping in more than one odorous mess, which only made them chuckle that much more. They were in an ethereal space that shut out all but themselves. Paul had never felt this way before. The touch of delicate human skin grasping his hand sent waves of warmth and electricity through his body. Every fiber in him relaxed and smiled. They did not even have to speak.

He did not know whether to kiss her. Especially in public, when their very touching each other was perilous if seen by anyone who knew them (given that she officially was married to LB), threatening to instigate a backlash, not of their own making. The love between Paul and Smiles was forbidden; if anyone caught them in their glances and touches and hand-holding, who knows what could happen next. Would they and LB be tossed out of Collin's apartment onto the street? Would Paul ever be able to see Smiles again? As much as he wished to smother her, he knew that he would die if he lost her, and she knew that as well.

So, they remained discreet, walking far away from their home in Cowpath before even daring to share a smile.

Paul thought about kissing her for quite some time but only when he knew it to be safe. He had never actually kissed anyone before, and, other than peeking discreetly at others who did, was not quite sure how to do it. He certainly did not want her to feel uncomfortable. She had been kissed by men of evil who had raped and tortured her. What if those flashbacks consumed her when his lips touched hers? Besides, holding hands was quite enough; in fact, it was mesmerizing.

After a while, Paul listened in on some of the conversations around him. He picked up a muddied copy of the *Herald* that had been nearly buried by dozens of shoes that had trampled upon it.

"It's amazing," he said to her, reading the front page. "*The Herald* is a tool of the Democrats and decries any hint of abolition. But even it is praising what happened in Virginia. I think half the people think that if Virginia stays neutral, then we will definitely clobber the Southern states in the event of war, and the other half hopes that Virginia's decision will make war less likely. 'If Mr. Lincoln has any love of Union,' it says, 'then he will accept Virginia's terms, which are reasonable and generous, and he will let the treasonous states leave unaccosted and allow the Union to dissolve so it can eventually be saved without spilling any blood.' Isn't it amazing that they still won't call him President Lincoln? Just Mr. Lincoln. So many people hate his guts."

Smiles put her head on Paul's chest. "So, what's next then?" she asked. "Virginia says it'll stays with the North if they let it keep its slaves and do what it wants. Then some other states, they do's the same thing. How does that help anyone if our president still wants to get those other states back?"

Paul did not know. But he was intrigued that Virginia took that path. "They voted two-thirds for Union. I mean, that's amazing. Without Virginia, the South will be a primitive country. I think we should just let the Deep South states go and maybe compromise with Virginia and work toward gradual emancipation. I always thought that's the right way forward."

"So, you's is saying let them keep their slaves and treat them any ways they wants, and we don't do's nothing about that? That's what you's is saying?" She yanked her hand away from his, as her face soured and her smile dissipated. "You wants Luke to stay a slave, that's what's you's is saying, Paul?"

"It's so complicated, Smiles," he said to her, stroking her hair. "I'm not saying that. I would be sick to my stomach saying that. But if President Lincoln doesn't bow to their demands, if he says he wants to get rid of slaves in Virginia, if he tries to take back the forts in the South like he is threatening, then Virginia is gone, and so is Tennessee and North Carolina and maybe even Maryland. We will have to fight against all of them. And if there is a war, God only knows what they may do to their slaves. It could get a lot worse. It's so complicated. There's no right answer." A tear dropped from his cheek. He worried so much about his brother. "I don't know the right answer," he whispered again.

She peered up at him, her large, inviting eyes washing away his pain. And then she kissed him on the lips, soft and quick. She smiled and lay her head on his chest, grasping his hand again and closing her eyes. "You's a good man, Paul. You a tortured man, but a good one. I'm heres for you no matter what's going to happen. I knows your heart is always where it gots to be."

Paul fell back onto his red raft, closing his eyes, breathing deeply, and enjoying every moment of her touch. They walked across the city, hand in hand.

Tomorrow, Paul would have an opportunity to perhaps do more for his brother. Tomorrow he would be going to church.

Before he could dwell on what he may say to the abolitionist ministers, Paul had other work to do. The sun set at 6:15 p.m. in New York, and once it did, his new employer, Abraham Strauss, planned to meet him at his clothing shop. "After Sabbath,"

Strauss told Paul when he wandered over to talk to him on late Friday afternoon. "It has to be after Sabbath."

Paul waved goodbye to Smiles at the bottom of their tenement; they had released their hands many blocks earlier lest a familiar face spot them engaged in a taboo act, and they walked more stiffly, barely even acknowledging each other. But Paul stood by for quite some time near the steps, gazing into Smiles's eyes, a silly grin on his face, until finally she said, "Paul, you's gots to goes."

In early April the sun's descent triggered a rapid burst of cooler air. He retraced his steps, back to the clothing district, along a street filling up with masses of white souls seeking rapid inebriation amid the clamor that surrounded them. He walked quickly; African Americans did not belong here.

Abraham Strauss greeted him with a suffocating hug and a huge smile that lit up his musty shop. A few candles illuminated rows of hanging shirts and scattered boxes. "Sabbath is a mixed blessing," he said to Paul, as he shuffled him into the cluttered back room. "On the one hand, it's a day of rest, when we don't have to work. On the other hand, all I do is think about work, and I can't actually do anything about it, so I am stressed all day! Hardly what God likely intended! But anyway, let's go through the books and plan your big day on Monday. I have several boxes of clothes all set for you to bring to the Negro districts. I want to review how to haggle. You seemed very naive about it when we talked last week. But it's what we do."

Like Izzy, he talked quickly, and moved in a haphazard way, leaping from one idea and task to another.

"When is Izzy getting back?" Paul asked him.

"Well, I hope before the war starts," Abe said. "They say Virginia is staying with the Union as long as the other Abe doesn't try to take back his forts. But if our president does take the forts back, which he should and will do, then Virginia's not a good place for a New York Jew to be, especially if he still has some of my merchandise. He will have to hightail it out of there! And your friend Izzy can't hightail himself out of a bathroom, let alone a hostile state. Which means that he will likely have to leave my clothes behind. Ugg."

Abe marched into his office and pointed to a spot near the wall. "Those four boxes are for you. Inventory the clothes, know the sizes and prices, know how much wiggle room you have to drop costs if you have to. Remember, the closer to production cost you sell this crap at, the less you make, and the less happy I am. You don't want me to be unhappy. With this war falling on our laps, I need these new markets to work out, and I'm banking on the Negroes to be our big new customers. Hopefully, it will be a quick war, as they all predict, but I'm still bound to lose business, and that I don't like."

"I started looking at your financial information," Paul said, as Abe sat at his desk and shuffled through a pile of papers. "I think that some of the margins can be reduced with a little bit of accounting prowess. What I am proposing—"

Abraham Strauss lifted his head and cut him off. "Son," he said softly, "I don't care. Fix my books. Do whatever you think is best. Just don't talk to me about it. Go through those boxes first. You need to know what you're selling Monday, and you have to be an expert in every sock and pair of pants you are peddling. Pull the clothes out and breathe them in and know them like they're your own two balls. And this is your time to ask questions, to write stuff down, to label things. Because once you hit the streets, if you hesitate or are not totally sure what in the hell you are doing, those people are going to find someone else to buy clothes from. Got it?"

Paul nodded. And Abe put his head back down, buried in piles of paper.

The night progressed slowly. Paul was both exacerbated and excited. Abe told him to keep it simple. So he priced the larger items twenty cents higher than the base cost, and the smaller ones ten cents higher. That way he would know just how much he could drop the price during a haggle. Abe also showed him quickly how to size people's waists and seams, how to find the right shirt for the right person, and shared some tricks to help buyers believe that they really needed "that perfect item," that it was a bargain, and other devices that a seasoned clothing sales- man had learned over decades of haggling.

Then, a little before midnight, Abe, who had been unpacking more boxes and hanging sundry items across his store, handed Paul a bag of change. "That's two dollars," he said. "The first installment of what I hope will be a small fortune for you. That's for doing my books, whatever the hell it is you are doing with them. Eventually, if I see some profit from your little accounting games, I'll certainly give you more. And if you do a good job on Monday, there will be a lot more coming your way. You bring that cart to me first thing Monday morning, I will load it up with your clothes, then you can head up town with your wares. Get back to me before sundown with your money and unsold merchandise, and I can load you up again the next day. If you need more prep time tomorrow, I'm here all day. But go home now. I don't need a dead salesman, and that's what happens to Negroes who cross through Five Points when those white bastards are too drunk."

The next day was Sunday, April 7. Paul yawned; he had slept only a few hours, and his mind buzzed with anticipation. He woke up and put on his blue-and-white striped suit. The blue flower, still full of vibrant life, made him feel special.

"You looks so fine," Smiles said to him as she stood up and stared. "I wish I coulds attack you here and now," she whispered with a devious smile. "Now you's go and be good, don't be a dumbass!"

"I promise," he said, staring at her, not wanting to leave. The crying baby finally pushed him away.

A warm, misty rain hovered over New York's muddy streets. They were empty but for a few families rushing from here to there. The thick smell of human waste lingered in the air. Paul walked quickly. His destination lay only a few blocks away.

For a while, he stared at Shiloh Presbyterian Church. It was 8:00 a.m. Morning services were about to begin.

"I know there's no God," Paul whispered to himself, as he slid between a line of well-dressed African Americans filling the small, wooden enclave. They were happy and smiling, from small families to the very old, bowing their heads to him, a stranger they did not know, and he bowing back. "But if there is one, I hope He's here today and He's got my back."

Reverend Pennington led the service today, which primarily consisted of songs and prayers that irked Paul in their simplistic and ritualistic monotony. His mind wandered, staring at crosses and the bloody body of a white Jesus painted and sculpted everywhere the eyes could see. Not having ever been in a church before, he contemplated how this race of oppressed people had found solace in so empty an institution and belief system as the Christian church. If anything, he knew, it distracted them from being more assertive and hypnotized them into accepting both their enslavement and their oppression, promising them a better fate after the horror they endured on earth. What a convenient tool for the white masters to toss around their necks! Yet the African Americans immersed themselves in blind faith and refused to step beyond its encasing walls. It was just sad. As the service progressed, Paul only grew angrier and more determined to fight against this vestige of white oppression.

When the reverend did speak, though, his words were inspiring, even if he had to sprinkle everything he said with "As God says," and "So said Christ," and "As we see in scripture," and other such nonsense. He talked about a holy war that may spread upon these lands. "And it is a war that will be bloody and horrid, as all wars are, but as Jesus lay witness, it will be a war of redemption, of salvation, of freedom from bondage. It will be the war we all must fight to undo the wrath of Lucifer that the Southern masters have wrought upon us."

"Halleluiah," the congregants all rang, whooping and hollering as the man spoke.

"They talk of compromise," he continued. "There can be no compromise. They talk of dissolving our Union so slavery can persevere in one part and freedom in the other. There can be no dissolving our Union. They talk of fighting for our pride and our nation. To that I say, amen! Know now, my Negro brothers and sisters, there will come a time in this war when father Abraham asks of us to make the most ultimate sacrifice—to take up arms and fight for this nation, to risk our lives so we can save our race. Both Reverend Garnet and I have already taken steps to make sure that the Negro man can fight in this war. We are working with the president to assure that there will be Negro troops. There is and will always be opposition to that pursuit. But I am telling you all, in front of the Father, the Son, and the Holy Spirit, that we will persevere, for our souls are strong, and our wills even stronger. And to that I say to one and all, amen!"

The tiny church erupted in a chorus of jubilant cries. Even Paul was swept away by the minister's words, that much more eager to lend his skills and passion to a cause that lay close to his heart. If an antipathy to the church and all it represented still festered within him, he at least had some satisfaction knowing that some men were using the pulpit to promote anger at the white slaveholders.

Paul wandered off to the side pews as the ministers greeted congregants after the service ended. The hugs and chats and handshakes went on for almost an hour. Reverend Pennington, who had been with the church for many years before relocating to Connecticut (apparently being pushed out by several church members who resented his radicalism, especially his protest over segregated streetcars), received the most adulation, as many in the crowd sought to give the man their greetings after several years of absence.

Finally, a well-dressed boy asked Paul his name and escorted him to a back room that was laden with books and a statue of a black Christ. Within a few minutes, the two ministers, laughing with each other as though they were old friends and not the bitter enemies Paul knew them to be, followed him in.

"Sit down, sit down," said Reverend Garnet, a smaller, more bubbly man than the tall, stern Pennington, who stood by the wall and was largely removed from the conversation. "I heard many great things about you, Paul. Maybe the next Frederick Douglass even! A man of great intelligence. An escaped slave from Virginia. And when we heard all of that, we knew we had to meet this man. I will tell you, I am already impressed, son. Already impressed." He smiled wide and shook Paul's hand firmly.

"I appreciate the opportunity," Paul responded. "I do think that I have a lot to offer. I have read a great deal about the movement. I can write quickly and well. I enjoy speaking and teaching. There is so much I want to do to help end the scourge of slavery, and the bigotry that I see even in New York."

"Amen to that," said Pennington from the wall, not paying much attention to the conversation. "Bigotry up North, that needs to be on the list of what we must fight for. It's too often neglected by our white friends."

"First things first, James," Garnet said. "First we end slavery, we join the war, and we become part of the solution. Our contribution to the cause will go a long way to achieving the other goal." He turned back to Paul. "Have you met Louis Tappan?"

"Not yet, sir," Paul responded. "Although I would like to. I am happy to engage in any role you think is appropriate for me."

They spoke for several more minutes, Reverend Garnet discussing some of the projects in which Paul might participate, none of which seemed quite as grand or worthy as he had envisioned.

Still, he smiled and demonstrated his interest in taking on any role the men felt to be appropriate.

Suddenly, quiet until now, Reverend Pennington twisted around and looked into Paul's eyes, almost menacingly. "What church do you belong to, Paul?" he asked.

Paul paused for a moment. "None yet," he said. "Frankly, since arriving here in the winter, I've been spending most of my time trying to eat, work, and stay alive." He laughed a bit, but Pennington did not. The reverend stepped a bit closer, his face some mere inches from Paul's.

"Wouldn't you want God as your shepherd in your struggles? I don't understand, son? Do you intend to fight your crusade without Christ by your side?"

Again, Paul paused. What was he getting at? "Frankly, sir," he finally said. "Where I come from, God and the church are not exactly allies in the cause of Negro freedom. In fact, religion is more a tool of our oppressors, and I have not been drawn to it for that reason. Please take no offense. I am very impressed by what you have achieved through your pulpit. Were it not for all the discussion of God and Christ, it would be a perfect vehicle for our people's escape from captivity."

As soon as he uttered those words, Paul knew it was a mistake. He tried to backpedal but did not have time. The two of them pounced.

"Are you an atheist, son?" Reverend Garnet snapped at him.

Paul shook a bit. He tried to talk, but words escaped him. He saw that these two men were irate.

"He is, Henry, he is indeed," said Reverend Pennington, who paced across the room. "I smelt it in him. He is exactly what we do not need in our movement. He will subvert it for sure. Frederick has done enough damage. This boy seems far more dangerous."

"I'm not," Paul pleaded. "I'm not, I promise. That's not what I meant at all. That all came out wrong. What I meant to say is that in the South sometimes religion is used by the very people who enslave us. But you and I, all of us, we are fighting the same battle. Does it matter what we believe in? What God we worship or don't worship? Is that really important, given the immensity of the sins that are being perpetrated upon us down South, and even here? I want to help with the struggle."

Henry Garnet shook his head. "Yes, it matters a great deal, son. We will not have an atheist in our ranks. A glib-talking atheist is nothing short of the devil himself. Son, are you sent here by Lucifer?"

"No!" Paul shouted, sweat started to bead on his forehead. "No, I am with you. Frederick Douglass, I'm sure, has the same doubts. I have heard his speeches. I know he questions how religion is used by our Southern oppressors to justify their vile acts. How can you not, when you come from the South, where the slave-owners quote Jesus and God every time they snap a whip into our backs, every time they say that our bondage is endorsed by the Bible itself, every time they tell us not to worry about our horrid lives because as long as we are good and subservient slaves God will reward us in the afterlife? Is it so terrible that I would harbor some doubt?"

"It is indeed," whispered Pennington, still smiling, and nodding horizontally. "You know, son, I knew Frederick Douglass when he was like you, when he escaped from his bondage. Did you know that I was the minister who performed his wedding, right here in this church? I know this much about him, even then. He knew that God ruled supreme. He escaped from the South like you, he heard the words of false prophets as did you, but never did he question the power and omnipotence of Jesus Christ, our Lord and savior. Never did he blaspheme the name of our lord!"

Paul sweated, turning from one man to the next. He could sense that the situation was spiraling out of control. What had he said to instigate this madness?

Reverend Garnet agreed with his friend. "You are not Frederick Douglass, my misguided boy. Your words are too smooth. You have no story that will inspire anyone. And now you speak in the devil's tongue. How would you presume to help us when you don't even accept the sanctity of Jesus?" His voice grew louder and crasser the more he spoke.

"Let me explain, please," Paul said, now drenched in sweat, his suit soaked.

"Get out of my church!" Garnet yelled. "Get out before I tear you from limb to limb. Get out!"

Paul stared at him for a moment and then turned, first walking, then running.

"If I see you in this city again, I will make sure you are killed!" he thought he heard one of them say, a mere echo against the din of his rapidly pounding feet.

Into the rain he darted, running as fast as he could, hyperventilating, his mind twirling in an uncontrolled tempest that consumed his every thought and emotion. He could not see or hear; he was moving forward, but to where he did not know. He was not sure where to go. Faces and voices shot by; he was oblivious to everything. What had just happened? How did it escalate so quickly? He breathed deeply. He was dizzy. Paul did not know what to do.

Before he knew it, he was climbing up steps, two at a time, and then three. And then he reached a door and pushed it open.

Smiles's face turned toward the door, and her grin quickly dissolved. "Paul?" she asked him, demonstrating a visage of pure fear. She was cuddling the baby. LB was by her side, his arm over her shoulder.

The image of the two of them together, the baby's cries, the stench, this horrible place in which he lived, his utter powerlessness, reverberating shouts from the mouths of the ministers—it all congealed and made him dizzy. He said something, he was not sure what. He needed her right now, he needed her forever, and yet could not have her, because there were rules, there was the ruse; he had to watch what he said, watch how he acted, pretend he was someone else, all in the name of the white master.

"What is wrong with this world?" he cried out. "Why can't I be the man I want to be? Why do I have to play so many games and fight so many fights just to be a man? What the hell is wrong with this goddamned world?"

Staring at these two friends who he loved so much, and not knowing what to do or say, he turned and ran away. Her voice trailed him, but he did not acknowledge it. He wanted to so badly but could not. So, he just ran. Past all these faceless people, across a barren desert, into the woods, up the mountain, filled with sweat and rain, warm from a piercing sun, his mind not able to stay still, he ran.

"Why?" he yelled out at his favorite tree. "Why in the hell is everyone a son of a bitch? Who is there left in this world with a brain and a heart? Why won't anyone let me be me?"

And then he broke down and cried, hysterically at first, and then in spurts. He was alone, isolated, in a jungle no different than his pear trees, not the savior he had always imagined. He thought about his job on Monday, the one that excited him so. After decades of reading and writing, developing a financial prowess that enabled him to manage a highly profitable farm, of mastering history and philosophy, he, Paul Conklin, would have to sell secondhand pants to a bunch of African Americans who likely would buy nothing. That was the job that excited him? Tears flew from his eyes. And then he thought of Smiles, the girl he could not have, a love he could not show. In a universe that could neither accept nor understand him, she did, and she loved him for everything he was. All he wanted was her. And yet, that too was stripped from him. So, he sat beneath his tree, tears rolling down his eyes, until finally, after a few deep breaths, he pulled himself together, gaining solace from his favorite tree.

"I guess," he said. "I'll just keep playing the game. What can I do? You have to know the rules." And he laughed and said to the tree, "What can I tell you that you don't know already?"

With that, he lifted himself and walked down the hill. So, things didn't work out in the church. There would be other doors to open, other opportunities yet to come. Why did he have to feign membership in a club he found to be reprehensible? Those men, those alleged men of God, were nothing but cruel to him. Why would he work with them? Abe, he was different, and perhaps that was Paul's best path to success, selling clothes. "Izzy does it," Paul reminded himself. "And look how smart Izzy is."

So, he lifted his head and hurried down the hill, back to the sea of white, back to all the pretense and ridicule. All he knew was that he wanted to see Smiles's face. That is what propelled him forward. If he doubted everything else, it was that one thing, his love for her, he knew to be the ultimate path to his happiness and success.

But, as is often true of forbidden love, it could also be his dagger, aimed right into the deepest part of his heart. For better or worse, Paul was smitten, and thus was he trapped, a fate that would soon be apparent to a boy who only wanted to be the man he knew he always could, but that the rules and vices of a hostile world refused to allow him to be.

20

I was traveling along the narrow strait between Scylla and Charybdis, knowing that my options were limited. Both paths were dangerous, and I could not navigate directly between them, so, I asked, should I move closer to the one or the other? Like Odysseus, I had but one path toward home, and thus I had to make a choice. On the left was Scylla, the six-headed beast, who, should I drift too near her, would snatch and bite off my head, taking from me my intelligence and values. Unwilling to relinquish that part of me, I took the more treacherous route near Charybdis, the enormous whirlpool that swallows ships whole, confident that with my skills and faculties I could get by. But despite all my efforts, it sucked me in, and I am in it now, spiraling down, unable to pull myself out, and unsure of what horrid fate it will take me. I long to be with you, Brother. I crave all that we had on our farm and in our lives with each other. Now the dice of war has been cast, and our fates are placed in the hands of others. But up here, in my oasis in my self-made hell, I will miss it all, as I twist down farther and farther into the deep black sea that has seized me and grants no opportunity for redemption.

Paul placed his pen upon the ground as he leaned on the large oak tree he called his friend. He couldn't deliver this letter to Luke, but he pretended that Luke might read it and say, "Brother, you should never have made the journey in the first place." Maybe Luke was right. Paul was alone and abandoned, forlorn by all those he knew, having retreated up to his mountain and now forced to hide here perhaps forever. He was hungry. He was cold. He had but two options: remain up here out of harm's way, or flee the city. But if he ran away and left New York, as they all told him he must, he would have to start from scratch, and certainly he would never see her again, the woman whose face and goodness swam incessantly through his veins every moment of every day. No! He preferred to die than meet that fate. So, he wrote to his brother, and wondered how it had all come to this.

His banishment from the world started a week prior, a day after his encounter with the two ministers.

By Monday morning, Paul wasn't able to shove the incident at Shiloh Church out of his mind. He and LB pushed their loaded carts uptown through a river of hustling bodies, chatting about Paul's predicament. Today was Paul's first day on the job, his grand opening in the African American district where he hoped to wow them and sell clothes. But his mind was on yesterday's melee at the church.

"You's goes in there like a bull who wants to tells these people that you knows better than them, and they ain't gonna take kindly to that," LB lectured him, as they meandered through a row of concrete tenements shoved so close together than they blocked all sun on the street. The complexion here was dark; African Americans of all stripes traversed the busy street, some pushing carts, others leaping over puddles and making haste, lonely souls mixed with larger groups laughing and talking. Paul had slid through this neighborhood many times on his quest to the northern Manhattan hills, but he had never stopped for even a moment to glance at its vitality.

"These preachers, they ain't gonna listen to some arrogant young Negro who then tells them that the very purpose of their life, their worship of God and Christ, that it's not's nothing more than the white man's tool. I mean, Paul, thinks about what you done, and then take their side for a second."

"I know," Paul said. "I know. Believe me. But it just strikes me as insane that these people can be so intelligent in one way, so forward-thinking, and yet attach themselves to this myth, and not even realize that the deception of religion is one of the major reasons that their people are so docile and oppressed."

"You's is doing it again, my friend," LB laughed, slapping Paul on his shoulder. "You best keep quiet, and then nothing like that will be spilling out from that brain of yours. You's gots to know when it's best to stay quiet and nod, and when you can open your mouth. It can't stays opens all the time!"

The two men parted ways and traversed different parts of the neighborhood. Paul pushed his old wooden cart along an uneven dirt street, calling out for people to come look at his wares. He barely looked up as the cart's wheels entrapped themselves on rocks and in puddles and cervices. He was not aggressive in his salesmanship; he did not stop people on the street or yell directly at any passersby. He just continually repeated, "Top clothes from downtown, good prices, come take a look," just like Abe had rehearsed with him. Other than a few eyes that pointed his way, no one migrated too close. And when his cart wedged itself into a puddle of mud soon after noon, Paul spent an hour unloading much of his stock of clothes and then reloading it, just to get his cart up and moving again, and by then a gnawing hunger consumed him.

He searched for LB, who had wandered several streets away pushing his cart of straw and buttermilk and having some better luck. They stopped for a moment and ate a small sandwich that Smiles had prepared for them and each gulped a swig of the buttermilk. It was chilly, but piercing sunshine struck them when they escaped from the interminable jungle of shaded concrete, making it just warm enough to feel comfortable. "Nothing?" LB asked him.

"Nothing," said Paul. "I got a few pants muddy. But not a single person came close enough to even look. I didn't even have an opportunity to wow them with my haggling skills!"

"Ha!" LB said to him. "That's where I's thought you would lose them. Follow me, Paul. Maybe I's can helps you a bit."

LB proved to be a bit more adept at attracting customers, accosting groups of people and pointing them to Paul's cart, his jovial manner and inviting smile persuading many to at least take a look. Paul then tried to make a sale. He spoke formally and stiffly, as LB told him when every single potential customer walked away with nothing. "You sounds like a schoolteacher telling them whats to do."

"That's how Abe told me to do it."

"Lighten up, son," LB told him with a smile. "You's got to look like you's is enjoying yourself and that you is friends to all these people."

But nothing Paul did seem to change the outcome. Not Monday, Tuesday, or Wednesday.

"When Izzy gets back, he'll help you out," Abe told him Wednesday afternoon, April 10, after giving Abe nothing but a bunch of muddied unsold slacks. "It's a hard business! Don't think because you're some genius that you know how to sell clothes. It's not going to be that easy."

When was Izzy coming back? With all the tension and talk of war rippling through the air, louder than ever, with newly formed Irish regiments marching through the streets and the New York Seventh Infantry conducting exercises on Riker's Island, with President Lincoln threatening to reinforce Fort Sumpter off the coast of South Carolina, Izzy's stay in Virginia was precarious at best. Why was he still there?

On Wednesday night Smiles had a respite from baby-watching; Sarah and John both came home from work and wanted to take the baby for a walk to Sarah's sister on the other side of Five Points. It was a warm and calm night. Smiles eyed Paul, who nodded, and the two stood to leave.

"Where are you two's going?" Bobby Jeffrey asked them. He had been sitting quietly in the corner, as was his habit, piling up a few stacks of coins, likely the loot from today's matchbook sales.

LB laughed. "They's probably going to fetch me a piece of chicken across the street. Smiles owes me that much for waking me ups last night with that baby, and Paul probably taking her there!"

BJ stood, his face uncharacteristically irate. He pointed his finger at Paul. "I seens him holding your wife's hands," he called out loudly. "And the word's out about him. He's an atheist. An adulterer. A sinner. A devil in men's clothes. May he rot in hell! There's be a bounty on his head. And only because I is a good Christian is the only reason I's not killing him myself, although may God be my witness, I shoulds."

Silence swept through the room. No one knew what to say; this sudden deluge of rage came from nowhere. Paul felt as though BJ had stabbed him in the chest. *Who saw us holding hands?*, is what he wanted to toss back before disputing it. Had they been seen? To Paul, that was all he heard; the chatter about atheist and bounty slid by him. But LB didn't much care about hand-holding. He immediately sensed something far more menacing in Bobby's caustic warning.

LB stood and looked at BJ. "What do you mean's by a bounty?" he asked.

BJ said nothing. He just flashed a stare in Paul's direction and marched out.

The next day, April 11, Paul quickly found out what Bobby Jeffrey meant.

They were pushing carts silently uptown. LB said nothing. His face was twisted into a frown. Paul did not know how to breach the subject of what had happened the night before. Since then, LB was uncharacteristically quiet and cold. So, Paul had to say something.

"Are you OK?" Paul finally asked his old friend when they were close to reaching their destination. Paul felt almost paralyzed by anxiety, especially when LB did not respond. In fact, James just pushed his cart farther ahead when Paul asked the question.

"James," Paul cried out, leaving his own cart and running in front of his friend's. "We have to talk. We can't leave it that way. I am sorry. I know I put us in danger by holding Smiles's hand, but we were so far away, I didn't think anyone would see us."

"Damned right you's did," LB shot back.

"I'm sorry," he said. "I didn't want to hurt anyone. It was my idea, not hers, I promise you."

LB paused for a moment. He then looked into Paul's eyes with a glance of both gentleness and hurt. "Does you love her, Paul?"

"Yes," Paul uttered.

LB simply shook his head. "Fuck, Paul," he said. "Fuck you. You knows she's my wife! You know what she's been through's. You's knows what it could mean to us if they think you's being adulterous with my wife, don't you, through your thick damned skull?"

"She's not really your wife," Paul said. "And I love her. I love her beyond anything I could have ever imagined possible. And I think she loves me too. We were careful. We haven't done anything more than holding hands once or twice, not even a kiss, or even a hug. I don't want to hurt you."

"She is my wife, Paul," he retorted. "And I loves her too. And that's where you's and me don't seem to be on the same page. I don't wants anything to happens to her. I swore to protect her, always. And now you puts her in danger."

"How can you love her?" Paul asked.

LB hit him hard on the side of his head. "Why you talking likes that? 'Cause I's an old man, and she is so young? I gots a news flash for you, Paul. There's lots of ways to loves someone in this world. And I loves that girl as much as one man could ever loves another person."

Paul, nodding, walked up to his friend and smothered him with a hug. "I'm sorry," he uttered again. "I really am."

LB nodded and lifted his head. "It's OK," he said. "I knows she loves you's. I's always has known. But you is so dumb that I fear for her safety when you's is with her. Look, Paul, I just gots to make sure that girl is happy and safe. And I don't know if you's capable of that, not yet, not now."

And then, within a few seconds, LB's words became prescient.

Paul spotted a small group of African American men approaching them from uptown. The street on which they stood was relatively quiet, nestled in an isolated and shaded outcropping from the neighborhood. And these men were clearly walking in their direction. Paul did not say anything for a moment. But as they quickened their pace and moved closer, he turned LB's head and showed him.

"What the shit?" LB muttered.

Paul did not know what to do or think. He had learned to stay away from white men, especially the Irish, when they approached him in a group. His instinct was to flee. But now, this was different. Perhaps they wanted to buy clothes? And then it came to him.

"The bounty," he whispered to LB, who instantly agreed.

One of the men, dressed in tattered clothes and a top hat, looking close to fifty or more in age, ran in the front. He called out to Paul, "You best stay still as justice is about to be dispensed."

The men fanned out to surround the two friends. A soft wind blew, and the sun was obscured by fleeting dark clouds. It was cold. But Paul started to sweat.

With Paul and LB paralyzed, the men, now encircling them, looked at them grimly. The older man in a hat spoke again. "Paul, you are hereby informed, by word of Louis Tappan and Minister Garnet, that you are given two choices. As an adulterer, and atheist, and blasphemer, we, by God's grace, give you one day to leave this city and never to return again. Or you can put your faith in Satan and try to fight us off and try to runs away. But if you fight us, we will kill you, and God will smile on us for that deed."

Was this all because of what he had said at the church? Had the two ministers sent these men to chase him out of New York? Or was there more to it? Perhaps they had caught him with Smiles, or he had done something wrong of which he was not even aware. Regardless, Paul knew one thing: this was the bounty to which BJ had alluded, and these people aimed to harm him if he did not comply with their dictate.

Paul stared at the leader. His heart raced. "What about this man?" he asked, pointing to LB. "He didn't do anything wrong. Can he leave in peace?"

The men all looked at each other and nodded. The man in charge, in a quiet and dignified tone, implored LB to take his cart and make haste. LB, peering peevishly at Paul, nodded and then took off, pushing his cart downtown, away from their destination. Soon he was out of sight.

One of the men approached Paul and hit him hard, right in the gut. "That is for my Lord, Jesus Christ," the man uttered. The others followed suit, landing one blow after another. Several fists bashed into his jaw, and he tasted blood trickling down his throat. His mind swam around. Flashbacks of that night on the farm shook his brain, as he stood by fecklessly, lacking all power and strength to resist the vicious passions of his accosters. He fell to the ground, not able to even fight back. And then the blows ceased.

The air was silent but for his hyperventilating lungs. He looked up at them through swollen eyes, hearing words like "praise the Lord," and "let justice be done."

And then, sucking in some wind that he knew lay within him, he pulled himself up, pushed one of the smaller men hard to the ground, and took off. He ran fast, blood and sweat marking his path along the uneven dirt road. Every muscle in his legs and gut hurt, every step caused knives to stab him. But he ran. Turning a corner, he fell flat on his face, tripping over a pothole and landing in a pile of what smelled like flowing excrement.

He looked back; the men were still pursuing him. And so, he pushed himself up and ran even faster, turning on one street, and then another, until the image of them faded far behind him.

He had arrived at Five Points, the streets much busier, the stares from strangers that much more piercing. Where was LB? What should he do? He limped forward, trembling, hurting. He could hardly even think. What had happened? What had he done to prompt such a sadistic reaction? He wandered up the steps, holding onto the wall lest he fall down, and pushed into his room. Smiles sat there with the baby, and she screamed when she saw him.

"Paul!" she cried out. "My Gods, my Paul, what they done's to you?"

She placed the baby down and darted over to him, as he crumbled to the ground, crying hysterically, hardly able to move. "What they done's to you?" she asked again. "What they done to my love?" She placed his head on her lap, using the baby's blanket to wipe away the flowing blood. She kissed him all over his face, rubbing his head, and then cleaning his face some more. He could do no more than cry, so thankful to be in her lap, to be at peace.

LB meandered up soon after. He shoved open the door and saw his friend. He just shook his head.

"Who done this, James?" Smiles asked him. "Who done this to Paul?"

"Is he OK?" LB asked.

Smiles nodded to the contrary. "He's hurting, James. He just cries and cries; he won't even talks. I don't know whats to do. We have to take off his clothes and see where they hurt him. We has to gets him help, a doctor, anyone. Who done this, James? Was it the people who been terrorized us before?"

"No," he said, sitting by his friend's side. "It was Negroes. Peoples sent by the church, I reckon. And they was dead bent on killings him. Let's get his clothes off and see what we's can does."

But that was not to be.

The baby howled its high-pitched shrieks, kicking its legs on the floor.

And then a flurry of footsteps rushed up their stairs. The door burst open. The men had returned.

"You leaves him alone!" Smiles cried out, standing up and walking right up to these men, some of whom now held clubs. She shoved one hard, the one wearing a hat. "Ain't we gots enough trouble that now you's gots to give us more? It's not enough to be whipped and tortured and raped by every white man who thinks we's no more than a piece of property? Now you's all got to get into the act? You walk out of here right now, or I swear, I will kills every single one of you devils!"

Other than Paul's intermittent whimpering and the baby's interminable shrieks, the room dropped into a dense silence. The older man with the hat then spoke to Smiles. "Are you his concubine?" he asked.

"You takes that back," she said, shoving him in the chest. "I ain't nobody's whore. I is married to that man there, and I is friends with that good, decent, wonderful man there, the man you felt you's needed to try to kill so you could satisfy some bounty you gots or something. Well, this man's only sin is that he talks out his rear end halfs the time and that he cares too much for this damned world to know well enough to lets it alone without trying to fix it. It's you's that's the whores, the whores of whoever told you to do this devilish deed to such a good man's as this one be. You ain't no better than the slaveholders who takes justice in your own hands and beats up the innocent because you thinks you's is God Himself. Let me tell you this, each and every one of you's. You touch this man again, and if I don't kills you, God will. God will punish you for you's all sins. He ain't one to be fond about people who take justice in their hands, especially when they is dead wrong in what they does!"

The men were silent. Smiles breathed hard, her vicious stare digging into one man after another. "You all gets out now!"

But before anyone could respond, another pounding of footsteps ascended the steps. Outside the door stood half a dozen white men, with more and more coming up every minute. The two groups stood face-to-face, with Paul, LB, Smiles and the baby between them. Paul stopped crying, and now he sat up. The baby wailed even louder. Smiles turned around and picked her up, rocking the baby in her arms.

This new group of men, a few of the Irish firemen who claimed hegemony over this district, insisted that the African American men leave immediately. The man with the hat looked at Paul, then at Smiles, then at the firemen, and finally gestured for his men to retreat. Quietly they descended the steps and faded away. From behind this group of white men stepped Collin Ryan. He glared sharply at LB. "You all have to leave," he quietly uttered.

"What do you means?" LB shot back. "We ain't done nothing wrong. Paul been beat up by those thugs. He's hurting. He needs help. We is the victims here."

Collin took in a deep breath. "Look," he said with an inflection of understanding, "we can't have this type of disruption in my buildings. I have gone out on a limb to even let Negroes live here. I've done all I could to help you people. But when I took him in," he said, pointing to Paul, "I knew that I was taking a chance. I know he's beat up. I can see it. But I'm guessing he did something to deserve it. Look, James, you are a good man. I wish you and your wife could stay. But my hand is being pushed. There is a war about to commence. This place is not going to be the same. There are a lot of people angry that I even let you in, and now even angrier that a group of Negro hoodlums invaded this neighborhood to go after one of their own. I don't know what's going on, James. But you have to leave. I will give you a week to gather your things and be gone."

Paul, who was now sitting, watching all of this unfold, finally spit out some words. "Kick me out," he said, barely audible between his swollen lips and a mouth full of blood. "Let them stay. Kick me out."

Collin nodded no. "I wish I could. You are the cause of all this trouble, and I don't want to hurt these people. But no, I'm sorry. I can't have Negroes in this building anymore. No one here is going to tolerate it. You all have to go."

The white men scattered away. Collin told LB that he would find him a place to live and that he had a plush job he could offer Smiles. "Ernest Biggelow, who as you know is the leader of the Sixth Ward, and the captain of Engine Company 21, he needs a nanny for his kids. John Campion gave Biggelow your wife's name, and Biggelow recently lost his help, and his wife is not up to the task—you know how these things are, James. It would be a good life for her, a steady income, a place to live. You can visit her there. With the war coming, this may be the best gift you two can have."

Smiles nodded no, vehemently. She started to cry. LB put his hand on her shoulder and whispered for her to stay quiet.

"What's about me and Paul?" LB asked.

Collin sucked in a puff of air. "I can't help Paul. From what I hear, there are others who want him dead; the list just keeps growing. Reverend Tappan is not in town. He is in Washington with other leaders of the movement, but I will speak for him to say that we are no longer willing to help Paul. It probably would be best if he leaves the city. I'll see what I can do for you, James. We'll find you something."

Smiles cried even louder. Paul lay back on the ground. His head was spinning, and he felt faint. *What have I done?* He peered at Smiles, whose inviting eyes bathed him in a soothing air of compassion. He wished he could kiss her. He dreamed of running away with her and leaving this horrid, unforgiving world in their wake. But he could not. His mind became blank, and soon enough, he passed out.

Two days later, word came that Southern forces on the coast of South Carolina, under the leadership of General Beauregard, bombarded Fort Sumpter into submission on Friday, April 12. General Anderson, the fort's commander, surrendered the following day. The war was now real. President Lincoln declared that he would use all force necessary to subdue the rebellion.

Paul quietly limped uptown to recover his cart later in the evening, when there was little chance to be assailed again by black bounty hunters or Irish mobs or whoever else wanted to harm him. After hours of searching, he and LB found remnants of it: two wheels badly mangled and few shattered pieces of wood. Every item of clothing had been stolen, save for one dirtied white sock that they found skewered by a large splinter of wood.

Now Paul had yet another enemy, Abraham Strauss, who berated and threatened him when he explained what had transpired. "It's bad enough there is a war hitting us, and I've lost my Southern business. But now a jackass has lost hundreds of dollars of merchandise! Do you know what this means? Do you have any idea what you cost me? You will be paying me back for this, Paul. You will be paying me back, or your friend Izzy will be paying it back for you. Now get the hell out of my sight!"

There were no goodbyes. Smiles was whisked away one day when Paul was wandering around looking for his clothes. Ernest Biggelow needed her immediately, and they could not wait for Paul to return. Besides, LB kept him away from Smiles, beseeching him to leave her alone. "Let her makes her new life, Paul," he said. "If you loves her, you will lets her be. She's is my wife, my charge. You needs to make your own life now."

On April 15, that Monday, President Lincoln called for seventy-five thousand volunteers to invade the South and bring the renegade states back into the Union. Mayor Wood declared that

New York would also secede, but his words were drowned out by the tens of thousands of New Yorkers who flocked to the make-shift recruiting stations, ready to join the fight. A few days later, the New York Seventh regiment would leave for Washington—part of General George McClellan's army, the biggest and most competently led fighting force the country had ever seen.

It was on that day, after shaking LB's hand, that Paul mean-dered up to his oak tree high on New York's hills, looking over the city and watching this nation prepare for war. He wrote Luke his letter and wondered if his brother's fate was any better than his own. At that moment, Virginia was still part of the Union. They would vote to join the Confederacy on Wednesday, April 17, although Paul did not know that, at least not yet. He drank the last few sips of buttermilk that LB had left with him, and he sat all alone, wondering how to escape from the whirlpool that was pulling him down fast. All he could think about was her. And, once again, he started to cry.

21

Except for one chilly night, when the temperature dipped into the forties and brisk winds blew up the valley from the south, late April proved to be an ideal time to plant grapes.

Luke marched up his line of twigs, inspecting each one. The irrigation ditches he had personally dug this winter now caressed his delicate French plants with the animating sediment that flowed from Old Rag. Just a few remnants of snow spotted the Blue Ridge range, with Old Rag largely devoid of any sign that winter had struck its tenacious rocky core. The rivers flowed heavy, the pond brimming with frigid water waiting to awaken hibernating trees that stood ready to produce an abundance of fruit.

"Why you so interested in making the harvest good this year?" Matt had asked him earlier that day. "You know, bubblehead, all we is doing is growing stuff for the Confederacy so they can eat well and bamboozle the Northern armies and make sure that slavery don't ever go away. We got to give half our fruit to the army; that's what the doctor told me. Don't it make more sense to have a bad year and not help them win their war?"

Indeed, after spending a week with Izzy, who escaped back up North as soon as Sumpter's guns shattered the fragile Union and instigated a civil war, and after reading Paul's letter and breaking down in tears, Matt battled his own demons. Likely too many dinners with the doctor had convinced him that Virginia's cause was his cause too. But then Izzy ranted to him about the fallacy of the doctor's theories and told him about Paul's embrace of his freedom. And an overt disdain of him by members of the now officially sanctioned Company B of the Seventh Virginia Regiment, still known to most as the Washington Grays—whose younger members were the very boys who had taunted Matt for most of his life and who ridiculed him now for being a Northern sympathizer, a "Negro" lover, and a coward—convinced Matt that he really did not belong in this place and time, at least not with those fighting to preserve slavery.

"I feel sick about the whole thing," he told Luke. "I just want to run away and be with Paul. This ain't our fight, and it ain't our place."

Luke smiled, his mind and soul completely tranquil. External clamor did not shake his confidence in their sanctuary. He admired the infant twigs that would one day produce the region's best wine grapes as they glistened in the warm Virginia sun, the blurry Blue Ridge Mountains painting a fitting backdrop to their impending majesty.

"Once the first grape comes off these vines," he told his brother, his mouth smiling with every word, "the war will be over. The fate of our Union will be determined, at least at this moment in time. One side will win or the other. And then the victor will go its own way or not, perhaps the two sides will reconcile, another crisis will strike them, and a new crop of politicians will have to change course again, and so will it go, far into the future—men and boys killed for fleeting ideas, with the ultimate foundation of the slave state never really breaking; our fate out there will always be perilous compared to our safety within these walls. Whether we are slaves in Virginia, or we are free and tortured like Paul in New York, why does it matter so much? Our only salvation is here, on our farm. The grapes, Matt, will outlast all of the wars and battles that are but insignificant echoes of people's egos and their inner hate. The grapes will be here, and the wine from them perhaps will quiet those voices, at least for a time, as they raise their cups to us and say, 'Thank God for the makers of this brilliant cup of wine.' That is what I live for, Matt. These twigs mean more to the world than the ensuing battles out there."

Matt just shook his head, not swayed by his brother's lofty ideas. "You know that Jude, that fat louse of a jerk who used to make fun of me alongside Jessie? You know what he said to me the other day when I walk by him in town? He and his pals was wearing their gray uniforms and holding their guns, and he lifted that gun up in my face, and he says, 'Matt, you best watch your back, because if you and your Negroes so much as fart the wrong way, we will burn your farm down and kill every Negro who lives there.' That's what he says to me, just laughing with the others. And now, with this war, they got the guns and the excuse to do all the things they been threatening me with all these years. They may just come here one day and torch the place, and I got news for you, Luke, those sticks of yours that you call grape vines ain't going to survive the torching neither."

Luke laughed at his brother's naivety! "The doctor will never let them burn the farm down. This is where his daughter lives, and it is the most productive agricultural resource in the county. That was our plan all along, Matt. Once you tied the knot with Jessie, you would be protected. And you will be. That is why too our crop must flourish this year. Our ability to feed the Confederacy is another means of assuring our relevance and survival."

Matt vehemently shook his head. "That ain't what I want," he yelled. "None of them boys care about that; they know that the doctor is protecting me, and they think I am like a baby who can't do nothing on my own. So, they mock me for it. And what I got to say in response?"

Luke slid toward his brother, placing his right hand on Matt's shoulder. "That is exactly what you want, Matt. You already said you don't want to fight for the slaveholders. You won't have to. In a few weeks they will be marching out, to Warrenton and maybe Gainesville if what Peter says is accurate, and then they can be extracted from your mind. You will be here on the farm most of the time, a meaningful cog in the war machine, and far beyond the reach of their contempt."

"I don't want to be no cog in the war machine," Matt countered.

"Then do you want to go with them, to fight in the war?" Luke wondered, unsure in which direction Matt sought to posture himself. "Or are you upset that we will be helping the war at all? Because, Brother, you have to do one thing or the other."

Matt's face seemed unsettled to Luke. He could hardly utter a word. "I don't know what I want," he finally said. "I just want to be together again, with Paul and Izzy, wherever that may be. I don't have the patience to wait for your grapes or even give a crap. We can grow them grapes anywhere. What difference do it matter anyway if the war flies through here and burns the whole thing down? I just want to get the hell out, Luke!"

"Well, Brother, there you are wrong. It does matter. This is the perfect spot for our grapes. There is none better. The soil and the flowing sediment are unique to this place. The pond is not easily reproducible. In a few years the war will be over, and you will walk up and say to me, 'Luke, it was worth waiting for these grapes. They have no equal in all the land.'"

"You know what," Matt said, "you are goddamned out of your mind. Paul is right when he says that. You and your damned grapes! I have a hankering to walk over to those pieces of sticks and just knock them all down so you stop your blabbing about all this grape crap! Don't you have a sensible piece of brain in that skull of yours? There's a war coming, Luke. A big war. And it's going to change our lives and our farm and maybe even put us in harm's way. It's way more important than your danged grapes!"

But was it? Luke did not agree.

Earlier, Jessie had wandered by with Matt and the doctor. Jessie wanted to show her father the farm's new crop, and she implored Luke to explain to him the art of cultivating grape vines. While Izzy was here, she had stayed away from the cabin, but last night she came back. She tore off her clothes and assaulted Luke. He was prepared and thus was able to perform to her satisfaction. He so convinced himself of the necessity of her allegiance that he was always ready and able to perform. In fact, having her stay away hurt a bit. He liked when she came last night. He thought of the farm and the raft and the wonderful summer that was about to greet them. Jessie was his conduit through which he expressed his pleasure. She even treated him somewhat decently, bringing him some lamb and a few sautéed vegetables, before running off into the night.

She was, in fact, his greatest ally, the one person who truly believed in him!

He showed the doctor his grape vine cuttings that were now well lodged into a firm and fertile patch of soil. The doctor marched back and forth, touching the twigs, even tasting a small bit of earth before proclaiming, "This is quite a sight for sore eyes in these dark times, the start of life even as we venture to shred our glorious Union into tatters. Luke, you are indeed a genius about such things!"

Luke bowed and thanked the doctor, even as he realized that the doctor's soil-tasting farce and meticulous scrutiny of the twigs were just another whiff of his chicanery.

The doctor then made a speech about the need to produce food that would feed the armies of the South, "a most heroic feat of patriotism that rivals what even our great generals will contribute to our battle against the forces of tyranny." Then, he pontificated about the war to Matt and Jessie.

"Horatio Moffett will be by for supper tonight, and I would like the two of you to join me," the doctor said. "He is bringing

Governor Smith, the great firebrand who is quite ecstatic about the upcoming hostilities, and you will like him Matt, a bit eccentric, but as it turns out, quite prescient."

"Then there ain't no other chance for peace?" Matt wondered aloud. "Ain't there the peace conference still going on, and lots of states still not committed to the Confederacy? It's not like the vote in Virginia for breaking away was unanimous or nothing. A war would be hurtful to everyone."

The sun shined bright on this April afternoon. Luke remained a few steps behind the conversation, waiting for the right moment to peel away.

The doctor stood statuesque with his folded palm beneath his chin as he smiled at Matt. "You can ask Horatio," the doctor said. "But I think we're well past peace. The only ones who voted for the Union were the poor souls from the West, who don't know any better. And Alan Magruder, the man who personified the so-called peace conference, is a naive man to think there will be peace; he is still talking to Lincoln, but no one from here is listening. No, Matt, we are well committed now. Several federal generals, including Robert Lee, have already declared for the South, and General Lee, who is a great man and a descendent of the Virginian Lighthorse Harry Lee—George's Washington's most admirable general and the man who gave the eulogy at his funeral—will be advising President Davis on strategy. Having Virginia in the Confederacy will add brains and chivalry to the cause. It is up to us in Virginia to make this second American Revolution a noble affair that will change the world for the good. Maryland, North Carolina, Kentucky, and others will join us soon enough. But we will talk more tonight. Let us see the state of your pear trees; your nation is counting on you to given them some juicy pears."

Matt lined up behind the doctor, as his wife stood with him arm in arm, turned quickly back to Luke, and winked. Their voices trickled away.

Luke sucked in a whiff of the sweet spring air. Wildflowers lined his path to the pond, as he fled from their irrelevant chatter. All he thought about was tasting his pond's fresh, cool water.

Earlier in the day he had overheard the overseer, Pete, telling an out-of-town friend his intention to join the Grays and fight for the cause of the South. The friend, a frazzled and poorly dressed man with an abstruse Southern inflection, said he had heard that all the Confederacy's military units planned to convene at Manassas and wait there for a federal attack.

"We don't want to miss out on it," the friend slurred, as though drunk, which perhaps he was. "General Beauregard, the hero of Fort Sumpter, he gonna be in charge, and we is gonna show them prissy brats from the North just who they is dealing with is what I say. Just imagine our situation. We don't got to do nothing. We just protecting our land. They got to knock us out; we just got to hold on. And they don't got the balls to stick with it. I want to be in on this at the start, 'cause this war ain't going on too long, and that Lincoln, he is a weak, ugly man who will be kicked out by the end of the year, that I promise you."

"I know, I know," Pete said, as Luke passed them, barely attracting their attention. "I plan to get out of here and join up by next week. Got to clear it with the doctor; he's the man really in charge of this place, but I think he will let me go. The slaves here are pretty docile, and the master here, and mostly his wife, they can handle this place. Tonight, me and you will feast and talk; the slave woman here can cook better than most. And the master and wife is going to be in town. Come back when you see them leave. We can put together a plan for my escape."

That was earlier this afternoon. Ever since the announcement of war, Pete no longer cared about pushing the slaves. He rarely even ventured to the fields or oversaw operations. The planting season had begun; Luke, Ruth, and her two boys knew what to do without Pete's interference. And so, for the most part, Luke had free run of the farm. It was like the old days. It was glorious.

Luke smiled, and imagined he was talking to Paul. *The war will free me, Brother. That's what you didn't understand. I just have to tolerate a few incursions by Matt's wife, and as long as I am dutiful and obsequious to her and her father, they will leave me alone. Their obsession with the great cause of Confederate victory made them less interested in the very slaves they were fighting to protect. How wonderfully ironic and liberating! I wish you had stayed, Brother! I miss you so much!*

The red raft floated near the shore, and Luke leaped upon it. The water was frigid, the air deceptively warm. A bright sun heated Luke's skin, and he closed his eyes, floating, emptying his mind, and enjoying the tranquility of a war that brought him everything for which he had ever hoped.

Later that night, Matt sat with the doctor, Horatio Moffett, and the former Governor of Virginia, William Smith, who had spent the better part of the past three months trying to persuade Virginians to join the Confederacy. Jessie, dressed in a frilled red dress that she had purchased from Izzy, served them iced tea and a plate of chicken with dumplings. Ruth, Matt's slave, had cooked it for her, but she took full credit, receiving great adulation from the two guests.

"We will outgeneral them now that we got the Commonwealth's best military brass signed on to our cause," said a burly William Smith, who spoke with spittle in his voice, and whose long brown beard occasionally dipped into his bowl of gravy. "We will outsmart them. We are fighting for a better cause, so our heart is in it, while they don't know what they are fighting for at all. We got better men. And we are fighting a defensive war. Case closed, boys. Case closed. Now, if I can just convince Governor Hicks in Maryland to go with his conscience and declare for the Confederacy, then we will have those bastards surrounded and this war may be over in a week."

"I don't know about that, Governor," said Horatio Moffett, eating a bit more slowly and daintily, even as Governor Smith called Jessie over for some more grub. "My sources tell me that since the Baltimore riots, and Hicks's reaction to them, Maryland is fully on the side of Union. They even have regiments moving into Washington for the upcoming Union offensive."

"They may be with the Union in fact," said the doctor, "but their sympathies lie on our side. They may be our best asset yet, an ally behind the lines."

"Precisely," said Smith with exclamation, food sputtering out of his mouth.

The empty words swirled around Matt, who sat silently, largely evading the conversation. He was bombarded by the same bravado over and over again. The same people saying the same thing. He felt as though his head was going to explode.

"What does our quiet young farmer say about all of this?" Governor Smith asked him, as Jessie cleared the plates. "I understand that your orchard is the best asset we have in Rappahannock County. You will be feeding the troops!"

"Yes, sir," Matt answered back.

"I sense that Matthew prefers to be fighting with the Grays," the doctor said. "He wants to be with his friends at the front, not back here with us old men and the women and young boys who are tending the farms. But I told him that every soldier in our glorious army will be thanking God for his bounty of apples and pears each time they lift their guns to drive those barbarians away."

Matt said nothing. He stared forward. The noise buzzed around him with its self-adoring and windy predictability.

"I'm lost," he said to Luke later that night, as the two of them sat in Luke's cabin, sharing some of Ruth's apple pie. "I hate this place, everything about it. Sometimes when I gallop up to the gates, I just stop before I enter and stare ahead. I feel sick and don't want to come in; it feels foreign to me now, like someone else took it over. I always pray Jessie is not around. I don't like being with her. Or the overseer. They both get on my nerves.

The doctor too. I just want things like they was. I hate it here now. It's like they own it, not me, not us. It's not ours no more. Especially with Paul gone."

"I thought you and Jessie liked each other?" Luke asked his brother.

Matt just shook his head. "She don't care a whiff about me. She is just stiff and boring, and I hate even when she is around. When I said I was going to the cabin to bring you pie, I don't even think she heard me. She was sitting by herself reading and drinking wine. And then I realized, she's always gonna be there. I can't never shake her. And all the sudden, the worst feeling of dread come over my body like I was going to explode. I am stuck with this girl for the rest of my life. She is going to watch my every move, tell me what I can and can't do, judge me and scold me. I am probably more of a slave now than even you, Luke. I am nothing on my own farm. I have lost my life."

Luke did not know how to respond. It was all part of the plan. The best way to save the farm was to entice Jessie to be here, to give her a stake in Matt's life and land, and then no one would ever threaten their oasis. And it seemed to be working brilliantly. Jessie was no easy customer. She twisted the screw against Luke, but he twisted it right back again. The secret was not to care about her motives or goals but rather to use her to achieve their own goals by any means possible. That's what he told his brother.

"Just go along with it," Luke said. "It's all part of the game we have to play to preserve what we have in this place. Make pretend you actually care about her. Make sure she spends time with her father. Soon enough you will be without an overseer, and you will have to stay here all the time. She won't be able to tolerate that level of isolation, and when she does leave for hours or days, we will grasp those moments and things will be like they once were."

A soft, warm breeze blew in. Crickets chirped, and bright stars glowed in the sky. The pie tasted good to Matt; he savored it. So much of what he ate lacked any taste at all these days. Ever since Izzy left, all joy evaporated from his heart. He knew that Izzy could never come back, at least not until this war ended, or maybe even beyond that. And, as he hugged his friend goodbye and watched his carriage meander away, that is when Matt realized that he was alone here, that everything he loved about this place had disappeared. It was a prison with new wardens. He had to play a game and consort with people he detested; he had to act in a way contrary to his true persona.

"I don't like this game of yours," he said to Luke. "The world is against us, Luke! It just keeps getting in our way and trying to destroy everything we got. It won't let us alone. I don't want to be in this crappy world no more. I don't want to never go back to that house. I want to stay here with you. I want to be with Paul. I miss Paul so much. And I ain't probably gonna see Izzy again. When he left. " Matt started to cry. He could not utter another word.

Luke held him in his arms, as he had so many times these past few weeks. His poor brother! Why couldn't he find solace in what they had accomplished to save the farm and its integrity?

"When all this nonsense ends, Paul and Izzy will be back, and everything we have together will be rekindled," Luke promised him. "They can't take our love away from us, as hard as they try. You just have to stay out of harm's way and be patient. Let's see which way the wind blows and dodge it when it gusts toward us. That's all we can do, Matt. We have no power over the world out there; it whirls around us, and it's up to us to dance around it and make sure it doesn't knock us down. It was Paul's choice to leave, and Izzy is watching over him, so that gives me the peace I need. I would rather Izzy be up there with Paul than down here with us. Me and you, we have each other. We will play their game when we must, and be careful, until the winds die down and our friend and brother can come back to us, and this farm will be ours again."

Luke paused for a moment, peering into space. He thought about the war, all those people killing each other over their fabricated ideas and passions. He thought about the grapes too, how quickly they might grow, how exciting it was going to be to nourish them and to watch them flourish. It was something tangible he could accomplish, something that required his own ingenuity and a hefty dose of well-mineralized water from the mountains above, the mountain that looked over them always and protected them.

"We'll survive this war," Luke told his brother. "And it will end quickly. You have to have faith."

Matt smiled, but he felt no solace. He thought a lot about his dad and his mom, how they raised him and his brothers, how they built this place, and how this place had ultimately destroyed them.

Izzy's parting words dug into him. *Don't trust the doctor. Don't trust his daughter. And promise me that if circumstances force you to fight for the rebels, if you have to leave this place in the hands of your wife while you join the troops, either you run with Luke and leave here, or you get word to me and give me permission to oversee the farm in your absence, and I will be here before you can even mount your horse. Promise me this, Matt! Promise it! What can I tell you that you don't know already?*

Izzy's words were like knives, and he seemed angry at Matt. But what could Matt do? What chance did he have to follow Izzy's instructions; his fate, it seemed, was out of his own hands.

"I think," Matt finally said, wiping his eyes and peering softly at his brother, "what I want more than anything is to be standing by Paul in a blue uniform and shooting every one of these rebel bastards until the lot of them is dead. That's what I want, Luke. That's my red raft."

Luke nodded and smiled. "Well," he said, "that's good! And that's what we will do. But in our own way. Let Jessie and the doctor think they own us. We know the truth; it's their blind arrogance that allows us to be free! We'll figure out a way to use this farm against them, Matt. They're very easy to deceive. We'll come up with something good! And that will be our blue uniform; that will be how we can fight with Paul."

Matt laughed. For the first time in quite a while, a small shot of pleasure rocketed into his head. Maybe there was another way to toss a cannonball back at them. "I can do that! It will be fun! And you is right. Jessie won't want to stay around here much. Too much work, too much of me. There won't be a man a hundred miles around who will be willing to oversee this place; Pete is leaving to fight the war, and everyone else will be too. So, I'll be stuck here. With you. And no one else to watch us or bother us! Just me and you. And they don't even got a clue! Ha! And then we'll come up with something good, something that would even make Paul proud!"

"I love you, Brother," Luke said, his arms on Matt's shoulders.

"Well, Brother," Matt said, "maybe I will get to taste them grapes after all!"

Luke nodded. "They will be the best grapes you ever tasted. That I guarantee!"

22

Preparations for war flooded the landscape as Paul watched helplessly from his perch upon Manhattan's wilderness mountains. Large wooden sailing vessels soared in and out of the harbor, as swarms of blue-clad dots cluttered along the shore. He wondered what they could be discussing, these soldiers who seemed ready to deploy, to where they might be venturing, and what was transpiring across the nation between the North and South. Did Virginia finally secede? What about Maryland and the others? Was there a Southern attack, or did the North intend to strike the first blow? Had President Lincoln made any statements about the abolition of slavery?

Paul was safely impotent on his mountain. Banished here due to the color of his skin and by those who shared the color of his skin, he was severed from events that swept across his adapted city and separated from his friends and from the girl he loved. He thought about her a lot, wondering if she had drifted away to another existence, one that did not include him. Maybe she had pushed him aside in the wake brutal necessity. Or maybe his actions had smothered her transient affection for him.

LB had wandered up earlier to deliver Paul some food and a blanket, items he salvaged from the streets near where the rich folk lived, he said. He could only stay for a minute; the war was increasing sales of his buttermilk and straw. "With me out of Collin's house I gots to make me some money," he told Paul, rapidly unloading a few jugs of his older buttermilk, a bed of straw he had assembled, and a bag of discarded bread and some carrots. "They's putting me uptown with four other guys, near Bleeker Street. If you think the Five Points was a bed of sin, you's gots to see this hell hole, and I gots to pay more rent, so I gots to earn some money. I doubt the Tappans is going to be helping us out now."

"Thank you," Paul muttered without inflection. "And I am sorry."

He barely looked at Paul as he blurted out words and unloaded his wares. Not once did he inquire as to how Paul was doing, and not once did Paul tell him. Paul asked him nothing, not about the state of the world, about Smiles, or about whether anyone had found Abe's stolen clothes. Paul did not care. He was happy to get some food; his gut had been gurgling for days. He knew that LB didn't care either.

Paul had screwed up. Now he was paying the price. And it was steep.

"Good thing you's gots no rain these past few days; I hope you finds someplace to hide if it comes," LB continued, his voice devoid of emotion, his eyes staring at the ground; not a single smile or puff of laughter crossed his lips. "It gets a little cold at night. Just stays warm."

Paul nodded. "Thank you," he said again.

LB nodded back. He forced a smile. "I gots to go," he said. "Me and Smiles, we's doing well. I haven't seen her since she moved in with Biggelow. They says she's doing good there, and I is happy for her. But I worry about her there. He's gots a reputation."

"I'm sorry about what happened," Paul said. "She wouldn't be there if it weren't for me."

LB nodded again. "Well, you can'ts beats yourself up all day, Paul," he said. "Just take cares of yourself. She's sick about you.

I know she is. And she don't blame you at all. I don't neither. People in this world are chunks of shit. Most of thems is. But we's got to survive." He paused for a moment, still looking past Paul. "You gots any plans?"

"Like, am I going to leave New York?" Paul responded.

"Or somethings."

"No," Paul said. "I have no plans."

"OK," LB said. "Then I'll comes up in a few days with more food. You be well, you hear me."

"OK," Paul responded.

There was a dense silence, and then LB turned and walked away, the fading crunch of old leaves slowly marking his exit.

More boats floated into the harbor. *There must be thousands of troops mobilizing to fight,* Paul thought. *Where could they be going?*

Then a fleeting thought popped into his head, and he chuckled. "With all the Irish leaving the city in droves," Paul said to himself. "Five Points might be the safest place in the city. What a great time to be a Negro in New York! And lucky me, I'm stuck up on this hill. How sadly ironic!"

In fact, he had no plans. No idea when or if he could return to the city or whether a bounty still sat on his head, or even what the bounty was or who had set it (although he had suspicions). No idea where he would go even if he ran off—maybe Boston, or Philadelphia, or somewhere to the West? He could not contemplate such weighty questions. For now, he had to grasp more mundane issues—for instance, as LB insinuated, the potential of rain.

Mostly, Paul sat and stared. His brain felt heavy, unable to even process logical thought. Every time he peered away from the harbor, painful images and recollections sliced through him. He saw Smiles's face, and Luke's, and his shattered pushcart. Haunting snapshots dashed through him without cessation; they refused to relinquish their grip on his brain. Through the night they kept him up as he shivered beneath his big oak tree, the bright twinkle of distant stars saturating the glorious night sky.

"All this because of fucking God," he laughed to himself. "Those people look into the sky and see God, and I look into the sky and see beauty, and because of that, I have a bounty on my head. Goddamn you, stars! And goddamn me for always opening my mouth. Goddamn those ministers who can't see past their myths to realize that I am their greatest advocate and soldier. All these damned men of God, fuck them all. And if there is a god, fuck you too!"

He placed LB's straw under the tree. He doubted it was any more comfortable than the hard dirt ground that he had been calling his bed, but when he lay on it, he was pleasantly surprised. "First good piece of news in a week," he proclaimed with a smile. "I have a bed and a blanket. And some carrots and bread. It looks like I am on my way to making a prosperous life for myself up here!"

He seized some chunks of hardened bread and covered himself with the blanket. A bright deluge of warm sun bathed him, and for the first time in a while, Paul felt good. Something LB had said elevated his mood. *Smiles doesn't blame me! I may never see her again, but if she doesn't blame me, somehow, I will make it up to her. Somehow!* And with that happy thought, and the morsels of bread easing the pangs in his gut, Paul drifted off to sleep.

The sun had started to fade when his eyes fluttered open. He felt completely rested, but a bit confused. For a moment he did not know where he was, or whether it was morning or night.

And then he heard voices.

He popped up, staring into the silhouetted trees. Maybe he was imagining something? Then he heard it again, a few voices, not too far away. The rustle of leaves. Someone was coming!

He yanked up his head just a bit and then peeked around. Nothing. It was getting dark enough for shadows to obscure his view. The voices gravitated toward him. Now what?

Paul maneuvered behind his oak tree. He sat still, hyperventilating a bit, peering forward, watching for who might emerge from the trees. Far through the haze he could pick out someone, maybe two or three people. Could it be Abe's men to beat him up as retribution for the clothes that were stolen or other African Americans tipped off as to his location and now hoping to collect the bounty? It could be almost anyone in this vicious city! Paul decided to wait and see their faces before he darted away. He would not confront them. The trees would serve as shields to any bullets they shot his way, and no man could catch him when he was in full stride. He continued to breathe heavily, watching, waiting.

And then, through the corner of his eyes, he saw an image, and his entire face lit up with a huge smile.

"Izzy!" he cried out.

It was Izzy! He must have returned from Virginia, and now here he was. But as Paul stood up jubilantly to greet him and smother the wandering Jew with a hug, he stopped cold. His heart started racing, and his brain spun around. He could hardly believe what he was seeing. A few tears rolled down his cheek. He was speechless.

An angelic image slid into his view.

"There is my man!" she called out, her eyes big and bright. She darted right up to Paul and wrapped him tightly with her long, thin arms. "I loves you, Paul," she whispered to him. "I loves you so much. And I miss you! Are you's OK? I feel so bads for you. I loves you so much!"

His arms slid around her narrow frame, and his eyes closed tightly. It was as if heaven opened up and all goodness rained down upon him. And just when he told God to fuck off! Tears rushed down his cheeks, a salty taste filling his mouth. And then both of them started to cry. They could barely speak. Every other thought and fear dissipated from Paul's brain; he did not even think of Izzy who was just standing in the cool and darkening air, smiling at them. Her body against his; that's all he knew. That's all he ever wanted to know.

"I am so, so sorry," he finally blurted out, his words choked up by his tears. "I so badly screwed up. I am so sorry, Smiles. I love you so much. I hurt all over from what I did to you."

"No, no," she softly said to him, pulling back just enough to rub his head and look into his eyes. "You ain't done nothing but be yourself. You is a passionate, smart, sensible man; it's all the reasons I loves you so much. It's everyone else in this world; it's them that's done this to my beautiful boy. We don't got a chance against them. They is all against us! They always is. But, Paul, my darling man, my beautiful and smarts and dumb man of my dreams, they can't's stop us. They never can. I promises you's that. A love like this, it can't be turned off by anyone. Even thems men of God!"

She peered at him and then put her lips on his. Her mouth opened and caressed his, and almost by instinct, he followed suit. He felt her hands rubbing his back and his hair. It was as if he was transported to another place and time. To perfection. To the very antithesis of his own reality.

"My God, do I love you, Smiles," he said to her, as he pulled away and just peered at her radiant face.

"You better be careful using that word God," she said with a chuckle. "It's getting you's in trouble all the time." She kissed him on the lips again. "I's spending the night up here with you, Paul. And all day tomorrow. I don't have to be back to work until Wednesday; they gives me a little break. Izzy Snout, this man, he did it all. He knows Mr. Biggelow's wife. He talks to her and tolds her what happened, and she's letting me off for a bit. She's a good woman, and I's working there will be goods for us both."

Paul looked over to Izzy, who just nodded. Sometimes Paul forgot all the goodness that still existed in the world. Trapped in purgatory, assailed by virtually every human he encountered, blocked from being himself on whichever part of the national divide he trod, Paul forgot that actual decency flowed around him all the time. He had his brothers, and Izzy, and LB, and Smiles. And even men like Collin and Tappan and so many others he had not yet met could be angels in a sea of pure hell.

The war was coming. He had a bounty on his head. Bigotry and intolerance slammed into him when he least expected it. He was forced to live either as a slave or as an impoverished creature afforded no opportunity to avail himself of the great American dream about which everyone spoke incessantly. But here on a lonely mountain in the worst urban jungle in the world, he was with these people, these amazing people, these beautiful people, people who loved him and risked everything for him, and how could he be anything other than ecstatic?

"What about Luke?" Paul asked his friend, as he and Smiles stood near each other, their hands clasped together. "And Matt? How are my brothers?"

Izzy put his arm on Paul's shoulder. "What can I tell you?" he said. "It's not good there. It's like a pile of dry kindling scattered around them, and people like the fucking doctor and his demonic daughter are holding the match. The men and boys are marching out to fight; the doctor made sure Matt could stay on the farm, at least for now. Luke, he's still got those damned grapes to talk about all day, thanks be to God for his imagination. He'll be OK. I mean, I don't know, Paul. As bad as it is here, you should be damned thankful you got the hell out of Virginia."

"Thank you, Izzy," Paul said to him, still holding Smiles's hand. "You are beyond a friend to us. You are our savior, every step of the way. There is no possible way I could ever thank you enough."

Izzy smiled. "You just did," he said. "You don't have to do anything more than that. I'm not letting someone with your heart and your brain be gobbled up by this city of assholes. I will always be there for the three of you boys. That was my promise to your dad."

Izzy dropped a bag he was holding. "Look, here's a blanket and some food, good shit—sandwiches, pickles, white fish, the best shit in this town. You two, you have a night and a day to spend with each other, probably the first one you ever had. Don't worry about anything; just think about each other. When I come to bring Smiles back, Paul, you and me, we are going to talk. I've been in contact with a lot of people. With Abe. With Reverend Garnet in that church. With the Tappan people. They are all consumed by this war that's about to blow up in our faces. They could give a damn about you and what you did or didn't do. I talked to them all, and I've got a bunch of plans all worked out. You'll live with me for a while. You'll apologize to Garnet, I know how. My people have been apologizing to holier-than-though Christians for the past eighteen hundred years! What can I tell you? So I know how to deal with them. And me and Abe, we have a plan for how you can pay him back. It's all covered. He is sorry he blew up at you; he's not in a good place with this war coming. He's not mad at you at all and wants you to keep working for him. I live in a crap tenement where people are going to stare at you and wonder why I have a Negro coming in and out, but I know how to tell a good lie, one that God is OK with because it's for a good cause. So Paul, you OK? Because after all the crap I just did for you, you better as shit be smiling for the rest of your god-damned life!"

"Izzy," Paul smiled, "I know you people don't have an afterlife—"

"We don't know if there's an afterlife; we keep all options open."

"OK, you don't know if there's an afterlife, but you and I know there probably isn't one, so this is my pledge to you. When all this crap ends, when the world becomes just a little bit more decent and inviting, you and I and Matt and Luke will sit down for a week, eat the best food you can imagine all at my expense, and we will just talk, like no one else matters. And then I will do something for you that will change your life for the better. I don't know what it is yet, but I will do it. That I promise. We don't need an afterlife, Izzy. Because I'm going to give you heaven on earth."

"My friend, you have a deal!" Izzy said. "I wish I could stay with you two as a chaperone. But I am not the nimblest Jew in the world, and I better get off this piece of rocky dirt before I break every bone in my body scampering down. I'll be back tomorrow at about this time. Just be decent when I show up; I don't want you two to embarrass me. Then we'll all come back down together."

Paul nodded, smiling big and happy. Izzy nodded back, turned, and retreated.

Paul turned his eyes to Smiles. Her face was majestic, its beauty—both in and out of her skin—struck him hard. He had never met another human being like her before. All that she had been through, so much trauma and hurt at the expense of other men; and now here she was, in love with Paul, giving all her heart and body to him, here in the woods, cold and damp, a hard dirt floor; and all she could do was smile and laugh and love him.

"I loves you, Paul," she uttered again.

And he just put his lips on hers, diving into his girl who had incited in him the most intense passion he had ever tasted. They lowered themselves down upon the straw, which Paul now knew that LB had brought just for this moment. His lips could not stop ravaging hers. His hands were touching everything. He had never been with anyone this way; he never wanted to, and he never could. But now he could not imagine anything more intox-icating. He was drunk in love, not sure what to do, but doing it nonetheless. A cool, dark wind blew against his naked body, as he lay atop her, his lips not letting go.

War was coming, and his world would change irrevocably. But for Paul, his dreams and hopes all congealed on a chilly April night in New York. He wished that this moment would never go away.

PART III

Deuteronomy

**"See, I set before you today life and prosperity,
death and destruction."**

23

lmost two years later, 1863
"I have been musing on an idea that has been percolating in my head, Matthew," said the doctor, who sat in his atrium, studying the contour of his left hand. "And I do believe that the time has come. When Jude and the other Grays came to town after the New Year, their exuberance was infectious; I am sure you sensed it when we met him. We have lost many good men and boys in defense of our nation, and there are too many empty farms to be filled and widows with tears in their eyes, but Kemper and his men, they have surrendered none of their confidence and fire. The rout of Burnside in Fredericksburg last month was the last nail in the coffin for the North. And they know it. Northerners have scant blood in their veins that can sustain them for the long defensive struggle that our great General Lee has orchestrated. Britain may well throw its backing to the Confederacy, and it is only a matter of time before the spineless Northern generals sue for peace. Lee's attack on Union soil at Antietam injected fear into the minds of every Northern soul, and Jude and our boys were instrumental in that decisive blow. We will be victorious, Matthew, that much I can assure you, and a new nation will be born, one more reflective of the America that Washington and Jefferson always intended, a true beacon of

democracy and freedom. And it will be led by Virginia. We must be ready to leap upon that mantle. Which is why, Matthew, your time has come."

As verbose as the doctor had been for all of Matt's life, these past few months had been that much worse. The doctor did not converse or talk; he made grand speeches. Even something as simple as inquiring as to the date of Matt's harvest could become an oration, one that touched on morality, God, and, of course, Thomas Jefferson. Now, the doctor's worship of Robert E. Lee, "yet another great Virginian sent by the Almighty to save our nation from the clutches of evil," inserted itself into every slice of discourse and conversation. The doctor was convinced that it was just a matter of time before the South won this bloody war. And now he had beckoned Matt to his home so they could discuss it.

Matt stood silently by the study's large bay window, a cold rain battering the doctor's wooden shingles. Just a few flecks of white snow fluttered in the sky, instantly dissolving upon confronting the warm dirt below. Matt peered outside, his mind drifting. He knew that he had a date with Jessie again tonight. She liked to call them dates; she scripted everything.

The evening started with a multicourse dinner, candlelights, and one of Ruth's sons playing the fiddle. Then the married couple retreated to the master bedroom, where Jessie peeled off his clothes and told him to lie on the bed until she was ready. After some time, she strolled in, lay beside him, and then instructed him to straddle her. For Matt, the encounter reeked of anxiety, and Jessie ended every night by rating Matt's performance. "Poor job, dear." "That was barely adequate." She wanted to have a baby! She had been pregnant twice, both ending in miscarriage. She blamed this on Matt's poor performance. She read books and talked to some people; she knew what the problem might be. And tonight, she had demanded another "date" so they could try again. She was "ripe and ready." If he followed her instructions to the tee, he might finally deliver adequate seeds to her fertile womb.

"Matthew," the doctor snapped, waking him from a trance, "I am talking to you, son. Be attentive." The doctor, who sat with his legs crossed upon his large throne-like easy chair, stood up and strolled along his back wall, where his skulls sat. He wrung his hands pensively.

"We witnessed the intentions of our Northern enemy during the dark summer of '62, a mere five months ago. They trampled our land boasting a misguided arrogance, one that they had not earned, and one that subsequent battles have erased. They had been beaten badly in Richmond by Lee and in the Valley by Jackson, and so they retreated here to torment the civilians of Washington, choosing to bully women and children after being beaten down by men and boys on the battlefield. They lived in our midst for well over a month, and I came to know them well. Especially General Banks, who revealed his nefarious intent many times in my presence, mistaking me for a friend. Finally, they left but have threatened us ever since, living off the land, encamping on our flanks, prepared to strike us whenever their whims so propel them. Despite defeat after defeat, they stalk us in the shadows, hovering. And now with Lincoln's proclamation of January 1, whereby he has clearly stated what we always knew—that he seeks to release and liberate every slave in the lands that his armies conquer—we can have no doubt. They seek complete and total annihilation of our way of life. What that monkey of a president does not realize is that he has only empowered us to resist even more vigilantly! The next battle may well be the one that decides this war, on the banks of the Rappahannock River, where Burnside so recently faltered. Now they will put General Hooker into the fray, another novice sent to fight against the great and sagacious General Lee, a gentleman, a wise statesman, and inevitably the next George Washington to the new nation that we shall soon proclaim."

The doctor did not stop his ranting there. He spoke about Washington and Jefferson and their legacy, how Virginia would dominate the new Southern Confederation and elevate it to the status of one of the great nations of the world and indeed of all of history, how it might take another war to keep rogue states like Mississippi and South Carolina in line, how the slaves might one day be freed and shipped to Africa, thus ridding the land of the black menace, "while the black-skinned hoards who infiltrated the North will reduce that land to an intellectual and economic wasteland that we will, with charity and compassion, allow to survive as a backward nation after the stain of self-castration emasculates it and renders it helpless in the modern world."

Finally, between references to Christ and racial biology, the doctor dropped his bombshell.

"I think it is time you join the Washington Grays and the Army of Northern Virginia," he said. "It is time, Matthew, for you to march to Fredericksburg and join Colonel Kemper and General Lee in their final battle of this war of Northern aggression. You must be there, Matthew, when General Hooker hands his sword to General Lee, and our new nation is born."

"Wait, what?" Matt asked, suddenly startled. "You want me to join the army, sir?"

"I do indeed, son, as painful as that idea might be to both of us." He marched to Matt and stood by his son-in-law's side. "We must think about our future, about our family's legacy. Those who don a uniform for the Confederacy will be the heroes of our new nation. They will regale their children about how they fought for the great General Lee, how they were there for the Northern surrender, how they participated in the creation of our new nation. While you have done so much for the cause on your farm, it will not be enough when the history books are written; it will not be enough if you—as I hope you will—enter the political arena and shape our national destiny after the war has ended. Our future is bright, Matthew, and it must start today. And for that to happen, you must wear the gray uniform and fight for General Lee with the Washington Grays."

"What about the farm?" Matt asked. "Who's gonna manage that, and the slaves? Ain't an overseer left in the land who can do that."

The doctor nodded and then resumed his pacing. "Jessie tells me that it essentially runs on its own. You have helped raise a loyal and obsequious group of slaves who know their jobs well. They need little instruction or supervision. She believes that she has mastered the operation, and along with our rotating over-seers who have assisted you and her, she thinks she can handle the farm until you return."

"Then she knows you want me to leave here and join the army?" Matt asked, somewhat taken aback. "She didn't say noth-ing to me. You'd think she'd be a little bit nervous and sad about it and say something."

"She knows, and she endorses it," he said. "I asked her to remain quiet. After our dinner with Jude, Jess met him again with some of her other friends who now fight beside him and General Lee. And she was quite enamored by their maturity, how they have grown emotionally and physically, how much fire now flows through their veins. She voiced concern to me that these would be the men destined to gain prominence in the post-war world and that you will be left behind, your deeds forgotten, your goodness buried by the battles in which you never were able to participate. And thus, Matthew, it is time. It is time for you to wear gray and march with our brethren and finish this thing. They are waiting for you and will be much pleased with your presence."

Matt started to sweat. What would come of Luke under Jessie's reign? He remembered the pledge he had made to Izzy. What now?

During the many days and weeks that Jessie abandoned the farm to be with her father, Matt stayed with Luke in the slave cabins, and only then could he be himself. Those nights were precious to Matt! He liked his life here. People in town respected him. He and Luke ran the farm on their own. Other than a few demands by his wife, she largely left him alone. He could not join the army now! He would not!

"I am so much more important here," he finally said. "They don't need me out there. Heck, I can hardly fire a gun or nothing!"

The doctor laughed. "During the dark summer, when General Banks invaded our tranquil lands, I learned that we cannot sit idly by while we let others fight for us. Indeed, had I been passive, Matthew, had I let General Banks's men invade your farm and countless other prosperous farms and orchards in our county, rather than simply arranging deliveries of food to him as I skillfully did, had I not understood his mind and so craftily manipulated him, we may well not even be having this conversation. I stood firm against a wall of danger; I did not relent, and so I saved us from imminent despair. Now it is your turn, Matthew. It is your turn to be a hero to our people, to my daughter, and to yourself."

It had only been five months ago that a large contingent of federal troops—scattered from their defeat at the hands of Stonewall Jackson in the Shenandoah Valley—convened here to regroup for the next battle. That is what the doctor and so many others called the dark summer of 1862.

The dark summer.

Tens of thousands of blue-garbed men descended upon Washington in early July under the command of Nathaniel Banks. Stonewall Jackson beat Banks badly in the Shenandoah campaign earlier that summer, chasing him up and down mountains, through tiny trails, across the valley that he knew so well, and taking potshots at the larger and better equipped federal army every chance he had. In fact, it was Banks's ineptitude that led to the North's defeat in the now-famous Battle of the Seven

Days, in which the Southern forces defeated the much larger army of General George McClellan outside of Richmond. Both Lee and Jackson made names for themselves at that battle, chasing away Northern forces and securing the Confederacy's capital against any future Northern incursions. This battle followed on the heels of the Southern victory at Manassas, and the Army of Virginia had not lost a battle since, chasing away one Northern general after another.

But when the smoke cleared from the Seven Days in the summer of 1862, exactly two years since the war of liberation started and the Washington Grays marched off to join the battle at Manassas, General Banks brought his fifteen thousand weary and defeated troops here, to Washington, planning to live off the land and evoke terror to avenge his loss and regroup from a devastating defeat. As his army marched into town, panic rung throughout the county, especially when it became apparent that Lee's Army of Virginia would not be intervening, nestled as they were in Manassas, preparing for another fight. Banks was a firebrand Northern politician, the former governor of the abolitionist capital of Massachusetts, and he intended to adhere to the orders of General Pope, his commanding general who had replaced McClellan and sought to stave off General Lee's momentum after the Seven Days. "The army will subsist upon the country in which their operations are carried on," said Pope, adding that "if any person, having taken the oath of allegiance to the Union, be found to have violated it, he shall be shot, and his property seized and applied to the public use."

And so, with Banks in their backyards, the farmers of this quiet hamlet trembled.

Until the doctor stepped in. He met with Banks himself, who with his copious bodyguards ate in the doctor's home on many occasions. As was his wont, the doctor charmed the bellicose Northern general. Rather than allow Banks's Northern troops to scavenge the land, the doctor offered to deliver food to them every day. He promised law and order from the virtuous Washington residents if only Banks promised to stay in a proscribed location, away from the farmers themselves. And when a typhus outbreak ripped through the Northern encampment, the doctor offered his services, providing advice and aid to the Northern physicians, as well as any supplies that they might need. The doctor gathered the town leaders and farmers together virtually every night, Matt among them. He told them how much they had to deliver to the army each day to prevent Banks from raiding their farms. It was a tremendous burden to the town and its farmers, but when Banks marched out in early August, his army had inflicted no damage, harmed no Washington citizens, and assaulted not a single home or farm.

The doctor emerged as a hero, the hurrah's and adulation swarming upon him when Banks's troops disappeared, and life returned to normal. And at that moment, the doctor's very demeanor changed, and his conversation morphed into speeches and soliloquies. He had saved Washington using charm and guile, he had outwitted a Northern general, and now he would help Washington be poised for greatness once the war came to its inevitable end.

After the Seven Days, the South and North battled again at Manassas, where Lee handed General Pope a cataclysmic defeat, prompting President Lincoln to sack the arrogant Western general and send him packing. McClellan again was given the reigns of the Northern army, as Lee and Jackson marched from Manassas and invaded the North, threatening to attack the nation's capital. The two armies struck each other in a tiny Maryland town on the banks of the Antietam River, resulting in tens of thousands of deaths and a military stalemate. McClellan failed to pursue Lee's march to the South, and Lincoln fired him for a second time. Lee and his army encamped on the Rappahannock River near the town of Fredericksburg; and the Northern forces, now under the command of a minor officer named Ambrose Burnside, whose long whiskers down the side of his face proved to be his most enduring legacy, camped on the northern side of the river. In early December 1862, Burnside's forces tried to dislodge Lee's, sending wave after wave of men into a well-entrenched brick wall on a cold and muddy landscape but finally abandoned the assault after losing over ten thousand troops and gaining no ground. And so, with a new year starting, Burnside was sacked and replaced by another general named "Fighting" Joe Hooker, whose last name proved to be more enduring a testament of his true persona than his first; and the two armies sat face-to-face, ready for one or the other to make a move.

Into that morass did the doctor intend to send Matt, believing that this next battle, this next victory for the South, would be the final nail in the attainment of Southern independence.

Throughout these battles, the Washington Grays had shown their bravery and skills at every turn. "You stick with Jude," the doctor said to Matt on that cold and rainy day. "He is a hero of our people. He will lead you down the correct path. You can ride the wave of his success to emerge from this conflict the most honored man in the country, one ready to be vaulted to great heights in our new and prosperous nation, one that will sit in the shadow of God and . . . "

Matt stared at drops of rain splashing in puddles of mud. It was almost dark. The doctor's interminable stream of verbiage faded into an innocuous buzz.

Just a few weeks had passed since several of the Grays came back to town for a brief respite from the two-year war in which they had been engaged. Many had perished, including Ned, the farmer who had whipped Paul on the farm, and at least five of Matt's schoolmates, as well as Matt's overseer Pete. But not Jude, whose feats and heroics bounced from mouth to mouth, both before his return and after. He led the procession home, and it was quite clear that he was the man in charge, the one with whom everyone in town sought to speak. A smile never cracked his stern face.

Matt sat with Jude, Jessie, and the doctor on a cold January day in the doctor's parlor, Ruth having come over to make her chicken and potatoes for the honored guest. Jude stared forward as though floating in a different plane. He wore a battered gray uniform with a line of silver buttons in front, a long red beard dropping from his chin to chest, and curly red hair sticking out of his floppy hat. He held a gun in his hands, tapping it from time to time, and occasionally squinting into its barrel. Two other men, young boys also in gray but not from the town or even recognized by the hosts, flanked Jude. They came with him at his request; *perhaps,* Matt mused, *they were his bodyguards.*

Jude was the boy that Matt most despised in all the world. The one who taunted him as a kid, who never stopped calling him "Negro lover," who had been Jessie's boy and best friend (and probably so much more) up until the time she started courting Matt. He could never be near Matt without tossing an insult his way, often striking Matt with some physical thumping as well.

But on this evening, as Jude sat on a pedestal surrounded by those who exalted his deeds and very presence, he was different. He hardly uttered a word; the other uniformed soldiers spoke for him. He barely acknowledged Matt's presence, looking past him, as though Matt did not even exist. His face was stern and focused. While the others laughed, his mouth remained firm. And whenever the doctor asked him a question, he turned to one of his subordinates, who provided an animated, thunderous response.

Matt's stomach gurgled as mindless banter flowed around him. He watched the faces of Jessie and the doctor seep with awe and blind admiration; the doctor said, "You, sir, make me and this town proud," while Jessie kissed him on the forehead and asked him to "tell me again, Jude, about that bridge in Maryland." For the first time ever, Matt did not even have an appetite for Ruth's chicken.

"Let me tell you about that bridge again, Ms. Jessie," one of Jude's underlings said to her, standing up, and using his arms to mimic the battle. "Company B, that's what we is really called, we was out of the action when the fighting in Antietam started. We was with A. P. Hill in Harper's Ferry, collecting cartloads of guns from the federal supplies. We didn't expect no battle. So Jude, he goes and talks to General Hill, and the general he says, 'You tell the men of Company B to get on their toes; we are marching to Sharpsburg to turn the tide of the battle there.' Ain't that right, Jude?"

Jude rubbed his small copper gun on his arm and nodded. "General Hill knew that we could be ready in mere minutes and could lead the march. I talked to my boys, and we were packed and ready to go before Hill was done shaving."

"So," the animated sycophant continued, pacing all over the doctor's room, as Jessie stared at him with an open mouth and blind smile, "we get there as the sun was dropping down. It was hot as hell, and we is in front of the line, and you could hear the cannon all over the sky, and the stench of sulfur and rotting flesh just drenched our nostrils. They was fighting all over the farm in Sharpsburg, and there was a bridge over the Antietam River, and that's where General Hill told us to go. And Jude, he said, what did you say, Jude?"

Jude stood, pointed his gun at Matt, and softly uttered, "It's our turn to win this war."

"Yes!" the boy shouted. "That's just what you said! And right then and there, we was all inspired! And we was so ready, just waiting for the word from above. General Hill, he gathered us on a line, and General Longstreet's men who had been fighting back and forth on that bridge all day, they was battered and getting pushed back. So General Hill told them to get behind us. Then I see Colonel Kemper up on his big brown horse, with bullets and cannon fire filling the sky, and he gives the word to charge. And them Northern people, they didn't see what was coming, did they, Jude? They thought they had our army beat, but they didn't know we was coming up from Harper's Ferry with fresh legs and more guns than they knowed we ever had, did they, Jude?"

Jude nodded. "A. P. Hill, he told me personally, 'Jude, you lead the charge and don't stop until every one of those invaders is either dead or is running back to their mothers up North.'"

"My goodness, Jude, you must have been so scared," Jessie said to him in a gleeful tone.

Jude just shook his gun back and forth. "You don't get scared in the heat of battle, Jess. You get brave. You know what you can do, and you do it. And that's what we done. That's what the Grays always do."

"So," continued the boy, "people start dropping dead on our side and theirs; they is dropping fast, a lot of the boys is scared, and you can smell death everywhere and just knows you can be the next one who goes down. But Jude, he keeps at it, running forward, and we right behind. If the Grays can do it, so can the others, and they followed us. We seen Jude just running, screaming the rebel yell, and we all followed him and yelled as loud as we could. We was running over dead boys, Blue and Gray, half our officers was screaming at us from behind telling us this and that, but Jude, he won't stop. He's grabbing guns from the dead soldiers on the ground and using them as his bullets is running out. He just keeps shooting and running right into the mass of the Northern army. Nothing even grazed him—the bullets just went by him, and the cannonballs exploded somewhere. Ain't nothing ever hits him, he's invincible. So, we follow because we want to be in his shadow, and soon enough we is rushing over the bridge, and the Union boys, they is turning and running away. But that don't stop Jude. He keeps at it, yelling, running and shooting, and we is all behind. Nothing scared him or slowed him down. It took the orders from General Longstreet himself to finally stop Jude, but even then, five people had to come over and hold him back. He was breathing hard, his face looked like some crazed horse you might see, and he had guns in both hands, including this one, the one he is holding now."

"I took it from the cold body of a Union aggressor, and I will never give it back until they surrender and leave us in peace," Jude said. "If Longstreet hadn't up and stopped me, I would have chased them down and ended the war right then and there."

"Which should be coming soon, my boy," said the doctor with a gleam in his eyes.

Jessie could hardly utter words. She just glared at Jude and nodded her head. "What a story," she finally cried out. "Can you tell it again?"

A wave of vomitus slid up Matt's throat that he swallowed with an audible gulp. He wanted—he needed—so much to leave this room and flee from these scoundrels. He thought about the dark summer, how close he had come to running over to General Banks's troops and just surrendering. On some warm nights he wandered there and sat in the woods, the lights from their camp-fires cracking through the dense star-filled skies, and he stared at those people, the people from the North, wondering why he found himself on the wrong side of this war.

And now, with Jude and the others marching back to Fredericksburg, the doctor told Matt that it was his turn to join them. Cold rain battered the doctor's house, and Matt just stared outside, into an intense sheet of darkness.

"When would I leave, sir?" Matt asked the doctor.

"In a week," the doctor stated coolly. "Now that the ape Lincoln has declared that he will emancipate every slave that the Northern armies encounter, now the moment is upon us to win the decisive battle. And you will be there for it, Matt. You will be bathed in the glory that so elevates Jude and the others to near God-like status. You will return a hero and regale us with stories, and Jessie will stare at you with awe and admiration, as will every-one in this town and beyond."

"What do I got to bring, sir?" Matt asked dispassionately, his eyes still peering into black nothingness. His heart was dead now. The very thought of engaging in this horrid deed wrested every bit of life from him. And yet, he knew that he had no choice

If you ever are sent away to fight the war, you get word to me immediately, do you understand? You have to promise me this, Matt. On your father's grave, you must promise me this! Someone has to take care of Luke. Don't trust the doctor or his daughter. Don't ever trust them with Luke. Izzy's words haunted him. He told Izzy that he would get word to him, always believing that this moment would never come. But now, it had come.

"I want to make sure my slaves is OK," Matt then said.

"Son, don't you worry. My daughter is there for them. She loves your slaves, especially that farming genius, Luke. She talks about him all the time, and her eyes light up when she does."

Matt nodded. "I will break him the news tonight. When I get home."

"Tonight?" the doctor laughed. "You can't go home tonight, son. The roads are caked with mud! No, Matt, you are my guest here tonight. We will drink bourbon and talk about the new world that will be born in this war's shadows. It will be a glorious rebirth of our national destiny." The doctor's mouth continued moving, as his arms made grand gestures and he paced back and forth along the row of skulls.

Matt nodded, still looking outside. He felt nothing. His mind was empty. "Your daughter and I, we got a date tonight," he said to the doctor when the man's soliloquy seemed to fade away. "She ain't too pleased when I break a date with her."

The doctor laughed again, in a calculated and stiff way. "My daughter will figure something else to do, son. She always does. She is very clever that way. Sometimes she can surprise you."

Matt nodded. In some sense, he was glad he did not have to go home and face her expectations and judgment. And yet, something pulled at him, something gnawing that beseeched him to be with Luke. He felt uncomfortable; even his skin started to crawl.

"Maybe she'll even spend the night with your slave," the doctor laughed. "She seems to like his company."

That didn't sit well with Matt. He turned again to the blackness of the world outside, as sheets of chilly rain washed away every bit of vigor left in him. He thought about Luke. And he worried. What would become of his poor, misguided brother if Matt went off to war? And what would become of himself? Matt had never been alone in the world before, never been off his farm for more than a day. Now he was being asked to risk his life for a cause, and with a group of people whom he despised, while leaving his brother all alone, his other brother already lost up North, and his farm in the hands of Jessie. The rains and winds blew hard into the window. Matt was trapped by forces of nature he no longer was able to control. His heart sank into the oblivion of the unknown.

24

A misty glaze hovered over the pond. Often in January, the pond was a glistening sheet of ice with fluffy white snow defining its borders and sharp snowcapped blue peaks providing a spectacular backdrop. But now the ground was muddy, and the mountains were brown. More often than not, thick clouds filled the sky and cold rain poured down upon the farm in this long winter of 1863. There was little for Luke to do here but watch and wait.

The word from Fredericksburg was that after suffering a humiliating defeat against the under-matched Confederate foes, General Burnside organized another offensive, but his troops became mired in a thick soup of mud. All the Confederates could do from across the river was to laugh and to hunker down for winter as the North found yet another general to subdue the wayward American Southerners.

"That's why they put in that guy Hooker," Matt explained to Luke. "Now they think he's got what it takes to break the line. But the doctor, he don't got any faith in Hooker or any one of the Northerners who they put up against General Lee. He says this is a done deal. That's why I'm going. He wants me there at the end of the war so I can come home as some kind of hero or something."

"Since when did you start listening to the doctor?" Luke asked his brother, as the two of them huddled in Luke's cabin, a fire crackling along the back wall, a chilly wet draft fluttering through the many cracks.

Frankly, Luke didn't care much about what transpired on the battlefield and the political stage these past two years. Nor did he believe any prognostications that the doctor declared. Did it really matter who won? Did Lincoln's emancipation proclamation of January 1 really signify anything more than the symbolic gesture that it really was? None of this ephemeral clutter mattered. Once the smoke cleared and the two sides shook hands, Luke knew that everything would settle back into what it once was. It always does; such is the law of inertia: staying the same is always an easier path than boldly changing course, even if the status quo is less than ideal. Whether slave or free, Luke knew that he and his brothers would be safer and happier on the farm than off it. He had already lost Paul. Now he had to bear with the imminent departure of his brother Matt, something that dented his already aching heart.

"I still don't see why you have to go," Luke said to his brother. "They aren't compelling you to do it. You don't have to listen to the doctor. If he is right, and the war ends early, then isn't it best you stay here and prepare the farm for the spring? And if he is wrong, and the war becomes interminable, why would you risk your life for a cause that you despise? It makes no sense, Brother; you must know that."

Matt just stood and walked to the door, peering out at the cold, dreary pond. "I don't know," he said. "You always is right, Luke; I know that. But if I mess with the doctor, he can make all our lives hell. He got big plans for me when this war ends. And Jessie, she ain't gonna be happy if I stay either. She told me so. She wants me to be brave like the others. Hell, Luke, you created this mess, you made me marry her, and now you want me to just say no to him? It don't work that way with the doctor. Once you sell your soul to him, he owns it."

"No, Brother," Luke said. "You own your own soul. You always will. You are the doctor's son-in-law; he will never turn his back on you. If you don't go, then he will make excuses for you and find some other way to prop you up. Besides, if he wants you to be a politician after this war, that's not something that makes sense for us. We need you here. We need you safe. Don't die because you are afraid to offend the doctor. That, Brother, would be the greatest folly of all."

Matt just shook his head. "You know what upsets me the most?" he asked his brother. "It ain't dying, which I promise I'll do my damndest to avoid, even if I am a coward in doing it. And it ain't fighting for a cause I don't believe in, because to be honest, I'll probably do more harm to the Southern cause by fighting with them than if I fought against them. But what worries me is that maybe I'll never see Paul again. And I worry about you too, being here alone, with Jessie in charge, with whatever they may do to Negro slaves if the war don't go the right way. I worry about that. And I'm sick as hell that I didn't get you out of here when I had my chance."

Matt had that chance in the dark summer of 1862. Every day and night Luke could hear the Union troops marching and firing weapons; he could see the smoke from their fires; he could sometimes even discern their laughter. The presence of these men entirely disrupted his life. The doctor set a quota of food that he had to provide, giving away some of the best apples and pears grown in Virginia to a group of men who probably chewed them up and spit them out. Paul would be shocked at the loss of income incurred by the presence of these men! Luke and the others worked hard to harvest everything quickly, to shine up the fruit, to prepare it in time. It was an exhausting summer, accomplishing nothing of value other than to sate these Northern invaders who parked themselves upon Luke's beautiful valley and refused to leave.

But Matt perceived the summer through a different lens. "They is our saviors," he would tell Luke, as he listened to their daily drills. "They could free every slave in this county if they wanted to. Hell, they could stay here the whole war and make sure no Negro ever gets whipped again."

Luke smirked when Matt said those things, and he gently reminded his brother that such fantastical thinking lacked a root in reality. That was five months before Lincoln's emancipation proclamation. "No, Matt, he is not able to free a single slave," Luke told him as they sat by the pond on a warm July day back in that dark summer. "If he does, he will instigate a backlash that might not only threaten his strategic position—because General Lee won't stand by idly if General Butler callously disregards the rules of war—but as collateral damage it might decimate our farm and all those around us. We can't allow war to be waged upon this hallowed land. Everything we worked for, our entire future, will be put in jeopardy. This one time, Matt, I do agree with the doctor. We should feed these men what they want and pray that they eventually move away. Their very presence here is disquieting to say the least."

"So, you just want the South to win then?" Matt shot back.

"I didn't say that, Brother," Luke smiled. "I only care about the farm. This spring our grapes will have their first full harvest, and I am optimistic that they will awe everyone who tastes their sweet excellence. And wait until we pound them into wine! Once Paul returns, he will help us to process and bottle the wine, to name it, and to market it. It will define who we are."

"When Paul returns?" Matt snapped back, kicking up the pond's cool water in evident frustration. "Are you damned deluded, Luke? He ain't coming back. Why would he? He's free now. And you should be too. I should march you over to General

Banks and give you to him, tell him to bring you up North and away from the slaveholders and all their sinister ways. You and your grapes! I don't want to hear any more about those damned grapes! Or the pond or the raft or nothing! You are a slave here, Luke. That's what these people here are fighting for, to make sure you is always a slave. And those people who are camped here, those soldiers that I go and watch every day, they is here to free you, to make sure that you are a person and not a thing. Don't you get that at all? Anyone can grow grapes, but down here, no Negro can be free."

"Not these grapes. These are special grapes."

"Christ, Luke, you are impossible to talk to!"

Matt came close to disregarding Luke's protestations and delivering his brother to the troops that summer. One hot day in July, General Banks organized a grand review, one that highlighted the spectacular power and spectacle of his army, one that half the town came out to watch. Matt said that he was going to take Luke to the main road near Sperryville so that they could watch it together. "And bring anything you think you may need in case we is there overnight," he told his brother.

Luke knew that Matt had ulterior motives; once Banks's army marched past them, he would send Luke over the lines to the Union formation and deliver him to freedom. Luke did not let on that he knew. When the day of the review came, Luke wandered out of his cabin and hid out in the pear orchard. For several hours he heard Matt calling to him, but he evaded his brother's feeble search. Finally, both Matt and Jessie left the farm, while a rented overseer named Ronald (a fourteen-year-old boy who walked around with an attitude, a gun, and a Confederate hat) remained behind to mind the slaves. Luke waited a bit, and once Ronald wandered into the main house to escape from flies and heat, he marched to the pond and leaped upon his red raft and floated upon his pond, listening to cannon shots and the synchronous cries of a thousand men, and watching the brilliant peaks of the mountains as they sparkled in a bright blue summer sky. No, he had no intention of leaving this oasis, not now, not ever.

Now five months later, in the pouring rain of a cold January evening, Matt regretted his failure to free his brother. The opportunity had come and gone. "I don't want you here alone," he said. "I don't want to leave you."

"Then don't," Luke said. "You don't have to. Stay here. Help prepare the farm for spring planting and cultivation. We have so much to look forward to!"

"I'm going tomorrow, Luke," Matt insisted. "I'm marching there to Fredericksburg where the soldiers is, joining up with the Grays, and you is gonna be here alone, with Jessie mostly, and I will be scared for you every day. If only I could get word to Izzy and tell him to come down here. If I had freed you last summer, none of this would mean nothing."

Matt simply did not understand. The North and their soldiers had no more to offer Luke than the slaveholders who patrolled this county. They would just dispense another form of cruelty upon him. Were the Negroes up North so much better off? Was Paul?

"I never been away from this place, my whole life," Matt said to his brother, sitting on a wooden bench beside Luke. "I'm scared of what's out there."

"You should be," Luke said to him, putting his hand upon his brother's shoulder. "You need to be careful. Don't get yourself killed. Just be inconspicuous. Stay quiet and smile a lot. Agree with everything they say. And when the bullets start flying, make sure to be at the end of the line. If you can fall down and pretend to be hit, that would serve you best. You have one goal, Brother, and that is to return here to me. I need you. I don't care who wins this war; none of that matters. I just care about you."

The patter of rain off the cabin roof isolated these two boys in a space all their own. For a while, they said nothing. Darkness descended quickly upon them. Tomorrow, Matt would venture toward the Army of Virginia and begin a journey that frightened Luke immensely. He could not even conceive that it was actually going to happen. It made no sense. And yet, here it was, just a few hours away.

"I suppose you are going to spend your last night here with your wife?" Luke asked his brother.

Matt just laughed. "She went to spend the night with her daddy," he said. "She gave me a peck on the cheek and said good-bye and good luck in the war and said that hopefully she would be pregnant when I next saw her. Now if that ain't love, I don't know what is."

The two of them burst into laughter. A few tears rolled from Matt's eyes as he nodded his head up and down. "I'll miss you, Brother. I'll think about you every day. I'll even think about your damned grapes and imagine you lying on that red raft of yours and staring into the sky and figuring stuff out in that crazy mind of yours. I think about Paul every day already. Now I got you to think about too. I ain't sure my brain is big enough to do all that thinking!"

"Then what are you doing tonight?" Luke asked him.

"I'll sleep here with you, like always. I got all my stuff together so I can march off at the crack of dawn. It's a two-day march from here they say, and no enemy troops to worry about on the way. But tonight, Ruth is making me a feast, and she's going to bring it to me here, and all of us, me and you and her and her boys, we all is going to enjoy it together. Like it should always be."

"Yes." Luke nodded. "Like it should always be. And like it will be again."

"I know what the doctor says," Matt told him. "And I hope he's right that this war ends quick. But I'm hoping we lose the thing. That this man General Hooker, he knows how to beat Lee, and he chases the rebel armies all the way back to Richmond and gets them to give up. That's what I'm thinking is gonna happen.

And then I can come back here and spend the summer with you. And eat your grapes and share a spot on that raft. And we will be doing it as free men. That's what I hope."

"I do too, Brother. I think about that every day. Every minute of every day."

The night passed quickly. Luke stayed up most of it. The rain had abated, and a soft, chilly wind bellowed through the porous cabin walls. He watched his brother, who snored often, tossing around the straw mattress, a visage of distress sewn upon him. Luke didn't know how he would function here without his brothers. This war of emancipation—the election of a president pledged to repress the brutal slave system—was ironically doing just the opposite. It was tearing the farm apart, threatening the tranquil fortress they had constructed, and tossing Luke to a fate unknown.

They hugged for a long time the next morning, both shedding far too many tears. They said very little. Luke beseeched his brother again to be safe. Matt told Luke that he loved him. Then finally, with Luke's prodding, Matt trudged away, turning back many times and waving to his brother, until his image faded into a soft fog that descended upon them from the mountains above. He was gone.

Old Rag stared down at Luke all day, its rigid rock core providing him with a whiff of hope.

Jessie came back from the doctor's house later that morning; Luke heard her carriage trumping toward the main house. Ronald, the young overseer, was sleeping in a guest bedroom, and Jessie likely would tell him to leave. In the past two years, she had barely come to visit Luke. She did on occasion when Matt had business in town. Sometimes she would rip off her clothes and implore Luke to do the same. Then she would tell him to pleasure her, because, as she relayed to him, "My husband is incapable of that. He's hardly a man. Hardly worth sharing a bed with." She could only be with Luke when her "womb was not ripe," as she said. "We can't take chances. I plan to have Matthew's baby, even though he seems to be entirely incapable of accomplishing that simple task. He is quite the idiot." After their encounters, she would dress herself and then tell Luke, "You are lucky. I still enjoy you. And you clearly enjoy me. As long as you can perform, you will be just fine. But the minute I tire of you, or you lose interest in me, or you can't satisfy me enough, then I will have no need for you, Luke. Don't forget that. Don't ever forget who owns your life."

Matt had been with Luke often in the past few months, and Jessie spent more time with her father. She was trying to have a baby with Matt, or so she said. She would still talk to Luke by day, often with Matt in tow, discussing mundane topics such as the upcoming planting season and her excitement about the grapes—she always patting Luke on the head, he always giving her a dumb smile and a mouth-full of thank you's and yes ma'ams in response.

After Matt marched off to war, Luke went about his day as always, trying to forget the empty hole that his brother's absence gnawed into his heart. There was not a lot to do on the farm during the winter. A cold, moist day confronted him, but it was saturated by bursts of the soothing sun that blasted through congregating clouds. He helped to grind cornmeal, and to assist Ruth's boys, he welded some metal nails in the blacksmith shop. Luke had some lunch that Ruth brought to him, and then he retreated to his cabin at a little after six, darkness already enveloping the farm, his belly just a bit hungry. He thought about Matt, happy that his brother had a dry, sunny day on which to make his journey.

Soon after six, footsteps approached the cabin, and Luke knew that it would be Ruth, bringing him something to eat. After dinner, he hoped to read a few books that he had stashed under his bed, using a candle to illuminate just enough of his cabin to enable him to peruse the pages. One of the books, written in

French, discussed the intricacies of making wine. The other was an English–French dictionary. He had learned a lot about the French language, but not enough to decipher this very complex manual.

A shadow from outside the door burst in, and Luke turned toward it, startled. It was Jessie!

"Take off your clothes," she barked at him. "I want to fuck you right here and right now."

"But, Ms. Jessie," he said to her with as feeble an infection as he could muster, "I isn't sure, because what do's I knows anyway, but isn't you's ripe now? That's what master Matt he says to me."

"Are you questioning me, Luke?" She snarled, slapping him across the head. "Do you want me to tell my daddy that you have the audacity to question my orders?"

"No, ma'am, no, it's not likes that. I's is just confused, that's all. I thought you's was trying to have a baby with master Matt, that you's was ripe, and always before you said, 'Luke, I know you wants to have me, but you can'ts haves me when I is ripe.' Isn't that what you always says, Ms. Jessie?"

"Take off your clothes," she demanded, as she pulled her pretty blue dress over her head. "Lie down on the ground, and you better be able to perform."

Luke was not sure if he could. He was scared. He felt nothing down below. He thought of other things, better things. He looked at her and imagined that she was an angel who had come to him in a dream; he thought of her as the sweet girl who patted him on the head and who was, without her knowing it, saving his farm.

She hovered above him. "I've been fucking a lot of people, Luke," she said. "Not just Matt. He is inert; he can't seem to produce. So, I'm upping my odds. When the troops came back last week, I offered my body to a few of them. Only Jude said no; he's been inside of me more than I can tell you, but now he's more in love with a flag than a woman. Let him fuck the Confederate flag for all I care. That's his loss. Matt had his turn too. And now it's yours. One of you will get me pregnant. At this point, I don't care who it is."

She pulled off her slip and leaped upon him, kissing him on the lips.

"But if the baby comes out black, Ms. Jessie, that's nots going to be good for none of us."

"Well, a Negro baby is better than no baby at all. Don't worry, Luke, I won't blame you for it. Maybe I'll say that one of Ruth's sons raped me, or one of the other slaves in town. I'll see how I feel. But if your master can't perform like a man, then I'll give other men a chance." She lay down on the dirt. "OK, I'm ready. Feed my womb with your best seeds. Fuck the living crap out of me, Luke!"

A wave of fear gripped him, but he knew that he had to perform, or God knows what she would do to the farm. He closed his eyes. And he gave her his seeds.

She came every night that week to see him and forced him into having sex. One night he could not meet her expectations, and she screamed so loud that a dozen owls howled into the dark, cold air. She told him that he would be hanging by the neck come morning if he ever did that again. But the next night she came back as though nothing had transpired. Luke lived in fear. He worried that his efforts would induce a pregnancy. And then what? A Negro baby? No greater scandal would have gripped this land for as long as he was alive.

And then it stopped, and everything became as it once was.

The winter was long, but a productive spring lay ahead. He watched to see if Jessie's belly grew even bigger than it was. And he sat down whenever he could and read about wine making in the original French. "I wonder what my brothers are doing?" he asked himself, flying as far from this reality as his tortured mind would allow.

25

"Henry Highland Garnet has earned the respect of every human being in this city and beyond," Paul shouted from a makeshift podium, as throngs of people cheered him. A cool wind whistled through his mop of dark hair, but he felt warm up here; he was glowing. This was his moment, this was his country's moment, and he was so proud and so thrilled to share it with those he most loved. He had finally achieved the morsel of success and recognition that he so desperately craved.

Locals lined an area of shops and shoddy tenement houses at Bleeker and Carmine Streets, where Paul lived and where his business had thrived for the past two years. Paul was but one of several speakers who riled up this small crowd before they would collectively migrate over to Cooper Union, where Reverend Garnet, Lewis Tappan, and other notaries planned to usher in 1863 with an Emancipation Jubilee to celebrate President Lincoln's proclamation. Finally, after so much suffering and waffling, the President of the United States declared an end to slavery in America at midnight of the new year. And despite the cold and damp weather, despite pools of icy mud and rivers of filth, despite the paucity of money for heat and food and affordable goods that the war brought to New Yorkers, this largely African

American crowd bathed in an intoxicating jubilation, cheering every one of Paul's words.

Near the front row, Paul peered at a white man and woman (the only dots of white in this black audience), who lay against each other and infused him with an inner fulfillment, being so integral to the arduous task that enabled him to be here today. The woman, with long orange hair and piercing blue eyes, exuded a glow that lit up the dreariness of this cloudy day. She wore a flowing yellow dress (secondhand, of course, purchased from Paul for just this occasion) and coddled a young toddler, not much more than a year old, with dark black skin, wide brown eyes, and a tuft of curly black hair. The boy laughed as the woman tossed him up and down, her smile radiant, her joy apparent, and her eyes peering proudly at Paul. The man near her cried out with a far more rambunctious and effluviant fervor, waving his left arm back and forth and shouting, "You tell those bastards, Paul," even as his concealed right arm seem to be rubbing her back. Occasionally, they would glance at each other, smile knowingly, and then immediately look away toward the speaker, of whom they were so proud on this amazing day.

"Reverend Garnet and I had a falling out a little less than two years ago, right around the time that the South chose its treasonous path toward war against our Union," Paul continued. "The fault for that breach was all mine, and since then, I have come to understand his greatness. Who can doubt this man's passion and resolve? Who can question what he has done for the cause? I was privileged to be at Shiloh Presbyterian Church last night when Reverend Garnet, among others, including Reverends Jocelyn, Leigh, and of course Gilbert highlighted the profound significance of what our most honorable President Lincoln has done, an act of goodness and courage as our soldiers struggle so mightily in the field. We heard these great men, these leaders of our cause, speak of the great deeds of Negroes in this country, and they reminded us that because of Father Abraham's declaration on the last day of 1862, slavery is dead and buried in America; our national sin has finally been erased.

"Yes," he continued, as he walked into the audience and snatched the small baby from the orange-haired woman's outstretched arms. "Reverend Garnet and I had a falling out. But no more. We speak the same language now, the language of freedom, and we help each other to achieve that very elusive goal. He is a man who, twenty years ago, encouraged slaves to rebel against their owners rather than continue to suffer the indignity of the institution, only to be assailed by liberal white and Negro men who advised caution. Reverend Garnet did not back down; he suggested that Negroes move to Africa, to Liberia, where at least they could be free. And then even more timid souls, whites and Negroes alike, told him that he was wrong to think that way. But to this great man, to this brave leader of our cause, all that mattered was that we would be free! Today," he said loudly, lifting the small boy over his head, "I hold my son, named after my father Jake, a white man, a slaveholder, but one who defied this barbaric system the only way he knew how, who educated us, who treated us as his own children and his equals. Today I know that Jake will never be a slave in America. Today I think of my dear brother Luke, still enslaved on a farm in Virginia, and I smile for him knowing that today and henceforth forever he too will bask in the light of freedom as I have felt the past two years in this great city and in this great nation under the shadow of a great man, my friend, my mentor, Henry Garnet. And so, let's all go to Cooper Union on this most glorious of New Year's days and bask in his glow, and in the glow of our fellow white and black United States citizens, free at last, living under a veil of democracy and freedom of opportunity, our chains broken, our lives finally able to begin. How wonderful that my son Jake is born into a world as this. Now, let's celebrate!"

The crowd roared as Paul hopped off his soapbox and kissed Jake on the cheeks. Unbeknownst to Paul, who had lost himself in the moment, Jake was crying hysterically, and Paul handed him to the smiling woman whose long orange hair fluttered in the soft breeze. She caressed the boy and then kissed Paul on the cheek.

"Smiles would have been proud," she said to him. "As I was. I told you that you would make a difference in this world! I had faith in you, Paul. I always will!"

He nodded. "Well," he said to Elana Biggelow, the long-suffering wife one of the most powerful men in the influential Five Points Irish community, the woman who had hired Smiles two years ago as her nanny and, in the process, saved Paul from himself, "it's not exactly the fame I hoped for. I won't be a speaker at the Jubilee, and Mr. Tappan doesn't even know who I am, nor does any mover or shaker in the abolitionist world. I'm not exactly Frederick Douglass. But I guess with my own people here, I at least made a bit of a difference, and that feels good enough today."

"As it should," she said to him. "Your friends and neighbors are the only ones you should care about. If they love you, then you have earned the love of the world."

The man who had been standing by Elana Biggelow's side slapped Paul on the head. "What can I tell you?" Izzy said to him, with a grin as wide as his receding hairline. "You were amazing up there, and for the first time in my life I had fun on the Christian New Year, although it would have been nice if a single white person other than me and Mrs. Biggelow were here to listen to you or to even care about emancipation. Other than that, it's a perfect New York day. And by the way, good fucking job."

Elana Biggelow gently handed the now-sleeping Jake back to the boy's father. She nodded at him. "I will go get your wife so she can join you at the Jubilee," she said. "If Smiles knew you'd be speaking, I'm sure she would have rather been here. But I will tell her how wonderful you were, just like we all would expect you to be."

At that moment LB pushed through a crowd of hovering men and women, many of whom now surrounded Paul to tell him that "it was the best speech I's ever heard," and other such acclamation. They hugged him and shook his hand and spoke to him as though he were their best friend. They all took their turns congratulating and thanking him, before marching a few blocks east to the jubilee. He knew most of them well and was thrilled to have earned their love and support. And then he turned to his good friend, who waited patiently for them to disperse.

"Hell, Paul," LB said to him, slapping him hard on the back, a big grin on his face. "You's sure is some kind of local hero around these parts, as shocks and surprised I is to even consider it. Think about it. Two years ago, me and you was running for our lives from these very people on these very streets; we was desperate, and you didn't have a friend in the world. And now look what the wind blowed in. It's like a whole different world started once this war began. You is a man who has risen again, just like the Son of God you don'ts even believe in."

"All I know, James," said Elana Biggelow, turning again to Paul and kissing him on the cheek, "is it that the people who know him the best are the ones who consider him their hero. Our poor Paul is always dejected because no one ever listens to him or gives him a chance to lend his voice to the movement. But look what happened today. Clearly a lot of people are doing just that, the most important people in the world, the ones who know him the best. You tell your friend that, James."

Paul laughed. "Without you, Mrs. Biggelow, I may still be up on that hill wallowing in my own misery. You and LB and Izzy and Smiles. Its takes good friends to make this world worth living. Good friends, and a day like today. We should remember this day. Because tomorrow may be another day of hell."

Izzy just laughed. "Spoken like a true Jew, Paul! You could easily be one of us!"

"Stop being so cynical, Mr. Snout," Elana Biggelow said to Izzy, as she stared deeply into his eyes, and he peered back into hers. For a moment they seemed transfixed and said nothing at all. And then she laughed. "We can't all be Jews all the time, you know. Some of us have to have some faith in the future and have a little bit of fun."

Elana Biggelow grew up in Five Points, an immigrant from Galway—a small town in Ireland—who arrived here at age two after the potato blight nearly extinguished her family. Her parents wandered the streets of New York and took what they could from garbage cans and handouts until her dad found more steady construction work and a small tenement in which to live. They nursed Elana through two bouts of pneumonia before losing an older boy to whooping cough a year later. Both parents worked twelve-hour days, her father climbing up the Irish ladder to a respected position in Fire House 21, where more opportunity for employment at the docks provided him and his family with enough money to live without fear of starvation.

Elana was pretty enough to attract the attention of some of the other Irish boys and smart enough to know what she wanted in life. Her heart was always big and welcoming; that was clear to everyone who knew her. She saw the good in every person, no matter what they thought or did. She defended "the poor, disenfranchised Negro," and fought hard for a bill to extend voting rights to African Americans in the state, a bill that failed to pass the New York State legislature at the end of 1860. She even insisted that women would make better leaders and citizens than men and that at the very least they deserved the vote. Despite how sacrilegious her views were in New York's Irish community, no one disparaged Elana, because she projected an incessant visage of kindness and decency, always smiling and immensely shy and, despite her often-abrasive positions, always courteous to all.

She met her husband, Ernest T. Biggelow, when she was twenty-two and he was twenty-seven. He too worked at Fire

Department 21, rose to become its youngest chief, and, by age thirty-five, he was an influential leader of the Five Points Irish community and a fairly wealthy man. He was known as a womanizer; he drank often late into the night with any number of men and women. She never asked him where he obtained his money and why he often did not come home at night. She really did not want to know. He claimed he was doing it all for his family. Together they had four children, two of whom survived, the last of whom was born in 1857, Ernest Junior, when Elana turned forty-two. Now, at age forty-eight, she was no less radiant, no less rosy-cheeked and happy, no less certain that every New Yorker despite their color or creed deserved a chance to succeed. Her views verged sharply from those of her husband's—the views that he could credibly elucidate if he were to retain his power base in Five Points. He publicly laughed off her naive ways as those of a pampered woman who did not truly understand the world, but privately he never berated her. Two years ago, he had hired Smiles as her nanny; he smelled the scent of war, and he wanted her to have help when he was gone. When the war started, he joined New York's Irish Brigade and, as a colonel, had helped lead his troops through some of the most devastating and bloody battles this country had ever known.

He wrote her letters often, at first extolling the war and the cause. As the months passed by, his words became less sanguine and more indignant and accusatory. He cursed all African Americans and claimed that he was fighting to bring the South back into the country and "kick all the damned Negroes out." Not once did he talk about her or whether he missed her, and not once did she write a letter back to him. In just a few weeks, his tour would be over, and he sent her a letter recently that he would be returning home. Many others had lost their husbands to the war, and Elana bled every day when she heard of yet another death. She prayed for her husband and for all the others. But she had come to enjoy being in New York without him, and she trembled about what life would be like when he returned home. That evening, as she walked with Paul and Smiles to Shiloh church, making sure to avoid any neighborhoods where she could be sighted by friends of her husband's, she told them her fears. She trembled a bit when she uttered the words. She did not know what to do. And then, as was her want when she felt sad, she changed the subject and sewed a smile upon her face.

"I remember hearing about you from Smiles," she said to Paul later that night, when they all ate together in the church's main hall, packed with small tables around which a few hundred black men, women, and children sat. Reverend Garnet, who hosted the event, was not present for the meal; he was called away to be with some of the other local abolitionist leaders where they would spend the evening with the Tappans. Henry Garnet, a short black man with a goatee and balding head, thanked every single one of his guests for making this day possible, hugged Paul, and bowed to Elana Biggelow, before rushing out to a more important calling. Paul felt a bit deflated to be left here with the "extras," as he called them. Still, he was with his friends and his wife. That really was enough.

"I took a liking to Smiles within two days of her coming to work with me," she said to Paul, as they ate a plate of corned beef and yams. "She was recommended to us by John Campion, who Ernie" (which is what she called her husband) "said was an up and coming member of the firehouse, and who praised Smiles's wonderful care for their baby when all of you were living together (and when Smiles, you were married to this other man, or so we all thought!)." She laughed and pointed to LB, who nodded and slapped Paul on the head.

And then she continued, "I immediately sensed her goodness, her intelligence, and her pain. She cried with tears of pure agony one day when I asked her why she looked so sad. She told me about you. I could see how much she loved you. What a wonderful man you must be for her to feel such intense passion for you, I thought! How much you had been through! She pointed me to Izzy, who I actually knew because I bought a lot of clothes from him; he has the best collection in the city of secondhanders, although I never took him as a do-gooder." She laughed and then stared into Izzy's eyes before turning her gaze again to Paul. "So, once I learned what had happened to you, I used my status as Ernest T. Biggelow's wife to talk to the right people, make some apologies, offer a few donations (money always talks!), buy a grand supply of used clothing from Mr. Snout's friend Abe (saying that it was to make up for the clothes that were stolen from you, and Abe forgave you that very minute), clothes that I wisely distributed to Reverend Garnet's parish, again in your name as an apology for what you had said to upset the reverend, and then I let it all play out. I put my faith in Smiles's love, and that motivated me to try to help any way I could. And today, Paul, and for the past two years, you have paid off my faith a thousand times over."

She kissed him on the head. He had heard the story far too many times, but he loved hearing it just once more and always enjoyed her maternal pecks that warmed his soul. Elana turned to Smiles and kissed her protuberant belly. "Two weeks until baby number two. I am guessing that Jake will have a beautiful sister this time." She winked at Izzy and then said, "Goodbye my friends, and Paul, you made me a happy woman today and so very, very proud to be your friend! But this Irish woman best get home before someone discovers that she's actually a decent person!" She walked out of the church's front door, turning around a couple of times and peeking in their direction.

Two minutes later, Izzy said he had to leave as well. "Being in a church for too long can be dangerous for Jews," he said. "Some have been known to spontaneously combust." He waved to everyone, kissed Smiles on her belly, and hustled out more quickly than Paul had ever seen him move before.

Paul just laughed. It had been a glorious day for him, and he basked in every part of it. He was truly happy. And, for this moment at least, he had not a worry in the world.

What is freedom? Paul wrote to Luke a few nights ago, as part of a series of letters he kept in a book that he hoped he could deliver to his brother once the war ended. *Freedom is pain. It is uncertainty. It is being exposed to irrational hate and having to figure out how to confront it. It is having your rights stripped away and fighting every day to retrieve them. Freedom is no holiday. But in my cold and drafty room three stories above a river of filth and human waste, I do have freedom. I have the ability to confront hate and fight for my rights. I can come and go as I please. I work for my living and use my industry and mind to earn money for me and my family. There is hope around every corner, and with my freedom I can work to achieve that hope. I may not have glorious mountains to peer at, or the quiet solitude of our pond and pear trees, and I so long to see your grapes and what they have become. But, dear Brother, the agony of freedom fills my veins and gives me life. I would not trade it for the world!*

As a dark and quiet night descended upon them, and the festivities faded back to the reality of the war—where inflation and incessant death flooded New York in the midst of a cold and miserable winter—three outcasts strolled away from Shiloh Church and up toward Bleeker Street. Smiles and her two husbands (as LB called the trio), arm in arm, traversed the dark and quiet streets of this suffering city. Tonight, they all were jubilant. Emancipation! The very thought of it weaved images through their own minds and generated thoughts of joy and hope of which none of them had previously conceived.

"It's just a gesture, really," Paul said, as his own thoughts trickled out of his mouth. "In truth, it doesn't change much of what is going on, and unless we win the war, it's really all about nothing. But, what the hell, it feels pretty damned good to know my brother is a free man in President Lincoln's eyes, even if he's not really free. I mean, that's a good thing, right?"

"There you go again," Smiles laughed, punching him on his chest. "You start spouting your views and don't have an idea how they affect other people." She punched him again. "You better listen to this pregnant lady, because I saved your hide far too many times, Paul Cocklin, and if I'm having this next baby with you, I better know that you is not going down another dangerous road, or I may has to find someone else to have it with."

Paul never spoke about how his wife's diction over the years had improved, although he marveled at the transformation. To him, it did not matter. Her beauty, her intelligence, her wisdom, and her love had not changed one bit! He stood in awe beside her as he always had!

"That hurts," Paul chuckled. "And I think it's too late to say you're not going to have this baby with me, don't you think?"

"I got more than one husband, Paul. Don't you forget that. Right now, that other one is looking pretty good just by virtue of his keeping his mouth quiet, something you not capable of doing."

A cool breeze whipped through some of the tall concrete buildings and struck Paul hard in his face. Under a shadow of concealed clouds, no stars twinkled in the night sky. Only a few people scampered by in this neighborhood bereft of any white faces, and so they at least felt safe. Elana Biggelow, who warned them to stay away from Irish enclaves tonight, offered to watch Jake and her own children; Smiles could spend the night with her men. Or her man, if LB offered to bunk with someone else, an offer he typically made, as he had many other friends in the building.

"And what's so wrong with what I said?" Paul asked Smiles's belly, talking to the child inside. "Why is your mother always criticizing me? I wasn't saying anything offensive! And I've been so good lately. Kept my mouth shut when I needed to. Played by the rules. Why is she complaining about this?"

"Because, dummy," LB said, slapping Paul on the side of the head, "you sounds like the arrogant bastard that you sometimes thinks you is. Emancipation is just a thing, right? Well, I gots to tell you something, and it aint's for the first time, and it's something you ain'ts should forgets. You was living on a prissy farm where they talked high and mighty to you, and you gots to learn about things and do things and live with the master and never get a whipping. In fact, it was the first time you did gets one is when you decided to up and runs away that day! Me and Smiles, we didn't gets that luxury. We had it rough; we barely survived. So, when we hear that the president of these United States says to all the people that he has just freed all the slaves, that when this war is over the bastard slaveholders will have to stop what they is doing and make us free, that's no fantasy to us. That's is a dream come true. And you better realize that from Reverend Garnet to every member of his church, we all's had that life in the South; not one of us had your prissy life, and we is all jumping and whooping and hollering, and we don't want to hear you say it's just a gesture. No, it ain't. It's everything. It's redemption!"

Paul nodded. "I know," he said. "I'm sorry. You know what I meant."

"This is what I know," said Smiles, grabbing Paul by his shirt and pulling him toward her. "I know that every Negro in New York is talking about my man. They all told me how amazing he was, how he put into words everything they were thinking. And I just listened to them, filling up with so much pride, and bubbling out with so much love." She kissed him on the lips, the passion of her embrace filling him with a warmth that seemed to burst through his skin.

And then she punched him again.

"Geeze," he hollered, pulling back. "What was that for?"

"Because, Paul, I love you, more than anything I could ever imagine. And we are having another child any day now. And when you say dumb things like you just did, I know your mind is starting to fart out loud like it did before, and that's when it got you and all of us in so much trouble. I need you to be good and keep those thoughts to yourself. You don't got to stop thinking them; just stop saying them."

Paul smiled. "I will. I promise. I only say those things to you two. And it wasn't even that bad!"

She punched him again and then started laughing. "When I say it's bad, then it's bad!"

They arrived at their tenement. There were no lights, hardly any heat. Smiles turned to her first husband and looked him in the eye. "I assume you are sleeping somewhere else tonight?"

He laughed. "Yes, dear," he said to her. "I will sleeps on the street if I must. I knows enough not to mess with the likes of you when you is in one of your moods, especially one of your pregnant moods."

"Good," she told him. "Although I don't want you on the streets. If you can't find a place to go, I'll toss you a few blankets and send you in the hall. I ain't cruel or anything! I treat my old husbands well!"

"That's be just fine," said LB. "It was a good day. Best day I remember in a long, long time. I am happy sleeping anywheres. Just glad that the world is now worth fighting for. Next, Paul, we got to convince the men in Washington to let us fights in this war. That's the only way we will really be free. But we can waits for that until tomorrow."

Paul nodded. Henry Garnet and others had been working toward the goal of Negro participation in the army. Paul knew that Smiles did not like hearing about it; it frightened her to think that her men would be in harm's way. So, he quickly changed the subject.

LB found a place to stay, and Paul and his wife walked hand and hand into their cozy little room. To Paul, this was the true reward of freedom. He would fall asleep in the arms of someone who had transformed his life and made him feel whole again. He would bathe in her love, as her hands caressed him and her lips washed over his. And when he woke up on Friday morning, he might be just a little late in getting to Abe's store to pick up his new supply of clothes, because her arms would still be around his body, her face against his, and the two would be entangled in a mutual knot that meant more to Paul than life itself.

Still, as the night progressed, thoughts did trickle in his mind. LB was right. Unless former slaves were able to take up arms for the Union, then all this would be for naught. Mrs. Biggelow told Paul that many men in the Irish community were not happy with emancipation. They resented "fighting a war for lazy Negroes who, once free, would come to New York to steal their jobs—their words, not mine," she said to him. Lincoln's proclamation triggered ire in the entire Irish community.

"In fact," she had said to Paul and Smiles earlier in the evening, before they all went to the church dinner together, "I wouldn't venture too far in Five Points or any of the Irish areas. I was down in Five Points, and people are very angry. I expect my husband will be irate when he comes home. He is going to say the same thing. That once our president declared that this is a war to free slaves, and not one to hold the Union together, then all of the men who fought for the Union and died for the Union will have been betrayed. I know that's how he will think, hanging out at the saloons with his other army buddies, talking badly about everyone other than themselves. I will have to keep my mouth closed when he comes back. And he is coming soon. I dread that every day. Sometimes I wish we could all just run away from here, to some cabin in a faraway place where no one can find us. Sometimes I do."

Her face dropped into an uncharacteristic melancholy, wrinkles and lines appearing where none had been before, and she stared into an imaginary space. Paul and Smiles did not know what to do, but within minutes her bright blue eyes popped open, and her glorious smile again leaped upon her ruddy skin. "We should get going," she said. "And get to the church. So much to celebrate. I told Mr. Snout that we would be there right at six. We don't want to be late."

Me and Mr. Snout. Elana talked about him incessantly. And when she did, her eyes exploded with an exuberant rush of joy. As did his!

Paul immersed himself in the night, his thoughts drifting away every time that Smiles held him. It might be weeks or longer before he could spend a night with her again, even after the baby was born, when she would likely be confined in the Biggelow house. Sometimes they could only share glances when too many of Mr. Biggelow's friends jostled around the place. None of them liked Paul or approved of his presence, and Smiles had few hours in the week when she was free to leave. As much as Mrs. Biggelow dreaded her husband's return, it was bound to be much worse for Paul.

LB was right. It was time for African Americans to arm themselves. But that thought would be more toxic in the minds of men like Ernest T. Biggelow than even emancipation. Biggelow and his cronies would fight against everything that men like Paul and Reverend Garnet had achieved in their absence. They would reestablish control over the city. Swarms of them were expected to return from the front. And of course, Ernest would regain control of his home, relegating his wife to a more menial role, and likely disrupt the harmony that now existed between them all.

He thought a bit about Mrs. Biggelow. *What would become of her once her husband did return? Would her fire and lust for goodness fall victim to his control? Would her ability to help those in need be muffled? Would she be putting herself in harm's way to continue her friendship with these people whom she had come to embrace during the two years of her husband's absence? And what about Izzy?* Sometimes the two of them seemed more attached to each other than could possibly be safe.

Now, though, he lay with Smiles, and that calmed his troubled thoughts. He knew that emancipation was a mere gesture, one that obfuscated the shackles that kept him and other African Americans confined to the lowest rungs of society. The return of the Irish Brigade would likely open festering wounds and show the limitations of mere words. As he told Luke, freedom never came easily. But he was free, in the most genuine meaning of that word, free to love and be loved, free to speak his mind, free to work for a living, free to change the world—if they would only let him.

Who would guess that the very next day he would be beckoned to do exactly that?

26

Spending a day in the neighborhoods of central Manhattan—where enclaves of African Americans gravitated and lived after being dislodged from their prior homes in the expanding island—proved both exhausting and exhilarating for Paul. Every day brought new faces, most of whom were refugees from the South, where they had escaped from farms and bondage; and every day other faces disappeared, usually relocating across the East River to Brooklyn or the Bronx. This was a tight community where people knew and protected each other. And all of them knew Paul.

"Which ways we heading today before the big storms hit us this afternoon?" LB asked his business partner as both pushed their wares upon wet, dirty streets in "Negro New York." LB peddled buttermilk and also an array of other more exotic products that varied, based on availability and pricing. When ripe fruit or overstocked staples or novel underpriced items hit the docks of Manhattan, they found their way to LB's cart. He kept his prices low and so his margins were small, but he sold a lot; people flocked to him when he had some new fruit or vegetable or staple. That was the business model that he, Paul, and Izzy adapted, and it was working. Last week he sold bags of white rice, something rarely seen here and something that generated quite a stir in the neighborhood. He sold out in two hours.

"I have a few deliveries to make, and then I may just set up shop down at the end of Bleeker," said Paul, shoving a heavy and lopsided cart laden with clothes, some hanging and some lying flat in open drawers. "Meet me there, and we'll have some lunch in Union Square. Smiles will be there at noon sharp; Elana can only watch the kids until one because she has an appointment. So, don't be late."

"Like I always says, Paul, Smiles can stay longer if she brings Jake and Elana's two kids, so why don't she just do that? They needs some outdoor time."

Paul just shook his head. "You know that's not happening, James," he said. "First, you're forgetting that she's pregnant and about to explode, and it's tough enough for her to drag herself around even if she didn't have to tow the other kids with her too. And you know that Elana, God bless her in every other way, doesn't like her kids out in the cold or on the streets, and she would be upset if she knew that Smiles brought them here. Smiles won't do it. So, I beg you, be on time. That's all I'm asking."

"I will tries," LB said. "But I gots me a flock of spices and crazy ass vegetables from India, and I knows there is going to be a mob trying to buy thems, so I might be a bit busy, my good friend."

"Twelve sharp," Paul repeated. "I want to see my son. And my wife."

"Yes, sir," James said, turning and laughing as he pushed his cart away.

The wind blew just a bit more briskly than usual, and large dark clouds hovered over the city. It was one of those days you just didn't know what might happen. It was cold but maybe not quite cold enough for snow. Either way, Paul did not want his clothes ruined by a burst of unexpected weather; he had burlap draped over his cart, but if heavy rain flooded the streets with mud and flowing garbage, there was little he could do to get his goods back downtown without them getting soiled. So, he moved quickly this morning; the goal was to finish all sales by noon, see Jake and Smiles, and then rush the merchandise back to Abe's shop before the clouds opened up.

Often on Fridays Jake would sleep over in the "husband's suite," as Smiles labeled Paul's and LB's tiny tenement room, but not tonight. Paul had been beckoned to Shiloh Church to meet with Reverend Garnet after work, so his boy would have to stay with Smiles and Elana in the comfort of the Biggelow mansion that sat a good twenty blocks from Paul's own home, near Union Square, where few black faces dared to wander.

The journey that brought Paul to this point in time, as an oft invited guest in Reverend Garnet's church, often surprised even him.

Paul came off his mountain two years ago under the auspices of his white saints, Elana and Izzy, who cleaned up his mess and cleared the way for him to reenter society and give it another shot. The war had started, and a large chunk of the male Irish community in Lower Manhattan, as well as many Germans and Jews and Dutch and British men, traveled to the front, which at that time was south of Washington in Virginia. No one could be bothered worrying about Paul or collecting bounties. The city was in a war fever!

From that point, Paul paved his own path to success. While stranded on his hill, he had pondered over novel means of improving Abe's business in the wake of Southern secession. Many clothing dealers thrived by supplying the military, but Abe, who stocked secondhand clothes only, made his small fortune by selling inexpensive merchandise to the common New Yorker. Inflation ran rampant in New York, curtailing the ability of many people to buy clothes, and the reliable Southern supply of cotton instantly ceased on the day that South Carolinians bombarded Fort Sumpter, thwarting the production of new clothing. This led fewer people to sell Abe old clothes that he could repair and resell, which was the very heart of everything he did.

"This is what I am thinking," Paul said to Izzy and Abe a few weeks after escaping from the mountain, as they sat in the latter's dark and cluttered back room, poring over a pile of diagrams that Paul had sketched. Paul had already discussed his ideas with Izzy, who needed several days to digest them. They verged sharply from standard business practice and seemed almost beyond pragmatic utility. But the more Izzy talked to Paul, the more they made sense, until finally he had the courage to tell his boss.

"It's a three-pronged approach," Paul told them, pointing to spreadsheets and figures. "It's predicated on the assumption that new supplies of cotton will be forthcoming, which I would imagine is what a reasonable capitalistic market is going to enable, probably from India and other Eastern lands, and that it may take a year or so for the larger clothing manufacturers like Brooks Brothers to generate a sellable supply of new products, especially given the government's requisitioning of thousands of uniforms to clothe the soldiers. That gives us a year to corner local markets and be prepared to compete favorably with larger distributors once their supply of locally oriented clothing is replenished."

Abe, his large head shaking horizontally, put up his hand. "Paul," he said, "I need you to slow down, speak in smaller words, and try not to brutalize us with your economic theories. What you just said sounds like Yiddish to an Irishman. I am a simple man. Izzy is an even simpler man. We don't want to feel as though we are going through an entire Passover service tonight. Just the facts, please."

Izzy hit Paul hard on the back. "This boy has got ideas flying through his brain at goddamned train-like speed. What can I tell you? Let the boy speak, and eventually it will make sense. He doesn't know small words, he doesn't know what simple means, and he just needs to talk."

"OK," Abe said. "Just, a little more slowly."

Paul smiled. "I know this is going to work," he said glowingly. "I am convinced of it. We will be thriving within two months. That's as simple as I can make it."

Abe looked at Izzy, who peered back, and they, along with Paul, started to laugh. "OK, son," Abe said. "Not quite that simple! I do appreciate your confidence, but from what Izzy tells me, you are asking me to change my entire business model. I won't interrupt you. Pontificate to your heart's content!"

Paul laid out his plan.

Part one: Establish costs to the consumer below market rates and flood the market with low-priced products. With fewer new clothes on the market—given short-term cotton shortages and the need for most manufacturers to focus on the production of uniforms—customers could be convinced to purchase secondhand clothes if they were priced appropriately low, especially given the inflationary constraints that most New Yorkers now experienced. "That means we give our customers firm, low prices; no more haggling. The people in the Negro neighborhoods don't like to haggle," Paul suggested. "Imagine that we have prices that are on the low side of market value," Paul said, pointing to a diagram of three boxes with arrows connecting them to another box. "We can have three tiers of pricing, based on the condition of the product: good quality, high quality, and near-new quality. Of course, most of what we sell will be the latter, but we need some inexpensive items too for those who cannot afford the high-end merchandise and for those who want a bargain. In all cases, our charge will be 10 percent above cost, and we will split the profit fifty-fifty between Abe and the salesman."

Abe raised his hand in protest, but Izzy shushed him. "Let him talk," Izzy said, waving Paul on.

Part two: "We sell our clothes locally. Most neighborhoods are divided ethnically, and each neighborhood has particular tastes and needs when it comes to which clothes they want to purchase. Also, people in those neighborhoods may like buying products produced within the neighborhood itself. Thus, let's say we are talking about the Negro neighborhoods off Bleeker. We will hire several people in that neighborhood, all Negroes; we teach them how to repair and improve used clothes, we pay them, and then we sell those clothes in the very same neighborhood. Customers will appreciate buying something knowing that Bessie down the street, or Sally who lives on Carmine, or others they might know actually did the work to improve these clothes and are being employed by us."

Abe shook his head up and down and put his chin on his fist. "Hmmm," he said. "Very interesting. Who exactly are Bessie and Sally?"

"Shhh," Izzy said to him again. "Go ahead, Paul, what's your third part?"

"Diversification," he said. "We sell more than just clothes. In addition to clothing salesmen, we have other carts peddling useful and interesting items that we can buy cheap and sell at higher profits. Without a Southern source of crops and cotton, other nations will be flooding our harbors, as I've said, bringing not only cotton, but also items from their nations that many common New Yorkers have never before seen. Through a process of trial and error we will find the ones that have the largest potential markets, or which are inexpensive because they are in oversupply or not perfect condition, and we sell them to our customer base, marketing them in novel ways and repackaging them to make the customers feel like they are getting something unique at a bargain price, which in effect they are."

It took Abe a week to buy into Paul's scheme. "Six days to figure out what the hell he was talking about," he told Izzy. "And then a day—when I was in the temple praying to God for some help in deciphering it all and wondering if it could work—to realize that it's actually the most brilliant idea I have ever heard in my life."

And so, for the next two months, Paul, LB, and Izzy assembled the many cogs of their new business. Paul and LB found willing assistants in the Negro communities of Manhattan to repair used clothing. They talked to some African Americans on the docks (who worked there in larger numbers now that the white supply of labor had dwindled from so many volunteering for the war) to get advance information about which boats were arriving in port to sell which goods. They spread the word that a new breed of pushcart operators was coming to the neighborhood, one that offered high quality and low prices all without any haggling, with all clothing produced by neighborhood residents. Izzy did the same for many of the white ethnic communities in Lower Manhattan.

Paul devised an advertising campaign. They hired local residents to spread the word.

By the end of the summer in 1861, Abe's new business exploded upon the city. He hired over twenty salesmen and spread his web across the entire island. Every night he met with Paul to look over trends and numbers and devise new strategies to increase market penetration. When Abe regularly wondered whether, given their success, they should increase their prices to above the 10 percent profit that Paul had originally suggested, Paul never budged. "Low, consistent prices," Paul reminded him just a month ago. "High volume. That, combined with quality, local production, and exotic goods, is why we are successful. People are hurting all over the city. A dollar now buys half of what it did a year ago. People count on us to give them a good product at a good price. We don't make much for each sale, but we make enough given our volume. And our reputation for integrity and honesty is a huge asset. You're doing pretty well, Abe. We all are. Let's not change direction now."

As always, Abe shook his head, smiled, and wrapped Paul in a giant bear hug. "My wife thanks you too," he whispered in Paul's ear. "We just bought a new dining room set. Ha!"

Now, two years later, as clouds swarmed across the darkening sky, Paul pushed his cart, saying hi to so many of the African American residents who lived and worked here, all of whom enjoyed chatting with this "smart-talking and funny Negro" who was glad to stop and engage any and all those who greeted him. Some looked over his clothes, a few purchased an item or two, a few more placed orders for the future when a paycheck may come in, but most just wanted to talk. They chatted about emancipation. About General Lee's successes and whether any Northern general could possibly turn things around. About President Lincoln's chances of winning a second term in 1864, just a year away. About the muddy streets and rats and whether a certain woman and man down the street would tie the knot, about how their employment opportunities might dwindle when many of the white soldiers returned to Manhattan at the end of their tours of duty, and whether the government may have to resort to conscription should the soldiers decide not to reenlist, as many were threatening to do.

"If we has a draft," said one elderly man with a well-trimmed white beard and a short tuft of mostly black hair, and who purchased a pair of brown socks for a few pennies, "no one is going to be happy. There will be trouble for sure; the whites is already blaming the whole war on us, and too many people is dying, and they is not happy—no, sir, not one bit. Since the emancipation proclamation was announced by Father Abraham, lots of white folk I runs into, they is not wanting to fight for our freedom, and I don'ts blame them. It's our fight, not theirs. I don'ts know why they isn't just let us Negroes to fight. I would even does it, even though I can'ts walk from here to there without my feets hurting."

"Your feet will feel much better with those socks, I assure you," Paul smiled at him. "Joan fixed them herself. You know Joan, a few blocks over? She said they have a lot of cushions now."

The man nodded and smiled. "I do's appreciate that, Paul, I surely does. Still," he said, "there is nots a man who lives here who isn't willing to put his life on the line and fight for the Union. Them white folk is right. This be our fight. We's should have a chance to fight for our own freedom. They's done enough. Enough of them has died already. Now it's our turn. We's gots to be able to fight; that's all I's is saying. And not one other Negro man or boy would think any different."

As it so happened, that is exactly what Reverend Garnet wanted to discuss with Paul later that night.

They sat in a well-manicured office behind the church sanctuary, the very room where Henry Garnet and James Pennington had berated Paul two years ago, driving him away and threatening his life. Now, having befriended Paul without ever discussing that past indiscretion, Henry Garnet frequently summoned him "for advice and counsel," to ponder issues about which he had been thinking. These two men had an implicit understanding not to discuss God or religion and not to ask Paul to come here when services were in sessions. It was a very cordial and formal relationship, one Paul had hoped would vault him into a more meaningful role in the abolitionist movement, something that never did occur.

Deep down Paul knew that Reverend Garnet would never forgive him for his atheism and for assailing those who used scripture to achieve positive ends.

"That's the price you pay for staying true to your values, my friend," Izzy had told him almost two years ago. "My people paid a hefty price for staying firm and not rolling over to suck the assess of our Christian masters, but what can I tell you? We're still hanging around, we're prospering, and we still can hold our heads high. One day, you will be rewarded for not crawling in the reverend's ass to help you rise up in the world, and believe you me, it's better to live as a lowlife in this world than to rise to the top covered in that kind of shit."

Reverend Garnet, with a deep and thundering voice, wearing a blue striped shirt that he purchased from Izzy just a few days ago, stood up and paced. "You may know this already, because you seem to know almost everything," he said to Paul, staring at a colorful piece of stained glass. "But soon before his emancipation proclamation, Lincoln's Congress passed the Military and Confiscation Act at the end of 1862 that frees all Negroes who are runaways, while at the same time allows, for the first time, Negroes in the North to join the Union army. It's gone quiet in the press, because there's no real mechanism for it to actually happen yet, and our cautious President isn't pushing the issue until he thinks it will fly. Word is, he wants a Union victory first, and God only knows when that's coming. But my good friend James Pennington and Fred Douglass and others are down in the capital now using whatever influence they have with the president to push the issue to fruition."

Paul was stunned. He had no idea. "I was just talking about this with my customers today," he told the reverend.

"They are trying to get our president to set up a Bureau of Colored Troops to manage Negro enlistees and encourage volunteers. We all know that the bulk of the Negro community will all enlist, every free Negro in this country wants to turn the war around and gain our own freedom. That's where we are." He swung his head toward Paul's and looked him in the eye. "And that's where I need your advice."

Paul peered back at him. The prospect of joining the Union cause had always excited Paul. But now the prospect frightened him. He was married with one child and a second on the way. His business was thriving and would continue to grow as long as he remained at its helm. Leaving New York now and putting himself in harm's way sent chills down his spine. He said nothing to the reverend.

Henry Garnet continued, "In some ways, Paul, you know the pulse of the Negro community, perhaps more than even I do. They tell me what I want to hear, but they talk to you with brutal honesty. And you have good connections to the white community—your best friend is a Jewish merchant, and your wife works for one of the more powerful movers and shakers in the Irish community."

"Elana Biggelow?" Paul asked. "She's not really a mover or shaker."

"Her husband," Garnet said. "Ernest T. Biggelow. I have met him several times. His reputation is not a good one, that I know. But I have heard other things about him that make me question whether the man himself is far better than the image he has had to paint of himself. The Irish have a reputation in this town, Paul. It's not a good one in our eyes. But I know many fine Irish men and women who have helped the cause, who are sympathetic to our plight. I need to know how they will react to a colored military regiment in this city. I need to know how the Negroes will react. If we want to build a regiment of Negro fighting men, we must do it, as much as we can, under the umbrella of cooperation between the city's Negroes and the Irish, two groups that have had their differences, but who pray to the same God, and who we hope to support the same cause. "

"I can tell you this much, Reverend: when the Negroes tell you that they are ready to fight, they are. I hear it every day. With passion and resolve. They all know that by entering the army they will jeopardize their own financial security and that of their families, and despite that, every one of them will put his life on the line for our president. We," Paul said, "we will do what it takes to win this war and do our part."

"And how do you think Ernest Biggelow will react?" Reverend Garnet asked, placing his right hand on Paul's shoulder. He looked deeply into Paul's eyes. "Is he the ally we are looking for? Is he a bridge to the Irish community? Your wife and his wife are friendly, or so I hear. Will that help our cause?"

Paul did not know how to answer that question. Elana did occasionally speak about her husband, but with tight lips and few words. Paul never knew what she really thought about this man whom she had met at a young age and who now had been absent for two years fighting in a war that had killed so many others from her close-knit community.

Paul remembered something Elana had told him and Smiles. *Ernie is not the man they make him out to be," Elana said to Paul and Smiles one day. "He is a good and smart man. He has never treated me poorly, and he puts up with my unorthodox ways. He is a good Catholic. They say he has been with many women, but I know that he hasn't. I just know it. He drinks with all the men in power, but I have never seen him drunk. He kisses our children goodnight, even if he seems at all times distant. But my husband only has one love in this world, and it is not me. It's his work, his community, his love of power. I think he will be a good leader. I am nothing to him. I am just one of his constituents. He even doesn't fully trust me to raise our children. But for his constituents, he is much more generous.*

"The Irish community isn't the monolithic entity that it was before Sumpter," Paul told the reverend. "Its leaders are split about the war, about emancipation, about where they stand politically. Elana Biggelow tells me that many support Mayor Wood and the Peace Democrats, while many others are firmly on the side of the Union and squelching the Southern rebellion. Archbishop Hughes told the Catholic community to oppose emancipation; he said it's a plot hatched by radical Protestants who have no regard for property rights or for God's natural order; to him, God created slavery, and it's not up to secular men to end it. That's what's making men like Biggelow—men who are fighting to support the Union—waver a bit. They feel as though they have been sold a bad bill of goods, and they want to keep control of this city once the war is over. That's what Biggelow's wife told me. They fear a swarm of Negroes coming here and displacing their political base. To me, sir, the idea of Negroes fighting in the war will only elevate their political power, and I don't think the Irish bosses like Ernest T. Biggelow will support that at all."

Garnet chuckled. "You had to toss one zinger at me about God's support for slavery, didn't you, Paul?"

Paul smiled. "No, sir," he said. "I'm mocking Catholics. I thought you wouldn't mind that!"

Henry Garnet laughed. "Well, these days, we'll take all the allies we can find, Jews, Catholics, even you vicious atheists. But it sounds like Bishop Hughes won't be one of those allies. And it will be hard for men like Ernest Biggelow to support Negro conscription unless the Church does. The only thing in our favor is if Father Abe passes a draft, as he has threatened to do, we can use Negro conscription as a viable alternative to drafting white men who have already fought. We will have to see."

"I understand that Biggelow and a lot of the Irish soldiers are coming home soon."

Garnet nodded. "It will be very interesting, Paul. Most New Yorkers joined the army for two years, and my understanding is that few are reenlisting. Too many have died. Others have deserted and left the city. These men coming back, I don't know what their thinking will be, and whether they may be willing to help us arm Negroes to fight the next round of this war. But I think that Biggelow is a window into any dialogue we may be able to have with them. Can you help open that window, Paul?"

"When is he coming back?" Paul asked.

"Soon. Very soon. Some from the Irish regiment are trickling in already. It is bound to be any day now."

The thought of Ernest Biggelow's imminent return struck Paul hard. His absence had been a blessing to Paul. Elana allowed Paul to visit every day, she encouraged Smiles to eat lunch with her son and husband out of the house, and she helped them to spend several nights together every month. It was far less likely that the master of the house, a leader of the city's Irish community, would be so accommodating. And with a new baby coming, Paul wondered how much he would see Smiles and the children at all. As the reverend continued to speak, Paul's mind wandered. He thought about his wife, her face, her smile, the way she instinctively understood everything about him and always knew how to make him laugh. She was his heart and soul. What if he couldn't see her every day? What if he couldn't spend nights with her? His gut dropped. Suddenly, the prospect of creating Negro regiments seemed far less important to Paul than the fickle reality of his life.

27

On a frigid February day, bouncing along the East River, the red raft floated through Paul's mind. He could think of nothing else.

He remembered one cold and rainy day back before the Old Rag junket, before the whispers of war brought fear to white men and lashed scars upon his skin, back when his most pressing concern was shoring up sufficient markets for their fruit at harvest time. On that day, Paul dashed by the pond and saw his brother floating on the red raft. It was raining hard, but Luke basked in a warm contentment that seemed incongruent with the state of his frigid body.

"Brother," he called out, "are you insane? You'll get sick out there!"

Wind whipped across the pond, creating ripples that thrust the raft toward a downstream dam. Luke causally propelled himself to the pond's center by paddling with his arms. He seemed oblivious to Paul's words; he just floated there, staring into the sky, smiling. He did not respond.

Later, Luke wandered into the cabin and did not seem a bit cold or wet. His omnipresent smile wrapped around a wide face beneath an almost hypnotic stare. "Thank you," he said.

"For what?" Paul asked him. "What did I do?"

"Everything," said Luke. "You do everything, so I have to do nothing. You worry about everything, so I can worry about nothing. I live in my own thoughts and deflect reality far away because of you, Brother. On that red raft, in Old Rag's shadow, on our oasis that is severed from this world's depravity and chaos, I find a certain peace that could not transpire anywhere but here and could not be possible without you and Matt tackling the horrid reality of life that I choose to eschew."

"You're not even wet," Paul said to him. "That's not possible."

"And yet," he laughed, "it must be possible because it is a fact. I formulated some ideas out there that could substantially improve our agricultural productivity. Are we going to the main house tonight? I would like to discuss them with you and Matt."

"Of course," Paul said him, never fully comprehending how his brother remained so at peace on that flimsy raft in a tiny pond and how he stayed dry in a rainstorm when he sat on it. The raft shielded Luke from a reality of storms both real and virtual, one that, if fully scrutinized, could never inoculate him and his brother from the cognitive dissonance that hovered incessantly over them. Paul, who grappled with truth and angst every day of his life, could not fathom the lure of Luke's raft.

But now Paul understood.

Even as his life seemed finally to be on track, gnawing apprehension bit at Paul almost incessantly. He could think of almost nothing but his wife and two children, how much he craved them, how he wanted to lie with Smiles in some peaceful spot— the babies by their side—and stay there forever without any choices or stresses or obligations pulling him away. That was his red raft, and every day, even as his successes multiplied, even as he achieved the esteem he had always sought, he felt increasingly distant from it, alienated from what he needed most in this world: his red raft. He understood his brother, and he envied him. He so coveted being on his red raft.

The water was choppy on that mid-February day as Paul and Izzy crossed the East River on a ferry bound for Brooklyn. His mind drifted, and he felt he was on the pond, floating, oblivious to reality. Even the sharp chill of the river's wet wind barely penetrated his hide.

"So why Matt?" Izzy asked him. The two had been silent for quite some time as they waited for the ferry to commence its brief journey. It was unusual for Paul's loquacious friend to be so muted, but he had been so for several days now, sometimes staring into space, seemingly lost in his own thoughts.

"You mean why did I name my son Matt?" Paul responded. "Why do you think?"

"How do I know?" Izzy asked. "What, am I some mystic who can jump in your totally screwed-up mind and figure out what the hell is going on in there? I thought you were going to name the baby after your mother."

Paul just looked at him and shook his head. "He's a freaking boy, dumbnut," Paul said. "Your little girlfriend Elana, with all her wisdom, says she was sure Smiles would have a girl, and yea I was going to name her after my mother, but, what do you know, out pops a boy, and I don't have any names ready, and so Smiles say, let's name him after your brother Matt, and that's what we did."

Izzy blushed after Paul spoke, and he turned away. Had Paul said something to upset Izzy? Was it the girlfriend quip? "Look, say what you want about Matt, but since I've been around all these white people in New York, I have an amazing appreciation for my brother. These people here, even the best of them, are either uncompromising bigots, or they have to work to not be. To Matt, me and Luke and Ruth and her boys were all his equals, an idea that was totally normal and natural for him; he couldn't imagine it any other way. Where we lived in Virginia, that was a gutsy and selfless way to think. I owe him everything I am today, and if naming my boy after my brother helps give something back to him, then I am thrilled that Smiles suggested it, and embarrassed that I didn't."

Izzy nodded and said nothing, staring blankly at the rocky river below them. The ferry landed at the Brooklyn pier, and they rushed onto a plank and up some rocks to reach a small dirt road. Brooklyn had grown rapidly over the past few years, and scattered across farms and ponds and seascapes, small, ethnically homogenous neighborhoods had emerged. When you made something of yourself in Manhattan, or you just wanted to escape from the city's unrelenting tumult and grime, you moved here, with your own people, in much cleaner and newer homes that barely cost more than the filthy disease-ridden tenements of New York.

Today, Izzy and Paul sought to open new markets for their thriving business, their first forays away from their Manhattan base of operations. They set up meetings in both an African American and German neighborhood; Paul would speak with representatives of the former and Izzy of the latter. The goal was to promote their concept and offer to hire people from the neighborhoods to help repair clothing, as well as generate some buzz for the products they planned to bring here. Abe had already lined up several salesmen to serve these new neighborhoods: one a young Jewish man with a wife and two children who had just returned from the war, and another an African American from Paul's district who was one of many young men who had befriended Paul before moving here and then apprenticed with Abe to learn the trade.

But Izzy said barely nothing as they traversed the quiet, muddy road that meandered through Brooklyn's more populated center.

"I didn't mean to mock Elana," Paul finally said. "She's a great person. You know I know that. I was just making fun a bit.

And I didn't mean to call her your girlfriend. I was just messing around."

Izzy smiled. "It's OK," he said, looking away. "She is an amazing person."

A tear trickled down Izzy's cheek. He wiped it inconspicuously and then turned his head to completely conceal it from Paul's view. But Paul saw it, and he was immediately concerned. Izzy never cried!

"Probably we need to split up at the next intersection," Izzy said, his voice choked up a bit. "You know who you are meeting, right? We have about an hour before our meetings, so don't walk too quickly. Getting to meetings early is worse than being late; you may seem too anxious to the person you are hoping to impress. And then let's meet back here in a few hours, right at this spot. Don't let them keep you too long. That looks bad too."

Paul hardly heard what his friend said. In all his years knowing Izzy, since being a small boy on the farm, through some of the most horrid ordeals that he had to endure, Paul never saw Izzy cry. He never saw his friend so dejected, so flat. He did not know what to do.

"I'm sorry if I said something wrong," Paul said again. "You know you are about my best friend on this planet. I would have named my baby after you if I thought about it, although, you know, as a Negro, that's not the most normal name, just saying."

Izzy smiled, just a bit. "It would be a ridiculous name, what can I tell you? Matt is a perfect name. I'm not upset about that."

"Then was it the girlfriend quip? I didn't mean it. I like Elana a lot. Seeing you together, it's just, I mean you both are so amazing. I guess I got ahead of myself. I know you are both friends, that's all."

"She is amazing," Izzy said again. Then he twisted his face toward Paul's. Tears were streaming from his eyes. And, out of nowhere, he started to cry. "She is amazing," he managed to say between his snorting crying fit. And then he fell on Paul's shoulders, bawling uncontrollably.

"What's wrong, Izzy?" Paul asked him, his heart sinking with every teardrop that saturated his shirt.

Izzy looked up at him and forced a smile. "It's just," he said, barely able to utter words, a deluge of salty water flowing into his mouth. "It's just, I'm so damned happy. So happy. I never felt this way before, Paul. I never imagined I could. I'm an old man, I'm married to my business, but with her, with that girl, I am transformed, I am, I am—" He held his breath for a second. "I am in love."

And then he just burst into tears, placing his head on Paul's chest again.

Paul rubbed the man's thin, graying hair. He smiled. "With Elana?"

Izzy nodded. Then he peeked up and wiped his face. He smiled. "It's not supposed to happen, I know. It's wrong, on so many levels. But it did happen. What can I even tell you? I've known her for a long time, she bought clothes from me since from long ago, and I always enjoyed chatting with her. I thought she was beautiful, and she always seemed to enjoy talking with me, and she is funny and down to earth and so beautiful. Did I tell you she is beautiful? My God, that long red hair! But she was Ernest Biggelow's wife, and so even though I thought about her a lot, and always couldn't wait for her to come back to buy something (and Abe said that when she came in the store to buy something she never did unless I was there, which should have told me something), I couldn't imagine anything like what happened. And now," he said, as more tears poured out, "I am the happiest man in the universe. People are dying all around us, the country is embroiled in a civil war, she is married to a man who likely would kill me instantly if he knew even what I was thinking, and yet, when we are together, none of that matters. We are apart from everything; we are on our own island where nothing else matters."

"The red raft," Paul muttered. He smiled and hugged his friend. "How did it even happen? And how are you pulling it off? My God, you have been doing this right under my eyes, and I had no idea." He put his hands on Izzy's moist cheeks. "You have no idea how happy I am for you!"

"I didn't know how you'd react, Paul. But I needed to tell someone, and I'm glad I did, although I didn't expect to." He dried his eyes and took some deep breaths. A contented smile drifted onto his face, and he seemed to almost come alive again. "You're my best friend, Paul, even though you're a hot-headed jackass far too often; I hope you realize that. I respect you more than any person I know. I figured you'd call me a fool, because I get it, I'm putting Elana and me in danger. I'm threatening even Smiles, and Elana has two small kids who she cherishes. So how do I have the effrontery to threaten everyone else for a whim and a prayer? God forbid we get caught, so I didn't know what you'd say. You have no idea how happy you make me for understanding."

Paul nodded. "Understanding? My God, Izzy, if I've learned anything in my short and precarious life it's that you can't always worry about how the world is going to react when you do what you know to be right. You two belong together! I can see that. The world be damned! But how? How'd you pull it off? And is she, like, is she just as infatuated? Is Elana in love with you? Are you two, you know, you know what I'm trying to say."

Izzy smiled. "Yes, she is, and yes, we are. And as to how we leaped from friends to adulterous convicts, what can I tell you, asshole? It's your fault. I just want you to know that up front."

Paul just put up his arms and laughed. "It's always my fault! I never know why, but it always is!"

They walked a bit more slowly, dodging puddles of water and long stretches of mud. Horses and carriages slid by them, houses and shops passed behind. They were encased in their own reality, Paul engrossed in this startling news. He was utterly shocked;

he was both surprised and excited. What a perfect couple! How fortunate that they garnered enough courage to buck convention and find love in each other! Time ticked away; their meetings were approaching quickly. But neither seemed to care. This was far more important.

Izzy continued, "When you were in trouble after the church fiasco, she came to my shop, Smiles told her to, and we both said we had to do something, so we laid out a plan to save you. I had just come back from Virginia, so I had no idea what had happened. We were with each other almost continuously for days, and we laughed and smiled and stared at each other through glassy eyes. And at the end, when we brought Smiles up to see you, we were just so happy, and then we hugged, and neither of us wanted to let go. We looked into each other's eyes, we were like dumb teenagers, her eyes were inviting me in, and then we kissed. It came out of nowhere; I don't think either of us knew what the other was feeling, and yet, that's what we did, both of us, together, at the very same time. It lasted for hours. I can still feel her lips and face on mine, as though it just happened; it filled me up like nothing ever did before, not even a full plate of smoked salmon and white fish. We were well hidden, far away from where her and my people live. It's not like we thought about what we were doing; it just felt so right, so fulfilling. She stroked my hair (what little of it there is, what can I tell you?), and I hers. Her luxurious long hair; it was like manna from heaven for my fingers to glide through it! We stayed there into the night, said almost nothing, just hugged and kissed and rubbed each other's backs and heads. I think we both knew the danger. She was risking her life and her family. And if I was caught, I'd lose everything too, be ostracized by my community, be fired instantly by Abe, likely have to leave Manhattan. But at that moment, I didn't care, and neither did she. We didn't even mention it; we still haven't. Love replaced good sense and logic. We, neither of us, ever felt that way before."

"Wow," Paul uttered, a huge smile growing on his face. "Good for you! Good for you, Izzy." And he hugged his friend tightly, tears dropping from both of their joyful eyes.

Happiness is a fleeting illusion in this world; Paul knew that well. Even as he attained a modicum of success, the deeper did fate trap him, and the farther he drifted from what he really wanted: his wife, his family, his brothers, his red raft. Paul craved Luke's disinterested tranquility, and he dreamed of it every day. Now Izzy had found his own slice of personal contentment, his own red raft that floated upon a pristine pond away from the rules and restrictions that sought to entrap him in a manufactured misery. And, like Luke, he was not looking beyond the pond, not worrying about the rain, not thinking about what danger lurked beyond the perfect insulated world he had sewed for himself and Elana. Good for Izzy! How difficult it had to be! Screw everyone else! Izzy and Elana dived into each other and discovered what both of them needed the most! Paul exploded with volcanic joy!

"So, how are you guys even doing it?" Paul asked.

Izzy smiled. "I'm a crafty bastard, Paul, you know that. And there's not much I'm afraid of; I've been selling to Southerners for years even though they hate me down there, and as a Jew, I have to always stare danger in the face and then run fast once it turns on me; I'm good at that, good at knowing when to run and hide. Elana is much timider and more frightened, but she trusts me, and she wants to be with me, so she goes along with everything I suggest. Because she has always been a very flighty soul—wandering around the city on her own, exploring various shops to look for bargains, meandering through neighborhoods just to see how other people live—no one questions it when she disappears.

"We usually arrange a meeting on one of the days she is going out on her little trips. We meet somewhere where none of my people or Biggelow's people live or gather, and we find a spot where we can be safe and alone. We've even been up on your hill and used that straw mattress of yours! What can I tell you, Paul, I've done things with her that I never did before, wonderful and sensual things, and no matter what, no matter if we are naked or clothed, no matter if we are just holding hands or passionately kissing, she makes me so happy, beyond anything I could imagine. I think about her every day. I dream about her. We meet when we can; it's never enough. Sometimes she talks about her husband and her family, and that's like a knife through my gut. I let her do that, because what can I do? I know she loves me, and I know she doesn't love him, but she is tethered to her life with him, to her children, and I know she just wants to talk to me about it, because, I guess, I'm her best friend. I don't know, Paul. This tiny bit of happiness of mine, this forbidden love, it will likely end one day. Her husband is coming back eventually, and she may decide that it's too dangerous to be with me. That would be the sensible thing for her to do, and so I will understand. But if that happens, if it happens Paul, I don't know what I will do. Because I am addicted to that girl! I am in a deep pit of love, what can I say?"

"It won't happen," Paul said. "I have always known that you two belong together; that you are soul mates is as plain as day! Fuck convention, Izzy! Just because you each feel stuck in your own stupid worlds, who gives a fucking crap about that? I'm an atheist, Izzy. I know one thing: life is short, the world shits on you every chance it gets, and so it's up to you to grab happiness every time that opportunity comes, even if it doesn't fit into society's conventions and often doesn't make sense. And you know what, asshole, you're the one who taught me that!"

Izzy laughed. "I know it, you bastard, I just didn't know that you ever listened to me."

"Luke gets it, you know," Paul mused. "He knows how to shut out the pernicious babbling that our deranged and self-interested society tosses at us—letting us know that we have to do this, or worry about that—and he floats in his own reality. Maybe we both are best to learn from him."

"The red raft," Izzy said.

"Yes," said Paul, "the red raft."

It was now getting very late, and Izzy told Paul that they had better hustle to get to their meetings before everything collapsed.

"We still have to do real shit," he said to Paul. "We can't totally abandon the planet earth like your brother seems to get away with. We need these markets. So, let's go there, make the deals, and meet back on the hill in three hours. And Paul," he said, putting his hands on his friend's shoulders, "thank you. From the bottom of my cynical and jaded heart, I thank you. I am a happy man today, and it's all because of you." He wiped another tear, smiled deeply, and then dashed off along a small side road.

Paul moved in the opposite direction.

By the time they reconnected, a large orange sun had begun to set across the distant city. They stood on Brooklyn heights; the ferry would arrive in about half an hour. People were starting to line up. Both men had success in their endeavors. They would have no trouble starting up branches in each neighborhood. They talked a lot about the logistics of their next steps. They did not discuss Elana at all. But Paul could see that his friend was beaming, chatty, and back to himself. Opening himself up to Paul had relieved him of a great burden. And Paul could not be more pleased!

Across the river, in Manhattan, the din of drums and trumpets drifted over toward the heights. Paul squinted; a band was playing, and there seemed to be a mass of blue-clad men marching near the shore, sliding off one of the docked boats. There were so many of them! More soldiers moving to the front? They both looked at each other and shrugged. It was time to hurry down to meet the ferry.

Paul and Izzy climbed into a seat, chatting about what they would tell Abe.

"What's going on over there?" Izzy asked a woman who sat across from him as the boat embarked.

The woman turned to him, flashing a disparaging glance at Paul, who felt her piercing animus instantly. She spoke in an Irish accent. "We're heading over to see our boys," she said gleefully. "It's the Irish regiment. The war is done for them. They're coming home. At least most of them. Some stayed with the army and reenlisted. Some are in hospitals and prison camps or in heaven. But we're all going out to greet them. It's wonderful news!"

Paul watched Izzy's face sink instantly. "It is," he said to the woman. "It is."

For a moment, neither said anything. The band faded into the background, and Izzy looked up at Paul.

"Well, that sucks," he said.

Paul nodded. It certainly did. For both of them.

Ernest T. Biggelow had returned.

PART IV

Numbers

"The people rise like a lioness; they rouse themselves like a lion that does not rest till it devours
its prey and drinks the blood of its victims."

28

"And so, I hereby declare that, pending review by General Lee, commander of the Army of Northern Virginia, you, Matthew Cocklin, are hereby condemned to death by musketry, to be executed tomorrow at 8:00 a.m. in the central garden. As in compliance with the Confederate Articles of War, 'all officers and soldiers who have received pay, or have been duly enlisted in the services of the Confederate States, and have been convicted of having deserted the same, shall suffer death or such other punishment as, by sentence of a court-martial, shall be inflicted.' You are convicted of desertion, you have been declared a traitor to the cause by your comrades in arms, and you will therefore suffer the consequences of your actions. God save your soul."

Under a cold and misty April sky, draped by thick fog, Matt digested his sentence with a stern visage and a mind devoid of emotion. A small contingent of grey-clad youths who stood before him, including the young boy who read his verdict, similarly reacted flatly. Two of them gestured a handcuffed Matt toward a ratty tent beneath a forest of oaks, and he passionlessly complied.

He was happy to have this ordeal finally end. His only regret was not being able to say goodbye to his brothers, whom he missed terribly. He felt empty, blank, dead already. He had hardly spoken for months. Tonight, he hoped to sleep at least a bit so he could wake up and meet his maker with a clear mind.

How had it come to this?

Nothing went right from the day he joined the Washington Grays in late January. Jude and his loyal contingent of sycophants greeted Matt with a deluge of disdain, calling him "Negro lover" and spreading a rumor that he had tried to lead a slave rebellion in Washington. Jude commanded unfaltering obedience; what he said was gospel among the troops of the Grays and its commander, Colonel Kemper. His achievements on the battlefield—his absolute devotion to the cause—left no doubt about his loyalty. Colonel Kemper listened to Jude unquestioningly; the Gray's leader refused to even meet with Matt when he complained about Jude's perfidiousness.

"You have the audacity to come to me?" Kemper said in late February, as a bruised and battered Matt appealed to him. "After all you done? You come to me? If it were my choice, I'd pull out my musket and shoot you in the gut here and now, and I would shoot you there because you lack a spine, you lack a heart, you lack a brain, and I don't got nowhere else to shoot you but there. I think Jude, he's being kind when he kicks you and tells you to lick the latrine clean with your tongue. Yea, he told me everything he did, he keeps nothing from me, and I think it's all rightful punishment for the vile person you are and always have been. You are an embarrassment to Virginia and the Confederacy."

Matt gasped. His hands trembled. He had nowhere left to turn. "I ain't done nothing!" he cried out. "I am just here, fighting for Virginia. I didn't lead no revolt. I ain't a Negro lover. I helped everyone in the Rappahannock County; that's all I done for all these years, everything to support the army. And now when they finally told me that I could fight for Virginia, which is what I aim to do, as best I can, now Jude and the other boys, they are using their old grievances against me, nothing related to the cause or nothing. It's not that at all; they are using their old grievances against me and my family to put me down and to soil my name. Can you move me to another unit? I just don't know what to do."

Kemper stared into Matt's eyes. He just shook his head and marched away disdainfully.

The fog grew thicker. Matt's mind darkened day by day. He ate and slept by himself; he avoided eye contact. He tried to march with the Grays during maneuvers and to follow protocol, but no matter what he did, Jude was there to disparage him, to embarrass him, to induce a comradery of laughter—all at his expense. So, he lay awake at night, swimming in a painful fog, in mental agony, knowing that the next day and the day after would be as harrowing as what preceded it. There were no battles in sight. General Hooker of the North marched his troops on the other side of the river as General Lee, whom Matt had only once glimpsed from afar on his majestic white stallion, did the same on the Confederate side. Matt prayed for a battle! Anything to shift attention away from these people's focus on him!

February passed quickly. More drills and cannon blasts and self-congratulatory bravado skipped across the Rappahannock River like a flurry of rocks tossed from one side of the other. There were great speeches; many were made by Jude, or Colonel Kemper, or once by Stonewall Jackson himself. And then the routine resumed, and the beatings.

One lonely afternoon he lay in his tent when footsteps approached. And then it happened, as it had so many times before. Boots struck his side, and they started kicking him. One, and then another, in his flank, his chest, the top of his head, his legs. Someone stepped on his left arm. He said nothing; not even a squeak of his torment crossed his lips; not even a grimace escaped from his lungs.

"You are a disgrace to our cause!" one of them said, as his boot tip hit Matt in the ribs. He was so bruised at this point that nothing really hurt him very much.

"You will be as dark as your Negroes once we is done with you," said another.

They chuckled and chatted as they kicked him, and then they drifted away into the fog, their voices and laughter slowly trailing into the silence of a dark winter night.

Matt lay there a few minutes, and then, without so much as a thought or idea, he stood up and strolled to the river, limping with each painful step, dizzy and confused, not quite sure where he was going. The river lay on his right; he could barely see through the fog. At some point, he dropped his musket and kept walking. He was in a deep patch of forest, crunching over leaves in a sea of bare trees.

Night's darkness fell upon him, and he could barely perceive a path ahead. Before he knew it, he was in the river, floating on its chilly surface, the current pulling him along. He hit a rock, and then another, twisting around, his face briefly submerged. His numb state shielded him from pain. And then, in an instant, he struck the other bank of the river, the one on the North. He smiled, even as he shivered, and then stood up and started walking.

I guess I is where I ought to be, with the fighters against slavery. Maybe I is a Negro-lover after all, just like they said. Maybe this is where God wants me to be, and He sent me here.

He laughed out loud and then strolled along the river's edge, back toward the mass of men. With each step, he tore off a part of his gray uniform and tossed it in the trees. A soft, frigid wind whipped through the forest. He was virtually naked now but for a pair of boxers. His naked feet slid over twigs and rocks; they bled profusely. It didn't matter. Suddenly, Matt felt alive again, as though he was somewhere familiar; Izzy and Paul lay just a bit up North, men and boys not apt to beat him. Freedom!

Happy thoughts flooded him. *These is my people. Maybe I will go up to see Paul. Or I can stay and fight for the army. Fight against Jude and slavery. And I will get that letter to Izzy, so he comes down and takes care of Luke. That's what I will do first.*

And then, without warning, he tripped, splattering on the muddy ground. Something lay below his legs, an object over which he became entangled. He looked at it. It was a dead soldier. A Northern soldier! This boy could not have died long ago; he was barely cold. Without much thought, Matt pulled off the boy's uniform and slipped it on. It seemed to fit fairly well.

"I'm now a Union soldier," he said, as he resumed his march forward. "Ain't no one's gonna kick me again, not now, not ever." The din of the Northern army grew closer.

A day passed. And then another. Matt did not utter a word. He passed through the sea of blue-clad soldiers, finding food, sitting with some, moving from tent to tent.

"You lost, son?" asked an older-appearing Union soldier. "You feeling OK?"

Matt peered at him with glassy eyes. He nodded yes. He remained mute, partly because he was not sure if he could even speak, partly because he did not know if his voice and accent would divulge his subterfuge.

"Can you talk, boy?"

Matt nodded no.

"You get hit by cannon fire or something? You hurt from the battle?"

Matt nodded yes. His expression was fixed as he stared into the man's hazel eyes. The eyes seemed to be gentle, inviting.

"Let me help you," the man said. "You look like you are from the Eighty-Seventh Volunteer Infantry; you have '13th Brooklyn' embroidered on your lapel, you see that? You know where they are, your people?"

Matt nodded no.

"You are certainly confused. You may want to seek medical help, son. Let me walk you to your unit. I know Colonel Dodge. He's a good man. Your unit is part of the Fortieth New York now. That's where I'll take you. You must have been hit pretty hard, son. You may want to see the doctor. And get some shoes. Your feet are a bloody mess. You got bruises everywhere."

He was led to his unit, to a group of boys who laughed and giggled and did not seem very interested in Matt or even care who he was. He found an empty tent that perhaps had been abandoned by another soldier who had died or deserted; both were rampant these days, or so his new comrades told him. His unit had merged with several others and now was led by the energetic and fiery Colonel Tom Eagan, who galloped every morning past their tents and called out for everyone to wake up and start drills. Because this was a merged unit, many of the boys didn't know the others. They all spoke with thick accents; Matt could not place them. And as the days and nights merged, as Matt marched and drilled with these people, he sat around the same fire with the same few men, and he silently listened to them talk.

They called him Quiet Boy and did not press him to speak. On one of the first nights with them, Matt was able to gesture to one of their pads and pens, and he successfully communicated his need to write a letter and send it North. A tall man named Slim provided him with an envelope and showed him where to mail it.

"To Izzy Snout, New York City," he addressed the envelope.

"That's all you got?" Slim laughed. "How in the hell of God's creation do you expect this here letter to get to that person, Izzy Snout, if the only thing you know is that he lives in New York, the biggest city in the world, if not the universe? No street or nothing? Geeze Christmas, Quiet Boy, you are asking for a wing or prayer that this gets to your friend, although I never heard a name like that. Maybe he's the only man named Izzy in the whole damned city?"

Matt nodded and smiled.

Slim laughed. "Well then, OK, let's send it off and see where it goes! I'll bring it to the post. We got drills in half an hour, Quiet Boy. You best grab a musket and meet there before Colonel Tom starts whooping and hollering like he always does. Izzy Snout? What the hell kind of name is that, in all of God's creation?"

The fog barely lifted, day after day, night after night. Matt's brain cleared a bit, but he still dared not speak, and no one seemed to care. They sat around the fire, these same three men, as they did every night, and Matt listened as they pontificated about the war and their philosophy of the universe.

"Fighting Joe, he's got a big job ahead of him if he thinks he can knock out 'ol Robert, for Christmas' sake," said Slim, referring to Union General Joe Hooker and, of course, Robert E. Lee. Slim worked in Hooker's general staff as a secretary; in his old life in Brooklyn he was some kind of lawyer, or at least that's what Matt surmised. "Joe talks a big game, but he doesn't have a plan from what I can tell. He says, 'Well, 'ol Robert, he don't know what's coming his way,' and 'Wait till Robert sees what we got in store,' but he says nothing else, and then he says, 'Make sure the men keep drilling and staying fit.' If we get any more fit and any more drilled, then God himself may come down and call us angels, for the sake of Geeze and Christmas!"

"It don't matter no how," said Stogie, who chewed on an old cigar. Apparently, Stogie, which is what the men called him, found the cigar on the body of a dead Confederate soldier at Antietam, and he put it in his mouth, promising to light it once the army finally wiped out the Confederate foes. Once he learned that Lee's army had slipped away that night, he vowed to keep the cigar in his mouth and only light it when the Union finally beat Lee fairly, which still had not occurred, and so the poor guy kept chewing on it. "What we fighting for anyways? Since Lincoln announced his emancipation proclamation, it seems we is fighting to free the Negroes. Oh, the poor Negroes, who the fuck cares about the damned Negroes? Is that what we is fighting for, so all the Negroes can be free and we get even more of them in Brooklyn? I think we got more than enough of those animals up there already, stealing our jobs and making havoc for us good

Christian folk, and if it was up to me, we'd ship 'em all out back to Asia or something."

"Africa," Slim corrected him.

"Who the fuck cares, Slim? Jesus, you got to constantly impress us with all your fancy learning?" He spits some old tobacco into the fire, and Matt could smell its wretched stench.

"This is how I see it," said Trump, who usually sat by the fire poking the embers with a stick as he placed his left fist on his chin. Matt could quickly surmise that Trump, with his thick tuft of yellow-tinged hair greased back over his scalp, thought himself a great intellect. "We're not fighting for any Negro freedom. We are fighting for Negro expulsion. This is how I see it, boys. If 'ol Robert wins the war for the Confederacy, all the sudden the South's worst Negroes will come flooding over the border to our land up North, and the South will be happy to let it happen, because most Negroes are criminals and rapists, plus they are lazy and lack mental capacity. We don't want them, but if we lose the war, we'll have a trainload of them in every city stealing and robbing and taking our jobs. But if we win, this is what happens. We throw all our Negroes down there, right in the South, right with all those people who made war on us and killed so many of our boys. Then we build a wall between us and them, and we let them stew in their own shit. That's how I see it all, boys."

Stogie stood up and slapped Trump on the back. "You is some genius for a crazy ass loon, that's what you is, Trump! If you was running for president, I'd vote for you, not the Negro-loving Lincoln."

Trump smiled and nodded. "I am damned smart," he announced. "I may be one of the smartest people that you boys will ever meet."

Fog slid between them, mixing with their words and the crackling fire, the booming of cannons in the distance, scattered laughter and inaudible voices far away, in this frigid patch of earth that seemed less real and hospitable in each passing day; Matt hardly listened, rubbing his hands, trying to stay warm.

"What do you think, Quiet Boy?" Slim asked him. "How we going to use this war to get rid of the Negroes? Looks like you got something to say. You guys see Quiet Boy, his face is all contorted; he may have something to say after all this time!"

Matt just shrugged, although his head filled with explosive indignation. They talked this way day after day. They trashed everyone, especially African Americans, but everyone, including generals, politicians, and especially Irish. *If we were leading the army, Ol' Robert would be running his ass back home, that's for sure!* That's what they said. Too many of their friends had died for a bad cause led by bad men, so they proclaimed, over and over. This was the North? This is where Paul had fled?

"Come on, Quiet Boy, say your thing," Stogie goaded him.

But Matt said nothing. He stood up and started to walk away. The fog dropped down upon him, and all he could hear was fading laughter and the trailing iterations of Trump.

"Leave him alone, boys," Trump said. "He's mental. He's no harm to us. He may be the smartest man, other than me, in this whole army."

"Maybe your running mate when you run for president?" Slim laughed.

"Could be, boys. Could be."

Often Matt wandered down to the Rappahannock River and stared across its banks, smelling the whiff of familiar foods and soothing voices from the other side. He took off his shoes and stepped in. The chilly late-March waters stung him a bit, but also caressed his wounded soul, and he smiled. Images danced before him, of his brothers, the farm, his father. In its ripples, its soothing current, Matt seemed to perceive Luke's serene face, to taste some of the grapes whose vines this water likely had passed through on its journey to this horrid spot of hell. This river emanated from the mountains, from no less a holy perch than Old Rag itself, carrying the ingredients of love and life that he and his brothers had known so well and for so long. Where had it all gone? On both sides of this river lay pain and hate; only the waters themselves brimmed with the purity of the soul. The river flowed past him quickly; it chose not to stay here too long, not in this place, not with these people.

There was a time, several weeks ago, that Matt thought about leaving the army and going up North to find Paul and Izzy. But paralysis consumed him, and he found himself unable to talk or move. He relished the routine: nights around a crackling fire with the three "wise" men, marching with his unit, his trips to the river, restless sleep in a dead man's tent. Soon he relinquished any thoughts of going North, where he might find even more vile people like the men he met here, people who treated him kindly and did not beat him like those on the other side, but whose words and thoughts stabbed him day after day, night after night. This was not the paradise he imagined. It was just another slice of hell.

Only the river gave him peace, so most nights he sat there, often engulfed in a dense and frigid fog.

A few cannon blasts shattered the blank tranquility. The army was preparing for something. March turned to April, and the days passed by in monotonous similarity. It was still quite cold and dark. But something was happening.

A new man had joined the fire to replace Trump. One day Trump did not return. Slim learned later that he had died of dysentery. Like so many other of the boys here, dysentery and typhus proved more lethal than bullets. There were dozens dying every day.

"We told Trump not to drink the water right below where everyone was shitting," Slim said. "But he was insistent, said it was all a hoax that shit can get a man sick. Well now, that's Trump for you. I guess he won't be president after all."

Stogie laughed. "Well, that makes you next in line, Quiet Boy," he said. "You better work on your speech!" He chewed on his cigar. "What's up with Fighting Joe, Slim? You said you'd have news for us tonight. We going to take on Ol' Robert or not?"

"Well, Stogie, let's just say that you may be smoking your cigar soon enough, if Christ and his disciples have anything to say about it," Slim said to him.

The new boy, they called him Jersey, probably because that's where he was from, he lit up. "We fighting, finally? General Hooker got a plan?"

"He's got one all right," said Slim. "But it's top secret. I was privy to it today at our staff meeting and was told to keep silent. Now, I know I can trust Quiet Boy, because who's he going to tell, and I know I trust Stogie, because he keeps secrets to himself, but Jersey, I don't know you well enough to really trust you on this."

"You can trust me!" Jersey shot out with obvious excitement.

"You're not Irish or part Negro, are you? We don't talk to people like that," Slim said.

Jersey nodded no. "Italian and German, them my two folks. The most trustful kinds of people you can have, I assure you!"

Slim nodded, as everyone leaned over the fire staring at him, transfixed. "Well then," he said smugly, "I'll tell you what I heard. Fighting Joe aims to cross the river ten miles up North with most of the troops, but keep enough here so Ol' Robert is guessing what he may be up to. He is going to march up to Robert's army and then stop there, checking out the situation. He plans to scare Robert into attacking him head-on, or running away across the river, in which case Fighting Joe will cross behind him and crush him. He's counting on Robert's arrogance to be his undoing."

"His what?" Stogie asked.

"Arrogance," Slim repeated. "You know, it's like Trump was. It means you try to do more than you are capable of doing. Ol' Robert won so many battles that now he thinks he's invincible.

That's arrogant. So, Fighting Joe's going to stand in front of him and egg him on, let him do the attacking this time. Robert will fall for the trap because of his arrogance. And Joe plans to be ready; once the attack starts, the reserve troops will cross the river behind his lines and crush him once and for all."

"So, General Hooker just going to take half our troops across the river and do nothing? Just stay there and wait?" Jersey asked. "Then why the hell they call him Fighting Joe?"

"It sounds smart to me," Stogie smiled. "Force Robert to make the first move, and then we up and squeeze him between the two parts of our army. Hell, we have so many soldiers that each half of our army is bigger than Robert's whole damned thing. Finally, I can light this damned thing!"

"Then we burn every farm down there," Jersey said. "We chase Robert all across Virginia and burn everything in sight. We torch the place and leave no one alive."

Stogie smiled. "I like you, Jersey. You think smart. And what would you say we do with the Negroes?"

Jersey thought for a moment. "You mean the ones we don't burn?"

"You is one smart boy, Jersey. Maybe even as smart as Trump!"

With that, Matt stood and made his customary trek to the river. The fog was thicker than ever. He walked down quickly and waded in the tide. But this time he wandered in deeper. And deeper still. Until, with hardly a protest, the current picked him up and yanked him away from this side of the war. He floated in the river, feeling only its warmth, hoping to be finally and ever-lastingly consumed by its totality, to be submerged beneath it, and to leave this horrid world behind.

But that was not to be. Within minutes Matt found himself on the other side, back where he had started over two months ago. He stood up and stared forward at campfires, at cannons. And then, someone grabbed his arm.

They had been looking for him it turned out. They thought maybe he had tried to run away. Scouts regularly monitored the banks of the river. That's who found him that night. And that's who brought him in for the trial that would ultimately declare him guilty of desertion and put him on death row.

It was mid-April now; just a whiff of warm air blew across the land, flowers popped up by the river's banks, and bits of green grass covered the landscape. *Nothing makes no sense.* He wished he had died in the river that night; only then would he have achieved the catharsis for a life that had been blessed before this war invaded his land. The banks of the river were poisoned he knew; their venom stretched far and wide, beyond where any eyes could see. It spared nothing sacred. And so he emptied his eyes and dived in the waters, thinking of his brothers. And the pond. And their days together in a sheltered peace. That made him smile.

The door swung open, and a burst of light struck Matt's eyes.

"Matthew Cocklin?" a young gray-clad private asked him.

Matt interrupted him, with the first words that slipped between his lips for many months. "I know," he said with a crackly voice but a happy one. "You is telling me that it's time I meet my maker, that I pay the price for my desertion. And I ain't gonna tell you that it's not deserved. I was there all right, over on the North side, and it's just as shitful as this side. So, even though I don't believe in no maker or any other of your made-up crap, as my father taught me good, I am damned well ready to meet him and get this over with. I don't want to live another minute in this place or nowhere else, nowhere but with them, with my brothers. So, shoot me, I'm ready!"

The boy seemed taken aback. He just shook his head. "No," he said quite calmly. "There's going to be nothing like that. It seems there's been a change of plans. Follow me."

29

As Luke fondly remembered, Dad always said that in Virginia the weather was as fickle as its politics. April could be especially disconcerting: heavy rains, dry heat, cool nights. You just never knew. Before Luke designed the pond and its tributaries, a single deluge of dire weather at an inopportune time could threaten the entire season's fruit yield. Now though, because of the pond and dams, water distribution remained stable, ground moisture was consistent, and temperature swings did little to impact the bounteous fruit their farm had produced for the past decade.

Luke peeked at his grape vines. Would this be the year that they spawned an edible crop? Last year was very close, and now the vines seemed ready to burst with glorious red fruit. They had grown immensely! Even as Ruth and her sons prepared vegetable beds and cleared debris from the orchards, Luke sat on his red raft, contemplating the growing season, allowing the cool, pure water of the Thornton River and the sediment from Old Rag and the majestic world above them trickle upon his skin and awaken him from winter's slumber. He always enjoyed floating upon his creation, watching the dam's flawless precision, reveling in the capacity of an intelligent and creative mind to transform a troubled piece of dirt into an oasis.

"Matt's gone missing," the doctor whispered one day, as he and Jessie meandered through the vines, following in Luke's trail. It was late afternoon, as Luke carefully trimmed branches and mulched the grapes' carefully engineered soil. He had altered the irrigation to provide more sediment, and he had added some of his French-inspired fertilizer into the stream that bathed the vines in proper pH.

Tears flowed down Jessie's eyes. "We don't know where he is, Lukie," she moaned. She rubbed the top of his head. "We are so scared!"

Luke barely reacted, although he hoped her salty tears didn't sully the soil. He continued to trim a few of the lower branches. One mistake could cost him bunches of grapes, if not the entire crop. These were fragile beasts.

He didn't worry about his brother. *Make sure to hide, Brother. Don't get into harm's way.*

"They think he could have deserted," the doctor said coldly. "That is utter nonsense. I have contacted the highest authority I know there to make sure his name is not smeared and that he is found instantly. I fear that he may have become disoriented and lost his way."

"My poor husband," Jessie cried, very obviously ingenuously to Luke's ears. "He is such a simple soul. He was never meant for war!"

In a few weeks, Luke would test the soil and adjust the mineral content as was necessary. Even now, when he held the beautiful black dirt in which his grapes flourished, when he sifted the soil through his fingers, it felt right. So, he knew in his heart that he had done a good job. His dad would have been proud! How incredible the farm had become under his tutelage, with this as its crowning glory.

"Who would accuse him of desertion?" the doctor continued. "You know, when Matthew's father Jake moved here, many of us were suspicious. The land itself was barely productive, and to have a Northerner settle in Washington, one with little knowledge of our ways and customs, one without any farming experience or any idea of how to purchase and utilize slaves, that caused consternation among us all. I came out to meet Jake, and he produced a letter from the man who had sent him here and arranged for him to purchase the land. Jake called him Bob, his friend from the army. That time, all we knew was that Bob was a prominent landowner in Northern Virginia, a man with a good family name, the son of none other than Light Horse Harry Lee, General Washington's favorite commander in the Revolutionary War and one of Virginia's most notable governors. When Jake produced that letter from so prominent and distinguished a man, I knew that he had to possess great character, and that it was my obligation to afford him an opportunity to succeed and to succor him in any way that I could."

"You remember, Daddy, what Light Horse Harry said at George Washington's funeral? Those famous words that always make you cry when you hear them?"

The doctor nodded, and a tear did flutter from the corner of his eye. "'First in war, first in peace, and first in the hearts of his countrymen, second to none in the humble and endearing scenes of private life.' That's what he said, Jessie. He was a man for the ages, that is who Light Horse Harry Lee was. And his son is who sent Jake Cocklin here and gave him this farm. Yes, Jake made some mistakes, of course he did, we all do, but he became one of us, and so too did his son Matthew, a boy so noble and virtuous that I allowed him to have the hand of my only daughter. And now they accuse him of desertion? I will have no such slander perpetrated on my son-in-law, on the son of Jake Cocklin, the man who Light Horse Harry's son bestowed upon us and upon this hallowed land."

Luke reached under one of the lower branches. He had read that it was best not to allow any branch to touch the water. He snipped it carefully.

"Can you help him, Daddy?"

The doctor nodded and wiped his eyes. "I will indeed. My word has certain authority in the Commonwealth, and I will contact who I must to assure that your husband is found and that his name is cleared. Such slander! Such foul play! General Lee will surely help his old friend!"

A warm breeze fluttered through the branches. Leaves had popped from the orchard's trees, and the landscape glowed with vibrant color. After the doctor and his daughter scampered off, mumbling and crying on the way out, Luke lay upon the raft and smiled.

Luke never really knew if his father's origin story was more fable than truth, but regardless, he enjoyed hearing it. The townspeople exclaimed how Jake obtained this malnourished farm from the son of one of George Washington's most favored generals, how Jake embraced the Southern way, how he transformed a plot of dying dirt and trees into the most prosperous orchard in the county. What they left out, of course, was that the farm only thrived after Jake married a "troubling" and intelligent slave whom he loved dearly. Jake Cocklin ultimately sacrificed his wife and his heart to achieve his goal, and for that pact, he lost his life. But on this land, Luke's parents sprouted from every tree and every blade of grass, every drop of water, and every burst of sunshine. Dad had never embraced the Southern way. He only trod on that fiction to arrive here, to this small bastion of heaven apart from everything else.

"It's all my choosing," Mom had said time and time again. "Your father treats me like a free woman. He values my ideas. And he knows that I have chosen this path so that you and Paul can have the life that you deserve. Never blame him. He is distraught. But it is the only way I know to save everything we have worked so hard to create. I am but one person in a vast world, Luke. So too are you. Often we must sacrifice ourselves for the good of the whole."

Is that what Matt was doing? Had he run up North to find Paul? Or was there some other design to his flight from the Southern army? Luke lay on the raft, staring upward, severed from the war and the doctor and all the clutter that sewed unwanted cacophony upon this paradise. He smiled as he thought of his mother and father and the stories they told. Matt was his father's son. He joined the Southern army reluctantly. He could never remain with those people and fight for everything he found detestable. And so likely he just ran off. What they called desertion, Luke knew to be liberation. Matt was Dad's son. And Dad became a Southerner, a member of acceptable Washington society, only in the service of something much greater than himself.

There was a fine line between legend and fact.

"Yes, Luke, your father's friend Robert was the son of George Washington's favorite general, the very general who gave the soliloquy at Washington's funereal," Mom told Luke when he asked about how Dad had found and settled on the farm. Luke had been curious from the time he was very young. How did his father end up here? How did he defy all the rules and fall in love with a slave, while still having the town's protection and blessing?

"It is because of Robert's status that few dared threaten your father," she said. "Your father has to be careful. There are certain lines even he cannot cross. But because of his friend Robert's lineage, because that man vouched for your father, there is little they can do to him, as long as he keeps his sins behind the fences of our sacred land and plays their game when he wanders outside our borders."

"What sins, Mommy?" Luke asked her.

She just laughed and hugged her precocious boy. "The sin of loving me, of loving you and Paul, of treating us all as equals, and making sure our lives are full and prosperous."

"How is that a sin, Mommy?"

"Inside our fences, it is a blessing my son, it is the very shadow of goodness itself. But out there, it is a mortal crime, because out there the rules are created by those in power, and all goodness must be sacrificed to elevate them and suppress us. That is their way. Never forget that, Luke. But it is not your father's way. That is why you must always stay within our walls. Were it not for your father's friend Robert, the wall would not exist at all."

And so it was for these many years; the farm was blessed and protected by a powerful force, one that even the doctor could not penetrate. Matt would be fine, he knew. There was very little that could ever threaten Luke here, or Matt there. Not the doctor. Not the Southern cause. Nothing. Ultimately, his brothers would return behind the farm's fences, the grapes would grow and prosper, and despite what madness ravaged the world beyond the outline of their oasis, they would be forever happy and free in this one spot of heaven. Such was the gift of Robert. Such was the magic of their farm.

That night, while reveling in his own creation, Luke heard footsteps approaching. He darted up from his bed and stared outside. A soft, warm breeze blew through his cabin, as crickets sang and leaves ruffled. The crunching steps gravitated closer and louder. Luke's eyes opened. It had been a few weeks. But he knew what was next. This was part of the game. Sometimes society's most vile creatures popped their head into his world, and it was his obligation to assuage them. And so he smiled and welcomed the imposition. One day she, and all she represented, would be extirpated from his soil. Old Rag would not allow such weeds to flourish here. But for now, Luke had to play the game. All Cocklins had to make a sacrifice to this sacred land. Luke's was no more onerous than that of the others.

Jessie walked in and tore off her shirt. "Now, slave, I want you now, and I will tell you once and for all, if you disappoint me, if you don't satisfy me to the level I expect, I will tell my daddy all about you, and you'll be hanging by your neck!"

Really? She shouted the same threat every night. It had become laughable by now. What power did she possibly have over

Luke, over this farm? Robert's stock had risen so high, his influence so broad, that neither she nor the doctor could threaten this land that Robert had bequeathed to Jake's sons.

Jessie watched as Luke undressed. He said nothing. He thought of the grapes and the pond and a marvelous future in which he and his brothers were reunited upon this land. That excited him enough, and so that night, like so many others, he performed to Jessie's satisfaction. She raped him, and he allowed it. What choice did he have? He was doing it for the greatest cause known to humanity.

But he did have a certain power over her. A power she could never comprehend. As long as he remained on his father's farm, in the shadow of Jake's good friend Robert E. Lee, Luke remained invincible.

30

A peek of the sun spread across a muddy, squalid horizon of tents and fires and filth. Few of the men here had eaten much the past month or two; even before Matt plunged into the river to reach the other side, rations had been cut dramatically, and every morsel of food proved to be a feast.

"The damned Union blockade, that's what's doing it," Colonel Kemper had told the Grays a few days before Matt bolted. "They got the whole east coast in their grasp. We still got the Mississippi, and we still got hope that England or France will come to our side and break the blockade; we still got hope of that. Our best men are over in Europe negotiating with them now."

"Not our best men," Jude shouted above the din. "Our best men, they be here, here with the Grays, fighting the enemy. We don't got to rely on no one but ourselves. We'll beat them ourselves. That's what General Lee says. He says a victory on the field is worth a thousand times more than what any diplomat or politician can accomplish to get the Yankees out of our backyard. And we got the best men, and the best generals, to do the job. Right here, on the Grays!"

The hollers and whoops and the Confederate yell shook Matt's ears.

Kemper nodded. "We do, Jude, we do. And General Longstreet, he's in North Carolina now fighting the enemy and collecting us wagonfuls of grub. That's how much faith General Lee has in our troops, and how little fear he has of theirs. He dispatched a third of our army with Longstreet and doesn't tremble at all. When Longstreet returns, then we'll all eat, men. Then we'll all fight!"

General Longstreet had not returned. Food was even more scarce. And succulent odors from the river's northern bank flooded across their encampment every day just to remind them how poorly supplied they were. Matt ate well during his month up there across the river. Here on this side, his stomach growled day and night as he awaited his fate.

"Where you taking me?" Matt asked his guide, a youthful redhead in a meticulous gray uniform. They traversed the tent city in which many of the officers lived. Matt could hardly speak, hardly walk. He had thought he would be shot by now. This delay proved more painful than an executioner's bullet.

Walter Herron Taylor, as he introduced himself, was General Lee's chief of staff, and he had been dispatched to collect Matt and bring him to the general. "The general is in a foul mood," he said. "He hates the snow, and this winter's storms have made him angrier than I have ever seen him. He spent the last few weeks in a convalescent tent; he started to have pains in the chest, and the doctors told him he had to rest. The general doesn't like to be told what to do, and according to what I hear, he was yelling and biting at everyone until finally they let him go. He aches all the time; I see it in him, but he never complains. And he has personal issues with his family, his wife, his children, his farm; I know that all weighs on him every day. So, what does he want from you? Why did he take you off the list of the condemned and demand to see you? I don't know, Soldier. Maybe he just wants to kill you himself."

Walter Taylor uttered those last words with profound conviction. And Matt swallowed hard.

They passed by several soldiers who saluted Matt's guide, and then they entered a large tent, actually a series of many large tents connected to each other. This isolated tent village sat at the edge of a pine forest, with the sweet scent of pine needles caressing Matt's nostrils. Birds chirped; little of the clatter and chaos of the ordinary soldier penetrated this far. This was central headquarters, Matt learned. Walter Taylor pulled Matt through one tent after another, chatting and saluting as he went, until finally he entered a large, cluttered structure to his left. There were two men in there, both standing and peering at a table. They were tall, towering many inches above Matt and his guide. One wore a very groomed gray uniform, his hands behind his back, a distinctive gray beard neatly trimmed on his face. The other slumped a bit; he was more disheveled, a thick brown beard and a curly head of brown hair covering him. The latter man was biting on what seemed to be an onion.

"General Lee," Walter Taylor said with a salute. The gray-bearded man turned around. "I brought you the boy."

Robert E. Lee turned and nodded, dispatching his chief of staff. The general's eyes were dark, his face devoid of emotion, a grimaced smile sewed upon it. Matt had no idea what he could be thinking or why he had called Matt here on the morning of his execution.

The other man started to laugh. He bit into his onion and chewed as he spoke, walking up to Matt and nodding his head. His eyes were steely blue, piercing, and his entire body reeked of onion and garlic. "Well, Robert," he said with a smile, his twisted teeth sliding between his tongue, "you want to kill the traitor, or should I?" Then he laughed and slapped Matt hard on the back. "Don't worry, boy, you look like you're going to pee your pants. You want a swig of buttermilk? It calms your nerves. We are glad you are here. The general isn't in the best of moods, and you, son, you made him smile this morning, and that was a sight for sore eyes."

The disheveled man put out his hands and introduced himself. But Matt already knew him well, by reputation, and by his occasional visits to the Grays. Thomas Stonewall Jackson. His name had become a legend both here and in the town of Washington; the doctor worshiped him almost as much as he worshiped Lee.

General Jackson grabbed Matt's hand tightly and shook it. "What were you doing up with the Northern troops?" he asked Matt. "And before you answer that, let me tell you what we want to hear, and what we need to hear. You were spying. You were gathering information. You did it on our instructions."

"Thomas," General Lee said in a gentle, soothing tone. "Leave Matthew alone. He is frightened and confused enough. We will get to that later. Tell me, Matthew, do you know who I am, other than being the general of the Army of Virginia?"

Matt nodded no. "I mean," he said, "the doctor says you is the son of George Washington's favorite general during the Revolution, that your wife is the daughter of George Washington's adopted son, that you is the best man this land has ever produced. That's what the doctor says."

Stonewall Jackson laughed and spit a piece of onion across the tent. He then grabbed a bottle of white buttermilk and swigged it down. As Matt would learn, Stonewall suffered from many ailments and treated them all with hot baths and a concoction of medicinal foods. He never touched alcohol or tobacco. Never ate any food prepared by anyone other than himself. And he hated doctors! "See what I told you, Robert," he said with a smile. "The doctor says you are the best man this land produced. What did I tell you about doctors?"

"The doctor to whom you refer," General Lee said, pacing across the tent and staring at Matt, "is who saved your life.

He came here when you were on death row and pleaded for you. He knew enough rotten politicians in the Virginia legislature to make me take a look at your name. And that's when I saw who you were, something that doctor of yours confirmed. Do you know who I am to you?"

Matt shook a bit. What was going on? What did he mean by that?

"Did your father ever tell you about his friend Robert, the man who sold him the land that you call your farm? Did he tell you about that man?"

And then, like a flash, it hit him. Had he been that dumb? Did he really not know?

Son, you have nothing to worry about over there. Your father's old friend, the hero of the Confederacy, will be right in your backyard should you ever need a helping hand.

The doctor knew. Everyone knew! Even Luke knew.

Brother, if you want to stay safe, go find Bob, and tell him who you are, that you are Jake's son; there is no greater angel to watch over you!

Of course! Bob! Robert! A wave of dizziness rushed through Matt's head, and he stumbled. He could barely look up at these men. This is whom his dad had saved, who brought Dad to the farm, who helped him through the darkest of days? Robert E. Lee was Bob?

Matt always revered his father, always perceived him through glassy—if sometimes smudged—lenses. But now, this connection, it vaulted his father to an entirely different plane. With Matt on the brink of death, Jake Cocklin resurrected himself on this hallowed field of holy war and brought Matt to God Himself. He saved his son yet again.

"You look like you're going to faint boy!" said Stonewall Jackson. "Have a swig of this milk."

General Lee pulled up a few chairs, and they spoke. Matt stared into the general's welcoming eyes, and it didn't take long for Matt to feel as though he was in the presence of his father, of family, of someone who loved him. The general seemed genuinely concerned about him, asking about the farm, his father, even the slaves. And Matt spoke openly and freely to him.

He told the general about what had happened to his mother, about Luke and Paul, about how the orchard was thriving, even about the grapes. Stonewall came and went, always having something glib to insert; Matt and his father's old friend chatted and laughed for many hours. All along, Robert E. Lee's tender eyes did not falter, his mouth and face poised in a gentle unwavering smile, and several times he rubbed Matt on the back and uttered, "Just like your dad. You are just like Jake. I see him in you."

"It's obvious that you love your slaves," the general said at one juncture. "Luke and Paul. The way you talk about them. It's like they are your brothers."

"They is my brothers," Matt said. "My dad and new mother, they are their kids."

The general hardly flinched. "Well," he said, "you put a New Yorker in the South, and that's what you get! Poor Jake could never feel comfortable with the values and morals of the Commonwealth. It probably killed him to live there, under those rules. He and I had many, many heated conversations. Did he tell you about our time together?"

"A little," Matt said. "My mom told me more. My dad didn't talk much. That was just his way. But all along, I didn't put two and two together. I never knew it was you who he was talking about. I just thought it was some lowly soldier from New York who had some land in Virginia."

General Lee nodded. "He and I were assigned to Fort Hamilton," he said, to which Stonewall Jackson made a quip about how much the Lees hated Alexander Hamilton and how it was God's will that Robert had been assigned to the very fort that bore his nemesis's name. General Lee let Stonewall always talk, softly listening but never responding. And then, he continued:

"I was there five years. We were both engineers in the army, me and Jacob, your dad. He was under me. It was horrible, menial work on the edge of a desolate land called Staten Island, Satan's Island your dad said, which to this day makes me laugh. We were doing masonry, painting, laying down the drainpipe, and then the storms would come and destroy everything we did, and we would start from scratch. The army never gave us enough resources or people to get the job done right; me and your dad, we just laughed about it, but it frustrated us to no end, and I think it's what turned my first hair gray.

"I was thirty-five at the time. I had five children and Mary, my wife, was pregnant with the sixth I didn't know where my life or career was going then. I was as confused as a man could be. Mary and I lived in a small home in Brooklyn. She never adjusted. So many of the soldiers had their wives there too, and those wives could cook and clean and take care of things. But not Mary. She had been brought up with slaves to do it all for her, the spoiled daughter of George Washington Custis, President Washington's adopted son, saying every day that she just wanted to go home and be with him in Arlington, far from the drudgery of New York. I know now just how much fortitude and strength Mary has, especially as this war has taken from her everything she holds dear, even as she is crippled and can hardly walk from one chair to the next without a cane and yet never complains or talks about herself. But back then, entering midlife, I didn't see it. And I had thoughts of another life, a different life. If it weren't for your father, I would not be here today. I was ready to do something terribly wrong, and Jake stopped me."

Stonewall Jackson came back in and pored over some maps that lay on a table in the center of the tent. Darkness started to descend upon them; already Matt had been offered a bowl of soup and some chicken, which he almost instinctively slurped down. He was drawn to these men; it was not like he felt he was in the presence of greatness or evil, as different people described them, but rather that he was in the bosom of goodness and concern. He simply listened and drifted into a trance.

"Do you know why we are in this war, Matthew?" General Lee asked him.

"Slavery," said Matt. "To preserve it."

"Would you ever fight for that cause?" the general asked.

Stonewall laughed from the corner.

Matt turned toward him, and then back to General Lee. Should he tell them the truth?

"I know the answer, Matthew, and, between you and me, I understand," General Lee said to Matt before another word could be uttered. "You and I have different views on the issue, as did your father and I. I think that bringing Negroes to this nation stained who we are as a people and is our greatest threat. The fact that we freed them from the backward lands where they lived, that we taught them the word of God and made them into His loyal servants, those are worthy achievements. But bondage can't persevere, and it will ultimately disembowel us as a people and as a nation. Ultimately, we have to teach the Negroes how to be free and to be rid of them. But how? It's a problem that George Washington couldn't solve, even though he freed his slaves upon his death. Even his son and my father-in-law, Mr. Cutis, toiled with the paradox of being a slaveholder in a free nation. Both were deists; they believed that man could do as he pleased, that God has left us alone to make our own decisions. But my wife, Mary, has great faith in God Almighty, as do I. She and I know that there is a God above judging our actions and guiding our hands. We believe we have an obligation to the Negroes that we have enslaved. Mary taught all her slaves to read, even though it was against the law to do so."

"A bad law," Stonewall Jackson said. "All of God's creatures have to be able to read His scripture."

Lee nodded. "Mary believes that. But she, like I, does not think that these people are capable of being on their own, at least not yet. They are indolent. They are not wise to the world. Their brains are not fully developed. When I inherited the Custis farm, the slaves had no discipline. Mary's father let them do as they wanted, they had their own plots of land, they came and went at will, and they did not listen to the overseers. I had to change all that. I had to set down the law. I was tied to that farm, to its slaves; it was an inheritance that I would have sooner discarded. It was a chain around my neck."

"Ask Robert what he did with his slaves," Stonewall chipped in. "Ask him, when that man Lincoln made his emancipation speech in the start of this year, ask Robert what he did."

There was a silence in the room, and Robert E. Lee shook his head. "Thank you, Thomas, for reminding me of that." He then turned to Matt. "My father-in-law did not have the courage himself to free his slaves, although he contended that is what he wanted to do. So, he placed the burden on us, on me and Mary. When he died, he willed all of his slaves to be freed five years after his death. We fought it in court, we tried hard to delay that, but we had no recourse. And so, in January, as per his wishes, I freed all of my slaves. Perhaps, as Longstreet reminds me all the time, I am the greatest abolitionist of them all! By coincidence it fell at the very time that the baboon up North freed the slaves; believe me, it had nothing to do with that. I was merely being true to the law and to my father-in-law's misguided wishes."

"Then what are you doing with your farm?" Matt asked him.

"It doesn't really matter," he said. "My land was taken over by those people up North as soon as the war started. Everything we have is gone. And so I ask you again, Matt, why are we fighting this war? Because believe me when I tell you, I am a unionist. My father would be rolling in his grave if he knew I was fighting against the nation he helped to forge; I opposed Virginia's secession from the start, never wanting to follow the lead of the malcontents and ignoramuses in the Deep South. I was asked to lead the Union armies, and I did consider it, but I could not. Not because I wanted to hold onto my slaves, who I knew I would have to set free regardless. Not because I think slavery is right, which I don't. Not because I wanted to break this nation apart. But rather because, just like you, I am a prisoner to circumstance. I am more of a slave to my fate than any Negro ever was."

Matt stared at this man, not fully comprehending his point, but being drawn in nonetheless.

"You were with those people up there when you ran off," General Lee continued. "Do you think they should be our masters? Do you want them to be our rulers and to set our laws? Ultimately God will determine the fate of slavery, not those people. I had always hoped slavery would die a slow death, that the Negroes would be freed over time, that perhaps they could be shipped back to Africa with the knowledge of Jesus imbued in their souls and the gift of civilization sewed into their guts, and they could make a world of their own there. Ultimately, when this war ends, I will either be a great hero revered by the people of a new nation with statues of me placed all over the new land, and towns and streets harboring my name. Or, should we lose, I will be the greatest scoundrel this land has ever known, a traitor to my nation, a man who subverted the will of my father and of my father-in-law's father; my name will be spit upon and uttered as a curse and warning. I don't seek either such adulation or defamation, and I do not have such lofty goals. I am fighting for the same thing you are. Because we are both prisoners of the same cruel irony. We are fighting for our people and our homes, even if we detest those who pulled us into this war and all the despicable goals they seek to achieve."

Matt just nodded his head, not knowing what to say.

Stonewall jumped in. "Just for the record, Robert," he said, "when we do win this war, I'm not sure that the people of

Mississippi and Alabama will be putting up statues in your name. And I'm not sure there won't be another war between us and them. I'll tell you why I'm fighting this thing. When the politicians and crazies on both sides of the line decided to tear each other apart, I was on the bottom part of the line, and so, well, that's who I fight for. I hope God has put me where he wants me. I hope our cause is the right one. But frankly, I never was offered a place in the Union army, not that I would have taken it, but I'm here because this is where I am, and I aim to do my best here, God willing, and win this thing and see where it goes from there. That's why I'm fighting this war. Why are you fighting, Robert?"

Lee nodded. "Because, Thomas, as I have told you before, I live in Virginia. I don't want those people to tell us how to handle our own affairs. And I believe that they have brought our nation far from where my wife's grandfather and all the other founders wanted us to be."

"You mean, all the founders other than Hamilton," Stonewall quipped.

"Yes, Stonewall," Lee smiled. "Yes. We must live with the scourge of slavery. We will have to confront it. I don't want those people doing it for me. I don't want the South Carolinians doing it either. But I am not fighting for all that. I am fighting like you are, Thomas. I am fighting because I live below that line that someone drew long ago and which has cursed our nation ever since."

General Lee walked up to Matt and hugged him. "I am so glad to have found you," he said. "I don't expect you to approve of all of this. Just to understand. And I must find out what you learned up North and to devise a way to get you back to your unit a hero rather than a villain." He looked into Matt's eyes. "Your father saved my life. I know his heart. I know yours as well. I will care for you, Matthew, as long as I can. That is my obligation to Jacob. But now," he smiled, "this old man has to relive his bowels in the river and take a rest. I want you and Thomas to discuss what you learned up North. I don't know why you went there nor do I care, but since you have come back, we need to create a fib that you went there to spy for us, and that is why we need to learn anything you may have heard there. Tonight, you will sleep with us, and tomorrow he will bring you back to Colonel Kemper in a new gray uniform and a badge of honor. Jake's son will not be anything but a hero in my army. That is my promise to you and your father." He turned and left.

Matt stood and stared. Tears trickled from his eyes. It was as if he had found God.

That night he and Stonewall Jackson sat by a table covered by maps. Matt was served a bowl of rice with a small piece of beef and some broth. Stonewall ate what looked like a green mush with clumps of nuts and seeds, which Matt learned were acorns and sunflower seeds. He drank deeply from his jug of buttermilk, frequently offering some to Matt, who politely declined. The two of them laughed about Matt's adventures up North, about the fate of poor Trump, about Luke and his obsession with grapes. Stonewall was the most comfortable, humble, and endearing man Matt had ever met.

Matt told him what the three wise men said around the campfire. And something about their words struck Stonewall's ears. He goaded Matt on and asked him more specific questions; and Stonewall glowed, as though Matt had fed him exactly what he wanted and needed to hear.

"General Lee will be very pleased by this," Stonewall said. "It's more important than you may realize."

Earlier that night, Stonewall Jackson told Matt that Lee hoped to invade the North again, like he had at Antietam, but this time he hoped to do it more intelligently—send cavalry units to threaten Washington, and penetrate Pennsylvania and scare the Northerners into surrender. Only then would foreign governments, who were dependent on the South's cotton, support the Confederate cause, and only then would the Northern people demand that the war end. To fight a defensive war would only prolong the inevitable and enable the North to starve the South out. Lee argued instead that the South had to strike right at the North's gut, over and over again, until they abandoned the fight and left the Southern people alone. Rather than stay here and face General Hooker, General Lee planned to pull his army around Hooker's right flank and march up North unimpeded.

But what Matt told Stonewall changed all of that. There would be another battle to fight first, and it would occur right here, very soon. And it was a battle that the South could win as long as they understood the Achilles' heel of Hooker, something that Matt's information had somehow revealed to the generals.

"According to the men that Matt was with, Hooker aims to cross the Rappahannock upstream with half his army," Stonewall said to his general, pointing to the map. "He aims to attack us from that side, but only as a feint. He doesn't have the guts to go for the kill. Rather, he is going to wait for us to attack him, and when we do, he plans to pull the rest of his army across the river further south and then squeeze us in a vice. With Longstreet gone, we don't have even half of the troops he does. But with this bit of information, we have the edge."

"How do you have the edge?" Matt wondered aloud.

"Because," General Lee said, "according to the men you were spying on, Hooker will cross the river and wait. He will wait for us to attack. But if we are patient and clever, if we don't take the bait but instead wait for an opportunity to surprise him, then the advantage will be on our side. That's how we beat those people." And then he paused, and placed his firm, wrinkled hands on Matt's shoulders. "Matthew, God brought your father into my life, and now he has brought you. I am glad to have you on our side. We will, of course, speak again. You have helped us more than you could imagine. Goodnight." With that, he turned and left.

The next morning Matt walked beside Stonewall Jackson, whose six-foot frame barely fit upon his tiny brown horse, Little Sorrel. It was an awkward sight! But no one dared ridicule him;

all those who he and Matt passed cheered and saluted as the great general silently slid by. A man who disdained speeches, who preferred to be in the company of a few close friends rather than a squadron of strangers, who was considered one of the worst teachers at Virginia Military Institute because he simply did not like to speak to anyone he did not know, this humble general had silently earned the acclamation of every man whom he touched and indeed of the whole Southern nation. Matt felt nothing but pride while walking in his shadow. To Matt, this man and his father's good friend Robert were perhaps the two greatest men who walked on the face of the earth. This was their army. And now it was Matt's too.

Stonewall leaped off his horse, and someone ran over to tie it. He asked a private to retrieve Colonel Kemper and Jude and to have them meet him in a clearing by a large oak tree. He and Matt sat there under a bright, sunny April sky, and they waited. Neither said a word.

Within a few minutes the colonel and Jude arrived, somewhat disheveled. They saluted the great general and peered oddly at Matt, who smiled back.

"Colonel," Stonewall Jackson said without inflection, "this is Matthew Cocklin. I understand that there has been a great deal of confusion about his role and position in the Army of Virginia and in the Grays. Let me clear that up now. Matthew's father, Jacob, was a great friend of General Lee's, and Matthew too has been doing the general's bidding. He was sent North as a spy to acquire important military information, which he has accomplished brilliantly, and now he will be embedded back in your unit to fight with you in the upcoming campaign. He, of course, had to pretend that he was a Northern sympathizer so as not to endanger his mission, and he told us that he was much abused in this unit because of that fiction. He holds no grudges, nor does General Lee. In fact, Matthew told us to specifically include you, Jude, in this conference because of your bravery and your devotion to the cause. Hear my words, soldiers. The enemy is upon us and intends to engage us in the next few weeks. We will defeat him. And you in the Washington Grays, owing to your performance in our past campaigns, you will be my lead unit in this battle, if you feel you are capable of that well-deserved honor. If you do have questions, Matt will answer them for you. Matt, do you have anything you want to say to these men?"

Matt smiled. He looked at Jude, whose pale face sweated beads of salty water on this lukewarm day, and who trembled just a bit. "All I want to say," he told Jude, and then Colonel Kemper, turning finally to Stonewall himself, "is that it has been my honor to do my service to the cause, and to you and General Lee, two of the finest men I ever did meet in my life. But I am excited to be back with my people here, to fight with them, and to defeat the enemy with them. I only say I'm sorry for putting you all through this with me, and that I intend to make it up once the battle commences. That is my promise and oath to you and to the Grays, the greatest unit on the face of this earth."

Colonel Kemper nodded and seized Matt's hand, shaking it vigorously. Jude said nothing at all.

In these woods and with these people, Matt had finally found a home, upon whose land his feet could stay firmly planted and dry. He marched away proudly, back to his tent, past his comrades, and relished what the next day would bring, and all those that followed. His skin shimmered in the sun; his nose tasted the sweet scent of wildflowers. He had never felt more alive in his life.

31

"Stonewall stopped by," Jude told Matt, who had returned from foraging for wood with a few other Grays. "He wanted to see you."

It was April 30, a cool and dreary spring day, light mist saturating the air and keeping everything just a bit wet. Overhead were daunting yellow balloons, the latest Yankees' ploy to spy on Lee and ascertain his intentions. Cannons fired incessantly; the frequency of their deafening booms had increased dramatically in the past few days. Blue-clad soldiers scattered to the river and back with unnerving rapidity; horses scampered across the Northern horizon. Matt was both terrified and excited. Something was finally happening.

"What did he want?" Matt asked him. "You sure he came for me?"

Jude nodded. "Talked to Colonel Kemper first, then asked for you. His wife was with him. And he was holding their little daughter, less than a year old. First time Stonewall ever seen her, or so they say. His family comed just a few days ago. You should've seen him with that baby! He was all cuddly and cute; not like the guy who all his soldiers hate for running them ragged."

Matt nodded. What could he have wanted with Matt, especially now, on the eve of all this clamor from across the river and a potential battle looming on the horizon?

Colonel Kemper beckoned the Grays to his tent at 6:00 p.m., as the sun slowly descended in the west. A cool rain persisted, and most of the men shivered, not owning any coats that could keep them dry. Little food remained other than some horsemeat and hardtack. General Longstreet had acquired many weeks' rations, but he was still a few days away.

"Men," the colonel cried out, flanked as always by Jude, "Stonewall was here today to talk with me. General Hooker's troops are on the move. Four of his divisions under Slocum, Howard, and Meade crossed the Rapidan early yesterday and are marching east along the Orange Pike. Today they arrived at a small town of Chancellorsville, which is about eight miles west of us. Hooker is also crossing several divisions downstream, so he will be on both sides of us with superior numbers to us in each of his units. And he continues to have a sizeable force across the river."

The colonel paused for a moment and looked into the sky. Another balloon passed by. Matt saw it too as he flanked two of his newer friends, Pete's son Charley, and a more shy boy named Pat, who had joined the Grays soon before Fredericksburg "According to Stonewall, and this comes right from the mouth of General Lee, we need to look like we aren't frightened by the crossings, that we have sizable forces ready to confront the divisions to our east and across the river to our north, while we secretly move the bulk of the army west to attack Hooker's forces there. And men, Stonewall told me something else. The Grays will be leading the charge!"

Everyone, including Matt, whooped and hollered as Jude twisted his right arm over his head and the colonel stood silently by with a smirk on his face.

"How we gonna fool them Yankees into them thinking we got enough men to hold off all of that, especially since they can see us with their balloons and all?" one of the Grays asked.

"Stonewall, he says we just got to keep moving. We got to stay active. That's how a weaker army keeps up with a stronger one;

it has to make up in activity what it lacks in strength. If the Yanks think they see larger numbers than we got, since they are scared of General Lee already, then they will be hesitant to attack. So we have to have big numbers everywhere, so when those balloons spy on us they will look at one place and see a bunch of us, and then we'll run somewhere else and they'll see us there too, thinking we are bigger than we are. You see those?" he said, pointing up at the yellow balloons. "Those are who we got to fool. And we got to make us look scary to those Northern wussies by staying active, firing cannons, and giving them a good dose of the rebel yell."

His words triggered a loud burst of that very yell, until Jude gestured everyone to quiet down.

"That's the spirit, men, but save it for tomorrow. We will be leading Stonewall's army as we march west. That's where most of the troops will be headed to face the divisions that Hooker just crossed over, while we leave the diversionary forces behind to fool the enemy here. Our thrust will be in two parts, and we plan to hit Hooker hard before he knows what's coming. We need good rest. No sneaking spirits or telling stories tonight, men! As long as we stay focused and follow the word of our leaders, General Hooker is about to get a mouthful of the Grays when he wakes up tomorrow!"

Later, around the campfire, Matt sat with Charley and Pat, as well as another very quiet boy from a farm in Stanardsville name Bill—he seemed much younger than the other three—and they quietly poked sticks into the flame. The rain stopped, and a soft wind blew heated air past Matt's ears. He thought about the people up North, people like Slim, who were finally crossing the river and preparing to fight. What could they be thinking? They were so scared of General Lee. But did they smell the ruse?

It was a sleepless night for Matt. Cannons shattered any possible tranquility. He dreamed a bit about Luke. The farm. Preparing the pear and apple trees with the approach of spring. To Matt, this battle was all about Luke. It was about making sure those people across the river never got close to his farm. That they got pushed back and left him and his brothers alone. He so trusted General Lee and Jackson. He knew that whatever they were doing was the right course to take. Sitting with the Grays tonight and hearing the colonel talk, this was what it was all about. This was his family, his people. He could not even imagine that he had ever doubted that fact!

The morning was dark and cool before a few hovering clouds drifted away and revealed a bright sun. Matt's division, under Stonewall, marched to the right along the Orange Pike, a dusty old road with brush and leaves obscuring a clear passage. The other divisions were on the left, along the narrow Plank Road, a tiny overgrown path that paralleled the Orange Pike for many miles. This group would be led by General Mccaw. It was Stonewall's job to keep the two groups together, all fifty thousand of them, as they marched quietly through thick woods toward Chancellorsville. The general rode ahead on his tiny brown horse Sorrel, saying very little, but whispering to his commanders who shouted out his orders to the troops. Stonewall was biting an onion. He radiated the very visage of calm.

"General Hooker has advanced a few miles beyond the town of Chancellorsville toward our position," Colonel Kemper shouted. "He is waiting for us there. It will be an even battle; he's got about as many men as we do, but only a fraction of our heart. I don't think he knows what's about to hit him, men!"

The Grays all whooped, very quietly. "We gonna beat the crap out of them and chase them back across that river," Jude cried out. "They ain't ready to meet the Grays again, I can tell you that!"

The day drifted forward, punctuated by periodic cannon blasts. Despite a few days of light rain, the ground was fairly dry, enabling a facile and coordinated march toward the battle. Step by step. Matt hardly knew what to think. He was about to engage in his first battle, his life on the line, the thing he most feared about to transpire. And yet he smiled, so happy was he to be here with these people, with Stonewall Jackson leading him, and not back on the other side of the river with Slim and the others.

"You know what they says," Pat said to Matt as they slid by more trees. "They says before his wife showed up, Stonewall, he was living in a big mansion house at some estate, with a waiter and everything, but when he knowed that his wife was coming, he moved back to the tent. He's a Presbyterian deacon is what he is, and he ain't supposed to be living all highfalutin, that's what I heards at least. His wife would have whipped him one cross the head!"

Matt laughed. He had heard the same thing. Stonewall turned thirty-nine in January and, according to rumor, felt that he might not have much longer on this earth. Most of his relatives had died young. He put his faith in God, as he always did, and as a Calvinist he lived a very simple and unpretentious life. "Maybe he just wanted a taste of the good life, just to see what it was like," Matt said to Pat. "I'm glad he moved back to the tent. And that he got to see his daughter."

"Me too." Pat emphatically agreed.

Matt smiled and nodded. What had Stonewall wanted to see him about yesterday?

The burst of cannons grew ferocious, and from far to his right he heard gunshots. Everyone stopped.

"What's going on?" he asked Pat, who answered with a shrug. Matt looked forward, Stonewall rode around on Little Sorrel, back and forth between some of the commanders, and then he darted past Matt toward the back of the line.

"We've engaged the enemy," Colonel Kemper cried out. "Wait for your orders, men. General Mccaw is leading the attack to our left. We just have to wait for our orders until we hit them on the right. Apparently, their flank is well protected, so we will be making a direct assault."

It was midday. Just then a volley of cannons erupted, and Matt instinctively covered his ears, peering forward. He could hear the rebel yell from far away, and then there was a volley of gunshots all around him. He looked at Jude, who stood quietly, and then at some of the commanders, who also peered ahead but were hardly flustered. For the first time, he shook just a bit. What was next? He started to sweat.

Just like that, the gunshots faded and the cannon volleys ceased. Out of nowhere, Stonewall shot up front and again gathered some of the commanders and spoke to them. He then tapped Little Sorrel on the side of the head and hurried back into the mass of men.

"Men," Colonel Kemper called to them. He smiled and then giggled just a bit. "It seems that Fighting Joe Hooker, the pride of the Yankees, the man who plans to take his army right down General Lee's gullet without any fear of the man that all of his fellow generals tremble about, it seems that General Hooker up and ran away!"

The entire line of troops hooped and hollered and laughed, with people calling out any number of insults against Fighting Joe Hooker.

After a few long minutes of mumbling, word finally came from another source. The three divisions under General Slocum, General Meade, and General Howard were given orders to retreat several miles back to Chancellorsville, just like Slim said that they would. They were not ready to confront the Army of Northern Virginia, at least not yet.

"It seems that Robert's tomfoolery worked a charm on Fighting Joe," Jude bellowed as he wandered over to Matt. "They could of crossed the river and destroyed us back at Fredericksburg if they had a lick of guts in their blood, since they had us totally outnumbered there; they could have fought us here, hit us from the front and the back with overwhelming troops. But they don't got no guts. He's playing into our own hands, Matt. Just like you thought. He's gonna wait there for Robert to attack. And that gives us the advantage! It always does. Now we just got to see what's up Robert's and Stonewall's sleeves. Men," he called out, "we live to fight another day! Let's make camp and get ready for tomorrow."

And so, on May 1, Matt's first battle ended with a whimper.

He said very little that night; none of them did. Rumors and innuendos floated back and forth between the boys. The one that seemed to have the most credence was that General Lee might divide the army yet again, something, as Jude said, that flew in the face of all conventional military wisdom.

"It seems, old Robert is gonna leave a few thousand here to stand up to Hooker's four divisions in Chancellorsville, being so confident that Hooker won't start the attack until we do, while Stonewall takes the rest down a small road behind Hooker's back and leads directly to Hooker's right flank."

"How you know that, Jude?" Charley asked him.

"Seems," Jude said, "that a chaplain from these parts, he knows of a road that Hooker and his men don't know about. Fitzhugh Lee, he took the road, with some engineers, and he says that it's solid enough and wide enough to bring most of our army on it and surprise old Fighting Joe right where he don't expect to be hit. And you know what else he says?"

Everyone, Matt included, glared at Jude wide-mouthed, waiting for him to respond. Finally, he did. "Seems that Fighting Joe's right flank ain't even defended. It's floating in the air on the Orange Pike with not so much as a single cannon to protect it. He thinks that the woods is protecting his right side, because he ain't got no idea about the road and the fact that we can slip right in behind his back and hit him right there where he don't go nothing to protect his ass."

"Is that what we is doing?" Matt asked. "We taking that road tomorrow?"

Jude nodded yes. "And I wouldn't be surprised if the Grays is out in front again. They say Robert and Stonewall, they is putting it all together; they're gonna be up all night with this one.

But we got to get to sleep, boys. Douse those fires and get into your tents. If we leading the route tomorrow, we had better be awake and alert to enjoy it!"

The night was silent, a bright moon piercing the sky's darkness. They all found plots of dirt within the dense pine forest; Matt placed his bag and gun far from the others, within a virtual temple of chirping crickets and clamoring animals. Distant artillery boomed; the war left a residual din at all hours, day and night. He sat upon a bumpy tree, staring forward, smiling. It was chilly, but he didn't care. Tomorrow he would face battle, a real battle, for the first time. Tomorrow he would be part of a daring strike that, if successful, could land itself in the archives of history itself. The doctor had said that one more Confederate victory may mean doom for the Union army. Would tomorrow be that time? Just a few weeks ago, the thought of a triumphant Confederacy—the perpetuation of a state of vicious slavery, as Paul always said—would have made him sick. Now as he walked among his own people, as he had come to know these leaders, he was not sure what to think.

Suddenly the sound of an approaching horse shattered his trance, and Matt heard a thump like when a man jumps onto the ground. There was a loud neigh, and then footsteps moved toward him, closer, closer. Matt sat up and stared forward. The bright moonlight shined on his visitor. It was Stonewall!

Stonewall Jackson wore a shiny gray uniform, one very uncharacteristic of a man who relished clothing himself in garb sullied and dirtied by battle. Quietly, he sat alongside Matt and pulled out a tall flask, slurping down its contents with loud gulps and then a burp. Without saying a word, or announcing why he had come here, he pushed the metal jug over to Matt. "Buttermilk?" he asked.

Matt, stunned, grasped the bottle and sipped a bit, somewhat delicately. He handed it back to Stonewall, who drank a bunch more, closed the top, and then leaned back against the tree, closing his eyes. He slid his hand in his pocket and pulled out some round nodules and then stretched his arm out to Matt. "Acorns?" he asked.

Matt said, "No, sir, thank you."

"Well," said Stonewall, squinting and lifting his head. "This is the last of my stash from the fall harvest. Picked a few thousand, me and my troops did. Got to keep medicinal foods always with me, especially with all the garbage they feed us. My legs, they burn every night like fire. And my joints"—he showed his knuckles to Matt; they were large and red hot—"they are aflame day and night. When I eat food from God's nature, what He gives to us from the trees and the earth, I can quiet my ailments and be strong and vibrant. I will never complain. I am blessed to be as healthy as I am at age thirty-nine, to be able to behold my wife and beautiful daughter before the dawn of battle, and to hold God's sword for whatever purpose He has given me. For this I am thankful. Tonight, as the good general sleeps, me and Jeb and the engineers and artillery captains, we are preparing for what might be either the most brilliant maneuver an army has ever made, or the most stupid. Only God knows. But regardless of the outcome, I need a few minutes of rest, and I had wanted to talk with you after that night when we met. So I thought, why not now. I hope I'm not bothering you. Your Colonel Kemper said I would find you here, away from the others."

Matt said nothing, staring into the man's brilliant blue eyes that pierced the night's blackness.

"I do want to thank you for the information you gave us," Stonewall said, lying against the tree and chewing on an acorn. "Joe Hooker is doing exactly what you said he would do. If he were a smart man, which he most certainly is not, he would cross the river right now with his fifty thousand men and destroy the few troops we left in Fredericksburg and then move here and wipe out what remains. He's got balloons and other reconnaissance; he should know about his advantage, but he's motivated mostly by fear of defeat. Tomorrow when I take our troops down the farm road and surprise him from the rear, we will have just about ten thousand men to face his huge army here at Chancellorsville. If he were a smart man, he would hit us so hard that we would be splattered all over Virginia and cease to exist. The war would be over, and he would be the great national hero. But he won't. Do you know why?"

Matt nodded no.

"Because we scare Fighting Joe. He trembles in his boots. He doesn't want to be the next victim of Robert E. Lee. Fear motivates him more than facts. Robert is very apprehensive about leaving us in a state of such extreme vulnerability. But when I passed him just a bit ago, he was sleeping like a baby, snoring, a smile on his graying face. That is hardly a man who has respect for his enemy."

Stonewall sat up taller, his freshly-trimmed brown beard resting calmly on a serene face. He smiled. "You and I, Matt, we have something in common. Something extraordinary. Do you know what?"

Again, Matt nodded no.

"I lost my parents at a young age, as did you. We both grew up as orphans. We both had to rely on ourselves to become the men we are. We were not among the privileged few, not given handouts and provided a path to salvation. I found God as a young man and put my faith in Him, but also in others who I knew had love in their hearts and who cared for me as a person. Robert told me that when your father died that you were left with his two Negro sons and that you view them as your brothers. Are they the ones you turn to when you are in need, your two brothers?"

Matt nodded. He thought a lot about Luke and Paul lately. About the farm. He told Stonewall about them, and he smiled as he did. He talked about Luke's amazing genius, his perpetual calm, his attachment to the land. He told Stonewall about the pond and the irrigation ditches and the grapes. And then he talked about Paul, and when he did tears flowed from his eyes.

"He's the smartest man I ever knowed," Matt said of his brother. "I know Luke, he figures things out, but Paul, he knows everything about everything, reads every book ever written; he can talk about it all, any subject, he knows it, can bring up what the Greeks said about this or that one minute, and then what some scientist might say about something the next, can answer any question that anyone puts to him. And on top of that he knows everything about the finances of the farm, how to sell and buy and make it all work, and he can cook like you never seen before. And Paul, he would always make me laugh, always said the right thing. His heart is big, and I knew he loved me. That meant a lot."

"It should," Stonewall said to him. "Robert told me about them, and that Paul, he ran away. That must have hurt you a lot."

Matt nodded and wiped his tears. "I don't blame him, though. It's just, we had it real good until all this war talk started coming around, and when that happened, no one would let us be ourselves no more. They came on our farm and terrorized us. They whipped Paul. They invaded us and turned on my brothers. I hate every last one of them. I still do."

Stonewall put his hand on Matt's shoulders. "I know," he said. "Which is why you ran away to the North. But then you came back. Why?"

Matt looked deeply into the general's inviting eyes. "I is here now because of you," he said. "And General Lee. And what you said that night. That maybe I is fighting for my brothers after all is said and done. I is fighting for my own freedom and for my farm, fighting to make it like is used to be. That if we win this war, they will leave us alone, everyone will. And them people across the river, I hate every one of them too. I want to kill every last one of them for what I heard them say."

Stonewall smiled. "Still," he said, "you are fighting to preserve slavery. As am I."

Matt said nothing for a moment. "That's what they all say," he finally uttered. "But I don't know what else to do. I never wanted this war or nothing like it. I just wanted it like it was. On our farm. We was all free there. We done what we wanted, and everyone left us alone. We was no masters or slaves. We was just three brothers from Virginia, and it was a perfect world we made for ourselves."

"Maybe," Stonewall mused, as crickets chirped against a cool breeze that caressed them. "Ultimately, Matt, the Deep South will destroy us one way or another. That's what I think, and that's what Robert fears. Only Robert's celebrity may prevent that and put us on a sensible path as a new nation, but even that may not be enough. Still, God is granting us victories, so He must have a plan that includes us, and it is not up to me or you or anyone to question it. We all have to hold God's sword and fight His war. When He thinks that we are fighting on the wrong side of His plan, he will cut us down, quickly and definitively. Until then, I can only hope for more victories, starting with one tomorrow."

Stonewall peered up at the sky and threw a few acorns in his mouth, chewing them. "Do you know who John Brown is, Matt?" he asked.

Matt nodded. "The doctor says that John Brown tried to lead a slave rebellion and wanted to kill every white man in the South. Paul, he don't like John Brown neither, said he was a zealot who ruined it for everyone who is saner."

Stonewall laughed. "They both may be right," he said. "You know, it was Robert who captured him in Harper's Ferry. To Robert, John Brown was a rebel against the country, of course a bit of an ironic position given what Robert is doing now. I was living in Lexington, a young professor at the military institute there, and that's where John Brown was hanged. I went to see it. All the Virginians whooped and hollered when they put a rope around his neck. But I looked into John Brown's eyes, which were as blue as the sky, and those eyes held more conviction that any man I had ever known in my life. Even when the rope snapped, he was so sure of his way that his telling smile did not fade one bit. I can still see it in my mind. And on that day, I said to myself that if the North has another dozen or so John Browns, men who are committed to ending slavery and wiping the South off the map, then we have no chance in this war. We haven't seen any men like that yet. All we get are a bunch of Burnsides and Hookers and other such nincompoops who have nothing in their heads but protocols and orders. But one day a man like John Brown will face us, and that will be a day that we have to fear. That's why we have to have our way with Fighting Joe Hooker and finish these people off. Our luck won't last forever."

"At least John Brown, he was fighting against slavery," Matt said to Stonewall. "I know slavery, it's wrong. I seen what it does to people who are good and decent. Maybe John Brown was right."

"Maybe," Stonewall said. "God will make that determination. But I'm guessing that if the North does win, it won't be men like John Brown or even Frederick Douglass that writes the new rules. It'll be the men you met around the fire up there. When I was in Lexington, every Sunday me and my dear wife, we went into the Negro churches, and we taught young Negro children and men and women how to read. We talked to them about the Bible. I could have been thrown out of my job for what I did because teaching Negroes to read is against Virginia law. But it was the right thing to do. The Negroes I met, all of them slaves, were good and intelligent people. Maybe one day, if all Negroes can read and discover God's words, and if all the white men truly take God's word into their hearts, we might have a civil world instead of this civil war that is killing so many boys and may, in the end, settle nothing."

A few more cannons shot into the still night. It was getting late.

"Matt," Stonewall said, standing up and dusting off his new uniform. "I had better get back to work before they find out where I am. This was a needed break for me, and so I thank you. I look forward to many more such conversations once this battle is over and before the next begins. I feel as though you are a torn soul, a fellow traveler in a world that is not quite right for either of us, an orphan in search of a father. I am glad we had this chance to chat! Get some sleep, boy. Tomorrow we march before dawn. It will be a day to be remembered!"

Matt shook the man's hand, standing in his shadow, a good six inches shorter than the sleek general. "Thank you for all you do. Your men love you, and they would do anything for you."

Stonewall laughed. "That they don't, Matt. They often hate my guts. I drive them much too hard. But as God told us in Leviticus Chapter 19, 'Do onto others as you would have them do unto you.' I only treat my men as I hope they treat me. I will see you tomorrow, son. It will be a glorious day."

He leaped onto Little Sorrel and darted away into uncertain oblivion. Matt placed his head against the tree and smiled. He did not sleep that night. But that was OK. He had been bathed by an energy that excited every fiber in his body. Tomorrow was coming quickly, and, as scared as he was thinking about it, he could not wait for this new adventure to commence.

32

A bloated full moon hovered above the horizon, illuminating pine trees and the rapid movement of men on horseback. Faint, cool breezes bathed Matt, as he slipped away from his regiment and peered toward a clearing in the woods. There, General Lee and General Jackson sat on boxes of hardtack with maps in hands and spoke softly, while one man after another dashed toward them for instruction. Within the scent of pine lay just a whiff of sulfa, likely a residual from yesterday's brief battle, and that of ash. Fires lay scattered across the horizon, both near and far. The armies were sleeping. But not for long.

Stonewall had just nudged the general awake, and General Lee, looking as though he was shaved and wearing a freshly pressed uniform, popped up from his bed of pine needles and a saddle that served as a pillow. He looked at Stonewall and chuckled a bit. "Thomas," he said, "that uniform certainly does not become you! You look like a boy at a prom!"

Stonewall just shook his head. "Jeb gave it to me. He will be protecting my flank today, so I really wasn't in a position to say no."

Stonewall sucked on a lemon; he knew enough not to offer it to General Lee, who rarely even ate breakfast, especially before a battle. It was 3:00 a.m., or so Matt guessed by the position of the moon. A few minutes later, Jeb Stuart galloped upon his large gray mare named Chancellor. He looked dashing, with a sword at his side and a large brown beard that consumed most of his face. He wore a red-lined gray cape over his uniform, a yellow sash, his hat cocked to the side with an ostrich plume, and a red flower in his lapel. He immediately leaped off his horse and approached the generals.

"Their right flank is still exposed," he said. "Fitzhugh has been up and down the road; there are no Union scouts to be seen. Our artillery is in place. A. P. Hill is ready to go. Best we leave soon, General. It's a twelve-mile journey around the flank. We don't want to hit it at nightfall and waste our chance."

Stonewall nodded. "Send the word to get the men up. The commanders all know to be on the line by 4:00 a.m. And to stay quiet. We have almost thirty thousand men to put in place. We need to move quickly and orderly." He sucked on his wrinkled lemon and then threw the core into the woods.

Jeb Stuart galloped away. Engineers came and went, as did other soldiers and generals. Everyone had something to say to the generals, and despite the gravity of what bounced from mouth to mouth, Stonewall and General Lee seemed hardly shaken. Apparently earlier in the evening, before General Lee took his brief nap, federal sharpshooters from the Union position a mile away had spotted these two men and started shooting at them on the plank road, leading them to relocate here. *What would this war have become had the generals been shot?* Matt mused.

Matt knew that the Grays were slated to lead one of two columns that would march along the farm road in parallel; General Rodes would lead the army to the left with the Grays spearheading those fifteen thousand men, and General Colston would take the right. There would be two hundred yards or so between them, and Jeb Stuart, in addition to assuring that no one spotted the mile-long column of marching men, would coordinate the columns so they stayed together. Behind them would be A. P. Hill with his artillery and a division of Georgians in the rear to fend off any Union pickets who might spot them.

As the troops gathered, General Lee spit out orders to many of the arriving generals and cavalry. "You have thirty thousand of my men, Thomas," he said to Stonewall, who leaped upon Sorrell, "and you are leaving me fifteen thousand to face Hooker's seventy thousand a few hundred yards away. You are going up against General Howard on that right flank, the timidest of all of Hooker's men, with a reputation of having the worst troops. You better make this work."

"I plan to," Stonewall said calmly. "God is on our side, Robert. He always has been."

"I need to be sure that General Early keeps Sedgwick bottled up in Fredericksburg," Lee said to another man who had just ridden up. "Sedgwick has four times as many troops there as we do, and we can't let him come in this direction. If Hooker sends those troops at Early, I want him to defend that position as best as he can, and then, if he can no longer hold it, to have a rearguard retreat toward Richmond. I don't want him coming this way."

The man on horseback nodded, saluted Lee, and then darted downstream.

More clamor ensued. Time had slid past 4:00 a.m.; the sun was starting to peek up as the moon faded away. Matt peered behind, and he spotted Colonel Kemper. He stood up and moved toward his unit. He had his backpack with a bottle of water and some jerky, as well as forty rounds of ammunition. He held his rifle over his shoulder. In spite of not having slept in over thirty hours, Matt felt energized. There was a long march ahead, he knew. But nothing muted his exhilaration at this moment.

Matt found his way to his friends, Charley and Pat. They hovered in the chilly air as the sun rose ominously to the east. Pat was visibly shaking. "Ain't we supposed to be leaving already?"

he asked. "We been just doing nothing but standing. This ain't good."

Pat was right. Matt peered around for any sign of movement.

Stonewall, awkward in his shiny gray uniform as he sat upon tiny Little Sorrell, moved toward the front and spoke with Colonel Kemper. The air was warming, and in the distant horizon, Matt saw a yellow balloon drifting up into the sky. The Union's eyes had opened! Just then, General Lee dashed over on Traveler, the most beautiful white stallion that Matt had ever seen. Both man and horse merged into one. Jeb Stuart, in his flashy attire, galloped past him. Stonewall joined them and then gave the order; the troops started their march forward. General Lee tipped his hat and nodded to each of them as they passed. Cannons blasted behind them. The sun was bright and hot as it ascended into the intense blue sky. Within ten minutes, Matt and the others were encased by silence, the raucous din drifting behind them. General Lee would be active today, firing guns and cannon and keeping Joe Hooker and his balloons fooled, hopefully, long enough for these men under Stonewall to finish their twelve-mile journey in time.

The minutes and hours clicked away. Scattered shots fired from far behind the line. Matt and Pat looked at each other with a bit of trepidation upon hearing the guns rattling, but no one else seemed very alarmed. So, they resumed the march, a clump of men remaining quiet, connected by a solitary purpose, with each imbued in thoughts of the battle ahead. Jeb Stuart rode by and spoke with Stonewall and then veered over to the right. Other commanders and generals did the same. Stonewall simply marched forward, remaining perched on Little Sorrell, staring ahead.

At one point, as Matt's feet started to ache, and his mouth was dry and parched, Jude approached him. He said hi to Charley and Pat and then told them that Colonel Kemper said there would be a brief moment of rest, so they better piss in the woods if they had to; they were only a few hours away from their destination. The two young boys darted into the pines, while Matt remained behind; he could hold it in for a whole day if he had to. Jude stared hard at him.

"I hope you is right, with what you told to the generals," he said to Matt.

Matt peered back at him. "Excuse me? What you saying, Jude?"

"I was just thinking," Jude said, glaring menacingly into Matt's eyes, "I knowed the person you was back in town. And now all the sudden you is everyone's hero. You run away to the North and come back with a story, and you tell it to the generals, and they believe you, and because of it they divide the army and send all of us in the woods so we got no one back there to face Hooker's main army. And then I'm thinking last night, what if Matt made the whole thing up? What if he is using his tale to put the whole army in danger? Maybe he is Joe Hooker's spy, and he is doing this to destroy our army. That's what I was thinking last night."

Matt's eyes contorted, and he looked away. "That ain't true, Jude," he said sharply. "I ain't like that. Why you saying that? We are on the same team. We are fighting the same enemy!"

Jude just nodded. He slapped Matt on the shoulder. "Let's hope you's right. I suppose we will know soon enough. I sure hope you's right." He thrust a harrowing glance into Matt's eyes and then slid up toward Colonel Kemper and General Rodes, who trotted in stride behind Stonewall.

Pat and Charley hurried back on the line. They smiled like little children and chatted a bit before the movement resumed. Matt peered ahead into the empty sky. What if he was wrong?

Time drifted forward. A round and blurry sun hovered high on the horizon before rapidly starting its descent. Matt's stomach growled. An eerie quiet consumed them all, as though they were removed from the war, in some other place, some other reality. Matt's angst metastasized throughout his brain. What if he was wrong? What if this was all a ruse planted in his head by Slim and the others to split the Southern army and deliver a devastating advantage to Fighting Joe Hooker? Maybe General Lee's army was being demolished at this very moment.

"I hope General Lee ain't in any trouble while we is out here on our own," Matt said to one of the previously nameless boys who marched beside him. "It scares me to think of that possibility."

The boy, who introduced himself as Tom, had scars across his neck and a beard that could match Jeb Stuart's in its thickness. He was one of four brothers who enlisted from their farm just a few miles east of Washington, where his father was ailing from tuberculosis. His oldest brother had died in Antietam during the bridge assault against Burnside's troops. *His brain spattered right against my face; I was behind him, and those bullets would have been my doom if Joseph didn't bite them first. When I picked him up, it was if there weren't no head there at all. I cried for a minute, then moved on. When the battle was over, I went to find my two younger brothers. One had lost a leg; he died a few days later. The other one I sent back to the farm. We couldn't all die here, I knew. Dad is not long for this earth, and someone has to mind the crops for the harvest.*

Tom reassured Matt a bit. "If General Lee was engaged, we'd be hearing it, I assure you. There's ain't nothing going on besides what we is doing now. Anyway, we is marching right along the Union line. They all just sitting there doing nothing, so there ain't no battle. That's for sure."

Suddenly, the line stopped.

Fitzhugh Lee, who beneath his long, pointed beard possessed facial features and a serene grin that somewhat resembled his more well-known Uncle Robert, galloped quickly toward Stonewall on his muscular white horse. The two men spoke for a bit, and then they dashed into the woods up a hill that was to their left. Matt watched them fade into a grove of shaded trees until they reappeared as small dots on top of the hill, peering forward.

"I think it's about three or four in the afternoon," said Pat, who had a penchant for knowing the time by measuring the position of the sun. Matt continued to stare at the two men on the hill. They were up there for a long time, and then finally they hurried down. Jude walked up to Matt again.

"They got a good view of the whole federal right flank; that's what Colonel Kemper told me," Jude said. "See that church there?" Jude pointed. "It's the Wilderness Church, and Stonewall had expected to launch the assault from here. But Kemper says it would slam right into a more fortified part of Howard's division. They want to see if we can go a bit farther, right into Howard's exposed flank. Meanwhile, A. P. Hill's artillery is still about a mile behind us. It ain't going quite as planned."

Matt nodded. Each minute of delay made his heart beat that much faster. He was tired and hungry, his mouth reeked of dry spit, and his legs could hardly move. His brain worried whether this was all a trap. He just needed to know. What if darkness descended on them before they could attack? Why would Stonewall take a chance and march even farther, before the artillery could catch up?

"I think I got to take a shit," Pat said. "You think we got time for that?"

"Why didn't you do that when we were in the woods peeing?" Charley berated him. "You don't know who's in them woods. Could be sharpshooters. Just take a shit here if you have to."

"Nah," Pat said dismissively. "I'll take it on dead Yankees once we trample them."

They laughed. Matt did not. He just looked forward, waiting, wondering. What was the delay?

And then the line started slithering forward again.

"Two miles ahead," said the boy Tom, who had wandered up briefly and spoken with Colonel Kemper. "That's where we is going. Fitzhugh and Stonewall, they seen the whole army from that hill; and the right flank, it's just sitting pretty right at the edge of the Turnpike. All the men of Howard's army are making fires, sitting around, chatting up a storm. There ain't nothing between us and them once we get there, just a few trees. They ain't got a clue what's about to hit them."

The sun descended rapidly. It was getting chilly. Would there be enough time? Matt's feet burned like fire. He wondered if Stonewall had any of those acorns left in his pocket.

And then they stopped.

Nothing was said. Everyone knew to remain quiet.

"It's about half-past five," Pat whispered. "We still got two hours to sunset."

A few uniformed men wandered into the woods. The sun had already descended below the massive grove of pines that hovered over them and cast foreboding shadows. Matt could smell Union salt meat roasting over fires; he watched as thick gray smoke drifted above the trees at a fairly close distance. His heart thumped loudly in his chest. He had heard so many horrific stories about the savage desecration of battle—the surreal state of death and chaos that sewed fear into the bravest souls and that divided the meek from the bold. Which one would he be? He imagined Slim and the others sitting around a crackling fire, spewing horrid thoughts to each other, laughing, blinded to the onslaught that was about to strike them. He hoped he could be the one to silence them for good. That made him smile! He pulled off his backpack and placed his Springfield Model 1861 rifle on the ground, loading in a 58 caliber minié ball, just to be ready. Taking the ten-pound gun off his shoulder gave Matt a bit of relief.

"Where you carrying your rounds?" Pat asked him.

"Fifty in each pocket," Matt said. "Powder in both too." He slung the rifle back on his shoulder and then emptied his backpack of his minié balls. He did have a small jug of water, and he slurped it down. It was not enough. His heart raced even faster. *I could use some buttermilk around now!*

419

The officers popped out of the woods and ran to Stonewall. General Rodes and Colston were there as well. Stonewall shook his head. "Is the artillery in place?" he heard Stonewall ask rather loudly.

The response was a bit muted, but Stonewall shook his head again. "Well then, Rodes," he said, "you may go forward then. Let your lieutenants know. Stuart will be by once you are ready to coordinate the effort. He will let Hill know when to fire the cannon. I think everything is in place." Stonewall pulled a lemon out of his left pocket and sucked it.

Matt seized his rifle tightly. Everything around him blurred. Many of the soldiers in the Grays brought their own guns, some with bayonets, several more antiquated than the Springfield 1861. Matt received his courtesy of a nameless dead Confederate after the battle of Fredericksburg; Charley and Pat had similar weapons. There were not enough guns being produced by the sluggish Southern factories, and so many soldiers also carried weapons manufactured in the North taken from the lifeless hands of dead Union soldiers. It was the ammunition that was the most difficult to find. The Springfield's minié balls were fairly common, easy to load, and easy to carry. Matt had learned just in the past two weeks to fire three shots a minute, loading quickly even while running during drills. But now, as his hand shook and his heart thumped, he did not know how well he would perform.

He looked around at the Grays. Jude stood near Colonel Kemper, who himself sat tall on a proud maroon stallion. They were both directly behind General Rodes, who would lead the charge of Matt's column. Stonewall lifted his sword and then let it go down. The charge had begun! They dashed into the woods; it was exhilarating!

"The first thing the Yanks will hear is a stampede, then they'll see is a whole forest of deer, rabbit, and foxes darting at them," Jude had said when he passed by a few minutes prior. "Before they even know what's going on, they'll hear the yell, fifty cannons firing at once, and then a swarm of gray-clad killers falling onto them faster than they can even take enough breath to yell mercy."

And that is exactly what happened! Matt darted through trees, oblivious to roots or rocks, just staying behind the men he was following. The rebel yell burst into the previous still night; deafening, bone piercing, it shook the ground upon which he stood and made even the trees quiver. Then came the blast of cannons. The din was so overwhelming that it consumed Matt's every thought; he ran through it and in it, and it seemed to propel him forward. His heart's beat was muffled by its intensity.

Suddenly Matt emerged in an expansive clearing, and there they were, the Union army, lying on the ground, sticks in fire, playing cards, chatting obliviously, guns propped against the stumps of distant trees. The rebel yell intensified in its deafening clamor as cannons continued their incessant barrage. Matt lifted his gun. He saw a man peer up at him near the fire. Matt pulled the trigger, and the man fell back, blood splattering from his neck. In the face of every Union soldier on this cool night, Matt saw Slim. He shoved his hand in his pocket and pulled out a ball, quickly loading, finding another blue uniform, firing. He missed. He loaded and shot again, this time knocking down a horse from under a soldier who was clearly of higher rank. The process of loading, shooting, and then loading became easy. No one was firing back. His hands were nimble, his feet quick, his eyes clear. He did not think; he just shot. Occasionally he looked to his left and right. He peeked at Jude; he saw Charley run by, and a few other familiar faces were also close. Colonel Kemper sat tall on his horse, shooting with alarming accuracy, yelling for the men to stay together and push forward. In the distance, to his left, he saw Stonewall on Little Sorrell, sword in his hand, watching as the slaughter transpired. Blood was everywhere— mangled Union bodies, supine horses. They could hardly even get up to run away. It was a massacre.

"Forward, boys," Jude yelled. And Matt blindly followed, keeping his former enemy in his eyes at all times, continuing to fire mindlessly. The sun was falling fast, as a hint of moon showed its face beyond the trees. It was a full, bright moon. It cast a brilliant light on this field of holy redemption.

To Matt, all the world faded into a simple task. *Find, fire, load, find!* Three shots a minute. Four. Five! A dead Union soldier lay faceup near a deck of cards, his guts splayed upon a hand of kings and queens; from the periphery of his vision, he saw that the man held a Springfield in his lifeless left hand. He dashed to the man, shooting as he went, and then reached into the dead Union soldier's pockets. Handfuls of minié balls! He seized them and dropped them into his pants. Jude had gravitated left, and Matt followed. He kept loading and firing. He watched one man fall after another. His heart thumped, this time from the rush of adrenaline! He felt invincible. He hit one man in the head and watched his skull crack and brains fly out. All he felt was the desire to kill as many as he could as fast as he could.

Darkness draped the land. The bright, full moon guided his path. A few federals had turned around and started firing back. A ball whizzed by Matt's ear. It felt exhilarating! He looked left as Colonel Kemper stood on a frantic horse that neighed in every direction, screaming inaudible instructions and pointing forward to a clearing in the trees. A blast of a cannonball shook the ground near Matt. It meant nothing. He shot off a few rounds and then darted toward Jude, when something horrid happened.

"I'm hit!" Jude screamed, and then he dropped to the ground.

Matt ran as quickly as he could toward his friend, hyperventilating, firing off a few rounds into the guts of Blue adversaries even as his mind focused on Jude. This was the obnoxious boy from town who flirted with Matt's wife and taunted Matt time and time again, the boy who had become a superstar on the field of battle, almost eternal, untouchable, until now. He stood with Stonewall Jackson at first Manassas, turning back the surging Union army on Henry House Hill. He pushed back the federals again at second Manassas and held Rohrbach's Bridge at Antietam against all odds as flocks of men perished all around him. At Fredericksburg, he crouched behind the wall and picked off almost a hundred men from the infamous Irish Brigade without suffering even a powder burn. And now, with virtually no enemy near him, these Northern people finally hit Jude and he was down.

Most of the Grays had already moved forward with Colonel Kemper, and from his left Matt watched Stonewall himself dart by with several other generals on horseback, flooding into a gap in the trees. But a few of the boys (including Pat who clung to Matt like a glove) ran toward Jude with him. Suddenly a squad of blue-shirted goons popped out of the woods, firing. Matt turned and fired at them; the others did too. Within a few minutes, they scattered back into the darkness.

Jude, who grasped a bloody hole in his leg, peered up at Matt. "You saved my life," he whispered. "Those damned Yankees would have killed me for sure."

Matt pointed to Pat and two others. "Stay here and protect him; make sure he's OK," Matt told them, pointing to Jude. "He's too important to lose. I got more Blue guts to puncture."

He ran toward the clearing, catching up to a small group of Tar Heels from North Carolina. Suddenly, out of the dark woods, several rapidly moving mounted horses soared toward them, and the North Carolinians lifted their rifles and fired.

"Cease firing!" yelled one faceless man whose horse was shot out from below him.

"Who gave that order?" one of the North Carolina privates called out.

The unit's confused leader did not know; no one could see these men in the darkness. "It's a lie," he shouted. "Pour into them, boys!" And with that, the entire North Carolina unit lifted their collective weapons and fired several rounds forward at these mysterious soldiers on horseback.

Matt came up behind them, puffing hard, his gun loaded and ready, peering into a cloud of smoke. Colonel Kemper stood by his side and watched as a few of the horsemen slid out of the dark forest, pleading with the North Carolinians to stop shooting. Their voices were Southern. And then the moon shined down on them, and one of the men on horseback, familiar to everyone, emerged from the woods.

"My God," Colonel Kemper said. "It's Stonewall. He's been hit. The goddamned Carolinians hit him!"

The shooting instantly ceased, as a paralyzing silence swallowed everyone's thoughts. It was now too dark to see even a few yards away. The sounds of gunshot and blasts of cannon were virtually silent. A few crickets chirped again. Up ahead, not very far, were the lights of Chancellorsville. Stonewall's maneuver was successful. They had driven the Union army back toward the town and were now enveloping them on two sides. But at this moment, none of that seemed to matter.

Stonewall sat on Little Sorrell, writhing in pain. The left arm of his meticulous gray uniform was saturated by blood. A few soldiers ran over and helped him off the horse, his injured arm limply by his side. "My own men," he mumbled. "My own men."

Matt's heart sank. At least he was alive. Medics rapidly arrived and carted him away on a gurney. Little Sorrell neighed wildly as a Tar Heel private tried to hold him down.

Matt limped over to Jude, who lay on his back, holding his bloody leg. "They shot Stonewall," he said with an almost stuttering inflection.

"Who done it?" asked Jude. "Who shot Stonewall? Is he alive?"

"It was the North Carolina folk," said Matt. "He's alive but hurt." Then Matt paused a moment and looked into the majestic sky filled with twinkling stars and a bright moon. "You know what he told me, Jude, when he talked to me last night? What Stonewall told me. He said that in the end, people from the Deep South would do him in. He called them assassins."

"Well," Jude said, trying to sit up, "North Carolina ain't the Deep South, so it don't make no sense."

"They is pretty close, Jude. And you know what else he said? He said as long as God gave him victories, then he know that God was on his side. Maybe God switched sides. Maybe this was a sign."

Jude squirmed over to Matt, draping his arm over Matt's sweaty shoulder. "No, Matt, it ain't no sign. First off, we won a big victory tonight, so God was on our side. And it was in big part because of you. I seen you killing Yankees tonight. I seen a boy that was crazed and fierce. I was so proud to be your friend. And then, just to put me in my place, you go and save my life. My God, Matt, you was reborn tonight. This was your baptism. I hope to God Stonewall lives, and it seems that he will. But all I know is that you became a Gray right before my eyes. Jessie would be mighty proud."

Matt smiled. He lay down near Jude and awaited orders about what to do next. His hands slipped into his pockets, and he rolled a few minié balls between his fingers, caressing them, anxiously desiring to fire them off tomorrow, and every day after that. He needed more balls, more shots, more victims. He would search for dead men and find more rounds. There could never be enough for Matt after tonight.

The battle had not ended, not by a long shot. Fighting Joe Hooker did not go down quietly, even after so humiliating a defeat as the one inflicted on him by Stonewall that night. About seventy-five thousand wearied and defeated Union men faced a split but energized force of forty thousand Confederates at the Chancellorsville front. Jeb Stuart now led Stonewall's men, and the Grays stood tightly behind General Rodes at the Wilderness

Church. Few men slept, and at 5:30 a.m. the assault began the next day. One wave after another thrust itself into the Union flanks, pushing them farther toward the Rappahannock. Matt shouted furiously as he charged, dashing into bullets without a morsel of fear, feeling nothing but the mechanical act of loading and firing within his myopic perception. It was all a blur to him, even as boys and men fell all around him. Colonel Kemper stood tall on his mare, and Matt followed him with a pride he had never previously tasted. These were all boys from Washington: farmers, just kids, now fending off the largest army ever assembled in America. His boys, his friends, his soul mates.

On that day, as another battle brewed near the town of Fredericksburg, almost twenty thousand men and boys fell from fire, many of them perishing. Matt watched as a ball sliced through Pat's eye, splattering blood all over Matt's face; the poor, nervous boy dropped dead instantly. Charley met a similar if slower fate; several shots slammed into his gut, and he fell backward, living just long enough to ask Matt who won the battle.

"We did, Charley," Matt said to him later that night. "We pushed them back 'cross the river. They ain't gonna bother us no more."

Charley smiled, the only son of Pete, who had overseen Matt's farm before himself perishing at Antietam. And then Charley died. The best and the brightest of the South's youth, the future farmers and leaders of Washington, were dying, one after another, on these bloody fields. But it was a small sacrifice to make to keep those Northern people off of their land. "We won, Charley," he said to the corpse. "And we gonna keep winning, because we got God on our side."

An eerie silence overtook the Army of Northern Virginia a week later, as Fighting Joe Hooker sat fecklessly across the river, and Robert E. Lee rode along its banks with a saddened face and sulking soul. It was May 10. Soon after his spectacular flanking maneuver, Confederate doctors cut off Stonewall's mangled left arm. He vowed to fight on; what was one less arm on the body of a warrior? But days after the surgery infection set in and Stonewall contracted pneumonia. There was nothing anyone could do. He sucked one last lemon, and beheld his wife and daughter one last time, before finally succumbing to God's judgment. Just like that, Stonewall died. General Lee could barely breathe.

"We will invade the North and give those people a scare the likes of which they have never before seen," a defiant General Lee told his men on the day of Stonewall's death. "It is time we end this war, and we can only do that on their soil, so they understand that they can never defeat us. We will put fear into their hearts. Those people will buckle in an instant. Be ready to march. We are moving North."

Matt sat with Jude on a bale of hay, watching as Stonewall's funeral procession crawled past them, several subdued officers carrying the body of the South's great hero in a wooden casket. What would Stonewall's death portend? Matt clung to a flickering worry that God had made a choice on this day. But that did nothing to mute his resolve.

"You know what Stonewall told me, Jude?" Matt said to his friend. "He says, that me and him are just two orphans trying to do the best we can do. That we got to hope God is on our side and keep fighting until we find out that He ain't. Well, Stonewall done all he could do. Now, Jude, God is looking to us to finish the job."

Jude smiled and nodded. A bloody bandage lay wrapped around his leg; he could still walk and drill with the Grays. He too cherished the next campaign. "God surely gave us a great surprise when He give you to the Grays," Jude said. "You was such a fucking asshole. And now look at you! That you done what you did is a miracle for sure, one I never expected to see."

Matt laughed. He held his rifle tightly by his side. He played with the minié balls in his pocket, each one feeling smooth and perfect, each one with the power to do God's will. "I was an asshole, Jude, I give you that," he said. "But I ain't no more. And I ain't never will be again."

"Good," said Jude. And he lay his head on Matt's shoulder and peered at the grand procession that honored the South's dead and praised the living. For Matt, the war, and perhaps his life, had only just begun.

33

It was a mystery for certain, and he could not figure out what may have transpired.

A brilliant mid-June deluge of sun draped the Shenandoah valley, with a bright blue sky hanging over the crisp mountains that reflected picture-perfect off the pond. Having been banned from floating on his red raft, which now sat idly by on the southern shore, Luke enjoyed simply crouching on the pond's edge whenever he could and imbuing himself in thought.

Now he focused on the mystery that bit at his brain.

Yesterday morning he awoke early to check on his row of grape vines. They had begun to blossom and produce fruit, the tastiest grapes that had ever crossed his palate. All the vines were growing marvelously in this spot, all were equally productive, all had been trimmed and manicured to enhance both their beauty and productivity. But on this June day, when Luke traversed them, one of the vines had snapped at the base, cleanly cut, and it was lying on its side, dead.

There was no wind, no storms that could have severed the stalk. How odd if a deer or rabbit had struck it in this way, but of course that was possible. Or maybe one of Ruth's sons had inadvertently walked into it. In the end, he concluded that whatever happened was likely a freak accident that would not occur again.

The doctor was meeting with a few of his dearest friends tonight at the big house, and Luke was expected to be there to help Ruth.

"It is unconscionable," the doctor lamented several weeks ago after the "great triumph of Chancellorsville" was trumpeted throughout the land. "We cannot find an overseer for the farm; everyone is being called to battle. I fear I will never be able to leave here to sleep in my own bed again and see patients in my own parlor. You would think it imperative, especially on the heels of one Confederate victory after another, to care for those of us on the home front, especially those of us who are so passionately helping the cause. We need an overseer for this farm. How many more letters must I write to Richmond until they understand that?"

"I could run the farm," Jess said sweetly, rubbing Luke's head as she cuddled near her father. "I have Luke. He controls everything in the field. Ruth takes care of the domestic chores, and her boys do most of the labor. We are still the most productive farm in the county. Let me do it, Daddy!"

The doctor shook his head dismissively. "No, Jessie, it is not safe for you to be here alone. They may seem innocent and loyal, but the Negro is inherently more animal than man, and these brutes will soon sense that your innocence and naivety is their route of escape. They could rape and kill you before you even knew their intentions. I will stay here as long as I must. But I do hope that the scoundrels in Richmond hear my pleas and provide me with much-needed help."

It seemed that the doctor's central preoccupation these days was to complain about his untenable circumstances. Letters rolled off his hand on a regular basis, some to the army, others to procurement, some to the Virginia legislature, others to the Confederate government in Richmond. He saw himself as a prominent gentleman deserving of an audience with whomever he sought out.

"The food situation certainly must change quickly," he snapped one day. "The rations they expect us to subsist on are not fit for a horse, let alone a Virginia gentleman. I have guests to entertain! They would be appalled by the lack of civility I show them when my pantry is so empty."

The doctor bit into a pear and then continued, "They go on and on about the Union blockade of our coast, about losing the Mississippi to General Grant, about not having a market for our cotton. Any reasonable leader would convert our land to the production of food so we can be self-sufficient. How can we be starving when we have the most fertile land in the whole country? It is not a lack of resources. It is a lack of brains. It is having a Mississippi man running our young nation!"

The doctor, as was his wont, took matters into his own hands. With the help of Luke, he underestimated the crop output of the farm, thereby short-changing the procurement he was slated to provide for the army. With the surplus crop, he found a squadron of black market salesmen who frequently visited the farm and traded excess pears and apples for meat, wine, and other fine delicacies. How could the doctor hope to survive otherwise?

"I am giving more than my share to the cause of Virginia and our new nation," he said to Luke one day. "We should be rewarded for our diligence, not punished by having to supply more to the army than the other less-productive farms. That is all I am saying, Luke. I know that you are likely not understanding much of this, but just know that I am being more than fair here. I am almost a saint in fact!"

Luke understood quite well.

Despite his perception to the contrary, the doctor—who spent all day in Matt's home and "out of this horrid heat not fit for a gentleman"—gave his daughter run of the farm, and for the past several nights she had run of Luke as well.

"I want more than you have given me, Lukie," she said to him, pulling off her clothes and stroking his penis. "Your cock has been too limp. I know you can do better than that. And if you don't, I promise you, there will be a price to pay."

"I's doing the bests I can do, Ms. Jessie," he pleaded, even as he pulled down his pants and hoped for an erection. "I's more than anything wants to makes you happy, and it makes me so happy too, but sometimes I'd can't done it is all, as much as I wants to, and I promise it will be better soon. Just that old Luke is tired from all the work, and I needs to get the trees going right, and that's all, Ms. Jessie."

"I don't want excuses, Luke," she snapped, grabbing his testicles and causing him to whimper. "You are my slave. You do as you are told. Do you want me to tell daddy that you raped me? Do you want me to tell him that one of Ruth's sons raped me, so one of them can be strung up by a pole on a noose? I will be ripe soon and can't come here for a while. We only have a few days, and I want you to be able to pleasure me."

Once again, he did not, and she slapped him hard on the face before marching out indignantly.

Several days after the battle that cost Stonewall Jackson his life, and which resulted in the greatest Confederate victory to date, a few members of the Grays, young boys who knew Jessie well, came to town for a brief visit. They told Jessie and the doctor about Matt's heroics and about the army's plans to march up North to silence the Union for good.

"I knew that Matthew would prove his worth once given a chance." The doctor glowed, his daughter lying on his chest and smiling. "You tell Matt from me that he has made us all proud and that we are doing our part back here. We are more like slaves than gentlemen, but it is all for God and country."

The boys all nodded, and Jessie kissed her father on the cheek.

Later that night, and for almost a week after until they returned to Fredericksburg, Jessie had her way with the boys, sometimes fornicating with them one at a time, sometimes all at once. She was not ripe, or so she said, and she wanted as much as she could get. "You better not tell Matt any of this," she said to them, as Luke sat outside his cabin waiting for her to finish. "Or my daddy will hear my version!"

The boys seemed to enjoy what she offered. And for Luke, it provided a respite from her demands on him. But now they were gone, and now she wanted him. And for some reason, he could not perform!

A night after his grape vine snapped, the doctor hosted two important friends in the big house, Horatio Moffett, the local lawyer stationed in Richmond, and former Governor Henry Wise, the most virulent Virginia secessionist. Ruth prepared roasted pork, herbed potatoes, a loaf of crispy butter bread, and apple tarts for dessert. They drank from a selection of fine French wines that the doctor had acquired by trading a few large bushels of apples. Luke helped Ruth serve, while Jessie, wearing a frilled white dress and her hair tied back in a gray bow, acted as hostess.

"Horatio," the doctor mused, leaning back on his chair and sipping his wine, "I must protest! Why all the austerity? Why must we recruit every farmer and every overseer into the army, only to allow our agricultural output to diminish? If you ask me, we have morons from the Deep South in charge of our confederacy, and until that situation is altered, we will never be able to fight a respectable war. I would be most happy if General Lee marched to Richmond and took over the whole thing himself!"

Horatio Moffett stared at the doctor with a visage of shock. "Doctor," he whispered, "in some circles, those words could be construed as treasonous."

The doctor laughed and lifted his glass. "Not in these circles I would hope, Horatio. Here we can have honest discourse, unless you worry about what the slaves may think!" He laughed loud and hard and then swallowed his entire glass of wine.

Luke wandered over and filled it to the brim.

Henry Wise, a former governor of the state, a former federal representative, now a general in the Confederate army, sat upright, wearing a dulled gray uniform bereft of any medals. His face was thin and stern, his eyes tiny. He rarely exuded much emotion save a lack thereof. He bit into the pork and chewed slowly, his mouth closed, his eyes jumping from one man to the next. Only then did he speak.

"It is a complicated situation as you say, Doctor, and no, your words are not treasonous, although I would keep them quiet outside the safety of these four walls." He put food onto his fork and held it, continuing to speak. "I have spoken to General Lee about it. Because President Davis, who is a military man himself, has given full reign of its conduct on the Eastern front to General Lee, the general is fine with the status quo. Our worries are in the Western theater, where a drunken Union general has Vicksburg in his grasp and has routed the best we have to offer."

"Then, Governor," asked the doctor, "why do you think that our present leadership can effectively guide us through this war? The blockade is preventing us from getting needed supplies or selling anything abroad. If we lose the Mississippi, then we are strangled from both sides. Given that reality, why is the present leadership, these scoundrels from the Deep South, and I include Vice President Stephens among them, why are they not compelling the states of the Confederacy to be more compliant with producing food, rather than growing cotton for which we have no market? Does only Virginia have to comply?"

Horatio Moffett, who still sat in a state of uncomfortable irritation at the doctor's words, then said, "You are forgetting, gentlemen, that England may well join our cause. We have commissioners there now, and they are why we are still growing cotton."

"Rubbish!" yelled the doctor, who banged his fork on the table. "Miracles will not save our Confederacy, Horatio! Certainly, you of all people know that!"

"I'm afraid," said Henry Wise, "that once Lincoln announced his Emancipation Proclamation on the New Year, England has backed away from any pretense of allying with us. But gentlemen, I remain optimistic still. General Lee, who is already moving toward Pennsylvania untouched, believes that if he can defeat the Union armies on their home turf, then the tide will change quickly. Public sentiment up there is fickle at best for this war; many refuse to fight now that the war is about the Negro's freedom rather than the fate of the Union. The army is in disarray, and there is no leadership; Lincoln could well be impeached should a major battle be lost in the North. A victory in Pennsylvania and then a push toward Washington could well bring England back to the table." He swallowed the pork, chewing slowly.

The doctor shook his head. "In the end, gentlemen, unless Virginia can lead our efforts, then all this, even a victory by General Lee in Pennsylvania, will crumble. The leaders of the Confederacy do not have the balls to get General Lee enough crops and assistance. Between me and you, Henry, if General Lee does secure a great victory up North, I believe he needs to march to Richmond and replace our joke of a federation with a strong central government led by Virginians, as always it should be!"

"A coup d'état?" Moffett shouted out, still not touching his plate of food.

"That is not Robert E. Lee's way," Henry Wise said. "I will tell you, off the record, that it would be a sensible course to take. Many states in our Confederacy are not helping the cause and are more imbued by their own selfishness than with a nationalistic spirit. Yes, Doctor, the Deep South is not going to lead us down a proper path to victory. Still, if General Lee wins in Pennsylvania and threatens DC, we may not need that path at all; the North may let us win this war just on the back of their own ineptitude."

"Hear, hear," toasted the doctor, who sipped down his glass of wine. "I do still see victory in sight, I have no doubt about that. But it is after victory of which I fear. If we remain a loose confederation of states, if the Deep South has its way and refuses to contribute to the cause, then what is this war being fought for after all?"

Horatio Moffett grimaced. "Doctor, Governor, that is the crux of it all, is it not? We have created a nation based on the belief that our central government should not be able to compel each state to act in accordance with the whole. It's not that the Deep South is exerting poor control over the states. Rather, by the very design of our Confederacy, they are exerting no control over them. So, Doctor, as we sit here and consume a feast that somehow you have obtained despite all your protestations, I suppose we must ask, why are we complaining at all? As long as Virginia has hegemony over its own affairs in the new Confederation, then the sky is the limit as to what we can achieve. Don't you agree, Henry?"

The general nodded. "The pork is very good, Doctor. And may I say, your daughter is looking very fine in her dress tonight."

Later that night, General Wise and Jessie met for a nightcap in the general's room. She had originally come to Luke's cabin and asked him if he were ready to perform. "And I don't need you to tell me maybe. Either you can, or you can't. If you can't, I have other options. Which is it?"

Luke stared at her, and before he could even respond, she shook her head in disgust and marched out.

Later, after her father and Mr. Moffett took a coach to Washington to spend some time in the doctor's house, Jessie found General Wise reading quietly in the parlor. Within a few minutes, they were in his room, where they remained until the doctor returned.

The following morning, another brilliant sunshine draped the farm. The guests had left early, and Luke ate a breakfast of strawberries and bread along the side of the pond. There was a great deal of work today getting the orchard cleaned of vermin, fungus, and bugs. Despite scant rain, Luke's irrigation pipes furnished mineral-rich water to the trees and plants all over the farm. Hovering above him sat Old Rag, proud and firm, providing him with everything he needed in these dark times. He stared up at its craggy face, and he smiled.

By noon, having worked already for over seven hours, Luke wandered back to his cabin for some water and bread. Ruth had made chicken for the slaves, which they would eat later tonight. He decided to take a foray to his vines, just to check the soil and water saturation. All the mindless talk of these great men last night bounced in and out of his brain like a bucket of empty chatter. They spoke as if they could prognosticate situations and fates that existed out of their realms! Luke always laughed at such people. Why stress over situations over which we have no control? Best to fix and create only that which sat in our grasp. For Luke, that meant the farm, his trees, his pond, and of course his grapes.

When he arrived at the vines, he stopped suddenly. He dashed over to the northern edge, and near the severed vine from two days ago sat two more dead vines that lay on the ground, their shafts sliced in half, almost methodically. He stood stunned, as though someone had died!

"I know you know how to read, Luke," came a voice from beyond the vines. "But how much math did Matthew teach you?"

Jessie emerged, smiling with her crooked teeth, wearing the same dress from last night, and meandering to Luke very slowly. She rubbed his head and then grabbed his balls. He let out a very subdued scream.

"Do you know what it means to double things?" she asked him, not relaxing her grip. "Let's say one of your grape trees falls down. Well, if the next day, two fall down, that is doubling. And then the next day four will fall, which is double two. Then after that, eight. Does that make sense to you, Lukie?"

He could hardly utter a word. Then she let go.

"When you couldn't perform for me, I cut down one of your vines," she said with her devious smile. "I know you love these grapes more than anything, so I thought, that's a fair punishment for your impotence. Then last night you rebuffed me again, so now two more are knocked down. If I come by tonight, Luke, and you still can't perform, you will find four more on the dirt tomorrow. After I destroy all of your vines—or, more accurately, you destroy them, since they are dying because of your insolent behavior to me, your master—and I have no way left to punish you, then I will take the next step and tell Daddy that one of Ruth's sons raped me. That boy will die because of your insubordination. You see, Luke, it is far easier for you to pleasure me than to force me to resort to this."

Luke didn't know what to say. He nodded, powerless, shaking a bit, scared. "I will makes you happy, Ms. Jessie, I promise you that," he finally uttered.

"Good!" She rubbed his head again and then skipped away, whistling as she faded.

That night, Luke sat in the cabin, waiting for her to come. She did not. He ate nothing. He thought about sleeping out near the vines, just to protect them from her wrath. But if he saw her coming, if he witnessed her chopping them down, what could he even do? For perhaps the first time in his life, a sense of rage burned within Luke's head. He could hardly contain it. And then an errant thought drifted inside his cerebral sanctuary. *Why not kill her? Why not sneak into the house and murder the doctor as well?* He smiled when those images flashed before him. The world would indeed be better off without those demons haunting the only paradise left on this earth! But then what? Hope to pin the murders on someone else? Flee from the farm? If he ran away, he would abandon his oasis, renouncing the legacy of his parents and slaying the depth of his own soul. And if he stayed, he would live in perpetual fear; there would be consequences, perhaps the destruction of the farm itself.

There was no escape. There was no reasonable alternative to his current reality.

I will perform. I will make sure she is satisfied. That is the only sure path forward. Once Matt returns, then we will have achieved our goal. Until then, I will have to perform.

He did not sleep that night. The moon was bright, and it illuminated the pond, sparkling as its current glided across the land and fed everything that he had created. Old Rag glowed in the moonlight, reminding him of the value of the remaining firm. With everyone asleep, he climbed onto his red raft and floated into the center of this bastion of peace and safety. There, staring up at the sky, he started to cry.

34

Izzy perused the letter again and then let it flutter to the floor. Paul and Smiles stared at him intently; LB shuffled through papers along the back wall. It was hot! Stifling waves of heat strangled their small third-floor tenement room on the edge of Bleeker Street. Even with an open window, sweat poured off skin, saturating shirts and dripping on the grimy floor. Smiles fanned herself. Paul doused himself with a towel, occasionally wiping off Smiles and their two small children who slept on his lap.

A bright light shined through the one open window; heat could not escape from this place, as hard as they tried to persuade it. Out on the streets, the hustle of a thousand nameless souls bounced here and there, talking among themselves, searching for an evasive relief from the sun's sting. Most faces here were black, most of them lacked adequate food and money, some worked, others wished they could. In the past two months, their lot in life had declined drastically. But laughter and joy still permeated their sweltering misery. Paul glanced at them through the window, and he smiled.

"He wrote it two months ago," Izzy repeated. "Who knows what happened to him since. He could have fought at Chancellorsville. He could be up in Pennsylvania with the army now. He could be dead. He could have run off. I mean, what can I tell you? Matt is an idiot. Look how he addressed this letter? He has put *Izzy Snout, New York*. There must be a God in heaven just that I am reading it now."

"He is an idiot," Paul smiled. "But how could he possibly know your address? He just wanted to get you the letter. And here it is. We're lucky he remembered your name."

Izzy smirked.

"What you gonna do, Izzy?" Smiles asked him, gently rubbing his shoulder. "You can't be rash. You can't go and do something dumb just because he says all that. You say he's a dumbass. You always says that. You got so much here. The job. Us. And of course—"

Izzy cut her off. "Don't even say it, Smiles. For God's sake, don't you dare say it!"

Beads of sweat rolled off him like a river. He did not have an inch of dry skin or clothing on which to even wipe himself. When he spoke, speckles of sweat lodged on his upper lip shot out with his every word. And then he said what he was thinking. He said it without any hesitation. "I'm going."

Paul shook his head.

From the back wall, LB, rapt in his spreadsheets, said, "Wells, that makes a hell of a lots of sense. You's going to march down South, a Northern Jew at that, and tell thems people that you is supposed to be master of a farm you ain't got nothing to do with, just because some kid who you all agree is dumb as these here walls sends you a letter (that, by's the way, is probably too wet to read with all your sweating, I's just saying) telling that you is in charge of his farm now? You do that, and all the sudden I'm nots sure that Matt is actually the dumbest person in the room, is all I's is saying!"

Izzy ignored him. "I can get down there," he said. "I know how to do that. And the doctor, he is a man of honor; he'll tell you that every day, even as he kicks you in your balls. So, what can he do? It's Matt's farm, and here's a letter penned by Matt saying that Matt wants me to run the farm while he is in the war. The doctor has to respect Matt's word, as a man of honor."

"Or he's can shoots you and bury you in the backyard and pretends you never came there and just be done with the whole affair," LB chimed in again, not even looking up.

"Why would you go, Izzy?" Smiles asked him, grabbing his arm, peering deeply into his eyes. "You have everything here. And yes, you has a woman who loves you, evens though you hates me to say it!"

"Stop it!" Izzy barked. "I am sorry, Smiles. I don't want to yell at you; you are too good for that, but please, I beg you, don't talk about her! I am not a fool. Don't forget, I'm a member of a tribe that spends most of our lives getting screwed, and that's not in the sexual way, which, by the way, has not occurred with me since the great Ernest T. Biggelow has returned from war. I am lucky to even get a glance, even a smile, from her now. No, Smiles, I appreciate your concern, but don't paint a picture that makes a sewer look like a temple. It's not. It's a fucking sewer."

"Didn't you hear a word she said last night?" Smiles implored him. "She can only do's so much. I live with Elana. She don't love him. But she's gots to pretend she does. He is a powerful man, and she has two small children. She loves you! She tells me every day. She cries on my shoulder every day. She told you last night. And all you went and did is walked out and wouldn't even hear what she said. You made her feel terrible."

"Words mean nothing to me," he said with a crooked smile. "Some of the greatest villains will try to soothe you with well-scripted words before they shove a knife in your back. She speaks a good game, but then, I see what she does, and that says it all." He then paused and lifted the letter. "Besides, it doesn't matter. What can I tell you? God sent me this letter. Luke needs me on the farm. That's where I belong. I am not going to live a fantasy anymore, not one where there is no hope for anything but pain. I am not that strong. And frankly, she can go on with her life much better knowing that I am gone. I need to go where I am needed. Paul, what do you think?"

Paul nodded. "Yes," he whispered. "Luke needs you. You should go."

Smiles slapped Paul hard on the back of his head. But Paul could only shrug.

Paul felt the depth of his friend's purgatory. Since remnants of the Irish regiment returned to New York in early April, life had become brutal. Ernest T. Biggelow had made a name for himself. He had fought bravely in many battles, and now, from a position of notoriety, he allied with powerful leaders in Tammany Hall and the Democratic Party, demanding an end to the war. He bucked his former commander, General Thomas Frances Meagher, who asked for more recruits and just said no!

"Not after Fredericksburg," Biggelow cried out, as Paul and Izzy hid in the background, listening. "General Meagher is misleading you and convincing you to return to a certain death for a cause that is not our own. It's not our war. Not when our foolish generals toss us Irishmen into a wall of bullets and we still lose every battle! Not after our Negro-loving president delivered his proclamation, telling us that this war is not for our nation, but is instead for the Negro, a race of people who seek to take our jobs and corrupt this nation! Even the Republican *New York Times* stated, and I quote: 'The war must be between anarchy and order, between Government and lawlessness, between the authority of the Constitution and the reckless will of those who seek its destruction, not for the liberation of the slave.' We thought we were dying for America and Americans, not for Negroes and emancipation. And so we will no longer be part of this charade! I say, enough! Tammany Hall says, enough! This is no longer our war, and it's time we make sure that it ends!"

The crowds cheered him, and he waved to them triumphantly. Sensible Irish leaders like General Meagher and Collin Ryan faded into a tainted background. Now Ernest Biggelow spoke for his people, buttressed by William M. Tweed, the most influential member of Tammany Hall, who stood by him at so many of his rallies. He spoke for the Democratic establishment, for men like Mayor Wood, recently elected to Congress on a peace platform, and for countless others who raised their voice against the "Negro war." "We say no more," Biggelow cried out. "It's time we Irish help those who are willing to help us! We are Americans! We are not liberators! We are not tools! It is time we fight for ourselves!"

Izzy stalked Biggelow as he marched around the city. He was obsessed with the man. He virtually stopped working. He hardly slept. He lost so much weight that his pants slipped off, and he didn't care.

I see her there, giggling, someone else's fingers gliding through her long, luxurious red hair. The most beautiful hair. The most beautiful girl. His beautiful wife. His beautiful girl.

In early June, Paul pleaded with him to stop, to forget about Elana for a while.

"Smiles says she has to lay low for now," Paul told his friend. "But she says that Elana talks about you all the time. Asks about you all the time. Cries and wants to talk to you and touch you, all the time. She is just asking for your patience."

Izzy shook his head. "Last week," he said, his wild hair flagellating as he spoke, his visage lacking even a small whiff of his usual humor, "last week the Irish hooligans held a rally at Cooper Union, the very place our president made his great speech before the election. All the New York trash showed up, desecrating our president's words and deeds. Archbishop Hughes, the great Catholic representative of an ironically bigoted God, talked about how emancipation is not what God would want; turns out, God is a slaveholder, which I am sure you know! Then, Mayor Wood spit out his usual treason, how we should join the Confederacy, while Governor Seymour egged everyone on to boycott the draft when it starts in July. They were all there, all the racists and anti-Semites, all the haters who talk about their God and their values and then manage to trash every decent law and value that God has given us. They speak in the language they know best, the language of hate, of bigotry. And you know who else was there?"

Paul nodded no.

"Elana," Izzy said her name slowly, punctuating every syllable. "I saw her walking to the rally with her husband. Holding hands. Staring into each other's eyes and giggling. He spoke about how we must keep the Negro out of this city, and his doting, loving wife was there to cheer him on. That's who was there, Paul. That's what has come of the one person in my life that I dared let down my guard for so that I could finally find love. God is punishing me for my sin. He is laughing at me. And so is Elana."

Paul's heart dropped. "She wouldn't do that," he said to his friend. "That's not like her. I know her too well, Izzy. She would never do that."

"And yet," Izzy said with a smirk. "She did."

Manhattan baked as June turned into an even more stifling July; the city had become almost unbearable for its African American inhabitants. The anti-war, anti-emancipation Republicans joined with the Peace Democrats under a single banner, "the Society for Diffusion of Political Knowledge," whose motto declared that New Yorkers could no longer afford to substitute "niggerism for nationality." They wanted to stop the war, unseat Lincoln, and push African Americans out of the city. Ernest T. Biggelow, wearing his Union blue, was one of many Irish voices who allied with leaders who suddenly now embraced the Irish after disparaging them for decades. Collectively they labeled Republicans "anti-American Negro-lovers." Ernest Biggelow vaulted upon the powerful and corrupt political instrument that controlled Five Points and much of Lower Manhattan: Tammany Hall and its leader, William "Boss" Tweed.

African Americans paid the price of this unholy alliance. The expansive opportunities that war brought to the city's

African American community evaporated with the return of the Irish. They erected new walls to black employment. Paul's business withered; few blacks could afford to buy clothes or any other such luxuries. An atmosphere of fear and apprehension percolated with the summer's stifling heat in the tenements of Greenwich Village, becoming more toxic and scalding with news of more losses on the battlefield, new financial woes, a feckless government. Biggelow and others were igniting a powder keg in the city. Indignation among the city's ethnic whites accentuated. It was hot. Food and money were scarce. Everyone crowded into a burning can. Sometimes Paul could hardly breathe.

Izzy's incapacitating melancholy took from Paul a source of joy and optimism that always buoyed him in the darkest of times. He had never seen Izzy so down, so defeatist. There was nothing he could do to change his friend's outlook.

And Paul too fretted from another ramification of Biggelow's return. He could no longer visit his wife and children at the Biggelow home. "He can't let Negroes come here anymore," Elana informed Smiles. "It's not that he feels any ill will toward you or any Negro in the city. He just, well, he is trying to climb the political ladder, and he says we have to keep a certain image. I know Ernie will behave very differently once he has a little more security in the Tammany organization. At heart, he is not this way."

Paul felt as though he were talking to a total stranger. Elana's demeanor lost its buoyancy; she acted robotically, emotionless. She rarely smiled, the brightness of her eyes and her face had faded. She walked slowly and seemed to drag her legs. And rather than deride her husband's actions, she explained away "Ernie's" words as no more than politics. Izzy was right; she had changed, and the rapidity of her decline was frightening to Paul.

"She is a mess since he been home," Smiles tried to explain to Paul. "We all is. We don't know what to do. We just hope it changes. It's got to change. It can't go on like this. She is falling into a pit. She cries almost every day. But what can she say? What can she do? She got to pretend, just to stay sane."

Paul could only visit Smiles in his tenement a half-day a week, on Sunday morning. He missed his family and friends terribly. He started to feel more and more isolated and alone.

He and LB continued to push their carts through Greenwich Village; they worked long hours in stifling heat selling very little. They did what they could, and they earned enough to survive. LB felt the tension too. Often, they would sit by the East River for lunch and stare ahead silently. Business was better in Brooklyn, but still was not good. Everything had gone very, very wrong.

It was early July, and other unspoken tensions swept through the city like a dust storm, mixing with the heat and filth and hate. These tensions churned with the rivers of refuse that flowed down his street. Somewhere in Pennsylvania, the Union army under yet another general had confronted Lee's forces, putting everyone on edge. It seemed that nothing could stop General Lee; people feared that he would push away the North's army and assail Washington itself. Meanwhile, with an increase in desertions and a lack of volunteers to fill depleted Union ranks, the United States announced that it would draft tens of thousands of soldiers, whereby reluctant men and boys from the ranks of New York's disgruntled white underclass—mostly ethnics in Lower Manhattan who could not afford to buy their way out of the draft—would be forced to join an army and a cause in which they no longer believed. Many cried foul and vowed defiance, mixed with whispers of hate and racism uttered by opportunistic men like Ernest T. Biggelow and so many others. It was getting hotter in the city. Something had to give.

"Why don't they finally just allow us Negroes to fight?" Paul asked LB as they sipped buttermilk by the edge of a malodorous river. "Let us fight for our own freedom; let the Irish and the others stay at home and leave us alone. If they don't think this war should be about emancipation, then allow us who do fight for the only cause that matters. We could wipe out the damned Confederates in a matter of days."

"Ha!" LB said, slapping Paul on the back. "That's we could, I do agrees with you mightily. But there ain't won't be a day in hell that those Irish lets us Negroes march around in their city with guns and weapons, gets all the glory, and wins a war they's couldn't. It ain't happening. They's want the war to be lost and the Negro to be gone. That's the war they's is fighting."

"I know," Paul uttered. "And I have a very bad feeling about everything these days."

LB laughed. "In other words," he said. "Just another day in the life of a Negro in this great nation of ours!"

Matt's letter arrived on July 2. It came out of the blue, delivered to Abe by someone in the Jewish community who recognized Izzy's name on the envelope. "Looks like a Jew name," a postal man said.

On July 1, Elana Biggelow had walked quietly up to Paul's oven of an apartment, breathing heavily, moving slowly, afraid of being seen by her husband's watchdogs, afraid of how the man she loved would react to her visit. Izzy agreed to meet her at the insistence of Smiles, but he did not want to be there.

She wore a dark dress, sunglasses, and an oversized hat. Her red hair lay hidden within the hat, and she barely showed her teeth. When she saw Izzy she burst into tears, and then she ran to him and draped him with her arms. He stood like a statue, emotionless, not budging at all.

"I only have a few minutes," she whispered. "I miss you so much. I can barely breathe without you. I am so sorry for all of this. Every day I think of what I can do to make it better, to fix it. I only want to be with you. But if Ernie sees me."

Izzy pushed her away. His eyes were contorted. Paul saw in them both a sadness and a certain disgust. Paul did not know what he might do.

"Don't mention his name," Izzy slithered. "I don't want to hear that devil's name in this house, not with my friends who he seeks to punish just because of the color of their skin."

Elana looked flabbergasted. "I love you, Izzy," she said. "I don't want any of this. I will fix it. I promise!"

Izzy just shook his head. "I have to go."

"Please, Izzy, I beg you," Elana gasped, trying to hold his hand, which he snatched back from her. She fell down and cried hysterically. "He is not the man I married," she cried. "I don't love him at all. I just don't know what to do. He's not a bad man. I don't know why he is doing this, I don't, but I don't want anything to do with him. I am a prisoner there. I love you, Izzy, I don't know what to do!"

He tossed a stare into her gut and marched out of the apartment.

Now, on July 2, as heat and stench blasted through their window, as Northern armies battled against General Lee toward an uncertain fate of this nation and all of its African American slaves and citizens, as bands of white malcontents conspired to unseat the president and end the war and disrupt the draft, as the city's black community sunk into poverty and despair, Izzy Snout looked over a sloppy letter written by his good friend's naive son and made an impactful decision. Matt implored him to return to the farm. Luke was in trouble. The farm needed his help. Izzy had to go.

He peeked up at Smiles, then at Paul, and he forced a grin. "You know, I do love her," he uttered.

Paul nodded. "I know you do," he said. "If you didn't, you wouldn't be acting like such a jerk."

Izzy laughed. "I don't want to be this way. It's not who I am. Love feels pretty good, and I'm glad I had a sip of it. But you know what? Some love is just not kosher; what can I tell you? It doesn't fit into the scripted rules and laws that we are forced to follow. We were fooling each other to think we could escape our worlds and find a place together. Society doesn't permit such flights of fancy. And that's why God gave me this letter. To give me a way out."

Paul hugged his friend tightly, as tears dripped from both their eyes. "I don't know about all that God shit," Paul said. "But I do think that this letter came at just the right time."

"She do loves you," Smiles said to Izzy. "You know that, right? All that crap you says about how they be holding hands and laughing, I told her you says that, and she said to me, that Jew, he must be crazy. I ain't never did that, I ain't never laughed with him, I ain't never held his hand. She said that he dragged her to that talk, that he threatened to take her kids away from her if she didn't come, and that she cried the whole way there. She just hid it as best she could. She said to me, 'Smiles, he must hate me so much to make up a lie like that, and to think I would act that way or be a person like that.' And I says to her, 'Yes Elana, you is right. He is just another jackass. All men is, just some of them have a heart beneath their jackass skin, and I always thought that Izzy did, but now, I just don't know.'"

Izzy looked up at her, and he smiled. "I do love her," he said. "And I know she loves me. I don't know what I saw that day. My mind plays tricks on me; what can I tell you? Maybe I imagined it, like I imagine them sitting and eating dinner together, and laughing, and making love, and his fingers stroking her hair. I think about all of that. Because I love that damned Irish girl so much. And I can't ever have her. And I don't know how I can go on in this city knowing that I can't have her. With all the hatred and pain I've had in my life, this is the worst thing that has ever hit me. And I can't shake it."

"Then why you run out on her last night?" Smiles berated him. "She just wanted to kiss you and hug you. You know how hard we's all worked to make that happen?"

"Because," Izzy said, kissing Smiles on the head, "I'm a jackass. You said it yourself. But don't ever question my heart. It's in there. It's shattered into a million pieces right now. And that's why I have to leave and help my friends. They need me more than I'm needed here. We'll see what God has up His sleeves! He gave me this letter right now, so He does have a purpose and a plan. What can I tell you? The world is a mystery, and I'm just one cog in a much larger game."

"I still think you's a damned fool," LB shouted out from his perch against the wall.

"No, James," Izzy smiled. "I'm a jackass. You heard Smiles. Let's get our insults straight."

"I want you to take care of my brother," Paul said. "Both my brothers. I'm scared for them both. And I can't do anything for them here. If you can help, I'll buy you whitefish for life."

"That's a deal!"

Izzy gathered his things, and before dawn, he was on a ferry across the Hudson for a long and perilous journey to a belligerent land and uncertain reception.

"I love her," he uttered to Paul before leaving, as his eyes dropped tears upon a sullied ground. "And deep down, I know that somehow, despite all the crap and stink that God keeps tossing on my lap, that somehow we'll be together, because if we're not, then nothing makes sense."

Paul laughed. "Since when did things make sense?"

But Izzy just nodded side to side. "Sometimes, things just have to."

And he was off.

Paul and LB sat by the river, drinking buttermilk. It was July 4, Independence Day.

"It ain't our independence," LB bemoaned. They usually said very little during their lunches, and that was OK. Paul needed this time with his friend, even if most of it was encased in a soothing silence.

"No, James, it's not, never was, never was supposed to be. It's all for them."

It was hot. Bright sunshine pounded them from the sky, intense heat emanated from brick and concrete, a paucity of wind providing no ventilation. Both men swallowed sweat with their lunch. Boats traveled up and down the harbor; there was a certain peace out there, a serenity of the routine. Birds chirped overhead, sometimes diving in the dirty water for a tainted meal. They asked no questions. They just followed their script and survived the best they could.

"If Lee wins in Pennsylvania, we is in big trouble," LB said.

"Rumor is that he was beat," Paul uttered. "You saw the papers this morning. And Grant out in Vicksburg, he won too, closed off the whole Mississippi River to the south. People are happy in New York today, celebrating. Another big birthday for our country."

"Well," LB smiled, "I's ain't feeling none of that love."

Several minutes passed, as thoughts fluttered through Paul's head. He dreamed of rescuing Smiles from her purgatory with the Biggelow's, finding a way for them to live together as a real family, out of this city, away from the incessant hatred and the ubiquitous barriers that strangled him at every turn. In the end, Paul wanted to be free, to be the best expression of himself that he could be. His success in sales had vaulted him toward that goal, but he still sat here, drinking buttermilk with his friend, treading water, as his family lay imprisoned in an existence that excluded him, and the purveyors of power conspired to undo all the progress that the nation had extracted from a war being fought for freedom. It was Independence Day, and yet Paul felt empty.

35

"You mean like the Fifty-Fourth Massachusetts Division?" Henry Garnet asked Paul as they sat in the reverend's cool, stone-studded study in the basement of Shiloh Baptist Church, images of Jesus, some of them black, staring down from the walls. "Fred Douglas managed to get that regiment authorized in Massachusetts, which took a lot of guts and favors for him to accomplish, and rumor has it they are fighting battles down in South Carolina even as we speak. What they do may mean a lot to us and our hopes of getting our very own regiment authorized here in New York. But it's not going to be easy."

"If they can do it," Paul said, leaning forward on his elbows, "why can't we? It makes total sense; what a huge advantage for the North, to throw the weight of the entire Negro population at the secessionists, to beat them with the very men who they consider imbeciles and weaklings. How precious would that be! All our president has to do is make the call, and every black man will be there to serve. The South wouldn't have a chance!"

Henry Garnet, draped in a black robe and calm demeanor, paced across the wall, as was his wont during moments of contemplation. He usually spent a great deal of time digesting his thoughts before turning them into words.

"There's enough ire in this city to fuel a fire as it is, Paul. The draft is tomorrow. How about we get past that before we start talking about arming Negroes? You know, Paul, me and Pendleton have been on that crusade for many years; we've met with Greely, with Douglas; Reverend Pendleton has spoken to the president several times. All of them are receptive. All of them understand that it makes sense. But then they say the same thing: we're not quite ready for that. We have border states who still hold slaves. We have frightened congressmen and senators. And of course, we have New York."

"What if I put together a coalition here in New York, whites and Negroes both, across party lines, who are willing to support a local Negro military division? What if I find a commander willing to lead that unit, an established white man, maybe someone who is Irish and who has fought in the Union army already, and who has the trust of the New York whites? If we have all of that, then when the Fifty-Fourth shows some success in its battles, as the nation becomes more accustomed to the idea of Negro men fighting for our own justice, maybe then President Lincoln will approve of a division here?"

Reverend Garnet smiled. "Paul, although I know you and the Lord don't always see eye to eye, I do appreciate your gusto. I've done my own groundwork for a Negro unit, so perhaps together we could provide a united front. But I will tell you, our president, God bless his soul, he is hampered by forces that tell him to slow down, people close to him who say that his emancipation proclamation went too far already. Arming more Negro units may be enough to push people against him, and he has razor-thin support right now. With the victories at Gettysburg and Vicksburg, and with General Grant moving East to take over the Northern armies, President Lincoln may not think he needs to involve Negroes in the fight and risk the political fallout from doing something like that."

"We can at least try," Paul pleaded.

Reverend Garnet nodded. "We can," he said. "But Paul, it's only a day until the draft. Let's get past that first. I don't want to add any more fuel to the fire, not till the kindling is a bit less explosive."

"You know what's ironic?" Paul told him. "It's that if we did build up Negro regiments, we wouldn't even need a draft. We could fight this war for ourselves. Then what's to complain about?"

The reverend laughed. "Complain about? You want a list?"

It was Friday, July 9, and the first day of the New York draft would commence tomorrow morning. Congress passed a conscription act in the late winter to provide more troops to a depleted army, and now tens of thousands of people would be chosen to serve their country, whether they wanted to or not. In Manhattan, the draft commission was instructed to arbitrarily pick the names of two thousand white men and boys who were to serve for the duration of the war. For $300 a man could buy his way out of the draft or could pick another man to take his place (and of course pay that man for the honor). For those chosen, they had just a few weeks to report to the Army of the Potomac, now under Grant, that once again stood face-to-face with the Army of Northern Virginia across the Rappahannock River.

Already a group of Irish leaders, Tammany Hall politicians, and disciples of Mayor Wood vowed to disrupt the draft. "Haven't we done enough for God and country? How many more have to die for this Negro war?" Indignation eviscerated the city, with rallies and speeches burning everywhere. The city was hot, steaming with anxiety and stench. It had not rained for days. People were in a foul mood.

Paul worried less about the draft than others. It was just two thousand people. Who could care about that? The draft was just a blip that would come and go; after that, he planned to put all his efforts in trying to create the first New York Negro regiment.

Today would be a busy day for Paul, ending with some quiet time with his family far away from the heat and madness of New York. The Biggelows usually allowed Smiles to have time with her husband for several hours every Sunday, but last Sunday was Independence Day, when the Biggelows needed Smiles to watch their kids while they attended a rally and parade with the Tammany faithful, and this Sunday Ernest T. Biggelow wanted Smiles to stay put so he could partake in draft-related activities downtown. So, Paul was promised a few hours with his family later today. He intended to bring them up to his hill high on the island of Manhattan and to regale them with stories about his farm while watching the boats drift in and out of the harbor. Elana packed a dinner for Smiles to bring, as well as some blankets and water. Paul couldn't wait!

After selling some wares on Bleeker Street most of the morning, Paul deposited his mostly full cart to Abe's. He explained to Abe why he was calling it quits well before the workday usually ended. They spoke a bit about Paul's scheme to create a Negro regiment in New York.

"It won't fly," Abe warned him. "The possessed never will arm the dispossessed. Trust me on this one, son. Me and my people have a lot of experience in what it's like to live as an outcast in a land where they despise you. You should work on selling shit and not on the fantasy of arming yourselves to fight in this war. They will never go for it, I assure you. It will just blow up in your face."

Paul unloaded items from his cart and placed them on designated shelves in Abe's messy storage room. "I think maybe if we get the right people to endorse it, it could solve a lot of problems at once. I may even talk to Ernest Biggelow about it. Just to see what he thinks. If he has any inclination to liking the idea, that would really increase the chance that all his peace goons would support it too."

"Let me give you some advice, Paul." Abe sat down and motioned for Paul to do the same. "These people you want to talk to, they despise you and they always will, for reasons even they don't understand. If you start talking to them, they will do what it takes to make your life miserable; you've been in that position at least once before, from what I recall. Don't try to change the world in one fell swoop. Just worry about bettering yourself, and leave the world's problems to God, as sloppy as He is at fixing them. Your goal should be to be the best person you can be and to make the most of every opportunity you are given. I do have something to offer you that may be of some value in that regard."

Paul looked into Abe's bear-like eyes, his kind face buried by a quickly graying beard.

"Izzy is gone; we all know that," Abe said. "I admire his courage if not his common sense. He's a man in his mid-forties who sometimes acts like a teenager. I am not sure what the hell he is even thinking to be going down South during a war, although if he should establish a beachhead back in his old territory, that could be helpful to our business prospects once this war is over."

Paul just looked at him, wanting to unload his cart and then dash out. Usually on Fridays Abe left very early due to religious laws mandating his being home before sunset, but in the heat of summer, when the sun lofted high in the sky well past 9:00 p.m., Abe could sit here and talk all night.

"My point, son, is this. Izzy is my best worker. Now, with him gone, you are. And while Negroes can't do everything a white man can do in retail (not that it is any consequence to me what color your skin is, mind you, but to my buying public, well, some of them are not so enlightened and are not going to buy very much from a Negro!), you can have a very large role behind the scenes. Financially you turned my business around. You opened up new markets and know how to keep them open. I am getting old, Paul. I need a partner, one who knows the value of hard work and who has the smarts and common sense to understand retail. I've been thinking a lot about this, and I want that person to be you. The money will be good, very good. You will be able to get your wife out of that job of hers, which I know from Izzy is an albatross around your neck. Just think about what I'm saying, Paul. Don't be given to flights of fancy like your friend Izzy; a Negro unit may sound promising, but most likely it will leave you at best disappointed and at worst at the bottom of the East River. Your future is bright as long as you stick around with me. Good Sabbath to you Paul, and goodbye. And remember, tomorrow is the first day of the draft, and because of my well-grounded fears of human rubbish, and your Irish friends, we will be closed, no sales of any sort, not until the draft is over. So, enjoy your vacation!"

Paul thanked the man, who wrapped him in a bear hug. Abe's words tickled him, and he smiled; it was rare to be appreciated, to be rewarded, for anything in this world! Abe was a good man, and Paul reveled being in his shadow. Perhaps the future Abe painted would be a path toward salvation, but for now, Paul could not bank on it. He had a bigger purpose than retail!

Paul hurried uptown to meet LB. They planned to speak with a few of their most trusted friends about forming a military unit, just to gauge interest. Then, after the draft, they would approach some members of the white community, starting with Ernest T. Biggelow himself! "Best to start with the worst of them," Paul told LB, "because if you can get him on board, the rest will be easy."

That night, beneath a few clouds and a pleasant warm breeze, Paul enjoyed a picnic dinner along with his family, nestled in the hills of northern Manhattan, where Paul had hidden as a refugee after being hunted by both blacks and whites. He still wandered here often, sometimes to think, sometimes to enjoy the view, often with Smiles when he could wedge her free from her prison.

"Me and the boys, we going to stay in the Biggelow house until the draft is over," she told him, as they sat on a blanket eating slices of pork. Little Matthew lay near them, while Jake ran about, swinging sticks like swords and attacking nearby oaks and maples. "Elana she says the whole draft thing could get ugly. She says that her husband said some pretty nasty words at the July 4 mass meeting downtown. Even the governor talk at that rally, and he said to the people something like, 'Sometimes it takes a mob to change a bad law, and there's nothing wrong with that.' Anyway, Paul, you best stay away from the draft and white folk. I don't want none of your schemes! Me and the boys, we be safe in that house."

"It's nothing, Smiles. It will come and go. It's almost over; I think they already picked most names."

"It's not," Smiles said to him, rubbing him on the head. "It's only about to begin. So, you be safe. Because I love you more than life itself. And I know how stupid you can be sometimes." She leaned over and kissed him; they embraced for many long minutes, with sideways glances aimed at Jake as he ran through the woods, just making sure he didn't run off the edge of the hill.

Later, Paul gathered his boys on his lap and told them about their uncles and grandparents. He spun animated stores about the farm, about Uncle Luke's grapes, about their climb up Old Rag, and about the mean old doctor and his daughter who "think they can bully everyone even though they are the dumbest and laziest people the world has ever known. And ugliest too! Let's not forget that!"

"Uncle Luke seems like he's dreaming all the time," Jake said to his dad as he lay down on Paul's chest and peered at the sky. He spoke incessantly at age two; sometimes it was difficult to keep him quiet. And he liked to ask questions. "It's like he sees everything through happy glasses."

Paul smiled. Images of the farm danced within him. "Your uncle Luke believes that the world on our farm is perfect. It's his own heaven, his own reality. He likes to float on a red raft in the middle of his lake and imagine amazing things under the shadow of big mountains. And you know what? He always makes his dreams actually happen; he makes them real. I miss your uncle a lot. When you meet him, he will fall in love with you and show you all of his magic. And you'll fall in love with him too."

"He sounds like a wizard, Dad!"

Paul nodded. Indeed, he was.

Another balmy day descended on the city Saturday; heat rose from the pavement even before the sun ascended. At 6:00 a.m. the draft began. On a typical day, thousands of federal troops remained stationed in New York, but not today. With the threat of General Lee slicing through the North earlier in the month, most of New York's troops had been sent to protect the capital and to fight for the Union, leaving New York virtually defenseless. Until the draft filled its coffers, the Union army was profoundly understaffed; Gettysburg cost it tens of thousands of lives.

Fearing trouble, and having few sympathetic soldiers to assure their safety, draft organizers moved the draft uptown to Forty-Seventh Street and Third Avenue, well beyond the mass of Manhattan's irate working-class residents, and certainly out of reach of the Irish mobs that threatened violence and disruption. Paul snuck over with LB, and from a private perch, they watched the draft silently. There were a few protestors, but hardly enough to make a dent in the proceedings.

"All the talk of mobs and violence," Paul whispered to his friend. "I think it was totally exaggerated. There is no one here. It's all just going off without a hitch."

LB nodded his head to the contrary. "It's be early, my friend. It ain't over yet."

But, in fact, it was. By noon the provost marshal called out 1,236 names drawn from a hat; these would be the first set of draftees. The rest of the names would be pulled on Monday, meaning that they only had to pick a few hundred more and the draft was done. With little hoopla, the marshals and police closed up shop and went home.

The crowd became more raucous after they left. The heat grew more intense. Paul and LB stayed a bit to watch, and then they wandered back to their apartment several miles downtown.

Of course, no one from their neighborhood was eligible for the draft. No one with a black face could fight. "At least for now," Paul said to LB. "At least for now."

The next morning, Sunday, New York's many partisan newspapers printed the names of the men and boys drafted, many of whom were Irish, many from Five Points and the surrounding neighborhoods. No one with money or who lived uptown showed up on that list. White people from all over Lower Manhattan gathered in bars and churches and homes to digest what had transpired. Ernest T. Biggelow, among others, made speeches to the throngs, listing the names of the unfortunate Irish souls forced to "fight and die for the Negro." The heat intensified. Beer and whiskey only made the moment's boiling fury start to bubble over and froth. Small demonstrations were set up for the next day, Monday, when the draft would commence again. Paul wandered toward the edge of Five Points, just to smell any whiff of discontent. What struck his nostrils was a huge burst of indignation and vile stares from the mass of white men and women walking the streets. Frightened, he quickly turned up Fifth Avenue and meandered further north to his destination. It was getting hotter.

Today Paul would be seeing Smiles again. Elana had arranged it.

"She gots her husband (who has to act like he be a man of God now in front of the church people) to say that I can take my boys to church today, and he says you can come and we's can sit together and hold hands and walk back together. So, I get's to see my man on Sunday after all!"

"You want me to go to church?" Paul laughed. "Me? In church? What would I even do there?"

"You would hold my hands and pretend to care about all the stuff they be saying," she said. "And you would show respect to Reverend Garnet, who helps you every chance he gets."

461

Paul leaned over and kissed her, wrapping her in the depth of his heart. "Of course," he whispered. "You are my goddess. I will happily worship you anywhere I can."

And that is where Paul wandered on this steamy Sunday morning, veering far north of Five Points in his fancy (second-hand) blue dress shirt, already saturated with sweat and much too tight.

Shiloh Baptist Church teemed with parishioners on this sweltering mid-July Sunday. Paul found Smiles sitting toward the back with their boys. She was wearing one of Elana's secondhand dresses that Elana had bought from Izzy years ago, during their flirtatious years that had evaporated with the heat and hate now brewing in the city. It was a long yellow dress, simple and stylish, and, with her big bright eyes and warm grin, Smiles radiated in it. Paul slid near her, slapped her inconspicuously on the butt, and then kissed her cheek. She blushed. And then slapped him on the side of the head. "You be good in here, and don't make a scene," she snarled at him.

Jake laughed and leaped on his dad's lap.

"You going to find God today, Daddy?" his precocious son asked him, well knowing Paul's views on the subject, which he shared with his boys every chance he had.

Paul laughed. "Not here, Jake. Certainly not here. You heard your mom. We better be good, or we'll feel the back of her hand, which is far worse than the wrath of God, or so I am told."

The service began, and Paul, even as he grasped and caressed Smiles's delicate fingers, sewed a solemn glance on his face. He peered up at Reverend Garnet, who instantly spotted him and smiled.

"Well," the reverend said, "Look what we have here. My favorite prodigal son has finally come to our house of worship! Welcome, Paul. A finer nonbeliever I have never met."

The reverend, in a deep and methodical tone, preached about "the need for temperance in the Negro community, to avoid all drink, and to be responsible citizens of this nation that had not yet embraced us, but will soon find its footing, thanks in part to our president and to all the men and women, like my friend Paul, who fight for justice and dignity! For us to find our place in the white man's society, we have to be better than the white man, we have to be more respectful, we have to avoid all vices, and we have to be humble. With that said, God will watch over us, but we must also watch over each other."

He then referenced Paul again when he spoke about his hope to create "a hundred Negro battalions that fight for our freedom and show the world what we are made of and who we are. Already, the Fifty-Fourth Massachusetts is in South Carolina making a name for itself, the first Negro regiment in this nation, but not the last one. Once the draft is over, Paul and I, and others who have a similar devotion to the Negro's role in God's war, will do the same here. The draft they are holding tomorrow is not a fair one, because it excludes the Negro members of His flock, those of us who are most desirous of fighting His battle against enslavement. We pray that there is no violence tomorrow, and that from the draft we can move forward and accept the Negro into the army and the nation. And to that I say, Amen."

Smiles peered sharply into Paul's eyes. "You didn't tell me about no army unit you is creating!"

Paul just shrugged. "At least he's saying good things about me and not that I'm a vile atheist!"

"We'll talk about this later," she whispered, rubbing his back. "I is proud of you, but you are always a damned fool and only think about yourself sometimes!"

The service moved slowly, but Paul enjoyed it. Not the part about God, but beneath the veneer of that fabricated mysticism resonated a message dear to Paul's heart. These were good people trying to survive in a cruel world, and in Reverend Garnet, they had a leader who had the faith and skills to make that happen.

Sadly, although none of them knew it, this would be the last time they would be praying here with Henry Garnet ever again.

36

Heat sizzled off the buildings and sidewalks like water on a frying pan; Paul peered through his tiny window smeared with the stains of lives gone by and watched a mix of steam and smog float through the sky. The city had started waking up, pushcarts slid by, owners were opening their shops. From a corner of Paul's tiny room, LB snored loudly, a smile glued to his face.

"James, let's go," Paul nudged his friend. Accustomed to waking up at 4:00 a.m. to start their workday, Paul and LB decided to use their forced vacation to go spy the draft's second day uptown on Forty-Seventh Street and Third Avenue. "Hurry, we have to get there and find a place to hide before the crowds start showing up."

LB shook his head. "It aint's not what I wants to be doing on the one day that Abe tells me to sleeps in!" he snarled back. "Besides, what's there to be accomplished being up there?"

Paul smiled. "A witness to history," he responded. "Besides, it was your idea!"

"Yea, well, that was yesterday's idea. Now I's was having me a dream historical enough, I will tell you's that much, before you went and woke me up and ruined the ending."

The heat intensified as they trod uptown. Rivers of filth flowed past them, and heaps of garbage lay scattered about; Paul choked on the stench. As they hurried past the village, toward Fourteenth Street and beyond, they witnessed something ominous.

"All the shops are closed," Paul whispered. "Everything. No sign of life at all."

LB nodded. "They is all open by now on any usual Monday. To me, this don't smell good at all."

"Why?"

"Because, if all these Irish and Germans who owns these shops, if they aint's here, then where else do you suppose they at?"

From the west they heard a hum of distant voices echoing off the concrete. Clanging gongs accompanied the westward din, something LB recognized to be the beating of copper pans. "It's what the Irish do's when they wants to make a ruckus, or so I's been told," he said. "There must be hundreds of them marching up to the draft. This ain't looking good, Paul."

"The draft's not even starting for four hours," Paul said to him. "I guess we're not the only ones with the brilliant idea of showing up early. We better find a spot to hide. I don't want them seeing us. Can't you walk a bit faster?"

"I's old and been whipped a hundred dozen times, boy. Don't push me, or I's libel to just turn back."

At 8:00 a.m. the two men found a spot near Forty-Eighth Street and Third, hidden behind a pile of garbage cans, but with a full view of the Ninth District Headquarters where the second day of the draft would commence. A chorus of voices and the clanging of pans progressively accentuated, although no one was here yet, not even the draft commissioners.

By 9:00 a.m., as the draft officials set up their equipment, about five hundred white men and women arrived and surrounded the table upon which the draft would be held, some making speeches, all yelling and demanding for the draft to stop. They banged copper pans and shouted incongruently.

Paul sweated profusely, which stuck to him like thick honey; he could barely peel his shirt away from his chest. He wiped his hair, streams of water floating off it and deluging his back. It was hot!

"Look," he said, pointing, "that's Biggelow. He's talking to one of the groups. I can't hear a word he is saying, but he looks damned mad."

"I's can hear it," whispered LB. "He's says, treat the Negro well, let him be our equal, and let's all volunteer for the draft so we's can help fight for the Negro's freedom. That's what I'm sure he's saying."

Paul just laughed. "Yea, something like that for sure."

The few men who orchestrated the draft went about their duties without an apparent concern, despite the raucous mob swarming around them.

By 10:00 a. m., about sixty policemen gathered around the draft commission, guns and sticks in hand. They peered at the crowd, a gesture that only revved the protesters that much more. The noise had become deafening. Many held signs up high, "NO DRAFT," said one. "Down with niggers and Republicans," said another. Most were some permutation of those sentiments.

"Thems signs ain't making me too happy," said LB. "Just saying."

"No, it ain't," Paul repeated. "Just stay down. We have to be careful."

"It's your goddamned idea to be's here in the first place. I'd probably be in bed finishing my dream rights about now, which is right where I shoulds be. No nigger signs in my dream, I assures you that."

"Shhhh. Anyway, it was your idea to come here, not mine."

"That was yesterday, damn you!"

"Shhhh!"

The dignified members of the draft commission twisted a large cylinder filled with papers each with someone's name on it. One of them pulled out a name and handed it to the next.

"Collin O'Grady," one called, as another wrote it down. "Peter Rourke," the first one said, reaching in for still more names.

The cries and catcalls from the expanding crowds drowned out the commissioners' voices. A few rocks were hurled, by whom and to where no one quite knew. The police stepped forward. Loud boos and curses shot from the crowd. The stoic draft commissioners just kept reading names.

Suddenly, from downtown, a fire truck pulled by four horses galloped up to the proceedings, the firemen shouting and whooping as the horses came close. A few dozen men darted out, all wearing their full uniforms, and they stood in front of the police. On the side of the truck was written "Black Joke Engine Company 33." Ernest T. Biggelow broke from the crowd and approached some of the firemen. They spoke for several minutes.

"Maybe they're here to stop any violence," Paul wondered out loud.

LB just shrugged. "Oh yea, I's sure of that. I don't know what they's wants, but it ain'ts good."

The answer came soon enough.

"This draft is illegal. Cease immediately," shouted Biggelow, standing astride the firemen. "We don't want to intervene, but we will. You have five minutes to comply."

One of the policemen protecting the draft commission approached Biggelow and the fire chief. Soon a shouting match ensued, and then the fire chief of Joke Engine Company #33 pushed the policeman flat down on the ground with a thud. A few other police officers moved to assist their comrade, but the entire mob ran toward them, clubs in their hands, shouting. The police scattered.

Within minutes the entire street erupted into chaos. The draft men ran back into the building, as members of the mob tossed rocks at the fleeing men and police, and through windows. A group of them smashed the draft wheel; the papers, each with a name on it, drifted around like confetti lofting in the thick, steamy air. Then a few women in the crowd poured turpentine everywhere near the building and lit a pile of chairs and tables on fire.

Lofting flames consumed everything.

The heat instantly intensified, with a wave of fiery air nearly blinding Paul, who sunk lower to the ground. Both he and LB watched intently, neither saying a word, neither seeming ready to leave, but both just a bit frightened and more concealed.

The crowds grew denser and rowdier, stones and bricks flying through the sky. Ernest Biggelow and a few others shouted out commands, and some of the groups ran off, mostly downtown and to the west. Paul pointed down the street. A few people were cutting down telegraph poles, others were throwing debris onto railway lines. Paul watched as a small group of them pulled down a wooden fence, tearing off pieces to make clubs. More and more white bodies flooded into the area; it was if there was no end to the size and fury of this mob.

Suddenly, from the South, a few horsecars raced up to the area near Ninth District Headquarters, which was now fully engulfed in flames. A few policemen lay on the ground, unconscious, bleeding. Out from the horsecars came what Paul instantly recognized as members of the Invalid Corps: wounded soldiers who had remained back in New York for light-duty work. Likely, with the absence of New York's regular regiment, these men were told to quell the violence uptown, being the only soldiers remaining on the island. A few of them hobbled toward the crowd, where they were quickly greeted by a deluge of stones and a gang of men and women rushing at them with clubs. They turned and ran; a few fell to the ground, where members of the crowd pounced on them, bashing them with their clubs.

Minutes later, three newly arrived policemen bravely approached Biggelow and his minions. One had a bullhorn. "This is Police Superintendent John Kennedy," he shouted out.

"I'm as Irish as each of you here, and just as frustrated by the war. But we need order. This cannot continue. I will arrest or detain no man or woman if everyone just returns home and goes about their business."

"We want the draft to be declared illegal and to stop instantly," Biggelow shouted out to him.

"I don't have that authority," said Kennedy.

Biggelow smirked and then shrugged. "Then I can't help you, Officer."

The crowd leaped upon Kennedy and chased after the other police who bolted. They shoved Kennedy to the ground and beat him with sticks, five or six of the rioters striking him simultaneously until skin peeled off his face and blood rushed down the cracks of the dusty street. He lay still on the ground, seemingly dead, unrecognizable, blood everywhere. That sent the crowd into a frenzy. They picked up more rocks, pulled paving stones from buildings, lit fires, and then dashed into the unsuspecting city.

"Let's get the fuck out of here," LB finally said to Paul, as a few of the rioters moved in their direction.

Paul nodded and then ran uptown to the east, where none of the crowd seemed to be moving.

The heat intensified. Small fires popped up across the city, visible on the west side, on the 40th street, along the docks. The screams of rioters and the squeals of victims pierced the air. Accompanying these horrid sounds were clanging pans, gunshots, and explosions. Paul and LB marched tenuously down First Avenue near the East River, away from the destructive clamor. They peeked uptown; fires and smoke consumed the sky, and a vicious heat blew at them with an intensity neither had ever felt.

They ran toward Shiloh Baptist Church at a little after 4:30 p.m. It was so hot outside that it felt good just to move inside to a familiar place. Many of the congregants huddled near Reverend Garnet, who stood astride a well-dressed white man. Henry Garnet turned toward Paul and LB, as did the crowd.

"You been up there?" he asked them.

Paul nodded. "It's a mess. I don't know where the mob's headed. They seemed to be moving north and west. They totally massacred all the police."

The white man, who introduced himself as George Templeton Strong, nodded and spoke. Paul knew well of this man. A trustee of Columbia College (where Paul aspired to one day achieve a proper education) and vestryman at Trinity Church on Wall Street, Strong was a virulent Republican, an integrationist, and a man who Paul revered.

"It's gotten worse," the well-dressed man with a tuft of brown curly hair upon his receding scalp and small spectacles upon his eyes said to them. "They are targeting Republican establishments in a methodical way, as though they had planned this for weeks. I was with Columbia President Charles King when they knocked on his door and threatened to firebomb the house with us in it. Thank goodness two priests who recognized me came and intervened and scared them away by threatening them a visit to hell if they dared hurt us. But that didn't stop them. They threw rocks and lit clubs at Mayor Opdyke's house until some neighbors scattered them away, and they burned down over a dozen mansions on Fifth Avenue, where of course many of New York's Republicans live. I am hopeful that no one was killed in those homes, but I just don't know."

"Is they mostly rioting ups there, sir?" LB asked the man. "We's safe down here?"

The man nodded no. "I walked down with a small crowd of them, concealing my identity, right down Second Avenue, where you boys said you were; you must have just missed them. They were heading to an armory there, owned ironically by Mayor Opdyke's son-in-law, and then they attacked it. A few police came over to stop them, but I swear to you, all of you, that there were more than a thousand crazed Irishmen and women in that crowd, from laborers, to stalwart young vixens, to withered old hags, all cursing the 'bloody draft' and egging on their men to mischief. They pounced on those police, bashed them with their clubs, and then assailed the building, opening it up and taking hundreds of guns and more than enough ammunition to tear this city apart. I ran down this way, and when I looked back, I saw that the armory had been torched. It caused my bones to shiver and freeze."

Everyone waited for him to continue. But Henry Garnet stepped in, his voice cracking, his face haggard. "They said they were going to burn the Colored Orphan Asylum up on Forty-Third street. Said, 'Burn the nigger's nest,' and 'kill all the niggers.'" There are 250 children in that orphanage, and they have nowhere to run. We're sitting here helpless, no way to help those poor souls. That's where George saw the crowd running."

"There was another bunch of them," Templeman said, "led by an Irish cellar digger, Patrick Merry, who took charge of the group I was walking with. He was a pitiful man, hardly could speak a word of proper English, but he planned to get himself and his gang of Irish thugs guns and fires and clubs and show that he had more power than God had ever wished to grant such a dreadful people. He was taking the mob to the Negro neighborhood on Broadway and Thirtieth Street and was intent to kill every Negro and burn down every house. I don't think any of us is safe with this riff-raff now in charge of the city, with guns and weapons in their hands, with thousands of followers and not an ounce of goodness or pity among them. And there is no one in this city with the power or authority to stop them. God save their souls."

Reverend Garnet bid all his parishioners farewell. "Go to your homes," he said. "Staying here is a dangerous proposition. This house of God is known to be a haven for Negroes who speak up for themselves, the very target that these rioters seek to destroy. And stay off the streets. You are much more at risk out in the open than you will be in your own homes."

"What if they start burning all our homes?" a woman holding her baby cried out.

Reverend Garnet shook his head. "We can only pray they are not that cruel. Although if they can burn down an orphanage, only the Devil knows what else they are capable of."

It was still bright and hot, close to 6:00 p.m. Although Paul and LB lived below Tenth Street, they decided to wander further uptown, ignoring the Reverend's tocsin. They stayed west of Broadway, moving up Seventh Avenue, along a row of warehouses and closed shops; few people lived in this desolate landscape of filth and rot. When they passed Twentieth Street, they could hear the screams again, feel the intense heat of fire, and see flames flicker into the darkening sky. They looked in the direction of Madison Square. There were signs that the mob had been here. Broken clubs, bullet shells, a building that still smoldered from being lit on fire. And then they turned onto Thirtieth Street and saw a large contingent of them, just a few buildings away. "Kill the fucking niggers" was all that seemed to be soaring out of their mouths.

Paul and LB fell onto the ground, Paul breathing hard.

"Think they seens us?" LB asked.

"How the hell do I know," Paul said. "All I know is if they did, I hope to hell you run a lot faster than you claim to be able to."

"I does too," LB whispered. "I sures as hell does."

Finally, the echoes and cries of the mob drifted away. Paul stood up, straddling an old factory wall; LB walked right behind him. They moved cautiously toward Broadway. There was blood on the street, and up ahead fire and burning buildings lined the entire landscape. The thick heat of smoke and summer air suffocated Paul, who coughed and covered his mouth. For a moment, when the wind shifted, he could barely see or breathe, with ash striking his eyes.

"There's something up ahead, on the ground," Paul said to LB, who merely nodded back. "I don't know if it's a person, or a piece of a building, or what. I just want to see."

Between a few gathering clouds above and the thick hazy smog and smut, the sky began to darken. It was difficult to see far in front of them. Paul, with LB behind, slid toward the object and peered at it. Suddenly, he gasped. His heart sunk, and a sickening feeling slid through him, one that mixed with the day's terror and heat, shoving the moment's harsh reality right into his gut. He retched, turned around, and vomited. He was not sure what even came out; it was a burning acid, vile green. He had eaten nothing the entire day. And then he vomited again.

"What's you sees there, Paul?" LB asked from behind.

Sprawled upon the dirty street, a body lay lifeless, its limbs mangled, its swollen black face and bulging eyes splatted with blood, which continued to drip into a red pool upon which the body seemed to float.

"I know this man," Paul uttered, before vomiting yet again. He stood and limped away from it, then sat down, his back across the building. "I know this man," he repeated. "He's got three kids. I've sold clothes to him. He's a good guy. Funny guy. They must have beat him to death.

And then Paul looked up. "Oh shit, James. Oh shit!"

LB peered at a light post where Paul's eyes pointed. He fell to the floor beside Paul and vomited as well. Tied on the post dangled three black men, nooses around their necks, bodies, and faces charred as though they had been incinerated. They weaved back and forth with the wind.

"This aint's what I needed to see tonight," LB whispered. "This can't be happening here. Not again. Not like it did in the South. Nots here. We gots to get out of here, Paul."

Paul nodded and the two of them hurried downtown, without being accosted.

They paced across their small apartment in a frenzy. The floor creaked, and intense heat strangled them. They said nothing. Occasionally, another tenement resident wandered in, usually from an apartment not graced by a window, just to peek outside.

473

Fires flickered far away, engulfing the city. The loud howls of this unassailable crowd provided an incessant background din, one speckled with cords of terror. Paul imagined streets of dangling black men and women, crushed skulls, buildings burnt down with everyone inside—a holocaust that had no precedent even in the deepest part of the South. How long could it persevere? Who could possibly stop it? He wished he were with his wife and children. As much as LB tried to reassure him, he feared for their lives, and for everything he had achieved since escaping from slavery. It was all collapsing in an instant, so fragile was the existence he had built for himself here in New York.

"You hears that, Paul?" LB asked him, walking over to the window. "Looks at what I sees. It's raining out there. God be putting out the fires!"

It was almost midnight, and a pounding rain doused the burning city. They squeezed their faces against the tiny, smudged window that they shoved open, just a bit. A cool, moist air swam past them, easing some tension. But then LB spotted something. He pointed his hand out the window and Paul saw it too. Something was coming. A light, drifting their way. It bounced up and down, as though being held by a person. Closer, closer it approached them. Both men stared hard.

"They's people coming here," LB said. "What the fuck they doing coming this way?"

There were several people approaching, maybe five or six, even ten. They walked directly to the building in a tight formation. Rain dropped quickly, as a burst of lightning shot across the smoldering horizon, followed by a crushing blast of thunder. Paul looked hard. Who were they? His heart raced, his body trembled. What if they were coming to torch the building, to kill more people with black faces? What if they were coming to kill him?

Within minutes they stood below the building and stopped. They huddled and spoke.

Another flash of lightning illuminated the scene, and Paul gasped. He pulled back from the window, and motioned LB to do the same. He dashed across the floor to snuff the single candle that flickered.

"What you sees, Paul?" LB asked, his voice trembling a bit.

"I could see one of them," he said. "He was Irish for sure, red hair, white arms. And he was holding a gun; I saw him lift it. I couldn't see the others. But, James, I don't know. If they come here, I mean, what are we supposed to do? What can we do? What if they burn the place? What do we do?" His voice exuded accelerating desperation with each word he uttered.

"I don't knows, Paul," LB said, placing his hand on his friend's shoulder. "I just don't knows this time. I gots out of a lot of messes in my life, but this one, this one I didn't sees it coming."

Paul imagined for a moment being on the farm with Luke, sitting on the pond and planning out a perfect world. And then, in his mind, he saw the doctor's vile laugh and felt the slash of a whip against his skin. The pain of that moment saturated his hide. He no longer sweated. Now he shivered, he was cold. Rain pounded the building and splattered into the window. The winds picked up. It was freezing.

Both of these men looked at each other as they heard footsteps racing up the stairs. Paul had been here before, attacked in Five Points, on the streets of New York, in Shiloh Baptist Church. Would this be the final blow, the ultimate indignation of a white world not ready for someone like him? Step, step, step. They were coming.

LB draped his arm around Paul's shoulder.

And then, after a burst of thunder crashed against the building, there was a harsh knock against the door. "Open up," cried an angry voice.

Paul peeked at LB, who looked right back at him. They sat there, motionless, not knowing what to do, frozen in this horrible slice of time, helpless. Fires consumed the city, and they sat together, in the center of a raging holocaust, two soul mates, two refugees from the hell-pit of slavery, whose new and hopeful existence had suddenly been tossed into the flames.

37

"The world is not binary," Izzy said, staring hard at Paul. "It's not divided between good and bad, with good being up North and bad being down South. The more you say that, the dumber I think you are, and the more I worry that someone raised on books will be blind to the nuances of the real world and is apt to get himself killed by trusting people he shouldn't." And then he twisted his head at Luke, who leaned back, chewing on a piece of chicken. "And your common sense, and your view of this farm, is no better. What can I tell you? For two smart boys, the both of you are damned idiots."

Paul, his eyes closed, drifted into the past. He remembered a moment several years ago, the white-capped Shenandoah range hovering behind them, a crackling fire warming the most comfortable space that Paul had ever known. Three brothers isolated in their tranquility, as they were day after day, glimpsing life beyond the farm's walls only with jaded lenses and otherwise floating in the sheltered enclave they created.

"I'm expecting to hear more stories about your people, is that what's next, Izzy?" Paul laughed on that day. "Go on, tell us how it's all going to go bad. We're ready."

"What can I tell you? You're not as ready as you think," Izzy said. "You go on about the North, Paul, like it's some haven where you can make a man of yourself, and then you Luke, you tell him that the only

477

place he can thrive is right here on this crappy piece of dirt and that everything outside of it is a pit of hell, and then Matt here makes sure to keep you boys a well-guarded secret, because believe you me, if they knew about you, they would lop your damned heads off, and the irony of Matt doing that for you idiots is that he is the biggest idiot of them all, excuse my honesty Matt, but you are."

"I ain't saying I'm not," Matt laughed.

"Then what do you think, Izzy?" Paul pushed him. "What's the answer?"

Izzy smirked and leaned back against a large pillow. The room was warm, but unlike the streets of New York in July, its heat radiated a pleasant comfort. Izzy then sat up and stared at the three boys, one after another. "My people," he started, eliciting the laughter of all three of the brothers. "My people, we had illusions too. We were invited in and made to feel wanted in many places and many nations and by many people who seemed to be genuine and good, but as soon as the power holders decided it was in their best interest, we were kicked in the ass, time and time again. First it was in Israel, a piece of dirt like this farm, a chunk of land that we held onto because we thought God had given it to us, but after centuries of being slaughtered there by invaders and exiled and subjugated until the Romans finally kicked us out for good, we realized, shit, this piece of dirt wasn't worth it. God didn't give a damn if we were there; He gave us other skills and laws so we could go into the world and thrive. You are wrong about the value of this farm, Luke; it's just a piece of dirt in a land of monsters. Dirt can be trampled on by anyone. You're never safe here, because the world out there hates your guts, and that world can always find its way onto any piece of dirt and have its way with you. My people know that lesson well!"

Paul hit Izzy on the back. "I've been telling him that for years," he said.

"Well, Paul, you are just as much of an ass. Because you think that the world out there is better. What can I tell you? It's not! We Jews were invited into the Arab lands as doctors; we were invited into Europe and into Poland to help them with taxes and finances. We were made to feel

welcome, but then, in every case, a new leader emerged, or new situations occurred, and the next thing you know we were being slaughtered or expelled, because despite all their fabricated friendliness and their alleged need for us, in the end, we were scum to them (we killed their God after all, don't you know that?), and we were never safe in their land. Don't ever think that there is a safe place out there where you will be accepted. There's not. They hate you. They all do. And do you know why they hate you? One reason only: it's because you look different. Just like they hate us because we don't worship their god. As long as they have someone to hate who is different than them, then they can feel better about themselves. That's the way it is and will always be. What can I tell you that you don't know already?"

"Geeze, Izzy," Matt smiled. "You is like the grim reaper coming here to spoil all our fun. Then if we is damned if we stay and we is damned if we leave, what's the answer?"

Izzy looked at all three. "Watch your back, and always be ready to run." And then he smiled and chewed a piece of chicken with his mouth open and his lips smacking, causing Paul to cringe.

Just weeks ago, Izzy had tossed a similar tocsin at Paul before leaving New York to make his way to Virginia. "Trust no one with a white face," Izzy said to his friend, much of his humor sapped by the circumstance of his life and his flight. "You can trust Abe, and he can likely find you others who will never lead you astray. But trust no one else. No one with a white face. They are all the same."

"Not even Elana?" Paul asked him.

Izzy shook his head. "What can I tell you? I love her, I do, you know that. But she is Biggelow's wife, and she has two kids to protect. No, don't trust her either; she isn't like the others deep to the core, but she is beholden to their hateful world and to her marriage. Trust no one. This new life of yours that you feel so comfortable with, it can collapse in a second. And if you turn for support in the wrong direction you will be slaughtered. Be ready to run, Paul. Always be ready to run."

The knocks at the door grew louder and more frantic. Thunder crashed, and lightning flashed brightly outside. It was raining hard. Paul looked at LB, both of them sitting down on the floor, quietly, wondering what to do next.

"They're saying something," Paul whispered. "I hear them screaming something outside the door. If they wanted to, they could have just knocked it down by now. Maybe we should go closer and listen."

LB nodded. "I's agree. You go."

Paul scooted to the door. Between knocks he did discern words, some of them drowned out by thunder. And then he heard a woman's voice, which he instantly recognized. He smiled, perhaps with a bit of trepidation, looked over at LB, stood up, and unlocked the door.

The door swung open, and LB laughed good and loud.

It was Elana! She was dripping wet, concealed in a bright red coat.

"So you's is the man Paul here saw with the gun out there?" LB asked her.

"Man?" Elana said, hyperventilating. "You thought I was a man? That's a low blow."

"Well, the window is smudged and all," Paul said, smiling and relieved, before he draped her with a hug. "I am so glad you are here. So glad. Is Smiles OK?"

"Yes, she sent me out to find you. She is so worried."

Behind her, to Paul's and LB's utter surprise, came Reverend Garnet, his wife, and children, all of them hidden in dark cloaks.

They sat; Elana had brought some biscuits and meats, which Paul and LB ravished. The reverend and his family ate as well, although a bit more modestly. The thunder and lightning quieted a bit, and now there was just a cool breeze and steady rain.

"Smiles sent me out; it was horrible out there. Fires, roving gangs, dead bodies. I don't even want to talk about what I saw. I took one of Ernie's guns, just in case, not that I can fire it. I checked Shiloh Church first, just in case you may be there, and that's when I found Reverend Garnet."

Garnet looked shaken, and he could barely speak. His family, including his two young girls, huddled near him. "My daughter here, she is thirteen, and she did something that God would usually reserve for someone older and more sagacious," he said to them. "She heard us talking about how scared we were that the mob may target us, and so she went outside, took our nameplate off our door, and put it onto the door of an abandoned home nearby. Not an hour later, a mob of them came with torches, clubs, guns, calling my name. They walked by us; we were sitting and trembling inside, and that's when my daughter told me what she did. They walked right by us, Like God did to the Jews in Egypt, and they torched the home where she put the nameplate. She saved our lives. I saw the Devil's eyes in theirs. When they moved on, we ran to the church, and we found Elana there, another savior sent by God in this dark time. She said we would be safer here with you. And so, we followed her, and here we are."

"I don't know if we will be safer here," Elana said. "I hope so. I know that the church won't be safe, and I haven't seen the mob this far downtown. I can't stay, at least not tonight. I'm going to go back to Smiles; she will be too frightened if I don't return, and if Ernie comes home and doesn't find me, he may start looking in all the wrong places. I'll be fine out there. I'm white and Irish. These days, that's a shield of protection."

Paul nodded and hugged her. "That's the second time you saved me," he said to her. He peered into her face, which glowed a vibrant goodness that was so rare and special. "You be careful. And hug Smiles and the boys for me. Tell them I am OK."

She nodded. "I will," she said. "And don't worry about me. The worse that could happen is I get too wet. I'll be fine. Don't leave this place. I'll be back tomorrow." She kissed Paul on the cheek, bowed to the others, and slipped away.

No one slept that night, although the petering of rain gave them at least the illusion of serenity.

Tuesday dawned hot and dry. Gunshots ricocheted across the horizon. More fires leaped into the smoggy sky. Paul and the others crowded around their small window, trying to see what was going on. It was loud outside—cries of pain mixed with the boisterous clamor of the gangs, who seemed to be everywhere at once, some very close and moving this way before veering in some other direction.

Other residents who lived in the tenement had gathered here; it was as if Paul and LB's room was the watchtower where events out there could be monitored. The presence of Henry Garnet only made the apartment that much more coveted. He prayed with many of the tenants, even some from other buildings who gravitated over.

Paul and LB did not leave the window perch. Another boy, whose mother was praying with the reverend (his father died in last year's cholera epidemic), stood with them. He was in his upper teens, and had helped Paul sell his wares when not in school, always calling himself Paul's apprentice, although he was not very good at the job.

"I got a gun," he told them, pulling out a small pistol. "It was my dad's, but it's mine now. I'm going to make sure none of them ever comes up here."

"Just be careful with that thing, Ronny," Paul said. "You shoot them, and they kill all of us."

"I'll get 'em all first before they even got a chance," he said emphatically.

LB just nodded his head unapprovingly.

At noon Elana returned. She had nothing but bad news.

"There are bands of them; they seem to be everywhere," she said, sitting down, appearing calm. Her red hair was tied neatly back, and she wore a long blue dress, barely sweating despite the intense heat. "I don't know where Ernie is in this whole mess; he never came home, and I haven't seen him or anyone else who knows him. But I've been talking to people. And you all, you have to start worrying."

Henry Garnet had been out there too earlier in the morning; he visited the church, which had yet to be assailed. He wandered near the docks and Washington Square, where many of his congregants lived, and he told them all to stay put. He echoed Elana's observations. "There are groups of them with clubs and poles, screaming about niggers. They've been pulling Negroes out of restaurants, some of them close to here, on Bleeker and Carmine Streets, and said they were coming back to burn buildings and wreck Negro businesses. I saw Negro bodies splattered on the streets, young kids, old folks, women. Most were bruised and crushed beyond recognition. I saw," he paused for a moment, "I saw three Negroes lynched from a flagpole, a Confederate flag flying, two of them were on fire, the third was charred beyond recognition. I have got to get out there to keep our people safe. Something needs to be done, and I can't just sit here while such misery is going on."

Elana shook her head. "No, Henry," she said, with a face reeking of pure agony. "They've been raiding gun stores; they're well-armed. They have been erecting barricades and knocking down telegraph poles. One brave man, from the Eleventh New York Volunteers, a mostly Irish unit, he used a howitzer to clear them from the east-side docks, and he hit a woman and child. The crowd came after him and beat him to death, cut off his head, skinned his scalp, and put it up on a pole. I saw it there." Tears flew down her white cheeks, her voice broken. "There were dead soldiers on the ground near him, shot, clubbed, burned. I talked to some of the people in the mob; they have no thought about stopping. There are thousands of them now, all over. Some of them are going downtown, to the financial district, and to the clothing stores down there. Others are just looking to pluck

Negroes out of their homes and business. They have homemade bombs and guns. They're going to destroy this city before it's all over."

A jolt leaped through Paul's hide. "Why the clothing stores?" he asked.

"Those establishments are just another sign of the rich Republicans," said Henry Garnet.

"But Abe's shop is down there," Paul said as his gut dropped. "What has he done to these people?"

"Ain't no one has, Paul," said a solemn LB, who sat with his head poking out of the window. "Ain't no one's done nothing to these people. They's just mad as hell and is gonna take that out of the world, on everyone in the world, for no reason at all but for their anger and hate."

"Some of them could be coming this way," Elana said. "They're bombing and burning houses on Bleeker and moving down toward Canal Street. And," she said, pausing, looking away, "they've been lynching and beating any Negro they see. So, we have to be careful. I can keep watch outside, and if they come, then we can run. But, until then, I think it's best to stay put."

"Thens what's, wait here to be blown up?" LB asked.

The boy, Ronny, again flashed his gun. "I'll protect us," he said. "No one is going to get hurt here!"

His mother yelled at him to put the gun away and to stop talking like a fool. She walked back with him to their apartment two floors down, lecturing him all the way.

"I have to go," Reverend Garnet said, despite the cries of his children. "I have to see where they are and what I can do to keep my people safe. I am a servant of God, and He needs me to do His work now. I know it's dangerous, but if I can't help my people, then what's the point of me being on God's earth?"

"I'm going too," said Paul. "I'm going downtown. I have to see if they did any damage to Abe's shop, and to stop them if they try. I just have to make sure."

"There's nothing you can do, Paul," Elana said, draping him with a hug. "You have a wife and two boys. Don't take any chances. It's not worth it."

"No," he said, quietly. "I have to go."

Paul traversed the streets warily. He listened for signs that might indicate the proximity of mobs: hollering, screams, the clamoring of pots. He watched for fire, felt for heat. He was scared but determined. He walked astride old, collapsing wooden buildings as he meandered along Division Street to Bowery before moving south. There were blazing fires up ahead, billowing smoke; tremendous waves of hot air slammed into him. But he heard no fearful cries of gangs, at least not ahead. Just echoes of people far to his right, gunshots and explosions there as well. Sweat poured down his face and saturated his clothes. His heart beat fast. He held a wooden club tightly in his right hand; hyperventilating, he moved one step at a time. A vicious sun beat down hard on his head.

Soon he straddled Five Points, where he previously lived, the very heart of this rebellion and of Irish New York. He breathed that much harder and trod that much quicker.

Voices in his skull told him to turn back. But he needed to know. *What had become of Abe's shop, of Paul's livelihood, of the life's work of a good man?* The farther he meandered down Bowery, the closer he came to Division Street, and the more intense were the fires. Step by step, he moved toward the clothing district, where he came every day to pick up his cart and chat with Abe. Step by step, into a den of precarious uncertainty. He still saw and heard no one in his path; loud voices and shots were audible far downtown in the direction of Wall Street, an area said to be impregnable yesterday but which was burning today. He peeked in windows, looking for any people who might be lying in wait to accost him.

"Go away, nigger," came a cry from an apartment somewhere behind him.

He frantically twisted his head and held up his club, looking everywhere for the noise.

"Shut up," came another voice. "Haven't we done enough damage? Let the boy alone!"

"Yes, leave him alone," came another. "We've gone far enough."

"I don't want a nigger in my property."

The voices faded behind him, and he galloped more quickly ahead. Fires raged everywhere, and to his right, he saw the large and imposing Brooks Brothers factory burning down, a few poor souls futilely trying to douse the flames with water, men wearing suits and hats, none of whom paid any attention to him. Other buildings were lit up too, but some were not. Maybe there was hope that a few had been spared. He walked further, slowing his pace, afraid of what he might find.

And then he stopped. Far ahead, he saw Abe sitting on the charred ground of this once-prosperous and busy avenue, his hands over his eyes, his head nodding back and forth. A building in front of him was nearly all ash, with just a few flames within its rubble puncturing the sky. It was hot; the smoke was thick. Paul coughed and then darted in the man's direction.

"Abe," he cried out, barely able to make words. "Abe, are you OK?"

The jolly man looked back and saw Paul coming. His face was drawn, blackened by soot, his suit torn and sullied. His sallow eyes expressed no emotion at all.

"Abe, did they burn it down?" Paul's heart raced. He looked where the store had been, and now it was nothing but ash and flame. Nothing but dust. Everything was gone. The carts. The desk. Every piece of merchandise. All gone.

A wave of intense dizziness stuck Paul hard; his eyes became glassy, and he fell to the floor. All energy drained from his body. He looked up at the emptiness. "My God," he whispered.

"They bombed it, Paul," Abe said softly, not even peering at him. "I begged them not to. I told them that I voted Democrat, for

God's sake. I told them I was on their side. But they just pushed me away and threw in a bomb. It was a terrible explosion! I tried to put it out, and they pushed me down again. And they laughed. They just laughed. A man's entire life destroyed in an instant. And all they could do was laugh."

"My God, Abe, my God!" was all Paul could say. His brain could not conjure any cogent thoughts.

And then Abe's face contorted into a snarl, and he twisted to Paul, grabbing his shoulders. "You get out of here," he warned. "They are killing every Negro they see. They bash their heads, they shoot them, they throw them in the burning wreckage. They are wandering around, looking for Negroes. What the hell are you doing here, Paul? You have a family, you have a future, you can't fall into their grasp. Get the hell out of here, Paul. Run the hell away!"

"But Abe—' Paul started to say.

Abe stood and grabbed Paul's shirt, lifting him with a strength that Paul could never have imagined he possessed. He slapped Paul on the face. "Get the hell out of here," he said again. "I lost everything today. I lost most of my life. I don't want to lose you. Run, you son of a bitch. Run!"

What do you do? You do what my people have done to survive all these centuries. You run!

Paul darted away. His legs moved quickly, toward his home. Suddenly the stench of the mob seemed to surround him. As he moved up the empty, smoldering street, it was getting hotter. He sweated profusely. His heart pounded. And his brain turned blank. But despite that, despite his fear of what lay ahead, he just ran, right into the gut of danger. Everything was burning in front of him. Burning where he had been just a few hours ago. This was his neighborhood, and now it was on fire. The voices were loud—banging pots, shouts of nigger. They were there!

It can't be. It can't be! Was it possible that the mob had moved to his building so quickly?

His entire existence collapsed in an instant. He was powerless; he did not know what to do. As he ran, he looked back and forth, up and down. He slid along the buildings, grasping his club, fuming as heat draped him. *I'll kill the bastards! If they hurt anyone in that building, I'll tear their fucking guts out!* But what could he really do? He felt like he did on that day on the farm, whips hitting his back, powerless to stop them.

He passed two dead bodies on the ground, both black, both beaten beyond recognition. He was racing up Bleeker Street. Just two blocks away sat his building. The fires seemed more to the east. But a full chorus of angry voices chimed out right in front of him.

And then he stopped, hyperventilating, and confronted a scene of utter terror. Breathing hard, he slid behind some rubble, and he merely watched, helpless, even as he fecklessly gripped his club.

Fifteen to twenty crazed rioters, holding clubs and guns, were throwing bricks through the window of Paul's building, shouting "You niggers better come out now, or we will burn you out," and "It's time for us to bake some nigger." These were old men and women and kids; many were likely churchgoers and pious folk who talked about God and goodness; others likely were respectable businessmen and caring parents, all of them now part of a vicious mob, terrorizing people they did not even know, blood on their hands, hate in their souls, murder on their minds. One of them lit a fuse and threatened to throw it in the building if a "nigger or two don't come down now and face their makers."

Just then, the boy who had been in Paul's apartment, Ronny, the one who often shadowed Paul and hoped to be a salesman just like him, bolted out the front door, brandishing his gun. He swung it back and forth. "You leave us alone now, you hoodlums!" he cried out with a remarkable calm.

Paul gasped. He wanted to tell the boy to go back inside; he so much wanted to run out and help him. But he just cowered there, hidden beyond the rubble, unable to move or utter a word. The full extent of his impotence in this concrete jungle overwhelmed him. What could he do? He grasped his club that much tighter as he watched a harrowing scene unfold in front of his helpless eyes.

The entirety of the gang turned and laughed at the boy, even a small girl who was likely no older than ten, who pointed her finger at him and said, "Look at that nigger, acting all tough!"

"You put down that gun, boy, and no one will get hurt," one of the group's leaders said, approaching Ronny with his hand up like he was stopping traffic. "We won't bother you or yours. We just want you out of this city. You tell your folk to leave the building, and we're going to torch it. We don't want to hurt no one. We just want to burn the place down, and you spooks can find another city to haunt."

"I'm ain't leaving," Ronny said, pointing his gun straight at the man. "You all betters leave, though. I'll take as many of you out as I can."

"That's a one bullet gun, boy," the man said, as all the others laughed. "You shoot me, and the rest of my people will tear you apart and kill every man and woman in that building. You want that on your head, boy?"

Just then, panting and sweating, Ronny's morbidly overweight mother slumbered out of the door. The crowd laughed that much louder.

"Looks like your mommy wants you home," one of them said, generating still more laughter.

"You comes in this minute, Ronny," she said to him, grabbing the back of his shirt. "You comes in now."

Ronny pulled away and, as the crowd roared, he pointed his gun and pulled the trigger. The man who had been talking to him grabbed his shoulder and fell to the floor. Ronny and his mother stood still.

And then, to a person, every member of the gang descended on the two them, even as the injured man stood up unharmed but for his blood-soaked shirt.

Paul watched, aghast. He peeked up to see scores of black faces squished against his window, similarly paralyzed. *Maybe,* he thought, *if I hit them from behind I could knock a few down, and that would trigger LB and the others to swarm down and chase them away.* But he knew that the gang would just come back, with guns and bombs; there was no fighting this swarming band of evil, not today.

The scene played out quickly. They pounced on Ronny and tore him apart, dozens of feet and clubs pounding him to death. And when his mother tried to intervene, she was knocked down to meet the same fate. Neither had even a moment to scream. Their violent demise transpired in an instant.

Members of the gang showered the man who had been shot with concern and compassion. "You OK, Casey?" one asked after another, as the two dead black bodies lay bleeding on the street.

"Yea, I'm good. Let's lynch these bastards and burn them; then I want to find a doctor," the man said. "We done enough here already. These people learned their lesson."

"You're a brave man, Casey," a young woman said, kissing him on the cheek, after which the young girl ran over and hugged his legs.

They tied Ronny and his mother up on a post, although his mother's rope snapped, and she fell down. They all laughed. "She's a fat son of a bitch," one of them cried out.

One of the women poured turpentine on them and lit them on fire. They burned brightly through the smog, the putrid scent of human flesh assailing Paul's nostrils. Then, grabbing their poles and buckets and other sundries, and helping the wounded man along, the group marched away, singing and laughing as their voices faded.

Fires gathered strength across the city, the heat intensified, and the mayhem gravitated toward the docks before moving back uptown. It went on long through the night.

Two days later, it all ended. Six-thousand troops marched into the city on Wednesday night. They confronted the rioters and isolated them behind their self-made barricades, although many in the mob refused to give in. They threw bricks at the soldiers and even shot at them, but in the end, with dozens being mowed down and killed, they scattered back to their previous lives, fading into the concrete jungle from which they came.

Despite calls for reprisals, Lincoln did nothing to punish the perpetrators. To quell the fury, he placed Democratic military leaders in charge of the city until all potential violence was quelled. There were no arrests. No one paid a price for the death and damage. All of New York returned to what it had been within just a few days, as though the riot never occurred at all. Businesses reopened, churches filled with pious white faces praying for peace, and the typical summer heat flowed through the air and sea. Governor Seymour vowed that that state would pay for all damage; the city itself would bear no burden for what had transpired. He spoke to a group of New York Democrats in Washington Square, flanked by William "Boss" Tweed from Tammany and his reliable sidekick, Ernest T. Biggelow.

"The draft has been suspended in New York," Tweed said to the cheering crowd. "And so, we did accomplish our goal. We never intended there to be any violence. In fact, the lying Republican press that is crying about how many buildings were burned and people killed is, as is usual in their false news reporting, grossly exaggerating the facts. Most of the deaths were of innocent Irishmen and Irishwomen who were exercising their First Amendment rights to state their opposition to this unconstitutional draft law only to be shot and killed by federal agents. How ironic! But, thank you, Governor, for helping us to rebuild our great city. We will work with you, and we will continue our civic responsibility to this great city and all its inhabitants."

The crowds went wild.

Later in the week, in the overheated oven in which they lived, Paul and LB sat quietly, with Smiles, Matt, Jake, and Elana. They talked about the past few days and wondered what lay ahead.

"When you thinks about it," LB said, "that boy, Ronny, he saved our lives. He went outs there and fed them what they's wanted, a few Negroes to be sacrificed. That's what they needed to feed their hate. They killed him and his mom and then moved on. Without Ronny, our building, they would have blown it up and we's be dead men now. All of Reverend Garnet's family and his kids would all be dead; that's is all I's saying. Ronny saved us all."

"He was a brave kid," Paul whispered. "The only one of us who had any guts."

"He's a dead kid," Smiles said. "And he got his mom killed too. That's not so brave. It's dumb."

Paul held his children tightly, although they eventually squirmed away, especially Jake, who liked to run around with his arms outstretched, making buzzing sounds. Elana had left her children with her parents. "I couldn't even tell my parents I was coming here," she said. "Even they think you people are violent and ignorant and ruining the world. Not like the righteous Irish that my lovely husband led in the nonviolent protest that only turned violent because the Negroes and police made it so. That's what they're all saying, and everyone is buying it." She shook her head, drained and despondent. "I have to sneak out and lie all the time now. I have to listen to horrid things and say nothing in return. And most of the time, I'm lucky to be allowed out at all. I'm a prisoner in my own house."

"What's he been like?" Paul asked her. "Your suddenly famous husband? Has he said anything at all?"

"He's giddy all the time, that's what he's been," Smiles interjected. "He dances around the house, even says hi to me and the boys. Lifted up Matt and twisted him around. Told me that things are looking up. I felts like telling him to fuck off," she said, tossing out a word Paul had never heard her utter.

"He's been rubbing my back and even kissed me on the head," said Elana, who could barely even look up. "I smile at him and pretend I am flattered by his new attentiveness, and then tell him it is that time of the month, even though that time of the month ended a few years ago (which he, of course, doesn't know), just in case he wants to do more with me. He's been overly affectionate, which only makes me squirm. He said we'll be going to more dinners, and that I had better start looking more presentable. He told me I should lose a few pounds. It's quite the life he has in store for me."

"Then leave," Paul said. "Just leave. That's what I'm going to do. I'm not staying here. Not after this. I have nothing here; it all burned down, and the people who did the burning, the men like your husband, they rule the city now, and there's nothing we can do about it. But, thankfully, I'm not a slave anymore, and neither are you, Elana. No one can make us stay in New York. These people can commit the horrible murder and destruction they did, and still they are portrayed as heroes, the victors. And we lose everything. How does that make sense?"

"It don't," said LB. "But we gots nowhere's else to go. This is better than what we left; that's for sure. And there aint's some magic place somewhere else where all the sudden the white folks are gonna likes us. We can rebuild here and survive. We gots to rebuild. This is our home. It's all we gots."

"No, it's not, not anymore," Paul insisted. "It can't be. If we stay here, we have no balls at all."

Smiles just peered at Paul. She could say nothing to her husband and wouldn't know what to anyway. So, she scooted next to him and lay her head on his shoulder, holding him tightly.

"Well, Paul, I actually don't have balls, and I'm no less a prisoner than you," Elana told him. "I can never leave this place as much as I pray to every day. The love of my life is gone, and likely I'll never see him again. And I'm stuck with a monster who is pretending to coddle up to me because now he needs a doting wife for his public image. I love my kids. They are my gift from God. But they are also my chains. To protect them, I have to be with him, to be in his world, to go through the motions to please him. I will spend the rest of my life mired in a world I detest. Chained here. Just to protect them, my wonderful children, my curse. If it weren't for them, I'd stab him in the back tomorrow. I hate him and my whole life. I live in the biggest house in town. And it's just a giant prison."

Smiles put her other arm around Elana's shoulder. Trapped in a suffocating heat, fearful of leaving their protected enclave, they cuddled together, reflecting upon a sordid past and uncertain future. They mostly sat in silence. Smiles rubbed Paul's head and Elana's back. LB just peered forward, saying nothing, thinking everything. Jake continued to run around them, oblivious to anything except for the fantasy that was playing out in his mind. The fires were out. The war continued, and Tammany Hall had made its mark in New York. And here they were, alone, but always together.

38

Through the gentle patter of a late summer rain, Luke heard something rustle behind the grape vines, and he gasped.

Last night he was prepared to satisfy the wife of his brother; he believed he could summon his inner discipline to provide what Jessie most craved before she destroyed his few remaining grape vines. But then the doctor altered that plan; he would be dining with Jessie tonight, along with a potential overseer "who will finally release my chattels and enable me to return to my own home!" And he asked Luke to find a few bottles of Merlot in Matt's closet to make the evening successful.

"They usually say yes to me after a few glasses of wine and a few glimpses of Jessie's breasts," the doctor brazenly told Luke with a deep laugh. "I will make sure Jessie gets good and close, even rubs up against the young man, just so he knows what his fringe benefits may be."

Luke, while somewhat nauseated by the statement, nodded and smiled. "Yes, Doctor sir, I's knows where I's can find me some good reds and whites and makes that man very happy indeed!"

"Just red, boy," the doctor said. "We are having meat. Not that you would understand that, but regardless, white wine would simply not do. And I want Merlot."

Luke nodded. "Yes, sir, Doctor sir, reds Merlots it is, it is indeed!"

The doctor stared compassionately into Luke's eyes. "I have received many accolades from the Confederate brass, and you, Luke, have done honor to General Lee's army with your hard work and farming prowess. I am sorry that your grape vines have not survived some of our storms. That is a shame. Jessie told me that many have fallen down. It would have been a feather in our cap to provide good red wine to the new nation that will be born on Virginia's soil."

"Yes, Doctor, sir, Doctor," Luke said, still smiling and nodding. "It was the ugliest storm I's ever did see that knocked them vines down. The ugliest storm I thinks is in the whole world, if you asks old Luke."

It was a cool August day, dry and windy. Luke had diverted his dams to better hydrate some of the parched land; the surge from Old Rag continued unabated, flowing across his farm and enriching all that it touched. Luke made sure that it also fed his grape vines, although by now, he was quite dubious if any would survive Jessie's tempest. He was down to only eight now!

At some point later that night, as Luke watched the doctor inebriate and sexually entice a young boy from across the county to become his overseer, Jessie whispered into his ear, "My daddy told me that an ugly storm came to knock down your precious vines." She bit his ear hard, causing him to wince. "The storm plans to be by tonight to see if she has to finish the job. It's up to you, Lukie."

Luke did not sleep. He listened for footsteps, hearing nothing but innocuous wind. When dawn finally illuminated a foggy landscape, he caught a glimpse of Jessie marching toward the vines. It was cool and wet, and her face looked determined. She was whistling "Dixie," wearing nothing but her nightgown, her long hair frizzed in every direction. At some point a few weeks ago, Luke had accepted the fact that his grapes had no future so long as Jessie reigned over his land. She would kill them all in her rage—of that there could be no doubt. But her menacing threat would dissipate when Matt returned. He had learned how to grow superb grapes upon this once-barren land, and next time he could do even better, grapes bathed by the holy beauty of Old Rag itself.

He watched as Jessie, an ax in hand, meandered behind the vines to commit her final act of murder.

And then, from nowhere, a loud soprano shriek sliced through the morning's calm. "Daddy, Daddy, Daddy!" Jessie cried out, scrambling quickly out from behind the vines and toward the main house. She screamed the entire way, quickly disappearing into the fog.

Luke meandered to the grapes, and he heard rustling from behind the vines. He swallowed hard. What was going on? Who was there? His vines still stood erect; she had not damaged them before bolting away. Step by step he approached. The vines rustled again.

Suddenly Luke saw a body emerge from the bushes, and he stopped in his tracks. There crouched a man, short in stature, emaciated, wearing rags for clothing, with a salt-and-pepper beard engulfing his sallow face. Then the man stood and smiled.

And Luke almost dropped to the floor.

Luke dashed over and buried the man in a hug, as pent-up tears and wails of joy flew from him. Luke never cried, not when sad or happy. Now he could not stop!

"You are going to knock me over," Izzy said to him. "What can I tell you? I am in a weakened state! Don't break any more of my bones."

Luke laughed and cried and hugged him that much more tightly. He grasped the man with every drop of the emotional angst that flowed within him. He could hardly breathe or think. It was as if God himself had delivered a savior, and just in time. "Izzy," he finally said. He looked at his friend and rubbed his thick, matted hair. "Izzy, thank God! How did you come here? I am so happy! Come to my cabin. I have some apples and pears hidden away, and a few slices of bread with butter. You look like a beaten-down Jew! Ha ha. Izzy! Oh Izzy! Come with me, before they come back."

Izzy kissed Luke on the forehead. He smiled. "Luke, I never knew I had such an effect on you! I want them to come, the doctor and his daughter, so I can show them this." He lifted a piece of paper. "And don't worry about finding me food; I've been eating your grapes. You've outdone yourself this time! These are spectacular!"

"I think I can do even better with the next crop," Luke said, glowing, again burying him in a hug.

"Go back to your cabin, Luke. I will wait for the doctor and his vile daughter to return. I think she thought she saw a ghost when she found me back there! Rest assured, Luke, there is nothing they can do to me. I am here for good, with the blessing of your brother Matt."

"Is Matt alive and well?"

"He is," Izzy said. "I received confirmation two weeks ago. Apparently, he is some kind of war hero. What can I tell you? If your brother, who doesn't even know the difference between a bullet and a marble, can be a war hero, then maybe we can be the next president and vice-president of this country. What do you say about that, Luke?"

Izzy relayed a bit of his saga to Luke, about the letter mailed to him in New York by Matt, his journey to the farm, and the snags along the way. "As I came to find you, despite my crafty stealth, I was captured by some Confederate sentries, who threatened to shoot me as a spy. I showed them Matt's letter, but they didn't believe me, not until they received verification, or so they said. They threw me in a prison, crawling with disgusting bugs and other vermin, fed me mold on a good day, and waited to have the letter delivered to your brother—who was marching back from Gettysburg—so he could validate it, which he did only two weeks ago, giving me his stamp of approval. And he even had the letter signed by General Lee himself, which just shows you how far your simpleton brother has risen in these Confederate ranks. I'm holding the letter now. Let's see how the doctor, with all his talk of honor and obligation, takes this very unexpected turn of events."

Luke laughed; an uncharacteristic giddiness flooded his entire body. He could hardly stay still. "And how about Paul? How is my other brother?"

"We will talk later, Luke; you are being very impatient, when I have a job to do and you need to be back in the cabin. Rest assured, Paul is very well. He is a successful salesman and a father of two wonderful boys. He has a wife who would make you so proud, and he talks about you every day. Now, go to the cabin, you foolish kid! I don't want you here when Satan and his witch show up. If all goes well, we will have many days to talk about everything. Go! We always thought that Matt was the idiot in this trio, but you are quickly moving into the first place. Go!"

Luke gave him one more hug, stared into his eyes with unending happiness, and then scooted off, just far enough to be out of sight, but near enough to hear what might be said.

A few minutes later, the doctor, a gun in hand, flanked by Jessie and the very exhausted boy who was being recruited as an overseer, marched over. "Whoever you are, come out now," the doctor yelled. "I will shoot you if I don't see you in the next minute."

The boy then tripped over a loose stick, falling hard to the ground. "Who in God's name put this thing here?" the boy slurred.

Izzy stood, hands in his air, and approached the doctor. "I see, Doctor, that you are still consorting with the best minds in Virginia," Izzy said, pointing to the boy. "It's good to see you again. You may want to help your friend off the ground, and then we can talk."

The doctor approached Izzy, strolled around him, and then smiled. "Well, if it isn't my Jewish clothing salesman, looking a bit ragged these days. Did you come down to switch over to the winning side?"

"Yes," Izzy said. "That is exactly what I did. How did you know? You are much smarter than you appear, Doctor. I am moving to the winning side. I am here to take over this farm."

The doctor laughed; it sounded like a forced bark. Then he turned to his daughter. "What do you think, Jessie? Should we give this Jew our farm? I think he has made a convincing case." And he laughed again, not waiting for his daughter to respond.

A soft breeze sliced through the fog; August's sun rose high into the sky, burning through the mist and heating the air. Both men stared at each other for a few long minutes. The doctor played with his gun.

"You ever shoot one of those, Doctor?" Izzy asked. "If you give it to me, I'll show you how. We sometimes use these weapons to chase pests off our property. I see at least two pests now."

"Do you?" the doctor laughed again. "How ironic. Because we Christians do the same thing, especially when the pests are of heathen blood."

"Yes, Doctor, you are indeed a good Christian, and I am a heathen. I know you to be a man of honor as well. As a Jew, I have a lot to learn about all of that from men like you. What can I tell you?"

"That is true," said the doctor, beaming. "Then what does bring you down here? Are you trying to sell us some more pants?"

"No," Izzy smiled. "You wear your slacks so well that I could never hope to sell you better ones. But I do have something, and it's from Matt." With that, he handed the doctor his letter.

The doctor seized it, slid it out of the envelope, and started reading.

"I have another one of these back with Matt," Izzy lied. "Just in case you choose to damage this one. I told your heroic son-in-law that I would write him back just as soon as this matter is settled. As a man of honor, we know that you will most certainly adhere to what this letter says, but just in case, he had General Lee sign the letter too, since, after all, it was General Lee who gave this land to Matt's father, as you well know. Tell me when you are done reading it, Doctor, so I can look at the glance on your face. My people don't have as much honor as you do, and we also suffer at your hands, but we have a marvelous sense of humor, and I fully expect to have a good laugh at your expense in a few minutes!"

The doctor's visage twisted into a contorted mess, his cheeks slowly turning bright red. He looked at the letter, and then read it again, and again. "It can't be," he whispered.

"What is it, Daddy?" Jess asked from behind.

The young boy tried to peek over the doctor's shoulder, but the doctor shoved him hard to the ground.

"It's from your husband. It says that Matt has granted this Jew control of the farm's operation until he returns from the war, and grants him permanent control should he be killed in the war. That he has total ownership of the slaves as well. That you and I can stay here, but that we have no authority to make decisions. This is preposterous!"

"We just won't listen, Daddy," Jessie said. "What can they do?"

"Poor, misled girl," Izzy smiled. "It's a matter of honor. Hasn't your father taught you that?"

The doctor peered up at Izzy and tried to throw the letter at him, although it fluttered in the wind and fell to the floor, where Izzy scooped it up. "This is preposterous!" he again declared. "I will get word to Matt and General Lee. I will talk to the people I know in Congress. Don't get too comfortable here, Jew, because you won't be here for very long, I assure you that."

The doctor twisted around, as he and Jessie and the young boy (who lifted himself up from the ground, covered with leaves and twigs) marched away.

"Don't worry, Doctor," Izzy cried after them. "I'm staying in the cabin with Luke. You can have the main house. I wouldn't want to spoil your Southern comfort!"

That night, to a chorus of crickets, and a warm gentle breeze, Izzy and Luke sat quietly in Luke's cabin. Ruth wandered by to deliver a special meal she had conjured once she heard of Izzy's arrival. "It's ain't exactly what you's likes, Mr. Izzy, but it's pretty darned close, if you's asks me."

She handed them each a plate with marinated beef, melted cheese, and cabbage between two slices of dark bread. Izzy stood and hugged her. "The Izzy!" he said. "My favorite sandwich and my greatest invention. You remembered! I haven't eaten anything more than chunks of dirt for weeks. Ruth, you are a princess!" He bit it, chewing with his mouth wide open, smacking his lips as was his habit. And then he gave her a kiss. "Perfect!" he said.

"Well, we's just so happy to have you back; that is for sure," she said. "Me and the boys both. To see that doctor run off, this be a good day for us all as we's ever had! But he did do one good thing, the doctor did. He stole so much food from the army that he wasn't supposed to have that we have lots of good meals coming our ways. And you looks like you needs it, Mr. Izzy. You surely does!"

They ate in peace that night, as Izzy told Luke about his brother's life in New York—LB and Smiles, the boys, the business. He did not mention anything about Elana or Biggelow, but he did regale Luke about Paul's early spat with the African American religious community that pushed Paul to flee to the hills.

"He doesn't know when to keep his mouth muffled," Luke smiled, as he took the last bite. "I'm glad you were there to keep an eye on him. My brother just doesn't understand the precarious banality of this world and its inhabitants. I hope he finds his way back here, to where he belongs."

"I don't know," Izzy mused. "It depends on this war. It may be going on for many more years, Luke. What can I tell you? These people here, they started something terrible, and now they are fighting for their lives; I don't see how it will end. I will stay with you until then. The doctor is not going to give up so easy, of that I assure you. He will try his best to get this farm back."

"Well, Izzy, you have the letter!"

"We'll need to do a hell of a lot better than that," Izzy said. "This farm has to stay productive, so we can supply the army and make them happy. If we slack, then the doctor has ammunition to take the farm back from us. For now has to abide by Matt's letter, endorsed by General Lee himself. But that's not enough for the doctor. He'll keep fighting. He won't stop. It's a matter of principle to him."

"He's just a doctor," Luke said. "What can he do? This is our farm. It's Matt's. It's separate from the world, severed from this war and all the meaningless squabbles between—"

Izzy cut him off. "OK, Luke, enough of that. It's not an island; it is vulnerable. That doctor, he's a crafty devil. There is nothing worse than an idiot with a veneer of respect. He is the doctor, so all the people here respect him. I've seen this man treat his patients. He puts leeches on their legs, throws potions down their gullets, digs holes in their skin. And even though his patients die that much more quickly after being bestowed by his fine care, they thank him, because he is a doctor. They listen to what he says, because he is a doctor. Yes, Luke, he's a clever bastard, an idiot hiding behind a title that gives him instant respect and credibility even as he poisons everyone around him. My mother always said, the first rule to fight sickness is to stay away from doctors. The second rule, chicken soup."

"I don't know, Izzy, but if you ask me, I don't think you like the guy."

Izzy laughed and leaned back against the cabin's wall. "Well, he was a good customer. Always bought a bunch of clothes from me at inflated prices. I do give him that."

A whiff of silence blew through the cabin. It was dark, with sparkling stars filling the night sky.

"You OK, Izzy?" Luke asked. "How are you doing?"

Izzy's face lit up a bit, and he smiled. He sat up. "I was in love, Luke," he said. "Can you believe that? I was actually in love. But now I'm here with you. And that I love more than anything in God's creation. Because now, Luke, you are the purpose of my life."

Luke slid by and hugged his friend. "I'm glad you found love," he said. "And I'm glad you're here. I don't worry about the doctor. You are the answer to my prayers. We will always persevere."

"Prayers?" Izzy laughed. "Paul would be ashamed of you. We're going to need more than prayers. But as long as we use our brains, we won't need too much more than that. The doctor is an idiot. A crafty idiot, but an idiot nonetheless. We just have to keep our eyes open and be ready to make a move before he makes his." And with that, he put his head down, snoring loudly as his eyes snapped shut.

Luke laughed. He gently slid his friend onto a bed of hay and then sat by him. He had not been this happy in a very long time!

39

An early autumn mist lifted off the river like a harbinger of something grand. Matt sucked it in and felt revitalized. "Why we got to get up so early and drill?" asked one of the boys near him, one of the younger recruits who came to the Grays after Gettysburg. "Ain't nothing happening. They just sitting there cross the river biding their time, them Yankees is. Ain't no fighting. We got all day doing nothing. The least Colonel Kemper can do is let us sleep in. Is that too much to ask?"

"Yes," Matt snapped back, approaching the boy from behind. "It is too much to ask. We is always preparing. That General Meade across the river, he may look like a turtle and act like a sloth, but there ain't no way of knowing when he may hit us next, and we got to be ready. We're the Grays. We defended the bridge at Sharpsburg. We led Stonewall's rout at Chancellorsville. We charged with Pickett at Gettysburg. We drill early and we drill late. Lots of boys and men has died for the Grays. You dishonor them, and you dishonor Virginia and General Lee, when you talk insolent like that."

The boy's face turned to stone. "I ain't mean no dishonor, sir," he said to Matt.

Matt smiled and placed his hand on the boy's shoulder. "I know you don't," he said. "But remember. We got to stay strong and together. Ain't no time for dawdling. It's now or never. Don't matter if we is fighting or drilling. Every day we got to be together as the Grays."

Matt's status in the unit had escalated, and now he stood with Colonel Kemper for the morning drills. He came to know all the men and boys, and they knew and revered him. His shooting finesse and bravery had dazzled even the most devoted soldiers, and that he lunched weekly in General Lee's tent draped on him a certain air of holiness that lofted him above this mass of mere mortals.

"This morning we remember the boys we lost to illness in the last cholera outbreak," Kemper said, standing on a stump within the flowing fog. "We lost eight this time, God bless them all. We remember them and all the boys we lost in battle; the Grays will always honor their memory! When General Lee calls us, we will be the first and the best to answer his call. Matt? You want to add to what I said?"

Matt stepped on the stump and peered around. He smiled. "We do it for Jude," he said. "We do it for him 'cause it was him who gave us our heart and soul. We is not just a unit. We is a family. We is a force of good against a vicious invader. Lots of people died when cholera swept through us last week, and we mourn them. But then we look ahead. And we take Jude's spirit, and Stonewall's confidence in us, and we drill harder than anyone else. We is in Virginia, where our country was born, and where all of us is from. We ain't about to let those people take that from us! No one is taking nothing from the Grays! Especially not our home!"

"What's the word from General Lee?" came a call from one of the troops.

Matt smiled. "I'll be seeing him and General Longstreet later today. They is always thinking about how to bedevil those people across the river, how to push them in another corner and scare them off. Don't you worry. They got our backs! We just got to be ready, so when they call the Grays, we will be at the front. General Lee is the brains. And we is his brawn. Now, drill!"

Matt sat alone by the river. He watched it flow calmly from west to east, bringing with it water of Shenandoah and his farm. A burst of heat descended upon him from above, a wet and sticky heat, but the river kept him cool. He had thought about going back to the farm, if only for a visit, especially after he received word about Izzy. At the time he wrote the letter that Izzy brought with him—sitting with Slim and Trump and the others across the river in a corrupt and sickened place—he feared for his farm, and prayed for a Union victory. After Chancellorsville, all of those misplaced thoughts had dissipated into the fog itself. He stared at the river for many days before making his decision to turn over the farm to his old friend. He even spoke with General Lee about it. Ultimately, he authorized Izzy's temporary ownership of the farm, because Izzy wasn't like those other people over there. He was, well, Izzy!

The war to Matt was about saving the farm, rekindling the life he and his brothers had enjoyed there before chaos intervened. He knew that a victory by this army, by these people, by this general, would reconstitute beauty and goodness to the land. It was about more than just his farm, Matt knew. It was about something bigger and grander, just like the doctor had preached to him all these years. It was about the very core of America.

"So," General Lee had said, "the question, Matthew, is whether your friend Izzy will help you to fight here while not worrying about what is going on there. Do you trust him to be your surrogate? That's all you have to ask."

The answer, Matt finally realized, was yes. Izzy was the most loyal of men; he devoted his life to Matt's father's legacy. He would protect the farm as though he were Matt himself. And he would watch over Matt's brother better than any other person could!

Matt wished he could go home for a bit, sit with Izzy and Luke, regale the doctor and Jessie with stories and feats of this heroic battle. But he was needed here, especially after Gettysburg, especially after Pickett's charge. That charge haunted him day and night.

The Grays comported themselves well in the first two days of Gettysburg. Assigned to Longstreet's division, they sliced through Union formations on Cemetery Ridge and the peach orchard. Matt and Jude, they were a tandem, inseparable, spearheading every thrust forward through the Union rubbish. Jude knew where to go; he was resistant to enemy fire. Matt could load and fire faster than any man, knocking off Blue troops with accuracy and ease. During the fighting, Matt morphed into a spectral being, floating above the melee, seeming out of his body, bereft of fear, fed by the carnage.

"General Lee, he wants to end it tomorrow morn," Jude told Matt on July 3, after the second day of battle, sitting around a fire and staring solemnly across the Northern landscape. "Colonel Kemper told me that the general plans to send up a few thousand troops up Cemetery Ridge, where we almost knocked them bastards off before, and finish the job. Right up the hill to end this battle and war. And if we take them there, we will win the day."

Matt had seen the hill and the fortifications on top; he knew that a charge like that would incur massive resistance. Like Jude, though, he believed that he and his army were invincible. "What Longstreet say about it?" Matt asked Jude. "I know General Longstreet; he never wanted to come up and invade the North in the first place. He's much timider than Stonewall. I talked to him back before we left. He said we should stay put and let the Union army come after us, but that General Lee, he says we can't do that, don't have enough time with the Union blockade and all, and that the only way to get those people to stop the war, and to maybe even get England to back our side, is to give them one hell of a beating up here. So, here we is. But if we run up that hill and get mowed down, where do that leave us?"

"I don't ask them kind of questions, Matt, and you shouldn't neither. Longstreet, he's a good man, he surely is, but he don't got the balls to fight this kind of war. General Lee got instincts for this war. He ain't never been wrong yet. If he says charge, then that's what we is going to do."

And they did. Up the hill they charged, Jude and Matt leading the Grays, with several other units from Georgia and Texas, behind General George Pickett and a massive artillery barrage. Matt fired, but he had no targets. They all were behind a wall, tossing artillery and bullets at the charging soldiers. Gray soldiers dropped like acorns from a tree. And then, hearing a deafening whistle soar by him, Matt looked to his left and saw Jude had disappeared. A wave of panic overcame him, and all his bravado in this one-sided slaughter evaporated. He dropped to the floor to find Jude. At that very moment, a cannonball crossed the very spot where Matt had been standing, flying innocuously over his now supine head. More men dropped—blood and mangled bodies everywhere. Crawling beneath the bullets, Matt found Jude, lying lifeless on the ground, headless, blood squirting out of his raw neck. Matt fell back, stunned.

"Retreat, retreat!"

The cry came from below. Matt stood and ran as everyone around him dropped dead upon the bloody grass. He made it to the bottom with scattered few others. The Grays, and the entire Confederate army, had been decimated in a matter of minutes. Matt only lived because Jude had died. Had he not fallen down to look for his friend, he would have suffered the same fate.

That was many months ago. Now the Grays stood back across the river, facing General Meade's army on the northern side, both taunting each other with artillery and occasional gunfire, but neither seeming ready to fight again, at least not yet.

That afternoon, Matt lunched with General Lee and General Longstreet. The two generals spoke sparingly to each other since Gettysburg. They bickered constantly when in Matt's presence.

"If we stay here long enough," a tall, soft-spoken Longstreet said, his long brown beard hovering off his face like a gentle dog's, "it puts the burden of offense on them. A defensive position is our best hope."

"That seems to be your recurring mantra, James," General Lee snapped back. Although as meticulous as always, he had lost his soothing calm when he spoke. Especially around Longstreet, he was quick to yell and often marched out of the room, claiming to feel sick. "I know you blame me for Gettysburg, but frankly had you not been so slow, my strategy would have been successful."

"We've been through this a thousand times, Robert," Longstreet quietly retorted. "We can't relive that battle. It's over. We have to look forward."

Matt could almost see what General Lee wanted to say. *Had Stonewall been there, we would have carried the day.* But he never uttered those words.

"Regardless," Lee said. "Time is not on our side. The Union blockade of the east coast is complete; we can get nothing in or out. Now that Grant has taken the Mississippi and is massacring our troops out West, the entire Confederacy is choked. And what have we for a government? A bunch of squabbling states who refuse to lend anything to the cause, run by a president and administration that have no power to conduct this war or to force the states to act honorably. Why Virginia joined this band of turncoats is beyond me. If we lose this war, my name will be uttered with the likes of Benedict Arnold and other traitors. It's ironic that the ideal that links these states together—their utter disdain for order and central control—is what is going to doom us in the end. And it will be I who will be seen as the leader of these traitors. I will pay the ultimate price, losing my honor, my fortune, and likely my life."

"A lot of people say," Matt uttered, feeling very comfortable with these two men, "that you should take over the government and run it during the war. That's what I hear them say."

Lee nodded and laughed. "Yes, I have heard that too, Matthew. But haven't I done enough damage to this nation already? Were I to now destroy its democratic core and become a dictator, what they would history say about me? Besides, I do have some fight left in me, and I don't intend to allow these people to advance one step farther into the great state of Virginia."

Longstreet ate a piece of chicken quietly. Then he spoke. "With the new Union draft, their numbers are growing, Robert. They have a never-ending supply of troops. But if we build up our defenses here, I think we can hold them off indefinitely. My only fear is if the rumors are true, then that General Grant will be coming East to take over the Union army."

Lee banged his fork on the table. "Enough about Grant! He is a drunk and a mediocre mind who has no accomplishment behind him other than a few lucky victories at the cost of many of his men. Let him come. I will be happy to meet him on the field of battle."

"There is also the rumor that the Union will be using Negro troops," Longstreet said. "That is yet another supply of men we can't match. Our government will never consent to using Negroes."

"Negro troops," Lee snarled. "Let them put in Negroes. They are indolent people who lack direction and intelligence. When I took over my father-in-law's farm, I had to exert severe discipline on the Negro chattel there. These people cannot fight. They can barely piss without being told how. They are lazy and stupid." He then stood and threw his napkin. "Let them put in Negro troops. If we capture any of them, we will send them back to their masters and back to the discipline of the whip. That may put some fear in their willingness to fight us. If those people win, God forgive the world that will come upon us. God forgive our precious nation! My stomach aches. I will take leave of you, Matthew. Speak to James a bit. Then return to your unit. We have to be ready for those people. This war is far from over."

He stormed out, leaving the other two to quietly finish their meal. Poor General Lee, Matt realized. He carried the full weight of this nation on his back! Stonewall's death and Gettysburg deflated him. But Matt continued to believe in the man.

"I hear you know General Grant?" Matt asked Longstreet.

Finishing his chicken, James Longstreet nodded. "I more than know him, Matthew. We were in the academy together, and I was an usher at his wedding. We are very close, Ulysses, and me. And I will tell you this. Despite what you hear, he is not a drinker; he became inebriated at a low time in his life and for this, he has gained a very unjust reputation. Ulysses Grant is a quiet man, a learned man who reads constantly, a modest man who has justly earned the respect of all those who work with him, and a warrior who will not give up. And Ulysses has abolitionist blood in his veins. He will fight for the Negro and hit Robert with a passion and drive not yet seen in other Union generals. I fear for this war if Ulysses comes East. He will be Robert's first worthy opponent, and Robert knows it. Matthew, I have enjoyed speaking with you, but this will be our last time together. I have asked for a transfer West to be with General Bragg's army. I do not like what I am seeing here. Robert is a good man who I see becoming unhinged and loathsome. It is time for a change."

The Rappahannock flowed slowly at the end of August. Matt sat on its banks and stared upstream, at its source. The massacre at Gettysburg had scarred him; the image of a decapitated Jude lying beneath a dying heap of Grays flooded his mind night after night. They ran away from Gettysburg having been fully whipped; they retreated to this place with just a river, this river, between them and a hovering fear of a lost cause. Matt stared upstream and grasped his inner strength.

Izzy was back, and Matt was happy. Upstream lay his farm, his oasis, the source of all his joy. Upstream lay his brother Luke, the dreamer and the optimist, the one person who understood that nothing else mattered other than the farm itself. Their father had made the farm possible—their father who had fled from the vile North—and now the North sought to destroy it. Matt would not allow that to happen.

Luke's face and smile fluttered in Matt's mind, and despite all the despair around him now, that picture gave Matt a glimmer of hope. This is why Matt was fighting this war. He was fighting for Luke. For the farm. For his brothers. For the life he once had and which he wanted again. Matt lifted some pebbles and tossed them into the river, watching them skip across the surface and slide slowly downstream. While Izzy took care of Luke and the farm, Matt was going to win this war. He adhered to a purpose that transcended the bickering and the despondency of this moment and place. The war would continue, and Matt would make sure that the South would persevere. That he would persevere.

40

Paul remembered the first day he met LB in Frederick, Maryland, after his harrowing escape across the mountains. LB sat cuddled with Smiles in the home where they hid; a visage of trepidation and suspicion concealed everything else within her. Her eyes wandered across the room, to their hosts, to the quick-talking Paul, and, as she told him much later, she wondered if perhaps it was all a trap, that they had been led here to meet an even worse fate than from where they had escaped.

LB, friendly and loquacious from the start, asked Paul about his life, his farm, his situation. And then LB laughed, good and loud. "You ain'ts hardly a slave," he said to Paul.

Paul was aghast by the accusation. "I couldn't leave my farm," Paul pleaded. "I was trapped there. I couldn't use my education and skills to advance myself. I was at the mercy of renegades who could abuse me at their whim, whip me, kill me even. Being a slave doesn't mean I have to suffer what you did. It means I can't be a man, and I'm at the mercy of other men. That's what it is to be a slave."

As he sat today in his small apartment with Smiles, Elana, and their four children, he wondered if anything had really changed since his escape from forced servitude. The definition of slavery he uttered to LB on that day long ago applied to his recent life in New York where, by want of the riots and the subsequent depletion of any opportunity for African Americans to work, his very manhood had again been stripped from him. Many of New York's African Americans fled Manhattan, most migrating to other boroughs or out of the city itself. Even Reverend Garnet moved his family to Washington, purportedly to pastor at a new church there and to be closer to the ears of the president, but likely more from fear of more assaults and reprisals in this city largely run now by Tammany.

Elana's older daughter, with long red hair and a pleasant face, sang to little Matt, coddling the young boy in her arms. She was typically very quiet; Paul had yet to learn much about her, for she was a closed book who enjoyed the young children but otherwise sat by herself wherever they were. Elana's son was a bit more vivacious, but he clung to his mother, whispering questions to her, and often chatting with Smiles; he and Smiles could always make each other laugh. Compared to Paul's two spitfires of energy, Elana's well-dressed and well-groomed children were always sedate and cooperative.

"Your husband, he's treating you much better these days," Smiles said to Elana. "He comes by and kisses your head and rubs your back. He spends a little more time with the children. He takes you on walks and takes you to dinner. It must be nice to have that. I seen a change in him."

A soft autumn breeze blew through the window on a cool October morning. Leaves were starting to change color, and the summer stench of filth and sewerage largely faded away. It was not often they all could meet like this; Elana had strict rules to stay away from the "Negro parts of town." But Ernie was in Albany with Boss Tweed and several other influential Tammany men, loosening Elana's leash.

She nodded when Smiles shared her observation. "Do you see this dress I am wearing?" Elana asked Smiles. It was a somewhat tattered red dress that flowed down her body, adding to her natural grace and goodness. "I remember when I first bought it. I was taking one of my walks through the city, and I ran into a young energetic clothes salesman who introduced himself as Izzy, and he showed me some of his wares. He pulled out this dress and said, 'With your red hair, ruddy complexion, and tall frame, I think this dress is designed for you. I am so sure of it, I will give it to you for half price. I can't imagine it on another woman.' I laughed, accusing him of making a sales pitch, but he told me no, that he could see that I was more than worthy of having his most favorite dress.

"I kept thinking about him, about Izzy. I would sneak by his cart and peer at it from afar. And then one day I put on that dress and went to visit him. We chatted for half the day! I don't know what I was thinking, but I asked him if he would walk with me the next day through the upper parts of Manhattan, to explore the new park and some of the highlands. I mean, I was a married woman. Why would I do such a thing? But it felt so right. When he said yes, I was inflated with a joy I had not known in so many years. He asked me to wear the dress again, and I did. It was the best day of my life; we talked and laughed and stared sheepishly into each other's eyes. I'm wearing that dress today, with you, my best friends on this earth, because I want to think that Izzy is with us. I miss him every second of every day. And when I wear this dress, I think of him, and hope that he is thinking of me. I love him beyond belief."

"But Izzy is gone, Elana, and your husband is being so good and kind to you," Smiles said. "What are you going to do?"

Elana peeked over to her children, who were across the room with Paul's boys. They enjoyed coming here with their "blessed Smiles" and their "Negro brothers," and with Paul and LB who made them laugh, in this apartment where they felt comfortable and safe. They never told their father about these junkets; in fact, they told him very little. To Elana, these were her children; they were only his by birth.

"I don't care how he treats me, Smiles. Every day I wait for the moment when perhaps I can leave him," she whispered. "I am deeply in love with another man. All Ernie's gestures toward me are for himself alone. He wants someone to take care of him, and he needs a happy family if he plans to move up in New York politics. You think he is treating me well, Smiles, but don't be fooled by what you see. He's treating Ernest T. Biggelow well. There is no love tacked to his kisses and rubs and walks. There is no passion. All of my heart is tied to a little old Jew who is down in Virginia right now; he is the man who rekindled my passion and soul, and who excites every fiber of my being. One day I'll be with him. I have to believe that to survive! Until then, I will bide my time, and wear this dress, and hope."

"I've seen him change in another way," Paul chimed in about Elana's husband. "He seems willing to talk about helping the city's Negroes. About even creating a Negro regiment. He seems to be the beneficent face of Tammany, if there is one. Maybe he is rekindling that goodness you first saw in him."

Elana laughed and rubbed Paul on the head. "You have a big heart, Paul," she said to him. "But sometimes you are very naive. My husband is playing a game. Don't trust him. People don't change, Paul. Likely he never was the kind man I thought him to be. I simply imagined he was, because he treated me well, he was a handsome man, and he was moving up in the world. I wanted him to be that man. But he wasn't. He was always focused on himself, always pretending. Izzy is an open deck of cards. He is all goodness, all selflessness. He is funny and playful, and he loves me deeply. When I contrast the two men, it's hard for me to even look at my husband, let alone actually love him."

Slavery in New York, Paul realized, did not mimic its Southern counterpart. Slaves here were not in chattels, but they were beholden to others; they had little personal choice to do what they wanted, and at any time they could be assailed by those who held power. Elana was no less a slave than Paul; she could never leave this place and the man to whom she was betrothed. She wore her red dress as an act of defiance, a leap into an alternative world from which her captivity held her. It was, in effect, her red raft. Paul, too, seemed to be mired in a staid and repressive existence. He sometimes wandered up to his mountain and contemplated how he might escape and find the glory that he so briefly felt these past two years. He no longer spoke to Smiles about it, or even to LB; they both were tired of his grumbling. After all, he still had a job and a comfortable place to live, Smiles continued to be gainfully employed and appreciated, and they were at least free of the bondage that had strangled them down South.

"There ain't likely gonna be's no more riots," LB said to him. "Not with all the Negroes moved out of this place, and the draft over, and the Irish back to running the city and having jobs and nots having to fight for this war that they's don't even want. I even seen when I walks by Five Points, sometimes they even says hi to me and gives me a nice look or gesture. I'll take what we has here, Paul. It ain'ts half bad."

But Paul knew otherwise. Like in his early days on this island, a piercing angst gripped him; he felt hollow and inconsequential. He peered down from upon his hill at a vital city thriving without him being able to participate. But what was worse to him was a suffocating reality: white men fighting and dying for his brother's freedom, with him marginalized from this noble war. With Henry Garnet and most other abolitionist leaders now gone from the city, Paul had few allies in the cause. He, instead, swallowed a lethal dose of monotony and struggled simply to sustain his meaningless existence. Even his children gave him only temporal joy; he barely had time to see them, and he worried about their fate in life, even as freemen in a liberated Union. In the end, what chance did even they have to surmount the racial walls of disdain that had been erected everywhere Paul could see?

Paul and LB spent eight hours a day pushing carts in Brooklyn and the few remaining enclaves of an African American presence in Manhattan. They sold buttermilk, matches, and straw; occasionally they found an interesting item by the docks when the Irish let them in. Besides, most of the city's blacks themselves lacked any money to buy any more than the rudimentary necessities to sustain their lives.

Soon after the riots, Abe invited Paul, LB, Smiles, and the children to his home in Brooklyn for dinner. He lived in a modest two-story brick building in a neighborhood of fellow Jews; his large three-room apartment seemed lush compared to anything Paul had seen in Manhattan. The kids ran from room to room, peeking through large windows to a view of the East River.

Somewhere between a plate of herring smothered with onions and vinegar and a main course of corned beef with borscht, a congenial Abe paused for a moment and peered hypnotically into Paul's eyes.

"I'm not going to reopen," he said, his face solemn yet content. "Not after all that happened. The insurance barely covered anything. The city is being less than generous. I have enough money to live my life comfortably, and I'm an old man. What more can I accomplish? I think I'll devote the rest of my years to my people and my temple and my God and hope that I die a happy man."

Paul's gut dropped; essentially, after all his financial wizardry and business prowess, after a promise of promotion just a few weeks ago, he was now out of a job. All hope instantly evaporated.

But LB, who also was left barren by Abe's declaration, did not allow his own consternation to blind him from Abe's own struggle. "I think's what you's people would says is mazel tov," he told the man, and then he laughed big and loud. He stood and hugged Abe. "You deserves it, old man. You's done more than your share. What you's done for us, I can never thanks you enough."

A tear flowed down Abe's eye. He nodded and thanked LB.

"Both of you boys, but mostly you, Paul, the smartest damned man I ever met, no offense, James—"

"Ain'ts none taken," LB said with a deep laugh. "Aint's none at all! I's knows that!"

"Well," Abe continued, "my success came from your brains and effort and heart. I know that; I'm not blind. I sat there, and you did the work, and boys, we sure as hell created an amazing network of sales and products all over this damned city! When the war closed our Southern markets, I figured we were dead in the water, but because of you, Paul, we were more productive and profitable in the last two years, right as a damned war was going on, than I was in my last ten years before. I am retired now because of you."

Paul laughed, and Smiles hit him on the back. "What'd I tell you, Paul?" she said. "You done such a good job that now Abe don't need to work, and you's is out work!"

Paul kissed his wife on the cheek. "Believe me, I understand the irony!"

"Paul, James, I have something for you boys. I made a fortune on your backs, and I want to share at least some of that with you. I wish it were more. But take this." He lifted an envelope.

"What is it?" "Paul asked. "You don't owe us anything, Abe. You gave me freedom! You gave me life."

"True," Abe laughed. "But those don't put bread on your table. And freedom is better with bread!"

Smiles stood and kissed Abe on his cheek. "You is a good man, Abe. We won't never forget you. I know you people don't believe in heaven, that's what Izzy tells us every day, but if there was one, you deserve the best room in the house!"

"Hell, this is not goodbye," Abe said. "My door is always open, and we will eat together often, I hope. This is enough money for you to pay your rent for a year, buy a few more carts, and to get the business going again. It's a start, boys. It's not a lottery win. But, believe me, boys, it's well deserved. And I have faith that you will turn this into a great success. No, Smiles, we don't believe in heaven, but all of you have made this crappy world feel a little bit like heaven whenever I am in your presence. Now, eat!"

Paul and LB pushed their carts through the depleted African American neighborhoods. Summer turned into fall, and they spent more time gabbing than selling anything. Luckily, they were making enough to survive, especially with Abe's gift still in their back pockets.

"If we's moved to Brooklyn," LB said, "we's have a much better chance to expand and sell more. Most of the Negroes is there now, all the ways back near the bay. It's too far for us to gets there every day, but if we moved there, Paul, thinks about it, maybe we could be what we once was."

Paul just nodded. They had been down this road before.

"You know we can't move to Brooklyn," Paul told his friend, not for the first time. "That would put me too far from Smiles and the kids. And she can't leave that job. Just push the cart, James. Let's not jump to crazy conclusions and totally disrupt our lives. Izzy will be back eventually. Two Negroes aren't going to do much on our own. Push the cart. We'll wait for him."

Slavery prevents me from attaining my manhood, from being the person I have always wanted to be. How was this any different? Paul mused upon that question every day. *Society, it holds the whip. It keeps us in chains. How can we ever escape? Is there a way out?*

And so, as Paul sat with Smiles and Elana and their children in Paul's small apartment, watching colorful October leaves flutter past his smudged window, they chatted about other things.

Suddenly, LB burst into the door. He was sweating and hyperventilating. All faces turned toward him, but he stared directly at Paul. Squatting down, he smiled and then let a big, burly laugh flow from his gut. He held an envelope and pushed it toward Paul.

"What?" Paul asked him.

"Reads it," LB said, breathing heavily between every word. "They called me down to Shiloh Baptist, and they says, I's got a letter for you and Paul, it's from Reverent Garnet. He wants you's to read it. And so, I done read it, and read it twice, and then again, just because I ain't that good a reader and I wanted to make sure it said what I thinks it did."

"What does it say, James?" Elana asked him. "Please tell me it's good news for a change."

Paul grasped it, and, encased by a cacophony of silence in a room bursting with curious stares, he read it. Then he looked up at his friend, who nodded back at him, and the two of them rushed over and embraced in a hug, slapping each other's backs.

"What?" Smiles insisted on knowing. "You driving us all crazy!"

"It's from Reverend Garnet," Paul said. And then he read the letter:

Paul and James, I hope this finds you well. As you know, since relocating to our nation's capital after the unfortunate events that pushed me out of our city, I have used my contacts, and the grace of God, to gain the ear of our most reverent president, Father Abraham. I and others have implored him that, given all that we lost in the city, the Negroes of New York only want one thing: to fight for our own freedom and for our country. Fred Douglass and many sympathetic Congressmen helped me in pleading my case. Today, finally, after so much struggle, after testing our Lord's patience and our own, I received word from Secretary Seward that President Lincoln has authorized us to recruit and organize two Negro units in the city, the New York Twentieth and the New York Twenty-Sixth. The official word of this hallowed and momentous event will come in several weeks, as will the announcement of the unit's commanders. But be assured, boys, that these units will be organized, will train on Riker's Island, and will fight in this war. The day we have all been waiting for has finally arrived! I will be coming to town at the end of October, and until then I have received permission for you two to start recruiting Negroes for these units. The pay will be less than that of white soldiers, but it will be substantial enough, and we will be fed, housed, and fully equipped. Most of all, we will finally have a chance to show that we are capable of fighting for our own freedom. Paul and James, God bless you both, and we will all rejoice over such wonderful news! Yours always, the Reverend Henry Garnet.

Paul peeked up at Smiles. Tears flowed down his eyes. "I'm sorry, Smiles," he said. "But I have to do this. I am so sorry."

"Sorry?" Smiles said to him, walking over to her man and hugging him gently, rubbing his back. "Sorry, you crazy man? I loves you beyond belief, you stupid man! And I knows that you needs this more than you needs life itself. You gets to be a soldier! You gets to fight for your brother's freedom! No more being pushed down by people who don't has half your heart and brain. No, Paul, I love you, and I rejoice with you! You and James, you gonna turn the whole world around."

By now, Paul was crying. He nodded his head and kissed Smiles all over her face. "I love you, my wonderful woman. I love you so much. I need to do this. I need to do it for me. And I need to do it for Luke. I want to free my brother. He's down there, still in chains. I want to be the one who frees him."

"It wouldn't be right any other way," Elana said, as she slid over to LB and hugged him. "That's what I told you. That's why I wear this dress. It's to show us what is possible, that we are not prisoners to our fate, that doors will open. Everything will be right again. See? What did I tell you?"

"You is right," LB said to her. "You is always right. And we is going to do this for Luke and for Izzy and for all the people me and Smiles left behind. We is going to make the world right again, just like Smiles says."

"Yes," Elana said, beaming. "We will. It couldn't be any other way. What can I tell you that you don't know already?" She laughed and hugged LB.

Red and golden leaves fluttered past the window as a cool breeze trickled through the cracks. Children ran around the room mindlessly, as warmth of spirit and love burst through the hovering darkness. With just a few written words everything instantly changed, and Paul's drive and spirit again soared through the rafters. He caressed his wife's soft back, where so many horrid men had struck her with whips, and he shed salty tears upon her head. He thought about his brother, and he smiled. "I'm coming Luke," he whispered. "I'm doing this for you."

41

A year and a half later

Paul clutched his gun tightly, sweat dropping off his face and arms. He trembled. The piercing rebel yell bounced off every tree and off the clouds and dirt, swimming through the river itself. He stared forward, flanked by other men, white and black, their feet in a crystal-clear Saylor's Creek somewhere in the backwaters of Virginia, their arms outstretched with the butts of hundreds of guns looking forward at a mass of gray-clad men charging at them, now only a blur, but becoming clear quickly.

"Don't let them through," Colonel Henry C. Ward had lectured his troops a few hours prior, as his horse neighed on a cool April morning. "They are trying to break through and join General Johnston in North Carolina, but General Grant wants to stop them here. Now is the time, men. Now is the time for America to see what a group of well-trained Negroes from New York can accomplish. This is our war. Let's win it here and now, and then we can go home." Colonel Ward, the convivial commander of the New York Colored Thirty-First, looked like a boy, a scrawny mustache on a babyface, his gaunt frame and slight height seeming even more diminutive upon the large brown stallion he chose to ride and which he rarely could control. And yet, his men loved him, as did Paul.

Paul quivered. After so much time doing nothing and waiting for his moment, now he could only wish it would all evaporate, that he could be with Smiles in New York, with Luke on his farm. That mind-shattering yell suffocated his focus, his courage. The mass soared at him, and he trembled.

I know I'm going to die, he said to himself, his feet planted in a cold stream, his fate soon to be sealed.

"You's aint's much of a shot for all your bragging and all," LB had laughed with Paul in the winter outside of Richmond. "If we's ever does find action, if I's was you, Paul, I'd stay in the back of the line."

But now, here he was, out front. They were coming closer. Their yell, bone-shattering and ear-piercing, unnerved him. And then he heard shots!

The moment moved slowly, as though he were in a dream. Gray-clad men charging him; bullets flying everywhere; men dropping, crying, screaming. He held out his gun, looking up, back, down. He did not know what to do. He fired the weapon, its recoil pushing him back a bit.

A man to his side dropped, then another. Cannons blasted everywhere; it suddenly became very hot. Paul reached into his pocket, his hand shaking wildly, desperately trying to find a bullet to load, but unable to grasp it.

Then, through the din of chaos, he peered at the creek. It was bright-red now, carrying the blood of his comrades down to the ocean, washing away these proud African American men who had waited so long to join the fight.

More bullets slid past him, other men dropped. The Gray soldiers, their guns outstretched, moved closer, firing as they ran, the power of their yell silenced only by the crushing din that filled the sky.

"Damn you," he chided himself, and then he grabbed a bullet and managed to load it in his gun.

Paul raised the weapon and pointed it at the skull of a charging Confederate, knowing well that he had never hit a target in his life, but fearing what may happen if he missed. They were so close now!

He fired, and they kept charging. So, he loaded again.

He looked from one face to another, and then, in his dizzy state, in this nightmare from hell, he halted.

His eyes locked with one of the Confederate boys, who himself lowered his gun and peered deeply at Paul. The boy was bearded, his eyes fierce and hazel, his hair wildly disheveled. But Paul saw through all of that clutter, and it was if time suddenly stopped.

"Matt?" he asked.

How?

And yet, it had to be.

He wanted to walk over and hug the boy, but circumstances obstructed his way. The boy raised his gun, and then Paul felt a sting in his shoulder. He looked down, thick blood running through his uniform and dripping into the red creek below.

And then something slammed into his chest, and he gasped, collapsing into the bloody water, trying to grab one last glance of the boy who had shot him, the boy with the beard and hazel eyes.

"Matt?"

He splashed into the creek, gasping for air. A few bubbles gurgled out of his uniform, and he felt all of his strength and wind dissipating. Other men fell on him and near him, seeming to drown him, splashing him with tainted water. Feet rushed by, as the army in blue charged at the Confederates, oblivious to Paul's fate. He could not breathe, could not talk. Everything was turning black.

"Matt?"

He tried to get up, but fell immediately back down, landing on a stick that pierced his chest and caused him to wince in pain. More blood gushed from his wounds, and he dropped in the river, face first. He could see just a bit in front of him; the rebels scattered, chased by the colored troops. Had they won? Consciousness faded and his vision blurred. He saw the water, blood, bubbles rising from his chest.

Time was running out for Paul. This had been his moment. He had waited so long for it to happen. And now without accomplishing anything, his short and uneventful life slipped away in a bloody Virginia creek.

It was more than a year ago that the New York Twentieth Colored Troops marched down Broadway on a cool spring day. They started in Union Square, greeted by cheers of thousands of New Yorkers of all colors. Paul and LB, wearing their Union blue after so many months of training on Riker's Island, strode hand in hand, proudly holding muskets that Paul had barely learned to fire. They were moving toward the Twenty-Sixth street pier where many would board a steamship destined for the battles of New Orleans. Paul and LB were not slated to join this enthusiastic group of warriors; their destiny lay elsewhere. But at least today, Colonel Nelson Bertram, the unit's leader, and a man beholden to these two friends for their help in recruiting and training the unit, would have nothing less than including them in this moment of triumph and redemption. Only six months after the draft riots tore the city apart and extirpated its African American population, hundreds of African Americans marched through the city carrying weapons, and the same Irish mobs who had burned and lynched them stood along the sidewalks, cheering with a vigor that surprised even Paul.

Nothing demonstrated the moment's odd irony better than the two men who spoke to begin the parade. Together under a frigid sun stood Police Superintendent John Kennedy, who had been beaten by the draft riot mob and left for dead, flanked by Ernest T. Biggelow and his wife, the very man who led the riots but who now commandeered the role of "the Negro's best friend in New York." Both delivered brief speeches extolling the significance of New York's first black regiment about to join a war that had finally swung to the Union's side.

Paul waved to Elana, whose own exuberance, or so she later said, had nothing to do with standing by her husband, and everything to do with Paul's moment of triumph.

"You've grown so much," she told him before the parade, kissing him on the cheek. "You are a man! Everyone respects you! And you are so humble, leading by example. Izzy would be so proud!"

"If you's seen that boy shoots a gun," LB interjected, "you's of seen right off why he's so damned humble." LB laughed big and hard. He had never been happier. "I told Paul right off the start, I says to him, 'Boy, you keep your mouth shut with these troops. You just shut up and does what's they says, and you don't said nothing to no one that will gets us in trouble with all your big words and fancy ideas. You just stays quiet and smiles is all I wants you to done.' And this boy here, he done just that, even made the colonel proud is what he did done. But when it comes to shootings a gun, no ma'am, he's rightful to be humble abouts that! This boys done never learned that; that much I can tell you!"

"Well, all I know is that I am so proud of you, and so is Smiles. Both of you. To do this thing, to help create this moment, is an accomplishment that will live on for the ages."

They filed passed Elana, who stood beside her husband and quietly winked at them. They marched through their old neighborhood, with throngs of people of every color and nationality cheering them on. During the entire parade, neither man said a word. They traversed streets where men had died for just being black, where others were driven off and prevented from working, where sewerage and filth tainted so much promise. They marched through those places now with guns in their hands, uniforms on their backs, and power in their souls.

Smiles could not be here today, or so Paul thought. With Elana forced to accompany her husband on the podium, no one else could watch the children. But then, moving toward the Hudson through a misty breeze, he heard her voice. His head swung to the right, and there she was, shining against the background of black faces, her teeth big and white, shouting at her two "husbands."

Paul, consumed by an instant burst of joy, broke formation and darted over to give her a kiss. He did not want to let go. "How?" he asked her.

"Elana's sister, she came over to help watch the kids, to let me see my husband all handsome and strong, about to change the world, just like I knowed he always would." She hugged him tightly, kissing him all over his face. "Now go back there," she cried, "before you go and get in trouble again. Go back. I will see you tonight. And I will give you the best reward a man can get!"

"Yes," he said. "Yes! That is all I want. I love you, Smiles. I love you so much."

"Go!"

The Twentieth Regiment boarded their transport boats, and Paul watched them disappear into the sea. There was still more training to do, so he was told. More troops to prepare for war.

Just a few weeks later, it was the Twenty-Sixth Colored Regiment's turn to march through New York's streets on their way to another theater of war. Paul and LB joined them in their parade, but a violent storm burst through New York that day, and the troops were hustled instead of waiting for ships that would bring them to South Carolina. John Jay, the grandson of one of the nation's founding fathers, presented the regiment with a national flag and words of encouragement and hope. The ship departed on Easter Sunday, stranding Paul and LB back in the city yet again.

They still had one more regiment to prepare, the Thirty-First Colored Regiment, under the diminutive but affable Colonel

Henry C. Ward, who relied on Paul and LB to recruit troops from outside the city and help him train them on Hart's Island.

"I know you two waited a good long time to fight in this war," the colonel said to them one day after a sweltering day of drilling in early May. "And I think your patience will be rewarded. I just received orders. We will be joining General Grant's army outside of Richmond. We are slated to leave next week. Congratulations. Please let the men know." He hugged them each and saluted.

"No parade?" LB laughed.

Henry Ward smiled. "Not this time, James. General Grant is pushing Lee hard toward Richmond. Sherman is heading to the coast. We are needed right away. This war may soon be over. You men are going to be there too for the grand finale. You will be remembered as the ones who freed the Negro from bondage." He saluted again, turned, and scampered away.

Paul smiled. He would fight in Virginia. How fitting! Images of the thunderstruck day of his escape flooded his mind. He stared ahead, and he recalled it all. Up Old Rag, through the mountains, past pockets of danger everywhere, until he finally landed into a den of safety, where he fell into the grasp of white folk who were not inflicted with the vile sickness of hatred, and where he met Smiles and LB. He wondered if he would ever return to his home state that had both coddled him and enslaved him. Now, that moment had come. To Virginia, where perhaps he would expunge the epidemic of slavery once and for all, free-ing his brother and so many others. His whole being exploded with ebullience!

"I don't want no speeches," Smiles said that night, as the group of four friends and their children hovered in Paul and LB's apartment one last time. "I don't want no crying. This is a proud moment for us. You are going to free the slaves, all the ones we left behind. You are going to end this nightmare once and for all. I know the danger. But I have faith in you. I know that no harm is going to come your way. Paul, you don't believe in any God, but I do, and I know that He protect the righteous, and you two are the most righteous two men I have ever had the pleasure of knowing. I love you both. Now, make us all proud and then come back to tell us the stories of how you saved the world. That's all I want."

"Then that, Smiles, is what you's is going to gets," LB laughed, kissing her on the head.

"When you do get there, and if you see Izzy, please tell him that I love him," Elana said to Paul. "And please, bring him back to me. That's all I want."

"I will," Paul said to her. "I know he'll be back for you."

She nodded and then broke down in tears. "One day," she whispered. "It has to happen, one day."

That night Paul and Smiles lay alone for the first time in months. As their bodies entangled, their passion knew no bounds. Neither slept. Neither spoke. They lived a moment of pure bliss.

He stared at her face the next day as his boat floated out to sea. He was leaving one reality to join another. He missed her instantly, and her face and love swam through his heart. But now he had no choice but to look ahead.

The Thirty-First landed in Yorktown to join Grant's army. After Grant's debacle at Cold Harbor, Lee fled south, and Grant pursued. They dashed past Richmond, until Grant's huge army cut off General Lee's in the town of Petersburg. As he had done in Vicksburg, General Grant settled down for a long and arduous siege. That's when the NY Negro Thirty-First embedded itself in the army of liberation.

It was hot. Men perished from disease every day, some men whom Paul knew well. They drilled and marched, but little transpired. Slowly, week by week, the wall around Lee's patch of gray turf shrunk, although none of the colored troops participated in any action. They remained behind, waiting. Colonel Ward tried to keep their spirits up. Finally, he came back with a piece of good news.

"You won't believe this," he told Paul, LB, and several of his lieutenants. "But the Negro troops, us included, are being asked to be part of a scheme to break through the Confederate lines in the craziest way possible." He laughed, and slapped LB on the shoulder. "Wait until you hear this one."

An engineer named Henry Pleasants believed that a tunnel could be dug under the Confederate lines, and enough explosive could be ignited to split the line in half and cause a sufficient breach that would enable a Union penetration.

"It would likely totally surprise Lee," Colonel Ward said to Paul. "General Burnside has signed on, even if Meade is reluctant. And Burnside wants to use colored troops."

Paul beamed. "Well, good for Burnside! He's not such an ass after all!"

As engineers dug beneath the muddy ground surrounding Petersburg, Colonel Ward and the assault commander, General Edward Ferrero, drilled the troops. Paul and LB woke up at dawn and collapsed each night. The timing and execution had to be perfectly coordinated for the attack to work; half the troops would move around each side of the crater that the explosion was going to create, thereby hitting Confederate flanks on both sides. Paul's blood churned with excitement.

"Maybe this is it, James," he said to his friend as they ate hard-tack by a log one day. "Maybe this will be the attack that wins the war. And we will be the ones who did it. Imagine!"

"Maybe," LB said, breathing hard, his age starting to show. "All I's knows is I am glads we is doing something finally. This has been one boring war, if you asks me!"

General Burnside, whose reputation had been tarnished after Fredericksburg and who hoped that the crater battle would rejuvenate him, pushed the troops hard. One day word got out that Paul was a damned good cook. Paul liked to meander into the kitchen to help with cooking when time allowed. He could stare at a pile of ingredients and whip up something amazing. Rumor had it that the Thirty-First ate better than any regiment in the army, with fancy chicken dishes "and sauces that made the mouth dance," as Colonel Ward told General Ferraro, who relayed it to Burnside. And so, General Burnside came to visit one evening, indulging in a feast of orange chicken, fire-roasted vegetables, and a delectable honey-wheat bread that Paul prepared. The rotund general, his large whiskers obscuring the side of his face, sat back with a grin as he took one bite after another, smiling. "Best day yet in the siege," he told Paul, LB, and Colonel Ward, who ate with him. "My compliments to the chef."

They talked a bit about the pending battle. Paul, of course, initiated the conversation, although LB begged him to stick to small talk.

"Why is it, General," he asked, as he served an éclair to each of the men, "that the colored troops are relegated to a menial role in this war? I am so very appreciative of your confidence in us to have us spearhead the mine battle, but until now we have been cleaning up horseshit as the white soldiers are on their horses making all the shit."

Both Colonel Ward and LB choked on their food. For the first time since being in the army, the real Paul popped out, and at the least opportune moment.

But General Burnside, who licked his lips after the first bite of his dessert, a small glob of yellow custard stuck to his whiskers, hardly flinched. "A very good question, my friend, and one, unfortunately, sprinkled with politics. The only way I was able to convince General Meade to use you boys at all is because no one thinks that our scheme will even get off the ground."

"Politics?" Paul asked. "Or racism?"

The general smiled. "I suppose always a bit of both. No one really thinks you boys are capable of fighting; that is, of course, part of the problem. But I would say politics plays a bigger role. This is an election year; the Democrats are using a popular disdain for Negro recruits as one of their rallying cries to unseat President Lincoln. You know what one of the Democratic campaign slogans is? 'The Constitution as it is, the Union as it was, and the niggers where they are.' That's what we're up against! If you boys go in and this battle falters, that will give them fodder for their slander, and will also rile up the radicals in our party; they'll accuse us of sacrificing you for no reason. So, we're are all in a tough spot. But I have confidence in you and in what we are doing. And I don't expect that this battle will falter; I think in fact that it will end the war. That's assuming they actually let you boys fight and don't pull out the rug. Now, more importantly, is there another cream puff, or do we just get one?"

Unfortunately, Burnside's tocsin came to pass. Mere days before the battle was slated to commence on a hot July day, Colonel Ward gathered the troops. "Well, men, our roles have changed. General Meade has ordered that we take a backseat in the battle. We will now be supporting General Ledlie's First Division, who will lead the charge, and we will be in reserve in case they need us."

The First Division, of course, was all white.

Groans leaped across the lines of the eager New York soldiers who had been training for this for a month. The battle was days away. How? Why?

"Have they even prepped those white neophytes how to fight once the explosion hits?" Paul asked the colonel. "They don't have our training and knowledge of the battle; if they make even one mistake, it will be a disaster that is totally unnecessary."

"I have my orders," Colonel Ward quietly responded. "And you have yours. Dismissed."

On July 30, before the sun even rose, a massive explosion shook the land, heard as far away as Washington. General James Ledlie, apparently drunk and confused, led the unprepared First

Division into the crater created by the explosion, something that he explicitly was not supposed to do. It was unclear if Burnside gave him that order, as Ledlie later contested, or if Ledlie himself was too intoxicated to know to go around the crater and not in it. Regardless, the Confederates were ready, and they took potshots at the men trapped deep in the earth, killing thousands of them in an instant.

Paul and LB waited in the back, and then word came from Colonel Ward: Ferraro's Fourth Division would now attack. Smoke and fog obscured the landscape, and Paul ran with his rifle up toward the chaos. Some of the men followed Ledlie into the crater, others, like Paul and LB, flanked around to the right. Bullets soared by his head as he ran forward, but Paul persevered, almost blind to the danger, just following braver feet in front of him. He lost LB, who drifted to the back, breathing hard. They pushed the Confederates back, before being repulsed. Colonel Ward, sitting small on his colossal brown horse, called for a retreat, and Paul turned and ran. The battle had ended. It was a fiasco!

It was soon revealed that the Confederate army, under the orders of General Lee, executed African American soldiers who were captured. This caused public outrage by the radicals, and snickers by the conservatives, something that the now disgraced (again!) Burnside had predicted.

"It's too dangerous out there for you men," Colonel Ward told Paul and LB one night over a feast of duck, some weeks later. "The rebels will never treat you like humans; you'll always be in danger; you bring out the worst in them. It's unlikely General Grant will even let us fight."

"Can't General Burnside intervene?" Paul asked. "He seems like he gets it."

"General Burnside has been dismissed from duty," the colonel told him. "Someone has to take the blame for the crater disaster."

Paul shook his head. "It wasn't Burnside's fault," he exclaimed. "If we had just gone by the plan and used the Fourth Division instead of bringing in a bunch of untrained and drunk white soldiers at the last minute, this may have worked. If anyone should take the blame it should be Meade, or Grant."

"Perhaps," Colonel Ward quietly responded. "General Grant is a good man, but he simply does not want to take any chances with his Negroes. There is too much at stake. I wouldn't question his motives, Paul. He protested when he learned about the Confederate treatment of Negro prisoners, calling it a violation of the rules of war. He then told General Lee that any further prisoner exchanges must involve captured Negro troops. Short of that, he said, he will no longer exchange prisoners with the rebels, and as we all know, they need men more than we do. General Grant is not one to play politics or pursue abolitionist goals, but in his own quiet way he let Lee know that if Negro prisoners are in any way hurt, then there will be repercussions."

"Has you mets General Grant?" LB asked him.

"Once," said Colonel Ward. "When we first arrived in Petersburg. He spoke to a few of us who were leading Negro units, said how proud he was of what we were doing, and that he had faith in us. You can see in his eyes that he is a good man with a great deal of conviction. Not a single officer or enlisted man has anything bad to say about our general; only politicians grill him unfairly, no one else. He will win this war for us. It's only a matter of when and whether we will ever have a role in it again."

That question haunted Paul, who drilled for no purpose, as summer turned to fall, and little changed around him. He missed Smiles! He thought about her every day, wondering why he was even here.

On a cold October day, LB woke up with diarrhea. "What's you putting in thems potatoes," he chided Paul. "You wents and gives me the runs!"

But no one else was inflicted. It was not the food.

It became apparent within days that LB had dysentery, a killer of soldiers even more potent than the enemy's bullets. No one knew the cause, but the outcome was grimly predictable.

He could barely eat or drink, and he weakened fast. Paul sat by him, made him salty brews to keep him strong, tried to cook and then feed him Izzy's concoction of chicken soup with vegetables. But, despite the doctor's opium and other patent medicines that only seemed to make him less able to eat or function, his diarrhea persevered, and his body decayed.

Distant gunfire and cannon blasts fill the autumn sky, as colorful leaves fluttered down upon the city that these men had created in a small Virginia enclave. Paul took LB by a stream and put him on his lap. He stroked the man's hair and cried. LB looked up and smiled.

"You took away my only burden on this earth," he said with a weak and tremulous voice. He laid his cold hand on Paul's leg. "You took away all the pain from my Smiles; you let her be a woman again after all that she's done been through; you saved her life, Paul. And for that, my friend, you's saved mine too. You are the best man I knows, Paul, even if your oversized brain gets in the ways sometimes. But you is all good. And I love you more than I imagined I would ever love another man. Thanks you for a life well lived." He peered at Paul, and then his eyes snapped shut.

He was dead.

Paul buried him near a stream beneath a giant oak filled with red and yellow leaves. He would be back to retrieve him after the war ended, and he would put his friend in a more respectable last resting place. But for now, this would have to do.

Winter swept through the camp; more men died, and many new recruits replaced them. General Grant's army swelled. Slowly they tightened the noose around Lee. Word came through Colonel Ward that General Sherman had burned a path from

Atlanta to Savannah and was now marching up North to join General Grant. The war was almost over. Nothing could halt the federal advance now.

And yet Paul wandered through trees and over rocks feeling empty. He longed for Smiles; he missed her face, her touch, her kindness. He missed how well she understood him and how she always could make him laugh. He feared telling her about LB's death, what it might do to her demeanor as she never had a chance to say goodbye. And he dreaded this war ending like this. What stories would he tell her and his children about his role in the war? How could he take credit for ending Luke's enslavement when his most notable achievement was cleaning the crap from some of the generals' horses?

He befriended a group of soldiers from Illinois, some of whom were students there and who gravitated to Paul for his knowledge and banter. They came to visit him every few nights. It was striking to Paul how little they cared about the color of his skin. When the Thirty-First marched through the Union ranks, Paul always noticed far too many loathsome stares from the white troops. But to these boys from Illinois, Paul was just another guy, "one smart bastard, that's for sure," as one of them referred to him.

"Let me tell you about our president," one of them said. "I met the man long ago; he was my father's lawyer back then, and one night we invited him to dinner, and this man, you could see something about him that was otherworldly, something that lofted above the rest of us. He was gentle and made us laugh all night. He ate everything we served him, and then ate even more. And when it came time for my dad's case, he so humored the judge with his stories and warm logic that the case was dismissed almost before it began. I almost feel like God put him on earth for this purpose."

He spent a lot of time with those boys, as the clock clicked forward slowly. The war would end, and that man, President Lincoln, may just be the one to fix everything. God had not put him on earth Paul knew, but his presence here was surely a blessing. Paul wished he could have had a larger role and that he could have been the one to fix things, or a least be a small part of it. That—as he dreamed so many times—President Lincoln could have seen him for what he was, could have used him in this glorious fight.

As the first buds of spring burst forth, Paul met a few members of Maine's Twentieth Volunteer Infantry, some of whom had been history students at Bowden College and heard that Paul had a certain theory about how this war mimicked the early civil wars of the Roman Republic. Twentieth Maine was well known for its repulse of a Confederate charge up Little Round Top in Gettysburg and for its erudite and brave commander, Joshua Chamberlin, who had twice been left for dead only to be resurrected to rejoin his unit. The second near-death experience occurred just before Petersburg, and the unit's volunteers almost placed him in a grave before one of them noticed just a flicker of breathing. Now he had returned, back with his unit, and anxious to discuss history with Paul.

"What was it like?" Paul asked him, sitting by a fire, chewing on some boiled potatoes. "To be so close to death, twice, and then to come back? What did you feel?"

Joshua Chamberlin, his soft face and large hooked mustache floating in cool spring air, looked up at Paul. "You just move on," he said. "You don't know the difference between life and death. It all is one continuum, I suppose. When I woke up each time, I figured, what the hell, time to go at it again. It doesn't make me a hero. But I don't easily die, Paul. I have got just this one life. I aim to make something of it, and I don't aim to let go of it too quickly. As I am sure is true for you too."

Paul nodded. "My skin color seems to always get in the way. People don't let me live as I'd like to."

"They will," Chamberlin said. "People can't stay this dumb forever. One day you'll get your chance, and I know you'll take it and not look back. It's never worth looking back. If I did that, I'd be afraid of looking forward. But forward's the only direction that there is."

Paul nodded. Still, he wondered.

"More important," Chamberlin continued, "my boys told me that you think General Grant could be the next Caesar. That with our dysfunctional congress and with constant bickering in our national politic, the general who wins this war and has the full confidence of the army might well try to wrest power from the people. Is that your take of what happened in Rome and what may happen here?"

Paul laughed. He enjoyed speaking with these people, bathing in their warmth.

But did it matter? All the chatter, all the pontification. He just wanted this to end so he could get back to Smiles, find Luke, and then, as his friend Josh Chamberlin implored him, move forward, somewhere, and leave all this behind.

At the end of March, Grant's army completely surrounded Lee's. The New York Thirty-First finally mobilized and flanked around the city, its goal being to shut off any avenue of escape for the Army of Northern Virginia. Soon after, Lee fled to the west; he burned Richmond, which Paul could see flaming into the sky. The Confederate government abandoned the city and rushed south to a fate uncertain.

The Thirty-First stood firm against a rush of white Confederate troops trying to blast through and escape Grant's pincers. Paul held his ground, until a bullet pierced his lungs and sent him spiraling into the cold water below. He landed hard, and a stick embedded in the creek's muddy carpet penetrated his skin and rammed into his chest, exacerbating his pain and generating a flurry of bubbles that trickled to the surface as Paul lay dying in the mud.

And there he remained, in a red creek, as blood and air rushed from his chest and life fluttered from his body. He could not breathe at all, and he became unconscious. Through his hazy vision he watched his men, his friends, these African Americans who had been given a chance, push the Confederates back and repel their last gasp. He had made a difference in this war. He had stories to tell and accomplishments to revel in. Sadly, like with LB, fate robbed him of that opportunity.

Was it Matt who shot him? Could it have been? How strangely wry that fate would be. Poor Luke! Poor Smiles! If only, like Josh Chamberlin, he could grab back his life where it no longer existed.

A shoe kicked him, and he twisted to the side, triggering one last jolt of pain and another spurt of blood. He peeked for the last time across the bloody stream and saw air bubbles fluttering up, likely from his lungs. Those would be his last breaths. Paul Cocklin, a man beyond his times, a man who found both happiness and tragedy throughout his life, closed his eyes in a tiny river in Virginia, as the faces of his brothers, and the beautiful smile of his girl, danced in his dreams one last time.

PART V

Leviticus

Do not seek revenge or bear a grudge against anyone among your people, but love your neighbor as yourself.

42

Warrington Pike stretched interminably forward, a long row of blue mountains encroaching upon the landscape, and young trees with fresh buds sprouting out from all around him. Step by excruciating step, no one to greet him or accompany him, step by step, a horrible sense of grief and apprehension flooding his core, step by step, shaking and sweating, he finally stopped. Matt lowered his head and stared at the moist dirt below, he breathed deeply and rapidly, his head spinning, until he dropped down, right in the middle of the road, frozen in place and time, a million thoughts racing through his shattered brain.

I wish a carriage would come by and run me over now!

Clouds hovered above him, occasionally obscuring a hazy sun. It was getting warm. A thick brown beard covered his face, now beaded with sweat. His long hair was wet and greasy. His gray uniform was stiff and muddy, splattered with blood and chunks of food, a testament and reminder of all that he and his friends had accomplished during the glorious years now behind him. How could it end this way?

There were a few Grays left. Most had died; others had already returned home, a home conquered by Slim and his invaders from the North, a home now more of a prison than a sanctuary.

Why did we give up so quickly? So much sacrifice for so little justice. He sat on the road and peered ahead. Paralyzed, he could go no farther. Everything about his farm, his former slaves, the town and its people, his past life, all of it, it was poison to him. He had found his home with the Grays, with General Lee, with the thrill of battle and the sacrifice of cause. Now, what was left? Nothing felt right anymore. Every bit of joy evaporated. What was once his salvation had become his hell. He sat on the road and felt nothing at all. He knew only emptiness. It could never be what it once was.

When he closed his eyes, a glimpse of Paul's face fluttered by. He saw his brother holding a gun that was pointed at him, buried in a line of black enemies, the worst fate that he and his friends could possibly endure. He wanted nothing more than to blast through those people; rage and indignation seeped from every pore in his body. Negro soldiers! How low had they sunk? And then he saw that face. Paul? He stood frozen, until his brother grimaced and dropped. Was it Paul? Or a dream?

The black hoard pushed forward, killing even more boys and men from General Lee's once-glorious army. Matt tried to thwart a retreat; he yelled and fired his gun in rapid succession, but it was too late. They were surrounded. And then it ended in as ignoble a way as possible for the great and glorious army in which he had found a home.

They stood together in their gray uniforms, part of an endless line of vanquished heroes in a small town of Appomattox. General Lee informed the troops of General Grant's generous terms of surrender.

"We will all return to our homes, unmolested," he told them. "We can wear our uniforms and keep our guns. We merely must pledge to not fight against the Union, on our honor, which we hold most dear. I ask all of you to do that, for our nation, and for your general."

It was a cool April day, and Matt stood alongside a young boy he had met in Petersburg, a boy who liked to talk and who clung to Matt like a pupil stuck to a teacher. Matt's mind felt dead as General Lee rode past the troops, appearing worn but dignified as he sat upon Traveler in full uniform.

"You know what's crazy?" the chatty boy said to Matt, whispering in his ear. "The man who owns this farm, the one where they signed the surrender papers yesterday, he used to own the farm in Manassas, where the first battle was fought, the one that we licked the Yankees at; his house got all shot up and destroyed, so he moved here to get away from the war, and look what happened, like God put him at the beginning and the end, which really makes you think."

Matt was not in a thinking mood. The boy's moving mouth irritated him. He wished he could lift his gun and shoot the Northern generals as an act of final vengeance. Only his reverence for General Lee prevented him from doing just that. He peered at the faces of the Union troops, especially the Negro troops, who seemed to glare at him with prideful disdain. Matt tried to find Paul's face among them, looking everywhere for it. Was his brother dead? Was that even his brother on Saylor's creek, or perhaps someone else? The questions haunted him on this horrid spring day.

"You know what else is crazy?" the boy continued. "You heard of Josh Chamberlin, the guy from up North who almost died like a zillion times, and then came back to life? He's the guy just now who is accepting General Lee's surrender, see, over there." The boy pointed to a man with a handlebar mustache and a well-pressed Union blue uniform. "You know what his initials are? J. C. Right? Jesus Christ, same initials. And like Christ rose from the dead, so did this guy too, and now this guy, he is in the role of God; he is making a whole new world for us. Isn't that just so crazy?"

"Can you just shut up," Matt snapped.

"But you got to admit it's crazy, all these coincidences and stuff. It's just the Lord's way, I guess."

"So, you saying that the Lord wanted the North to win, that He was on their side? That what you saying? That your point?"

"Maybe," the boy said, gleefully. "I'm not in any position to know the Lord's intentions. But it makes you think, right?"

"It makes me think you is an ass and a traitor; that's what I think. You want the North to be in charge?"

The boy shrugged. "I don't give two damns about that," he said. "I don't own any slaves, and the slaveholders never did anything for me. I figure, once this war is over, things will be about the same for me anyway. Doesn't much matter one way or another."

"Then why the hell did you fight?" Matt growled.

The boy smiled. "'Cause they telled me to, and I fought for my people. That's what I did; that's what I was supposed to do. Still, that doesn't mean that the Lord didn't have His say in the end. The fact that Josh Chamberlin has the same initials as God's Son, well, that has to make you think."

Matt so much wanted to shoot the boy! He tried to ignore him, peering ahead. He wished he could be by General Lee's side. Instead, he was stuck with boys and men he hardly knew, remnants of the once-proud unit with which he served; even Colonel Kemper could not be found. His mind nearly exploded. "You know," he said to the boy, "my dad's initials were J. C. too. That makes him a Christ figure?"

"Depends," the boy said. "Did he die and come back to life? You got to do something else other than just have the right initials. But you got to admit, this man, Josh Chamberlin, he does make you think."

"Fuck you," Matt said and then slid away and stood alone.

He last spoke to General Lee many weeks ago, in the cold chill of Petersburg, when he was beckoned to the general's tent. Longstreet was not there, just the general, his beard trimmed neatly, his gray uniform as meticulous as ever, but a grim visage painted upon his face.

"I want you to know, Matthew, that whatever happens to us and to our people, I was proud to know the son of my friend Jake, and you paid back my faith in your father a thousand times over. The future is in your generation's hands, Matthew. You who fought here for our great and noble cause, only to see it stripped away by forces out of our control, you are the ones who will live with our choices and failures, and you are the ones who will have to repair the damage and restore all that we have lost. Don't let those people dictate your future. Stand true to the cause. God will reward those who are good and righteous."

"It ain't over yet, General," Matt pleaded. "We all got a lot of fight left in us, and we all going to follow you to the end of time. You know that. They can't beat us. They never will."

General Lee nodded. "I wish I could share your optimism, son. We will fight as long as we can; I promise you that, but I will not sacrifice my men for a lost cause, nor will I fight to appease the scoundrels who lead our government in Richmond, whose bickering and ineptitude cost us this war. We did all we could, Matthew, but forces out of our control sabotaged us. History will judge me harshly, as well it should. My punishment in the here and now is difficult enough; I have lost everything for me and my family, and I will be lucky to escape with my life. But in the eyes of history, I will forever be known as a traitor to my country, a turncoat no better than Benedict Arnold. That is how it should be and how it will be. Those people, and the Negro hoards who will overtake the nation that my father and father-in-law helped to create, they are the dispensers of justice now. My legacy is sealed. But your generation, you can still help to forge a destiny that is better than what our tormentors seek to inflict upon us. The next war, Matthew, is not one with guns, but one with brains and heart. God will judge me when I get to heaven, that I know. But here on earth, my deeds have led me to the pits of hell, and that is where I will live out what little life I have."

"Don't talk like that, General," Matt implored him.

General Lee hugged him, smiled, and walked away. They were never to speak again.

A cool breeze swept dust into his eyes along Warrington Pike a week after the surrender, and Matt looked up at the mountains ahead. Still empty and not wanting to move, he nonetheless lifted himself from the ground and started walking that way, slowly and painfully, step by step.

What was left for him there? Luke, Jessie, the pond, his house? He had no desire to see any of them. He preferred to be all alone far away from this foreign and conquered land. Nothing made sense.

Your generation, you can still help to forge a destiny that is better than what our tormentors seek to inflict upon us. The next war, Matthew, is not one with guns, but one with brains and heart.

He had to move forward. If not for himself, then at least for the general.

Everything Matt valued was incinerated at Saylor's Creek and Appomattox. But the general was right. Matt could never give up the fight, and he did have an ally who seemed to always understand and know what to do. It is to that man whom Matt ventured on this lonely, dusty road in the foothills of Virginia.

He did not want to see or talk to anyone else.

Matt slipped into the quiet town of Washington a bit after sundown. Crickets greeted him, as did a soft breeze and a full moon that glistened off the silhouette of mountains. But Matt noticed none of that. He walked step by step, aware of only the ground below him; he felt heavy and sluggish. He had to push hard to even get this far. Rather than a heroic soldier returning home, he floated in a desolate universe, with nothing but hindrances lingering all around him. He feared he may shoot anyone who dared greet him. He sought to see only one face. To hear only one voice.

He knocked on a pristine white door.

"My goodness, Matthew! My dear Matthew, you have returned. Come in, come in!"

The doctor hugged him and then backed off. "Your odor—" He tried to laugh. "It is pungent."

"I just need to know what to do next," he grumbled, his words barely audible.

The doctor, his demeanor friendly and embracing, put his arms around Matt's back and led him to his parlor. "Come with me, son," he said. "We will talk."

Matt sat on the chair that had always been his. The skulls were still there, and the books, and the windows, with moon rays shining brightly through. He felt safer here, although hardly comfortable. He didn't like to sit. He preferred to march, to shoot, to call for action. The chair was too soft. Within seconds he started to get antsy and started to shake just a bit. Breathing hard, he stood up and paced.

"You don't have to sit, Matthew. Walk around. Get it out. You have endured more than most men do in a lifetime. You have been unjustly defeated by an inferior foe. But the war is not over, Matthew, and your role in the ongoing fight is essential. No one can ever understand what you feel now. No one ever will. But I do. I feel it too. Together we will prevail, Matthew. Count on me."

Matt nodded. "How?" he asked. "How, Doctor? Tell me. Tell me how."

"First and most importantly, you keep on your uniform when you are on your farm. You wear it every day you are there. The less comfortable you feel, the angrier you are, the more you will be able to contribute to the cause and not be tempted to retreat to your prior life of accommodation. Your sacrifice will not be forgotten, nor was it in vain. You have more influence than you can imagine. It is crucial that right from the start you seize total control of your land, your servants, even your wife. You work on the crop, and you pay your slaves a small wage to stay, a wage that will primarily come back to you as a fee for their lodging and food; they will remain your slaves in all but name, I assure you. Your farm has done remarkably well in your absence. Despite my disdain for him, your Jewish friend from New York has done a fine job assuring its stability and productivity. My daughter tells me that he has been nothing less than honorable and true to his word. Despite his loyalty and efficiency, he will have to eventually be stripped of all power and authority, but for now his presence here is to our benefit, as I will later explain."

Matt nodded, his pace accelerating. He looked only at the floor, at each slither of wood, each crack and stain. "Yes," he uttered. "You will tell me how?"

"I will tell you everything," the doctor said in a soothing voice.

"Good," Matt responded.

The doctor continued, "You must keep your distance from your slaves. You have been too close to them in the past. That must stop. The Negro is now empowered, and you must not add to that unfortunate circumstance. To strip the Negro of his power, to shove him back into the harmless subservience from where he cannot menace the white race, we must treat him with both disdain and fabricated deference. We will play the Northern game well enough to satisfy our captors, while maintaining control over the chattel in a way the Northerners cannot comprehend. You cannot befriend your slaves. You cannot speak kindly to them. Do you understand, Matthew?"

"Yes," Matt said. "Yes, I believe you. I do." A sense of calm flowed through him. Slowly, much of his pain, his sense of not belonging here, drifted away. He stood still, and then he sat down. His eyes gravitated to the doctor's. He could see a powerful resolve and strength in the man. A purity of purpose. He was drawn to it and could not let go. "Tell me more."

The doctor smiled. "Go home tonight and become the man of the house. That starts with my daughter. Everyone on that farm is subservient to you, including her. They may feel differently after your absence. Do not allow that to persist. Fuck her. Impregnate her; you need her to be a mother to your children. Do not fraternize with your Jewish overseer or your slaves. Remain distant. Do you understand?"

Matt nodded. "I understand," he responded robotically. He had forgotten that Izzy was there now; that was the last person he wanted to see! But the doctor's words told him what to do.

It was now too dark outside to continue his journey. The doctor advised Matt to stay for the night and make his grand entrance in the morning. He had a bed prepared. He had a dish of chicken, made by the doctor's black servant, a former slave, now a paid employee, or so he told Matt.

"Bessie, you tell Matthew here what kind of life you have since the war ended."

"Doctor, you give me the best life; you are a good man, and the Lord, He smiles at you," the young, thin woman said gleefully. "Do you men need more food? Drink?"

The doctor nodded no and whisked Bessie away. "She had been a slave on the Peter's farm. They are all dead there. I took her in, and I provide her a wage sufficient to allow her to pay her rent back to me. It is an amicable arrangement for which she thanks me every day."

He walked with Matt back to the study. "The federal government will send men down here, soldiers and do-gooders, men and women to assure that we know our place and that we are properly taking care of the free Negroes. It is our job, our duty, to comply with their dictates both in the letter of the law and the spirit of the law. Do you know why, Matthew?"

Matt nodded no. But he was curious.

"Virginia is in a fortunate place at the end of the war. We provided the Confederacy with its capital, its best generals, the main theaters of battle. We sacrificed for God and country; even people in the North admire what we accomplished. And now we are free from the stench of the vile scum from the Deep South.

We can negotiate our future on our own. To do that, we must comply with those who have conquered us. We must be obsequious and thankful. And only then can we maneuver and script our own destiny."

"I trust you, Doctor. You has always been right."

The doctor smiled and slapped the boy on his back. "Sleep well, son. Tomorrow you begin the next battle. I will speak with you and instruct you every day; you will not have to take a single step without my guidance. This is a very exciting time in which we live." His face shined across stray beams of moonlight.

Matt wandered upstairs and lay on his first bed in many years. It felt good. He did not take off his uniform. He had grown accustomed to its stench. It reminded him of times gone by. His eyes snapped shut. He saw General Lee and imagined slicing through Union troops, Jude by his side, Stonewall encouraging him, Colonel Kemper, his friends, his comrades—they were all there. He lifted his gun and fired, one blue uniform dropping after another. Suddenly a black face appeared, staring hard at Matt, running toward him, screaming, lifting his gun. Matt shot at it, his bullet piercing it, its head shattering, blood everywhere, and there was Luke by the pond crying, his tears red with blood.

Matt sat up and startled. He breathed heavily. A cool wind blew through the room's open window. He looked at the walls. He thought of what the doctor said. But the images would not evacuate his brain. So, he stood and started to pace. The bed was too comfortable anyway.

It's time to drill, boys. Never stop drilling! We don't know when they'll cross the river again and try to push us back. But, boys, we never will let them. We never will!

It would be a very long night. As would every night from now on. Cold and empty, with the doctor's words nudged into his fractured mind, he paced back and forth, calling out to the troops. Paul's bloody face burst into his thoughts from time to time, forcing him to punch the wall and resume his march. There was no pond. No wife. No Luke or Izzy. He craved only purpose, and with General Lee now gone, the doctor gave him enough to get him through.

Keep marching, boys. The war ain't over. It's only just begun!

Stonewall sat by his side that night. His long beard neatly trimmed, his uniform tattered and loose, he sucked on a lemon.

"We're in this together, son," he said. "You don't worry. I'm not going anywhere."

And so Matt smiled as he continued his march. Back and forth. Back and forth. He saw and felt nothing else.

Keep marching, boys. The war ain't over. It only just begun!

Maybe there was hope yet. Matt was glad to be here, glad to be finally home.

43

ary held her son tightly. Poor Luke! This world was too
cruel for him. She wished she could coddle him forever
and never let the sting of humanity shake his fragile hide.

"He doesn't like those people, Momma; he only likes us,"
Luke said to her. "Why would he say he likes those people? Why
would he say that? It doesn't make sense, Momma. He is the best
daddy ever!"

"He is, Luke, he is," she said, kissing his forehead. "But he
has to make nice with all the people out there. When he says
bad things about them to Matt and you and Paul, that's how he
really believes. But out there, he can't be like that. And when you
have to pretend for so long, well, sometimes you start to believe
it. Sometimes you start to understand their point of view and
to even agree with it. Your daddy is a good man, the best man I
know. But even he is not immune from that."

"I wish he wouldn't go out there," he said. "It's bad out there.
He should just stay here, with us."

His mother laughed. "If only he could! If only we could close
the gates and stay here forever. Our own private heaven. Hide
from everything out there. They are nothing but distractions
from our happiness."

"Then," the small boy said, beaming, his eyes wide, his smile large, "just tell him not to leave the farm. He can stay here forever with us! Let's close the gates! Let's just be together!"

"Maybe," his mother mused. "Maybe one day. We can always hope."

Luke lay on her chest and smiled. Then he popped up, as though a stray thought dashed into his brain. "And why does that doctor keep coming to talk to Daddy?" Luke asked. "Is Daddy sick?"

His mother nodded no. "The doctor is sick. Not your daddy. That doctor, if that's what he really is, he is trying to pull your daddy away from us. Your daddy says that the doctor sometimes makes sense. I don't know, Luke. I wish we could keep him away. I wish we could keep everyone away."

Luke nodded, safely on his mother's breast, his eyes heavy, slowing drifting to sleep.

Luke smiled when he reflected on those times gone by. It was now May 1865, and a bright sun shined over the Shenandoah skyline. With the war over, slavery had been extinguished, but on the farm, nothing changed. How could it? It was planting season. Time to make sure the trees were properly watered and pruned, the debris from winter had been cleaned away, and the small vegetable gardens were weeded and fertilized. They had to chase away the vermin. Ruth and her two boys did what they always did, lived in the same cabins, and ate the same meals. Luke and Izzy shared a cabin, and they too minded the farm by day. Maybe they weren't slaves anymore. But did that really matter? They never left their farm; they engaged in their same activities. Who cared about the war?

One day, Colonel Stompmonger and two of his officers rode through the farm's gates to speak with Matt. Matt trounced out of the main house, having shed his Confederate uniform for the occasion, and, with Jessie's arms around him, invited the men in. His dark wavy hair and long beard concealed any emotion that may have crept onto his visage. Ruth cooked a dish of honey ham with potatoes. Luke served them wine, while Izzy remained outside to supervise the farm's workers.

Had anything really changed? Anything other than Matt?

The colonel, who hailed from Iowa and had fought mostly with General Sherman in the latter part of the war, greeted Matt warmly. Luke watched from a perch along the side wall, meticulously filling their crystal cups with wine. He only wished he had some grapes to make his own vintage, which would be far superior to the colored water spewing from these bottles. Perhaps in August, the crop would finally prosper, and he would have enough grapes to at least get started. By then, Paul should be back, and things would ease into what they once were.

"Where did you fight, son?" the burly colonel asked Matt, his oversized gut pushing through his uniform's lower buttons, his crooked teeth chomping on some of the fruits Ruth laid out. "You with General Lee in the East?"

Matt nodded yes, squirming a bit, saying very little.

"Well, it was a hell of a battle in the East," the colonel said, slapping Matt on the back. "I give you and Lee credit. You did your fair share of fighting and winning. But there is only so much you could do. I have been talking to the doctor. He tells me that you have the most productive farm in the area and that your former slaves have already signed a contract with you to stay on and that they are nothing but pleasant. He says that one of your slaves is a bit of a genius in fact."

"That'd be Luke," Matt said, pointing. "He helped me a whole lot getting this farm to be as good as it is. I'm glad he stayed on with me. He ain't the smartest slave in the world, Colonel. Lots of them ain't that smart, and most of them know that and stayed on their farms. It's better for them. And it's the only way we is going to keep doing what we is good at. We is trying all to cooperate best we can."

The colonel nodded. "I have been here a month, Mr. Cocklin, and I have seen no trouble from these parts. The Negroes are docile and willing to stay with their owners for the most part. Some of the others are looking to acquire unoccupied land, and we are working on that. The Freedman's Bureau has been helping out, and they got someone coming down next week to talk to the area Negroes. That's mostly what I'm here to tell you. The doctor said that I should come by and talk to you directly. He said it would be a good idea to have your Negroes there. That doctor of yours, he is keeping everything running smoothly. Washington's whites are just as docile and cooperative as its Negroes! No trouble from anyone so far. That's how the US Army likes it. We appreciate your cooperation. And this fine meal."

"It's our pleasure, Colonel," Matt said—Jessie sitting near him and smiling—his face flat, his words staid. "We want to cooperate. We is good people and just want to show you how good we is."

It was clear to Luke that Matt was reading from a script.

"My daddy," Jessie chimed in, "is so happy to have you down here with us, Colonel Stompmonger. He says you are a good and understanding Christian man. You will see how fine a place Washington Virginia is when you are here long enough. So much more hospitable and cultured than the other Washington, I assure you!" She laughed. "And right now, you are in the most productive farm in the whole county. I would love to show you around with Luke; he is the genius behind its success. Not all Negroes are stupid, and we don't treat them that way down here, and Luke is a testament to that. We respect our Negroes. We are glad that they are free to make their own choices, and as you can see, they choose to say right where they are. You tell him, Luke."

The sudden beckoning took Luke by surprise. He stepped forward and bowed to the colonel, who he had not yet met. "I's loves it here," he said timidly. "Massa Matt, he is so goods to me and all the other Negroes, and we is so glad and proud to be parts of this farm and to make it works, and we is so glad to still be here to live and work and be with Miss Jessie and Massa Matt and all the other good white folk."

"Well, son, that is very heartening, it is indeed!" the colonel proclaimed, as he shoved his face into a bowl of mashed potatoes, white specks cluttered all over his disheveled red beard.

Izzy had met the colonel a few times prior, speaking to him after some of the meetings that were set up in town. He didn't like him at all.

"The doctor got to him first," Izzy said to Luke a few weeks ago. "That vile doctor is like the snake from the Garden of Eden. He tells you what you want to hear. He charms you and convinces you that the world is actually not what you think it is. Then slowly he twists you to believe him and to doubt God's word. Next thing you know, you're kicked out of the fucking Garden and everyone is screwed."

"What did the doctor do that was so bad?" Luke asked. "If the doctor is keeping the peace, enabling the Negroes to work, dissuading the white men from any cruelty, if that's what the doctor is doing, what's so bad about that?"

"You don't get it, Luke," Izzy snapped. "My people have learned the hard way. Your enemies use this trick often. They let you think they are on your side until you let down your defenses, and then they pounce. You remember a few months ago at the end of March when we did the Passover Seder? Well, the deal is that the Pharaoh invited the Jews into Egypt because he led us to believe that we'd prosper there, that we'd get land and have jobs, but then, first chance he got, he threw us in chains and made us slaves. That's the way it works. The doctor is charming the colonel. He is making sure his own people behave; he is feeding the colonel and the Negroes just enough to make them happy, and then, when all seems good, and the colonel wanders off to another place and leaves Washington alone, then the doctor will tighten the vice and put all the Negroes in their place. That's how it works. It always does."

"I don't know, Izzy," Luke said. "Even the doctor doesn't gain anything from that. He benefits from everyone being happy and productive. Besides, we have Matt here to protect us. I'm not worried. Once Paul gets back, with his wife and kids, then it will be like it once was."

"Matt?" Izzy laughed. "What can I tell you, Luke? Sometimes your naive thinking scares the shits out of me. You start counting on Matt to be our Moses; then we are really going to be screwed."

Matt.

Luke's oldest brother marched around the farm incessantly donning his Confederate uniform, a dour face, not even making eye contact with Luke or Izzy. He rode off to see the doctor almost every day. Jessie barely left his side. He spoke without emotion or inflection.

When he first arrived on the farm, Luke ran out to greet him. He met Luke coldly. He said hello and then walked in to see Jessie. He did not reemerge from the house for many days.

"I heard so much wailing in there from that bitch," Izzy told Luke, "that either she was being attacked by a raccoon, or she was being fucked by him every hour day and night."

It turned out to be the latter. When he did emerge from the house, his agenda focused only on business, never peering into their eyes or interacting with them in any other way.

"I saw right away he didn't want to talk. I could see it in his face. There was nothing behind those hallow hazel eyes. Just emptiness. What can I tell you? That boy who left to fight came back to us as something else. That's not Matt in there. Behind his beard is some other creature. Don't trust him."

"Of course he is Matt!" Luke insisted. "He's just playing his role. He has to do that to survive here. In the end, he is doing it for us, for the farm."

Izzy grunted. "Something happened to him on the battlefield, Luke. Something profound. Has he spoken to you at all kindly? Has he been over to see you alone, without that bitch wife of his, to sit and chat, to talk about how you are, to tell you what he went through?"

Luke nodded no. "That's OK," he said. "He needs to play the role."

But Izzy had had enough.

A few weeks after Matt's return, when Izzy figured that the farm no longer needed him hanging around, he announced to Luke that he would be returning to New York to try to find Paul and Smiles, to perhaps resume his work, and to get back to his old life. Having Passover in Virginia away from his friends was hard enough; he was certainly not staying long enough to suffer through the high holy days down here. He wanted Luke to come with him.

"No," Luke flatly said. "Not during planting season. Not until the crops are secure and my grapes start to mature and bear fruit. I owe that to Matt and to the farm, and to myself. I don't ever want to leave, Izzy. I do want you to go up there and bring Paul back."

But the following week, after Izzy also told Matt of his intentions, Jessie came by the cabin to bring Izzy a letter. It was from Abe. And it was open. "Matthew told me to give this to you. He didn't read it; he opened it by accident. Then he saw it was yours." She peeked over at Luke. "Hi, Lukie," she said. "I hope he is treating you well."

The letter was not what Izzy had hoped to see.

Izzy, my misguided friend, greetings from Brooklyn,

Things have gone to shit since you left. I just wanted you to know that before you had it in your head to come back. The Irish burned down the business, and now I am living a life of leisure across the East River, having fully retired from the retail trade. There may be other work for you here, but with the war almost over, and with Tammany Hall having a firm grasp on every goddamned thing that goes on in the city, you'll have to do some major sucking up if you want to work at all. And by the way,

Elizabeth, or whatever her name is (I am old, so forgive me, I actually forget her name!), you know, Biggelow's wife who hung around with you guys, she may be the one you have to suck up to. Biggelow is the guy with power now, and she is forever by his side. I went to a function last week, and there they were, hand in hand. She kissed him on the head, and she walked away with him. I heard that they are an inseparable couple. So, maybe you can use your friendship with her to get in with Biggelow.

By the way, in case you didn't hear, Paul and James, they went off to fight with the Negro units. I think they went to New Orleans or some other shithole. Word also is that the Negro soldiers are in the army for three years, so we won't be seeing Paul for quite some time. Assuming they survive.

Anyway, good friend, you may have been smart to leave, and if I were you, I'd stay down there for a while until things settle down a bit. Nothing for you up here. I do have some money for you, gave it to Paul, so you'll have to get it from Smiles over at the Biggelow house, and I would love to see you when you do come. But no rush. I hope you had a healthy Pesach with the goyim. God bless you.

Abe

Instantly, Izzy dropped into an uncharacteristic silence. "That sucks," he muttered.

He informed Luke that he would stick around a bit longer, and he wrote a letter to Smiles, hoping it would arrive and that he could get more information from her.

"I guess I'll write the letter in care of Elizabeth, Ernie's loving and faithful wife," he sighed.

Izzy brooded over that letter for days, hardly eating, and often drifting alone in the trees. One day, Luke found him sitting the pond, staring. Luke joined him; there was no more red raft—Jessie destroyed it in one of her rages—but just sitting here was soothing enough, beneath the shadow of Old Rag.

"I don't want to stay here," Izzy said. "But I don't want to go back home. Not yet. Maybe never."

"I am glad you'll be staying, Izzy," Luke smiled. "Although in my heart I know that Elana still loves you, despite what your friend said about Elizabeth. How can she not?"

"I think Elana and Elizabeth are both lost causes. Just like Matt. I worry about Paul. I am all worries."

In the first week of June, when much of the farm's work was complete, a flier announced that Peter Marsh of the Freedman's Bureau would be meeting members of the Negro community on June 10 at the Washington Baptist Church. Luke, Ruth, and the boys agreed to go if Izzy accompanied them.

It was a dark and gloomy day, with large, drifting black clouds threatening to dump buckets of rain onto the travelers. A soft, warm wind whipped at them from the east, as they trod the puddle-infested dirt road on the way to Washington.

Inside the pleasant church, with its colorful stained-glass windows and neatly arranged pews, a few dozen of the area's former slaves gathered for the first time together. Most had never set foot in Washington, let alone being allowed in this church. But with the protection of the US Army, and an apparently apathetic white community, they filed in without being accosted or jeered.

Behind the altar stood the doctor in his Sunday best, Colonel Stompmonger with a few of his men, and a very tall and thin man with a Lincoln-like beard and tiny wire spectacles, who shuffled through a pile of papers as the colonel and doctor chatted and laughed.

After about an hour, when a pattering rain and some distant thunder broke an awkward silence, Colonel Stompmonger stood at the podium and spoke. "Thank you, my Negro friends, for coming here; I know for many of you, this is the first time you have seen each other. Let it be known that our job in the United States Army, under the authority of President Johnson and General Grant, is to protect you and to ensure that the Southern people treat you as United States citizens, that they free you from your bondage, that they do not harm or disrespect you, and that you have the opportunity to work and pray in your own way. To that end, I have invited Peter Marsh from the Freedman's Bureau. Mr. Marsh is under the authority of General Otis Howard and is instructed to help your assimilation into society as best as can occur. He is stationed in Warrenton, but his agents are available to be here as often as is needed and to meet with any of you who have grievances or concerns. The doctor here, who has been more than cooperative in the transition, is happy to work with the Freedman's Bureau as well to help all of you achieve what you seek. Having said that, I give the podium to Peter Marsh."

"Can you imagine this shit?" Izzy whispered to Luke, probably louder than he realized, since a lot of heads turned his way, including Ruth's, who put her finger over her mouth telling him to be quiet. "The doctor even got to the Freedman's Bureau rep. He is quite the clever snake!"

Peter Marsh stood as several sheets of paper fluttered to the ground. He reached to grab them and then dropped even more. His voice was muffled, even a bit tremulous, and he had a stutter. He rarely looked up and spoke with long pauses between words and sentences.

"Many of you have approached me—you came up to me, or you let my office know, some of you did at least, not a lot of you, some of you—about building your own Baptist church, with its own preacher. I'm a Congregationalist, and we do things differently, and also we want to start a school here too. The Freedman's Bureau is committed to educating all of you to be productive members of society, and I thought we can do that in the church. We can do all of that in the next few months, or get started at least. I can't make promises; there are funding issues and finding personnel; there are a lot of Negroes in need. You are among the luckiest being here; many of you have told me that, and some of you approached me about getting land. The Federal Government has promised all of you land if you want it, and we do have some abandoned farms here that are now property of the government that we do intend to give to you people, but that will take time. So until then you can work the farms here, and I do want to thank the doctor and the colonel for making my job so much easier, and I want to thank those of you who have spoken to me already, and I suppose even those who haven't. I don't want to exclude anyone. All of you should rejoice in your freedom, and we will assure your rights. . ."

"This is the longest sentence I ever heard in my life," Izzy laughed to Luke. "I'm not sure he has ever heard of a period. He is a pro at commas; that much I can tell you."

Luke smiled. "Imagine Paul's consternation if he learned that their first order of business is to build a church," he whispered

"You know what Paul would say," Izzy quietly responded. "That they're doing it just to keep the Negroes happy and to shut them up, so they don't ask for anything more substantial. That's the power of religion. Once you give the people access to God, they stop asking for jobs and food and power."

"Shhhh," Ruth implored them. She looked like she was ready to hit them over the head.

"Paul is usually right," Luke said, ignoring Ruth's plea but speaking very quietly. "When he comes back, he can interject his views. We don't need a church or school or land. We just need to do what we've always done and not have interference. Matt will be on our side in that task."

Izzy nodded. "For now," he said.

"Do you have a question back there, you in the fifth row?" the doctor shouted out and pointed to Izzy, interrupting Peter Marsh mid-sentence as he promptly dropped his whole pile of papers. "I see you chatting. Perhaps if you have something to say that would be instructive to all of us."

Izzy stood. "Thank you, Doctor, yes. I do have a question. I was wondering if you were planning on building a temple as well.

We do have a few Jews come here from time to time, and I'm hoping to convert many of these Negroes to Judaism, maybe even some of Washington's white citizens, as well as bringing many of my friends and my family to live here to repopulate the area as a Jewish haven. So having a temple would be very important, don't you think, Mr. Marsh?"

As the doctor grimaced and Luke chuckled, Peter Marsh stood stunned at the podium, reaching down to grab a few papers. "Well, I, this is somewhat new to me. We do have Negro churches, but this issue, well, it has not come up before, and I could take it up to General Howard, if it is something, I am saying, if it has consensus, or at the very least . . ."

His words knew no end. Izzy winked at the doctor, who just shook his head in disdain and then drifted away. Izzy put his mouth to Luke's ear. "If it weren't raining, I'd say me and you should get out of here, go to the doctor's house, and make ourselves at home there; he's going to be here for a while, and I understand that he has a lot of good food stashed away from the war, and no one is there to keep us out. We could have a hell of a feast at his expense."

"No ham though," Luke laughed. "We can't let you eat ham again."

"Thank you for looking out for me, Luke! I promise, no more ham. Although it's damned good. What can I tell you?"

Nothing, it turned out. Luke had known all along that there was no reason to leave the farm, not today, not ever. There never had been. The allure of freedom spit out by men like Peter Marsh meant nothing to him. Izzy was right; none of this would amount to anything of value. For Luke to achieve freedom, he needed to assure the integrity of his farm's gates so that no one came in and no one interfered. Momma was right. A tight fence around the farm was their best protection. Now, if he could only convince Matt of that, something he knew he could best accomplish after Paul's return.

Of course, what frightened him the most was Jessie's presence there, especially after what she had done soon after Matt's return. He could only hope that it amounted to nothing, just another painful violation of his freedom that he would have to endure periodically. This time, though, it was different. Very different. And when he saw Jessie vomiting by the pond the other day, and Matt comforting her and rubbing her belly, a bolt of fear shook his entire hide. It was probably nothing. Nothing at all. But he was glad that Izzy would be around this summer. He needed his friend's companionship and protection to be able to focus on his work and help Matt find his way home. And he couldn't wait to taste the grapes in August, him and Paul, sitting on a new red raft beneath Old Rag's domineering shadow! That thought is what made him smile more than anything else in the world!

44

Paul is dead.

That reality, about which he alone knew, reverberated across Matt's skull at the most inopportune times—when he sat with Jessie or the doctor, when he tried to sleep at night, when he ate or hid in the living room and phantom odors from Paul's cooking shook him to the core. Knowing what he knew, Matt could not even look at Luke or feel anything less than a ghost while he traversed the farm in a perpetual fog. His former sanctuary felt like a foreign land now, somewhere he did not belong, a place invaded by others and twisted into something different, something vile. Matt saw no mountains; he felt no joy. He wore his uniform and let that sew images and recollections in his mind of better times with his boys and the general, always a purpose, firing his gun and running through the woods in search of enemies.

But then Paul's face inevitably crashed into his thoughts— hovering by the stream, lifeless, pleading for Matt to help, his rifle aimed at Matt's head as he dropped dead into the shallow red waters of an obscure Virginia field. And then he saw Paul as a young boy, the three of them sitting by a fire, sometimes his dad and mom with them, laughter saturating the house. He shook off the images as best he could by marching and staying active, never sleeping, never dwelling on an extinct past.

It was a hot day at the end of August. The summer had been a blur to Matt, its searing heat bouncing off his hide fecklessly; he spent most of his time inside, in his room, often with Jessie lecturing to him, as her belly enlarged, the baby in it portending the next stage of his life, a father, a man with responsibility. He did not think much about it. He could stare at blank walls for hours at a time and contemplate nothing, even as she gabbed on and on. When needed, he evoked images of the war; it was his elixir, his alcohol. Often, he let himself descend into a state of pure fantasy.

"You're drifting again," Jessie told him, as she draped him with uncomfortable hugs and kisses. Her very touch rattled him, and he rarely made eye contact. "Do you want to make love to me again? In the uniform? You can pretend I am General Lee, like you did the last time. I don't mind. Our baby loves it when you fill me with your precious seed and smother my body with your fluids."

"No," Matt uttered. "I'm meeting with your dad and some other people later, in town. The colonel is coming is what they say. I don't know why, but your dad, he wants me there early, so I aim to leave soon. I got to get on regular clothes since the colonel will be there."

"I know, Matthew, but that is not for a while," she said, kissing him on the head and face as he grimaced. Her words tore him from a blissful dream state in which he was running with Stonewall through the woods near Fredericksburg, except this time Stonewall didn't die; he lived and then fought at Gettysburg. This time they won!

"Matt!" she snarled, slapping him hard on the face. "Stop your stupid games. And take that angry look off your face. Do you understand? Don't you ever be angry with me!" And then she smiled and kissed him. "I am going into town too; we can ride together. Daddy wants me to visit the Negroes who are building the Baptist church; a woman from the Freedman's Bureau will be in town to see our progress, and Daddy thought it would be good if I were there too, girl to girl, to tell her how well it's going."

Matt said nothing.

"We are starting the Negro school in September, in just two weeks, and this woman is going to be one of the teachers. Imagine having Lukie come too, to teach them about farming, and I can help. I want to help the Negroes. We live in a different time. I want the Negroes to be happy."

Matt did not budge. He stared forward, immersed in emptiness.

"Well, if you're not in the mood to make love to me, I am going to wander around the farm, maybe visit Lukie and see how he is; I hear that Izzy is out and about, and poor Lukie is all alone in there, probably working hard like he always does. He says this may be our best crop ever. And have you seen his grape vines! I am so proud of him!"

She kissed him and marched out. He did not migrate from his statuesque pose.

Later that afternoon a few men gathered at the doctor's house. The doctor offered them small sandwiches and sweet tea, his new servant happily tending to their needs. They were in his parlor. The doctor seated his guests, as he walked by his skulls, rubbing them as he spoke.

Matt wondered what Paul's skull would look like on display. He stared at the bones, the jaws, the eye sockets, hardly cognizant of what the doctor uttered.

Horatio Moffett and Governor Smith sat with legs crossed. Neither wore their Confederate uniforms, although Mr. Moffett garnished one that he slipped on from time to time.

"It is only a matter of time," the governor said, biting his sandwich. "Virginia will be back in the Union. The Negroes will be able to vote, and the Republican swine will have an advantage if they do vote. Our goal is to make sure that they don't."

"We don't want violence here, Governor," Mr. Moffett said. "It is not in our interest. I would rather lose a few elections than elicit the suspicion of men like Colonel Stompmonger. Right now, he is on our side, and he believes in our good intentions. If we make mistakes at this juncture, we could lose total control of our destiny."

"Then what do you suggest, Mr. Moffett?" the governor asked. "Do you think we should merely bend over and kiss their butts?"

The doctor nodded. "You men are both correct, but your vision is skewed." He paced along the skulls. "Negroes are not an intellectual challenge to the white race, and thus we should not fear them nor ascribe to them actions which they are incapable of taking. Our goal is to manipulate them, which is not very difficult if we keep our wits about us, gentlemen. Currently, they are very satisfied with building a church and having a school. There is a prospect of them getting land of their own, something that Colonel Stompmonger assures me is a promise that the Yankees will never keep, but the Negroes need not know that. Let them think they will be our equals in this place. Matthew has had a good name among the Negroes. Jessie has also suggested that Matt's slave Luke help teach them about farming. That will only further elevate Matthew's good name in their eyes."

"I don't see your point, Doctor," Mr. Moffett said from his chair. "First of all, I must remind you, we don't use the word 'slave' anymore."

The doctor laughed. "And yet, they are slaves in all but name, as we well know."

"But then I ask you again, are you making a point?"

"His point," said the governor, "is that we can manipulate the Negroes to do our bidding if we feed them what they want, and we can manipulate the Yankees to believe in our good intentions if we act like we support the Negro. I understand your point, Doctor. I simply don't agree with it. In other parts of the South, people are teaching the Negroes a lesson—men who wear white sheets and put fear in the Negro hearts, ruffling the Union soldiers and the visiting teachers and do-gooders from the Freedman's Bureau. We don't have to sit back like sheep, Doctor."

The doctor rubbed one of the smaller skulls. "Why be bombastic, Governor, when there are other solutions? The Negro is a lesser species. Eventually, we will have to marginalize or eliminate them, as I have always advocated. I have never been a supporter of slavery; it perpetuated a Negro presence in the Commonwealth, when our true objective is to extirpate them from our lands. But my point, Governor, is to use them to our advantage. We can let the Negro vote as long as we assure that they will vote for our man. Matthew is a war hero and is popular with the Negroes. He will receive widespread support. He will be our candidate. The Negroes will be doing our bidding."

Both Governor Smith and Mr. Moffett nodded. To them, that made great sense.

Matt stared at the skulls. *Could one of them be Paul's?*

"My daddy has big plans for you!" proclaimed Jessie. She kissed him all over his head. "A baby, a big place in the government, so many things. We will get everything we want!"

Matt wore his crusty Confederate uniform. He usually refused to even wash it. He wanted it to smell like gunpowder, like mud, like blood. He wandered around the farm, carefully avoiding contact with anyone. Sometimes he would carry his gun and run through the trees, firing rapidly, loading and firing, hitting tree after tree. At the end, he hyperventilated. Then he stood and stared.

Did he want to run for office? Serve in the legislature, perhaps in Congress? Hobnob with sycophants and Northerners, with men who breathed dusty air and had nothing of value to say or think? He detested his trips to the new black church being constructed. Jessie forced him to chat with all the African Americans, treat them with kindness, and offer his support. But he kept seeing that line of black soldiers charging at him from the small creek outside of Appomattox. And then he saw Paul, and he watched Paul die.

Izzy marched into the house one day, demanding to see him. He was indignant! It was early September; the days were shortening, the nights become a little less suffocating, and the trees were starting to bear fruit. Matt had carefully avoided Izzy during these many months, wondering why he even stayed here. Jessie did not want him to depart. She thought that his presence would convince Luke to remain on the farm. "Remember, Luke cannot leave. Ever."

"They is all free now," he reminded his wife. "Luke can leave if he wants."

"No!" she snapped, grabbing his collar and slicing her eyes into his skull. "Never. Do you understand me? He can never leave." She stared at him harshly.

"How can I assure that, Jess?" Matt asked, pushing her away. "He can do whatever he wants."

Jessie smiled, showing her brown, crooked teeth. "There are ways," she said, "to do anything. The Negroes are not as smart as us, and that includes Luke. Luke can never leave."

Matt just nodded; his mind floated elsewhere.

Paul is dead. What if Luke knew the truth?

Izzy marched into his home, irate. "Matt, I have sent five letters to the Biggelows, inquiring about Paul. I have received nothing back. What can I tell you? Something is very fishy about that."

"You accusing me of not sending them?" Matt asked.

"In fact, I am. You or your pretty little wife. Or maybe you received a response, and you burned it. You are all crafty devils. You lost the war, but you won't surrender. Look at you, Matt. What would your father think?"

"You better watch it, Izzy," Matt said to him, squeezing his gun tightly, feeling his crusty old uniform against his sweaty skin. "You got a lot of enemies around here. You better watch your mouth."

Izzy laughed. "Enemies? A bunch of idiots is what they are. My people have known a lot worse than the bumbling blabber-mouths who gather in the doctor's den every night. Are those my enemies, Matt? Let them talk all they want. I'm not afraid of the putrid gas that they spew from their asses."

No one in town wanted Izzy to stay. Not even Colonel Stompmonger.

"The Jew is riling the Negroes," the doctor told Matt one after-noon. "He is helping them with their quest to acquire land from Mr. Marsh. He is persuading them to demand more from us, more civic support, partial ownership of their former farms, repa-rations. We have docile Negroes, Matthew. We don't need this Jew twisting their vulnerable brains into thinking they need more."

"What do you want me to do, sir?" Matt asked the doctor.

The doctor smiled. "Just keep an eye on him. Colonel Stompmonger, who is a good and pious Methodist, he was appalled at what your Izzy said at the church when we first gath-ered the Negroes there, when he threatened to bring more Jews into the town. Your Izzy may have been joking, or he may actu-ally have a nefarious plan to do just that. But either way, it made the colonel uneasy, and I have fed that unease with other stories about your Izzy, stories that make him look like a rabble-rouser who is a threat to the peace and the harmony of this town. We will take care of Izzy. You just make sure he stays on the farm during the duration of his time with us. Let it be known too, Matthew, that under no circumstances can he ever return here with your other slave, with Paul."

Paul is dead. A skull on a shelf. A corpse in a stream. Would he have shot me first?

Izzy marched into Matt's room on a cool Saturday in September, sliding past the dozing Jessie.

"I want some answers," Izzy demanded.

Matt lifted his gun, startled by Izzy's sudden entrance. Slowly, he lowered it.

"I hear the harvest is coming in good; that's what they say," Matt uttered, turning away. "I'm glad for all your help. Sorry you'll be leaving us next month, but I know you want to get back home."

"I'm told that I can't take Luke with me," Izzy said, jumping into Matt's line of sight. "Your precious wife told me. But that's a discussion for another day. I think you people have a hard time grasping that you can't tell Luke what to do anymore."

"You can't neither," Matt snapped, caressing the muzzle of his rifle. "He can do what he wants."

Izzy nodded, a grimace sewed upon his face. "What do you know about Paul?"

Matt saw the line of Negroes firing! Instinctively he lifted his rifle, and Izzy slapped it out of his hand.

"Tell me, Matt. What the hell do you know about Paul? Your villainous wife made a comment to Luke that Paul was gone forever. All those letters you allegedly sent with no answers. What do you know?"

Matt grabbed his gun from the floor, his mind exploding with rage. He stared at Izzy. All he saw was the face of a traitor, an enemy to his father and to his brothers. "I seen him die," said Matt, seething.

Izzy's face dropped; his complexion became pale. "When?"

"I seen it on one of the last days of the war," he said. "He was in a line of Negro troops shooting at us, trying to mow us down. And then I look up, and I see Paul. And I know, in that instant, that he saw me. And then the next thing I know he grabbed his chest, and he went down into a stream. We got pushed back. But at the surrender, I looked at the Negro troops, and he wasn't there. He got hit in the chest. I seen him die." Somehow he felt great pleasure saying that to Izzy. He smiled and almost laughed.

Izzy paused. "Then you don't know he actually died?"

"I seen him die! If he didn't die, he'd of shot me dead. It was him or me. God chose him."

Izzy laughed. "Did you shoot him, Matt? Is that what happened? He never would have shot you. Do you know that he named his son after you? You do know that, right? Did you shoot him, you bastard?"

"I didn't shoot him," Matt said. "But he had no right to be there. No Negro did. He would have killed my boys. I was glad to see him die."

Izzy turned away from Matt. "And what about all the letters? You never sent them, did you?"

"Jessie, she ripped them up," Matt told him. "You is a pest, Izzy. You overstayed your welcome. Once the harvest is over, we want you gone from here, never to come back. And don't you dare touch Luke. He ain't going nowhere. This is where he belongs. It's his land. He got nothing in New York without Paul being there. I'm his kin; you ain't nothing. I'll make sure he knows that."

Izzy shook his head. "What can I tell you? What the hell can I tell you? The devil shows his face, and it's the very face that I trusted and cared for my whole life. What the hell can I tell you?"

"What, now you going to tell me all about your people and their suffering, Izzy? You know what? Maybe they deserve it. Maybe it keeps happening to them because they is nothing but snakes in the grass. After harvest, me and the men of this town, we is happy to escort you on the way back to your Jew home up North. And guess what, so is Colonel Stompmonger ready. Ain't no one here much cares for you. Well, maybe the Negroes, but that ain't exactly a ringing endorsement. And what can I tell you about that?"

Izzy laughed. "Well, Matt, I will be happy to take leave of this slice of hell. But rest assured, Luke will be by my side. Don't think I'm not telling him everything you just told me. And he's not quite as dumb as your little wife thinks he is."

Matt lifted his rifle and pointed it at Izzy's head. It would be so easy just to take care of this situation here and now. There would be no questions asked. No one would miss him. No one would care.

"You going to kill me too, Matt? Like you did to Paul?"

Matt put down the gun. He turned away. "Go," he whispered. Izzy nodded and slipped out.

"Paul isn't dead, Izzy," Luke told his friend after Izzy relayed the news. "Matt is just saying that. Matt is in a tough place right now. Give him time. Be patient."

"He shoved his fucking gun into my head," Izzy shouted. "What more do you need?"

"Be patient. He didn't pull the trigger. He never would. He's worried about Paul. But Paul's not dead."

"What are you, God? Is that what you think you are now, Luke?"

"I would know. I feel Paul's presence in me, in this place. I would know. And I feel him stronger than ever!" He paused for a moment. "I'll come with you to New York. I thought about it, and as long as you promise me we will come back, I'll come with you. I want to see where you lived, experience your life and world, meet Paul's wife. And I want to see Elana."

Izzy shook off that last sentence. He told Luke that he was glad of his decision to make the trip.

But now, on a cool night late in September, Luke was all alone. A soft wind rustled the trees. Near him sat the new red raft, almost complete, ready for a chilly dip in the pond once the harvest ended. A large bowl of red grapes lays half-eaten on his wooden table. They were sweet and almost perfect. Next year, with a few adjustments in the sediment distribution along the irritation stream, they would be even better. But as he sat there, Luke was uneasy. Where was Izzy? He did not like to be alone. And Izzy was never in town this long.

Suddenly something blocked the moon's bright illumination, and Luke looked up. Jessie stood in the doorway.

"I'm not here for fun," she said. Her blue blouse sat low on her chest, with her large breasts bursting out. Her protuberant belly was like a watermelon shoved over her gut, round and nearly perfectly dimensioned. The baby was due in January. She always seemed to know when Izzy would be gone.

"Hi Ms. Jessie," he said, reverting to his linguistic depredation that so irritated Izzy. "I's is so happy to sees you here. How is you doing? How is Massa Matt?"

"I need you to know, Luke, that if you garner any thoughts about leaving here with your friend Izzy, I want those out of your mind immediately. Do you understand me?"

Luke looked at her. "I's is thinking of joining him just for a bit, Ms. Jessie. I's be back before—"

"You shut up, Lukie," she snapped. "You are going nowhere. If you dare even try, there will be consequences that you may have a difficult time bearing. Don't forget what happened on that day in May. There is a baby brewing in my belly. I feel you in me all the time. I can't not have you. It's you who I want. You who I need. And I won't let you go. Ever."

Of course, Luke remembered that day all too well.

It was a warm May day. Matt had been back for only a couple of weeks, and Izzy was in town to speak with Colonel Stompmonger about a plan to sell the Union army some of their crops. Luke sat outside the cabin, enjoying a moment of sun and rest. And then Jessie came.

She told Luke to undress and then proceeded to rape him. She threatened many things if he did not comply. On this day, he was able to satisfy her, and she put on her clothes and smiled.

"You know, Lukie," she said to him, as she sat on his lap and kissed his head, "I am ripe."

"What's does you mean, Ms. Jessie?" he asked with some consternation in his voice.

"That I'm ripe, Lukie. That my womb is ready to be impregnated. That what you and I did today, that's why I wanted you so badly. Your seeds entered my womb today, and they have every chance of becoming my baby. That's what I'm saying, Lukie. You may be a father by next year."

Luke was stunned. She had always done just the opposite, only invaded him when she was not ripe. What could she be thinking? "Ms. Jessie," he said, "that's won't be good, not good at all. You can'ts does that. What if the baby is a Negro? What would you does if that happened? Ms. Jess, please tell Ol' Lukie here that it isn't true."

Jessie laughed. "We have to have some fun in life, Lukie," she said. "Adventure and uncertainty are what I thrive for more than anything! It's a dull life I live, with a dull husband and a dull existence. I need a little thrill. And this is it!"

"But, Ms. Jessie!"

"Don't worry, Lukie. We don't know if I'm even pregnant. And I've been fucking Matt day after day for the past two weeks, although his seeds can't seem to ever sprout. I can't take a chance of being childless by relying on his impotence. Maybe this time it will work. I gave him first dibbs. Yesterday, I fucked two of Colonel Stompmonger's men, nice young boys, happy for my company. And today I fucked you. And so, Lukie, if I do become pregnant, then we won't know who the father is until January, when the baby pops out and reveals itself. I hope it will be yours! You are my greatest conquest. You are the most satisfying of my men. I so hope it is yours."

"But, Ms. Jessie," he pleaded, although he knew there was nothing now he could do to change what had already transpired. "If it comes out black, what will you say? They ain't gonna allow that. They'll kill it. They'll kills me too. Oh, Ms. Jessie!"

"Don't you worry, Lukie. I will spare you. I'll just tell them someone else raped me. Some Negro from another farm. And then I'll offer to let you raise the baby. It will be a scandal, but it will pass, and we will have our baby. Besides, I learned from daddy that sometimes when a white and a Negro have a baby together, sometimes the baby still comes out white. That's what happened with Mr. Jefferson, or so my daddy says. Don't fret! Life is an adventure. And I want to always live it with you!" She kissed him on the head and slid out into the late spring warmth.

Now, five months later, a baby grew within her. *Whose baby was it?* Often Jessie wandered over for some "fun" and to tell Luke that she felt that the baby was his and that made her very happy.

Today her message was even more firm. "I know it's yours, Lukie. That's why you can never leave."

"Your friend Izzy is leaving us, and I for one am happy," she said, sitting by his side, chomping on some of his grapes. "But you won't be joining him. Do you understand me, Lukie? You will stay here with me forever. You will never leave. I won't let you. You are less free than you think. We still have power over you. I don't want to think that way, Lukie. I really would wish you'd want to stay. This is your land, and I am your girl. And I am carrying your baby, or so I hope. But if you think otherwise, or if that vile New York Jew tries to steal you from me, I do have a certain power to make sure you never leave."

"Ms. Jessie, please, I's will be back. I's just want to find my brother, is all, and I'll's be right back."

She nodded her head no. "Paul is dead. Don't you know that? I'm sure you do; Matthew told me that he told your friend already. But besides that, Luke, there is nothing up there for you. You belong on this land. You tell me that all the time. And I need you."

Luke said nothing. He just looked into her eyes, pleading.

"I will tell you this, Lukie. If you leave with Izzy and the baby comes out black, as I know and hope it will, I will tell daddy that Ruth's two boys raped me. That they always rape me. And you can be sure daddy will make sure that they hang from their necks. If you leave with Izzy, that's exactly what I will do. Their death will be on your hands. And if the baby comes out white, well, I'll still tell daddy that. If you stay, I won't be so cruel. Cruelty is not in my nature, Lukie; I only resort to it when I must. If you stay and the baby comes out black, I'll blame in on the Henderson slave, the one who died in July of dysentery. That way no one has to suffer for our love. I wanted you to know that you have a choice. You can leave if you want, since you think you are a free man. But if you follow that path, then two men will die because of your decision. Or you can stay, and all will be right with the world. So, you see, Lukie, you are still my slave in many ways. You always will be. I'll never let you go."

She kissed him on the head and slithered out.

Luke sat for a moment, and then he took a deep breath. In the end, did it matter? She was right. He belonged on this land. He could never leave. And yet, he so wanted to find Paul in New York, to see his nephews, to visit Izzy's world.

"We are stuck," he whispered to the red raft. "There is no escape. Such is my fate. Such is my life."

Paul was not dead, or so Luke knew. In the end, he latched his hopes and dreams upon that reality.

Now he longed for Izzy to return. Where could he be? He wiped Jessie's lipstick off his face and stared quietly out the window, waiting, wondering. Old Rag hovered above him, waiting too.

45

Four horses galloped along the dusty road as a hazy sun set over glowing blue mountains. A man dashed in and out of the woods, awkwardly, hardly knowing which way to go. It was clear he was confused, and afraid. The horsemen maintained their pursuit, keeping the man in their sight, following closely. The group's leader pointed to two of the horsemen, beckoning them to the left.

"Cut him off," he yelled.

His voice was muffled by the white sheet that draped his face, as it did all the riders. Two horses shot ahead of the running man, sliding past him as he disappeared again into the shadowed forest, falling more than once, getting up, running, stopping, and then running again. Suddenly as the man exited the woods, his path was blocked by the two forward horses. The other two horses came behind him. The man looked left and right, thought about running back into the protection of trees, but then just stopped and sat down.

The group's leader leaped from his horse and approached the man, his face obscured by a white sheet. The other riders followed. They surrounded him.

"Izzy Snout, stand up. We have a message for you," the leader shouted, his voice a bit muffled by the sheet. "We mean you no harm. We're here simply to deliver a message."

Izzy stood. "Haven't you idiots ever heard of just using the mail?"

No one laughed.

Izzy Snout had become a pest. He needed to be removed. Quickly.

Colonel Stompmonger agreed.

"Do what you must, Doctor," the colonel said two days earlier, sitting with the doctor, Matt, and Jessie in the doctor's study, slurping down a dish of chicken and dumplings. "We are instructed to protect the Negroes, and we will, under all our capacity, do just that. But as to Northern salesmen from New York who are causing you trouble, frankly we will leave those issues in the hands of local authorities to handle. I want no trouble in my district, Doctor. If this Izzy character is causing trouble, do what you must. All that I must insist on is that you cause him no physical harm. I don't want an investigation. You never know who he knows up North. People have connections. I don't want him harmed."

"Of course," the doctor said, smiling. "We do have a code of ethics here in the Commonwealth; we are Christians, after all. This man is not a Christian. He does not share our values. We simply would like to persuade him to go home and to not take any of Matthew's hired help with him; that is all."

With a mouth full of food, the colonel said, "Doctor, be my guest."

"I want you to know everything going well with the church and school we are building for our Negroes," the doctor stated, changing the subject. "A new teacher is on her way from Pennsylvania."

"I painted her bedroom myself," Jessie said, smiling. "It's very pretty. I look forward to meeting her."

"You have been nothing but pleasant to everyone, young lady," the colonel said. "You are a testament to your father's good rearing. A few of my men have told me that you have showed them great hospitality here. Thank you for that. Oh, and Doctor, that reminds me. Several of my men have completed their tours of duty. We have two new soldiers coming to us next month to replace them. One of them is also attached to the Freedman's Bureau and will be a liaison between the army and Mr. Marsh. There is something about him I think you need to know."

The doctor peered at him.

"He is part of one of the Negro units that fought in the war," the colonel said. "I don't know how I feel about it. He will report to me and to Peter Marsh. But you better tell your men to be nice to him. I want no trouble. I want him treated with the same level of authority as you give to me and my men. Do you understand?"

The doctor smiled, a snarling smile. "Of course, Colonel, of course. Why would we not? I am sure you know that we are good Christians and have a code of honor and decency that extends to all people regardless of the color of their skin. But this Negro soldier's presence in our town is even more reason for us to make sure that Izzy Snout is no longer in Washington when the Negro soldier arrives. Negroes are very susceptible to being manipulated by poisonous ideas; their brains are not as well-formed as ours, as I am sure you well know, Colonel; it is a scientific fact."

The colonel nodded. "As I said, you do what you want with the Snout man. Is there dessert today?"

"Of course, Colonel. As I have said, we are very cultured people. How could there be a meal without a good dessert to finish it off?"

Matt sat on his chair, his mouth closed, but his brain indignant. A black soldier? He didn't know how he would react. Images of that day on the creek flooded him again. He closed his eyes. He just wanted it to go away.

Now, two days later, four horsemen surrounded Izzy, having chased him down a dark dirt road as he was returning home from the church. Finally, after a good hour of running, they had worn him out. "Then what do you want?" Izzy asked. "What is this message you needed to send to me, to cover your faces for, to drive your horses into the night just to find me? And by the way, you idiots, I know who all of you are. I recognize your damned horses. How dumb are you? I see you there, Matt," he said, pointing to a man in the back. "Glad you are part of the message brigade. But really, couldn't you just walk over to my cabin and tell me in person? Was all this so necessary? And who made your sheet? Your devilish wife? You know, she cut out the eyes all crooked."

Beneath his white sheet, Matt grimaced. He grabbed his rifle and lifted it. Why not just shoot him? But of course, he was told not to. So, like a good soldier, he played his part. He said nothing, letting John Towson, a farmer from fifteen miles to the south, take control.

"Mr. Snout," the farmer said in a muffled voice, "your welcome in our humble town is at an end. We know that you declared your intentions to leave us after the harvest, and we are pleased for you to do just that. But we have some advice for you, and it's advice we all think ain't something you should ignore. First, we insist that you leave alone; you don't take any of the Negro workers with you from the Cocklin farm. They don't belong with you, and you won't get too far out of town if you try, if you get my meaning. Second, you don't never come back. Not never. And you don't bring no new Negroes back down here. And no Jews neither. That's all we ask, Mr. Snout. We don't need to purchase none of your pants and shirts no more. So really, there's no reason to come back."

Some of the riders chuckled.

Izzy stood and walked up to Matt's brown horse. He stared at the sheet on Matt's head. "You are brave, brave men with great Christian values and the pinnacle of Southern chivalry, of that there is no doubt," he said. "I do appreciate the message. Now, I will take leave of you. You must be tired after riding so long on the legs of other beasts. So, go home, eat a nice meal of lard and ham, take a bath, and be so proud of yourselves for the good deed you've done tonight. I so, so very much appreciate it. And Matt, your father would be so proud of you, of the man you've become. He must be farting in his grave now. I can almost smell it."

Matt grasped his gun.

The other men mumbled to each other. "Well then, Mr. Snout, what is your answer?" asked Towson.

"I already told you," said Izzy. "I received your message. It was well delivered. I must admit that the sheets do need more work, but I understand this is all new for you, and yet your performance was very sharp, and I applaud you. Good job to you all! Well done!"

More mumbling.

"Then is that a yes, Mr. Snout?"

"It's not just a yes," Izzy said. "It's a ringing endorsement." Izzy clapped his hands. "Well done to you all! I am very impressed. Very impressed indeed."

After some more mumbling, the farmer beckoned the riders onward, leaving Izzy in a dusty cloud.

After riding for about a hundred yards, Towson brought his horse by Matt's. "He did say yes, right? You know him the best, you must know."

"I guess," Matt said. Although he didn't really care. He just wanted Izzy gone. He wanted everyone to leave him alone.

The Shenandoah's mountains glistened with red, gold, and orange—just a hint of the magnificent rainbow that was to be. Izzy had picked the day on which he would travel back up North. It was going to be after Sukkot, the Jewish festival of the harvest, which ended in the middle of October. He floated in the cool pond near Luke, who finally completed his refurbished red raft. Jessie had wandered by to see it, but Izzy's piercing stare chased her away. Matt had been absent for many days.

It was Thursday, September 21, the day of Rosh Hashanah, the Jewish New Year. To Izzy, as to most Jews, a more important day did not exist other than Yom Kippur itself. On that holiday, the last day of September, when Jews fasted and prayed, God decided who would be put in the book of life and the book of death for the upcoming year.

"We have between now and then to convince God to help us," Izzy said, splashing the water and dunking in his head. "Once God makes His decision at the end of the month, He's probably going on vacation for a while, because there's nothing more we can do to change His mind. Either we get written into the book of life, or we get screwed. And the way things are looking here in the great town of Washington, we are royally screwed."

"It's OK, Izzy," said Luke, smiling from the raft. "You don't have to worry. Go up and get Paul. I will be fine here. You will find a way to make things right. I will be OK here with Matt. This is where I belong."

There was little Izzy could say to convince his naive friend otherwise, and so he didn't even try. After relaying to Luke the threat uttered by Matt and the other horsemen, Luke told him everything. About Jessie's repeated rapes. About his being the potential father of her baby. About her threat to murder Ruth's kids if he dared leave the farm with Izzy. At first, Izzy steamed, swearing to kill them all, to do something, anything, so that justice was attained. But the more he fumed, the less he could find any feasible ways to make it happen.

"They have us by the balls," he finally told Luke. "I never thought they were smart enough to do it."

"Don't worry, Izzy," Luke said, his smile serene. "I am safe on this land. I always will be. Somehow, everything will work out. I know it. I feel it. I feel Paul every day."

"You really think Paul is still alive?" Izzy asked him, grasping for even a slither of hope against the wave of odious misfortune and cruel fate that stuck him so voraciously.

"I do," Luke smiled. "And you will find him and bring him back home."

After the night of the four riders, Izzy left the farm only once to speak with Colonel Stompmonger, to let him know what happened.

The colonel's aide greeted him at the door.

"The colonel is not available," the aide said, in a thick Boston accent. "He said he heard what happened, but there's nothing he can do, because you don't live here, you are a visitor, and thus it's just a local matter. He advises you to talk to the doctor if you have a grievance."

"The fucking doctor?" Izzy shot back. "Really? He's the one who masterminded all this."

The young soldier merely shrugged. "That's all the colonel has to say. He says it's a local matter that the United States Army has no jurisdiction over. He advises that it's best to go back up North."

Izzy spurted out a barrage of curses, but then he turned and marched away. The gig was up. His options had been stripped away. The doctor owned this town, even the United States Army.

For the next two weeks, up until Rosh Hashanah, he stayed away from Matt and Jessie, never drifting from Luke's side. He would stay through the harvest. And then he would leave, all alone. In the back of his mind, he wondered if these people would even allow him that honor, of if they would instead pursue him beyond the town lines and turn him into a corpse, a forgotten visitor from the North who no one would ever realize had been murdered by their noble Southern hands.

"Ruth said she's making a special meal for you tonight, Izzy," Luke told him. "Apples and honey, egg bread, and then some chicken with potatoes. Matt is letting her cook just for you."

"Oh, he must be quite the saint, your brother Matt. We better make sure it's not poisoned."

Luke laughed. "Don't worry! Jessie would never allow him to poison me!"

Izzy splashed him and laughed as well.

They sat in the cabin that night as Ruth served them a feast. Its odor filled the room with succulent reminders of times gone by. Ruth's boys joined them, although they said very little and were quick to leave. Ruth did not stay long either. She had made an apple pie, and she brought out a bottle of red juice.

"It's from Luke's grapes," she said. "It's not no wine or nothing, isn't old enough for that, but the best darn juice I ever did taste, thanks to our boy Luke, best juice ever. The perfect treat for your New Year, Mr. Izzy. We sure is gonna miss you when you leave us."

"I'll miss you, Ruth. But I'm not leaving quite so fast. We've got a lot more meals ahead of us. And a lot more fruit picking. Which apples did you use for the pie?"

Ruth smiled. "When you go and eat it, you tell me Mr. Izzy. I wants it to be a surprise. You tells me. But here's a hint. It's more than one type. It may be my best pie yet."

Izzy hugged her and kissed her on the cheek. She smiled and then wandered out into the cool night.

Crickets chirped, and the fading glow of mountains filled a black sky.

"Three years ago, in New York," Izzy told Luke, as the two of them dived into the meal, "I think I had the best New Year's ever. I can't believe it was so long ago. I went to the temple as always, with my friends, with Abe and the others, and my mind was elsewhere. These were my people; this was my ritual; every year I had been with them, and every year I relished their company. But this time, it didn't feel right. I usually went to Abe's house for Rosh Hashanah dinner, but instead I went home. He seemed happy to let me go, even encouraged me to leave. By the time I reached my apartment, I quickly found out why."

Luke peered at him eagerly.

Izzy leaned back on a bale of hay as a streak of moonlight dripped through a crack and illuminated his face. He smiled serenely, as he chewed an apple with his mouth wide open.

"I walked into Paul's apartment first; he had told me to stop by. And there they all were. Paul, Smiles, James, the kids. And," he said with a pause, "Elana. Beautiful Elana. She yelled out, 'Surprise,' and then draped me in a hug. I can still feel it now. The touch of her body against mine, especially on that night; my God, Luke, what can I tell you! She was radiant! It was a time I'll never forget. As sad as I am to have lost it, to have lost her, I am glad to have had those precious moments."

"She loved you," Luke said to his friend. "And that means that she still does!"

Izzy shook his head. "It doesn't matter. That was three years ago. Before her jackass of a husband came back and swept her off her feet, stealing her from me. Who can blame her for making that decision? She had her people, I had mine. We were fooling ourselves to think we could change all that. What can I tell you? God likes to give you candy, and then when you bite too much of it, you get sick. He just wants you to taste it once in a while and then move on, back to hard bread and moldy cheese. That's the life of a Jew. I'm glad to have had some candy."

"What did you eat for Rosh Hashanah dinner?" Luke asked him.

Izzy smiled. "Your brother made a feast, right in Elana's kitchen. The best challah I have ever tasted in my life. A perfect spiral circle, crispy and brown outside, tender and sweet inside. It melted in my mouth. Like I never had before! And Elana brought apples and honey and fruit and a fruit tart for dessert. And Paul, he made chicken with apricots and prunes, in a sauce that danced on my tongue. I can taste it even now." He paused for a moment, a few tears trickling down his cheek. It was hard for him to speak. "I ate it sitting on Elana's lap. She rubbed my hair, what little I had. She liked so much to make me happy. And

I was happy that day! Those were my family. I never thought it would end." He paused for a moment and looked up. "Fuck you, God. You hear me? Don't give me that joy and then take it away. That just is mean!"

Luke laughed. "Well, here we are, having a wonderful dinner, you and me. And maybe next year Paul and Smiles and the children will be with us. And he will make you that bread again."

"Yea, and maybe your new baby with Jessie the demon will join us, and maybe the doctor will invite his skulls as well, and a few of Washington's finest can join us with sheets on their heads. It will be quite a gathering." He paused for a minute, then looked into Luke's eyes. "The next Rosh Hashanah after that one, two years ago, was maybe the worst one I ever had. I didn't even know when it was. I was in a Southern prison and just hoped I would get out alive. And now, here we are again."

"Yes," Luke exulted. "Here we are, me and you, having a feast in the cabin. For me, this is heaven itself! You came down here and saved me, Izzy. You gave up everything to do that. And you did! This year I'm going to fast with you on Yom Kippur. I'm not going to eat or drink anything! How can God not reward us if the two of us together honor Him in that way?"

"Well, thank you, Luke, but I didn't save you. I'm going to leave you here at the mercy of these people, with the devil woman who may spit out a Negro baby, and heaven only knows what will happen after that, especially with your brother being the lunatic he is, and the doctor in total control over Stompmonger and everyone else. I wish I could take you away; I wish you'd let me. I understand why you won't. They have us by the balls, but still, I wish you would. I don't know what they'll do to you. And Luke, I don't know if I ever can come back. They will shoot me if I try. They may even shoot you."

Luke stood and draped his arm over Izzy's shoulder. "It will be OK," he said. "I will see you again. Somehow, I will. I feel it!

And Paul too. And Matt will come back to us. We just have to be patient, Izzy. This is our magical place, with the flow of Old Rag bathing us and making sure that we stay together and remain safe and happy all through time."

Izzy nodded. "Damned war," he said. "Who would guess that freeing the slaves would turn the world into a pile of shit?"

"It didn't," Luke said. "It gave Paul a family and allowed him to finally put his talents to use. It gave you love, and that love is forever, despite what you might think. Matt and I, we are in the clutches of something sinister, something that snuck in here from outside the gates. We will fix it all! And then we will be together on our farm, free to do as we wish—to climb mountains, to grow our grapes, to wallow in the pond on clear warm nights, and to sit in the cabin and talk and eat and laugh and be a family again. You do have your family, Izzy. It's just as you imagined. You have to have hope."

Izzy smiled. "Well," he said, hardly convinced, "at least we have this apple pie. It smells wonderful. Although I may need your help to figure out which apples she used in it. I don't want to lose that challenge!"

"Don't forget," Luke said, "she could have put in some pears too."

"Ha!" Izzy laughed. "See? That's why I am glad you are on my side."

Crickets chirped throughout a still night. The shadow of Old Rag shined on the pond, bouncing upon its ripples, watching over everything. Two men laughed inside a tiny cabin, forgetting life for a moment, and simply enjoying the present. A new year had begun today. No one could know upon which roads it would send them.

"I sure miss Paul's challah," Izzy mused. "And Elana's blue eyes. And her touch. But I am glad to be here with you."

"Me too, Izzy. Me too."

46

S aturday, October 7. The third day of Sukkot. It was a pleasant day, with a bounteous rainbow of colors sprinkled across
the mountains. A pasture of tall, yellow sunflowers swayed
at the far side of the pond, planted by Paul many years ago, an
eternal reminder of the beauty that habituated this unique spot
on earth. Thick white clouds hovered above them; the air was
warm, and the sun shined brightly.

Izzy and Luke sat in a makeshift lean-to that they had constructed in honor of the holiday. This was a sukkah, a small
dwelling built out of apple twigs, hay, and vines, in which Jews
traditionally lived and ate for eight days at the end of the harvest. Izzy told Luke about the holiday, and Luke insisted that they
celebrate it together. They ate all meals in the makeshift dwelling, and sometimes they sat and peered over the farm from its
perch. Luke built it at the edge of the pond. Brilliant colors and
streaks of sunlight reflected off the pond's clear, cool surface.
Sometimes the two of them sat here silently, thinking. Often,
they leaped upon the red raft or flicked pebbles across the water.
There was not much to say. Both felt that despite nature's spectacular display, their world was coming to an end.

"I'm going to leave tomorrow," Izzy told Luke that morning.
"The doctor and his idiot friends expect me to leave next week,

and frankly I don't trust them. They'll probably chase me down and kill me if they can, although given their feeble level of competence I doubt they'll be able to do it. If I leave tomorrow, they'll all be in church, praying to their God, and they won't expect it. I've been practicing on my horse for the past few weeks, trying to feel a bit more comfortable on it at higher speeds. Anyway, I know you thought I'd be here for another week, but I think this is going to be best."

Luke nodded, staring forward. "I understand" was all he said.

"I wish you'd come with me, Luke. The harvest is done; the grapes are in our gut. You've got nothing here. You can't trust a damned thing Jessie says. She may kill you either way. She may kill Ruth's kids either way. Or she may do neither. And don't count on Matt to protect you. I hope you know that."

Luke peered deep into the pond. He smiled. Memories flashed through his mind and heart. He could not remove those recollections from the reality of this place. Somehow, in some way, it would all be right again. It had to be! What perverse universe would rob from its soul so perfect a world as the one that once flourished here?

"I admit I'm a bit scared," Luke told him. "You have been my protector, my friend, and my window into everything that is right and good. I will be alone without you, Izzy. But I haven't given up hope. I'm not there yet. I imagine that on a fine spring day, as I am irrigating the grapes, you will come through those gates with Paul at your side and embrace me. And Matt will join us. And we will all be together again."

"Yea," Izzy mused, tossing rocks into the pond, creating ripples that split Old Rag's rocks and blurred the mountainous colors. "Maybe. Maybe I will. We can always hope. But promise me this, Luke. Promise me that if things go sour here, you will run. You will run as fast as you can. I'll be in New York. I gave you my address. I want you to run there. Do you promise me that?"

595

Luke nodded. "I will bring a whole suitcase of grapes for you and Paul."

"Sure," Izzy said without any inflection in his voice. "That would be great."

"Paul is alive, Izzy," Luke insisted. "You will find him."

Izzy smiled and put his arms over Luke's shoulders. "This is sure a beautiful farm you built, my good friend. I'll miss it. And you. What can I tell you?"

In the early afternoon, Izzy brought his small, brown horse to the sukkah, and Ruth's sons fastened a pair of saddlebags on it. Ruth filled the bags with fruits, vegetables, bread, jams, and bottles of spring water. Izzy placed a few sets of clothes atop the treats, food for the horse, and several sundries that would be necessary to complete the two-week journey to New York. Little was said as Izzy packed up. They made sure to do it outside the view of Matt and Jessie, who were nestled in the main house with the doctor.

Time passed quickly, and soon enough Izzy's bags were almost full.

"I'll's be back tonight with the boys," she told Izzy after loading the last of her food. "We's going to have one last feast, rights here in this vegetable house, and I figure we can eat right off the roof! We will eat like kings tonight, Mr. Izzy, of that much I assure you."

Izzy hugged her. "I love you, Ruth. I can't wait!"

When she wandered away, a whiff of silence overcame the farm as Izzy and Luke sat alone on their perch yet again, quietly, their minds drifting, their eyes staring forward. Bright, warm sunlight bathed them as they enjoyed each other's company for the last time.

An hour or so later, a boy rode onto the farm. It was the milk delivery boy; he brought Matt bottles of fresh milk a few times a week. Izzy called him over as he rode by.

"Hey," Izzy said standing up and approaching him. "You have any extra bottles to sell me? I could use two or three."

"I'm afraid not," the boy said. "All I got is what is already accounted for. Why you need it? For the visitors?"

"No, for me," Izzy said. "What visitors?"

The boy looked at Izzy with wide eyes. "Well, you may have heard that there is a Negro soldier coming to town to work with Colonel Stompmonger? You heard that, right?"

"Sure, but what does that have to do with milk?" Izzy asked.

Luke pushed himself up and wandered closer to Izzy and the boy.

"Well," the boy continued, "turns out that the Negro soldier, he got to town this morning, and he tells the colonel that he is from this very farm. That he lived here before the war as a slave. And this is where he is coming, right now; I just passed him on the driveway. With his wife, I venture, and three little boys. Oh, and there's a white lady with him, very tall, with red hair, and she's got two kids too, and she was running ahead as fast as I ever seen anyone run. She fell right in the mud and threw off her shoes. She's probably right at the gate now as we speak. She was running so fast by me and called out, is this the farm with Izzy Snout? And I said, who in God's name is Izzy Snout?"

As soon as he heard those words, Izzy dropped to the ground. His face turned white, and tears streamed down his cheeks; they dropped from his eyes like an open spicket, trickling upon the leaves below, scaring the milk boy away. He looked up into the sky. He seemed almost delirious. "Please, God, promise me, promise me that this is not one of your cruel jokes! Promise me that!"

Luke peered at the gate. It swung open, and through it dashed a tall woman with bright red hair that swung back and forth, her yellow dress splattered with mud, water pouring out of her eyes as well. She was running fast right at them. Luke almost exploded with joy.

"Izzy," Luke yelled at his friend, tugging him up. "Izzy! Get up. I think that's Elana! What a glorious day! It's just like I have dreamed all along. My God, Izzy, get up; she's almost here."

"Is it her?" Izzy asked, his tears so thick that he could barely see. "It can't be her. It can't be. How could it? And Paul? All of them? It can't be, Luke. I won't look. It just can't be. This is just a dream. It's a cruel joke. I can't even look!" He was crying hysterically.

Luke lifted him up. He turned his head toward her. "Look," he said. "It's not a dream. It's just like I said."

And then, she pounced on him, crying hysterically herself, kissing every part of him—his head, his face, his lips—as Luke looked on. They fell to the ground, and she kissed him all the more. He was crying so hard he could hardly breathe, choking on his tears. He kissed her too, his arms rubbing her long red hair, crying and laughing, touching her everywhere his arms could reach.

"My beautiful, beautiful man," Elana cried out. "The love of my life. Thank God! Thank God!"

"Oh my God, Elana, my Elana, my beautiful Elana," he said, his face wet, his arms draped around her. "How? How can this be? My beautiful, wonderful girl? How can this be?"

She pushed him away for a moment, her face smeared with mud and tears, her bright smile and piercing blue eyes digging into his heart. "Because, my dear man, my beautiful man, it has to be. I always knew it had to be. Love is a rare gift that you find if you're lucky, and I found it. I found it in the heart of a kind and wonderful man. And let God stab me in the chest if I'm dumb enough to ever let it go. I love you so much, Izzy. I love you like life itself. Thank God I found you again!" And she leaped upon him, kissing every part of his head and face, as their tears saturated the warm ground below, and they both fell upon the leaves, rolling around in the dirt.

Luke stood over them, grinning. Every fiber in his body filled with pure joy. He had known all along that they would return. And now, upon this hallowed land, on this perfect day, it had come to be. What a turn of events! He stared at Izzy and Elana. And he glowed!

Elana stood up, holding Izzy's hand, and walked to Luke. She smiled at him, a smile reeking of pure goodness. And then she hugged him. "Finally," she said. "I get to meet Luke, who everyone always talks about. Thank you for taking care of my Izzy. Thank you. Thank you so much."

Just then the gates flew open, and a woman came through, holding a small baby. Four children followed, two white, two black. Luke marched toward them, his heart beating fast, his mind dancing upon the clouds. What a day this suddenly became! Tears dropped from his eyes now. He could not stop them. He was filled with such powerful emotion that he had never known before. He felt dizzy, as if he was floating; he was smiling. It had all happened so quickly, right on the precipice of despair. But still he walked toward the woman, so beautiful she was, and then the woman saw him.

Her face lit up, and a huge toothy smile filled it. She handed the small baby to an older, white girl who lagged a bit behind, and then, with gentle strides, she walked over to Luke. Still smiling, she put her arms out and held his shoulders, looking into his eyes, staring.

"Luke," Smiles whispered. "Luke. How long I have dreamed of meeting you! You are Paul's guardian angel, his better half; all he talked about was getting back to his Luke. My God, you are just like he described. And this beautiful farm! I want to see everything! Your grapes! Your red raft! Everything you created here! The mountains! Old Rag! I heard all the stories. And now here I am, with you, here in this place that you and Paul created." She wiped the tears from his eyes, her smile not fading even a bit. "You're just like I imagined you to be. It all feels so right now. Everything is right and perfect."

"It is," Luke said, nodding. "Everything is. And you are just like I hoped. My brother's wife. And his children."

She called the boys over. "This is Matt," she said of the small, rambunctious one. "And Jake here, say hi to Uncle Luke," she said, as the boy waved, seeming just a bit stunned. "And my little baby, he was born when Paul was off in the war; this is James, named after my guardian angel, who as fate would have it died just when my baby was born." The baby chuckled. "And he is in the very image of my James. I need to tell you all about him. About everything! And I want to hear all the stories. I want to know everything about Paul! I only get his version. I need to know the Luke version."

"You mean, the true version?" Luke laughed, now wiping his own tears, his mind still spinning. "Where is my brother?"

At that moment, Paul appeared at the gate.

It had been four years since the brothers had last seen each other on that rainy November day when Paul darted off the farm to a fate unknown. Now here he stood, just like when Luke last saw him. Paul stopped for a moment and peered at his brother, a tranquil smile on his broad, powerful face. He wore a blue soldier's uniform that seemed to suit him just fine. It lay on his body and chest as if it were meant to be there. His posture, his very demeanor, spoke a confident pride that now coursed through his veins. He had returned here a free man, a man of accomplishment, a father and husband, a man whose every passion and skill that had been thwarted by these fences and the heinous forces that locked him in this place finally budded and flourished after he ran away and found himself. Now he was back, a man and not a slave, here to be with his brother again, as he had promised.

They looked at each other for many minutes, neither knowing what to do or say. Finally, Luke stepped toward his brother, and then Paul ran at Luke. He grabbed Luke's cheeks and nodded, peering deep into his brother's eyes. And then he buried Luke in a hug, squeezing him, and Luke did the same; they could not let go. For the first time in years, Luke was where he so needed to be. In an instant, just as the world seemed ready to collapse, in an instant on this glorious day, everything became right.

"I love you, Brother," Paul said to him.

"I love you, Paul," he said back. "They said you were dead. But I never believed it. I knew you would be back."

Paul nodded, not relaxing his grip. "Of course, I'd be back. I promised I would. I was a bit dead, but death can't get in the way of what I knew I had to do. I had to free you, Luke. That's all I ever wanted to do. You are my other half. I'm nothing without you."

"Me too," Luke whispered, crying. He then slipped out of the hug and looked at his brother.

"I saw your wife," Luke said, holding his brother's broad shoulders. "Your beautiful children. I want to get to know them all. Mom and Dad would be so proud of you! Just like I am! And Izzy's Elana, she came with you. He loves her so much; he was sure he lost her. Just like he was sure we lost you."

"No," Paul smiled. "Izzy is a cynic. He should have learned more from you. You can't get rid of us that quickly. I don't die easily. And love doesn't die easily either. Just like you taught me, Brother; dreams sometimes do come true. This is the moment I had been waiting for. And here it is! I hope Izzy is OK; he must have been so sad. I'm just glad he came down to be with you."

"He was ready to go up to New York tomorrow," Luke said. "He had given up hope."

"Well, you can't imagine that man in love," Paul laughed. "He is a different person. Elana swept him off his feet. She helped Izzy to laugh and smile like I have never seen before!"

"And then her husband came back," Luke said. "He told me that it all fell apart after that."

Paul nodded. "And of course, our Izzy, as is his wont, gave up hope. But there was never doubt about what Elana wanted.

She just needed the opportunity. She's like you, Brother. She is a dreamer. She has faith that goodness will always triumph. I used to laugh at people like you and her. But not anymore. Life tried to piss on us, Brother, but here we are despite that. Screw them!" He hugged Luke again. "I love you so much, Brother. I want you to get to know my family; I want them to be part of your life too. They have heard so many of my stories."

"So," Luke smiled, "I suppose it's up to me to actually tell them the truth."

"I suppose it is!" Paul laughed.

"Have you seen Matt?" Luke asked. When he uttered those words, Paul's grip loosened, and he went just a bit limp.

Paul pushed himself away. "There's a lot we have to talk about," he said to Luke. "About Matt, about so many things. Has he tried to hurt you? Him or his evil wife?"

Luke nodded no. "Not Matt," he said. "He is playing his role. But he can't ever hurt me."

"His wife?"

To that question, Luke had no response.

That night, they gathered under the sukkah. A bright moon shined down upon them, the visage of Old Rag dancing off the pond. There was so much laughter, the patter of little feet, and a burst of color and joy that rivaled even the leaves of Virginia's peaks in early October. Ruth was there; she had prepared a feast. She ribbed and joked with Paul, shared stories with Smiles that sent her on the ground hysterical, held his baby, and ran around with his boys, telling them how shocked she was that the crazy little boy she knew was now their father. "Just to proves miracles are still possible in this world," she said. She brought out the last bottle of Luke's grape juice, which she had been saving to slip into Izzy's cache early tomorrow morning before he left.

"These are your grapes, Brother?" Paul exulted, throwing his thick arms over Luke's neck. "So, you finally did it. You grew your grapes. This is the best damned juice I ever tasted!"

Elana walked by, holding Izzy's hand which as far as Luke could tell she had never stopped grasping since they fell on each other this afternoon, and she kissed Luke on the cheek. She smiled brightly. "You grew these grapes?" she asked. "Paul told us all about it, but I never have tasted anything so rich, so full of love. Now I know why he always talked about the grapes. You poured yourself into them. Luke, you are everything I imagined you to be. You are someone very special."

Luke nodded. "As are you," he smiled. "Anyone who is wise enough fall in love with this misunderstood man and whose heart is ten times bigger than he is willing to admit, is a special person."

"I know," Elana said. "Now, if we can only get him to eat with his mouth closed."

"That is a much bigger challenge!"

"Tell me about it!" Elana laughed.

"Tell me," Luke asked her, "how are you here? Izzy received a letter from his friend that you were fully back with your husband. Izzy was sure of it. He said that you could never leave New York, your husband, your family, and your way of life. And then, you came. You came to be with him. I don't think he believes it even now. Look at him. He is stunned. He is smiling again! Things are rough for us here; I won't lie to you. He was ready to give up. And he had no intention of trying to find you in New York. I almost think he was afraid to go back there just because he was scared to see you. He loves you so much, I could tell, but he had given up all hope."

"When does Izzy not see the dark side of everything?" Elana asked him.

Luke smiled. "Never! That's because, as you know—"

"I know," she interrupted. "His people don't ever catch a break."

Luke laughed. "Yes, exactly. That is precisely what he would say!"

"Well, Luke, I don't blame him. Once my husband returned, every freedom Izzy and I had instantly disappeared. It was hard for both of us. And I had to play a role; sometimes it was very public; I had to hold his hand and smile with him and be by his side. I begged Izzy to understand; it was all for show. I didn't love my husband, and he didn't love me, as much as he pretended to. I only love one man, one precious gem of a man, a man who I want to smother with hugs and kisses every day of his life, but which fate and circumstance prevented me from doing."

"Then how did you come here? How did you change that?" Luke wondered.

Elana shrugged. "I knew that it had to happen, that I had to be with Izzy. Unlike your brother, I am a religious enough woman to at least believe that God would not fill my heart so deeply with passion and then take it all away. When your brother and Smiles decided to come back to Virginia, after your brother had shored things up in Washington to make sure he could come here safely, at that moment, I knew what I had to do. Ernie was in Albany, elected to the legislature. So, I wrote to him to tell him that the children and I would be helping Smiles and Paul move down to Virginia, and he seemed not to care. My children don't know their father well enough to care either. All they knew is that they wanted to go wherever Smiles was going. They love her more than almost anything else. And they knew all about Izzy. They didn't quite know how much I loved him, but I told them both on the way down here. I told them that I did not expect we would ever go home, and they just hugged me and told me that as long as we stayed with Smiles and Paul, with Jake and Matt, and as long as I was happy, they would be happy. It was much more diffi-cult to leave my sisters and parents, and so I left things open with them. They don't know about Izzy, nor that I am staying down here forever. I hope to see them again. But all I know is that every mile I drifted away from New York and every mile closer I moved to be with Izzy, the happier I became, the quicker my heart raced, and the bigger my smile grew. Just being with Paul and Smiles and the kids away from all the clutter and garbage of New York filled me with a pure happiness that I don't think I've ever felt before, only matched by that moment this afternoon when I laid eyes on my Izzy for the first time in almost two years."

"I can see it in your face," Luke said. "Your joy."

"And I can see it in yours too," she said, hugging him. "To have your brother back."

A few soft shrieks burst through the gathering. It was little Matt being pestered by Elana's daughter.

"Excuse me for a second, Luke," she said.

Elana gathered up the children, making sure they had enough to eat and that they didn't wander into the pond. They all seemed to be having a wonderful time! Luke remained with Smiles and held James. He kissed the small boy repeatedly, and the boy just laughed and laughed.

"Just like my James," Smiles told Luke. "Laughing all the time, always happy. Let me tell you about him. About my James." They meandered by the pond and sat on a rock beneath the moonlight.

In the corner of the sukkah, Izzy and Paul sat down. They feasted on Ruth's hens.

"If Matt lets me into the kitchen," Paul said, "I'll make you that bread you like. I learned a lot in the army. We did more cooking and eating than actually fighting."

"Matt told me that you died," Izzy said, bridging that subject for the first time. "He said he saw you on a creek; your gun was pointed at him, and then someone shot you; you grabbed your chest and fell down dead in the creek."

Paul looked down, and he smiled. "That, my friend, is partially true," he said. "Although I couldn't shoot Matt, that part isn't true. Frankly, I couldn't shoot anyone or anything; I had no idea how to aim the thing let alone shoot it. And I was shot in the chest. I lay there wondering if Matt pulled the trigger."

"He said he didn't," Izzy told Paul. "Although he said he wished he did."

"I'm sure," Paul said. "Or he did and doesn't want to admit it. I would have been here months ago if it weren't for Matt. There's a lot I have to tell you, Izzy. A lot of shit going on."

"Then," Izzy probed, "how the hell did you survive getting shot in the chest? Are you the second coming my people have been waiting for?"

Paul nodded. "I was dead, as far as I knew. I was bleeding, I couldn't breathe, I had no life in me. The last thing I remember was falling on a stick and watching air bubble out of me. Turns out, that saved my life."

"The stick? How?"

Paul smiled. "There was a Negro doctor embedded in our unit; he had been trained in Europe, but he couldn't get a job in this country. So he worked as a train coach steward and was just an infantry man in our division, not even a medic. You know, you have to be a moron like our doctor here if you want to practice medicine in the United States. The last thing they want is smart doctors telling them that using leeches and potions is not how you save someone's life, especially if that guy is a Negro."

"How about getting to the point," Izzy laughed.

"So, there I lay in the river, pretty much dead, and this man, William Peach, from Ohio of all places, he sees what happens. And he immediately knows what to do. He takes a shell casing, which is pretty much just a hollow tube, and shoves it in my chest. Suddenly all this air flies out, and I wake up. I don't remember it, but he said I was cursing Matt. That's the first thing I said, talking totally out of my head. It took me days to actually remember what was going on, long after Lee's surrender, which, unfortunately, I couldn't even attend; I was still lying in a bed."

"How the hell did a stick and a bullet casing save your life?"

"What Dr. Peach told me is that when the bullet pierced my chest, it cracked a bunch of ribs. Those ribs popped my lungs from inside, and the air escaped into some cavity around my lungs and filled it up, like a balloon, and put pressure on my heart and lungs and started shutting me down. Then, when I fell on that stick, some of the trapped air escaped and relieved the pressure. By a lucky break, Dr. Peach was behind me and knew exactly what to do. When he put in the shell casing, he let all the air out, and he kept that casing in there for several days until the lung puncture healed itself and stopped leaking. I'm sure any other doctor would have put a sheet on my head or a leech on my leg, but this man knew what to do; and even though they tried to kick him out of the hospital tent, he told one of the nurses what he did, and she made sure to keep the casing there, hidden from the idiot doctors, who certainly would have pulled it out. I haven't seen him since that day. But I owe him my life, and one day I'll be sure to repay him."

Izzy patted Paul on the back. "Well, I'm glad for it, you lucky bastard! That's all I can say. Paul, I hope that Matt didn't pull the trigger, but I wouldn't put it past him."

"I know," Paul said. "Believe me, I know. I have a lot to talk to you about, Izzy. A lot of shit has gone down since I came home." He lifted an envelope from his front pocket. "This is what it's all about. This is the only reason I am back here. Matt did everything in his power to block me. And there's a lot of shit still to come. I need your advice. Luke, he still loves his brother. I can tell just talking to him for a couple of minutes. But you have lived with Matt and that bitch of his, who I hear is pregnant, so I need to run it all by you. I want this to be a happy night. I don't want to ruin it. But there's a lot of shit that's still ahead of us. We really have to talk."

Izzy nodded. "There's a lot of shit on this end too, Paul. What can I tell you? Matt is not to be trusted. And his wife has done things that might make you choke her right here and now if I told you about them. When we talk I may need Smiles there too; I know she's the only person on earth who can tame your passion and stop you from doing what your heart and brain tells you is right. They have us by the balls. Maybe you and me can figure out how to get out of it. But you have to promise me that you'll approach it calmly. That's all I ask."

Paul smiled. "Come on, Izzy. You know me. I'm always the paragon of restraint."

"Ha, yes, always; you never get yourself in trouble. But what I am going to tell you, it's far worse than anything you could probably imagine."

"Then don't tell me tonight," Paul said. "Today is a day that I want to remember for nothing other than the perfect day it is. When we tell our children and grandchildren the sagas of our lives, October 7, 1865, will rank as one of the great days of our family history. We will celebrate it with song and food and happiness. I don't want anything to get in the way of that."

Suddenly a twig snapped in the woods. Paul stood up, Izzy right behind him. They walked toward the trees. A bright moonlight shined down, illuminating a man standing there, slumping, in a tattered gray uniform, holding a gun. As Paul came closer, the man barely budged, just a silhouette devoid of any perceivable emotion.

"You want to join us, Matt?" Paul asked the specter. "You can bring your wife too. It is a family affair."

"I don't want you here," Matt's voice called out, quietly. "I want you to be gone from my home."

"Matt, Brother, you know that it's my home too. You talked to Colonel Stompmonger, to Mr. Marsh. You know what's going on. Why not come by and join us?"

But for the chirps of crickets and the distant banter from the pond and sukkah, Paul's request was greeted by silence. Then, he saw the figure lift his gun and point it at him.

"You going to shoot me again, Matt? You tried once and failed. You plan to try again? You know that if you kill a Union officer your ass will be in jail for the rest of your life. Is that what you really want?"

"Maybe it is," the figure called back in a crackled voice. "Maybe I don't even care where I end up, just to get rid of you; that's all I want. I didn't shoot you the last time. Although I wish I did, 'cause whoever did it sure as hell didn't do a good enough job to finish you off."

Paul laughed. "Well then, shoot me. At least then I know that Luke will inherit the farm, and your wife will be tossed off it like the piece of garbage she is. The papers are all filed, Matt. Do what you want. I would be happy to take a bullet for my brother. We both know what the outcome will be."

"I hate you, Paul!" he cried out. "And you too, Izzy. I hate you both."

With that, the specter turned and retreated to the woods.

Izzy and Paul stood silently for a few minutes until the footsteps dissipated into the night.

"Well," Izzy said, draping his arms over Paul's shoulders. "I'm so glad Matt came to join us and spread his joy all around. What can I tell you? As you can see, we have very interesting times ahead. And that's just the tip of it. Believe you me. It goes deeper than you can imagine. But that's for tomorrow, not today."

Paul put his arms around Izzy. "My friend, seeing you, seeing you with Elana, seeing Luke, being back here—nothing can damper the happiness I have today. Let's go back to the party. Let Matt wallow in his miserable life. We have so much to be thankful for. I feel sorry for that bastard; that's all."

Izzy nodded and chuckled. "Thank God Luke fasted; that's what I have to say."

"What does that mean?"

Izzy laughed. "For Yom Kippur, he fasted. He said that if he did it and I did it, God would have to reward us! And now look at what He has done! To see Elana again, to be in her arms, and to feel her love. My God, Paul. Even I am blown away by today. Maybe my people do have a chance after all. What can I tell you? Thank you. Thank you for everything."

"No, Izzy, thank you. For taking care of Luke, and of me. It's no wonder Elana loves you. Who wouldn't? My father would be so pleased to know how faithfully you stayed true to your word. Elana is lucky; she knows that. And so are we. To see such a hard ass like you melt like a little baby, wow; that makes it all worthwhile."

The moon seemed to shine all night. When October 7 morphed into October 8, no one noticed. Not even the kids. Young James continued to laugh. The boys threw sticks into the pond. And food continued to slide into everyone's guts. Luke sat back and watched it all, sitting on a bale of hay, smiling, as serene as he had ever been. Paul was back. He could hardly even believe it! The world could never be wrong again.

47

Paul stomped into his house bursting with fury, beckoned here by Ruth, who told him that his father wanted to see him right away. "For the terrible thing that you done," Ruth said, "I hope he gives you a spanking you may remember for the rest of your days!"

Paul stuck out his tongue and marched away. He didn't care. He didn't care about anything! He would never forgive his father for what he did. He told Dad that every day. He refused to listen to his father's explanations, just covering his ears and yelling whenever Dad tried to talk. *He can't just send my mamma away like she's nothing and say it's OK! He can't do that!* So, Paul didn't care about what Ruth or his dad or even Luke or Matt had to say. He was not OK with it, and he never would be.

The previous night, Paul had chopped down a bunch of baby pear trees. He was mad, and he did it in a rage. He hoped his father found out. It served him right. He wished the whole farm would burn!

"You put that tongue back in your mouth lest your daddy cut it off," Ruth screamed at the defiant boy. "You get in there now, or God be my witness, I will drag you in by your hair, you terrible, ungrateful boy!"

"There is no God," Paul said to her. "And you couldn't catch me even if you tried. You're fat and slow."

"And you is pigheaded and dumb," Ruth countered. "Get in there now!"

"Make me!" Paul lost himself in the fields for a while; it was a cool autumn day. He slid through a patch of rotten pears and apples. He threw a few. Finally, after enough time had passed, he turned around and entered the house.

Dad was in the main room. He called Paul in and asked him to sit down. He was kind as always, more tired than usual it seemed, thinner, maybe a bit sad. He stood up and looked Paul in the eyes.

"I don't care about anything you have to say," Paul said to his father. "And I don't care about you!"

Jake nodded. "I know," he whispered. "And you are right. You are always right, Paul. I'm not here to punish you about them pear trees or nothing else; I'm here to say I'm sorry."

Paul peered sideways at his father, not knowing how to respond. He breathed hard, still angry, but now a bit confused. "About what?" he finally asked.

"For doing a terrible thing," Jake said to his son, pacing across the room. "When I think about what I done to your mom, what the doctor and some of the others told me I had to do, Paul. I can't sleep at night. I had a choice. We could have left this place. It's just a place. That's all it is. Your mom, she begged me to let her be sold away. She wanted you boys to be raised here, to make a life here. But she was wrong. I was wrong. I let them force me to do something horrible. The doctor, he has a way of convincing you to do something that deep down you know isn't right. But it was wrong, Paul. And I want to tell you that. I'm going to get your mother back; I'm working on how to do that right now. And then we will deal with the consequences. If we have to leave here, we will leave as a family. We're not a family without your mom. I can't even breathe without her being here. I am sick every day."

Paul stood stunned. This was not what he expected. He said nothing at all.

"A few weeks ago, I drew up a will for the farm," Jake continued. "I divided it between you three boys in case I ever die. I gave it to a lawyer in town I know, Horatio Moffett, who looked it over and said he would register it. Next thing you know, I'm called into the doctor's study. He had the will in his hands; Mr. Moffett had given it to him. The doctor ripped it up. He said if I ever try to do something like that again, he would make sure that my life would be hell from here on in. So, you know what I did, Paul?"

Paul nodded no, listening in rapt attention. "What, Daddy? What did you do?"

"I'm only telling you this, Paul. You are my only son who really understands the world and the only son who I really trust. Do you understand me? You can't tell no one else. Ever. Not Matt, not Luke, not Ruth. No one. Do you understand?"

Paul nodded, staring intently at his father.

"I took my horse into Warrington," he said. "There is a lawyer there named Silias Gondard. I know him to be a fair man; my friend Robert told me about him, and I trust Robert like he's my own brother. So, I showed Silias my will. He said, 'Jake, there ain't a man in the county who will honor this will, who will allow a farm to be given to Negro children. It's just not the way things are. But tell you what I'm going to do. I'm going to file it. I'm going to file it under your son Paul's name. If things change, if slavery ever does end, if circumstances allow it, it will be here, at my office, and Paul, because that's who you name as the beneficiary and arbiter of your will, if he is of age, and if Negroes have any rights in the future, Paul can come get it. It will be officially sanctioned by our office, and he can execute it. I don't think that day will ever come, Jake, but if it does, and you are not alive, then make sure that your son Paul knows, knows to find me. It will be here.'"

Paul stared at his father. He was speechless. Every bit of fury and indignation melted from his veins. He only saw the man he had always loved, the one who had betrayed him, but who now had come back. He loved his father so much. "So, you going to try to get Mom then?" he asked.

"I'm gonna try," his father said. "But if the doctor gets wind of it, I don't know what will happen. And Paul," he said, walking over and putting his large hand on Paul's tiny shoulder with so much affection that it felt like an angel's touch, "if something does happen to me, you have to remember the name I told you, Silias Gondard, in Warrington. The will is there. You can't get it now. But should some miracle happen that gives you freedom, then you need to get it and claim your right, and Luke's right, to share the farm with your brother Matt. Do you understand?"

"Yes, Daddy."

"You remember the name?"

"Yes, Silias Gondard."

"Good. Commit it to memory. Never forget it. Hopefully, you will never need to even think about it. Hopefully, I will retrieve your mother, and we will all be together, away from this terrible place, somewhere where we can just be a family and live our lives together. But if not, I don't want you ever to forget. I love you very much, Paul. You are the passionate one among us, the one who knows right from wrong and is willing to fight for it. Don't ever lose that quality. I was so wrong in what I did. I hope you can forgive me."

Paul leaped over and hugged his father. He was so filled with joy. He loved his father very much.

Two weeks later, Jake developed a respiratory illness. The doctor treated him, and within days he was dead. Paul sat in a corner of the farm and cried. "Silias Gondard," he said, over and over again. He would never forget that name. Maybe, he hoped, one day, he would need it, to make his father's wish come true. *Silias Gondard, Silias Gondard, Silias Gondard*—over and over again he said the name through his tears.

It was a cool October day many years later as bright leaves dropped rapidly upon the long dirt road to Warrington. Paul rode alone upon his brown horse, wearing his bright blue Union uniform, to meet with Peter Marsh. He had an envelope in his hand, one he had been holding tightly for weeks. It took a lot for him to secure this. He met with Reverend Garnet, who introduced him to the head of the Freedman's Bureau, General Otis Howard, a burly jovial and pious man who seemed genuinely interested in Paul's case, and he tracked down the law office of Silias Gondard, run now by a man named Joshua Beachum, as Mr. Gondard died in the war. Jake Cocklin's will was there, addressed to his son Paul, sealed with a legal stamp, unopened. General Howard passed the letter to his legal experts, who informed Peter Marsh that Paul would be reassigned to Colonel Stompmonger's unit in Washington to be a liaison with the Freedman's Bureau; and that until the matter was settled, Paul would be a legal owner of Jake Cocklin's farm, along with his two brothers; and that Paul's family would be permitted to stay there as well. Only then did Paul gather up Smiles and his children and march down to Washington.

"No word yet," Peter Marsh told him, referring to the matter of the will, a copy of which Paul carried with him wherever he went. "It's in the legal weeds, or so I hear. There are so many other things going on with the bureau and with some of the other districts that I'm not sure how long it will take."

Paul nodded. "What about my mother?" he asked the lanky man sitting behind a tall, wooden desk cluttered with piles of papers. His heart beat fast when he uttered the words. His mother. Her image flashed across his eyes; the love and intelligence that seeped from her pores filled his heart with both hope and melancholy. How much he wanted Smiles and his children to meet her! How much he wanted to see her after all these years, to embrace her, to thank her for everything, to tell her how sorry Daddy was for letting her go.

He had done some preliminary research to ascertain where she had been sent when she was sold, and he passed that on to General Howard, who sent word to his agents in North Carolina to search for any slave bearing her name and who had arrived from Virginia. It was like trying to find a needle in a haystack, or so General Howard told him. But Paul was committed to doing whatever it took to find her, even if it meant galloping down there once the matter of the farm's ownership was settled to do some investigation himself.

Peter March shuffled through a few papers and then pulled one out.

There were two papers clipped together. The top one was white and crisp, the bottom one yellowed and tattered. He handed them to Paul.

"On that matter, my friend, I do have some good news."

Paul's heart pattered. He stared at the awkward man, who smiled and looked at Paul in the friendliest of ways.

"We found her," he said. "She is alive and well, on a farm outside of Ashville, in the mountains of North Carolina. We sent word that you and your brothers are safe and sound and that you are looking for her. Like you instructed us, we told her not to go anywhere, that you would come get her once you could. According to the agent, she laughed and then said that you probably already got yourself in a heap of trouble trying to find her, if she knew you like she thought she did, and that she couldn't wait to see her boys, but that she wanted you to wait at least until November so she could put her affairs in order." He held his hand out to Paul and gave him the two pages. "On the top is her location, and on the bottom is a letter she wrote to you and your brothers. This is very good news. Very good indeed!"

Paul seized the letters and nodded. He could not utter a word. He wiped his eyes before any tears might smudge the precious papers he now held. Finally, he squeaked out a "Thank you, thank you so much," before crying just a bit and turning his head away.

Peter March nodded. "If only everything was as simple and satisfying as this," he said. "Can I give you a piece of advice, Paul?"

Paul, still emotionally overwhelmed, hardly able to think, anxious to leap on his horse and go snatch his mother away from the voracious monsters of the Deep South, peeked up at the kindly man and nodded.

"Listen to your mother," he said. "Obviously, she knows you. Don't get yourself in trouble in Washington and then be unable to get her. This is such an important moment in our history as a country and a people. That's why I am down here. But it's even more so an important moment for you and your family. This is a wonderful piece of good news, and I am so happy for you. But not all the news is going to be so happy. That's just the way it is. Reconstruction is not as seamless as any of us would hope. There will be ups and downs. Be willing to accept that, Paul. Don't be rash. Don't be angry. You've just been given an amazing gift, one that few will ever experience."

"And," Paul said, smiling, holding the papers tightly, "you're telling me not to blow it by doing something dumb or shooting off my ass to some of the bastards in Washington who are going to inevitably piss me off. I know. Believe me, I know. But I'm also not going to sit back and let them shit on me and my brother. I thank you for this, I really do Mr. Marsh. I will try."

Peter Marsh nodded. "The doctor, he has warned us that you are a troublemaker, that you could ruin the peace that has been established in Washington. I assume you and the doctor have a history?"

"Do you think I'm a troublemaker, Mr. Marsh? Is that how I've come off to you and to other people who work for General Howard?"

Peter Marsh, buried in his pile of papers, simply laughed. "You, Paul, are an intelligent, thoughtful, and forward-thinking man who is nothing of the sort. You know that I'm on your side, and I'll do anything for you, because you represent everything I am fighting for. But when it comes to the peace and the good-will in your town of Washington, I don't think anyone, especially Colonel Stompmonger, will be willing to threaten it; and to keep the peace going, we do need the support of the doctor."

Paul stood up and thanked Peter Marsh again. He left with these parting words: "It's not a peace in Washington. It's a deception. It's a rouse. The doctor is not the man you and the colonel think he is. I won't disrupt your precious peace, Mr. Marsh. But I won't sit back and let that man reinstitute slavery when so many of us fought and died to destroy it. Thank you, sir. I'll be back next week, hopefully for some more good news about the farm."

His mother was alive. He could hardly believe it!

That night he sat with Smiles and baby James. Cool winds blew from the mountains, and the soothing splashes of pond water and the echo of laughter had not faded a bit from the slave cabins. This place was alive! Paul felt so comfortable here with his family, with Izzy and Elana, with Ruth and the boys. Matt and his bride had not again showed their faces, nor had the doctor. Sometimes Paul peered at the big house, at the lights that flickered in the windows, and he thought of Matt. He wished he could have a minute with his brother, a brief time just to hug him and to say that all is forgiven, to tell him that their mom was alive and well. But then he felt Matt's ire and tasted the venom of his wife Jessabelle; he saw Matt with his gun pointed at him and firing, and he strayed away. He could not shake the deep hatred he had for everything festering in that house that had invaded his daddy's lands within these fences.

Smiles lay her head on his chest, as he rubbed her thick, luxurious hair. Her breath, her warm touch, soothed him as much as the wind and his joy of finding his mother. With her so close to him, he could only be happy. But there was so much out there of peril, so much that tugged at his very soul.

"I'm powerless, even now," he said to her. "I guess I always will be."

"Why would you say that now?" she asked him. "You found your mother! My goodness, what a blessing that is, for you and Luke, for all of us. Your mother! I can hardly believe it!"

"I know," he uttered, watching as little Matt ran through the cabin and then out the door. "And I should be happy. I'm an ungrateful son of a bitch, I know that. Just tell me so I can dig it into my head!"

"You are an ungrateful son of a bitch," she laughed. "But you're my ungrateful son of a bitch. And I love you more than love itself. And I love your heart and I love your passion and I would not have you any other way!"

He looked up in her eyes and kissed her, smiling. Then he placed her head back on his chest. "I love you, Smiles. You save my life every day."

"Someone's got to!"

"I don't like what you told me about the church," he said. "How they treated you. You know I already have a whole thing about the church in the first place! There are so many more productive things they can be doing. I talked to Peter Marsh about a grain exchange, an agricultural school, a farming co-op. Luke can help lead it and build it. And we should have a school that actually educates people to go to college and to be productive citizens here and outside of this piece of shit place; they are just learning the alphabet and how to rake up manure. It's time that the Negroes here stop sucking up to the doctor and his cronies and, instead, stake a claim of their own, do things better than the whites here ever did, get some political clout and education, and tell the doctor where he can shove his pills and potions. I will need to go talk to them; they're buying a bill of goods couched in the veil of a manipulative God, designed only to keep them subservient to their white masters."

"That's my Paul," Smiles said. "But I will tell you, they are very excited about their church. That's all they talk about. It's an AME church, a denomination of freedom, they say, and a pastor is coming from the North. That's all they can talk about. Colonel Stompmonger, he's a Methodist too. He's very excited about the church and the new pastor. Even your General Howard is a Methodist; that's what I learned today. They all think that this church will be a bridge to freedom. How you think they will react when you tell them how misled they are? Paul, I love you, but maybe it's best we focus on us and not worry about everyone else, at least not until we get the farm and your mother back."

Paul laughed. "You have no idea about my mom; she's worse than me," he said. "She'll really be pissed off if she learns they're putting all their resources and energy into a church."

"You know what I think?" Smiles said, kissing his chest. "I think all she'll care about is her three boys being alive and well and having grown into such wonderful, smart, and thoughtful men."

Apparently when Elana and Smiles visited the African American church in town—marveling at the spectacular stained-glass windows recently installed—some of the townspeople berated them.

"You tell your husband," a few of the white farmers said to them, pointing to Smiles, "that if he starts trouble here, that we ain't responsible for what might come next. And you tell your friend," he said, referring to Elana but not looking at her, "that we is a good, Christian community here, and we don't want no Catholics or Jews making a home here, bringing all their kin, and then turning this den of God into a home for heathens. You seem like a nice Negro girl, and we don't have a grudge against you, but we don't want no trouble here, and neither does the colonel or any of the Negroes. All has been good until you people showed up, so that's all we got to say."

"Thank you," Smiles responded. "As a woman of God myself, I certainly appreciate all your kindness and good words. As the Bible says, Leviticus chapter 19, according to my Jewish friend, 'God says you should treat your neighbor like you want your neighbor to treat you.' Words to live by, don't you think?"

"I wouldn't know, ma'am," the farmer said. "I don't read no Jewish bible. I just don't want no trouble. That's all. Have a blessed morning." And they rode off.

"So, they don't like Catholics down here either," Paul said with a laugh. "All of us must be quite the threat: Jews, Catholics, and a Negro in a Union uniform. These people are probably peeing in their pants at the sight of us."

"Everyone was nice after that," Smiles said. "The Negroes are so happy about their church. And they are setting up a school and also working on getting land. Give them some credit! Just because they want a church doesn't mean they aren't taking care of themselves. Remember how you treated Reverend Garnet when you first met him? Sometimes you make some pretty arrogant assumptions, Paul." She stood up. "I'm heading out to be with the kids. It's too nice to be stuck in this cabin. I love you."

"I love you!" he said, kissing her on the lips.

The afternoon darkened as a few leaves blew into the cabin, dancing down the walls. Luke wandered in from the fields and stood over his brother. His face was firm, almost devoid of emotion.

"They found Mom?" he asked. "That's what Izzy just told me."

Paul nodded. "Yes," he said. "She's alive and well. We can get her, Luke."

But that didn't make Luke smile. "Paul," he said, standing aside Izzy, who entered the cabin with him. "Me and Izzy, we have to tell you something. It's something very bad, something that may set you into a rage, that may push you to act in a way that will not be good for any of us, especially for mom, if she should come back. I need you to promise that you will listen to me calmly, that you won't rush out and start killing people after I tell you, and that we can all talk about it, the three of us, and how we should handle it. We need to figure this out before we think about getting mom."

Paul stared at his brother, his face dropping. "What is it, Luke?"

"It's not good, Paul," Izzy reiterated. "We may want Smiles here when we tell you. It has to do with your brother, and your other brother's wife. What can I say you don't know already? This world, just when it gives you candy, it throws a poison dart into your heart and takes everything away."

Paul forced a smile. "I've seen shit the last few years that has shaken me to the core," he said. "I'd like to think I'm a more reasonable man these days. Do me a favor. Luke, before you throw more shit on my head, let's both read mom's letter. She wrote it for us when they found her. I waited for you until I read it. Can we do that first?"

Luke nodded. "Of course," he said. "Can you read it to me? Then I can close my eyes and imagine her face and eyes. I so much want to see her again, Paul! I do. I can't tell you how overwhelmed and happy I am that you found her! Don't think I'm not. I'm just . . . I'm just scared."

"We all are, Luke. Every single day."

"How about if I read it to both of you," Izzy said. "And you both can drift off and think of happier days. I remember your mom so well. I see her in both of you all the time! I'd like to read it."

Paul and Luke sat by each other upon a small log, where they had shared space so many times before. Paul felt his mother's presence; he remembered his father on that day when Daddy told him that he had made a mistake and sought to rectify it. He put his arms around his brother and closed his weary eyes. Izzy read the letter.

My dearest boys,

I suppose I always knew that you would come for me. I just wondered why it was taking so long. Your father, I have heard that he passed away, and that the three of you built the farm into something majestic, something that reflects all that we tried to instill in you, and that the three of you worked as one to make that happen. That's all we ever cared about; that nothing would drive the three of you apart, not slavery, not the doctor, not this war. As I have said, the world outside our fences is one soiled by the dirt of history and humanity, but what lays inside, that must remain pure and untouched. I am not sure what state it is in now, and I don't care, as long as my boys have stayed true to each other against all odds and against a world that is filled with hate.

I will be waiting for you late in November. Don't come sooner; I need to shore up my life here. I have many attachments to whom I must say goodbye, many who I love and cherish, many who I have come to rely on and who rely on me. That will take time. When you do come, I want to see all three of you; I want to look at each of your faces and behold the men you have become, and I want to kiss you and hug you and make up for all these many years when circumstance pulled us apart, a pact I made with a cruel society, but one which paid off dividends beyond what I could have even imagined.

My dear Paul, my passionate and emotional son, have patience. My dear Luke, my pensive and thoughtful boy, have faith. And my dear Matt, the one who had to bear the greatest burden to keep our dream alive, and who lost so much at such a young age, know that I love you. I will see you all soon. And on that day, my life will begin again.

With all my love,
Mamma

Izzy put the letter down. "Does that mean we have to show it to Matt?" he asked.

Neither of the brothers uttered a word. Their eyes remained closed, as tears trickled down their cheeks.

48

"All of that is meaningless," Jessie said, her smile enlarging, her crooked teeth all the more visible. She peered hard at Paul as Matt looked on from the woods. "You think you have so much going for you that you come here with your fancy talk and your blue uniform and you can change everything. Well, I have news for you, boy. My daddy has one thing that you can never have, and that one thing means more than everything else, more than anything you can ever have."

"And what's that"? Paul asked, barely able to contain his rage.

Jessie showed her teeth. She couldn't wait to tell him.

Matt wandered through the farm stealthily just like he had done in the war, hiding behind trees, crawling along leave-cluttered moss. He wore his uniform and carried his gun. All for the Confederacy. All for General Lee and the Grays!

"Pick up your guns, men," Colonel Kemper shouted out. "The enemy is everywhere."

Matt slid by rotten pears, pine cones, tiny rocks. He lodged himself behind a large tree with a panoramic view of the landscape—the pond, the fields. He breathed deeply and watched.

Small boys chased each other, laughing. The tiny one kept falling down. A tall, white girl called the small boy over to the pond and splashed him. He chuckled and darted away. Two women sat on a log, chatting. Both had pleasant faces. He stared at them, drawn in. The boys ran all around them, hardly disrupting their conversation. Matt watched for a long time. A smile crept upon his face. His brain lightened; he felt a glimmer of joy.

It was long ago that he too had chased two small black boys around the farm. He pelted them with apples; the bigger one was always angrier than the other. And then he ran off. It was long ago that another man and woman sat upon a log, that same log, talking, smiling. He darted across an endless landscape of so much wonderment! A small stream trickled through the trees, twisting around rocks and along the fence, flooding the ground in places; Matt jumped over; he chased the boys, and they ran after him. A bright sun bathed him. He smiled; it was the best time of his life!

"When this war ends," a boy said to Matt as they sat in Petersburg—hungry, wet, cold, incessant mortar being tossed at them, their hope fading— "when it ends, and we go back home, it ain't gonna be the same. Not that I much care about slaves or that stuff, but I know, it ain't gonna be the same. We got to make something of it, make something new, make sense of all this fighting, make it so it made a difference."

"It did make a difference," Matt told him. "It has to. We didn't go through all this for nothing. General Lee, he'll make sure. It ain't like we lost yet either. We got a lot of fight left in us."

The boy nodded. "Maybe. But it will end, and it won't end good for us neither. Still, we got to go home and make a new world there, maybe a better one. Who knows? That's what I hope at least."

"Maybe," Matt said. And then he walked away

He peered again at the pond.

Both women stood and gathered the children. They faded away, their voices and laughter dissipating into a brisk breeze. He watched a bit longer. Where was Luke? Paul? He closed his eyes and imagined.

"How could you not have told me?" Jessie yelled at him after he wandered in the house. He peered at her, his mind squeezed by too many thoughts; he wasn't sure where he was or what he was. Did the war mean anything? Is this what it was all about? Is that what the boy in Petersburg was trying to tell him?

"What you talking about, Jessie?" he asked, perhaps a bit too snippety for her, because she shoved her face against his and wagged her finger sharply.

"You know damned well what I am talking about!" She hollered, her protuberant belly jiggling against his legs. "Your bastard brother Paul comes down here talking like a white man. An educated white man. My daddy says, looks like you educated yourself up North. And he says, no, he always talked this way; he just faked talking dumb so we would understand him."

Matt smiled a bit. That was a pretty good comeback by Paul. "What you want me to say, Jessie? And why do you even care?"

"I care because you were deceiving us all those years," she snarled Her breath reeked of sulfur. "You taught him how to speak, how to read? You educated him? And then you had him pretend he talked like the rest of them? What were you trying to accomplish, Matt? Just to make fools of us?"

"Luke talks the same way, Jessie," he said. "He's just as educated. He been fooling you all this time all by himself. And you went and fell for it."

She slapped Matt hard across his cheek.

Matt squeezed his pistol that sat by his side. He prepared to lift it.

"How dare you teach the slaves to read! How dare you! If I tell Daddy, he will be furious. And Luke? I will give Luke the punishment he deserves."

Matt shoved his wife away and walked to the edge of the room, staring at the wall. "What you think, Jessie? You think I taught them anything? You got to be kidding. You hear me talk? I'm an idiot compared to my brothers. While I was going to school and being educated by the morons of Washington, they was being taught by Mom and Dad. I would say they got the best of the bargain." He walked out the door and then turned to his wife, glaring at her face. "And don't you dare touch Luke. You stay away from him. He is my concern, not yours. You understand me?"

"I do what I want on this farm," she snapped back. "Don't you forget that. Don't you ever forget that."

He shook his head and then turned and walked away.

"Where are you going?" she cried out. "You get back here right now, Matthew!"

"I got an appointment with your dad," he said, wandering away. "Should be another enlightening experience for me."

Is this what he fought for? To spend his life with Jessie and be under the tutelage of the doctor? Estranged from his past, his brothers, everything he once knew to be sacred?

To be by the pond with those women, to chase the children, to embrace Luke in his arms! His mind drifted to the past; he saw his brothers in those boys; he could not shake it. His body trembled.

"We have a few matters to discuss," the doctor told him. A beam of sunshine splashed through the library windows, blinding Matt a bit as he attempted to look at the doctor and listen.

The doctor's docile black servant handed Matt a glass of tea and a small sandwich.

Last night he hid behind trees and watched them all eat, a tranquil smile sliding upon his hardened face. He had never seen Ruth happier, not for many years. He lay along the edge of the pond, slowly crawling forward, observing the boys. One of them was crying; he could hear Paul's voice. Izzy said something to make everyone laugh, and then the red-haired girl walked over and kissed him. The other woman laughed the loudest. She seemed so kind! He could not see Luke, could not hear him. Was he there?

Succulent odors flooded Matt's nostrils. Barbeque? He remembered time gone by, eating with Mom and Dad. This was their playground—Matt and his brothers, eating and then dashing away for another adventure. Sometimes, Momma would call them over for a nightly lesson; it was always something from history. She had a penchant for ancient Rome. Paul and Luke listened intently while Matt glanced away, wondering where he could find a good apple to toss.

"Matthew!" the doctor chided him, yanking his attention back into this time and place. Matt stared at the line of skulls; he imagined where he might be among them. "Are you listening to me?"

"Yes, sir," Matt said, squinting through the bright sunlight. "You was talking about Paul."

"I was," the doctor said, as he paced around the room, sipping his tea in a very dignified manner. "Paul. We will forget for the moment the fact that you deceived us about his education. That is no fault of yours; we will ascribe blame to your dear misled father, who sits six feet underground, hardly able to defend himself or acknowledge culpability. But, perhaps his educating Paul will be to our advantage."

"What you mean, sir?" Matt asked him, trying hard to stay focused.

"In his short stay here, Paul has managed to alienate virtually everyone. Highbrow talk in a Negro even alienates other Negroes!" He laughed at his own clever observation. "The Negroes do not like him; his arrogance and his disdain for the church rub them the wrong way. I had Jessie spread word to them that he is a heathen who denounces the very existence of God, which indeed he is. Paul is digging his own grave with the Negroes. And to Colonel Stompmonger, he is equally repulsive. He brings a Catholic and Jew into our community, he blasphemes the word of God (quite an affront to a pious Methodist such as him), and he threatens to undermine the peace that the colonel has established here with my succor. Paul is the best tool we have to keep the colonel on our side. The last thing anyone wants to see is an arrogant, educated, atheist Negro." The doctor laughed, sipping his tea.

"Paul is pretty persistent, Doctor," Matt said. "He got my daddy's will, and he got some big people on his side. I don't think he's leaving all that quick. Unless you want me to do something to help him to leave, if you know what I mean, Doctor."

"No, dear Matthew, I want nothing of the sort from you!" the doctor said, sitting down. "Paul will orchestrate his own doom. You need to stay clear of him; you can have no blemishes on your record. I have big plans for you, son. In a few weeks, I am bringing you to Warrington to meet some people who will help you to launch your political career. That is your only concern. We will take care of Paul. I have gathered many letters from prominent Washington citizens to declare that will a forgery."

"Is it a forgery, sir?" Matt wondered. "It sounds like something my daddy would do."

"It is a forgery if we make it so," the doctor said. "Truth is merely the image we choose to show to others. Let that be a lesson to you, Matthew. You will need that piece of wisdom when you enter the realm of politics." The doctor chuckled and then sipped his tea. "In just a few weeks, all those people will be off your farm; they will be banished from our sacred lands, and you will begin a new life, with a child and an influential career. Be patient. The reward for your loyalty and sacrifice is soon to come."

Reward? Is this what the war was for? To be trapped in a world that he abhorred? Sitting here, near the doctor, sunlight blinding him, a line of skulls at the edge of his vision, Matt felt like a slave to a different owner, the joy and promise of his youth having faded into some noxious fog that engulfed him.

All those people will be off your farm.

Those people. He slid past the bare grape vines. With his tattered gray uniform, he concealed himself well, the hovering sun blinding any who might otherwise reveal his stealth. The laughter of children intoxicated him. He could hardly get enough! It was as if his childhood had been transposed upon the very dirt where he and his brothers trampled. Despite all the battles and death he endured, all the confusion that dug at him after Appomattox, all his discomfort when with Jessie and the doctor, all his fears of the future, here with these people he found some solace. Lying here, hidden, he watched the children run and play and the adults affectionately embracing each other; this one thing made sense to him, and it pained him to be severed from it. He needed it so much right now. His eyes fell into a trance.

"Matt?"

A voice sliced through him from behind, and he gasped, grabbing his gun, twisting around. He looked up, into the sun, and there was the tranquil face of Luke staring down at him.

"Matt," his brother said. "I see you found my grapes. I told you that I would grow them. Next year the crop should be spectacular." Smiling, a gentle wind caressing his hair, Luke sat beside his brother and peered at the pond where the children were playing.

"You know," Luke said, "one of the boys is named after Dad; that's him, Jake. The other one is named after you, little Matthew, see him? Paul loves you. He always will."

"It don't matter to me," Matt snarled back, trying to look away. "Paul and them kids don't belong here. The world is different now. They ain't welcome. I want you to stay, Luke. I want you with me all the time. But not them. Not Paul. Not none of them!"

Luke's smile did not fade a bit. "You remember when we built this pond, Matt?" he asked his brother. "We owned our own existence then. And we still do! Nothing changed, Matt. We are still brothers. I love you, and so does Paul. You have to believe me. Those kids, they would want nothing more than to see their uncle Matt. Paul tells them stories about you all the time!"

"Like how I shot him and fight for slavery," Matt cried out. "That what he saying to them boys?"

Luke laughed. "No, he knows you didn't shoot him, and he knows you weren't fighting for slavery. We all know what you were fighting for. You were fighting for this place. And for us. We know that. Paul knows that. The stories he tells the boys are about Daddy and Momma, about us and what we did here, about how you did everything to save our lives and make us into the people we are."

Matt's head started to ache. He hardly knew what to do; he felt the need to flee. "I don't care what he says or does," he told Luke. "I just can't have him here."

Luke then turned and peered into Matt's eyes. Matt seemed stunned, hypnotized, angry, afraid, confused. He saw only his beautiful brother who did not have a bad bone in his body!

"Paul found Mamma," Luke said softly, handing Matt her letter. "She's down in North Carolina, healthy and well. She says that she wants to see all of us, all three of her boys. We should never doubt the love that flows around us in this place, Brother. It can't die, Matt. We are brothers forever; nothing will change that. Momma and Daddy are always watching over us."

Suddenly, Matt's head exploded. He felt himself running across the fields of Spotsylvania, friends and comrades dropping all around him. Guns and cannons blasted through his peace. The din deafened him. He stood up and tossed the paper back at Luke. "This is all your fault," he cried out, as a few of the adults near the pond peeked over. "I blame you for everything! You is the one who told me I had to play a part, marry her, pretend to like her and her jackass daddy. Well, look what it all did! Look what you done to me! You call that love, Luke? What you put me through? You get off my farm! I don't want to see you or any of them people again! You understand me? You get off and leave me alone!"

Matt rushed into the woods, dodging bullets, dancing around the trees as though they were enemy combatants. Cannon blasts shook the sky, frightening away the approaching darkness.

He ran fast, far away, breathing deeply, not knowing where to go, not knowing why. Why? What was it all about?

We got to make something of it, make something new, make sense of all this fighting, make it so it made a difference.

Where were the children? They had scattered away, frightened by his outburst. *Come back! Go back to the pond! It's OK!* The gunfire rattled him. So many dead! And for what? What was it all about?

And then he stopped, snapped awake by an incongruent sight. Jessie stood near the house, screaming at Paul, holding his brother's collar and spitting into his face with her every word.

"I just want to tell you, because my husband doesn't have the balls to do it," she told Paul through her spittle. "You will lose. And when that happens, I will pour myself a bottle of your brother's red juice, as putrid as it is, and I will toast your defeat and will cheer! And there's not a thing you can do about it!"

Hardly shaken, Paul slid out of her grasp. He seemed calm, so much different than the Paul Matt had known for so long. "You would like that, wouldn't you?" he said. "To stay on this farm all alone with Matt, you, and whoever's baby you are carrying in that gut of yours, whichever one of the people you raped and screwed being the father. Let's hope it's not black, Jessie. But regardless, you will never win. I have forces with me that you and your moronic father will never be able to defeat. In the end, I will prevail, and it will be me drinking that wine as I wave goodbye."

Matt stared hard as the words flew back and forth. What did Paul mean by that? By all of it?

"I'm glad you feel so confident, Paul," Jessie shot back, slicing through Paul's eyes, not demonstrating an inkling of fear from the husky man wearing Union blue. "This farm will never be yours. You see, my daddy owns this place. Not just the farm. But everything. Everyone. They all answer to him. Even the Union army, even the ones I didn't fuck, all of them, because my daddy has what you can never have."

"You mean deception, lies, race-baiting, fearmongering? Your daddy does have all of that. But those won't save him from the contingent of high-ranking men who have my back, men from the victorious side, not from the side of the losers."

"All of that is meaningless," Jessie said, her crooked teeth shimmering through her sinister smile. She peered hard at Paul as Matt looked on from the woods. "You think you have so much going for you that you come here with your fancy talk and your blue uniform and you can change everything? Well, I have news for you, boy. My daddy has one thing that you can never have, and that one thing means more than everything else, more than anything you can ever have."

"And what's that"? Paul asked her with a smirk.

Jessie showed her teeth. She couldn't wait to tell him.

"My daddy is white. You are a Negro. In the end, that's all that really counts."

Paul's face dropped a bit, as though she had hit a nerve. She spat at him and then marched away.

Matt darted off, deep into the grove of naked pear trees, breathing hard, his head pounding.

Along the edge of the trickling stream a man sat on a rock, chewing an onion. Matt wandered over.

"What did it all mean, Stonewall?" Matt asked the man, who looked into Matt's eyes and smiled.

"Well, Matt," he said, his face serene, his eyes a piercing blue. "We put up a good fight."

"But for what, Stonewall?" Matt asked him. "What did we fight for? I mean, here I am, and nothing makes sense. Win or lose, I ain't done nothing. I ain't where I want to be. It all feels wrong!"

Stonewall laughed and put his arm over Matt's shoulders. "You know what I fought for, Matt? It's really very simple. There's this line that splits the country in half. The people on top of the line and the people below the line, they couldn't seem to see eye to eye. And so, they went to war."

"And what? What you saying, Stonewall?"

"Well, Matt, it turns out, I was on the bottom part of the line, so that's who I fought for. I think it's pretty much as simple as that."

A bloated sun set over a monotonous line of mountains, each one the same as the other, each the same before the war as it was after. Nothing had changed. Not for Matt at least. But for his brothers, it was as if they were alive in a way like before! Matt was the slave now. He was trapped and miserable. His brothers, they were free and happy! Matt looked to his side; Stonewall disappeared. *What was it all about? What was he supposed to do now?* It was getting dark. He had nowhere he wanted to go. So, he sat here. And he dreamed. And all the children came alive again!

49

O n an early Tuesday morning in November, when the brightest leaves still swirled in a cool autumn sky, Sam Bredridge died. Sam was a vibrant man who said little but who enjoyed his family and his life; he spoke often about how he hoped he could flourish in the newfound freedom that had finally come his way. But suddenly he hurt his leg and got sick, and they said his life was in the hands of the Lord and the doctor. Sadly, neither of those folks could prevent his eventual demise. And so, he died.

While others wept, Paul snarled. Because he knew that Sam had been murdered, killed to send a message to Paul and to the entire black community of Washington.

"He was all I had," Paul lamented to Smiles, as he lay nestled on her breast, beside the pond that glowed from a brilliant setting sun. "It doesn't make sense."

"Which part?" Smiles asked him, rubbing his hair as she stared across the horizon. "The part where he died, or the part where he was the only one?"

"I guess the part where now we have no life or future on this farm."

"You know what I know about you boys, what I learned just from the little while we been here?" Smiles said to him, turning her head and peering into his melancholy eyes. "You've all been living in a fantasy world your whole lives. While we were whipped and beat and held down, while the Negroes in New York went cold and hungry and were treated like dirt and not even able to find a job, you were here, a whole wonderful world at your disposal, beautiful mountains looking over you, nothing ever to get in your way, all the food and money you needed, and pure love all around. The only one of you whoever had to face the real world and the one who kept you away from all its troubles was your brother Matt. You and Luke, you worked hard, I grant you that, but you were free to live a life that almost no one else will ever know. That's why you came down here and tried to make it work for all of us, why you wanted to revive that world you cherish so much. That's also why it can't ever be the same. The ugly, real world spilled in your gates. Your fantasy just went and dissolved. You used to tell me that every day up in New York."

"Well, it's gone, Smiles. After what Peter Marsh told me. And Sam's death. Or murder. Whatever you want to call it. That is the nail in the coffin."

"I am sorry, my beautiful Paul," she said sweetly, her warm heart beating into Paul's ears. "But we never had a chance to live here. Never. I'm glad we got to taste it though."

"If it weren't for Matt, maybe we'd have had a chance."

At that, Smiles grabbed Paul's head and twisted it so he could see her eyes. They were firm. He knew that he was about to get a talking-to. "You give your brother Matt a break, Paul," she said. "From everything you told me, he was as close to you and Luke as anyone could be. He saved your butts countless times. He was, and I am sure still is, totally in love with you. You named your son after him, Paul. That's because you know your brother's heart. You say he changed. You say that the war changed him. But deep down, Paul, people don't change. Not that much. It's not even possible to do."

Paul paused and took a deep breath. "I changed, Smiles. I'm not the man you met in Frederick. People do change."

"No, Paul," she said more serenely, rubbing his hair. "You are the same passionate fighter as you always were, the same loving man, the same brilliant and relentless man who will work your butt off to do what you know is right. The only way you changed is that now, most of the time at least, you know when to shut your mouth. Not always, but mostly! In your core, though, you are the same man that I saw in Fredrick that first night after we all escaped. I felt all your goodness the first time I laid eyes on you. I think I fell in love with you at that very moment. No, Paul, you didn't change. And I'm sure neither did your brother. He is waiting for you. I see him in the woods, watching us. I see him with that wife of his, wishing he wasn't. He's just waiting for you. Ask Luke, he knows. Even Izzy said it. You got to go to him, Paul. We have precious little time left. You don't want to leave here without telling him how much you love him."

Paul knew that at some point the meeting of the two brothers was inevitable. The brother in blue and the brother in gray. He had come close to engaging Matt, but always backed off, harboring some excuse, seeing Jessie nearby, or just losing his nerve. He dreaded it. But it had to be.

First, though, he had to grapple with the ramifications of Sam's death.

"It was the day after I talked to him, the day he spoke to some of the others that Sam fell down and got hurt. Just a piece of twig in his leg. A splinter. They took him to the doctor. Next thing you know, he's dead. If you ask me, it seems that the title MD means master of death when it comes to the doctor."

"You think the doctor killed him?"

Paul knew that he did. *I'm sure he killed Daddy too.* There were probably countless others.

Sam's death sent a message that reverberated around the entire community, black and white.

Sam died on a Saturday. The following day, First Washington AME Church held its first service in a partially completed building with logs and straw bales as chairs. There were no Bibles yet and no minister, just a few prayers and several black community leaders directing the proceedings. Sam—a deeply religious man—had been one of them. Today the doctor offered to give the sermon. Insisted!

"The Lord punishes those who defy the will of the righteous," smiled the doctor. Colonel Stompmonger stood at his side, as did two prominent black farmers from just south of town. Elana was there that day and relayed the doctor's speech to Paul. "Sam was a good man," the doctor continued, "but his soul was sullied by diabolical influences and by men who tried to turn him away from his Lord, from his people, from his town. As all of you know, I have never owned a slave, and I am working tirelessly to assure that Washington is a model of what we can accomplish together. This church is a testament of what we have achieved so rapidly already, in harmony and in peace. But others would seek us to fail. Others have come into our town and have tried to disrupt our collaboration. Papists, Jews, atheists; some of them are even here with us today in the Lord's sanctuary. They have come here to sew disharmony and dissent, and their venom slayed poor Sam. I tried to save him, but the Lord would not have of it. See his death as a message. Let us not repeat his mistake. Let us all move together as one."

"At that moment," Elana told Paul when she returned to the farm, "I peeked around, and everyone's eyes glared at me, not in the nicest of ways; so I grinned, bowed, and got the heck out of that place. I don't think I am going to be welcome back there, Paul. I don't think any of us are. It's such a shame."

Sam's funeral was slated to be on a Wednesday, and, despite Elana's and Izzy's stern warnings, Paul rode into town to speak with Sam's widow. He had met her many times and had spoken to both Sam and her about the doctor's perfidy. Sam agreed with Paul, and so too did his wife at the time.

As soon as his horse trotted down the lanes of Washington, Paul felt an icy vibe. Whereas the townspeople typically ignored him or flashed a half-hearted wave—the benefits he derived from wearing a uniform of blue—now they did neither. They held their ground and glared at him. At least some of them did. Enough to make him feel ill at ease. He grasped the revolver in his holster. He did not know how to shoot the thing, at least not accurately, but he thought that it may be necessary to ward off whatever stench brewed in this vanquished town that now seemed to have empowered the people of Washington to defy a Union soldier.

What had changed?

As Paul moved toward the AME church, a black man jumped out and beckoned him to stop. This man, somewhat old and worn in appearance and thin in hair, was also named Sam; although most called him Samuel. They had been friends, the two Sams, at least since the war ended; before that, they had been locked onto separate farms, never crossing paths. Samuel's master died in the fighting, and his master's wife and children left Washington and relocated with her sister in Charlottesville. Samuel and the other slaves managed the farm on their own this summer; they grew apples and some wheat, and they earned a salary. The doctor, with a few of his men, managed the farm's operation and finances and paid the workers a fair wage, or so Samuel had relayed to Paul when they spoke a few weeks prior. Samuel was one of the doctor's men, a fierce advocate for the church's construction, a man who believed in Washington's future so long as there was a firm spirit of cooperation under the guidance of "our goods doctor."

"Don't go no farther," Samuel said to Paul. "Get off your horse, and let's me and you talk a spell." His voice was calm, almost welcoming. But that demeanor evaporated within minutes of Paul's dismounting.

Samuel stood erect, almost statuesque. "It's not's gonna work, Paul," Samuel said. "Nothing you's is doing is going to help us. Nothing. I talked to Sam before he went and died. He told me all's that you said. We is not interested in your ways, Paul. I know you talk fancy and is smart, you have your New York ways, but we is not interested in that down here. Don't comes here no more, Paul. That's all's that I am saying. It's not personal or nothing. We love all your people, your wife, the others. We love them all. But, don't comes here, not none of you. It just won't work."

Paul, though, refused to simply accede to the man's verdict. "I know your views, Samuel, and I respect them," Paul said. "But I want to talk to the others too. You are not their spokesman. This is an opportunity that will not come again. We can't just accept the doctor's word. We can't cheat ourselves out of making substantive changes that will protect us for decades to come. We need to be bold."

Samuel simply shook his head. He was not in a talking mood. "I ain'ts gonna debate all this with you, Paul. Just 'cause I don't talk all fancy don't mean I is dumb or gullible. I know the score, I know what we's is doing, I is not as naive as you may think. And I do think I talks for most of the people in this place. A big chunk of us Negroes is scared of going against the doctor and all the white people, that I grant you. But a bigger chunk, me included, think that the doctor is doing all he's can do to help us, and there is a lot he is doing, and there is a lot he just can't do. We is willing to be patient, to works with him, and you is not helping the situation at all. We know you have your heart in the right place, Paul, but we, all of us, we don't wants you here. Not to make trouble. We don't want none of your people here. That's all's I is saying. Sam died, and we don't want that to happen to none of anyone else."

"Then," Paul said caustically, "you admit that his death was not accidental, that he was killed because he was willing to listen to me? If you admit that, then you fully acknowledge that you are working with people who will quickly turn on you unless you follow their script."

Samuel shook his head and moaned. He turned around. "Just, don't come back Paul. That's all's I is saying. Go home. Go to your family, be with thems. We don't want you here. Sam should never have talked to you. None of us should. Things are going good for us. Real good. We got our church, our pastor, a teacher, and good jobs. We got the white folk treating us kindly. Things are good. Leave us be. That's all I is saying." He leaped upon his horse and disappeared in a puff of dust.

Paul stood for a bit, stunned, uncertain. Part of him thought, *The hell with him! I'm going to make my case to the others.* But part of him was tired. He had waged an incessant fight for too many years. He just wanted to lie on Smiles and go to sleep. Luke's words also reverberated in his brain.

Why are you spending so much effort on people who don't care? Just worry about us, about our family, our farm. This is our moment, Brother. We can't let it get away. It's not our job to save the world.

So, he rode home, despondent, unsure. Did the doctor wield so much power that he owned every human being in this town, black and white? Even wielded power over the US Army? He even had the authority to kill? There seemed no defeating the doctor. Izzy had warned him; the doctor was far cleverer than any of them realized. *He's got us by the balls.*

"Sam was the one guy among them I could talk to," Paul said to Smiles as they lay near the pond. "We need land, and credit, and agricultural education, and higher education. We need and must demand reparations. Sam was one of the few men of any influence who heard me out; a lot of the others—the ones who think that the doctor is their savior—they are convinced that I'm a devil from New York who came down here to cause trouble. But I could talk to Sam; he said he would try to convince a few of the Negroes that I made some sense. And then a piece of wood gets lodged in his leg, they bring him to the doctor to fix it, and he drops dead. Either the doctor is a totally shitty doctor or a pretty good killer."

"Or both," Smiles added.

"Yes, both," he said. "Then the very next day Colonel Stompmonger calls me in and tells me that he hears I am causing trouble in this town; he orders me to stay away from the Negroes and not to go near the church; he said that he is going to reassign me to another district out of Virginia."

Smiles laughed. "Is that the moment you middle-fingered him and resigned your commission?"

"Ha ha, yes," Paul said. "It was about then. I threw a few things first and then yelled out some choice words at him in concert with his religious values, like 'you goddamned moron' and 'Jesus Christ, how can you be so blind.' And then I resigned my commission, effective next week. He seemed relieved! I guess it doesn't matter. It's not like we can stay here anyway Smiles, not with what Mr. Marsh told me earlier today, and not with everything that happened since Sam died. It limits our options if I'm married to the army. It's hard enough being married just to you! It's time to find our freedom, real freedom this time, to get Momma, and then to find a place for us to live. I only volunteered to extend my tour in the army so I could come here with a blue uniform to confer some protection us; I knew this wasn't going to be a welcoming place. But now, it's time to move on. The fight is over; I know when it's time to say, uncle."

"You are a good man, Paul," she said. "You had visions of this farm, of all the people, which may have been true before the war. But not now, my lovely man. Not now. You did try, and I thank you for it!"

"I thought we could do it, Smiles, I really did."

She kissed him and then lay down, soaking in the shadow of imposing mountains and a warm autumn sun. "I fear for you," she whispered. "I want to get out of this place just as soon as we can."

"Me too."

Paul's meeting with Peter Marsh had not gone well earlier in the day. The mountain of papers on Marsh's desk buried him, his face obscured from Paul's view.

"It's not looking good with the will," Peter Marsh said to him. "We have so much going on in the bureau, Paul. So much to do, so many snags at so many levels; it's not been an easy task to free the Negro while at the same time we avoid violence with the Southern people, and the Northern Democrats, and our President. It's been hard. So hard."

He shuffled some of the papers as he spoke.

"Then," Paul asked him, deflated by the man's apparent apathy, "what? What do you mean by saying it's not looking good with the will? I am assuming we have lawyers looking at the will now, verifying its authenticity. Isn't that all we need? It should take a couple of seconds to verify it."

There was a pause. Then he spoke again. "It's not so simple, Paul, not so simple at all, because a lot of people of some repute, they sent letters to General Howard; they told him that the will was a fake, that you were trying to steal Matt Cocklin's legitimate land, and that you came down here to cause trouble. A lot of people wrote letters smearing you, even some Negroes, but mostly men of repute in the town."

"You mean the doctor? That's the man of repute? That's who they're going to listen to now? Are you fucking kidding me? This is how the Freedman's Bureau dispenses justice to the Negro, to a Negro who fought and almost died for the Union? You would rather take the word of Confederate sympathizers than of a soldier in the Union army?"

He shuffled some papers. His voice became soft, somewhat tremulous, disheveled.

"Others in the town too wrote letters, even the state's former governor; they call you a swindler, an atheist, a troublemaker; they say that you brought infidels from New York—Catholics and Jews among others—to cause disarray. This is a good town, a town where there is a good working relationship between the whites and Negroes, where we are making progress; and General Howard, he can't afford to cause trouble in a place like this. I know all of what they say about you is slander. I told the general so myself, but his word on the matter is final, and I'm afraid he wants us to drop the matter for now; the land is going to remain in your brother's hand. It's up to Matt if you can still live there."

Paul felt sick. Powerless. He wanted to stand up and push all the papers away, grab the man's shirt, and demand that he do something. Anything! The entire process was a sham.

"Then I will talk to Reverend Garnet," Paul finally said. "He will take my side."

Peter Marsh stood and approached Paul, a visage of melancholy drenched upon his face. He looked tired, worn, and defeated. He shook his head. "They called you an atheist," he said. "That you ridicule those who wanted a church. Reverend Garnet won't back you on this, I assure you. He has other battles he is fighting right now. He and General Howard are very religious people; they want the church. Paul, you are a good man. Want my advice? Move on. Leave here. You don't belong here anymore."

Paul smiled and nodded, placing his hand on Peter Marsh's shoulder. Somehow, those words allayed him just a bit. It was over. He had to accept that reality. "Promise me this," Paul said. "Don't tell anyone about this. At least not for a while. I need time to get ready; if you tell them now, they'll kick me out before the moon rises tonight. Promise me that."

Peter Marsh smiled and nodded. "Of course," he said. "That's the least I can do. I promise."

And so, Paul lay by the pond on a glorious autumn day, basking in an explosion of colorful visions of past joy, resting quietly upon his wife's chest. As a young man, all he had ever wanted was to run from this place and be free. But during his darkest moments in New York and in the army, the only thought that seared his angst was the prospect of coming back here. Now he would have to forge another path forward. He had found his mother. He had everyone with him that he could ever want. It was time.

"Hi, Brother."

Paul lifted his head and saw Luke hovering over him. Smiles stood and then, after a bit of chatting, left the boys alone to talk. She needed to tend to the children anyway.

Luke's entire being exuded pure serenity. He sat with his brother near the pond he had built, a dream that had become real. He sat and smiled. Paul would have to tell him. But how?

"It is a beautiful autumn, Brother," Luke said. "I miss Matt. Have you talked to him?"

"About what?" Paul shot back. "About how his wife raped you? About how his father-in-law keeps skulls in his study to prove our inferiority? About how our brother tramps around here with a gun and Confederate uniform and has threatened to kill me? That's the one you want me to talk to?"

"Yes," smiled Luke. "That's the one. He is waiting for you. He needs to know his brother loves him."

Paul moaned. Sometimes his brother drifted too far from reality, and it irritated Paul's skin.

"We can't stay here, Luke," Paul said, staring forward, past the mountains, as the shadowed edifice of Old Rag dominated his view, a pile of misplaced rocks apart from the blue ridge chain. "It's been a good run, Brother. What we did here, it was beyond imaginable; it was extraordinary. But, Brother, the game is over. Dad's will, it is not going to be accepted; we are going to be kicked out. And I have been told to resign my commission, to leave Washington, not only by the doctor and his group of snakes, but by many of the Negroes too who have come under his spell, and by the US Army. They want Izzy and Elana gone too. It's over, Luke. This place is corrupted. Look what Jessie did to you! What may be brewing in her gut! How could you imagine staying?"

Luke's smile did not diminish. His eyes peered forward too, to the same edifice that filled Paul's eyes and thoughts. To Luke, Old Rag represented life itself. It nourished his farm and bathed him in eternal hope. It was a constant reminder of his past, his accomplishments, and all that made life worthwhile. He was not ready to bid it farewell.

"I've been thinking, Brother," Paul said. "I befriended a lot of people during my time in the army, people from all over this country, black and white. There is a place in Montana, the Bitterroot Mountains; it seeps minerals into a rich and fertile soil; it is an ideal location to grow fruit trees, a place quiet and distant, perhaps a new place we can make home."

Luke nodded. "Too cold for grapes," he said with a smirk.

Paul persevered. "I hear there is a land in California, just north of San Francisco, which is so fertile and laden with the runoff of grand Pacific mountains that trees and grapes and every crop possible will grow better than anywhere in the world, with, of course, the right touch. Brother, you have that touch."

"Too far away. We would have to cross through Indian territory. Over mountains that kill men much stronger than us. Not feasible."

A soft breeze blew between them.

"I'll talk to Matt," Paul finally said. "But, Brother, there is nothing I can do to change reality. He will likely want us to leave. Are you willing to stay here alone? Is that really what you want?"

Luke nodded no. "I have faith in our brother, Paul. You have to approach him with love and kindness. You cannot blame him for deeds that were not of his own volition and for the wife we forced upon him. I have seen him watching us, your children; he wants you to tell him you love him. Give him a chance. At least do that for me."

Paul nodded. "But, Brother, even if he agrees to let us stay on the farm, we are prisoners here. We've been banished from the town, and we will be vulnerable to attacks. It's not safe here."

"All that will change, Brother," Luke said. "In time it will change. Once you stop preaching to them, when you accept who they are and focus on yourself, they will accept us. Let our example be one that all the others seek to emulate. That is all we can do. With time, and with a trust that will come, you will be invited back into their lives. These are good people."

Paul stood. He smiled at Luke, and then he wandered toward the big house. Jessie had been gone for the past two days, nursing her father through a cold. Against a darkening sky, Paul marveled at the house for a while, peering inside, remembering so much, so many good things; this was his haven for so long—a crackling fire, sitting and talking with his brothers and parents and Izzy about every subject imaginable; designing a better world, a perfect one! And now, it was so hard just to walk in.

He knocked a few times, and then he entered the vacant downstairs. He wandered into the living room. The fireplace was empty. It seemed cold, almost sterile. He called out Matt's name. He could hear footsteps upstairs, so there he went, climbing to the rooms where he and his brothers slept, step by step, wondering what would greet him when he arrived. Matt might shoot him, might tell him to leave, or might simply ignore him. But Paul had to talk with him. Luke and Smiles were right.

"Matt," he called again, walking to his brother's bedroom door. "Matt, it's Paul. I need to talk to you."

He could hear footsteps inside. Cautiously, as he started to sweat, Paul nudged the door open.

"Hi, Paul," Matt said, sitting on his bed, staring at his brother, in his Confederate uniform, holding his gun. "I seen you coming up the steps. What you doing here? Come to finish me off?"

Paul shook his head. "No, Brother, I am here to talk with you, brother to brother. I am here to talk with you not as a soldier or an enemy, but as a brother. Can we talk to each other that way? You are still that to me. You are my brother. I love you, Matt. We both faced our share of shit. But that doesn't change anything between us. We should have talked the minute I returned home."

Matt stared forward; his face grimaced, his hands grasping his rifle that much more tightly. What was Paul's game? "You can talk," he said. "Ain't no one stopping you."

Paul stared past the boy with whom he had once shared a life, but who seemed so distant and vile now. He breathed deeply. "I need to tell you something that will make you happy, and then tell you something that will be difficult for you to stomach. You just need to promise me that you won't react to any of this rashly. I am trying to be calm, and if a hothead like me can be calm, I hope you can be too!"

Matt remained firm, staring forward. His head seethed. Every word from Paul dug into his hide.

"We are going to leave," Paul said. "All of us. I am giving up my claim on this land. It's yours now, to enjoy with your family, to run as you want. I've asked the Freedman's Bureau to rip up the will that Dad drew up. I don't belong here. There is nothing left here for me or my family. For Izzy and Elana. For Luke. But before we leave I want to say, I just want to say, I want to try to make sure me and you, that we leave as brothers, as friends. That's what I'm trying to say."

Matt's heart raced. He could not even look at his brother. So many thoughts burst through his brain. Images. Recollections. "The children too. They is leaving?"

"Of course," Paul said.

"But I never met them. Not even the one you named after me."

"I can introduce you to them," Paul said. "It would be my honor for them to meet their uncle, and for my wife to meet her brother-in-law who she heard so much about. All good! All good stuff, I promise!"

Matt paused. "You aim to take Luke too? Ain't no way Luke would leave here."

"He has to, Matt. He has to leave. We all do."

"No," Matt whispered firmly, still evading Paul's glance. "You ain't taking Luke!"

Paul breathed deeply. "Matt," he said quietly, "there is something I need to tell you. This won't sit well with you, and I beg you, don't react rashly. Don't shoot me. Don't even shout me down. But it's why Luke has to leave. Do you promise me? If not for me, then at least for Luke?"

Sweat beaded on Matt's scalp. He nodded up and down. What more could Paul say to upset him?

Paul looked away. He just didn't know how to tell his brother. The words, they would not come out. Finally, he just said it. "Your wife," he whispered, "Jessie. I am sure she loves you. But Matt, while you were gone, she took advantage of Luke; she did it many times. He has not wanted to say anything to you. He is ashamed of what happened, and he wants no ill harm. And even I don't want to tell you, because it is likely to hurt. But she raped him many times, including after you returned. And she told him that there is a chance that the baby in her belly is his, that it may come out black. That's why I have to take Luke away. Matt, I beg you, don't do anything rash. But you had to know."

Matt sat silently on the bed. His mind twirled around violently. He could not at all make sense of anything. He loosened his grip on his gun. He felt nauseous. Then he said, "I don't think so."

"Well, that's what Luke said. He said it, and we know that Luke says nothing short of the truth. He does not want to leave you, leave this place. But, Matt, I hope you can understand, if that baby comes out black, my God, Matt, if that happens, what will become of Luke?"

A tear trickled down Matt's eye. He looked at the ground and nodded. What could he do? Every fiber of his being believed what his brother uttered. But what could he do? He was trapped in this prison, with these people, because of Luke. The children, Paul's children, they were all going to leave him here alone, abandoned. He never even met Izzy's wife; how much he wanted to greet the woman who fell in love with Izzy! So many thoughts raced through him, none of them making any sense.

What was it all about? What do I do?

"All I ask, Matt, is two things. That you let us go and prevent anyone from pursuing us. Make up something; tell them we are returning to New York. Just please, I beg you, protect us; you've done it all your life, and I'm asking you to do it this one last time. And please too, if the baby comes out black, make sure you don't let Jessie blame Luke for it, or blame any Negro who is alive; tell her father that it was some Negro who died, one who came here after the war, anything, just promise me that. Matt, this is a lot for you to bear. You've done so much for us; you are Dad's most wonderful reflection. He would be so proud of you, and I do love you, and so does Luke. I just ask this one last thing of you."

Sitting on the bed, Matt nodded, up and down. He did not look up.

Paul nodded too and turned and walked away.

A strong wind blew that night, whipping around the mountains, scattering leaves and debris across the farm. Paul and his extended family sat together in the cabin; there were no songs, no laughter. It was a solemn night. In the big house a single light illuminated the sky, from a room upstairs, where a boy sat on his bed, not having moved from where he had been since Paul left. He could not think. He could barely breathe. But he knew what he had to do. A gun sat firmly in his hand. Matt had not missed many targets during his time with the Grays. He just had a few more targets left to hit before he could say that the war was finally over. He played with some minié balls in his pocket and seethed. "Time to end this thing," he whispered. He understood now what this war was all about.

50

"I hate all doctors," Matt sniveled. "They ain't so smart as they think, and all they do is spout off, and everyone just listens. They don't cure nothing. They just tell you how brilliant and enlightened they is, everyone follows what they says, and then they make nothing but trouble. I hate them all."

Stonewall laughed, seeming oblivious to the crisp wind that blew around a few maple trees in which Matt embedded himself on a dark, frigid November morning. Frost glistened off the dying foliage, visible through the intense light of a full moon that hovered over him ominously. Matt shivered, holding his gun with a numb hand, staring forward, as the town of Washington slept innocently, oblivious to his intentions. They thought of him as nothing more than the doctor's pet, a foolish sycophant, a plaything for the doctor's men. *We have plans for you, Matt. Now you are with us, with the righteous and the decent; you are fully part of the world your father rejected but which you embrace; now you are here to do our bidding, and we will reward you with flattery and a sip of tea.*

Stonewall slapped Matt on his back. "There's a doctor in every town," he said. "They are North and South, East, and West. They were with us, and against us, in the war. They are all the same; it doesn't matter what color they wear, what ideas they proclaim. They all tell us they are going to cure our ills and fix us. Which they can't. And they prosper by lying like that. But what can we do about it, son?"

"I aim to start doing something," Matt said, staring forward through the darkness at the town of Washington, which lay sharply in his view. "I ain't gonna just sit here and let him and his people pull me on a leash no more. We fought the wrong enemy, Stonewall. If we had won the war, it'd be no different than the fact we lost. Just like that boy said to me at the surrender, win or lose, other people is in charge of us now. The doctor, he wins either way, and we is the losers; we is the ones who do his bidding and have to heed his cures, either way. How many good and innocent men did I shoot dead in that war, men who just was there because they had to, or they thought they was doing something right? And they got all caught up in the moment. How many of the survivors came home thinking somehow all their sacrifice and passion would lead to something good? Instead they come home, and all they find is their very own doctor telling them to do this or do that, and they is nothing, all their sacrifice for nothing, no different than the people I shot dead, all for no reason."

"They have their lives, the men who returned home, their families, their homes. Isn't that enough?"

Matt nodded vigorously. "No, they don't, Stonewall. They return to nothing, like I done. I had the perfect life, I know that now. I said to Luke long ago, 'How we going to protect this place from the doctor and all them people?' And he said to me, 'Brother, he said, you been doing it all these years. You been protecting us, and we will prevail. Don't you worry.' That's what he said to me. But then Luke goes and lets the doctor right on our farm, makes me marry his daughter, and it's like all the diseases that the doctor holds in his pocket to get people sick, the ones we avoided all those years. Now he lets them loose on our farm, and it's like a tornado sweeping through a beautiful garden, a garden we took years and years to grow and protect; and in a second, a tornado of my own making sweeps over it and wipes it out, and then all the doctor's people they run in and say, 'It's ours now; we will save it!' And they do the opposite. That's what my farm is now. It ain't special no more. It's just like the land around it. Dust. Filth. Nothing. Only Paul had the sense to run away. He's the only smart one among us."

Stonewall lay against a frosted tree, chewing on a few acorns he found on the ground. *I had to fight a family of hungry squirrels for these, he had told Matt earlier.* His face darkened a bit, his demeanor contemplative, and for a moment he sounded more like Paul than Stonewall. "Brother," he said, "back in ancient Rome, Cato, who fought hard against his own versions of the doctor, against people who threatened the republic he cherished, he sat in his tent when he knew that the battle was over, knew that evil had triumphed and that his precious society fell prey to self-interested men of power, he lay in his tent, and he took a dagger and sliced his gut, all of his insides falling out onto his bed. It was his last act of defiance, the only way to escape from those who decimated the paradise he had helped to create. And you know what happened next?"

Matt nodded no, wondering what Stonewall was getting at.

"His servant came in, saw what Cato had done, shoved his guts back into the hole he had cut, and got a doctor to sew it up. So, there lay Cato for days and days, suffering immensely, unable to escape from an evil and voracious world, from the fiends and scoundrels who now everyone revered and who desecrated everything he revered—there he lay, cured by the doctor, only so he could suffer. Matt, you won't change anything. The doctor will always win. Your battle is futile. You fought the war. Now it's time to find peace and follow the only path you have left. Don't suffer at his hands. Not worth it."

"But," Matt said, his heart beating fast, "my brothers ain't my enemy. None of the boys I shot were my enemy. We fought the wrong war, Stonewall. I can't just sit back and do nothing."

Stonewall had fallen asleep against the tree.

The faint, illuminating Shenandoah glowed in the distant horizon. Matt looked up at the mountain range, waiting for the sun to rise. He was not a smart man, not a man who always could figure things out, but he had to finish the war he was meant to fight, the only one that really mattered. He held his gun in frigid hands and just waited.

Time passed slowly in the early-morning darkness. Washington slowly woke up.

Somewhere beneath those mountains, beyond Matt's vision, a carriage and several horses trotted forward, carrying a family of exhausted and sleeping inhabitants to another gasp of freedom.

The moon shined brightly, as craggy rocks of Old Rag grew larger and closer. Thin, frozen mist blew out of the horses' nostrils like smoke stacks, as children huddled beneath blankets and adults stared forward in tranquil and perplexing silence. Every mind churned its own perceptions. Paul looked over at his brother, who peered back at him smiling, each wondering what the other was thinking.

"You know," said Elana, from inside the carriage, yelling to Paul who rode a horse astride it, "Izzy is asleep in there. He is scared to death of going up this mountain of yours; he can't stand heights. He is sure he's going to fall off the edge. He just kept saying it until he finally fell asleep. I can't imagine what kind of terrible dreams he is having now; his whole face is grimaced."

Paul laughed. "After all his people have gone through, this is what he is scared of? I have been up this thing in the dark, in the rain, running for my life, not knowing where to go. He will be fine!"

"Well," she said snarkily, "we are not all you, Paul. Give us mortals a break once in a while."

"It's so beautiful up there, Elana," Paul said. "You will be so engrossed by it all that you won't think of anything else but how amazing it is. New York has nothing that comes close."

Luke nodded. "You are about to see God for the first time," he smiled.

Elana nodded and hugged Luke, who sat beside her in the front of the carriage. "Well, I am glad you are showing it to me. I just hope your God is a bit kinder than Izzy's. It was hard for him to leave. And it will be even harder to say goodbye to you when we get to the top."

"It's not goodbye," said Luke. "It's the beginning of something new and wonderful."

Elana nodded. Then she turned to Paul. "When you woke us up this morning and shoved us into the carriage," she said, her face a bit more contemplative, "I swear I heard a horse dart off the farm. Did you hear that? It was 3:00 a.m. Was I just dreaming?"

"No," Paul said. "You weren't dreaming. It was Matt."

"Where was he going?" Elana asked.

Paul just shrugged. He had no idea.

Slowly, as a bright if not particularly warm November sun drifted into a clear blue sky, the town of Washington woke up. Matt peered across the horizon, comfortable knowing that he had concealed himself from anyone below. He had found the perfect spot from which to peruse the comings and goings of Washington's inhabitants and to have a direct view of the only house that had any meaning to him.

Near the doctor's house was a barn, one in which his most prized horses lived a pampered existence, and where a few of the local farmers had been keeping their horses as well.

"Daddy told all the farmers to gather their horses in our barn," Jessie told Matt when she visited the farm briefly yesterday, before returning home to take care of her father, who had recovered from his minor illness but still needed her company, or so she told Matt. "The men are all talking. They say that Paul is going to be kicked out of the army, and when he goes, the colonel gave Daddy permission to chase him away. All the farmers, they got their horses here and are staying with Daddy so they can join him in the chase. They are so excited about it! That's all they can talk about."

Matt said very little when Jessie revealed this. "You gonna chase way Paul's little boys too, his wife, all of them? You gonna hurt them?"

Jessie laughed and hugged her husband, kissing Matt on the cheek. "Silly boy," she said. "Daddy won't hurt anyone, just put a scare in them, so they don't come back again. It would be good for those young Negroes to learn a lesson and have some fear put in them. They are being told lies by their horrible father, and they need a good dose of the truth, and Daddy is the perfect person to give it to them."

"And what about Luke, and Izzy?"

Jessie rubbed her body on Matt's, her large belly jiggling against his groin. She kissed him all over his face, her putrid odor seeping into his nose. "Let's make love, Matt!"

He pushed her away. "What about Luke and Izzy?" he persisted.

Her smile twisted, as her crooked teeth filled the entirety of her face, or so it seemed. "Daddy doesn't like Izzy or that Catholic Irish lady he brought down here. I don't know what he plans to do to them; whatever it is, they deserve it. But not Luke. Lukie wants to stay. I talked to him; he will never leave." She kissed him, over and over. "Luke will never leave," she continued to whisper. "I love Luke," he heard her say. "I love Luke so much." The words, whether real or not, pounded Matt's ears.

He shoved her hard upon the bed. "Luke ain't a slave no more, Jessie," he said. "And Izzy is my friend. You leave them alone. You tell your daddy to leave them alone. Now, get the hell out of here!"

Jessie stood up, kissed Matt, and then pulled off her dress, her pendulant and engorged breasts dangling beside him. She thrust her body against his and eased him to the bed. Then she kissed him, and he snapped his eyes shut. He was impotent to fight her. He imagined her on top of Luke doing the very same thing, as poor Luke, frightened beyond belief, succumbed to her powers. Luke created a monster by bringing Jessie to the farm, and now everyone was going to pay the price.

But today, under a rising sun, Matt held the upper hand. He aimed his rifle at the doctor's door. Washington's people started to meander along the main street and engage in pleasant conversation. They were mere blurs to Matt. His eyes focused straight ahead. His hands were blue and cold, but they grasped his gun tightly and were prepared to fire. A bag of ammunition and powder sat aside him; he could fire, load, and re-fire faster than any man alive, with an accuracy that stunned even the most seasoned soldiers and hunters. He could knock ten people off in a minute before anyone knew where the shots were coming from. And his path to escape was secure; he had made sure of that.

Now he just waited for the door to open.

You can't fix the woes of society with a few bullets. We learned that in the war. The doctor can never die. There's always another one right behind him.

"Well," he whispered to Stonewall. "We'll see about that."

A tiny, barely visible trail that led up the underbelly of Old Rag rose gently for several miles, with few hazards either dangerous or worrisome. Paul traversed this sanctuary effortlessly, strolling with Luke at his side, knowing every tree and rock as though he had been here a thousand times. The others drifted behind them, occasionally imploring them to slow down. Paul held James in his arms, and the other kids scuttled up and down, left and right, although Elana's oldest daughter seemed to be snoozing as she held her mother's hand, occasionally tossing out a protestation like, "This is so dumb."

"It is exactly that," Izzy said to the girl. "Dumb. Idiotic. Moronic. Suicidal. We could have picked a nice spot near a waterfall and had a decent breakfast and then taken a road over the mountain; there are roads, you know. There are other ways to get to the other side. What can I tell you? Keep telling us how dumb this is, young lady; you are absolutely right. Your uncle Paul can be very dumb."

Smiles (who held her two boys' hands, seeming to drag them at times, and then at other times barely able to contain them when they dashed over to some huge boulder or stream) patted Izzy on the back. "Let the two big boys enjoy their fantasy in peace," she told him. "Look how happy they are! All they want is to share this place with us. We should at least pretend to enjoy it."

"Enjoy what? It's still dark. It's cold. I can barely see ahead of me. I just hope the sun comes up by the time we hit the cliffs your husband always talks about. You won't be in such a good mood when we all fall off the edge of the mountain; that much I can tell you."

"Can you keep your mouth quiet for just a few seconds, Izzy?" Elana pleaded with him. "You'll scare away the bears if you keep yapping like that."

"Oh, the bears, I forgot; if I'm lucky they'll maul us before we have a chance to plummet from the cliffs."

Elana's daughter laughed. Izzy rubbed her head.

Slowly, this band of unwanted misfits ascended to the sky. The sun opened a majestic landscape in front of them, with glimpses of a vast horizon visible through bare trees and a plethora of colorful leaves and green moss. Even the most cynical and dubious faces peeked leftward to witness the open wonderment of everything around them. This place's majesty, its holy aura, extinguished the banter. Soon, but for the chirps of birds and crunching of sticks and leaves, all fell silent, as so should it be. Luke smiled and breathed in the clean and refreshing air that encased him. He had been here but once, and yet this mountain lived in him; it coursed through his veins; it ticked his every sense. With each step he vacated the other world behind, and his very soul and vitality exploded in a nirvanic state of bliss.

The two brothers said nothing, and yet they were fully attached to one another. At one point Paul held Luke's hand, and Luke refused to let it go. Step by step they walked into the sky, relinquishing the land below, rising above it all, looking down as though the farms were mere toys at their disposal, until finally they stopped, a huge rock obscuring their path—nothing but rocks all around. Paul turned to others.

"We're here," he whispered, smiling just as innocently and brightly as his brother, as though both were hypnotized and in an otherworldly state. His smile reeked of pure tranquility. "We're here. It's all rock scrambling from here on in. Keep the kids close. Just follow us. You are about to be amazed."

"What's up there, Daddy? Is there candy?" Matt asked him.

Paul laughed. "Is there candy, Luke?"

Luke nodded. "Everywhere. There is candy everywhere." He glowed against a rising sun.

Matt clapped his hands and smiled at Elana's son, who smiled back.

"Who's going to hold my hand?" Izzy asked. "I can't even get over that first rock."

"I'll help you, Izzy," Elana's daughter said to him. "It looks like fun!"

Paul and his brother leaped over the first boulder. The trees disappeared; all that was left were open vistas and bounteous rocks ascending into a bright blue sky. And so they went, helping the others up, showing them the way, stopping and peering over the edges, admiring the stretches of farms and the endless landscape in every direction.

"We own the world from up here," Luke told them at one stop, placing his arms over Izzy's shoulder as his friend, drenched with sweat, hyperventilated. "They can't hurt us from up here. We are masters of the universe. We are free. Don't you agree, my friend?"

A cool breeze caressed them. "It's nice," Izzy acknowledged. "Are we almost there yet?"

"Not even close," Paul said. "Not even close. Let's forge ahead!"

Smiles kissed him on his neck. "It's beautiful," she whispered to her husband, glowing. "Thank you for sharing this with us. I love you. I love you so much."

Paul kissed her lips. "I could tear you apart right here and now," he whispered back.

Smiles nodded. "I wish you would."

Luke leaped from rock to rock. The children followed him, then Izzy and Elana. Paul and Smiles drifted just a bit behind. They stood locked together under a bright, enticing sun.

At the very periphery of their vision, just a dot to them from this elevated perch, another boy sat aside a tree holding his gun, waiting, hoping. He breathed in the same wind that fluttered past his brothers and soared into his lungs—an air of hope, a whiff of redemption. *Now I know what it was all for.*

He felt the touch of General Lee beside him. *We need to make sure we get the best of them. Get them before they get us. Grab the upper hand. Be on the offensive. It's the only way to win a war against an enemy that is stronger than you are.*

The doctor's pristine white door opened, and two figures slid out. Matt smiled; he aimed his gun. They wandered toward the barn, as he knew that they would. He could see them, their wily faces and their corrupted souls—a well-dressed man with his noble air about him and his fabricated bravado and his hypnotic power; and a pregnant girl with her doting innocence that masked cruelty and evil that grew even larger in her protuberant gut. They spoke to each other and giggled, seething of sinister intent. How shocked they would be to know that their fate now sat in Matt's frigid hands! He wore his Confederate gray, continuing a war that had ended prematurely, against his real enemy this time.

They opened the barn door.

And Matt fired. He got off two quick shots, instigating chaos on the street as his victims fell hard upon the ground below. He quickly loaded, aimed, and fired again, as more creatures came in his view. Bodies dropped in rapid succession, blood splattering everywhere; there were shrieks from below. Others ran toward the slaughter, and he shot them all, one after another, five dead, ten, fifteen. The more that came, the more he shot. Smoke fluttered from his gun's barrel. He loaded, fired, loaded. With each bullet another body splattered upon the frigid ground, now running red with blood—a river of vengeance—signifying the completion of this war, a war that he intended to win.

A few faces peered in his direction, and he shot at them, causing everyone to scatter away. Blood was everywhere. Fear swept through this once-tranquil place. And Matt smiled.

He waited; there was nothing else left to kill. So, he mounted his horse and rode away, pausing for just a moment, taking it all in, relishing the courage of his conviction.

"It's for you, Stonewall, you who was killed by your own men, by scoundrels from the Deep South. And it's for you, General Lee, because even if you would have won the war, them people from the South, the doctors in every town, the crooks and fiends who ran the Confederacy and couldn't even give you enough food and soldiers as your men lay dying on the field, they would have beat you in the end; they is the real enemy, and now we is finishing the war against them. The first battle is ours, the battle of Washington. Let them remember this day for as long as they is allowed to exist."

Matt lay against a tree, listening to cries and shrieks from below, as he sucked on a lemon. He had struck the first blow. But he was not done yet. He grabbed his gun and bag of ammunition and prepared for the next battle. Mounting his horse, he rode forward, toward his farm, where he would finish the job he started today.

Far up a distant mountain, Paul and Smiles emerged from behind a rock, both encased in a smile. The children scuttled everywhere upon the upper ledge of Old Rag. They ate some sandwiches that Ruth had prepared and found a bag of candy that Luke had hidden under a tree, telling them that the mountain always provided sweets to those noble enough to climb it.

Luke wandered over to Paul. "I thought I heard gunshots below, Brother," he said.

"Well," said Paul, "as long as they're not aimed at us, I'm good with it."

"It sent a chill down my spine," Luke continued.

"Don't let it," Paul said. "We're safe up here. No one can touch us. This is where we belong."

But Luke felt uneasy, as though the shots were a tocsin of something profound.

Izzy and Elana sat upon a ledge, one that did not drop but ten feet down, affording them views across mountains to their west. Their arms around each other, they kissed gently beneath a piercing sun, Izzy's angst dissolving amid the tranquil breezes that caressed them high in the winter sky. Smiles ran with the kids, telling them stories about mountain ogres that lived here beneath trees and in caves.

"It's the first time up here that I wasn't pummeled by rain and almost hit by lightning," Paul told his brother. "It must mean something."

Luke nodded. He paused for a moment. "I think California would be our best chance, Brother," he said to Paul. "I've been thinking about it. We could go up to Illinois after we get Momma, make a home there for a while with the people you met in the war. Izzy, he can start his business, bring in some money. Then we will see. When the time is right, when the children are old enough, we will make our way to California. I think we can do amazing work out there. I think we can change the world."

Paul smiled and buried his brother in a hug.

As morning faded upon Old Rag's peak, it was time to say goodbye. After many hugs, Paul led Izzy, Elana, and her two children down the mountain's back side to a tiny path in the woods.

"This was the path I took to freedom," Paul told them, pointing to the right. "It heads right up North, over the mountains; it was so long ago." He paused, staring into Izzy's eyes. "You will take this other path. It's a fire road; used mostly by mountain people. It's an easy trail. There's only but one way to go; you should get down before it's dark. Once you get to Luray, you know what to do. Just be careful."

"After surviving those rocks, this part doesn't worry me," Izzy said. "You be careful. I will be nervous and sweating until I see your face in a few days. I'll be ready for you. That much I can tell you."

"You have all the money?" Paul asked.

Izzy nodded. "It's a virtual fortune," he said. "I don't know how Abe earned so much that he could give me and you such a hefty bonus. We owe a lot to that old man. One day, I hope I can thank him and sit down for a dish of white fish and chicken soup."

"One day," Paul whispered.

They nodded to each other, and then Izzy gathered the troops and meandered down the mountain, carrying a backpack with food and water. He did not even turn to say goodbye.

Up on Old Rag's summit, Paul told the others that it was time to descend.

"They'll be alright, won't they, Paul?" Smiles asked him about Izzy and Elana, her arms around his waist, her lips kissing his cheek. "You know, I'll be worried."

"I'm more concerned about us," Paul said. "In a way, our fate is in the hands of Matt. If he chooses to, he can do us in quicker than even if we drop off the edge of the mountain."

"He won't, though," Smiles said. "I just know that he won't."

Just about then, in the valley to their east, a boy on a horse rode quickly into the town of Washington. He held no gun or bullets; he had left them back on the farm, after completing what he needed to do there. It was time to orchestrate the grand finale of his plan, the last barrage of the last battle. Matt smiled, but he knew he had to shed his grinning face and replace it with a visage of distress. "I heard gunshots," he would tell them. "I came over as fast as I could. And then I saw someone riding away, a Negro, holding a gun. So I chased him down, and he told me the grim tale of what unfolded here today. I come back here as fast as I could. My God, so much blood. So much blood!" He laughed as he rehearsed it. Night would descend upon him soon. It was time to finish here, before completing his task on the farm. "So much blood!" He laughed so hard that he almost fell off his horse.

As they scampered down the mountain, Luke seemed worried, more pensive than usual.

"What is it, Brother?" Paul asked him.

Luke wasn't sure. Something about those gunshots. They didn't seem right. He could not tell exactly why. But they didn't seem right.

"I worry about our brother," Luke finally said to Paul.

To that concern, Paul offered no response.

51

It came to pass that the cities of Sodom and Gomorrah were tainted by sin, their societies corrupt and their people not worthy of God's protection. God said to Lot, who lived there with his family, that He must now destroy those cities, and that Lot and his family must flee quickly and not look back, or they would meet the fate of the inhabitants of those who lived there. But as fire and brimstone was thrust on those bastions of sin, Lot's wife turned back, so sad to be leaving the only land she knew, and she was turned into a pillar of salt, deprived of being delivered to the promised land because of her lust for a sullied past. Thus, as Izzy told the others as they sat above Old Rag peering down at the world, we must flee from the corrupt society where we find ourselves; we must not covet what we are losing, but rather we must move forward toward a place that is pure and peaceful where we can thrive, and never look back, lest we all turn into salt. What can I tell you? Genesis 19:26.

Something tugged at Paul, something visceral. They scampered down the rocks, a bright sun slicing through crisp winter air, the sky blue and welcoming, his children giggling as they played, Smiles nudging them away from the edge. Paul's mind spun. He felt uneasy, even a bit outside himself.

"What if Lot's wife had left something really important back in the city?" Luke asked Izzy.

Izzy smirked. "She should have thought of that before she left," he said. "God is telling us that when we choose to abandon bastions of sin and evil, we should not dwell on what we gave up, but we do need to make sure to take our sandwich meat and bread with us; this much is what I can tell you."

Luke peered at Izzy. "I fear we are leaving something very important behind."

"What do you mean?"

Luke smiled. "A table can't stand with two legs. We can't leave the third leg behind."

Paul knew exactly what he meant, even if Izzy stood perplexed. Luke's query was aimed at him.

He felt sick for having to tell Matt about Jessie's indiscretions. Matt's tepid reaction surprised Paul, who had expected a violent rebuttal from his altered brother. What Paul saw in his mind's eye was not Matt the Confederate, but rather Matt the brother, the brother always at his side, always doing the right thing. Just plain old Matt. Matt's eyes were sad, they were tired, and they expressed not a morsel of animosity or hate. Those eyes bit at Paul's psyche. The eyes of his brother. His companion in life. His savior.

A table can't stand with two legs. Once we leave, like Lot's wife, we can never turn back.

But what could Paul do? He felt Matt's presence in him; it suffocated his very soul as he saw those sad eyes. Peering ahead, he tripped over a rock, and then he quickly pushed himself up before anyone noticed. His palms were bleeding. What could he do? The question spun through his mind.

We gave him Jessie. Don't ever forget that. We created the chattels that now enslave him in a world that he wants no part of. He is a lonely leg apart from the table. Do you think he wants that?

What can I do? How can I make it right again before it's too late?

Matt galloped hard upon cold, crunchy earth with an aura of contentment and conviction the likes of which he had not felt

since his days with the Grays. A tranquil smile encased his stubbly face, and a happy song danced within his brain. All alone
he had done this deed, and with it, his angst evaporated into a
clear blue sky, the angst of a war that had gone so horribly wrong
and lost its purpose. He had been fighting for one reason and
one reason only; his role in life was predicated on protecting
his brothers, while preserving the sanctity of his father's legacy
and of his mother's sacrifice. Today he achieved that goal in the
final act of the war he had been waging these past so many years.
Despite his dull intellect and pestering incertitude, he had done
this thing without any help, any guidance, or anyone telling him
that he must. He did it because it was his job, and he did it with
a gusto and exuberance that elevated his soul. So, he smiled and
hummed a tune, preparing to slice the final dagger into his victims, into his real enemies—those who most threatened everything his father had ever struggled to achieve, those who sought
to deny his brothers the freedom they deserved.

"Fuck you, Doctor," he yelled to the trees.

Somewhere from above the branches, Stonewall winked back
at him.

He stopped briefly at the periphery of the town, upon the
perch from which he had fired two-dozen perfectly placed shots
several hours before, and peered down upon the altered land
below. They were all there, Jessie, the doctor, the doctor's posse,
and scattered townspeople, all there, gathered together, bewildered and frightened, meandering astride the carcasses of innu-
merable dead horses. The stench of rotten flesh drifted into the
woods, and Matt sucked it in with succulent ardor. Finally, he
darted down to them, wiping the smile off his face, prepared to
finish this bit of theater, to erase the sins that had haunted him
and his family for far too long. For Matt, the war was finally going
to end, and for the first time it made sense to him; he knew what
it was all about, and he knew that he would be victorious.

Far to the south, Paul and his brood had reached the valley and were making their way home. The kids slept as the sun slowly drifted down. It had been a long and exhausting day.

"Then we leave tomorrow?" Luke asked his brother.

Paul nodded. "Yes," he said. "Early. Same time as today. Before the town awakens. Before—" He was going to say, before Matt wakes up, but he could not utter those words of abandonment.

Luke, though, would not let it go. "What about Matt?" he asked.

Paul turned to his brother and snapped, "What about him? What do you want me to say?"

Luke did not respond. Somehow, he knew that it could never just end this way.

"I know we can't bring much," Luke said. "But I will be sad leaving all of my books behind. They all mean something to me and could be of use. I wish somehow we could stuff the pond into our baggage. And, of course, the red raft. And—"

"It will always be with us, Luke," Paul interrupted his brother. "The red raft, it lives inside of us. It always has. It always will. We don't need anything else. No reminders. We'll build a new world, Brother. Let's just take what we need. Like what Izzy said. The rest we will create later."

"You know what Elana said to me," Smiles chirped from the back of the carriage. "I asked her what her and Izzy and the kids were taking with them, since I knew I had to pack up their stuff; they surely couldn't take it with them over the mountains. She gave me some clothes for her and the children. A few books to read. Nothing more. She said that Izzy had packed a few things, some clothes too, not much more, a menorah, which is something dear to him from his homeland; that is all. He had sent a letter to Abe to collect everything from his house in New York and to put it in storage. One day, he said, he might come back for it, or else maybe he would not. He wasn't sure.

"'I think of my past life often,' Elana said to me," continued Smiles. "'Images flash past me. Of me and Ernie when we were young and innocent, two fools in love, when we had our children, the heartbreak and happiness of each birth. I think of Christmas with my family, with my sister Susan O'Rourke—Aunt Susie as my kids know her; I can see them laughing together, all the children, my family all in one place. It was so joyful. I think of all that—of when Susan and I wandered along the piers, of my two brothers who made something of themselves and I was so proud of them. I think of a warm bath and a raging fire in the hearth. I think of all those things. And then I turn my head to Izzy, and all those things just disappear. They were mere flashes in a long life. Just a few bright spots. Ernie and I drifted so far apart, God bless him. He tried so hard after he got back from the war, but I knew deep down that he was trying not for me, but only for him, and besides, I didn't see him the same way. I didn't love him, and that emptiness stabbed at me. And my brothers moved on, just like my parents who gave up everything in Ireland to follow their dreams.

"'Before I left New York with you, I spent the night with Susan, and she hugged me and wished me well. Izzy said that wherever we end up, there will be only a train between me and her, and that he will make sure that we see each other again. That would be nice. And that is why my life and my heart are with him, because he doesn't just give me a flash of light; he gives me eternal light. He is full of love for me and has a heart that knows no bounds, day after day, night after night. Sometimes my children ask about the cousins, about Daddy, about Aunt Susie, about the house. I tell them we will see them all soon. And then they forget and enjoy their new life, the people we are with, and the adventures we are living. I don't want mementos to remind me of a few flashes of joy in an otherwise dreary life. I don't want to pretend that the world I left was more than it actually was.

669

I chose to leave it behind and inhale the intense love that Izzy and all of you have given me. I will never turn around and regret what I had to give up to achieve the exhilaration that I feel now every moment of my life.'

"Then, I asked her," Smiles said, "I guess you are not packing more than your clothes? And Elana hugged me and said that a few dresses would be good enough. She is right, you know. Everything here that you hold precious, all of that can't be put in a bag or a carriage. You will always cherish your flickers of life from here. But what's ahead of us, we don't need to drag old rubbish behind as we move forward. We got each other. We don't need a red raft or some books. We just need clothes on our back and the love we all share. When we meet Izzy and Elana in Luray in a few days, we'll have everything we need. And then we take everything else as it comes, knowing that we are all in it together."

Paul kissed his wife on the head.

But Luke glared at his brother, a knowing smile drawn upon his face. *We got each other. But that's not all we need. A table only stands with three legs. Right now, we only have two.*

The carriage darted forward along a cold dirt road toward the farm, the sun setting quickly behind them over glowing blue mountains.

Matt's horse dashed into the town, and he stopped it in front of the doctor, kicking up a puff of dust. He leaped off, a visage of consternation drawn upon his face, and immediately he hugged his wife.

"You OK, Jessie?" he asked her. "I was so scared for you. I seen what happened. I was scared that they was shooting you!"

"What do you mean you saw it, Matthew?" the doctor asked, striding toward him with grace and a furrowed brow. "You were here when the assassin shot all our horses?"

"Yes, sir," Matt said, his eyes wide open as he looked hard at the doctor. Others gathered around; they listened too; the town's din quieted as a glowing darkness spread over them. "I was riding over to see how you was, to check on you and Jessie, when I heard gunshots, lots of them. I rode fast, so fearful and scared, and then I seen down that someone was behind a tree shooting up all the horses. I yelled to him, 'Hey, you, what in the hell is you doing?' Because that was crazy, a man shooting up all our horses. And he turned and looked at me all startled, and then I seen him. He was a Negro, not one I had ever seen before, and before I could even pull out my rifle, he jumped on his black horse and headed west to the hills, as fast as I ever seen a man ride a horse."

"We assumed it was your slave Paul," the doctor said. "I sent Colonel Stompmonger and his men out to look for them. They have yet to return. Did you happen to see who it was?"

"I ain't smart like you, Doctor, but I know it wasn't Paul, most of all because he was still on the farm when I left it, and he could never have gotten here that fast, which you would know if you ever seen him ride a horse, and he can't shoot worth a lick. No, I didn't see who it was, but as soon as he took off, so did I, and I chased him for two hours into the woods, up through the thick trees, far up the mountain. I seen him all the way, and I chased him like probably he never been chased before."

Matt nodded as the town's collective eyes stared into his. They were biting at his story, rapt by his every word. A gush of adrenaline pushed him forward.

"Then what, son?" the doctor asked, exacerbated. "Go on, tell us."

"Well, all the sudden I get to this spot in the mountain, I don't even know where it was, and the Negro, he stops and turns around, and then all sorts of others come out from the trees, lots of men and women, white and black, little kids, a whole bunch of people. And they all got guns, and they point them at me, until I drop mine and go cold; don't know what to do."

"Negroes and whites, in the woods, living together?" the doctor called out. "Preposterous! How can that be? It's not even possible or feasible."

"I ain't so smart as you, Doctor. You is a sagacious and brilliant man, and you may be right, but there they was, the lot of them, and they tell me they is called mountain people. They been there a long time, well before the war—runaway slaves, discontented farmers, making a life for themselves apart from all of you, apart from everything. And now that I found them, they tell me, they got to kill me, even though they don't like killing nobody other than jackrabbits and deer and the like. It just ain't their way. So, I say, why you come into town and shoot all them horses? Tell me that at least! And the Negro, he says he did it for protection. He was afraid that all of you would go in the woods and try to find them, and since they ain't not fond of killing people, well, they figured they will just kill your horses so you can't come get them, and that's why they did what they did. But then, the Negro who did the shooting, he told me something that I hesitate to even repeat, and I think maybe Jessie and the lady folk best leave here before I tell you all what he went and said."

The doctor nodded his head. "No, they can hear whatever it is you have to say, Matthew. Already your tale is far more dubious than I or anyone else can feasibly believe."

Matt nodded. "Well, I will tell you what he said to me, and all the other mountain folk, they backed him up on it. And his face was so full of truth and emotion that I couldn't but help but believe him, even though I don't, because of the slander it was. So, he says to me that very often they sneak into town and steal a few things when they need them; not so much food, because they have enough of that in the mountains, but more like stuff, like blankets and seeds and all. And they do it quiet and all, just one thing here and there, so they never get noticed. Well, the Negro says, one night he is in town, and he spots Jessie fornicating with one of Colonel Stompmonger's soldiers, two actually. That's what he says at least, and the sight of it stunned him. So rather than being careful like usual, he walked too close, and one of the men, they see him and they grab him from behind before he could dart away. They bring him to Jessie, and she says to him, 'You got two choices, to either get shot, or to fuck me right here and now.' That's what he says Jessie says to him."

"Matthew!" the doctor shouted, interrupting him and slapping him across the head. "You stop this idiocy right now. I warn you, you stop this instant."

But Matt, his face still innocent and vibrant, just shook his head and looked at all the eyes that continued to peer at him, hungry for more. "It ain't what I said, Doctor. You is a smart man, so you know that what people say ain't necessarily the truth, even if they do look truthful and sincere like that Negro did, even if every person with him backed up his story. I is just telling you what he said. So, he goes and fornicates with Jessie, and then she tells him that she is ripe to have a baby, and there is a chance now that the baby, if it grows in her, maybe his, maybe black, and that he can go now but to never come back, or she will say he raped her. And I say to him, you is insulting my wife to say that. You dishonor her and her father, who is a righteous and decent and brilliant man, a healer and a leader, the very pinnacle of Southern values. That's what I says to him. And he says to me, 'I will make you a deal. You can leave here if you promise never to come back until your wife has that baby.' And he says to me, 'If that baby comes out black, then you know I is telling the truth. And if it don't come out black, then you can call me a liar.' 'And know this,' he says, to which all the others agree, 'if you do come back, it ain't likely you will ever find us, 'cause we don't stay put for long. But if you do find us, we will fight you tooth and nail, and we got so many guns and ammunition left over from Stonewall's valley campaigns that we could shoot up a whole army should they come looking for us. So, you tell your people that.' And then he let me go, and I come riding back here to make sure you is all OK."

He hyperventilated after telling the tale, peeking from face to face. The doctor, for the first time in his life, stood silent, staring at Matt with an open mouth, wanting to utter some words of venom but not knowing what to say. A dense hush hovered over a darkening street strewn with rotting horses.

"Anyway, I know that Negro ain't telling the truth, but I aim to give him the benefit of doubt for not killing me right then and there, and to wait to make sure that the baby comes out white, which I know it will since it's my baby, and it ain't like Jessie would have other men but me. But just to honor his word I'll wait, like the good Southern gentleman I is, and if it does come out white, which I know it will, well then, that proves he's a liar, and then I will lead a whole army after them people and kill them all for such horrible slander. But if it does come out black, well then, I guess he was telling the truth after all."

Jessie at this point had fallen to the ground, crying hysterically. She shouted, "Make him stop! Make him stop!" even as Matt continued to speak, a soft grin growing upon his face.

"Matthew!" the doctor shouted. "You tell us right now where these people are, and we will find them and slaughter them. I am sure that Colonel Stompmonger and his soldiers will help us. Now, Matthew!"

Matt smiled and nodded. "I know you is smart and wise, Doctor, and I don't question your anger at all of this slander and the dead horses and all, but due to the honor you instilled in me as a man of the South and a citizen of the Commonwealth of Virginia, I want to wait for Jessie's baby to come out. So when we go after them, we got good cause, and I can do it with a pure heart, like I did when I served valiantly with General Lee in our army. And besides, Doctor, and I ain't questioning your wisdom or sagacity, but we don't got no horses to chase after them now anyhow. They is all dead on the ground; so we best wait anyway. They ain't going nowhere so fast. That's all I is saying."

The doctor banged his fist on the ground, peering at his hysterical daughter, then at Matt, and then at all the townspeople who remained silently rapt in a darkening trance.

"My father always said," Matt continued, "that the mountains, they have eyes and ears and a soul. That they look over us, they judge us, they make sure we is following a righteous path in their shadow. Well, I been thinking, maybe those mountain people, maybe those are the eyes and ears and soul of the mountain. Maybe that's what they is. And they is trying to tell us something. All them people living in harmony in the mountain, black and white, young and old, all living together, that ain't something that's supposed to happen, as you told me so many times, Doctor. And that Negro, he shot faster and more accurate than any man I ever seen, and he was smarter than even me in how he talked to me. And I know how wise and decent you are, Doctor, and I do believe everything you tell me, but what I seen today, well, it means there is another way, not just the one you always talking about. And maybe it ain't a right way or maybe it is, but it ain't up to me to judge it, at least not until that baby comes out."

"What are you implying, Matthew?" the doctor shot back at him.

Matt smiled and nodded his head. "You is a smart man, Doctor, so I hope you know what I is saying. But, anyway, I have to leave you all now. My brother, he aims to leave the farm in the morning. I heard him talking about it, and he aims to take Luke with him, which I ain't too pleased about. I aim to chase him down, get Luke back, and then dispense some justice on them, justice they well deserve. That I will do myself, first because it is my fight and mine alone, and also because none of you got enough horses to even help me. Let me do that first. Then, Doctor, we will go after those mountain people right after the baby is born. I promise you that. I am a soldier of the Confederate Army of Northern Virginia. I know General Lee and Jackson personally. You know my word is good, and that's all I have to say."

The doctor, his face now obscured by darkness, did not respond.

Matt mounted his horse. "You all got a lot of horsemeat to cut up, should keep you busy for quite some time," he called out. "I will be back. Jessie, you be well; take care of that baby. I can't wait to see what it looks like when It comes out. I know it will be a spitting image of its daddy!"

And with that he bolted away, leaving a wall of dust between him and all those he knew, a wall so inviolable that even the guile of the doctor could not knock it down. He smiled as he rushed to the farm. He had done his deed. Stonewall lauded him from above. As did his dad.

The moon hovered high above the mountains, illuminating their blue peaks as they reflected off the glistening pond. The children were all asleep, and Smiles wandered out to give Paul a kiss before grabbing a few hours of sleep herself.

"You gonna talk to him?" she asked her husband.

Paul just nodded no. "I'm waiting for Luke to come back. He went to talk with Ruth."

As if on cue, Luke strolled over. He smiled at both of them. "Ruth loaded up the carriage with crates of food and drink, almost everything that was in the house. She wished us well. She does not want to come say goodbye, not again. She said it would be too painful."

"You sure she doesn't want to come with us?" Smiles asked him. "You want me to talk with her?"

Luke nodded no. "She says her and the boys, they are happy here, happy with the new church. She is helping out with the school. They say they are too old to leave. But she wishes us well."

"How did she get all that food out of the house without Matt finding out?" Smiles asked. "I don't want her in trouble."

"Matt told her to," Luke said. "He told her to give us everything we may need, food, clothing, anything. He is standing there, Paul. You must have seen him. He is standing on the other side of the pond."

"He's been there all night," Smiles said. "Just looking at us. And Paul is just sitting here, looking at him. I told Paul a hundred times, go there, go talk to him, make your peace before you leave. This is your last chance. But your brother is stubborn, Luke. He's got one way of thinking, and he can't get past that. You try. I'm going to sleep. Wake me up when it's time. This is a pitiful scene watching them two obstinate boys just staring at each other." She kissed them both and wandered to the cabins.

Luke sat by his brother, staring forward. "He is just standing there," Luke said. "Watching us. Hoping for one thing. Just one thing."

Those sad and painful eyes.

Paul kicked the dirt. His brain jiggled uncomfortably in his skull. He didn't know what to do.

A soft breeze swept through the bare trees as they fluttered. The waves on the pond rippled, blurring the moon and mountains. It was cold, but dry. Matt stood still, like a statue. He wore his gray uniform. He did not hold a gun. He watched them all pack. He made sure they would be safe, be well fed. That's all he ever wanted, to take care of them, and he smiled knowing that they could now be free. He wanted so much to tell Paul what he had done, how clever was his ruse, how he had outwitted the doctor, how he had made sure that Jessie would pay for the horrid sin she inflicted upon Luke, and how he had instilled fear into this entire town. Matt watched them with a heavy heart, paralyzed, knowing that when they drifted off this farm, forever gone, everything he was and every fiber of his being, of his past, of his parents' hope and prayers, all that would drift away with them. His was in a purgatory of no escape. He had fought his final battle and defeated the enemy; he had freed his brothers. He had completed the war. But now, despite all that, he lay dying, with no hope but for a lifetime of pain.

Suddenly he saw Luke tug at Paul, and the two of them stood. They exchanged some sharp words, until finally, with Paul raising his hands in disgust, they moved toward him.

He followed their approaching shadows, the moon bouncing off them like flashes of light. A great unease filled Matt with every step. He shook a bit; he did not know what to do, what to say. Slowly they came, Paul first, Luke lagging farther behind.

For several awkward moments, they greeted each other with deafening silence.

Finally, Paul uttered a few words. "I just want to tell you goodbye, Brother," he said, his voice soft and crackly. He could barely glance into Matt's sad and unselfish eyes. The eyes of his brother. Those eyes grabbed Paul, and he started to melt. He wanted so desperately to hug his brother, but something held him back. So, he spoke flatly, the words slipping out, more from his heart than his head. "And to say, thank you, thank you for everything, for everything you always did and always do. Thank you, Matt. I just need to tell you that. And tell you again, I love you. I always will."

Paul's eyes welled up, concealed by the night's darkness. "I wish you came with us," he whispered.

Matt did not know how to respond. He peered past Paul, speaking more to the trees than to his brother. "I want to say, I hold no grudges. I know we done some things, and we both did what we thought was right, and maybe it was, maybe not. But I want to tell you this, Brother. I love you too. I always will. I want to hug your children more than I can even tell you. I watch them; all day I watch them, and they make me smile! I want to see Momma again. I want to be part of the life we once had. I do. But I know we can't shake the past and what we done. And I thank you for giving me the farm. But without you, without Luke, it's just a piece of dirt, like you always said. We is the farm, all of us together. With you gone, we got nothing here but dirt and water and filth."

A table cannot stand on two legs.

"You can come with us, Matt!" Paul pleaded, grasping the spark of hope that his brother released. He was desperate. He wanted so much just to hug him!

Matt deflected his brother's plea. "I just want to tell you this before you go," he said, trying to remain distant, even as tears rushed from his eyes. "I did something today that I think you and Daddy and Luke and Mommy would be proud of, something to make sure that when you leave, you will be safe. That Jessie ain't gonna blame anyone but herself if that baby it comes out black. I got to take care of you to the end, Paul. That's what Daddy always told me to do. That's all I ever tried to do, and that's what I done today. I wasn't always good at it, because I ain't that smart and ain't that crafty, and maybe sometimes it looked like I wasn't on your side, but I always was, and I always will be. That's all I want to tell you, and to say I love you too, and I want you to find your freedom, and to get Momma, and—" He stopped, as he choked on his tears. "I got to go. That's all I had to say." With that, he turned and disappeared into the darkness.

Paul chased after him. And then, he saw Matt staring into the sky, having stopped beside the edge of the pear trees.

"You see that, Brother?" Matt said, pointing upward, his back to his brother. "The moon, it is showing it to us. I ain't seen it since I been back. But now, the moon, it's showing it to us. Look!"

Paul looked up. As if struck by a spotlight, the craggy rocks of Old Rag shined brightly in the sky.

"I see it, Brother," Paul called out, his face consumed by a smile. "I see it!" His heart raced, as a tranquil deluge of peace filled his mind and body. It was if he were floating in the mountain's shadow. Old Rag would not let it end this way.

"Remember when I took you there, Paul?" Matt whispered. "That's all I ever wanted. To take my brothers up into the sky. I wanted to share it with you, to show you what Daddy always showed me. And then look what happened? That trip, it turned everything bad. It caused a flood of filth to ruin our world. It was the worst thing I ever done. All I was supposed to do was protect you. And look what I done. I ruined everything."

Matt dropped to his knees, bawling. He lost himself to the moment. Paul rushed over to him and kissed him on his head. *My big brother! My big brother Matt!* Tears dropped from his eyes as well. He held his brother tightly, so imbued by a love for this boy that deflected all other thought.

"No, no," Paul pleaded. "You saved me that day. You freed me! You showed me a life beyond what I ever could have known. That was my moment of redemption, Matt. From that moment on, all I dreamed of was running off with you and making a new life, far from this place, far from everyone but you and Luke. Now, Brother, that is what we are doing. Come with us! For all these years, you watched over us; you took care of us. You did more than any human being could possibly do to make sure we were happy and safe. But now, it's time for us to take care of you. Let me free you, Brother, like you did to me! Matt, I love you beyond anything that I could ever imagine. You are part of who I am. I am barely alive without you! My family, they need you. Come with us. I beg you. It's time for me to be there for you, to take care of my big brother. Please, Matt, Brother, please, come with us. We can't survive without you."

Matt turned his head, his face more water than skin. He buried himself in Paul's chest, bawling uncontrollably. For the first time in so long, he felt free, totally free, totally happy. All of his pain drifted away. He placed his arms around Paul and just cried. He nodded up and down.

"I want to go with you," he finally blurted out through his tears. "But first, I have to make sure you get away. I got to! Go without me, Paul. Just tell me where you will be. I will find you. I promise. I want to leave this place behind. To find Momma. I just want to leave this horrible place. It was so good to us. It was everything we prayed for, but now it's my prison. I want to be with my brothers in peace. With your kids, with Luke, with Izzy. My God, Paul, can you ever forgive me?"

"For what?" Paul asked him.

Matt shrugged and forced out a laugh. "For being so dumb."

"You? Dumb? No, Matt. You are brilliant. You are amazing. You are my hero. And you always will be."

The two brothers dropped upon the chilled dirt of their sullied sanctuary, bawling tears of love as a watchful mountain hovered over them and glowed with pleasure. Luke emerged from the trees. He too cried profusely. He lay his head on Matt's, and the three of them lay beneath the pear trees, beside their pond, in the glow of moonlight that reflected Old Rag's shadow across the land, embraced in a grip that could never be broken. It was a table with three legs, and all of them felt alive again. Their tears mixed together and dropped upon the land, trickling along frozen dirt and into the pond, where they joined with the holy water of the mountains and grew effervescent and strong. The water flowed into the river and saturated the land, past farms and forests, and into the sea, where it brightened everything it touched and, at least for a moment, made the world perfect.

They were three brothers standing alone, standing as one, three brothers standing against the world. Each had endured persistent hardship and pain, each had drifted in and out of different lives, but together, together in the shadow of Old Rag, nothing could stop them, for they possessed a power that transcended convention and the staid mores of a corrupt society. Together, they radiated pure love, a love that bucked everything thrown against them. A love eternal. The love of three brothers, joined by mankind's last and final hope.

PART VI

Luke

"There was a rich man who was dressed in purple and fine linen and lived in luxury every day. At his gate was laid a beggar named Lazarus, covered with sores and longing to eat what fell from the rich man's table. Even the dogs came and licked his sores.

"The time came when the beggar died, and the angels carried him to Abraham's side. The rich man also died and was buried. In Hades, where he was in torment, he looked up and saw Abraham far away, with Lazarus by his side. So, he called to him, 'Father Abraham, have pity on me and send Lazarus to dip the tip of his finger in water and cool my tongue, because I am in agony in this fire.'

"But Abraham replied, 'Son, remember that in your lifetime you received your good things, while Lazarus received bad things, but now he is comforted here and you are in agony. And besides all this, between us and you a great chasm has been set in place so that those who want to go from here to you cannot, nor can anyone cross over from there to us.'"

EPILOGUE THANKSGIVING, 1865

A brown horse trotted rapidly across the empty landscape on a chilly December day, desperately seeking its home at the crest of the mountains. Its rider had leaped off and sent it on its way.

It was Thanksgiving Day, December 7, 1865.

President Abraham Lincoln, Father Abraham to Paul and to so many others, had declared the fourth Thursday of November a national holiday, a day of Thanksgiving, a day to dwell upon our nation's journey toward attaining its status as a city on hill, a beacon for all of humanity. Thanksgiving was a day of reflection and of appreciation for what this country represented, especially after undergoing the horror of a civil war that nearly tore it apart at its seams. It was a testament to the bravery and conviction—the passionate desire to seek liberty and fulfillment—of so many daring people who abandoned the comfort and security of their homes and sacrificed their lives to find something better, something that transcended the shackles of the societies from which they escaped. These were the dreamers, those who embraced America's mission to better the world.

But as with all things good, the spirit of those who forged a new nation with transformative words and thoughts, with guns and sacrifice, was drowned by a new normal, one whose strings the rich and the powerful held—those who preferred the status quo. The old world co-opted the new, the oppressed became the oppressors, and those who sought something better than a society of rules and stations and prejudice found themselves again in peril, having to flee from that which they helped to construct.

Nothing exemplified the fickle nature of the country's aspirations than Father Abraham's successor, President Andrew Johnson, who massacred all that the former president and so many visionaries had struggled to achieve; he even had the audacity to change the date of Thanksgiving, if only to prove that he, and not Lincoln's legacy, ruled the roost now. And so, in 1865, Thanksgiving was not going to be the fourth Thursday in November, but rather the first Thursday of December. It was on that day that a few pioneers drowning in the nation for which they fought and in which they struggled gathered to rewrite the rules, redefine their vows, and undergo a pilgrimage of redemption and discovery, to remake an America that had drifted away from itself.

"How much longer?" Elana's daughter asked, as she shivered in the back of a carriage.

The others too expressed their protestations.

"Give it time," said Luke, smiling. He had never seen this side of the mountains before. He stood with the others under intensely bright stars that twinkled with a magical aura against the backdrop of endless darkness. They gathered a few miles south of Luray, Virginia, in the Shenandoah Valley, along a pike that stretched far to the south, to North Carolina and beyond. It was from here that their journey together would commence—propelled by a common love and hope—to Ashville, where their momma waited after so long. It didn't matter where the roads led them after that, as long as they were together for its duration. Luke felt the energy of the moment. His smile could not fade. He did not look back at what he had lost; his vision now was only forward. This was his dream, and he had finally achieved it.

Except for one thing. He stared into the woods, waiting, waiting.

As the riderless brown horse sped rapidly back to its home, its owner climbed over some rocks and descended toward a path that would lead him to that very spot where Luke peeked into the woods. The rider stood up, hyperventilating, cold and wet, and stared down into the valley. He saw a few distant lights at the nadir of the path, and he smiled. Everything vile spilled out of his gut as he descended, and instantly he felt light and nimble. He ran now. Ran fast. He laughed as his legs propelled him forward. It had finally happened. The war was over. A glorious peace would now begin.

"I think we have to get going," Paul said to his brother, his hand draping Luke's shoulder. "The kids are getting restless; they're going to fall asleep. We have to get an early start tomorrow."

"Give it time," Luke repeated, patting Paul's hand. "Give it some time. We have waited this long. We can wait a little longer. The kids can handle being tired. They've been through much worse."

Paul nodded. He wandered over to Izzy, who stood cuddled with Elana below a tree near a small fire, shivering in the December frost.

"He wants us to wait a bit more," Paul told his friend.

Izzy shook his head. "What can I tell you? Who's to say he will ever come? Who's to say he won't come with the doctor and kill us all? He is crazy, you know! Before he slaughters us, at the very least I would like to get married first, to join myself to this girl who I love and have been waiting for my whole life. So when the doctor and his fiends riddle us with bullets, I will drop holding her soft and caressing hand."

Elana smiled and kissed him on the head. "Matt isn't going to do that," she said to him. "He will be here. Let's just wait. It wouldn't be the same without him."

Smiles wandered over and draped Paul with a hug. She kissed him all over the face. "I just love this beautiful man, and I am happy to say it over and over while we wait! Who doesn't love him?"

"I don't," Izzy said. "In fact, right now, I don't even know if I like him. I am freezing, you know! Has anyone thought of that?"

"I'm sorry to contribute to your people suffering even more," Paul said with a smile.

Elana and Smiles laughed.

"Tonight," Smiles said to Izzy, "under these stars, freed from the burden of being owned by the rules of other people, Paul and I are going to get married, to get really married, by our rules this time, in our own way. I'm going to marry my darling man who I love so much, and you, Izzy, are going to marry the love of your life who has given up everything but her heart to be here with you. How can we complain about something as meaningless as being cold on a night like this? Tonight, we are going to be reborn into our new world. I agree with Luke. The kids can deal with it. I am willing to wait."

"Me too," Paul whispered to her, kissing her on the lips.

"Me too," Elana smiled. "I'll hold you and snuggle you, Izzy. I'll keep you warm."

Izzy nodded, but he did not look happy. His skin crawled with trepidation. Even as Luke peered beyond the dark valley toward an obscure mountain path, waiting for Matt to emerge, Izzy harbored ample doubt. What had ever gone right for his people? "Why should this night be different than any other?"

"Because," Elana whispered to him, "today we are free from all of that, from the past and the present, from our history and from our fates. Today is different. Today belongs to us. Today we are in charge of our own futures." She wrapped him tightly in her arms and kissed his stubbly face.

Luke stood apart, peering into the woods, up the mountain, waiting, waiting. *Where was Matt?*

From the mountain's edge, Matt hustled down, doing his best to evade rocks, guided only by the bright stars above. Their focused illumination led him to his salvation.

He had left late because it took him longer than he hoped to write one last note, one last expression of his freedom. He tied the note to the saddle of his brown horse and sent it on its way, back to the farm, back to his wife and father-in-law—one last statement to share with them before leaving the place of his birth, the place where he and his brothers grew together and then were torn apart. He did it for his father, whose bones were buried within that piece of dirt, but whose soul and spirit floated with his sons wherever they may be, somewhere meaningful and ephemeral in a place beyond.

So, he wrote one last note. He imagined Jessie reading it; he could see her face, her consternation. Would she show it to her father? Would she finally acknowledge her defeat? She had bested Luke and Paul and Izzy. She had swindled and subdued Colonel Stompmonger and his men, the town's black inhabitants, and the other farmers and their children. Her power knew no bounds. But would she finally acknowledge that Matt, of all people, had been the one to slay her? He could only hope! As he ran down the mountain, he entertained that vision, that last glimmer of joy that danced upon his empty piece of land, before he dived into a future that he hoped would sow the seeds of what once was.

He wrote the letter and sent his riderless brown horse on its way home with the note tacked to it.

My dearest Wife,

As I went out to do the bidding of you and your sagacious and pious father to stop my brother Paul from running North and to rescue my other brother, a terrible fate befell me. Suddenly from the woods, the mountain people, they come out at me, and they abducted me. They took me to their place, hidden and separate from everyone and everything around them, and they said I can't never leave. I would be there forever, they told me. All they says is that I can write one last letter to you and tack it to my horse and then send my horse galloping home so you can know what happened to your poor, misled husband. So, that's what I is doing now.

First off, I want to tell you that I know what you done. I know everything you done. The mountain people told me, and I believe them. And I know that Luke ain't just a slave to you, that you made use of him in all different and sorted ways, and that you disgraced me to all variety of men. It don't bother me though, Jessie, because in the end, you was never anything to me neither. I seen through you a long time ago. I used you for what I needed you for. Poor Luke, he had to pay the price, but even he don't care, 'cause we got what we wanted, and you got what you wanted, so everyone is happy, and I guess that's what's best of all. So, I will say this, my dearest and most loyal wife: if you have a baby and it is black, which I reckon it has a fair chance of being, you take care of that baby like it's your own, or you let Ruth care for it if you can't, and you supply her with everything she needs to do that. You don't blame anyone excepting the mountain people for doing that to you, and no one else pays for your sins. I will be watching you, my lovely wife, from up here in the mountains, and if you don't do like I says now, well, let's just say, it won't be good for you or for anyone you love, if you do love anyone, which itself ain't something I is sure of one way or another.

And this I say too, so long as we is talking about it. You better take care of Ruth and her boys. I will be checking on them too. And if you hire other Negroes in town to help with the farm, you better be good to them, all of them, lest the wrath of the mountain folk come down on you so hard that you won't be able to see it coming, even through your slimy little eyes.

I am giving you what you want, dear Wife, and for that you should forever thank me. Under this letter I got the deed to the farm, and I signed the whole thing over to you. It's yours now. The only thing I took is my brothers and all the intelligence and goodness that my brothers have in their hearts and brains. I took my daddy's spirit too; it is what makes the farm thrive, and I took it with me, because here with the mountain people, that's what I need to make my new life meaningful. So, we both got what we want. You got the dirt, I got the soul. You do with it what you want. I wish you nothing but luck.

I fought a war for the South. I fought because your daddy told me to, and I listened to everything he said. But when I fought that war, I found deep inside me a purpose and meaning that I never knew before. It wasn't about slavery so much, but it was about freedom and about who I am and where I came from. About freeing myself and my brothers, and on this day, when the mountain people took me away, I finally got what I wanted. I am finally free, and my brothers, they is too. Even as you and your daddy lived the high life back home, while me and the others were fighting and dying for you, even as you and your daddy took control of the peace and turned what we did into only what you wanted, it was me in the end who was fighting for a righteous cause, fighting alongside General Lee and Stonewall, fighting for everything you claim to believe in, but actually you do the opposite. I fought the righteous cause, and now I will keep fighting for the righteous cause, fighting alongside the mountain people and my brothers, fighting with the power of my father's and mother's souls, while you languish on the empty piece of earth I left you. You and your daddy can't never understand the war I fought; you are everything I was fighting against, but it's OK that you is ignorant of all that, because me and the mountain people, we know the truth, and in the end, even as you fool everyone else and make the world like you want it, we will be happy knowing we don't got to be in that world with you anymore, and we will keep up the good fight against you and yours and everything you claim to be right and good.

With that, my dear Wife, I bid you farewell. It was a marriage I won't soon forget and one I am happy to be rid of. Say hi to your daddy. I will be watching you. Both of you. Forever.

Your loving husband Matt.

Luke peered into the woods. It was getting colder. The children were getting inpatient.

Where was he?

"We have to start," Paul finally acknowledged.

Luke nodded. It was time.

They gathered beneath a canopy of trees, carrying lanterns and candles to illuminate the bare branches that twisted in unusual shapes and encased them within a cavern of emptiness. From above, the mountains shined blue, hovering, watching. The children, yawning and tired, lined up along a rug of moss, led to their proper positions by Elana's daughter, who smiled as she held little James. The baby was asleep—snoring, dreaming. Everyone fell silent.

Izzy, who held Elana's hand, handed Luke a bag with two glasses inside of it. This one ritual from his faith he sought to retain, even as he modified it; each glass symbolized their individual selves. Elana's was a tall wine cup, Izzy's an old, chipped mug he had brought over from Poland. Luke nodded to them, his effervescent smile not fading, even as he continued to peer into the woods.

Paul and Smiles also stood arm in arm, each rubbing the others' back, staring into each other's' eyes, a solemn glance drawn upon their faces, one of tranquil happiness.

The two couples moved under the arch, side by side, as Luke stood in front of them, his arms crossed, thinking about what he might say. It would be simple, brief. Just enough to express the magnitude of this moment. Marriage was many things to many people, but for Luke, as for those whose bond he would consecrate, it was a manifestation of love, bereft of all the ritual and legality that cluttered its essence beyond this place and time. Astride these ancient trees, beneath the protection of God's mountainous paradise, all rules evaporated, and all that remained was a glue of infinite adoration.

It was an affection identical to the one Luke felt for his brothers. It was no different. Not for him.

He peeked again into the woods. Did he hear something?

"Are we going to start this?" Elana's daughter asked.

"Not yet," a distant twang cried out.

The voice came from the woods. Luke laughed, jumping up. He abandoned his perch and dashed in the voice's direction. He could hear footsteps running toward him. Somewhere, in the depth of the forest, they met, grasping each other tightly, kissing each other on the head. There they hovered for many long minutes, unwilling to let go. Now it was complete. Now everything had become right, here on the other side of the mountain, here in a virgin land of their own choosing.

"Did I miss it?" Matt asked, breathing hard. "I came just as fast as I could. I seen you from up there and ran as fast as I could and kept saying, damn, why in the hell is it taking me so long?"

"No," Luke smiled. "I delayed them. We are just getting started."

Matt nodded, smiling. Whatever fear he harbored being here, embracing these people for the first time, these radiant souls whom he had watched from afar and coveted, melted away in Luke's presence. This was where he belonged. It was where he had always belonged. It was home.

Young Jake, restless, was pacing back and forth until Elana's daughter berated him to get back by her side; he stopped and stared into the woods. He pointed his finger.

"Look, Daddy," he said, causing other heads to turn. "A Confederate soldier got Uncle Luke! Look, here they come now."

Paul twisted toward his son's finger, his transient fear instantly disarmed. "That's no Confederate soldier," he said. "That's your uncle Matt."

"Then why's he wearing that uniform?" Jake asked.

Paul laughed, peering into Matt's eyes gently. "Because, Jake, your uncle is a dumbass."

"I ain't so dumb as your daddy says," Matt countered, walking toward the boy and kneeling down. He stared into the boy's eyes, marveling at a spitting image of Paul from days gone by. Tears rolled down his cheeks. "This here uniform, it may do us good on the journey ahead. Your daddy don't always know these things. He don't got quite the common sense brains that all his book learning gave to him."

Jake laughed. "Daddy, he talks so funny!"

Smiles approached this man she had heard so much about, the man after whom she had named her second son, the man painted as hero and villain by her husband, who she knew loved him beyond belief. Now, here he was, a gentle soul, a stunning reflection of Paul. A tear popped into the corner of her eye as she walked to Matt and kissed him on the head. Then she looked at him. "Your brother, every time I said one word that's not grammatically right, he looks at me like I am ruining the world. Why is it he let you get away with talking that way?" Then, she laughed.

Matt smiled broadly, peering into Smile's large, inviting eyes. It was as if he had known her all his life. "It ain't so much as that," he said. "It's more that I had to be with the people in the town and mingle with them, while Paul and Luke got a real education at home, one deprived to me. That's been my job in life, going out among the people and having them accept me, protecting these two, while your husband and his brother can sit around and read their books and talk about fancy things."

"I know," Smiles said, kissing him on the head. "I always told Paul he was one lucky slave to have you."

"He damned well was," Matt said, glaring at Paul.

Izzy then approached Matt, nodding up and down. "I'm glad you found your way out of the shithole you were in for the past few months," he said. "Now, if you don't mind, I want to marry this girl over here. It's already damned late. What can I tell you? These kids will be asleep before I can say I do. And right now, that's the only words that I want to be saying, because if we wait too long, this girl may well get second thoughts. As well she should!"

Matt had so much to say. He wanted to tell them how he had fooled Jessie and the doctor and how he had escaped and made sure that everyone in town believed that Paul and the others were heading North to New York. But, in this place, with these people, he knew that he could wait. "You go get married, Izzy," he told his old friend. "But you ain't right about one thing. This girl, she's got a good sense about her. She sees you for what you is. Just for once, you and your people ain't getting the raw end of the stick."

Luke gravitated to his brother Matt, his arms draped around Matt's shoulders. "Can I say this first?" he announced, looking around at the others. "I look at you, and I am happy with what you each have found in the other, and yet, there is something missing. As soon as I laid eyes on Matt, I found it."

"Jesus Christ," Izzy muttered under his breath. "What now?"

Luke's face glowed in this lighted chapel of trees and mountains. The stars punctuated his every word. He stood larger than life, and instantly all the others quieted as he spoke.

"It's just that, we're paving a new direction with new rules," he said. "As we march from here, we are entirely the masters of our own lives. The gauges of our success are our love, our happiness, our ability to reach our potential, and our goodness without and within. Paul, Izzy, Elana, Smiles—you have found that love in each other, in your children, and in all of us. I suppose that marriage, in our new world, is a means of bringing you together in a spiritual way. Well, I don't want to be left out. Marriage can be any bond of love, and so, here, on the other side of the mountain, at the inception of a journey that will bring us to a new and exciting paradise, I want to marry my brother Matt, to declare my love for him, for all of you, so that the two of us are also included in this ritual we are performing tonight. That's why I can't officiate. I want to participate. If you, Matt, will agree."

Matt laughed. "I don't love no one more!" he said. "And hell, you is even prettier than Jessie."

"Wait," Elana's daughter interrupted. "Uncle Luke, you're going to marry Uncle Matt?"

"Yes," Luke said.

"Ewww," her daughter said, and all the other children laughed.

Izzy peered at Elana. "To hell with Luke. I've been waiting for this moment my whole life. I think I can do it on my own, after all I've been through. Luke, give me the bag with the two glasses in it."

Luke happily complied. Elana and Izzy stood together under the arch of twisted trees, mystical light glowing upon them. They peered into each other's eyes and held hands gently. Matt had never seen this side of Izzy. He stared intently, so happy, so glad to have arrived here on time. Paul held Smiles and kissed her. The children all looked on.

They sang their vows to each other—their vows of passion, of hope, of love. Each of them kissed the other, and then kissed everyone else. A cool, gentle breeze caressed them. Even the children stared wide-eyed at such uncommon glee.

Izzy and Elana smashed their glasses in the bag and laughed, their individual cups breaking and mixing, becoming entangled forever, as were they all, all these people, these pioneers, these dreamers.

Many trying days passed after that night—days when only Matt's Confederate uniform and some clever thinking on his part kept them from being massacred by men on horseback, days when Paul's pretense of still being in the army helped them past checkpoints and through encampments, and days of snow and winds and freezing rain. Not every minute brewed with happiness, and many days sowed doubts in even the most sanguine and robust among them.

But then, on Christmas Day, they hobbled into a valley beneath the most glorious mountains that Luke or any of them had ever seen—snowcapped, overpowering, enticing.

A woman stood on her stoop, watching, waiting. The ravages of time and age had hardly dented her visage or spirit; she was not so old, not so worn, not so beaten down to appreciate what finally sprouted from the seeds she had planted so long ago. All these many years she knew that this day would come. She looked upon them all as they poured out of the carriages. There was Izzy! And holding the hand of a redhead at that! And there were Matt and Luke, just like she had always known them, together, their bond so strong that she felt it from afar. And there was Paul, big and strong, his arms clasped with those of a beautiful and powerful woman. My goodness, Paul, he had grown in so many ways. And she saw three children pop out, one in Paul's arms, the other two scampering around, three brothers, swimming in a sea of love.

She stood still, waiting, looking within her soul. "Jake," she said. "My dear Jake. It all happened for a reason, my dearest man. You had to let me go, or else this moment could never have occurred. Look at them, Jake! Look at what we created, beacons for this new world, a new world of freedom, a world where they have a chance. Look at what we have done! If you hadn't let me go, my dearest man, even though it caused us so much pain, then this day could never have occurred."

A cool breeze whipped around the mountain, and Mary stepped forward.

Suddenly, as if in a gust of wind, they ran at her, the three brothers, her boys, her wonderful boys, safe at last, about to again fall into her chest that had been empty for so many lonely years. She opened her arms, and they leaped in, buried by her grasp, bawling as one, until all the others came as well and the world—her world and theirs, the world of her husband and of her every hope and dream—once again came alive.

The End

Made in the USA
Middletown, DE
22 December 2020

29809658R10423